MYSTICS OF FORTUNE

MIKE CARLOZZI

MYSTICS OF FORTUNE © 2022 by Mike Carlozzi
All Rights Reserved

Perfect Bound ISBN: 978-1-0880-1765-4
Library of Congress Control Number: TXu 2-291-729

Published by Mike Carlozzi

First Edition, Paperback January 2022

Cover illustrator by Robert Williams
Interior Design by KUHN Design Group
Edited by Jonathan Starke
Proofreading by Scott Pearson

PROLOGUE

In 2029, Dr. Sabrina Maria Reeves, a young physicist attending MIT, completed and published a theory on faster-than-light (FTL) travel. With funding and logistics assistance from the German aerospace company Space Gen Y, Dr. Reeves started a journey that forever changed mankind. Adhering to business advice from her father, Sabrina founded the Reeves Corporation, a holding company that later merged with Space Gen Y, and together they launched the first manned asteroid-mining mission in 2039. Revenue generated from subsequent expeditions funded future FTL projects, though Dr. Reeves wouldn't live to see the full fruits of her work.

In 2049, an asteroid storm, whose composition absorbed all light, tore through an unexpecting Earth, leaving the once beautiful planet in pummeled ruins. Nine and a half billion unsuspecting people looked on in horror as the 4,200-mile-diameter storm, roughly the width of Mars, rained death, killing 80 percent of the planet's population by direct impact, starvation, rioting, and disease. Crops and livestock perished, water reservoirs became irreversibly tainted, and humanity turned on itself. Friends, families, and neighbors contrived against one another, often resorting to cold-blooded murder for necessities such as water and bread. Disease and viruses blanketed regions.

The most brilliant minds left on the planet speculated that humanity would not survive.

Then, in 2054, rumors of a mysterious virus circulated through the

African scientific community, bringing more distress. Scientists soon discovered the devastating asteroids contained organic compounds that sickened humans when exposed at close contact. The extremely contagious Kupita virus passed from person to person, bringing with it an extraordinarily high mortality rate.

As scientists struggled to contain the virus, Dr. Shalini Oyenusi, an astute hematologist from Seychelles, studied thousands of blood samples at her small lab in Cape Town. An ordinary day for Dr. Oyenusi turned extraordinary after analyzing blood samples from a man living only a few miles away.

Rakeem Simphiwe Hill, a South African musician, was one of the few blessed individuals to survive the virus. His resilience reshaped his cellular makeup, an outcome that Dr. Oyenusi discovered during her analysis. By the time the excited hematologist found Rakeem, the little-known musician's name was fusing into history.

Similar to a caterpillar morphing into a butterfly, Rakeem's near-death experience while fighting the virus forged something akin to a sixth sense. When Dr. Oyenusi caught up with him, the musician-turned-saint was already using his arcane abilities to heal the sick and dying. Records indicate his first patient was his younger brother, who was dying of bone cancer.

Dr. Oyenusi and several neurologist peers studied their patient as he traveled throughout Africa, using his new abilities to heal those in need. The probing doctors concluded that Rakeem's abilities stemmed from organic compounds within the meteorites reacting with his DNA. The interaction created a sixth sense, seemingly centered within the brain stem, and a capacity to project energy through thought.

Facing extinction, the human race needed a catalyst of hope and found it on the backs of Rakeem Hill and others who slowly emerged. For the next hundred years, Earth unified behind these so-called mystics and started rebuilding their once beautiful planet. An uncredited historian later disclosed that Mr. Hill's middle name, Simphiwe, means "We Have Been Given Him" in Zulu.

No cure or vaccination exists for the Kupita virus, which continued killing nearly everyone infected. As the masses died, the number of mystics grew along with their knowledge and capabilities. Historians disagree on the exact time, but around 2139 a rift developed between a small but growing sect of sages who believed their abilities were granted by a supreme being who demanded they rule over humanity.

In 2143 a civil war erupted between the Argos, mystics fighting for the good of humanity, and the Nein or Dark Mystics, who maintained their superiority and destiny to rule nonmystics. After a bloody eleven-year war, a small, unknown group of nine Argos mystics with uncommonly powerful abilities emerged and single-handedly turned the tide. Nameless, with no known origins, these staff-wielding saviors vanished after the announced peace accord.

Frequent skirmishes and casualties overshadowed the accord as years passed. Clusters of vindictive Nein targeted nonmystics, deeming them Thoba because of their affiliation with the nine Elders who spearheaded the Nein's defeat. Thoba, referencing the number nine in the African language of Xhosa, sought refuge with any Argos willing to fend off any lurking arcane threat. As many predicted, the armistice slowly dissolved, and the rising death toll mimicked the days prior to the civil war. Leaders of the Thoba, Nein, and Argos met in the scientific hub of Cape Town to discuss strategies to avoid war. Hours after the first meeting ended and it was clear the Nein would not compromise, four members of the Elder Nine appeared to the committee members.

The Elder leader presented a solution: exile all sages, Nein and Argos alike, to the recently discovered planet of Ojult. The Elder mystics promised to govern the planet but would not tolerate Earth's intervention.

To prep for the settlement project, Earth formed the Planetary Governing Union (PGU) to oversee off-world projects. Having never settled a planet, PGU leaders met behind closed doors to consider the recommendation. Of chief concern was safely transporting the sages and supplies to Ojult. The Reeves Corporation, now run by Scott Reeves, was a shadow of its former self but still retained the exclusive FTL patent. The astute businessman approached the PGU with his proposal.

Mr. Reeves demanded exclusivity over intergalactic trade, planet settling, and governance, and a monopoly over all transportation to and from all planets. Having no obvious alternative and with skirmishes between mystics escalating daily, the PGU reluctantly agreed.

Years passed as the Reeves Corporation fine-tuned their FTL technology and built the infrastructure needed to undertake the endeavor. With company profits at the forefront of his mind, Scott Reeves provided only the bare necessities to the newly exiled sages of Ojult. The corporation's fees charged to Earth's governments were limitless as their leaders begged to rid their lands of the treacherous mystics. With under-the-table deals prolific, Reeves developed another lucrative revenue stream by *persuading* the PGU to declare Ojult a penal colony for not only mystics but anyone found guilty of criminal activity.

Decades into the mission on Ojult, it became clear to Scott Reeves that the Elders were no longer overseeing their exiled brothers. With the comfort of Elder oversight gone, Reeves feared his expanding empire would suffer if war were to break out again among the mystics. Away from the prying eyes of the PGU, Scott Reeves developed an elite policing sect called the Celje whose charge was to covertly monitor the mystic population on Ojult. Scott Reeves passed away before seeing the first Celje set foot on Ojult, yet his sons and successors would continue the company and his ideology.

Fifty years after the first mystic exile set foot on Ojult, the greatest fear of the long-deceased Scott Reeves materialized. A second and even more horrific civil war among the mystics broke out, collapsing the universal economic market. The Elders never appeared, though rumors of their presence were rampant. Reluctantly, the Reeves Corporation activated their clandestine Celje agents who slowly and systematically assassinated key mystic leaders on both sides, eventually bringing Ojult back to order.

With a new Reeves descendant at the helm, Ojult's future once again remains uncertain.

PART I

CHAPTER 1: YEAR 2389

Jayden Vaut sat in a metal recliner aboard the *Night Scope* surrounded by Kupita-infected strangers, violent criminals, divided families, and captured mystics. He was alone, wearing a pale-yellow virosuit that filtered the exterior air into his full-body ensemble. He had nothing and was nothing according to the Planetary Governing Union. He had been exiled to Ojult because the PGU's Debt Services Act stated "if a family's debt, regardless of employer, reaches more than 10 percent of the household income, a violation of the law occurs." Two notifications were required before the PGU Taxation Service could take action.

Jayden got no such notification.

Three days ago, his mother had succumbed to the Kupita virus. She was a nurse at the regional hospital in the infectious-disease unit and had put in twenty years of incident-free work with the sickest patients modern medicine had ever seen. Then, after walking out of the clean room, her four-ply gown had torn on the disinfectant tube that released the cleanser. She'd taken only three breathes of the infected air, but that was enough. The virus took her six days later, leaving Jayden alone for the second time in his life.

Yesterday, a PGU taxation agent knocked on the front door. Jayden tried explaining that his father was a fleet-mining pilot for the Reeves Corporation but had died two years ago in a collision out in deep space. But neither his father's service to the corporation nor his mother's service to humanity exempted him from the PGU's exile clause.

The agent grabbed him by his shirt collar and slapped kurint cuffs around his wrists. Better known as k-cuffs, these electrical handcuffs shot a twelve-thousand-volt charge through a victim's body whenever the smart chip inside detected resistance. Each consecutive charge lasted five seconds longer than the first and would eventually render its victim unconscious.

Jayden's hands burned and itched. Under the virosuit, he was still wearing the same sweater and pants he'd worn in the hospital when his mother had died. Rows of adjustable metal chairs filled the enormous cargo bay. Crew members wearing green-and-khaki uniforms escorted the soon-to-be exiles to their designated seats. The crew didn't wear virosuits but instead opted for expensive, surgically implanted filters designed to neutralize the proteins protecting the Kupita virus. Warren Vaut, Jayden's father, had taught him such things before his death.

His father had often taken him to the launch station outside Fort Worth, Texas, showing him ships like the *Night Scope* and its scientific breakthroughs. The ships were inspiring, but it was the drive from their house to the station that always fascinated Jayden. Beautiful tall oak trees, wheat fields, cornfields, and a single Reeves Corporation golf course were seen along the route. The closer to the launch pad they got, the more the landscape had changed into its post-Event terrain.

Barren trees, cavernous craters, and gray-dirt-sprinkled craters the size of sports stadiums. Crews in full hazmat gear operated large cranes, dump trucks, and tankers full of decontamination foam. Pockets of pressurized hydrogen gas hidden within meteorites erupted spontaneously, sending plumes hundreds of feet into the air. The spectacle might have been worth watching if the air molecules spreading over the decontamination crews weren't loaded with virus droplets.

Two hundred and fifty years since the Event, and Earth still hadn't fully recovered.

Yellow lights around the cargo bay started flashing while crew members double-timed passengers to their iron chairs.

"Hey, *cad*, you don't speak English or something?"

Jayden's mind returned to the present, and he had to turn his entire body to see who was speaking to him. Through his face shield that misted every time he breathed, Jayden took in his neighbor. Clean shaven, black hair, and small eyes was all Jayden could make out.

"I speak English. Sorry, other things on my mind."

"I get that. You a mystic?"

Jayden leaned back into the sharp-edged chair. "Not a mystic."

"That makes two of us. I'm Rystral and this talkative man next to me is my older brother Cort. Don't worry, he won't hurt you, he's probably the weakest mystic ever to be exiled to Ojult."

At the word *mystic*, Jayden's heart double thumped. "You're a mystic?" whispered Jayden. "Can you get us out of here?"

"My brother just recovered from the virus," Rystral said, mimicking Jayden's soft tone. "The agents tried to k-cuff him while he was still in the hospital bed, so I punched the first guy, and next thing I knew, we're both in these torture chairs. How about you?"

Jayden's hope of escaping the ship had long faded. He was entranced by the magical essence of mystics, but the thought of the Kupita virus only drummed up more memories of his mother. After a few minutes of peace, speakers embedded in the ceiling and floor came to life.

"Good afternoon, everyone. My name's Captain Garvin Donato, and you're on the *Night Scope*. Now, most of you are scared, which is understandable. But you can blame the PGU for that, not me or my crew. I've just secured the bay doors, and we'll be taking off shortly. If you need water, find one of the many fountains located in the sterile rooms throughout the bay. Food will be distributed first thing tomorrow morning, then again tomorrow night. We'll drop the artificial gravity and turn on the skimmers so you can eat without your suits on. You'll have ten minutes of this freedom per meal, so don't waste it. Our journey to Ojult will take about two weeks, with four SKIPs. For those of you who've never been in space, a SKIP is like launching a pebble with a slingshot and will make any first-time space travelers vomit. So, fair warning. Also, stay in your seat as much as possible and keep the peace around you; it's a long flight, and violence isn't tolerated. Finally, I get that you're likely upset for having been treated like cattle. Again, not my problem, but your safety is my responsibility, and I take that seriously. I'll get you to Ojult safely. What you do from there is up to you. Prepare to depart."

In school, Jayden had learned that SKIPs really were just like the captain described. The ship lined up on an invisible runway in space near a mass-force generator (MFG). The MFG station locked on to a ship that contained an equal charge and pulled or pushed the object depending on the circumstance. MFGs worked on a line-of-sight basis, and field equilibrium was necessary or the object would be torn apart. Heating and cooling hydrogen atoms and introducing them to the electromagnetic field helped maintain field equilibrium for short periods, thus keeping the ship from falling apart at incredible speeds.

A gradual humming of the engines vibrated throughout the bay. A few minutes later, the ship started shaking as it lifted from the launching pad. Jayden felt fine until the ship left Earth's atmosphere and the captain turned on the artificial gravity. Everyone in the cabin experienced the same loss of equilibrium and lurched forward as the hull magnetized. Dozens of nearby exiles wretched in their virosuits, including Jayden's neighbor.

Jayden took pity on him squirming in his soiled virosuit. "Plug into the siphoning valve," Jayden advised.

Rystral turned, exposing his grimy face shield. "Wha… what? This… isn't what I—I need to take this off! I need to take this off!"

"You want to breathe in the virus, take a chance on leaving your brother alone? Below your seat, there's a hose that plugs into your virosuit. It fills your suit with some sort of gas, then sucks it back out. Like a car wash for the inside of your suit."

Minutes later, Rystral was breathing normally and chatting Jayden's ear off again. "How'd you know that? You been exiled before? I owe you, but we've got nothing. How can I repay you? That gas was purple! Purple's my favorite color. Thought I was high or something. You ever tried jashinto?"

Rystral didn't seem to have an *off* button, and Jayden didn't have the strength to quiet him. Silence didn't settle again until their first SKIP, when most of the same people who got sick earlier once again found their virosuits swamped in muck.

While Rystral was emptying his suit, Cort reached over and tapped Jayden on the knee. "Thanks for helping out my brother. He's all I got."

Cort had reddish, stringy hair with a nose that looked like it had been broken several times. It was hard to believe these two were brothers.

"Where are your parents?" Jayden asked.

"Once the hospital notified the PGU I was a mystic, my parents didn't have a choice. The only reason Iron Stomach here got exiled was because he punched the first agent that tried to k-cuff me."

Jayden's response was interrupted by two large men, dressed in virosuits, who walked up to Cort.

"Did I hear you say you're a mystic?" asked the larger man.

"I'm pretty sure he did, Broden," said the portlier man, joining in.

Broden snatched Cort by the throat and lifted him off his chair. "I don't like mystics, and I don't like you. How about you find yourself an airlock and do us all a favor."

Prejudice against sages was frequent, but direct action against them by nongovernment agents was rare.

Cort's windpipe was being crushed, and Rystral's face shield was full of purple gas. Jayden stood and realized how much shorter he was than both goons. "Let him go before he shoots lighting out his eyes."

"Clive, take care of this shaman lover," Broden barked.

Clive's virosuit jiggled when he stepped toward Jayden. "How about I space you along with your shaman, *cad*?"

He palmed Jayden in the chest and sent him crashing back into his chair. Jayden expected the move and cushioned the fall. Clive outweighed him by a hundred pounds, but Jayden was about to bet he was stronger and more capable in a fight. Shooting into a standing position, Jayden over-hooked Clive's left arm, then used his free arm to lock onto his head. The takedown was quick.

Broden dropped Cort and lunged at Jayden's kneeling figure, but the trap was already laid. Jayden lunged at the larger man's left leg and executed a perfect single-leg takedown. Broden's head smashed against the metal floor, dulling his senses. Thinking of his school's wrestling coach and every morning practice he'd attended for the past six years, Jayden climbed over Broden.

"It's not like he chose to be mystic, you *cad*. Let's see how you like it." Jayden reached around Broden's neck and yanked the flimsy straps free.

With another heave, Jayden pulled off Broden's protective mask. "Back at school, we called racists jerks like you *soras*. So listen up, *sora*, take a deep breath of that Kupita air, and don't you ever step our way again."

CHAPTER 2: YEAR 2389

For the second time in as many days, Jayden felt the clamps of buzzing k-cuffs around his wrists. He followed the arresting officer through the rows of exiles, who watched through fogged face shields, until reaching the doorway leading to a wide passageway. Behind him, Cort and Rystral followed uncuffed, the pretty female officer deeming them innocent victims in the brawl. In the corridor, they were met by dark skinned man with rugged muscles and scars running up his neck and cheek.

"Bardolf, take these two down to cargo bay nine," the female officer ordered. "If they cause any more trouble, procedures say we can eject them."

Bardolf wore a large badge marking him as the ship's security chief. His voice drummed in a deep, drawn out, accent. "What about this one and the two he beat up? Airlock?"

"The two injured brothers are, or were, VIPs. Captain wants them brought to medical to make sure they didn't pick up the virus. This kid here, the reason we're all busy babysitting—the captain wants to see him personally."

Jayden looked at his escort. She was shorter than him with olive skin, dark-pink highlights twirled within her space-black hair, and earrings that glinted black or white depending on their angle.

"Why? What does he want with me?" Jayden asked, still steaming from the fight.

"Easy, Jayden," Rystral whispered. "I think you're supposed to convince them *not* to toss you out."

Kass shook her head. "Bardolf, take the brothers. Jayden, is it? Follow me."

Cort's hand landed on Jayden's shoulder. "I was a complete stranger to you, and now you may get a permanent space nap. I'm no fighter, and I don't think I even have powers. But thanks, Jayden, really. I hope I can repay the favor one day."

Jayden nodded, and Kass tugged at his restraints. The brothers headed down the corridor while Jayden shuffled in the opposite direction. When his father had taken him to visit the launch stations, Jayden knew the ships were big. Now, having to walk through one, the enormity of the vessel didn't seem possible. They passed cargo bays, hangars, more cargo bays, a cafeteria, barracks, animal pens, a recreation room, some sort of maintenance bay, and more storage bays. Hundreds of crew members worked the ship and all reported to the captain who was about to sentence him.

Kass stopped in front of a sealed metal door labelled *PRESSURE EXCHANGE BAY, ENTER ONLY WHEN GREEN LIGHT IS ILLUMINATED*. Up until that point, Jayden's conscience hadn't accepted the reality of being fired out into space by way of a depressurization chamber.

Kass typed a seven-digit password into the keypad mounted above the door's latch, then pressed her thumb over the biometric scanner. With the green light above the entrance illuminated, the door hissed opened.

"If you think I'm going in there willingly, you and Captain Hook in there have another thing coming." Jayden stood cemented in place despite the officer's modest efforts to pull him.

Kass lifted her wrist showing off a 3DI watch that, among other things, controlled the k-cuffs. "We both know that with a wave of my hand, I can send you to your knees. Those cuffs aren't just for show, now put on your big-boy briefs and get in there."

Jayden stayed put, and Kass didn't hesitate. The jolt seemed to skip from his wrists directly to his knees. The muscles in his feet and calves lost contact with his brain and gravity took over. Jayden crashed to his knees.

The trauma lasted only a few seconds, but Kass had proven her point. Ahead in the pressurization bay, heavy footsteps thumped toward them.

"Kass, come on now, he's a kid," said the stranger. "Come, get those archaic things off him."

"That's not a good idea, Captain. He's already taken out two passengers and refused to enter the bay."

Jayden's eyesight came back into focus, and he marked the captain's soft smirk. "Alanah, come on, now. Besides, I think he's got fleet blood in him."

Kass's brow creased, but the remark convinced her. She tapped a series of buttons on her 3DI, and the k-cuffs unlocked. "From fleet, huh?"

Jayden coughed and tried to take a full breath.

"Easy, kid. I'm the captain of this ship, and I hear you've been beating up my passengers. That true?"

Kass took the cuffs off Jayden's wrists, but his legs were still frozen. He looked up at the captain, a less-than-commanding figure. The captain wore a black leather jacket over his green-and-khaki uniform, not unlike the one Jayden's father had had. He kept his hair high and tight along with a finely trimmed mustache. He looked more like he belonged in a biker gang than commanding a stadium-sized ship.

"I don't think putting a bunch of soras back in their place merits a death sentence. They threatened my… friend, and I reacted."

"Death sentence? Listen, my name's Captain Donato, and this is Lieutenant Alanah Kass, but just call her Alanah. Your FOCC says your name's Jayden Vaut; any relation to Warren Vaut?"

An FOCC (free optical communication chip), was a small implant most everyone in the Unified Western Powers region got when they were born. Jayden wasn't surprised to know the captain had already scanned him.

"Yeah, he is… *was* my father. He died years ago in some sort of collision."

Donato looked down and raised his hands. "I read the accident report. There was a glitch in the MFG software that sent your father off course. His mining ship clipped an uncharted asteroid, damn shame. Funny thing, I also knew the MFG fleet tech the corporation blamed for the accident. Cruz was his last name, good man, family man. The corporation didn't finish that investigation until a few years ago. They exiled Cruz and his whole family. The whole situation is sour."

Jayden's legs were tingling and coming back to life, but standing was arduous. "Yeah, well, lots of sour stuff happening these days."

Behind Donato, a virosuit was being loaded into a chamber. The attendant locked the motionless exile into the compartment, then closed the
hatch. "Captain, need the corridor door closed before I can expel the body."

Donato gave him the thumbs-up, then stepped into the corridor next
to Jayden, closing the door behind him. The door locked automatically,
and the green light above the entrance flashed red. The captain looked
from the door to Jayden, then back.

"Yeah, I knew Warren. We'd have a beer together on Lent if we ever
crossed paths. I was sorry to hear of his death. The fleet lost a good man
that day. But, Jayden, I brought you up here to talk, and seeing that dead
body being ejected has given you the wrong idea, I think."

When his father had died, Jayden felt like all the happiness he'd ever
had drained from him. With his mother gone too, he felt numb, a void in
his core that could never be filled again.

"The reason we have everyone wear the suits is because of the virus. We
get active cases on these transport jobs all the time. Unfortunately, many
of the infected die enroute, and I can't risk keeping them on board. Burying them in space is our only option. Jayden, we still have at least a week
before we get to Ojult, and this is only the start of what I can promise will
be a difficult life. I may be able to help you once we get there, but if I were
you, I'd take time to let everything sink in. I know about your mother
and why you're being exiled. Keep wearing that suit, no more fights, and
don't give my crew any grief. You do that, and I'll see what I can do when
we land."

Restless nights, nauseating SKIP jumps, and melancholy summarized
the next week of Jayden's isolation. His misery quickly turned to depres-
sion, and Jayden began looking for a way out... permanently. There were
plenty of sturdy ceiling rods but no rope or sheets. Drowning was another
option, but there wasn't a large enough bucket to even consider it. Jayden
even tried sneaking to bay thirty-two, where they'd ejected the Kupita
corpses, but he couldn't get past the sentries. Seeing no way out, Jayden
resigned himself to whatever future Ojult had in store.

A nearby speaker sputtered before the captain's voice broadcasted over
the ship.

"This is Captain Donato. We're approaching Ojult. There are a ton of asteroids around here, so we'll be making quick maneuvers. Stay in your seats and hang on. Once we've entered the atmosphere, we'll descend quickly or risk catching the attention of a vengeful mystic. Keep firm, and we'll be on the ground in a couple hours."

Jayden reclined in his iron throne, wondering what curveball life would throw next. The ship rocked and jerked, inducing more vomiting episodes from the passengers.

The cargo bay lights flickered, and the thrashing continued for an hour. The ship landed with a loud thunk and bounced several times before settling.

Lieutenant Kass's voice came over the intercom. "Exit the ship and follow the red lines out of the station. Once you exit, you're free to do whatever you want, but don't attempt to reboard the ship."

Following the crew's instructions, muddled passengers shuffled toward the exterior bay doors.

The rumors were true then: the corporation just left people to fend for themselves. Unsure what to do, Jayden remained seated.

A few minutes later, Kass emerged from the hallway. "Captain asked me to grab you. You okay? You're not going to try and fight me are you?"

Jayden looked at the pretty woman whose tone sounded more empathetic than their last encounter.

"I'm scared out of my mind, nauseous, and hungry. Fighting isn't on the list right now."

"For what it's worth, I'm sorry. The corporation and PGU aren't all bad, but I suppose I'm not going to convince you of that today. Before we landed, the captain got in touch with some of his contacts around town. I think he's got some options for you. You ready? You can take that suit off now."

Jayden stood and unzipped the two-layered suit, happy to be rid of his polyurethane prison. The gravity was different now that they'd landed, and Jayden felt woozy while his body attempted to adjust. He used the corridor wall to keep himself steady as he followed the lieutenant down the ramp.

At the end of the ramp, Jayden made out Captain Donato speaking to his crew.

"Welcome to Ojult, kid," said Captain Donato. "This place will try to kill you in more ways than my ex-wife, so listen carefully."

Jayden nodded, noticing the captain and Kass exchange an offbeat glance.

"A few of my pals came through, and I've got a couple choices for you. We don't have much time so listen up. Your first choice, become homeless like what most of these folks will do and likely die within a few months. Not a fan? Okay, next, live in a halfway house associated with the local mob and probably die within a year. You could also head to Meridone, the continent east of here, but you'd probably get shot or enslaved by the Celje. Last and perhaps least, but it's what I recommend, I can put you in touch with the Nein. They're always looking for... helpers... and will at least give you food, water, and a roof."

Jayden didn't have a clue where Meridone was or who the Celje were, but he'd heard of the Nein—a sect of mystics that rebelled against the Argos after the reconstruction effort began on Earth. It was the classic tale of good versus evil, and the Nein took up the role of the powerful villain. Only because of the Elder Nine, a small group of extremely gifted mystics, did the light prevail. They defeated the Nein, then brokered a deal between all mystics and Earth's governing authorities, suggesting the mystics henceforth exile to Ojult.

This seemed like a big decision, one that Jayden had to get right. "But Captain... the stories said the Nein hate us, the Thoba?"

"The Nein are ruthless, and yeah, they don't like nonmystics, but life here is going to be uphill no matter what, and you can't stay on the ship. The Nein are your best shot for survival, but I'm no compass. Decide for yourself."

Several gunshots went off outside the station, and Jayden dropped to the ground. "What... what's going on? Who's shooting!"

Donato was still standing and hadn't cowered. "This is what the locals consider normal. The entire planet is anarchic, chaotic, lawless, and fractional. Pick a side, stick to it, and keep your head down. Oh, and you better learn how to fight and shoot a pistol too."

Jayden got back to his feet and took a breath. "Okay, what's a Celje?"

"A secret organization that many folks don't know about, but their rap sheet is longer than the cads on Meridone and the Nein put together. Getting involved with the Celje, other than just dying, is the worst option I gave you. And before you ask, Meridone is full of killers, hookers, and killer hookers, basically."

Thirty minutes after making his decision, Jayden stood outside the launch station, taking in the alien world. It was flat, dry, and hazy with two moons that glowed purple and gold. The air was thin and tasted sour. The captain's comments on the trip over about asteroids around the planet was no joke. Even in the daylight, Jayden could plainly see the chaotic black dots sailing above the clouds. Half-dead trees with car-sized leaves and root systems above ground scattered what little horizon he could see between the wooden buildings. Dust devils kicked up dirt, whirling over gravel streets littered with beggars, dogs, and human waste. What really got his attention was all the children begging with their hands out to the new exiles. They looked gaunt and malnourished. The sight vanquished all self-pity he'd felt earlier.

"Holy hell, Garvin, he's like ten," said a ruffled woman walking toward him.

Donato smirked. "He's eighteen, my dearest ex-bride, and he comes from good stock. Life's handed him the wrong end of a polecat, and the PGU dumped him here. Was hoping you might be able to help. Maybe get him in with the Nein?"

Jayden was stunned by the woman. She was tall with strutting hips, long legs, lustrous black hair, tanned skin, and a confident narrow face. Her brown boots looked worn, as were her faded pants and dusty shirt. Jayden guessed the planet had turned this once beautiful woman into a dispirited killjoy.

"The Nein? What the hell are the Nein going to do with this rat except sell him into slavery?"

"I don't ask for much—"

"Nor should you, Garvin," she interrupted. "We're divorced and ex-husbands don't ask favors from ex-wives."

"First of all, I haven't signed the papers. Look, I'll throw in dinner and a nice bottle of wine, just see what you can do for him."

Under different circumstances that didn't involve his mother dying and him being stranded on a penal colony, Jayden thought he might like Captain Donato.

"Dinner, wine, how many women do you have lined up waiting on your ship? How many kids you have now? Never mind, I don't care. When I replied to your message, I didn't promise anything. Things are getting bad around here, and I mean that. I'd say send him to me, but my people are coming under attack more and more. I might be able to get an intro with the Nein, but this will cost you. Say no and I walk."

Donato looked to Jayden, then to his ex-wife, then back to Jayden. "Jayden, this is my ex-wife, Nencia. She's runs Appian Shipping, a logistics company that ships goods across Ojult. As you can tell, she's a brute that knows everyone and everyone knows her. She'll help you out. From there, you need to make your own way." Donato looked Nencia in the eye. "Don't let her kick you around either, she's not that much older than you."

"Not that much older than him? You think you married a Meridonian dancer right out of the orphanage? I'm twenty-five and have bigger balls than you!"

More gunshots and screams rang out.

Jayden dove into the dirt again, covering his head.

"A little yellow, huh?" said Nencia. "Welcome to Worall. No computers or video games, no toilets, no cars or planes, no technology to speak of. We're able to smuggle a few things onto the planet, but for the most, what you see is what you get. And you best get used to guns, killing, and a hell of a lot worse. Now, come on. A Nein's here picking up supplies. I know him, good slaver, always gets good prices. Perfect for your first introduction."

CHAPTER 3: YEAR 2389

Elasus Reeves, chief executive officer of the Reeves Corporation, sole owner of the Reeves Holding Company, and the most powerful person on any known planet, stood at the podium, preparing to end his speech to the Planetary Governing Union.

Descendants of powerful executives sometimes inherit corporations because of nothing more than lack of options. When it came to the Reeves lineage, nothing could be further from the truth. For nine generations, the firstborn male child took over the company following the death of the family patriarch. The sons were bred for leadership, from their first days in preschool and all the way through college.

Elasus relished in the power. Everyone from the PGU prime minister to the global regional governors bowed to his demands. With his self-proclaimed exceptional leadership, Elasus glorified every financial statement that illustrated new record profits.

With intellect and family history on his side, Elasus also looked the part of the cold-hearted, successful business tycoon. His head was shaved bald, and his full gray beard resembled Greek paintings of powerful gods. His godlike appearance bolstered his constant callous expression that fused with his perfectly tailored vintage black suits, nanofabric dress shirts that intuitively formed around his chest, and ties made of Lent silk.

Inside the Scott W. Reeves Conference Hall sat the most powerful people in North America, which meant they were government officials, most of whom Elasus had helped get elected. Back in its prime, the Las Vegas

Strip lit up the sky with high-rolling casinos, professional sports, and the who's who of entertainment. Everything changed after the Event, and like many metropolitan areas, most of the Strip still lay in ruins. Not all was lost, however, and through strategic corporate real-estate investments and a few closed-door meetings with PGU officials, areas like the SWR Conference Hall were a shining example of what capitalism could achieve.

"I'm not one for long speeches, so I'll end with the following," Elasus said, his commanding voice echoing through the artistic room. "The number of exiles transported to Ojult is at an all-time high, and mystic violence on Earth is at ten-year lows. Our new pharmaceutical operation on Ojult grows exponentially per quarter and will reach profitability this year. Lastly, Ojultan ore is trading at a fifty-two-week high. From these business interests, among others, the Reeves Corporation is now more profitable than ever." Elasus pointed around the large chamber. "The women you see walking in have your distribution checks."

Shouts of *hear, hear* and *well done* echoed throughout the room.

The chants and applause gave him no sense of pride or of a job well done. He'd seen and heard all this before and waited for the commotion to quiet before continuing.

"When my ancestor, Dr. Sabrina Reeves, developed the working theory behind faster-than-light technology, it changed humanity's vision of the future. The heart of her dream was to conquer space and expand her newly formed company, and now, here we are, more than two hundred and fifty years later. Riding on the back of Dr. Reeves's successes, we've developed tourism to new planets, discovered new ores through mining, new metals for space transportation, and new sources of energy that burn completely clean. You sitting before me have put your belief in me and have been generously rewarded. Members of the PGU, continue to trust in my vision for the future, and you will not be disappointed. Good night."

As his audience did every quarter during the same ceremony, they stood and gave their de facto leader a standing ovation. Elasus acknowledged the praise with a nod. He couldn't care less for their gratitude or input. Their presence was necessary to keep the universal economy stable, nothing more.

"Excellent speech, Mr. Reeves," said the recently elected PGU prime minister, Joshua Kennedy. "But I question your logic allowing junior members the opportunity to invest. What can they really offer?"

Mrs. Irelyn Reeves sat on the opposite side of her husband and gave him the obligatory cheek kiss and faux smile. "Well done, darling. Excellent speech. They love you."

Elasus nodded and sipped his nearly empty bourbon glass, ignoring Kennedy's ignorant comment.

"And, Elasus, thank you for taking care of our former minister. I promise I won't be so foolhardy," Kennedy said with a slur to his voice.

Elasus's eyes wandered to his wife's red dress and well-defined upper thigh. Irelyn was in her mid-forties, with shoulder-length, brown hair, and easily passed for someone much younger. Elasus still found his wife attractive, but the passion between them had left long ago.

"Former Prime Minister Carter's death last week was tragic, and your insinuation that my organization, or perhaps me personally, had something to do with it is ill advised." Elasus's voice sounded as if death itself was speaking.

Kennedy began pawing back his remarks, but the damage was done. "Mr. Reeves, I'm sorry, my mouth ran away from me. Must be the wine."

Elasus looked Kennedy in the eyes, ready to pounce. "From a leadership perspective, where Carter failed, you will prevail. Attempting under-the-table dealings with the regional governors behind my back while simultaneously accepting my company's distributions is bad business. Biting the hand that not only feeds you but pumps blood through your heart and breathes life into your body is moronic. I'm sure you'll agree, Mr. Prime Minister?"

Elasus didn't care to listen to the minister's response and casually stood from the table, offering his wife a hand, signaling his wish to leave. He ignored the continued apologies coming from Kennedy, knowing the man would probably sleep with one eye open for several nights.

Once outside the conference center, an older man with furry eyebrows and a full head of white hair opened the black town-car door for the executive. The gesture was antiquated given the car's automated features, but Elasus reveled in these types of obsolete customs.

"Thank you, Hewitt," said Elasus to his longtime driver. "Drop Irelyn off at the house, then I need to head into the office."

As soon as both wife and husband were in the car, Irelyn started in on him. "You're just as evil as those shamans! You had him killed, didn't you?"

Elasus sipped from the awaiting glass of bourbon. "I'm not in the business of assassinations, even of those sleeping with my wife." The sudden revelation had the desired effect, bringing an inward smile to him. "Yes, I know many things, both within the family and outside of it. But I didn't kill him. Carter made many enemies throughout the FIAS and the Sovereign Asian Alliance, and he brought about his own death."

"I... I only did it to help find Marilla," conceded Irelyn. "And, god, you're an evil man. How long have you known? And you continued to sleep with me?"

He crossed his legs, touched two buttons on the armrest, and a holographic notepad appeared in front of him. The image was his agenda for his meeting tonight. "Do you know why my company has only been governed by men after Sabrina founded it?"

Irelyn looked out the window onto the empty streets and broken skyline of Las Vegas.

"The Reeves ancestors gave no specific direction as to who should lead the corporation upon succession, yet it's always been passed to the firstborn son. And now, after your betrayal to not only me but to my family's legacy, it will be passed to our son, Ruven. How do you feel about that?"

"I don't care about your money or the power that comes with it. I want my daughter back. You claim family's so important to you, then why aren't you helping me find her!?"

Elasus handed her a glass of champagne. "One of our children is a rising star, the other made a poor choice. I don't beg or plead with those competent enough to understand the consequences of their actions."

———

An hour later, Elasus sat in his corner office, observing the fragmented city to the east and the alluring landscapes of Red Rock Canyon to the west. AI-managed cranes, tattered cybernated autonomous dump trucks, and other commercial construction equipment littered the region, but their progress was slow. The only habitable buildings in the area were owned by the corporation or PGU.

In the spacious office closely resembling a high-rise apartment, Elasus looked upon the corporation's senior officers. It was after midnight, and everyone was tired, but his senior staff knew better than to complain. Elasus called the meeting to discuss the ongoing suspicion that the PGU had planted a spy within the corporation.

"I expect you all to remedy this situation in the very near future," said Elasus. "For now, let's move on. Commodus, please begin."

"Yes, sir." Commodus Vrabel put down his scotch and stood to address the other executives. He looked the part of a chief operations officer, though slightly shorter than his colleagues. Commodus's buzz cut, goatee, graying hair, and temper reflected the character Elasus wanted in his number-two man. "I've narrowed down candidates for Idca's planetary resource officer and will have the names submitted to you tomorrow morning. Next, survey teams down in Florida hit another hotspot. A couple guys went down with the virus, others got toasted with radiation. And in case you're keeping tabs, that was the last spot in Florida our surveyors marked as safe, so basically the whole damn state is now untouchable."

"I've seen pictures of Idca; it's attractive, no doubt," said the heavyset chief intelligence officer, Rico Crouse. "The hotspots you're seeing, it's the same all over Earth. The Sovereign Asian Alliance minister just reported one twenty miles away from their capital. But we need to think about terminating our efforts in Florida for the time being, maybe refocusing on FIAS?"

Security Chief Tanner Sands shifted uncomfortably in his chair, which did not go unnoticed. Sands was a tall, muscular, intimidating man with a full head of gelled hair. He customarily wore short-sleeved shirts that exposed his well-defined, tattooed forearms and engorged veins.

"The Free and Independent African States is too unstable right now," corrected Tanner. "We should also remember that FIAS Governor Drohar still thinks we killed his defense minister, so don't expect any sort of warm welcome from them."

"Your job is security, Tanner, mine is intelligence," advised Rico. "My people tell me we can enter without problem."

"Did your people also tell you that the Las Vegas coroner's office just reported that the death of Prime Minister Carter was ruled a murder-suicide, with his wife, Anita, committing the murder?"

Rico stroked his thick mustache. "No, they did not."

Tanner continued. "The former minister's children are in hiding, according to the media. They have two sons, Broden and Clive, both in high school. We couldn't come up with a reason Anita would kill the kids, so I shipped them off to Ojult a few hours ago." Tanner anticipated Elasus's next question. "Sir, Anita was having an affair, and so was Raymond Carter with… well, he was sleeping with another woman, so the motive we set up is easy to justify."

CHAPTER 4: YEAR 2389

Elasus waited impatiently at the elevator door on the thirteenth floor of the executive level. Doug Kranzer, the doorman for the Reeves building, called Elasus a few minutes ago, informing him of the arrival of Tayla Cruz.

The elevator doors opened, and Elasus watched the homely looking woman step out. She was well dressed, in her mid-twenties, with short brown hair, little makeup, wide hips, and small breasts.

"Ms. Cruz, my name is Elasus Reeves."

"It's an honor to meet you, Mr. Reeves," replied Tayla with more confidence than he'd expected.

"My COO, Commodus Vrabel, interviewed you and recommended I meet with you before formally offering you the position. We'll spend time together, see if there's synergy between us, then I'll make the final determination whether to hire you on as my personal secretary. Any questions?"

"No, Mr. Reeves, I'm ready when you are."

They entered his elegant office through a large, artificial oak door.

"These are my ancestors," he said, pointing to the dozens of portraits hanging along the walls. My expectation is that you'll know each of them by name. Here you see Petya Amurski, a cousin of Sabrina Reeves. Petya discovered the relationship between the sudden appearance of the Amurski tree and asteroid-impact sites. A mystic herself, she found the branches amplified her own powers."

Tayla stopped in front of Dr. Petya Amurski's portrait. "Yes, I'm familiar with Dr. Sabrina Reeves and Petya. Similar pictures line the information-technology offices where I currently work."

She sounded intelligent, not cocky, and Elasus appreciated her forwardness. Her resume included substantial work in the corporation's cyber-defense department and in the flight department as a network administrator. She'd received multiple accolades in both sectors and came with experience other applicants lacked. Many of the fleet's pilots sent endorsement letters, all of which complimented her skills in networking the flight department's dispatch systems with their ships' navigation equipment.

"My organization, along with our global partners, have worked very hard to prevent the export of the Amurski tree, or at least its branches, to Ojult and any other group with links to the mystics." Elasus continued down the hallway, pointing out different portraits. "This one here is Rakeem Hill, the first-known sage to appear after the Event. From all reports, he used his powers to heal; too bad the rest of his kind didn't do the same."

"And what of these last two, Mr. Reeves?" asked Tayla, ignoring the comment and pointing to two young adults.

Elasus starred proudly at the first picture. "That is my son, Ruven. This was painted before he left for the PGU Defense Academy. He graduated with honors a few weeks ago."

"And the redheaded girl?"

"My youngest, Marilla. She's bright and was in medical school until recently."

It was apparent by his tone he didn't want to elaborate on his daughter. "My apologies for bringing up the subject, Mr. Reeves."

They continued walking down the maroon-carpeted entry, Elasus commenting on portraits until stopping in front of his mahogany desk.

Elasus turned and fixed a scrutinizing gaze. "Ms. Cruz, loyalty to me and my company is of the utmost importance. Lying or manipulating me or mine in any way will not be tolerated. I'm acutely aware of your family situation and will, if necessary, exploit that condition if it serves my purposes. Your predecessor retired when she turned fifty because this is a young-person's game. Do you understand what I'm saying?"

For the first time since meeting Tayla Cruz, he noticed a hint of anxiety in her unassuming posture. "Yes, Mr. Reeves. I understand fully."

Elasus led her through his private apartment adjacent to the office, then through the conference room, and back to the elevator. He waved his wrist in front of the screen and moments later, the elevator door slid open. They shot downward, past the ground floor and into the subterranean levels that very few people knew existed. Like master and servant, they remained silent during the ride while Elasus contemplated his plan for what was about to come. The doors opened at sublevel six, and Elasus led the nervous woman onto a floor resembling a high-tech prison.

The stained concrete floor reflected the soft-white imbedded lights above. Small rooms with thick concrete walls and reinforced steel doors dotted the hallway. Each cubicle-sized room consisted of only a small bed, toilet, and sink.

They rounded a gentle curve and were greeted by a familiar, handsome young man.

"Hello, Father," said Ruven Reeves.

Ruven resembled more of his mother than his father as he grew older. He wore his brown hair blown out and combed over and kept a hint of stubble around his attractive features. Ruven was by no means a big man but he kept in shape. The one feature Ruven and Elasus shared was their intense, accusing stare.

A hug or any other expression of emotion wasn't Elasus's style, opting instead for a simple handshake to the son he'd not seen in over a year.

"Ruven, congratulations on your graduation."

Ruven pointed down the hallway. "Tanner was showing me some of your handiwork. Seems like Marilla got herself into trouble again."

Elasus motioned for Tanner and Commodus to join the group. "Your sister doesn't have the foresight that you and I possess, but before we get into that, let me introduce Ms. Tayla Cruz."

The group exchanged brief pleasantries, but Ruven's handshake lingered.

"My father only chooses the pretty or loyal ones," remarked Ruven. "You must be loyal. If you ever need someone to show you around Las Vegas, or what's left of it, call me." With his hand extended, his pinstriped-suit sleeve slid up his forearm exposing a tree with burning branches.

Elasus watched Tayla glance at his son's forearm, then with surprising forwardness, she rebuked him. "Thank you, Ruven, but I've lived in Vegas for many years, and if I'm going to work for your dad, best not get mixed up in other family business."

Ruven jerked his hand away, preparing for his own reproach, when Elasus interjected.

"We're here for two reasons," explained Elasus, setting the tone. "First, I have an announcement regarding the Celje. Second, to show you all the danger mystics pose, not only to society but to our family."

Ruven eyeballed Tayla, then turned his attention to his father. "What's new with our personal *soldiers of fortune?*"

Elasus was pleased to see his son let the woman's jest go and focus on the business that followed.

"Your instructors at the academy provided me with reports of your successes in nearly every subject," said Elasus. "Now that you've graduated, it's time for your first assignment." Elasus ignored the imperceptible look from Commodus, to whom he'd not told this revelation. "As of tomorrow, you're the new planetary resource governor of Lent and commandant of the Celje training institute that's hidden on that planet."

Ruven inhaled sharply. "The PRG post? I suppose it's deserved. But the Celje? I thought that was Commodus's hobby?"

Elasus had not shared this news with his senior staff and caught the knowing eyes of Commodus and Tanner but ignored their concerns. "What you hear today never leaves this room, and this goes for you as well, Ms. Cruz." His leverage over the young woman was substantial enough that she'd do whatever he wanted, when he wanted it. "After the Elder Nine banished all mystics to Ojult, the PGU unwisely assumed the Elders would follow and govern the colony. As we're aware, the Elders haven't been seen in some time, and Ojult has become a haven for violence. Civil unrest on Ojult, or any other planet, hurts business and decreases profits, thus, in 2208, Scott Reeves, then CEO and owner of the Reeves Corporation, founded the Celje. They're a relatively small group of highly skilled soldiers, trained to fight mystics. The Celje operate in the shadows, not even the PGU know of their existence, and it must remain that way at all costs. Some are trained on Ojult, but the elite teams train on Lent."

"I'm heading to Lent tomorrow and can escort you there, Ruven," said Commodus. "I've been managing the Celje for several years; glad to finally pass the torch. You're inexperienced and young, and there's a lot to catch you up on, but the trip should give us enough time."

Elasus studied Tayla and Ruven, watching for any sign of dissent.

"The Celje ensure the mystics never organize into a body the PGU Defense Force can't handle," continued Elasus. "They also protect the nonmystics on Ojult, something I think you should take comfort in, Ms. Cruz."

"And I guess they keep a pretty close eye for staffs," added Ruven.

"Of course they do," said Commodus. "Those shamans get their hands on an Amurski staff and our agents are going to have their work cut out."

A brief silence fell on the room. "Ruven's business is settled then, so let's continue. Mr. Sands, I'd like Tayla and Ruven to see our detainee."

The group followed Tanner down the rest of the corridor, passing empty holding cells, until reaching the end of the hallway. This cell housed a young man, roughly Ruven's age, his face bruised and covered in dried blood. The mostly naked captive sat strapped to a metal chair, facing away from the door. Tanner unlocked the door and stepped inside.

Tayla gasped and moved back into Elasus who felt the woman's rear end against him.

"You asked earlier about my daughter," said Elasus, staring at the prisoner. "The man in there is Cadoc Alzer, and up until recently, he was dating Marilla. Once things started getting serious between them, I asked Mr. Sands to investigate the young man. Though it took some time, we've discovered Mr. Alzer is a mystic employed by a terrorist cell based in the FIAS region. It seems this mole was going to seduce my daughter in order to infiltrate the family. Evidence suggests he planned to assassinate me and perhaps my wife. When I tried explaining this to Marilla, she didn't believe me. We're trying to figure out if he was working alone, and in order to expose the other potential culprit, I told Marilla we executed Cadoc. Marilla made a scene, as we expected, and has not been seen since."

Inside the cell, what negligible light the room afforded reflected off Tanner's gelled hair. With a mastered hand, he slapped the prisoner across the face. "Wake up! Mr. Reeves is here to see you."

Elasus motioned for Tayla and Ruven to remain outside while he walked into the cell. "I'm glad to finally have the privilege of speaking with you in person, Mr. Alzer."

Cadoc's eyes altered from scared to calculating. The frail man lurched against his restraints, but the kurint chains kept him inert.

"Trying to use your powers? Right about now you're wondering why your attempts to break free aren't working."

Cadoc's glazed eyes looked murderously at his target. It was clear he was attempting to conjure something.

"I don't care about your little band of shamans in whatever no-name tribal village you come from," continued Elasus. "What I care about is your plan to kill a member of my family, my blood. What you need to know now is that I'm going to kill you, then have one of my officers air-drop your body onto whatever wasteland you're from."

By his frustrated look, Cadoc clearly expected something to happen.

Elasus smiled, enjoying the dominance over the helpless fool. "There will be a note attached to your corpse, threatening your entire village if any threats are made against my family again. If you had stolen from me or threatened one of my staff members, then perhaps a deal could have been worked out." Elasus walked behind the prisoner and whispered in his ear. "No one threatens my family, ever."

With a signal from his boss, Tanner grabbed an amber-glass liquid dropper from the nearby table. With gloved hands, he carefully unscrewed the top, pinching the rubber cap to fill the neck. Tanner yanked the man's head sideways and placed three drops down his ear canal. Cadoc began choking and thrashing against his restraints until an emptiness overtook his eyes and he slouched forward. The mystic assassin was dead.

"The poison was made from the veleno plant," said Tanner. "It's native to Ojult and highly toxic. One drop paralyzes you, two stop brain function, three suffocate you. The eustachian canal connects the ear, nose, and throat. Placing the drops down the ear canal accelerates the poison, making it impossible to trace. This *shaman* can't heal because those chains are made from African Ore."

Elasus exited the room in time to see Tayla sprint toward the hallway trash can and vomit. He gave her time to gather herself before continuing.

"Ms. Cruz, I run a tight ship and demand the utmost out of my employees. Mr. Sands is going to take you upstairs, debrief you, and get your final word as to whether or not you'd like to accept the position."

Tayla's ghostly face peeked out of the trash can. "My apologies. Mr. Reeves, I... wasn't expecting that. I'm prepared to do whatever's necessary."

Elasus watched Tayla follow Tanner around the corner, paying special attention to his future assistant's hindquarters. Once the elevator chimed shut, he turned to Ruven. "As both the PRG of Lent and the Celje commandant, you'll be pulled in many directions."

"I can handle it, Father. I'm ready. These *shamans* want a fight, we'll give it to them." There was a yearning in Ruven's voice.

Elasus turned and peered at his victim's limp body. "Ruven, I wouldn't have assigned this to you if I didn't have full confidence in you. War is bad for business, remember this. We need to speak about the management of the Celje before you leave."

Ruven slumped against the cell's reinforced plexiglass window. "If I'm about to get the speech about the Elders, save it. I don't believe in them."

"As the leader of the Celje, you'll believe what I tell you. The purpose of the Celje is to maintain order, not prance around like an army. You'll keep the numbers small, their existence a secret. Few know they exist, even less know their specific purpose. The corporation employs officers on Ojult, let them handle the details while you maintain the larger picture. Whether you believe in the Elder Nine or not, our job is to protect the corporation and ensure mankind's existence. Am I clear?"

"Sure, Father."

Elasus nodded. "Good. Chat with Tanner when he's finished with the girl and dispose of that body before it starts to smell. I want it dropped in the center of wherever this trash came from."

CHAPTER 5: YEAR 2389

The sunrise reflected through the aircraft's tinted window, momentarily concealing the rows of decontamination equipment blotching the toxic earth below. They were over Florida now, its terrain littered with small craters containing the Kupita virus and exploding hydrogen bubbles. Since the Event, food supplies were a constant worry among Earth's regional authorities, and given Florida's climate, the region was the perfect place to invest if the meteorites could be removed.

Over the past decade, Elasus sent cleanup crews to the Florida region, each as unsuccessful as the next. Eleven of sixteen crews were dead or unavailable, with the corporation's last crew withdrawing the week prior because of numerous hydrogen pockets erupting, causing a severe oxygen deficiency in the area.

"I'm talking about *our* daughter, Elasus. Your own flesh and blood. At least look at me!" Irelyn was red from yelling, her normally glamorous face retreating behind the crazed mask.

Elasus sipped his coffee, noticing the distinct flavor that only Ojultan beans emanated. Agriculture was a small but growing piece of Ojult's export business compared to the highly sought after Listo brandy. Ojult could not support the food requirements of Earth, its soil not capable of yielding the volume required, but perhaps another off-world planet could. "Marilla didn't tell me where she was going," he said.

Irelyn's red sundress threatened to fall off her shoulders. "That's it!?

That's all you have to say? You have spies and access to everyone, everywhere, and you're simply giving up?"

Elasus continued thinking about the commodities venture. Lent was a small planet with excessively fertile soil. It was also starting to become a hub for the corporation's pilots to fix their ships. "I won't assign resources to a task that will neither make money nor lead to the betterment of my organization or family."

His new secretary walked down the cabin aisle with a slight swagger.

"Who the hell is this?" said Irelyn, scanning the professionally dressed woman.

Elasus said nothing, opting for Tayla to address the situation.

Tayla walked up to Elasus and handed him a black folder before addressing Irelyn. "Mrs. Reeves, good morning. My name is Tayla Cruz. Mr. Reeves hired me last week as his personal assistant. I've been working on a brief for Mr. Reeves this morning. May I get you something to drink?"

Irelyn looked the assistant up and down. "Tayla, are you aware that our daughter is missing?"

The plane hit light turbulence, nearly forcing Tayla into Elasus's lap. "Pardon me, Mr. Reeves," she said, holding on to the seat for leverage. "Mrs. Reeves, I'm aware of your family's situation. I worked with Commodus Vrabel over the weekend to locate Marilla. Our most likely guess is that she's retreated to the FIAS region. The Free and Independent African States are known to be sympathetic to the mystics, and given your daughter's tendencies, it seems the most logical place."

Irelyn looked from Tayla back to Elasus. "Then… then call Drohar. He's still the governor? Have him start searching!"

Elasus signed the medical affidavit and power-of-attorney forms and handed them back to Tayla. Steam from his cup wafted in front of the holographic projection where a report showed what he already knew—Florida, as with most of the southeast region, was uninhabitable.

"You want me to contact the current FIAS regional governor who publicly announced that he believes we recently assassinated his defense minister? You believe this man will be motivated to help me on a personal matter? No, dear wife, I will not stoop to that level of idiocy. Now, if you'll excuse me, Commodus and the others are waiting for me in the conference room."

The Falcon 13z jet was the top of the line of corporate travel and, in contrast to everything surrounding Elasus, was not built by the Reeves Corporation. With one engine over each wing, plus another in the rear, the range of the Falcon was never in question. The aircraft's main fuselage contained a full-size bedroom and bath, a conference room, first-class seating for up to thirteen people, and a full bar with accompanying bartender. Elasus invited Tayla to sit in on the meeting, taking roll call as the holographic display projected three people around the table. Their names and positions sat below their virtual self: Sasha Burmistrov, Ojult Celje Leader; followed by Misora Souji, Deputy Celje Commander; Commodus Vrabel, COO; and Nikoli Sokolov, Celje Lieutenant.

Around Elasus sat Rico Crouse and Tanner Sands, each with virtual notepads projecting in front of them. This was the corporation's standard weekly meeting on Ojult, and it started like all the others, each man giving an update on their situation as it pertained to Ojult. Elasus listened intently as his senior officers stated problems, resolutions, and statuses of various projects pertaining to cash-flow-positive colonies. A little over the two-hour mark, Commodus Vrabel wrapped up the last of the updates.

Commodus was enroute to Lent with Ruven Reeves, thus his picture flickered in and out of focus. "Mr. Reeves, that about wraps up the agenda. We've got a lot of work ahead, but we're moving forward and making progress."

Elasus waved his hand across his display, scrolling through pages of dictated notes. "A couple announcements, gentlemen. First, my son will be Lent's new PRG and commandant of the Celje. He's with Commodus on his way to Lent. Sasha, what's the size and state of the Celje on Ojult?"

The older man in his mid-fifties looked tired, his appearance exacerbated by his receding hairline and unkempt beard. "Funny that our confidential killing squad has their training base on a planet named by a former Catholic priest during the weekend of Easter, is it not?" Sasha was from Russia, and his thick accent sometimes made it difficult for others to understand him.

Misora and Nikoli laughed.

Elasus crossed his arms and even his digital representation showcased his annoyance. "The Celje aren't assassins, and you're not dealing with gods, you're dealing with mystics."

Sasha sat back in his chair. "We have roughly one hundred and twenty-five operational agents, and as you said, all undercover with most of the population unaware. Regarding the mystics, they number less than a few hundred and are unorganized. They clash with one another constantly but stay mostly on the continent of Listo."

Elasus scrolled down Ojult's recent financial statement. "Top domestic products and services on Ojult are, in order of value, Ojultan ore, prostitution, Listo brandy and other alcohol, drugs, water, food, and various agriculture. I've also heard of an underground slave trade, Sasha, what of it?"

"That's on Meridone," said Nikoli.

Elasus looked over at the screen picturing the dark-haired man. He didn't much care for Nikoli, his small eyes, chevron mustache, and egocentric grin giving the impression that everything he said was a lie. He was Sasha's cousin, however, and that meant something.

Elasus contemplated the three continents of Ojult. "You govern Meridone, Nikoli, so tell me why slave trade only exists on your continent?"

But Sasha spoke in place of the sometimes dull-minded leader. "It's been taken care of, Mr. Reeves. A young woman who runs a logistics company called Appian Shipping got wind of the underground operation between Listo and Capintesta. She's got some muscle and put an end to it, then a couple idiots tried restarting it in Meridone, but like I said, we handled it."

"I'm less interested in the moral aspect of the deal than the financial piece," replied Elasus. "If the Reeves Corporation doesn't make money off the transaction, then it doesn't happen." He paused, letting the silence further his point. "The woman running Appian Shipping is Nencia Donato; make sure you keep peace with her. She's a middleman in most cases, but it prevents us from having to worry about logistics on Ojult."

Static flickered across the virtual projections. "Asteroid interference again," complained Sasha, hitting the display. "Lots of asteroids around Ojult, Mr. Reeves. They keep knocking out your satellites."

The stream adjusted and went back to normal. Elasus stood, the camera following his movement. "Our connection won't last much longer, gentlemen, so let me conclude with this. My daughter is missing. This isn't so much a family issue as it is a security matter. Mr. Sands will fill you in on the rest."

Tanner Sands tapped his virtual keyboard in front of him. "Understand the information I'm uploading to you is confidential." Two pictures emerged on everyone's screen. "These images indicate that Marilla Reeves smuggled herself through port security in Las Vegas, traveled to Texas, and likely boarded a vessel heading to Ojult. She has a history of showing sympathy toward mystics, and we believe she's heading to Ojult. Sasha, you and the rest of the Celje will keep an eye out for her and alert us if she's spotted. Any questions?"

Commodus leaned in toward the camera. "How long have you had this information, and why wasn't this shared beforehand?"

Rico Crouse joined the rebuke. "I agree! We could have manipulated all launch-station surveillance systems to look for her, but if she's left, we don't have that type of technology off-world. She's obviously deactivated her FOCC, so we need all the human intel we can get. Why compartmentalize this information, Tanner?"

"What's done is done," said Elasus. "You have the information, now use it. This meeting has gone on long enough. We'll connect again next week."

CHAPTER 6: YEAR 2389

Ojult was neither beautiful, temperate, peaceful, nor a vacation spot for the wealthy. One-third of the planet was missing, full of jagged cliffs, endless caves, and void of life. In the habitable zones, clay made up much of the soil composition, and when added to the temperamental climate, made farming tricky. Mystifying animals and aquatic life peppered the broken planet. News of outlandish wildlife brought sport hunters from Earth, though many found the vicious creatures too much and never returned to their blue planet. Sea creatures and other marine life across the Altum Sea were rarely seen, resulting in claims the massive saltwater sea could not support living organisms.

Ojult revolved around its only sun every 328 days and spun upon its axis every twenty-one hours. Orbiting satellites controlled by the Reeves corporation dotted the sky but were most often seen burning up in the atmosphere after crashing into errant asteroids littering the space around the planet.

Life on Ojult was difficult, dangerous, and often fatal. Living on the planet wasn't impossible with off-world trade and bartering between the continents using tonze as the primary currency. Tonze was a low-grade ore mined on Ojult; its poor quality made it unsuitable for crafting, so the original exiles used it as currency.

As a sixth-generation Ojultan, Markus Fonte knew the intricacies of the planet well. He was the town steward of Dalth, located in the middle of Capintesta. A religious man and single parent, many revered him for the trials he'd overcome.

"Daddy, are you still praying?" asked his preteen daughter, Bélise.

The immediate prairie outside their small abode was empty minus a fenced-in cemetery. Kneeling, Markus stared at the marker covering his wife's burial site. The slab was made of Ojultan ore, a poor substitute for the gravestone she deserved, and already showing signs of erosion. There was an imprint of his wife's hand on the stone, followed by her name, *Bianca Fonte*. She died giving birth to Bélise, leaving the strong-willed leader to bring up a daughter on an unforgiving planet.

Markus's ancestry blended Native American, South American, and Italian into one thinning, silver-haired, fifty-year-old man with glasses and drooping eyelids. It was the anniversary of Bianca's death and the pain still pierced his broken heart.

Bélise wrapped her slender arms around Markus's forearm. "Daddy, Mommy sees us, right? How come we can't see her?"

Markus looked at his daughter, a spitting image of her mother. "I think so, yes." A rooster crowed, the second one in as many minutes as the sun edged over the tall tree line to the east.

"Come on, Daddy, can we please have breakfast with Uncle Kun?" begged Bélise, tugging on her father's arm. "Remember, we didn't have dinner last night and I'm starving."

Markus put two fingers to his lips, then pressed them to the grave.

Markus plucked the petite girl off the ground, placing her carefully on his neck. He'd pay for it in the morning, but hearing Bélise's belly laugh as she played with his hair was worth it.

Dalth was a small town located in the central-east region of Capintesta, earning a reputation for being removed from the daily violence that blanketed the southernmost continent. Kun Nguyen, or Uncle Kun to the kids, owned Dalth's only pub. During the day, the small pub served breakfast and lunch, consisting of whatever ingredients were available from the week's trade. At night, it turned into the town's watering hole and perhaps some gambling, though never prostitution. If people wanted that sort of thing, they could wander up north to Worall or Pa'Gran.

Markus's farm rested on the far west side of the town, making the trek to the centrally located pub about twenty minutes. When they arrived, Bélise begged Uncle Kun for his famous pancakes.

"Yes, yes," said Kun with a heavy Japanese accent. "How can I say no to my most favorite customer? But today will be the last day of pancakes until I get more supplies from Appian."

Kun was a tired-looking man with wavy hair who was rarely seen without his stained cooking apron. His wife, Liao, wore her hair up in a ponytail and had sweat dripping off her forehead as she tended to customers, cleaned dishes, and manned the bar.

"Hello, Mayor," said Liao. "The usual?"

Markus embraced his longtime friend. "Good morning. Yes, kaldi, please, and water for Bélise. I'm guessing Appian hasn't shown yet?"

Liao poured a steaming cup of kaldi into a chipped mug. Kaldi was an earthy drink with caffeine and a cherry aftertaste. "Here you go. No, Appian hasn't shown up. The list I gave Zakar last time said specifically when we'd need these supplies. Then I ran into Celine last night. She's used our last vial of hovrol on little Diego; he came down with a fever. She's having to use bourbon as an antiseptic and reusing the few syringes we have, it's a mess. I know Celine isn't going to complain, but food storages are running low, medical supplies are out, and the harvest is months away. We're not in good shape."

Markus knew everyone's backstory in Dalth—why they were exiled, their family, kids, and what skills they could put to use. Kun and Liao Nguyen were nice, hard-working people, but they hadn't confided in him why they were exiled almost a decade ago.

"Dalth always finds a way, and Nencia's never failed us. But I understand your concern, and if Appian hasn't shown by tomorrow, I'll head to Worall. We've rationed food before, and the people are ready to do it again if needed."

His comforting assurances calmed Liao who bent down and kissed him on the cheek. "Thank you. You've always taken great care of us."

Kun flashed a currish glance at his wife before returning to the stove. Surely a meaningless gesture like a kiss on the cheek wouldn't set him off, Markus figured.

Soon the kitchen master delivered three fist-sized pancakes as promised, earning Bélise's widest smile in days.

Markus quizzed her over various math problems during breakfast as he did most mornings before school. Celine Dubois worked as both the town's nurse and teacher, but the kids needed more schooling than what she could offer alone. When Bélise aced all his questions, Markus couldn't help but feel proud of his young daughter.

"You're just like your mother, bright, pretty, and full of hope." As a single parent, Markus constantly checked himself before becoming too overbearing or too strict. But life on Ojult was hard, and to survive, you needed more than just book smarts.

Markus changed into his work clothes after seeing Bélise off to school and headed toward his field. He'd planted his winter wheat a few weeks ago and prayed constantly for a successful harvest. When the harvest came, Markus would barter with his own townsman first before selling off the rest to Appian. If enough money and help ever came to the town, Markus planned on growing kaldi beans and tobacco, primarily to sell off-world via Appian Shipping. For whatever reason, the high-class executives on Earth liked off-planet commodities and paid a premium for them.

Markus walked the peaceful field, looking for signs of disease and pulling finger-sized, transparent toso-worms off tiny stems peeking through the dry soil. The tranquil silence was broken when several horse-drawn wagons rolled down the rocky north road. Dalth was several hours from the nearest town and rarely received visitors. Markus pushed his glasses up and focused.

"Nencia, Zakar, good seeing you," greeted Markus, welcoming his old friends into his small home. "Please, have a seat." A worn couch and table decked the tiny living space inside Markus's home.

Nencia accepted Markus's hug and made herself at home. The man accompanying her was Zakar Qualis, the unofficial number-two man at Appian. On the outside, Zakar put on the facade of a brutal, uncaring authoritarian, but Markus knew the Englishman better than anyone on the planet.

"I need to help Aldrich unload the supplies," said Zakar. "But first, I've got a gift for you."

Nencia snorted. "Between old man Aldrich and your tubby butt, Zakar, I'm probably going to be visiting both of you in the clinic. Get some of the younger guys to help before you break your back."

Markus ignored the remark and accepted the box. "Ah, Zakar, thank you." Markus slid the box halfway open. "Listo brandy. I'm almost out of the last bottle you gave me. Great timing, my friend. I'm sorry I have nothing for you."

Zakar shook his head and walked to the door. "I owe you many things, and this is a small token of my thanks. Boss, I'll be in town if you need me."

Zakar shut the screen door behind him and Nencia turned toward her longstanding ally.

"You look tired, Markus, and where's that little girl of yours?"

Markus headed into the kitchen, pouring two glasses of brandy. "Bélise's at school, though when she sees Zakar, she'll probably tackle him and try to help unload supplies."

"Thank you," said Nencia, taking a sample of the expensive brandy. "I'm afraid I'm not just here to deliver supplies."

"Okay. I'll do my best to help you out."

"I appreciate it, but it's not like that. You know the kind of business I run and the network I must keep happy."

Markus's gut told him this conversation wasn't going to be as simple as he first thought. "Of course, and while I don't like the Celje, the Reeves Corporation, or the PGU, I appreciate your position."

She finished the remaining bourbon in one shot and declined his refill. "Unlike most people on this junk planet, you know about the Celje, so I'll keep this brief. Things are heating up between the Nein and the Celje. One of Sasha's goons, Misora, came into the warehouse yesterday and suggested I was providing weapons and ammunition to the mystics. After I threatened to hang him by his testicles, he left, and I contacted a friend of mine who confirmed that buffoon's story. You know me, I play a neutral game here, and I'm not the one selling this crap to the Nein."

"I know Sasha and Misora, but I'm not following you. Have I done something to offend one of these groups?"

Nencia frowned. "You know I have spies everywhere, including Dalth. I know you have mystic friends, and the Visconti family has a reputation."

"I try to befriend as many people who share the same principles as I do, and that sometimes rubs people the wrong way. Perhaps some people might react negatively if they knew how much I value your friendship, but nevertheless, I consider you a close confidant and wouldn't lie to you."

Nencia wasn't buying it. "I believe that someone in Dalth is smuggling guns and ammunition to the mystics. That's why I'm here. I need to know what you know about this."

Arcane attacks by mystics were largely confined to the Nein who carried guns and melee weapons like everyone else. "Appian, the mystics, the Celje, the Reeves Corporation are all playing a ruthless game of chess here. I don't play favorites in this game, Nencia, and I keep Dalth out of their line of sight on purpose. So, to be frank, I have no clue what you're talking about, and Dalth is small enough to where I think I'd know if something like that was going on."

Nencia nodded. "The Celje aren't stupid and they can be sneaky bastards. If they find out who it is, they'll hang 'em and burn down the whole town. Markus, I believe you, but if someone in Dalth is responsible, you need to take care of it immediately."

Nencia was only doing what she was obligated to do, and Markus held nothing against her for it. "I know of no one dealing in that sort of thing in Dalth."

Nencia's expression turned brighter. "You're a good man; an uncommon trait on this planet. For your sake, I hope you're telling the truth. Take a look here. I was able to snag a box of hovrol and a few other goods off the Celje last week. Most of it went to an orphanage I'm trying to put together in Pa'Gran, but I saved you a box. Zakar knows to give it to Celine."

Part of the tension building within Markus eased. "Thank you. We ran out a few days ago when one of the children got sick. I know you keep strange company, but God has sent you to this planet for a reason."

"Ha. Markus, if God has seen half of what I've done, he's already bought me and my crew a first-class ticket to hell." She put her empty glass on the counter. "I'm going to check up on Zakar, then head to your pub. Meet me there and I'll buy you a drink."

Markus opted not to join Nencia and everyone else at the pub that evening, choosing instead to read through his bible and pray for guidance. The familiar giggle of a young girl around dinnertime brought a smile to the proud father.

"How's my little girl?" said Markus, greeting Bélise and her guard.

Bélise ran full speed into him. "Hi, Daddy! Look what Aunt Serena gave me. Ham sandwich! You want some?" Bélise darted toward the kitchen.

"Hey there, Mayor," said Serena Visconti, walking in behind Bélise. The only child of the Visconti family was covered in black grime and dust. Markus wasn't an elected official and by no means political, but people often called him *mayor*.

"Been helping your parents at the mill, I see," he replied.

Serena, at fifteen years old, was the daughter of Marco and Erika Visconti. Her parents got into trouble with the PGU and were exiled to Ojult a few years back. "Yes, sir. Dad's been running the forge day and night for the past couple weeks. He's got Mom and me helping, and even Bélise pitched in."

"Thank you for seeing her home safely. Tell your mom and dad I said hello." Then something dawned on him. "Serena, have you eaten?"

"No, sir, not today, but that's okay. Dad has no money right now, and the pub only has beer. I heard people from Appian showed up today, so we'll eat tomorrow. I gotta run, Mayor. Thanks!"

Markus watched the young girl rush off into the dimming evening, then turned his attention to Bélise. After brushing the bread and ham out of her teeth with baking soda and boiled water, he lit a small candle in her room, then knelt beside her bed. They prayed together to a God that continually provided obstacles for their survival, but Markus's faith was an integral part of his life, a fuel for his psyche that fostered his ability to raise a daughter by himself and manage a town full of criminals and innocents alike.

CHAPTER 7: YEAR 2389

Syrus Tokarek walked around the city of Carendra, glimpsing his Nein mystics, working hard to keep the town functioning. Syrus was tall, broad, and dark-skinned, with a deep voice to match his authoritative position. Even in cooler weather, like today, Syrus went shirtless, wearing only loose-fitting black pants, leather sandals, and a large sheathed Amurski staff across his back.

The Nein and their slaves bowed to their liege as he passed, not daring to speak or make eye contact. Syrus demanded this type of respect but often wondered if his people revered him out of respect or out of fear for the weapon he carried. The prolific mystic weapon came from the Amurski tree that grew on Meridone and Africa back on Earth.

Despite the hundreds of mystics shipped to Ojult each month, very few survived their first few months on the hostile planet. No formal sect of Nein or Argos existed on the northernmost continent of Listo, or anywhere on Ojult. Syrus's goal during his reign was not domination but survival. Congregating in the small tent village of Carendra, the few dozen mystics lived under his rule, following the old Nein ways.

The Nein believed their powers came from a higher being for the betterment of mankind. They were not meant to hold back or rule in a gentle manner. The Nein of old took what they wanted at the expense of lesser beings. Perceiving themselves as the next stage in mankind's evolution, their power was all the authority they needed to plow over the Thoba.

Only two groups ever stood in the Nein's way. The Elders and Argos were formidable adversaries during the mystic civil wars, but their presence no longer concerned Syrus. The Elders had not been seen in some time and the Argos were nothing more than a footnote in today's world. Today, the Nein fought against a new modern enemy, the obscure Celje.

Syrus's Nein did not seek violence but often fought against the Celje and other mystics who followed a warped ideology seeking revenge against the Nein, whom they blamed for their exile.

The cool weather and strong westerly winds brought dark clouds over the morning horizon. This was common weather, even during the fall.

"Premier," said a deep Irish accent from behind. "Good morning."

Syrus continued walking, already aware of Giles Murphy and Kavil Siller following him.

"Why are two members of my senior council stalking me this morning?" said Syrus.

Both men followed in behind their liege. "My premier," continued Giles, "we have re—"

"I'm the guard captain," interrupted Kavil Siller. "I'll make the report. Premier Tokarek, my scouts report a small band of mystics approaching Carendra from the south, most likely coming from Port Naok."

Syrus stopped, angling his head just enough to see his advisors. "You're implying that Levi's coming to visit?"

"Undoubtedly," replied Siller. "Shall I order my men to intercept them and put an end to this constant bickering between the Capintesta Nein and our own?"

"Alternatively, I volunteer to greet him personally and escort him to town," suggested Giles. "After all, you and your sister were once the deepest of friends with Levi Anjou."

Giles was the more moderate of his two advisors, with curly hair, buckteeth, and a chubby nose. Siller, on the other hand, was in constant need of battle to satisfy his appetite for violence. Though a ruthless killer in combat, Siller's short stature, patchy beard, and balding scalp intimidated no one.

Syrus was in front of a small lake on the northern side of Carendra, a tranquil spot his sister frequented when needing a moment away from her young daughter. The cool, soft dirt settled between his toes and reminded him of Mea who frequently played in the sand near the water.

"There are too few of us left to shed blood, and Levi's dreams of unity against the Celje will only reduce our numbers further." Syrus sighed, regretting the dissolved friendship. "Giles, escort him to the courtyard; I'll meet him there."

Syrus continued his walk, indifferent to his advisor's guidance on the matter. He rounded the lake and started back toward his pavilion, the upcoming meeting with Levi burdening his conscience.

In front of his dwelling, Syrus looked upon his strikingly beautiful sister. Her soft features would tame the most ferocious sarcto, while her long black hair swayed low enough for her daughter to play with. Her clothes were knitted by slaves using only the finest fabrics Ojult could supply. Standing with perfect posture, she donned an informal blue-and-gray dress.

"Hello, Helia," said Syrus, ignoring the bleeding slave kneeling next to her.

Helia Tokarek didn't return her brother's blissful greeting. "Do you see this?" she exclaimed. "Your filthy radicals beat this boy as soon as he got here. He volunteered to be here Syrus!"

Syrus stepped toward a drinking bowl and sipped from the ladle. "My men may do as they please to Thoba; you know this." He looked down at the teenager. "Leave us, boy. I have something I need to discuss with my sister."

"He's hurt badly Syrus, he needs healing not forced labor."

Syrus pushed the teenager over with his foot. "What's your name, boy?"

The teenager coughed blood all over the parched dirt. "J... Jayden Va... Vaut."

"Well, Jayden, we've buried thousands of slaves like you, and I suspect you'll be another unmarked grave soon enough. Now leave before I make that decision for you."

"Three... three against one, and they attacked from behind, brave... real brave."

The kid had more vigor in him than Syrus expected. Still, he back-handed the boy. "You're a slave and will not speak without permission."

Helia jumped between Syrus and Jayden. "My god, Syrus, what's gotten into you? Where's he supposed to go?"

"Dismiss him, Helia. We need to speak. Levi's on his way."

Helia's poise ebbed as she edged closer, gripping Syrus's arm. "Is he alone?"

"No." Syrus was satisfied his sister was comprehending the situation.

Helia released him and opened the door to the nearby stone home. "Mea, come here." Moments later, Helia's daughter peeked out.

"Mother! My powers, I think they're—"

"Mea, I need your help. Please take Jayden here and get him cleaned up. He's got the rest of the day off. See him back to the slave quarters after you're done. You can use my sink if the slave quarters are full, but make sure Brady's with you."

"My niece won't be tending to any slave while I'm alive," barked Syrus. "If you—"

"This boy was playing with Mea before your thugs clubbed him from behind. If he wanted to hurt her, he'd have already done it. Now, Mea, do as I say."

Shifting gravel behind Syrus gave way to an alarmed Irish accent. "Premier," said Giles, "Levi and his cohort are awaiting you in the courtyard."

Syrus turned and read the expression on Giles's flushed face. "What is it?"

Giles bowed. "I escorted Levi and his cohort as requested, but I don't think Levi's here just to talk. I believe Captain Siller may have been right."

"Was there a battle. Is everyone okay? Was Levi hurt?" asked Helia.

Syrus's eyes fell upon his sister. "I'm not sure Levi's well-being is our primary concern. Giles, do nothing to provoke them. I'll be there shortly. Helia, stay home. Levi seems to get anxious around you, and that's not something we need right now."

Syrus didn't bother changing into his armor and instead loosened the straps around his staff. Taunts were already being exchanged between the two mystic sects when Syrus arrived. He knew Levi well, and seeing his former friend dressed in full battle armor with staff already unsheathed wasn't a good sign. Levi had been born in London, England, the only country in the Western European theater that didn't join the Incorporated European Syndicate (IES). The reasons behind his exile were a mystery, but he was raised among the mystics on Ojult. He had dark, tousled hair and a tangled beard.

"Quiet," ordered Levi, taking a few steps toward Syrus. "The almighty Syrus Tokarek has finally blessed us with his presence."

Syrus ignored the condescending remarks. "You're troubled more than usual, Levi. Let's speak in private, away from the provoking voices of our fellows."

Levi slammed the butt of his staff on the ground, causing a small ripple of energy. "Enough of this. The time has come to bring our tribes together. The Celje assassinate our brothers and sisters while you keep the power of your people locked up in this pathetic village. Join me!"

Syrus kept his staff sheathed. "You've come knocking on the wrong door if you're seeking an ally for such a foolish venture. Our numbers, even combined, are too small to stand against the Celje. Come, Levi, let's talk in private."

Syrus caught the change in Levi's stance moments before a fire-engulfed sphere launched from Levi's staff. Syrus sidestepped the warning shot and again kept his own staff sheathed.

Levi adjusted his posture, readying himself for a counterattack. "You sit quietly while your own die at the hands of outsiders. You sit behind your wall of soldiers while others, real Nein, continue the fight our ancestors started."

Syrus circled Levi. "Levi, my old friend, the Nein's glory died long ago when the Argos and Elders butchered our sect. The Celje are incognito and outnumber us six to one. They're organized and well trained. No, I'd admire your courage, brother, but our goal now is survival and rebuilding."

"Please, listen to Syrus," said Helia, walking through the ring of armed guards. "Settle this with words, not bloodshed."

Syrus watched in apprehension as his sister attempted to calm their old acquaintance. For a brief, hopeful moment, Levi lowered his staff, pointing the weapon away from Helia.

"Helia," replied Levi in a soft, controlled manner. "It's... it's good to see you. But... you need to leave. I can't allow your brother to continue this division."

Syrus sensed the amplified tension growing within Levi. "Helia, step away." His voice carried the severity of his concern, and Helia stepped back, keeping a heavy gaze upon Levi.

Three rows of thin flames jetted out from Levi's staff. Syrus rolled out of the way, his own staff now in hand. Giles grabbed Helia and rushed her away. Levi's hatred toward Syrus was pure, but he'd never allow harm to come to Helia. With his sister safe, Syrus put his full attention on his opponent. Two fire-spheres shot toward Syrus, but he sidestepped the first and used his staff to bat away the second.

Syrus took two long strides toward Levi before slamming the butt of his staff on the ground, letting lose a cataclysmic energy wave that sent Levi somersaulting backward. Syrus launched himself into the air, intent on ending the fight, but Levi regained his footing in time to raise his own staff, and the two weapons clashed. Erratic strikes, parries, and combos were unleashed, sending smoldering sparks flying as if their staffs were made of metal.

A dozen meters away, another fight simmered between Siller and Levi's own guard captain, Jenna Dimare.

"Step down, Kavil!" yelled Syrus after connecting a well-timed knee to Levi's stomach. "Don't escalate this!"

Levi's staff blocked Syrus's at its base, giving way to a bone-snapping counterstrike that fractured Syrus's forearm and sent his staff tumbling away. Syrus spun and threw out a veiled side kick that caught Levi in the chest. Ignoring the pain, Syrus lunged toward Levi with a conjured ice spike protruding from his good hand. He plunged the dagger into Levi's shoulder.

"This insanity is over, Levi," Syrus said, telekinetically calling his staff to his uninjured hand. "You've lost… again. Order your people to back down."

Levi yanked the spike out of his shoulder, tossing the melting projectile to the ground. "You… should have killed me, Syrus. Take my people, conquer the Celje, take Ojult for your own."

Syrus sheathed his staff and knelt in front of his former friend. "Someone could have died here, Levi. Our people killed, for what? Our two orders have different ideologies, unity is not the answer. It may come, or it may never, but now is not the time. Take your men, go back to Capintesta, call off whatever attack you've planned on the Celje before it's too late!"

Levi's hardened face mellowed. "If we don't act now the Celje will grow too strong, we won't survive. Initiate my guard captain Jenna into your forces, take the fight to them."

Syrus still felt a tingle of danger, though the battle was over. "I know you care for our people, Levi. Don't let that passion die here. You've got to see the bigger picture and—"

Precognition, clairvoyance, perhaps just intuition. Few mystics possessed the natural talent, but the feeling was unmistakable. Both mystic leaders paused as the sensation rolled through their senses.

Behind Syrus, a woman's blood-curdling scream tore through the crowd.

"Helia!" shouted both men. They sprinted toward Syrus's home, their bleeding appendages leaving a grimy red trail. Syrus, followed by Levi and dozens of armed mystics, burst through the door.

Syrus surveyed the living room, ready to massacre any threat to his sister. On the far side of the tent, near Syrus's bed, Helia sheltered Mea. A few feet from them lay Giles, facedown with only a faint hint of life. Beside him, two dead Nein guards lay atop one another with burn marks across their cheeks and throat. On the opposite side of the room, an unconscious stranger and teenager were propped upright against the wall, both bleeding profusely.

Syrus went to his sister's side while Levi knelt next to the unconscious man. "Syrus," said Levi, "I know this man. He's… one of mine."

A quiet rage formed within Syrus. "A lesser man than me would have you executed, Levi. Explain yourself."

Helia intervened. "He said you both were weak, that the only way to unite was by forcing your hand, Syrus. He wasn't acting on Levi's orders."

"Is this man… is he Mea's…?"

"Of course not!"

Levi touched the renegade soldier's hemorrhaging neck, checking for a pulse. "His name is Genest, one of my aides. He's been with me for years. He's alive, only just. Why… why would he?"

Syrus's broken forearm was beginning to throb, but it paled in comparison to his blistering rage. An uncontrolled part of him wanted to slay Levi, but the logical side of his mind knew his former friend had nothing to do with this. Syrus stepped away and rolled the motionless teenager over, recognizing him from their earlier encounter.

Helia pulled Mea closer. "His name is Jayden Vaut, he's the slave you backhanded earlier."

"This boy fought Genest? Managed to get a knife into him?" Levi was taken aback.

Helia nodded. "Jayden and Mea were on the other side of the room when that man barged in. Your aide took the guards by surprise, killed them, then bounded toward us. The boy grabbed a knife from one of the dead guards and leapt onto him when he was on top of me. Syrus, please, help him. He's not going to make it if you don't. He saved our lives."

Syrus considered the circumstances. "This ordinary boy, with no power, and a slave to my people, guarded you when I did not," said Syrus.

Faint, whistling pops came from three stabs wounds across the boy's chest.

"Please, Brother. Please, save him," pleaded Helia.

"Uncle, please, he's my friend," Mea said.

Mea's innocent plea tore through Syrus's mental armor. He looked over to Levi who held the attacker's knife. He didn't think Levi would attack, but the day had been full of surprises already.

The scenario resolved itself when Levi slit his traitorous man's throat. More blood leaked from the severed artery onto the floor. Levi knelt and whispered into Genest's ear. "I hope you're still alive and feeling the life leave your worthless body. I will find your family, your children, everyone you've ever loved, and they will suffer for what you've done here."

Syrus was glad Helia and Mea didn't hear Levi's last rites to the dying assassin. Syrus knelt over the teenager and placed a hand over his chest, closed his eyes, and introspectively commanded the cells in Jayden's body to mend. A purple aura escaped Syrus's palm, and the boy's wounds began to scab over. Blood stopped flooding Jayden's chest and the hissing from his punctured lung sealed. The medicinal trance lasted until the boy's eyes opened.

"Say nothing, boy," ordered Syrus. "You sacrificed yourself to save my sister, now I've saved your life. The customs of my people prevent slaves from that honor, but, if you live through this, you'll have a place with my people." Syrus rose, ready to move on. "Levi, take your troop, leave, and never return. I don't believe you would have killed me today, which is why you still stand. But listen closely, my Nein brother, because I'll not grant a second chance. Never show your face on Listo again unless I send for you."

Levi looked to Helia, then Mea, then rested on Syrus. "I'm defeated. I know it, but I don't need a lecture. Seeing my defeat, my followers will leave me, perhaps some may choose to join you. But I understand, and you'll not see me again."

Syrus watched as Levi bowed respectfully, not toward him but to Helia. "I'm sorry for all this. It wasn't supposed to happen this way."

PART II

Ten Years Later

CHAPTER 8: YEAR 2399

Inside the recently built stone structure, the Ojult Celje leader, Sasha Burmistrov, warmed his frigid body around a crackling firepit. Smoke plumes withdrew upward via a ventilation system built by a recently exiled engineer to whom Sasha pressed into service. Most in Limeth were either Celje or pressed exiles working for them. Sasha chose Limeth as their de facto headquarters on the continent of Lent because of its approximation to Carendra, a well-known mystic town.

Today, Sasha gathered his senior advisors to discuss the increased mystic activity on the continent. Attending this meeting were Kain, Merle, and Waylin, all dependable and loyal members of Sasha's inner circle. The fourth man, sitting opposite Sasha, was Misora Souji, deputy commander of the Celje forces. Misora was tall, with thin eyes, burnished-gold stud earrings, and constantly worried about his appearance, which conflicted with the Celje ideology of staying incognito and blending in with the rest of the exiles.

"The mystics are a joke these days," said Misora. "It's been a decade since Levi and Syrus tried to ally, and it didn't work out well, did it? The idea of it, especially now, is absurd. It's time to relax."

Sasha looked at his cohort, who had adorned himself with sunglasses atop his abnormally stylish hair. "You believe we should… relax? Perhaps you have already started this since you look like you just got out of a salon." Sasha's heavy accent was even more difficult to understand since he'd been drinking most of the morning. "We do not relax here. Our job is to protect humanity from the sages, there is no greater purpose. We will stay vigilant and hidden as we have always done."

Around him, Kain and Waylin, two of Sasha's most trusted senior officers, nodded in agreement.

Sitting next to them was Merle, a true roughneck of Ojult. The native Ojultan looked rough, like a man who'd lived off only what the land provided. He wore his hat low and kept his beard thick to hide his scarred face.

"Off the grid, right," said Merle. "I was in Worall a few days ago, and Appian's not the small shipping company it used to be. That group knows us too well. The Nencia woman, I'm not sure if I want to screw her or kill her. If we want to stay in the shadows, might be best if we take out Appian's leadership."

Misora pointed at Merle. "He's got a point, Sasha; that woman's nothing but trouble. Kill her, take over Appian, save ourselves the trouble later. We've allowed her too much leniency, and they're too powerful. Take them out before they outnumber us or start running their mouth."

Sasha lifted his mug of gorilka and reveled in the spicy, burning aftertaste. The stiff drink was difficult to come by unless you were with the Reeves Corporation or Appian Shipping. "They already outnumber us, a fact I'm surprised you missed, Misora. Yet with our training, advanced weapons, armor, and leadership, Nencia's people pale in comparison. But Appian isn't our concern at the moment, and we must keep our focus on the mystics."

Misora swiped his hand over his wrist, sending a digital document to Sasha's watch. "I know you think I'm an overzealous idiot, Sasha, but take a look at this."

Sasha produced a small holo-image of the document, which showed population statistics on Ojult. Since the intense asteroid activity prevented satellites from orbiting the planet, most intelligence came from those on the ground. After reading over the sheet, Sasha worked out what Misora was getting at. Since their spies had discovered the fight between the two continental leaders ten years ago, the Nein on Capintesta had disbanded, leaving almost no trace of the sect. Conversely, the Nein on Listo had organized and expanded, but not beyond their claimed city of Carendra.

"The Amurski staff in the hands of a mystic is alarming, but I've already seen this." Sasha locked eyes with his deputy. "There are two staffs on Ojult. I already know the location of one, and the second is with Syrus Tokarek. A strategy is in place to retrieve it."

A knock on the door interrupted their conversation. Waylin walked over and opened the door. "This be a private meeting, and you needs to get going before—"

Sasha glanced at the woman before turning his attention to his council, intrigued on how they would respond to the staff attached to her back.

Waylin stood dumbstruck, while Merle and Kain drew their high-energy beam projectile sidearms (BPs). Misora, on the other hand, looked from Sasha to the woman, then back again.

Sasha raised his glass toward Misora, appreciating his deputy's confusion. "This woman is here at my request; stash your weapons."

Sasha's command was not well received, considering the woman wore an Amurski staff across her back.

Merle was the first to holster his pistol. "Good enough for me," he said, sitting back down to the fire.

"I suppose you want us to leave," said Misora with a hint of irritation.

Sasha nodded, and Misora escorted the others from the room.

Sasha stood alone with the stout woman. She had short, additive magenta hair, salient cheekbones, and wore a constant expression of annoyance. Sasha embraced the woman, kissing her passionately but resisting the urge to undress her.

"Ah, my lover, I have dreamed of you every night," she said, her accent mirroring that of Sasha's. She unsheathed her staff and placed it against a nearby chair.

Sasha gazed into her eyes. "It's been months. I worried for your safety," he said, staring at the staff. "Were you successful?"

Achilla pointed at the staff. "Obviously. The lovesick fool was easy to seduce. I poisoned him, took his staff, and he now rots in Misora's prison."

She stepped back from Sasha and looked to the door. A quick innate command locked the door, sealing the two from interruption.

"Come closer," said Achilla. "I have a gift for you."

Sasha's eyes wandered to her chest and waist. She simpered and pushed his head up so he looked into her eyes. "Not that. No, my love, I have something to tell you. I have found something, or someone, who you will be very, very happy to see. It will change everything."

"Who?"

With another muted command, the candles extinguished and the shutters closed. "The fate of Ojult has just fallen into your hands."

CHAPTER 9: YEAR 2399

The Nein council building inside the town of Carendra was exceptionally ordinary. The exterior was made of gray, fractured stone, massed together unevenly by exhausted slaves. The interior was almost as dull. Several fireplaces lined the perimeter with the occasional window that remained shut during the winter months.

A large disjointed table tilted to one side in the middle of the mostly empty hall. At the far end of the room, a high-backed chair made from a large sarcto rested next to a fatigued desk and bookshelf. Flaring candles seated in animal bone oozed down tall metal stands providing barely enough light for reading and conversation.

Thoba slaves regularly cleaned the mundane hall, but today, beads of blood soiled the concrete floor, originating in the entryway and pooling at the feet of a callous-looking bearded man. The man, a gunfighter, wore a wide-brimmed black hat, faded dark overcoat, burly dark pants, hand-crafted boots, and a broken-in revolver resting inside a thigh holster.

Ten years ago, the gunslinger saved the sister of the most powerful mystic on Ojult, sending his future into a labyrinth nightmare. Syrus Tokarek had enslaved him, not as a servant changing bedsheets, but as an assassin. For two years, Jayden Vaut spent night and day training with Kavil Siller, captain of Syrus's Nein guard. A long way from playing golf back on Earth, Jayden found himself excelling in the abhorrent profession.

Tonight, Jayden stood against the perimeter of the great hall having just returned from a six-day journey into the northern forests of Listo.

Syrus's assignment for his tenured killer—track down a former Nein named Sonus who fell asleep while on watch duty. This simple mistake should have warranted a day without food or a week cleaning the animal pens, not death.

Jayden's presumptive clean kill with a sniper shot turned into a bloody melee after he mistakenly believed Sonus's still body was deceased. A lucky strike by Jayden's short-blade ended the affair, but not before Sonus's dagger took three deep chunks out of his arm and leg.

Syrus was in the middle of court proceedings when Jayden arrived, ordering him to wait in the corner while he finished.

Around the center table were Helia Tokarek and her daughter Mea. The father of Mea remained a mystery to everyone, including Syrus, but the enigma of the situation didn't bother Jayden. Helia stole a quick glance at him, but Jayden waved her attention back to Syrus.

Jayden also doubled as Helia's bodyguard. He loved Helia and Mea like they were his own blood, and Syrus understood this. It was also the central grounds for allowing Jayden to carry a weapon among the very people who had enslaved him. Helia was different from all other Nein; she treated him as an equal and defended him rigorously against frequent indignities brought on by Captain Siller and others.

Jayden's blanching face rattled into focus upon hearing Syrus's deep voice. "Next."

Syrus sat erect in his high backed, grand chair. His loose-fitting, black robes draped over his brawny chest like water streaming over a smooth bank. Next to him, Captain Siller stood at rigid attention in full red-and-black light armor made of woven scrap iron.

Syrus glanced a menacing eye toward Jayden as they waited for the next prisoner. Moments later, Giles Murphy, scarred from his near-death experience ten years ago, dragged a pale-looking old man to the opposite side of the table.

"Premier," said Giles, holding the handcuffed man. "This Thoba was found attacking a member of our order this morning. Three of our number witnessed the account."

Syrus gazed at the man. "You had no hope of injuring my men, why attempt this?"

The man trembled as he told the story of trying to protect his young daughter from the Nein attempting to bring her into the slave quarters.

Captain Siller smirked at the trembling father. "My men were escorting her back to the slave quarters where she works in the pantry. Kill him and be done with this garbage."

"This man did attack one of our own," stated Giles. "However, the girl in question is only nine years old and showed signs of multiple cuts and bruises when I questioned her."

"Which she received at the hands of your brutes," argued the father, so distraught that his entire body was shaking.

Syrus's eyes crossed Jayden again. "The act of an ordinary attacking a mystic for any reason is against our laws. Giles, have one of his hands removed, but allow him to stay within the city to look after his daughter who will remain at her post. Next."

Two more men and a woman were brought in, Syrus finding each of them guilty under Nein law. Their punishments were severe, one losing a foot, another both his ears, and a woman sentenced to death by veleno injection.

After Giles escorted the last criminal from the room, Siller spoke to Mea. "This is our way child. We're their betters, and they will obey us or suffer the consequences."

"My daughter is seventeen, Kavil, and doesn't require parental advice from you," said Helia. "Jayden, I know you just got back, but I need to speak with my brother alone. Can you—oh, Jayden, you're bleeding!"

"Nothing to worry about," said Jayden. "You want me to take Mea back to your quarters?"

Captain Siller raised a hand. "You haven't given us your report, Slave. What of Sonus?"

Jayden looked to Syrus who signaled him to answer.

"Sonus's dead. His body's out front."

Helia ran an anxious hand through her long hair. "Mea's heard enough of this nonsense for one day. Jayden, if you're able, please escort her home, then please see to your injuries."

Jayden stepped toward the table, but Captain Siller blocked his way.

"Was there something else you wanted to waste our time with, Captain?"

muttered Jayden. The words were out of his mouth before he knew what he'd said.

The captain looked him up and down, then grabbed his injured arm, squeezing tightly. Jayden collapsed to a knee, groaning in pain. Siller knelt next to him, pressing his thumb into the hastily wrapped wound. "You're just a slave," he whispered. "You're nothing but a pet for our entertainment. I could kill you right now and no one would think twice. I own you, Vaut, own you. Remember that the next time you raise an attitude toward me."

Throughout Jayden's ten years with the Nein, he'd enjoyed the limited protection of Helia and Syrus. All too often, however, Jayden bent and sometimes broke Nein law, especially when it came to the treatment of women and children. He was on thin ice with Syrus and Captain Siller already, but it didn't stop him from seriously considering ripping out the captain's throat.

"That's enough," Syrus said. "You're bleeding all over the floor. Do as my sister commands."

Siller let go, and Jayden took a moment to collect himself before daring to stand. "All… right… then. Mea, you… ready?"

With her shoulders back and posture erect, Mea stood and headed toward the main door. She brushed passed Siller as if he was an insect not worth noticing.

Once outside, Jayden used his good arm and helped Mea put on her heavy sarcto coat. She pulled the hood over her curly hair and brushed errant strands away from her amber eyes. She was no longer the little girl who slipped food to him in the middle of the night. She was a woman who carried the burden of a goddess on her shoulders, but her face still carried hints of youth.

Mea put a gentle hand on Jayden's arm. "Come on, Jayden, let's get you outta here before you pass out."

He nodded and followed her across the grounds, his eyes scanning for threats even within the walls of the village. Carendra wasn't exactly the booming night town like Worall or Port Fiesta. In fact, the arteries of the town were empty save a handful of firepits lighting the area.

"Let me heal this," said Mea inside her quarters. Her servant took her coat, and she turned to Jayden. "Take off your shirt and pants. Let me see the wounds."

Mea's servant took his overcoat and shirt, but Jayden held up his uninjured hand. "Wouldn't be a good look if your uncle walked in here with my pants off."

Mea smiled. "I can still heal it without seeing it, but it will take longer. Sit, please."

She knelt beside him on the bare floor and placed a graceful, calloused hand onto his forearm. She'd healed him dozens of times, but Jayden had never gotten used to the icy, tingling feeling. The sensation was invasive, like someone trying to climb inside his body after swimming in a freezing lake. A purple brume flowed around their melded bodies.

Mea's eyes transitioned from slits to full awareness. "Every time you come back from a mission, you're injured. One day I might not be able to put you back together."

Jayden stood and started dressing. His wounds felt tight and scabbed, but experience told him the mending would hold. "Thank you." He reached over and pulled out a small rectangular object wrapped in brown paper. Jayden handed it to her as if expecting her to know its contents. "Consider it payment for your troubles."

Mea smiled. "You've been doing this since I was a child when you started hunting for my uncle. Always chocolate when you come back from a mission. Why?"

Jayden winced while contorting his arm into his coat. "I don't have many opportunities to show my appreciation to you and your mother. If sneaking into Pa'Gran during missions and buying chocolate for you brings a smile to your face, it's worth it."

"Is that why you saved me all those years ago?" reasoned Mea, "because you think I'm one of the good guys?"

His vision was becoming blurry. "You and your mother are special, like a bright light in a dark room."

Mea pursed her lips as if contemplating her next question. "You're sure you're not… my dad… right?"

Jayden grinned. "God no. How old do you think I am? You need anything before I leave?"

Jayden checked the grounds around Mea's home before he staggered back to his own quarters. His wounds were healed, but he'd lost a lot of blood, perhaps too much. Although a mystic could heal the most terrible injuries, they couldn't replenish the important life-giving substance.

The four dozen slave pads were on the southwest side of Carendra, out of sight from the Tokarek family and other respected Nein members. The quarters resembled little more than tents, often blowing over in high winds or flooding during the rainy season.

Jayden managed to find his cabin, letting the tent flap fall behind him as he stepped inside. In the far corner of the room stood a portly woman wearing a maroon-and-gold saree, round gold earrings, and a bindi tattooed on her forehead.

Jayden fell to his knees. "Janice, I… help."

CHAPTER 10: YEAR 2399

During Jayden's first months on Ojult, he dreamed vividly about his family and former life. Whether playing golf with his father, board games with his mother, or dominating his high-school wrestling matches, Jayden sometimes awoke believing his exile was just a bad dream. As time passed and his subconscious accepted its fate, the lucid dreams became infrequent, and Jayden stopped dreaming almost entirely.

Jayden knew the difference between waking from a normal night's sleep and awakening from unconsciousness, and this was definitely the latter. His body tingled. Something warm and slightly moist touched his lips, bringing him further out of his slumber.

"I'm disappointed it only took one kiss to wake you up," Janice, his servant, said. "You look like hell, by the way."

Jayden recognized her distinct Indian accent before his eyes adjusted. "How much jashinto did you give me? I'm not sure which one of you is speaking right now."

She placed a wet rag to his head forehead, dabbing the edges. "I am your servant, I do what I am commanded of course." There was a pitch of warm mockery in her voice.

Jayden placed an uncoordinated hand on her inner thigh.

She moved his hand further down. "You were gone nearly a week this time. Thought you might have found another servant." She looked at his hand. "If so, she apparently wasn't very good. And before you start imagining me naked, know that I've given you enough jashinto to keep you laid up for a week."

"Tease," he said, sitting up on his elbows. It was then Jayden realized he was naked, his arm and leg wrapped in medimesh. The mesh wrapping was expensive and difficult to get on Ojult, but its adaptive skin-replacement therapy and hovrol coating prevented infections and quickened recovery. Jayden loathed thinking what it cost her to acquire such an expensive item, for a slave no less. "How long have I been out?"

She pulled the sheet back, exposing his full manhood. "Two days. Your leg wasn't bad, but your arm was torn up. I'm guessing Mea put you back together? One day you're going to learn that you need blood to survive. You should have come straight here when you got back." Janice sounded genuinely worried.

"What would I do without you?" he said, taking her hand and kissing it.

"Ha," she said, crossing her legs and yanking his hand away. "You'd be dead, considering how many times I've patched you back together. I thought assassins were supposed to be stealthy."

Jayden shrugged. "Every time I get hurt, you undress me; how else am I supposed to get laid around here?"

"I'm your servant, don't you know you're supposed to beat me and humiliate me in public, not actually treat me like—"

"Like what? A human being who deserves more than the cards she's been dealt?"

Janice got up and walked over to a pot of boiling water sitting over a small fire. Her saree covered everything up to her collar bone, but her purposeful strut kept him snared to her backside. She placed the bloodied rag into the pot and fetched a broiling new one. "We all serve a purpose, and mine is to care for you. I take that responsibility seriously."

Her sincerity sent a rush of appreciation through him. "I know," he replied. In the far corner of his quarters, ascending steam from his bathtub caught his attention.

Janice started scrubbing his chest and neck. "The bath was for you, but your wounds are too fresh. If I let you get in, you'd likely get an infection, and we can't have Mea playing doctor for you all the time."

She finished cleaning him, then slipped off her dress. Jayden wanted desperately to jump into the small tub and join her, but the muscle numb-ing effects of the jashinto still had him bonded to the bed.

After an hour of small talk and explaining the details of his mission, Jayden made his move. "Am I sleeping alone tonight, Ms. Mangal?" he asked, rubbing the empty space beside him.

Janice stepped out of the steaming tub, flashing him before wrapping a tattered towel around her. "How romantic," she sassed, walking toward him. "You're a very pretty man, but perhaps one day you'll actually try to woo me into bed instead of using dumb one-liners."

The cool night gave way to the sounds of prey and predators. Chirps from rodents scurrying along the tent walls were so common Jayden didn't notice them. Frantic squeaks made it clear the zibars were hunting and having a successful night. Flocks of in-flight phoenixes chirped and sang at the moonless night. Then the night air froze as the petrifying huff and roar of the native sarcto silenced the land. The rarely seen animal walked on four legs with one razor-sharp claw on each paw. It hunted only at night and its chameleon fur kept it well hidden during the day.

It was the first night in nearly a week he'd slept on something other than rocks, but the palpitating tenor of the sarcto muddled his slumber. When sleep finally found the mystic assassin, it wasn't meant to be. When Jayden awoke, he recognized two problems. First, the jashinto serum had worn off, and his arm drummed with pain. Second, and much more prob-lematic, someone was holding a knife to his throat.

"Call for help and we kill you both," dared Nester.

Jayden recognized the jittery voice, and then heard Janice whimpering from the floor beside him. A slender, bald man, held Janice by the throat.

"Okay, you've got us, what now?" asked Jayden calmly.

"Kill him now, Nester," said a familiar voice.

"Shut up, Brady. We do it how she and the captain ordered. You two are going to follow us outside the town gates. Either of you tries to run, you're dead."

Kavil Siller was a giant prick, but sending two of his own men to do a job like this didn't add up. Jayden looked into the ugly, toothless, stinking face of his captor. "Who's 'she'? And I'd have thought Captain Siller would've wanted to do this himself instead of sending two *brave* soldiers like you."

Nester backhanded Jayden, then dragged him across the bed by his beard.

Boiling pain shot through Jayden's arm, sucking the air out of his lungs. "Arrgghh."

Nester sailed a full-knuckled punch into Jayden's face, sending him to the floor. Jayden felt something wet creep down his leg and looked just beyond his briefs to see his bandaged wound bleeding freely.

"Screw it, we do it here," said Nester. "Do what you want with her, then kill her. I'll take care of Vaut."

Insulting Nester proved to be a painful decision, but it served its purpose. The oblivious Nein had dragged him near his pistol and short-blade.

"No, no, please, no!" cried Janice over the sounds of tearing cloth.

Hearing her cries jump-started Jayden's adrenaline. In two swift moves, he unsheathed his blade and swung it across Nester's leading knee. The convex edge cut cleanly through the mystic's flesh, launching the extremity across the room.

Jayden sprang into a crouching position, pushing the excruciating pain from his mind. With a well-trained skyward strike, Jayden slammed the blade through Nester's jaw, which exploded, sending junks of bone, flesh, and teeth across the floor.

Jayden turned his attention to Janice. "Get off her, admit to all this to Syrus, and you'll get to live."

Brady was still on top of Janice and only now seemed to comprehend that his partner was on the floor with half his face missing. "I'm admitting to nothing, Vaut. The captain's got our back. You're hanging for this."

"Which means killing you costs me nothing more." Jayden eyed Brady's posture carefully, looking for clues that might prelude an attack. The giveaway came when Brady pivoted, preparing for a quick turn. Jayden's shortblade spun end over end as Brady conjured a protective shield. Jayden's weapon caromed off the ward, slamming into the wall.

Brady laughed at the clinking weapon.

Adept at fighting mystics, Jayden understood their weaknesses. Dense metallic objects, like a blade, couldn't penetrate a mystic's shield, but something like a fist or knee could pass through without issue. It was one of those odd rules governing mysticism that boggled the mind but had worked to Jayden's advantage before. The mental fortitude needed to conjure and keep an arcane shield up was taxing and didn't allow for much multitasking by the user.

Even before the blade bounced off the shield, Jayden was already leaping toward his adversary. Brady lowered his shield and went for his shockblade, but he wasn't quick enough. Jayden plunged an elbow into Brady's chest and something inside his cavity popped as both men crashed to the ground.

Janice scurried into a corner, terrified.

"You mystics can't handle close-quarter fighting," mocked Jayden. "And what the hell were you thinking, bringing only two men to kill me? Did you forget who trained me?"

Brady wheezed, struggling to catch his breath while the nerves in his diaphragm. spasmed. "We... accomplished... our goal. You're going... to hang... for this."

"Maybe," Jayden said, and without reserve, he pushed his palm into Brady's windpipe. The sickening crack brought Jayden to the realization that, for only the second time, he'd killed a mystic without Syrus ordering it. The feeling was less gratifying than he'd expected.

"Jay... Jay... Jayden, is it over?" Janice cried.

Jayden helped her back to her feet, tenderly embracing his frightened servant. "They're dead." But in truth, it wasn't over, and she knew that as well as he did. Once Captain Siller found out about this, he'd probably hang Jayden or at the very least exile him. Jayden wondered who Syrus would send to hunt him down if he was banished.

"Are you hurt?" he asked, checking her puffy cheeks and bruised wrists.

Janice broke away and checked herself. "No, I'm okay."

"Then we have to move fast. Get dressed and head back to your tent. Avoid everyone. It's still the middle of the night, so there shouldn't be many wandering eyes. If someone asks where you were, tell them in your quarters, understand? And keep an eye out for a sarcto, he's been prancing around town all night."

Janice dressed and scurried out the door, leaving Jayden with the dead bodies. He decided honesty was probably the best course. Tell Syrus before Captain Siller found out and took matters into his own hands.

Dressing quickly, he felt a peculiar draft against his bare back. Too focused on dressing and what he would say to Syrus, Jayden never noticed the intruders looming behind him.

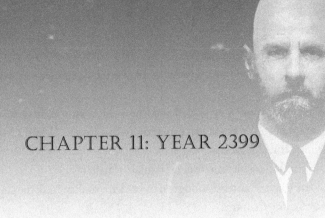

CHAPTER 11: YEAR 2399

Sharp metal cuffs dug into Jayden's wrists, which carried his entire weight. His shoulders felt dislocated, but it was the smell of his own excrement that pushed him fully back into awareness. His wounds were scabbed over, suggesting he'd been in the cell for some time. He caught the reflection of a fist coming toward him in time to close his eyes.

"You traitorous, power-broke *cad*!" yelled Captain Siller, rearing back again.

The second blow connected above Jayden's left ear, rattling his senses, and permeating a loud clamoring in his ear. Using the pain as fuel, he lashed out against his chains.

Siller readied for another swipe, but Jayden was done playing victim. As soon as the captain came into range, Jayden hoisted his untethered legs around Siller's neck. The sudden parry took the guard captain by surprise, and Jayden had him in a rugged choke. The muscles in his legs burned from the pressure, but Jayden watched with pleasure as Siller's face reddened.

"Release him," said a familiar voice from the far side of the stockade. "Release him Jayden, or you'll have no hope of leaving this building alive."

Jayden wavered, wondering how much longer he could continue the hold. Reluctantly, he released Siller who tottered backward, gasping for air.

Syrus took a few steps closer, his face illuminated by what little light entered the prison. "You've again taken advantage of my leniency, Jayden. Choose your next words carefully."

"Water," croaked Jayden.

Syrus motioned to a slave who splashed gray, murky water down his throat.

"Give me your story Jayden and know this is your only chance."

Captain Siller stood erect, massaging his throat. "Death. He should die immediately for this!"

Syrus bid his captain silent. "Explain, Jayden."

The water restored a smidgeon of Jayden's vitality. "Ask the captain; he knows more than me."

Captain Siller gut-punched Jayden, knocking the wind from him. "Answer him!"

Jayden heaved several times before his lungs refilled. "I… was… asleep. The captain… ordered Nester and Brady… to sneak into my tent. They… tried to kill me."

Siller swung again, but Jayden shoved his knee into the captain's chest. He thought he heard a rib crack as the mystic fell back.

Syrus looked at his long-time captain with dismay. "Leave, captain." But Siller didn't move. "Leave the room Kavil, before this tied-up, beaten, ordinary Thoba beats you to death."

The defiant captain bowed and shuffled out of the room clutching his stomach.

"Jayden, answer my questions. What you've done cannot be undone."

Jayden waited for Siller to leave before angrily countering Syrus's accusation. "This is all a setup. I was unconscious from all the blood I lost from trying to kill Sonus. I woke up with a knife to my throat. Nester and Brady admitted they were acting on the *captain's* orders. What else is there to say!"

"It's your word against Kavil's, unless you have a witness who can attest to your story."

Jayden's eyes darted to the floor. Janice was there, but the word of a servant wasn't going to help him. There was also the cold truth that if he was found guilty, they'd probably kill her just to show supremacy.

"How long did it take for the captain's goons to show up?" asked Jayden.

But Syrus's intellect matched his battlefield prowess. "Redirecting the conversation isn't going to help you, Jayden. If you can't find a witness, then it's Kavil's word against yours, and that's not going to end well for you."

"Fine!" shouted Jayden. "Kill me, banish me, end this fantastic life!"

"You may not care about your life, but Helia does. Have you thought about Mea and what your death will mean to her? You're like a father to her and my sister likens you to a brother. Do not toss your life away so easily."

The ringing in Jayden's ear started to fade. "I'm telling you, I'm innocent."

"Saving my sister's life all those years ago has spared you many pains, but I cannot save you from this. Is there anything else I should know?"

Jayden smirked. "Your sister and Mea are the only things worth saving in this town. I'd do it again, but maybe I should have killed a few more of your Nein along the way; it might have saved me some trouble later on."

Syrus sighed, looking over Jayden's scars. Unexpectedly, Syrus placed a calloused hand upon his cheek. Jayden braced himself, but instead of pain, he felt a cold tingling engulf his body, akin to diving into a chilled bathtub.

Jayden's injuries numbed and his pain diminished.

"Helia and Mea spent most of last night begging me to spare your life, and I've decided to accept their pleas. But our laws are steadfast and cannot be broken, not even for you. You killed two of my people for a purpose I will never know. You will be punished. For now, I've healed your wounds, the rest is up to you."

That was it, no second option or plan B. Syrus's decision was final and he walked away.

"That staff on your back, Syrus, imagine what you could do for the people on Ojult if you'd just open your eyes."

Syrus stopped and looked back. "It's not the Nein's job to bring peace to humanity. We're preordained to rule, and that's why we have our powers." Syrus paused for a long moment. "There are days, like today, that I look upon you not as a slave, Jayden. You and her, it could have been… together, you would have been unstoppable. I… regret what's to come."

Jayden began to question the cryptic statement when Helia's light footsteps passed Syrus as he exited the stockade. "You stupid, stupid, stupid man!" she said, unlocking Jayden's chains and helping him out of the enclosure.

Her beauty, fragrance, and aura were ecstasy to Jayden's spirits. "I'm sorry. I didn't mean to—"

"Shut up and listen," snapped Helia. "I've begged my brother to spare you, but Kavil is going to push for your execution. I... I don't think..." Her earlier brashness faded. "I don't think I can do anything for you."

Jayden resisted the urge to hug her. "It's important that you know all I did was protect myself. They came in and put a knife to me and threatened to kill Janice. I didn't have a choice."

She accepted his story as truth and wrapped her arms around his neck. "I owe you my life. I wish I could do something for you. Mea even begged Syrus, which she's never done. You're like a brother to me. God, I hope you know you're special to us."

Jayden tenderly returned the affection. "Well, don't go sizing me up for the catacombs yet. Whatever happens out there, you and Mea mean everything to me. Thank you for all you've done."

———————

Dusk settled over Carendra when Helia handed Jayden over to Janice. "He needs to be back in the common hall in an hour," said Helia. "Get him cleaned up, and make sure he's got a bag packed."

"Yes, Lady Tokarek," said Janice with a bow.

She undressed Jayden and guided him into the metal tub. "I didn't think I'd see you again. You don't look good, but your wounds are mostly healed."

Jayden sunk into the water, resting his head at the bottom. Fully submerged, he relished the tranquility of the soundless ambiance. The serenity was cut short when Janice yanked him up by his beard.

"Lady Tokarek told me to have you in the common hall within the hour."

Jayden patted his beard. "Easy on the whiskers. It took me ten years to grow this thing." With fleeting speed, Janice scrubbed him clean and pulled him from the cloudy bath. Jayden's naked body showcased the brutal life of an assassin working for Syrus. As she'd done countless times before, Janice helped him get dressed and packed his bags.

Looking like an antiquated criminal, Jayden adjusted his overcoat and hat. "How do I look?"

"Nothing like a prince who's ready to sweep me off my feet and take me to his castle."

He raised his hands in defeat. "Good, that's what I'm going for."

"How can you be so calm?" She extended his pistol belt to him with a shaking hand.

"No need for that," he said, waving the weapon away. "If they execute me in the hall, those won't do me any good. You take them."

She looked at him uneasily. "They still might execute you?"

Jayden nodded. "Listen to me, Janice. If they execute me, you've got to get the hell out of Carendra. If they kill me, you're next. Don't head to Port Naok, they'll expect that. Follow the main trail to Limeth, it's less likely you'll get caught. Got it?"

Her lip quivered, and Jayden regretted unloading all this on her at once. She nestled up under his chin.

"Please take care of yourself."

He kissed her on the forehead. "They're mystics, not gods. We can survive this."

CHAPTER 12: YEAR 2399

Light snow skirted Jayden's face as he walked by the north-side pond Helia frequented. The possibility of execution didn't frighten him like he expected. The front door of the great hall came into view when hurried footsteps from behind stopped him cold.

"Jayden," panted Mea, skidding to a halt. "Tell me… tell me it's not true… what they're saying."

Jayden flashed his best smile. "Your uncle told me what you said to him, thank you, Mea. You and Helia, you've made my time here, better."

Mea latched onto his arm. "My uncle's never found anyone innocent."

"Yeah, I know."

Her eyes mushroomed. "Then… why are you going? Run! Get out of here while you still can."

"Your uncle just wants to talk right now, it's just a conversation Mea, nothing more." Jayden patted her shoulder. "With the Nein, just because you didn't do anything wrong doesn't mean you're innocent. Either way, I need to speak with Syrus."

Mea was lost for words.

"It's cold and an ungodly hour, head on back to your home and don't worry about me, I'll be fine." He kissed her forehead and headed toward the great hall.

He walked confidently into the dimly lit room, not bothering to clean his boots or remove his hat. Jayden stopped short of the rectangular table were Syrus so often handed out his judgements. Helia and Giles sat next to one another while Captain Siller stood next to Syrus in his customary position. There was a newcomer in the corner, a girl he'd never seen before, doing her best to hide in the shadows.

"I'm here upon your request," said Jayden, not bothering to bow.

Syrus stood from his kingly chair, showing off electric-blue and black armor. Jayden's heart froze in alarm.

"I trust you understand why you're here," said Syrus in a terrifyingly low voice.

"Because I didn't die. I mean, because I didn't let Kavil's assassins do their job."

"Mind where you are, Jayden," demanded Captain Siller. "Address him as Premier Tokarek, and those men you killed were Nein, our brothers. Your accusation that I sent them is pitiful."

Helia adjusted uncomfortably in her chair. "It's ridiculous to believe Jayden went looking for this fight, Kavil, but I admit that I don't think you'd order such a thing either. There's got to be an explanation for all this."

Jayden's hopes of Syrus heeding his sister's perspective nose-dived before even gaining traction.

"I've raised you among my family and senior council for years, and there's no question you know our laws." Syrus leaned against the desk in front of him. "You've acted carelessly and without thought of the consequences. What do you expect me to do?"

Captain Siller's head jerked toward Syrus. "The punishment is clear, my premier. Our laws demand his death. This ordinary slave, regardless of his previous services, is an outcast!"

"Quiet, Captain, or it'll be you on trial next," said Syrus.

"Brother," pleaded Helia, "Jayden saved Mea and me from certain death. He respects you and our people. These accusations don't make any sense. Surely you agree?"

"It's obvious where my sister and Captain Siller stand on this matter," said Syrus. "Giles, do you have evidence that may affect the trial?"

"My premier, the case does not appear cut and dry," suggested Giles. "Perhaps Jayden was just in the wrong place at the wrong time. We should also consider the Celje killed two of our own yesterday and left their bodies hanging off the main road to Port Naok. If things escalate with the

Celje, we'll need every available man. Allowing persons like Jayden to execute our people without recourse, it isn't advisable."

"Wrong place?" said Jayden, unable to keep his emotions in check. "I was asleep in my tent and woke to a knife at my throat. What the hell was I supposed to do?"

A snicker came from the strange woman in the corner. Jayden locked eyes with Syrus.

"Syrus, please... don't," whimpered Helia.

Syrus raised a hand, and Jayden felt everything stop. "Because of the affection my sister holds for you, Jayden, and my personal feelings on the matter, you will not face execution."

Helia's sobs met Captain Siller's silent outrage, the hollow walls magnifying the tension. Jayden's temporary relief faded when Syrus paced toward him.

Syrus leaned in and whispered in his ear. "I'll give you a one-hour advance, then I'm allowing Kavil to do what our laws dictate. If you get off the island, I'll call them off."

"You're exiling me," said Jayden, much louder than he'd meant.

Helia's hands went to her mouth. "No!"

"You are indeed a great leader, my premier," said Siller. "Might I suggest sending your new apprentice for the chase?"

The woman hiding in the shadows stepped into the light. "He doesn't look like much of a threat," goaded the young woman. "Is it really worth my time? Seems like a—"

Syrus slammed his fists onto the table. "Be silent! Phaedra, you would not survive the encounter. Kavil, this is your responsibility."

Jayden checked Captain Siller's dumbstruck expression before examining Phaedra. He'd never known Syrus to have an apprentice. Her hair was bright silver and came down past her shoulders, where two short swords crossed over her back. Her three-piece black armor looked heavily used and matched her grungy appearance. What gave Jayden pause was the woman's cold, piercing eyes and aristocratic brows that warned anyone near her to approach with caution.

Exile meant leaving Carendra, the continent of Listo, and Syrus Tokarek. It also meant never seeing Helia, Mea, or Janice ever again. Expulsion from the camp also gave Siller full consent to kill him like any other exiled member.

"Please, Brother, don't—"

"One hour, Jayden. I suggest you use the time wisely."

Jayden looked from Syrus to Helia. "Tell Mea I said goodbye. And... Helia... thank you."

CHAPTER 13: YEAR 2399

Elasus Reeves sat at another Reeves Corporation quarterly dinner with prominent PGU officials. Soft classical music played in the background, Chopin's Ballade No. 1. Elasus was ever the classical enthusiast. His wife sat across the table next to PGU Treasury Secretary Vijay Zhang, a rising star within Earth's governing authority. Elasus didn't care much for the young man, but large governing establishments like the PGU must always have a young up-and-comer, and this generation's candidate was Zhang.

Elasus surveyed his audience of PGU representatives, far fewer in number than in years past. Each were passive equity owners in various subsidiaries of the corporation and had several billion reasons to be in attendance.

The Medallion restaurant attracted only the richest and most prevalent Las Vegas guests, one of the reasons Elasus purchased the business in the first place. For tonight's meeting, the Medallion closed its doors to outside customers.

Feeling the evening coming to a close, PGU Prime Minister Joshua Kennedy leaned over to speak with his neighbor. "So, Elasus, your most recent financial report shows continued success. I hope our distributions and other monetary exchanges reflect this."

Elasus didn't appreciate the personal-space violation and stared down the pointed nose of the smaller man. "Mr. Prime Minister, my company rewards its investors when appropriate. Regarding other monetary exchanges, this isn't the place for that discussion, and I trust you'll not bring it up again."

Kennedy's face blushed, not accustomed to being told what to do. "What of our other dealing? Have you taken possession of him?"

Elasus expected Kennedy might unwisely bring up the subject. "It appears that you want to discuss private matters in an inopportune environment." Elasus nursed his chilled drink. "But if you must know, my people picked him up in the eastern region of FIAS two nights ago."

"And? What did you find out?" Kennedy said, catching the attention of his neighbors and Irelyn Reeves.

Elasus wasn't fazed, despite the attention. "The intelligence your office provided was accurate. That's all you need to know."

Kennedy rubbed his brow. "In Elasus speak, that means you killed him? Did you at least get anything useful out of him?"

Elasus turned his entire body toward the prime minister. "The Reeves Corporation is a private company. You, like many officials at this table, have various tiers of investment shares but nothing that constitutes disclosure of how I handle the operations of *my* company. The successes, failures, and strategies behind how I deal with these obstacles are private and will remain so."

"Damn it, Elasus, I gave you that information so your people could investigate and find out more about that group. We don't even know what they're called. You're worth a lot of money to me but only if you're breathing. Killing him was risky no matter how powerful you think you are."

"I'm not an Elder who can see into the future, nor do I feel the overwhelming need to explain my actions to you. Having said that, your point is well taken. I *am* worth more dead than alive, especially to the investors here tonight. This fact begs one, very important question. What scared our recent captive so badly that he'd swallow an SMD pill seconds after we took him into custody?"

Kennedy took a hasty drink of wine that left a red stripe across his upper lip. "You don't just accidentally have a Silver Mystic Dancer pill in your pocket. They knew we were on to him?"

Elasus went back to staring at his wife and sipping his drink. "We each have our spies lurking in the offices of our competitors Mr. Prime Minister, we should expect no different from this mysterious group. Of course, one alternative rests in the hands of the FIAS, a regional power that has reason to dislike my corporation."

Kennedy finally started connecting the dots. "You're concerned the FIAS are bankrolling this group?" He began tapping the table, faster and faster. "You... you found out something?"

"Like I already mentioned, I take care of my investors." Elasus gave a slight nod to his wife letting her know to wrap things up with Zhang.

Irelyn smiled and pinged the side of her wine glass. "Good evening, everyone," she said to the seated PGU representatives. The table of all men immediately went quiet. "Thank you all for attending tonight's quarterly investment meeting. Elasus and I thank you for your time and patience as we work hard to bring you the highest possible return on your investments. My husband and I will retire for the evening, but please stay and enjoy the fabulous services and spirits. Let us all give thanks to Elasus for filling our pocketbooks and calorie counters. Have a wonderful evening."

Elasus stood, nodded to a few guests, then followed his wife toward the front of the restaurant.

"Mr. Reeves, a moment of your time, please," said a young man.

Irelyn and Elasus turned to see Treasury Secretary Zhang behind them.

"I'll call for the car while you finish up," said Irelyn, walking outside.

"How can I help you, Mr. Secretary?" asked Elasus.

Zhang, a short man of Chinese descent, walked up to Elasus, thus avoiding the need to shout over the dinner guests opening Reeves-engraved envelopes. "Mr. Reeves, my apologies for interrupting. I wanted to congratulate you on the financial successes your report illustrated as well as increased criminal-exile transportation all while decreasing your overhead."

Elasus nodded.

"I noticed the report said very little about Lent however. How goes that operation?"

Out of all the PGU guests, Zhang was likely the only official to catch the purposeful omission. From what Irelyn told him, Treasury Secretary Zhang was as intelligent as he was good-looking. To match his fitted suit and athletic disposition, Zhang aired flawless eyebrows and frosted white teeth.

There was a good reason Elasus wanted PGU eyes off Lent. "Very observant, Mr. Secretary. Lent will one day produce revenue on the same scale as Ojult, but not yet. I want my minority equity partners focused on Ojult for now. Once my son gets Lent operating to my standards, you'll hear more."

"My understanding is you hope to convert Lent into a giant farming planet that will perhaps one day furnish all of Earth's food supply. Is that correct? Your son has been there some time; I wonder what's holding up his progress."

An attendant approached and let Elasus know his car was ready.

"Correct, Mr. Secretary. Allowing the off-world growth of a substance needed for all human life would guarantee transportation fees for my company and expand upon the real-estate strategy I brought to the PGU last year. Pertaining to my son, he's setting up a comprehensive economic system from the ground up, *on another planet.* This particular model requires a corporate fortitude that takes time, but I have the right leader in place to efficiently accomplish the goal. But, as you can see, my car's here, and I'd like to leave. Good evening, Mr. Secretary."

———————

With Mr. and Mrs. Reeves in the back of the sleek sedan, Tayla Cruz navigated the cybernated autonomous vehicle (CAV) back to their primary residence.

"As you requested, Mr. Reeves, I've adjusted the location of tonight's meeting," said Tayla, adjusting her newly acquired wavy blonde hair.

"Where's Hewitt?" asked Irelyn.

"Tending to a sick relative, Mrs. Reeves. I offered to drive for him until he returns."

Elasus began working on the holographic display in front of him. "We'll drop Irelyn off at the house, then head into the office for the meeting."

"Yes, Mr. Reeves," replied Tayla.

Irelyn removed her heels with a sigh. "What did Zhang want?"

Elasus continued typing, ignoring his wife's sculpted legs. "He inquired about the delay with Lent and why I didn't put more information into the quarterly report."

"And what lie did you tell him this time?" spat Irelyn, her disgust at an all-time high.

"I told him about the farming idea."

"You don't think Zhang's smart enough to see through your bullshit? Or are you so pompous that you don't think anyone sees through you? The most powerful person who ever lived, and you can't even find your own daughter on a planet you practically own."

"Our daughter left the family years ago, speculating about her whereabouts a decade later is foolish. Let it go."

"Not a day has gone by that I haven't tried to find her and you ask me to let it go? She's our daughter! If Ruven had gone missing, you'd send your entire army to find him!"

Elasus cracked his neck. "I have no army, and our son's loyalty has never been questioned. Marilla made her decision a long time ago, but if it makes you feel better, I'll ask the council for an update tonight."

While the they argued, Tayla watched the HUD as the sedan navigated the faintly lit residential streets. When the car pulled up to the gate house, she scanned her ID card and submitted to a retinal scan. Five guards in total, all armed with radial energy rifles (RERs), stood at attention as the familiar sedan waited outside the gate. Only a few people, including Tayla, knew the guards were trained Celje, there to defend the family in case of a rogue sage. If someone managed to get past the guards, the automated defense systems—including auto-turrets, self-targeting taser mounts, and mechanical dropdown barricades—would meet the intruders in force.

The guards cleared them onto the property, and Tayla watched the husband and wife say their goodbyes.

"Back to the office, Mr. Reeves?" asked Tayla, pulling away from the home.

Elasus tapped the flashing connect icon on his display. "I should be done with this meeting by the time we get to the office. You're planning on staying the night?"

"Of course."

Two flat-panel monitors dropped from the ceiling, and after a brief flicker, the meeting attendees came into focus.

"Evening, Elasus," greeted Commodus Vrabel. "How was the dinner?"

Elasus waved to his old friend. "As expected. How was Idca?"

The two had attended Wharton together before heading their separate ways. After spending a few years with the PGU, Commodus accepted the COO position with his old friend, and neither man seemed to regret the decision.

Commodus Vrabel looked part business executive, part cowboy barbed in a sport coat, jeans, and polished boots. "Yeah, I'm back on Earth, and Idca's basically one giant volcano," replied Commodus, earning laughs from the other executives.

The car turned and hit a bump, nearly spilling Elasus's drink. "Please continue."

"Initial reports had Idca as uninhabitable with nothing to offer from a commodities perspective. By luck, however, one of the exploratory teams found something. Now hear me, this is preliminary, but check your monitors." Commodus tapped the display and an object appeared in front of everyone's display.

A pale-yellow diamond, smaller than a tennis ball, reflected brilliantly on the screen.

"Should I ask how much?" asked Rico Crouse.

Faces flickered back on the displays. "Oh, somewhere around twenty-six," said Commodus.

"Twenty-six million isn't going to cover the fixed overhead of the operation," disputed Rico.

The ends of Commodus's mouth danced up and down in a failed attempt to restrain a smile. "Yeah, that'd be billion. Twenty-six billion in the thirty-three-square-mile area we've surveyed."

Elasus's eyebrows went up. The precious metal and stones market had been decapitated after the Event, driving prices toward the heavens. Virus-laced craters prevented mining corporations from excavating old and prospected sites, bankrupting the industry.

Elasus had already calculated mining, packing, and shipping costs before his next question. "How preliminary is this information?"

Commodus shrugged. "Give PRG Kaoru Oishi another two weeks to add to the sample size, then we'll have a better estimate."

"All right, then, two weeks. Misora and Sasha, I see you joined. I just left our quarterly meeting with the PGU. We've been able to meet or exceed projected distribution values to our investors, which primarily consists of PGU officials. North of sixty percent of our revenue comes from operations involving Ojult. In short, all this means is that you two are doing your job. Commodus, put through the proposed bonuses to them tomorrow morning."

"Will do," Commodus confirmed.

Both Misora and Sasha acknowledged the gesture.

The men's indifferent response caught Elasus by surprise. "As Commodus and I have mandated, positive profit-and-loss statements directly correlate to the peace, or relative peace, on Ojult. As my onsite managers on Ojult, you will continue to manage in a manner that promotes peace, thereby increasing profits and your own bank accounts."

"Speaking of peace, why's your arm in a sling, Misora?" asked Rico.

"Training accident," Misora said in heavily accented Spanish. "Horse bucked me off, dislocated my shoulder."

Elasus deduced Misora was lying but disregarded the issue. "Ojultan ore, Listo brandy, and jashinto seeds still rank in the top-three most-profitable exports from Ojult. Is that your conclusion as well, Commodus?"

"Yes. Appian Shipping, or Nencia, more specifically, sent her quarterly balance sheet last week. What she's got on the books suggests nearly fifty percent of her operation consists of those three items. Black-market demand here on Earth for the jashinto leaf, or at least the hallucinogenic seeds, are going up, so expect a price increase at some point this quarter. The corporation gets one-third of the revenue from Nencia's operation, plus full transport fees; it's turning out to be good business. We expect the normal seasonal decline with Ojult in the dead of winter, but outside of that, it's all looking good." Commodus scanned several tabs making sure he covered everything.

Elasus touched his display, which modified everyone's screen. "Regarding imports to Ojult, both mystic- and criminal-exile numbers continue to increase at six percent a quarter. With steady numbers heading into

Ojult, the overall population there is declining. Recent mortality numbers, as indicated from Nencia, speculate nearly seventy-five percent of sages exiled to Ojult are dead within six months. Please explain, Sasha."

Sasha cleared his throat. "I am not convinced Nencia's numbers are accurate, Mr. Reeves."

"I *am* convinced, Sasha, so please answer the question."

Sasha wisely stopped protesting. "As I have stated for months, the local mystics seem to be organizing more so than in years past. Those who don't join the Nein are usually killed by *them* within a few months. There is evidence that some of these sages were killed by a staff-wielding mystic."

The car speakers amplified Commodus and Rico shifting nervously. "This isn't the first time we've heard rumors of a staff on Ojult, so please explain what you've discovered."

"Some of the corpses show the unmistakable sign of being hit with what the mystics call *purple rain*. This type of attack can only be conjured using a staff. We've also heard rumors that a staff-wielder is roaming Listo," said Sasha, "but it comes from a trusted source."

Tanner Sands, who rarely spoke during these meetings, said, "A source? You're suggesting that none of your men have seen it yet?"

"You're correct, Mr. Sands," replied Sasha. "This only furthers my previous requests for more men and the African-ore element."

African ore was a rare substance that, among other things, resisted all but the most powerful mystic attacks. It was mined from the same asteroids that devastated Earth during the Event. For a reason unknown, only those asteroids mined in Africa contained the rare element. This unique quality made it a favorite material for the Celje. Quarrying for the ore was often deadly and thus very little of the element existed in its extracted form.

Elasus pondered the request. "I don't appreciate having to probe my frontline managers for information, Sasha. You're holding back."

Sasha fidgeted with his shoddy jacket. "My men are constantly attacked by the Nein. We need supplies to keep the odds even."

This was Sasha's way of telling the senior staff that conflict between the Celje and Nein was escalating. "You'll speak with Commodus after this call and sort out the details," said Elasus. "Bear in mind that skirmishes with the mystics sparks unrest among the general population, which hinders trade and impacts profits. Peace and profits are the goal, gentlemen, ensure you remember that."

Elasus heard confirmations of his decree and continued with the agenda. Topics like weapons development, FIAS relations, and Prime Minister Kennedy's leadership failures took up most of their time. According to recent polls, public sentiment toward the corporation was at a record high. The general public didn't care how the corporation made its money, as long as it continued to subsidize school tuitions, building repairs, medical bills, and other widely used utilities.

He concluded with recent real-estate plays in the most heavily damaged regions of South America. Sterilization crews would need to ensure the Kupita virus was killed off before construction crews entered these sites, which meant significant delays in potential returns. Decades might pass before the corporation reaped the fruits of these investments, but this was the Reeves family's formula, always looking toward future generations.

———————

Tayla parked in front of the thirteen-story Reeves Corporation after passing through three heavily guarded checkpoints.

"Good evening, Mr. Reeves," greeted Doug Kranzer, opening the executive's door.

Elasus stepped out with his black briefcase in hand. "Thank you, Doug, did you receive my envelope?"

"Yes, Mr. Reeves. Very generous and thoughtful. Thank you very much, sir."

Tayla followed Elasus into the executive-only elevator and waited until the doors closed to speak. "Your schedule for the next three days is on your desk, Mr. Reeves."

"Thank you, Ms. Cruz. Start putting together an inventory report for the upcoming African-ore shipment out of FIAS. I suspect we're going to need a larger shipment after tonight's meeting. Make sure finance accrues for the life insurance payments that will result from the additional mining expeditions."

He inspected her white skirt, then moved on to her new curves. When she'd taken the personal-assistant position, Tayla planned on keeping her hair naturally brown and didn't think twice about her breast size. A few weeks after taking the position, she found that Elasus had already scheduled her enhancements. Today, her long, fake-blonde hair fell over her fake breasts and low-cut top. To maintain her figure, Elasus had hired a personal trainer.

They stepped off the elevator onto the elegant executive floor, Tayla's heels clicking with the motion of her slim hips. She locked the elevator, which prohibited uninvited guests from reaching the floor.

"Yes, Mr. Reeves, I'll have it on your desk in the morning." She paced ahead of him and opened the main office door.

Elasus walked down the wide hallway leading to his desk, passing the portraits, photographs, and paintings all representing some aspect of his family or the corporation. Tayla sat at her desk outside the main door and started the inventory report. She powered on the holographic displays and adjusted outdated pictures of her two children and husband.

It was well after midnight when Elasus called her into his office. Understanding his expectations, she'd changed into a short white dress after finishing her work.

Tayla tapped the flashing icon on her desk. "Yes, Mr. Reeves, are you finished for the evening?"

"Not yet Tayla," he replied, hanging up before she responded.

Tayla picked up on his use of her first name, which meant her role switched from assistant to mistress. She shut down her office and turned off the lights, making sure to lock the main office door behind her. Elasus drank straight bourbon while she preferred vodka soda, the only drink that seemed to help put her mind in the right mood.

"It's late; shall I turn down the bed?" She placed the straight bourbon in front of him and sat down on the nearby couch.

Elasus looked up from his display, locking onto her hiked-up skirt. The game of give and take with the most powerful man in existence was nothing short of nauseating, but it was imperative, a necessary evil to keep her children safe.

CHAPTER 14: YEAR 2399

Jayden jolted through the tent door, ready to kill any man ordered to slay Janice. In the corner, a note lay atop his weapons and backpack.

> *I listened to the verdict and followed your instructions. It's unlikely we'll both make it out of this, but I hope you know that I consider you my closest friend and confidant. Godspeed Jayden.*
>
> *Love Janice*

"Good girl," Jayden said. Her head start might mean the difference between living and an excruciating death. Jayden fastened his pistol belt and short-blade, shouldered his rifle, and checked his backpack. Four filled canteens of water, salted beef, and dried vegetables.

With Janice on the run, Jayden bolted toward the stables, following the plan he'd already turned over repeatedly in his head. He hoisted himself atop a saddled horse and shot toward the southern gates of Carendra.

Sleet fell around the galloping horse, sticking and accumulating against Jayden's beard and garment. The six-hour journey to the southern harbor of Pork Naok was his best but most obvious option. Appian trade ships frequented the port, casting off toward Meridone and Capintesta every few days.

Pacing the horse, Jayden followed the well-worn path south, passing the occasional frostbitten traveler. Snow-covered limbs hunched and snapped from their burdens while visibility continued to diminish.

When small barrel fires dotting the entrance of the port town came into view, Jayden freed the exhausted horse and scanned the area. Layers of falling snow reduced visibility, but unlike the furtive Celje, the Nein were easy to spot. Jayden tipped his hat low and walked into town. The sun crept up behind him as he passed through the main gates by dozens of early risers.

Jayden knew the port town well and headed for the docks, bypassing the single pub and motel. Docked in the harbor were three snow-covered sloops and one large, two-masted brig, crowded with crewmen.

Gusty winds drove the boats into the docks while twirling snowflakes danced to the rhythm of Mother Nature. Jayden recognized the larger ship as an Appian cargo ship, meaning Nencia's people were here too.

Jayden headed away from the brig. He'd not seen Nencia since his arrival on Ojult and knew what her group did to those they did not call friend. By contrast, most independent ship captains on Ojult were easily bribed and would take the occasional passenger for a steep fee.

From the Appian brig, a man with a British accent barked orders. "Schedule change, men, we're heading back to Rindo within the hour. Get that cargo on board fast, or this storm will keep you here for a week. That's a week with no booze, women, or money! And did I mention, no women!?"

The three sloops didn't look in any condition to leave within the week, let alone within the hour. Still, Rindo was the northern port town of Capintesta and rarely frequented by the Nein.

Fluttering with the risk, Jayden walked toward the brig. Less than thirty meters from the ship, he pondered his options. Sneak aboard? Perhaps ask for passage? Or try to work for the violent group?

"Take one more step toward my boat, and you'll be just another souvenir for the sea," said that same British voice behind him.

Feeling a gun barrel aimed at his back, Jayden raised his hands. "I'm not a bandit or thief, just looking for a ride is all."

"Hasn't anyone told you that creeping around an Appian ship is a good way to get dead? Your weapons tell me you're not Celje, but you've got plenty of them, and you ditched your horse beyond the gates. You're coming with me and the boss can decide what to do with you. Leave your gear here and mind your movements."

Disarmed at gunpoint, Jayden's plan was crumbling with every step. Sweating despite the frigid temperatures, Jayden crossed the planks onto the boat, urged on by the barrel in his back. He marched down three flights of stairs and through a dimly lit hallway until pausing at the entrance of a small room. These quarters were obviously used as an office, adorned with digital navigation charts, paper charts, trade manifests, and other business accoutrements. Behind the small desk in the corner sat a familiar, dark-haired woman.

"Apologies for the interruption, boss," said the British man. "We found this crook taking his jolly time looking over our ship and cargo. Thief or spy is my guess. You want us to put him at the bottom of the sea?"

The woman looked up from her digital board. "Put a bullet through his head, Zakar, then tell Captain Green to hurry up and get us out of here. I can hear ice scraping against the hull."

Zakar grabbed Jayden by the collar and thrust him back into the hallway.

"Wait," said Jayden, failing to shrug off his captor. "I wasn't trying to capture your ship. I need a ride to Rindo, I can pay, and I could care less about your black-market trade."

Nencia didn't bother looking back up from her notes. "So, you know what we're hauling and our destination," she said. "Not exactly helping yourself out, are you?"

"Let's go, fish bait," Zakar said, dragging Jayden out.

The ship suddenly lurched, sending both men into the wall and Zakar's pistol skidding onto the floor. Jayden snatched the weapon and pointed it at Zakar's head.

"I'm not a thief, a criminal, or anything of the sort," said Jayden. "Ten years ago, Nencia, you and your husband handed me over to the Nein, and now I'm running from them. I'm looking for passage to Meridone or Capintesta, any place but here. I've got money and will pay whatever you're asking, but I need to leave today."

Zakar stared down the barrel of his own pistol while Nencia stared at them.

"You pull that trigger and you won't make it to the foredeck before my men cut you into pieces," said Nencia.

With practiced ease, Jayden flipped the pistol around so the handle faced Zakar. The Appian man skeptically seized the weapon and turned it against Jayden once more.

"No, Zakar, not yet," Nencia said. "Running from Syrus Tokarek, not good at all. I'll hear you out. Give us a moment, Zakar. If he gives me trouble, I'll kill him myself."

Zakar slowly holstered his pistol and backed out of the room.

Nencia shut the door and motioned for Jayden to sit. He sat in a nearby chair, thinking how beautiful this woman might be if she showered and combed her hair.

"What's your name or should I call you dumbass going forward" she asked.

"Jayden Vaut. I work... worked for Syrus Tokarek up until last night. I need to—"

Nencia waved him silent. "You, a slave for the Nein? Didn't know they kept the pretty ones. I figured they sold them all." She paused, appraising him and taking a sip from a small cup on her desk. "Maybe I do remember you, Vaut, but if you've pissed off the Nein, the last thing I want to do is help you. I'm in the business of making money, and upsetting my clients isn't a good way to stay profitable. I'm sure you understand. Unless, of course... you wouldn't happen to be Syrus's rumored assassin, would you? Shadowy man, good at killing mystics?"

This woman was as clever as she was beautiful. "The Nein trained me as an assassin. I'm a quick learner and loyal. Whatever you need done, I can take care of it, but I need to get off Listo first."

She leaned back against the desk exposing her upper chest through her coat. "I've got plenty of killers working for me already; try again."

Rapid knocks on the door. "Boss, need a minute," said Zakar.

"Come in."

The door snapped open and Zakar's wide frame stood in the door. "Five Nein on the docks looking for an escaped slave. They want to search the ship."

Jayden eyed Zakar, then Nencia. "I'm not a normal slave, Nencia, and they'll kill to get to me. Give me my weapons back, I can help, you'll need me."

Nencia ran a calm hand through her tangled hair. "You want us to fight the Nein? Over you? I'd rather hand you over, or better yet, sell you." She twisted a dull wedding ring in contemplation. "Zakar, keep them off the ship, and tell them I'll be up in a minute."

Zakar nodded and left.

"I'll fight before I let you turn me over," countered Jayden, feeling a tinge of adrenaline pulse through him.

"I expect you would," she replied, her lips turning up into a mischievous smile. She stepped toward him, stopping so close he could feel her breath. "I see you as an investment, Vaut, so starting now, you work for me."

For the next twelve hours, Jayden hid inside the cargo hold fighting off seasickness and closing his mind to the constant shouts of *Iceberg ahead!* Loud thumps against the hull followed by high-pitched screeching sounds sent Jayden's heart into overdrive. Drowning or heart attack, neither sounded like a good death.

An abrupt horn from above nearly did the trick.

"Get those lines ready, secure the jib, and keep an eye out for ice and traffic. This forsaken fog and snow is covering up everything, and if we hit something, we'll go down like a whore on Meridone." Jayden recognized Captain Green's Irish accent.

"Captain Green, we're tied off!" yelled Zakar several minutes later.

"Make sure they get all the ice off the hull and lines, or the weight'll drive us right into the sea," replied Captain Green.

The dark cargo hold smelled like spoiled meat, churning Jayden's already weak stomach. Unable to stand because of the short ceiling, his back and knees roared in agony. He heard heavy boots stomping down the stairwell.

"Boss wants you up top, Vaut," bellowed Zakar. "Your gear's with her. Get going!"

Jayden hadn't heard from Nencia since she'd shoved him down into the cargo hold. Whatever she'd said to the Nein got them off his back for the time being.

Jayden stepped onto the deck and froze. If the weather in Port Naok was foul, the conditions in Rindo were apocalyptic. High winds, blizzard, freezing fog.

Zakar skidded to a stop beside him. "You afraid of the cold, Vaut? Get going!"

Jayden tipped his hat and beelined off the busy deck.

The ramp off the ship was slick and covered with snow, blasting Jayden with the realization of the gruesome death that awaited him if he fell into the icy sea. He walked carefully down the lantern-lit dock, searching for Nencia or any signs of the Nein.

Nencia was at the end of the dock, checking off her inventory list against the unloaded cargo.

Jayden coughed but she ignored him.

"You see your husband, the captain, very often. He seemed like a good guy. Can't imagine why he'd leave a beautiful woman like you alone on this half-cracked planet."

Nencia looked up from her handheld, brushing snow off her knotted hair. "Flattery only gets you so far, especially with me. And for your own good, don't mention *the captain* again."

Jayden turned and took in his surroundings. "So, I'm in Capintesta? This is where my new life begins?"

Nencia rolled her eyes and motioned behind her. "Your gear is back there. Regarding your future, you're no good to me with the Nein looking for you. They're a client, a shitty one, but their coin is as good as the next. You need to disappear for a few months, get off their radar, then we'll talk."

Jayden fastened his pistol belt and grabbed the rest of his gear. "How about Worall or here in Rindo? Not many Nein around."

"I operate out of Worall and Rindo a lot, so that's not going to work. Go somewhere else, a smaller town, find a job, go get laid, make a few tonze, try to not starve to death, and stay off the grid. Stop assuming the Celje aren't looking for you either. They have spies everywhere, and you just spent a decade working for the Nein. If they think you're Nein, they'll kill you. They've changed their beat over the past few years, not the clandestine people they used to be."

Jayden didn't think the Celje knew of him, but her advice made sense.

"I'll keep that in mind, thanks. Peace and quiet sounds like a good idea. Any decent small towns around here with gawdy tourist attractions?"

"You're not funny, Vaut. If you want peace, or at least don't want to end up in pieces, then get a new appearance and try to find some work in one of the small villages down the coast. The Celje and Nein generally stay away from small towns."

Find a small village, become a farmer, get a haircut, didn't seem too complicated. Still, jobs were nearly impossible to find, even in the larger towns.

Jayden stuck out his hand. "You saved my life, and you're right, the Nein won't stop looking for me, maybe ever."

Nencia returned the handshake and locked eyes with him. "My people tell me there's only one Celje patrol tonight, and we haven't been able to pay them off, so be wary. Once outside the city walls, head southeast and follow the coast. It's mostly dense forests and cliffs. Remember, I expect repayment for saving your ass. Stay alive long enough to pay me back."

This wasn't exactly the new beginning he was hoping for, but it was a start. "I appreciate what you're doing. Tell your husband I said hello."

"I'm not married to that man," she said gritting her teeth. "And you're too young for me, so don't get any ideas. Now, get going before the Celje come wondering around."

Jayden tipped his hat one last time and left to find his new life. Vigilant of the Celje patrol in town, Jayden holed up in an abandoned stable near the harbor. It smelled awful, not as bad as the ship, but bad enough. Jayden checked the grounds between him and the barely visible city gates. Large wooden fencing surrounded the busy town full of shops and small huts. Hundreds of people crowded the seaport, but Jayden ignored them, except for a group of four men walking past a water well from the east.

Working for the Nein taught him many useful skills, such as how to identify a Celje agent. The Celje dressed shabbily, like every other citizen on Ojult, except they traveled in groups of four and generally carried pistols at the small of their backs. These four were dressed for the cold, but Jayden could still see BPs bulging from their coats. BPs shot depleted uranium rounds with a magnesium coating, which produced the beam.

Using both a beam and projectile, the pistol was quieter, kicked less, and could still be used in an oxygen-deprived environment, like space.

Unlike the oblivious citizens around them, these Celje continually scanned their surroundings. Jayden took no chances and headed for the front gates once the group faded into the blizzard. Outside the gates, Jayden headed southeast as Nencia suggested. Trudging through the dense foliage and deep snow wore him out. Used to life outdoors without amenities, Jayden built a small fire the first night, using kindling and a flint lighter. Under a canopy of woven branches and twigs, Jayden warmed some of the prepared food Janice had stashed in his backpack.

Trusting the fire to keep the smaller of god's critters away for the night, Jayden slept dreamlessly.

Snapping twigs from two furry zibars woke him at sunrise. Many on Ojult believed these animals were a scientific experiment of the Reeves corporation brought to the planet for hunting purposes. Ojultan lore told a different story. Patriarchs of Ojultan told of the zibars hunting in packs to take down the berserk sarcto beast.

Either way, these harmless-looking cotton balls were carnivorous with teeth sharp enough to shave a man's beard. Jayden hunted zibars on Listo and found them to be good eating and easy to shoot. After a healthy breakfast of zibar and orange berries, Jayden extinguished his fire and set off down the coast.

Jayden traveled three more days down the eastern coast of Capintesta, encountering nothing but more snow, hard-packed mud, and frozen fresh-water streams. It was easy to see why Nencia recommended this path, especially during winter. Yet his ecstasy in escaping the Celje and the Nein faded by the fourth day.

Tired, drenched, and with no signs of any villages, Jayden decided to make camp at the end of a nearby tree line. He doggedly pushed through the dense brush until he fell face-first into muddy slush.

"Damn it!" he cursed, getting up and brushing himself off.

The crack of a pistol sent Jayden diving back into the soggy mud. With practiced fluidity, Jayden flung his backpack ahead and rested his rifle atop. He scanned the open land ahead, his eyes and thermal scope struggling to adjust with the dimming sun.

"He's not dead yet, fool," said a man with slicked black hair, sunglasses, and his arm in a sling. "Merle, you fool, shoot him again. Hurry up already, he's bleeding all over the place."

"I am, I am," said Merle, standing over a severely bleeding man. *Crack!* The shot ended the man's life.

Finally seeing the field clearly, Jayden spotted two armed men with two bound women.

"Mind if I have a little fun with the younger one?" asked Merle.

Misora, the man with the sunglasses, shook his head. "It's below freezing and all you're thinking about is screwing? We're getting back to camp first, then you can have the mother, but the daughter's mine."

Jayden crawled forward, ignoring the cries of the gagged women.

"You see, Erika?" said Misora, pointing to the dead man. "You see your husband down there? This is what happens when you support the Nein. We warned you, we even offered to buy ammunitions off you, but your stiffening husband over there just had to play hero."

"Wheel's fixed. We're ready to go," said Merle. "What we doing with them once we get to camp? We killing them or shipping them off?"

Misora rubbed his hands together. "Sasha wants to send a message by killing the mother himself, then sell that piece of ass to Meridone." Misora waved to his partner. "Load 'em up in a hurry; the villagers and that damn mayor probably heard that gunshot."

The women wore torn clothes and fresh blood smeared their faces. Jayden inspected the area to ensure the men were alone, then made his move. Staying prone, Jayden clicked the safety off and readied his kill shot.

Merle suddenly screeched as the older woman leapt off the wagon into him. She'd broken free and clawed Merle's exposed face.

"Run, Serena!" she yelled, but the younger woman struggled against her bonds.

The brawling woman blocked Jayden's shot. He leapt to his feet and charged, covering the distance in seconds. He swung his rifle like a bat, hoping to kill Merle with a single strike.

Bam!

An invisible fist slammed into Jayden, sending him sprawling onto his back. He reached for his rifle, but his shoulder wouldn't move. He looked down, baffled, and found his left shoulder covered in blood.

"Merle, you okay? Get up!" Misora ripped off his sling and fired several unsteadied shots at Jayden, who rolled away. Bullets kicked up mud and snow as they impacted the wet ground.

Merle threw the woman to the ground and raised his pistol.

Two loud cracks pierced the air.

Smoke bled from the end of Jayden's revolver as Merle fell to the ground.

"No!" yelled Jayden, seeing the mother collapse, blood oozing from her chest. His shot was milliseconds too late.

Sobs beat through the younger woman's gag, but Jayden didn't have time to tend to her. More rounds came from Misora, one zoomed centimeters from his ear.

"You're gonna die slowly for killing my guy!" screamed Misora. The murderer bolted to the opposite side of the wagon for cover. The unmistakable sounds of *chinks* revealed he was reloading. "You've made an enemy of the Celje today."

Jayden fired a shot that missed wide, then called to the bound woman. "Can you move? Can you run? Get out of here!"

Through tears of fear and grief, she shook her head. The bonds were firm, and she was still on her knees, frozen. Jayden changed tactics, climbed to a knee, and charged around the carriage. If he could surprise Misora and get a quick shot in...

Underestimating his opponent's prowess nearly cost him his life. Misora's shot slapped against his already disabled shoulder.

"Arrgg, shit!" Like someone held a torch to his arm, Jayden's wound burned, but he kept fighting. He repositioned himself for a clearer shot, but his foe had disappeared.

Twigs cracked from around the wagon, and Jayden whirled to face the threat. Misora's rifle was aimed high, and by the time the Celje adjusted, Jayden had fired three rounds at him. Misora staggered back, blood beginning to soil the front of his shirt. Like himself, Misora was on the ground now, clutching his side. With only one arm and darkness narrowing his vision, Jayden reached for more ammunition.

Hardened to the unanticipated realities of combat, Jayden used his good hand to reload while he slid toward the roped girl. He scanned the area, but had lost the man again. "You hurt?" he asked. She was panicked, confused, and in shock, but otherwise appeared uninjured. Shouts in the distance yanked his attention away from the battle zone. "You need to get out of here, now, before his friends arrive." Jayden pulled a pocketknife from his belt and sliced through the ropes. "Go!"

Over nearing shouts and rumblings of a fleeting wagon, Jayden saw the girl unravel herself and scramble over to her motionless mother and father, hunching over their bodies. She shook as tears poured down her cheeks.

Jayden's opponent had escaped, but a new group had appeared over the tall, sky grass beyond. His shoulder was completely numb and his body started to shake, a side effect of shock and blood loss.

"Look girl," shouted Jayden. "They're dead! You need to get out of here, now, before this new squad arrives."

She didn't respond or even react to his warning. Jayden thought about dragging her away, but the logical side of his mind took over. This young woman had just witnessed her parents murder, and the demands of a stranger weren't going to move her.

Jayden positioned himself between the girl and encroaching crowd. They were armed, with rifles raised, ready to kill. Jayden raised his pistol at the front man and took stock of his enemy. The man leading the group was dressed like a farmer, with silver hair, glasses, and aged skin. An adjacent man was wearing a greased stained, white apron, with a sword raised in a defensive position.

If these people were a Celje squad, then he was a mystic Elder. "Stop!" shouted Jayden, his steel sight still focused on the lead man. "You may have the numbers, but I promise you, I'm not your ordinary stranger. Back off and leave this girl alone."

The older man halted the group, but their weapons remained leveled on him. The silver-haired man spoke something to the pack, then advanced, alone, toward Jayden. He carried his rifle with one hand, and the elongated weapon swayed with each step.

Jayden's experience told him not to relax and to anticipate the unexpected. Yet, he found himself steadily lowering his pistol as the man neared. "What is this?" demanded Jayden. "Who are you people! What do want with her?"

"Easy son," said the man earnestly, then directed his words to the girl. "Serena... Serena, look at me. I need to know what is going on here. Who is this man? What has happened?"

For the first time since the ordeal started, the teenage girl looked up. "Misora, he... he did this. This man, he saved me and tried to save... them. They're dead... they're dead... they're gone."

PART III

CHAPTER 15: YEAR 2400

Mystics are frequently confused with wizards and genies capable of producing unimaginable feats with a simple wave of a wand. Tales of such chimeric beings made popular during the twentieth and twenty-first centuries helped fuel the stereotype of mystics into the post-Event society. While mystics did help society rebuild from the Event, many Thoba believed they could do more but were unwilling to show their true power.

A frequently told story among exiled mystics tells of a father murdering a mystic for refusing to cure his daughter's cancer. Akin to the Salem witch trials of the seventeenth century, the Thoba revolted against mystics who refused to use their powers for the good of the world, helping forge the current-day Nein.

Dr. Petya Amurski, whom historians would later find was a distant relative of Sabrina Reeves, is credited with much of the knowledge known about mystics today. As a biologist and mystic, Dr. Amurski took a different approach toward the mystic phenomenon. She kept her abilities a secret and ran tests on herself, the asteroids, and the strange gray trees sprouting near impact sites.

Her discoveries included healing powers, the manipulation of fire and water, and perhaps the most important, how branches of the Amurski tree amplify a sage's powers. Like comparing a lighter to a blowtorch, the appropriately named Amurski tree became a popular commodity among mystics during the post-Event rebuilding efforts.

Knowing the limitations of mystics and their history was important to Syrus Tokarek as he trained with his twenty-one-year-old protégé, Phaedra Lillea.

Syrus effortlessly blocked the silver discs coming from Phaedra's staff. "Change your attacks, Phaedra, keep your enemy guessing."

Phaedra's silvery hair bounced as she shot alternating projectiles at her master. "I will defeat you," she said, firing off spells one after another.

Syrus blocked the attacks with his free hand. "Your mind determines the power of the attacks, not all this grunting. Slow your attacks and add fortitude in their creation." An ice spike he narrowly blocked scraped his hand and drew blood.

Phaedra ceased the exercise and hunched over, gasping for breath. "I... still don't know how you... I'm throwing everything I have at you."

He healed the minor scratch with a mental command and walked over to his apprentice. "I'm closer to seventy than sixty and have been doing this a long time."

"And I'll get your staff," she said, tossing the weapon back to her master.

"If you prove worthy, then perhaps. If that day were tomorrow, would you be ready?"

"Teach me more. I can handle it."

With a simple command, a translucent energy wave burst from Syrus's hand, knocking Phaedra to the ground. "If you wish to lead the Nein, you must train your mind as well as your body."

The ease and power of the attack seemed to knock some sense back into the youth. "I understand, *Daska*."

Daska meant teacher in the old native tongue of the Nein. An advocate of the ancient Nein teachings, Syrus demanded these customs be followed.

"You're only scratching the surface of your power, Phaedra, and you're already a match for any Celje."

The training-room door creaked open. "Lady Tokarek," said Phaedra, bowing.

Helia walked into the room and smiled. She could have anything she wanted, the best clothing, fine jewelry, anything the planet offered, yet she dressed like a common villager, never wearing trinkets or gems. "Hello,

Phaedra. I hope you're not hurting my brother too much. Everyone in Carendra can hear your training."

"Your brother's powerful; I hope to one day match it."

Syrus hugged Helia. Phaedra bowed and dismissed herself from the room.

Helia's smile broadened. "I came from the kitchens, where I met Andreas. You really didn't have to go to all this trouble. I don't know where you found enough sweets for a cake, but I'm sure the town's children will love it. And I had no idea Giles was such a master in the kitchen."

"There's nothing more important than you and Mea."

She placed a gentle hand on his face. "You take such good care of us. If only you'd show this side of yourself to others."

"I'd kill every sole on this planet for our family, but blood is different. Being the Nein leader, different rules apply."

Helia hugged him again. "I love you, and thank you for allowing Giles to help with the food. It's going to be a wonderful birthday."

As one of Syrus's senior advisors, Giles led the probe into the recent Celje incursions into Nein territory. The Celje were becoming more aggressive, even attempting to kidnap his people if found alone on the road to Port Naok.

Helia must have sensed his hesitation. "Is it as bad as Kavil says?"

Syrus felt the conversation pulling his sister's mood down. "Our people will never succumb to the Celje, not while I still breathe. But enough of this, let's go celebrate my niece's birthday."

———————

Children on Ojult celebrated birthdays with no luxuries. A day without chores, perhaps drinking berry juice or eating a piece of sweet cake, was considered a rare treat. The party started off with singing, dancing, and a large pork-belly roast. Mea enjoyed the attention and the momentary withdrawal from the realities of her life.

Yet all was not as it should be. Looking around, Syrus noticed two of his senior staff missing. "Captain Siller," said Syrus, "where are Phaedra and Andreas?"

Clad in maroon armor, the nearby commander stepped toward his liege. "Scouting, my premier. Phaedra felt that with the recent Celje incursions, an extra set of eyes during the party was prudent. Andreas was already scheduled to lead the evening patrols, and I expect him back shortly."

"Uncle, I could benefit your patrols. I'm ready to do my part," Mea said.

Ojult's two moons, Genesis and Durum, shined brightly over the teenage girl. "You'll be a powerful mystic one day. Keep up your training with the captain, but for now, you stay within our walls."

"Are the Celje hunting Jayden?"

Mea often brought up Jayden on random occasions, but Syrus remained patient with his young niece. "The banishment of Jayden was complicated, and all I can say for certain is that we are not searching for him. He escaped our land and earned his freedom."

"Jayden Vaut was nothing more than a slave who murdered two of my guard," said Captain Siller. "His name should be banished from our lands and your niece's mouth sterilized for even—"

In a flash, Captain Siller was skidding across the ground, bringing the party to a sudden halt.

Syrus raised a reassuring hand. "All is well," he said to the stunned crowd. He approached Siller who spun on his back and kicked back up to his feet.

"Forgive me, Premier, I spoke out of haste."

"Speak that way to my niece again, and you'll be the one hunted off the continent."

Captain Siller was an astute fighter, able to match any mystic, yet even he trembled before Syrus. "Yes, Premier, of-of course, it shall not happen again."

Mea stepped beside her Uncle. "Jayden was good to our family, I miss him."

"One day, Mea, you will lead our people," said Syrus, choosing his words carefully. "What happened to Jayden was the result of his own misgivings, not the captain's ignorance or my judgements. Sometimes the decisions we make have unintended consequences, but we live with them. The Nein rule with a firm hand. It's our way."

"Perhaps we'll see Jayden again one day," chimed Helia, walking into the conversation.

Syrus didn't regret Jayden's exile, but nevertheless, the young man did have an impact on the family.

That night, Syrus slept soundly with the knowledge his family and people were safe—he'd accomplished his function as a leader today. Texts from mystic scholars foretold of powerful sages able to see the future, like premonitions of impending danger. Like an itch within his subconscious, Syrus awoke moments before Andreas Palada knocked on his bedroom door.

"Come in, Andreas, what is it?" asked Syrus, sensing the urgency from his freshman advisor.

Andreas extinguished his lit hettle and cautiously opened the door. Andreas was a pale-faced man with a handlebar mustache and a pistol hanging from a shoulder holster. His dull gold and dark-blue armor blended with the darkness of the room.

Smoke consumed the air in front of Andreas as he spoke. "Premier, it seems that my letter to the runts next door didn't work," he said in a prolonged drawl.

"The Celje," confirmed Syrus, putting on his black armor.

Andreas nodded, lighting several candles around the room. "Our distant cousins are roaming the woods as we speak, and they're armed this time. It seems they want to dance."

For the first time in many months, Syrus, enrobed in his ebony leather armor and sheathed his staff. "It's nearly morning, and the odds of Sasha launching an attack in daylight is low. Where's Kavil and Phaedra?"

Andreas ignited a wooden match and puffed another hettle stalk to life. "Jenna went to scout the incoming group. Siller's organizing the troops, and Phaedra's having a look at the incoming party."

Outside his home, Syrus was met by his advisors. "No organized group on Ojult is dumb enough to attack us; this is something different. I'll go alone and discover their intentions."

Siller's eyes bulged. "Premier, I must object. If this is an assassination attempt or all-out attack, then walking out there is paramount to death."

Syrus's premonition of danger grew stronger, and he could almost smell an upcoming battle. "Giles, find Jenna and see to the safety of my sister and niece. Kavil, continue organizing the guard. Andreas, follow me."

His advisors bowed in unity, Syrus's tone leaving no room for contradiction. The sun peeked over the eastern tree line, and the residents of Carendra were now aware of the approaching force. Since becoming the Nein leader three decades ago, Syrus focused on rebuilding the Nein to their former glory. As in years past, Syrus would deescalate the situation, but if a fight started, he knew his people would relentlessly slaughter the enemy with no thought of mercy.

Syrus approached the outskirts of Carendra, Andreas in tow. The enemy was only a few hundred meters to the north. Soon the sounds of horses and men echoed through the forest.

"Guess we can scratch Levi off the list," prattled Andreas, tapping the butt of his pistol.

Syrus sensed more troops than just those approaching. With the safety of his people of utmost concern, Syrus unsheathed his staff and trekked forward. "Stay here, Andreas."

Sasha Burmistrov dismounted from his horse just ahead of Syrus. He wore common clothing, a wide-brimmed hat, and a cloak that didn't quite cover his two BP pistols. There was something about the Celje leader's arrogant walk that foretold of a fight.

"Mr. Tokarek," said Sasha, raising his hands in greeting. "I see your spies did their job, yet you are alone. Should I feel honored or scared?"

Sasha's accent was so thick, Syrus barely made out what he said.

Syrus counted about a dozen well-armed, plain-clothed soldiers and guessed each wore special armor underneath. Their dull-black radial energy rifles used enhanced, *intelligent* scopes that guided nanoprojectiles to their targets. "You and your people aren't welcome here, Sasha. Leave, now."

Sasha shrugged and looked past Syrus. "We are Ojult's peacekeepers. It is our responsibility to patrol the land and make sure all is well."

Syrus shook his head. "Those rifles auto-target vital organs, hardly a peacekeeping weapon. My scouts tell me you've been raiding supply lines, kidnapping Thoba, harassing my people, and growing your *peacekeeping* army for months. Have the respect not to lie to me."

Sasha waved the accusation away. "We are peacekeepers, but you don't seem in the mood to chat, so I'll get to my point. Your staff, Mr. Tokarek, please hand it over."

The saddled Celje behind Sasha widened their formation.

"Nothing but the slaughter of your people will come of this. Take your fellows and leave my people be. Do not return."

Sasha hooked the sides of his cloak over his pistols. "Drop the weapon, Mr. Tokarek, and retreat back to your home. No reason to make violence today."

Sasha's ploy was just as obvious as it was ineffective. He went for his pistols just as his men raised their rifles. Syrus expected the move and was faster, twirling his staff and slamming it into the ground like a sledgehammer. The earth around Sasha exploded, sending the mounted Celje flying. Sasha blew back several meters, his hat spinning off. Startled horses bucked their riders and fled while Syrus began a methodical retreat toward his own people.

The Celje were shocked but not down, and with surprising quickness, they returned fire. Syrus deflected their concentrated attack with a conjured shield while falling back.

"We spill blood today," shouted Sasha, dusting dirt off his chest. He tapped his earpiece and opened a channel. "Unit Two and Three, focus on staff-wielder. One and Four, smash their borders. Force them together!"

Along the Nein lines, glistening wards reflected the morning sun. The mystics who preferred projectile weapons let loose their barrage straight into the Celje vanguard.

"Celje reinforcements coming in from the right," barked Andreas.

Captain Siller was on the front line, casting shields around his men. "They're widening their formation. Expect a quick advancement."

Andreas ducked behind one of the captain's shields and reloaded. "Why the hell would they do that?"

Energy bolts pinged then dissolved off the captain's shields. "We hold the advantage while fighting at a distance. They'll want to engage us in melee to take away that edge. Some of their energy-blades may be made from African ore as well, so be mindful."

Syrus's augmented vision narrowed on a flanking squad. The Celje's energy-blades were forged by bonding two slender, closely set swords with a plasma current enshrouding the weapon. The luminous weapon bloomed ginger as rushing air streamed against the current.

The enemy's rapid-bounding tactic came abruptly, but Syrus readied himself to halt the advance. At the front gates of Carendra, small spheres engulfed in raging fire slingshotted from Syrus's staff and onto the incoming Celje. He guessed that most of Sasha's forces had never encountered a staff-wielding mystic before. A devilish smile painted his face when the advancing Celje halted their charge and dived for cover.

From behind Sasha's line came another weapon, a silver-haired ghost moving swiftly through the ranks. Phaedra cut down three soldiers with her two blades before the Celje realized they were under attack from their flank.

"Unit Five, kill that witch!" said Sasha, aiming his own BP at the silvery hair. "Use suppressing fire while the others advance. Kill her!"

Phaedra spiked one of her blades into the ground and conjured a burly shield that put her into a defensive position.

Syrus raised his staff, concentrating on the four men closing in on his apprentice. Out of the tip launched three thin, purple tracers rocketing out like fireworks. The missiles struck their targets, but only one soldier fell lifeless.

Andreas was back on the attack and noticed the result. "Seems like our friends got some new armor."

Captain Siller used a sequence of hand gestures ordering his rear forces forward. "Premier, we're at a stalemate unless you continue the onslaught. What are your orders?"

Syrus surveyed the battlefield, first noticing Phaedra moving slowly forward, shield and sword still raised. "Order your men to attack in pairs; they're not to venture out alone."

"Premier," said Andreas, pointing ahead. "Phaedra's in trouble."

Syrus marched forward a few paces, enraged at the thought of his apprentice falling to these cowards. Centering his mind within the heart of Sasha's formation, Syrus unleashed an arcane salvo upon the Celje forces. Fire spheres, ice javelins, razor-sharp silver discs, and purple-streaked rain tore into Sasha's ranks.

With blade and shield, Phaedra exploited the distraction and continued her assault. Her first opponent managed to unsheathe his energy-blade and block her first combination, but the man's skills carried him no further. Phaedra's next sequence took the soldier's forearm off, followed by a neck strike.

Syrus gorged on the pride pulsing through him upon seeing his apprentice's success. Around the battlefield, most of Sasha's men were injured or seeking cover.

From his flank, Andreas rang out a warning. "Incoming!"

Syrus turned in time to see several dozen Celje kneeling and taking aim. Bullets slammed into the Nein line, striking vital organs and cutting them down like dominos. Four rounds struck Syrus in the arm and shoulder, wheeling and throwing him to the ground.

Andreas avoided the salvo and advanced to Syrus's aid, unloading his pistol and placing a protective shield in front of them. "Siller, need a healer here!"

Captain Siller ordered his line to adjust their fire and limped over to Andreas. Javier and Nigel took up firing positions on either side of Syrus and fired at will.

"Continue the battle!" Syrus ordered then turned his arcane powers inward to begin healing his torn flesh. Scratches and small wounds were simple to heal, but bullet holes were another matter.

The sounds of battle dissipated while Andreas worked one-handed to reload his pistol. "And I was hoping he would stay for a smoke. Sorry Captain, guess the fun's over."

"Shut up!" barked Captain Siller. "They're pulling back. We must press our attack now. Nein, follow me!"

Syrus watched his men pursue the retreating Celje, no doubt hoping for melee combat.

"They're just giving up?" said Andreas. "They get one good swipe in and retreat?"

Syrus stood, blood streaming down his arm. "Order our remaining forces to scout the area, kill any surviving Celje, then man the perimeter."

Andreas gaped at Syrus's free-flowing wound. "Premier, that arm looks like it's ready to come off. Perhaps we should tend to that first?"

Phaedra approached from the shaded trees. "Cowards! What the hell was the point of that? They just like wasting soldiers?"

"I'll heal once inside our walls," Syrus told Andreas, turning his attention to Phaedra. "You showed great prowess and strategy during the battle."

"Don't think they liked you much, Phaedra, sneaking up on them like that. I'm guessing you just went to the top of their bad-guy list." Andreas grinned until noticing she was wounded. "Phaedra, you're shot!"

"I'm fine; it went straight through," she replied, but her eyes flirted with something back toward the village. "Something's off. I can feel it."

Syrus turned with the group, following Phaedra's gaze back toward Carendra. He diagnosed the situation first and sprinted toward the village. Phaedra and Andreas followed close behind, unsure what was amiss. Syrus shot past three dead arcane guards, an inert Jenna, and Giles who was crawling on his hands and knees, bleeding and mumbling for help.

Nearing Syrus's home, the battle cries of Mea rang out from inside. Syrus crashed through the door, eyes alert for the enemy. He caught a flicker of movement from the hallway before a crushing energy wave blasted him back through the entrance. Syrus tumbled, taking out Andreas, knocking the advisor out cold.

A hooded figure holding a staff stood in the doorway. "You ought to guard your family a bit closer. This is the second time you've left them unattended." The voice was ruthless, cold, and female. She sheathed the staff and dragged Mea out the front door. Mea's face, neck, and forearms were bruised and bloody, no match for the assassin.

"One of three is dead, but I want you to watch as I finish your lineage. Look upon the world you helped to create, Syrus Tokarek."

Syrus tried pushing away the stars in his vision, but he'd taken a hard blow. His arms and legs moved in slow motion. The cloaked woman shoved Mea to the ground before placing an ice spike to her neck.

Syrus breathed heavily, his powers divided between healing his bleeding shoulder and repairing his concussed mind. "Are... you such a... coward that... you would take... another mystic's life? One of your own kind?"

For the second time that day, Syrus caught sight of a silvery haired silhouette, readying to pounce. Phaedra leapt from atop the home and collided with the hooded assassin. Mea jostled free in time to miss the plunging ice spike and crawled to her uncle's side.

With her opponent caught off guard, Phaedra called Syrus's staff to her hand and went on the offensive, maneuvering the staff like an extension of her arm. The assassin blocked the incoming blows, but Phaedra kept up her attack.

"Foolish girl," spat the assassin, using only one hand to block the attacks. "Give me that staff before you hurt yourself."

Phaedra changed her style, using a mix of arcane projectiles and melee strikes. "You've betrayed your own people!"

"There is only one side in this fight but you won't live long enough to discover it." The assassin's staff suddenly glowed molten red, and the sage went berserk. Three silver discs launched from the staff, one tearing through the side of Phaedra's armor.

Two fire spheres then exploded at Phaedra's feet, lifting her off the ground and slamming her down near Syrus's wounded body. Dirt and dust obscured her vision, but Phaedra heard the *whooshing* of the assassin's staff sailing through the debris in time to block the attack. The impact forced Phaedra onto her back, and the assassin readied her killing strike.

Thundering footsteps from the center of Carendra forced away the assassin's attention. The hesitation opened her defenses long enough for Syrus to launch an energy wave into the killer's chest. Syrus floundered to his feet and charged the staggered woman. The assassin recovered quickly from the weak attack and sidestepped him, using his own momentum to flip Syrus onto his back, once again forcing bright flashes into his vision.

With an unobstructed line of sight, the Nein guards fired at the assassin. With masterful agility, she invoked a shield, then a strange, heavy mist engulfed the area. She escaped under the veiled fog, leaving only a swirling mist in her wake.

"M-Mea!" yelled Syrus, still unable to stand.

Mea appeared through the haze, her nightdress torn and covered in blood. "I'm okay, Uncle, but ..."

"Stay next to me," he ordered.

"Uncle... I think my mother..."

"That rogue may not be gone," said Phaedra, kneeling next to Syrus. "I can run her down. I can beat her."

Syrus went to one knee. "Keep my staff and guard Mea. I must find my sister."

Syrus staggered to his feet, ignoring the appeals from Nigel and Javier to sit and allow them to begin healing his wounds. Moving sluggishly into his home, Syrus noticed blood marks and broken furnishings, likely from Jenna, the guards, and Giles's clash with the hooded woman.

Past the living area and into the bedroom, a pair of feet extended off the bed. Using the wall for support, Syrus shuffled into the bedroom where Helia lay faceup, clutching an ice spike that had pierced her throat.

A week later in the catacombs under Carendra, Syrus stood stiffly in front of his sister's stone vault. Andreas and Phaedra stood behind him, awaiting his next command. Giles and Jenna were still in the infirmary, clinging to life, like several other Nein mystics who fought in the battle. Captain Siller and several guards stood watch around Mea's quarters while the young woman coped with such a devastating loss.

Syrus told Mea the truth. The assassin was there for her, Helia, and himself. She was mature enough to understand the consequences, but grief still overwhelmed her reasoning.

Before the entombing, Captain Siller submitted his resignation as guard commander and offered to self-exile after falling for the fake Celje retreat, but Syrus dismissed the idea.

Syrus stared at the stone structure holding the remains of his beloved sibling. Only he knew she wasn't a mystic, not a true Nein. His fist clenched, then eased, knowing what must be done.

"Sasha's attack and the assassination of Helia weren't random," said Andreas, seeing Syrus's visage change. "It was meant to draw us into an all-out war with the Celje. There's a reason Sasha wants a fight with us."

Sweat trickled down Syrus's head and onto his chest plate. "Too many leaders have marched down the warpath because they were impassioned by the loss of a loved one. I will not do so."

"Siller inspected the dead Celje left on the battlefield. Many have tattoos and clothing from Capintesta and Meridone," continued Andreas. "Sasha's getting recruits from the planet, not just off-world now."

Staring down at his sister's forever resting place, Syrus reflected on Sasha and his motives. Helia and Mea were not strategically important and worth more alive than dead. Kidnap and ransom made more sense. Moreover, the Celje were supposed to operate in the shadows and in small clandestine groups, not flagrantly attack a village in broad daylight with dozens of troops.

Syrus stepped away and headed for the surface. "Sasha wants a war, and I'll have my revenge, but on my terms. We will not walk openly into the Celje's hands."

"Helia was well liked," said Phaedra. "Your people will obey any command you give."

Syrus nodded. "Nothing is more important than blood. My sister and Mea, they were easy targets and will continue to be unless we respond in the way Sasha expects."

"Which, if taken one step further," replied Andreas, lighting another hettle stalk, "means Sasha will continue coming after Mea if we don't retaliate."

"Correct."

Andreas tapped the butt of his pistol. "I think I could find it within myself to put a bullet through his eyeball."

Syrus looked back at his sister's vault one last time before exiting. "This fight taught us the Celje are willing to fight us head on, to die on Sasha's orders. We also know they've recruited a sage with a staff, which makes them even more dangerous. Right now, however, safeguarding Mea is the priority. After that, we'll give Sasha his war."

CHAPTER 16: YEAR 2400

For seventeen hours straight, snow thumped against the thirteenth-floor window of the Reeves Corporation building in Las Vegas. The unusual weather phenomenon had thus far dumped sixteen inches of snow, virtually shutting down the city. For Elasus Reeves, the weather was nothing more than something that affected other people, those unprepared for the most unlikely of events.

Chopin's Ballade No. 3 played in the background as Elasus stepped out of the shower and began to dress. He kept a full closet, plush with dark suits and other business attire, yet not all the clothes were his. Tayla Cruz, who left the shower a few minutes before him, sat in front of the bathroom mirror, putting on fresh makeup, a white towel wrapped around her body.

"What's my schedule for the morning?" Elasus asked.

She put the finishing touches on her makeup. "You have a conference call with Mr. Commodus Vrabel at eight, then a meeting with Prime Minister Kennedy at ten. I took the liberty of sending a special car for Kennedy due to the weather."

Elasus straightened his suit coat. "Very well. I need to review the fleet's balance sheet and their projections before speaking with Commodus. I'll be at my desk."

"Do you like it?" she asked, stepping up behind him and slipping on her new outfit.

Elasus turned and stared at the formfitting white pantsuit that spotlighted her perfect physique. He funded most of her wardrobe and had given her certain criteria about what to wear around him. "It's nice," he said. "The earrings, my Christmas gift?"

Tayla rotated, showing off her suit and pushing her blonde hair back to expose the diamond earrings. "It's hard to imagine these came all the way from Idca; they're amazing."

"Those are the first ever exported off the planet, I'm glad you like them," he said. "When you're done, please separate the weekly projections. I'm more interested in Ojult this morning."

"Yes, Mr. Reeves."

Thirty minutes later, Elasus stared at his chief operating officer through the holographic projection on the opposite side of his desk. "Our connection isn't great, Commodus. Where are you?"

Commodus sounded nervous. "In orbit around Chden, arrived a few hours ago."

"In orbit?"

"Long story. I'll send you the full report, but we damn near got ripped apart coming out of SKIP this morning. Our EM field spiked as we neared Chden, and the ship took serious damage. Donato performed another miracle and saved the ship and cargo."

The usual result of an imbalance in the EM field toward the end of a SKIP jump was deadly unless quickly corrected. Such a variance ordinarily crushed the ship or sent it off course at incredible speeds, generally resulting in a high-velocity impact.

"Captain Donato's a loyal man. Glad he kept you and our cargo in one piece."

"That makes two of us."

Elasus pulled out his summary of the newly discovered planet of Chden. "Tell me what you've learned so far about Chden."

"The initial exploration team was wiped out, but the second is still here, exploring during the day, getting drunk at night. They've only scanned a small portion of the planet, but their first report about the new metal, *parforlium*, is holding up. It's stronger than diamond and more pliable than nitinol. This could be used for everything from nanobots to ship hulls if it's true."

Elasus continued studying the briefing document, already piecing together returns on the new metal. In addition to parforlium, exploration scouts and internal business developers put forth the idea about Chden becoming a tourist destination. Chden was uncommonly beautiful among the habitable planets discovered to date. About half the size of Earth, tiny islands and one large continent covered most of the planet, which was discovered by accident by a mining team working in the Edwards asteroid belt. The captain of the mining rig refused to name the planet after his wife after intense pressure from his crew, so his executive took the last letters of their vessel's identification number, thus naming the planet Chden.

Reeves scrolled down to the section labeled *Risks*. "I see that one of our meteorologists thinks weather might be an issue."

Commodus nodded. "Yes, sir. I brought Jasilla with us for a more hands-on perspective. Historical probe logs suggest massive storms make their way over the entire planet a few times a year. The exploration team just rode one out, and they weren't in a laughing mood afterward. The team lead mentioned he preferred an asteroid storm to what just hit them."

"I want two proformas on the planet by month's end, each assuming tourism revenue. One will assume bad weather and no natural resources, the other supposes all is well with good weather and the new metal. Anything else you want to report?"

Commodus still sounded shaken. "No, like I said, haven't had much time to catch up. Give me a few days."

After the call, Elasus scoured through updated financial statements and balance sheets pertaining to his operation on Ojult. Whenever problems surfaced, he usually tried to follow the money, or lack thereof, then branch out his investigation.

Tayla's voice interrupted his review. "Mr. Reeves, Prime Minister Kennedy's here. May I bring him in?"

"Yes, please."

The purpose of the meeting was to bring Kennedy up to speed on the corporation's discovery of Chden and its business opportunities. Elasus wouldn't mention he'd already given Treasury Secretary Zhang the same information last night.

Kennedy entered through the main door, and Elasus detected a spring in the man's step. He'd colored his hair.

The prime minister extended a friendly hand. "Elasus, hello there. Good to see you're still up and running with all this weather."

Elasus skipped the small talk and spent the next hour explaining the discovery of Chden to the prime minister, including details such as logistical needs, trade strategies, resource-export projections, and the likely capital investment needed for the resort concept.

"Yet another trillion-dollar idea," said a wide-eyed Kennedy. "Unbelievable." He swiped at his watch and started typing on a holographic keypad. "I'll contact my broker tonight and have him buy up the hotel stocks. And what about you, Elasus? How do I repay such a favor? Cash, power, women? How do I repay a man who has everything?"

A steely expression overcame Elasus. "I have not asked for favors in the past, nor will I today, or at any point in the future."

"I'm sorry," said Kennedy. "I never know how to act around you sometimes."

The prime minister sounded sincere, and Elasus moved past the issue. "To your second notion of buying stock in lodging corporations—no, Minister, that's an idea I've already suggested to Secretary Zhang."

Kennedy's jovial demeanor turned. "Zhang? You've already met with one of my cabinet members? That seems like a backhanded move. I presume there's an explanation? I thought you didn't even like the guy?"

An icon on Elasus's screen flashed red. "Liking is a poor emotion to base future profits on. Zhang will be a valuable ally in the years to come, and it was prudent I give him this information. My proposal to you is different but no less lucrative. Tonight, you'll receive information on a construction company I purchased last year. I've purposefully slowed down their sales volume to diminish their value. This company will be the sole builder on Chden when the project begins."

Kennedy folded his hands, grasping the situation. "I see. May I assume no one else is getting this advice? I'd like to think I hold a special place on your special-informant list."

"I have no list. You hold a prominent position within the PGU, an organization that I require to side with my interests on occasion. This is networking, nothing more."

"Under-the-table payouts and insider trading, you mean," said Kennedy with a smirk.

Elasus glared and decided a well-timed interruption was needed. He reached over and pressed the flashing red button. "Yes, Ms. Cruz?"

"Sir, your wife is here to see you."

"Please send her in." Elasus stood and glowered down at Kennedy. "Call my goodwill whatever you like, but I know that I'm not the only one in the room exchanging favors."

Irelyn Reeves walked confidently down the hallway. She was dressed for the weather, wearing jeans, a gray sweater, and furry boots. "Hello, darling," said Irelyn, giving her husband a gentle kiss. "Josh, how are you? I hope I'm not interrupting. Do you have time for lunch? I'm sure we can find an open place around here. Can you believe the weather? Absolutely horrible." After a quick look at the two men, she took a step back. "Would you like me to come back? I've obviously interrupted something."

Kennedy made little effort to disguise his head-to-toe inspection. "No, not at all. Elasus just finished his report, and I was on my way out."

Kenney stuck out his hand, but Elasus didn't return the faux gesture. "Good day, Minister."

Irelyn waited for Kennedy to leave before changing personalities. "I see you had to work late again last night. I hope you didn't have too hard a time getting up."

Elasus ignored the comment. "I've already checked up on Ruven this morning, and everything's going fine on Lent. He doesn't plan on visiting but suggested he'd message you today or tomorrow."

"Too busy training your guard dogs to even visit his mother," Irelyn spat.

Elasus went over to the wet bar. "Drink?"

"It's not even lunchtime, something stressing you? It's obviously not our children."

Elasus poured bourbon into a chilled glass and walked over to the window. The snow was creating near-white-out conditions. Even the PGU headquarters wasn't visible. "Preliminary figures indicate trade output from Ojult is down for a third quarter in a row. I reviewed the numbers last night and again this morning."

"It's always about money with you. I guess I worry about our kids enough for both of us."

Elasus savored the taste and burn down his throat. "I have other things to worry about. Ruven's a grown man and deserving of his role. With Marilla, I don't want to hear about her again."

"What if she's still alive and imprisoned? What about a ransom? You care so much about money and people know it. You may not be willing to pay up for her, but I would. Ever think about that?"

"If money could solve this matter, I would have already taken care of it. I know what people would do to get to me, and it's not about money."

"Marilla Evelyn Reeves, captured by mystics. I can see the headline now. I wonder what the story would say. Ransom Paid by Loving Parents or Daughter Executed Because of Obstinate, Power-Lusting Father? God, I hate you."

Elasus turned his attention to his office door.

Tayla strode down the hallway. "I'm sorry, Mr. and Mrs. Reeves, but I heard shouting. Is everything okay?"

Irelyn whirled on her husband's mistress. "When you're needed, Tayla, you'll be summoned like the pet you are. Leave!"

If Tayla was offended, she showed no sign of it. "Of course, Mrs. Reeves. Please, let me know if I'm needed."

This wasn't the first time Irelyn ridiculed his secretary, and it wouldn't be the last. Irelyn understood his relationship with Tayla, and pretending it didn't exist wasn't worth the time.

Elasus poured another three-finger glass. "She got involved with a mystic whose network still poses a threat to this family. She compounded her error by running off without regard to her situation. I have thousands of sons and daughters working for me; what about their interests? If I divert attention to my own selfish needs, they suffer. What would you say to them?"

Irelyn's tone settled somewhat. "When Marilla took the summers off away from med school, she was devoted to community clinics. She gave a lot back, and so have you in an eccentric way. People would have understood it, but it's… I suppose it's too late now… isn't it?"

Family came first, and if that trust was betrayed, Elasus didn't let you back into the circle. "Relations with the FIAS are eroding by the day. Across the universe, clashes between the Celje and Nein have increased over the past year, which, as you now know, has impacted trade to and from Ojult. It may be necessary to send Ruven and his team there."

Irelyn pulled a tissue from her purse and dabbed the corner of her eyes. "Great, what better way to keep our only remaining child alive than by sending him to a war zone. Can't the Argos straighten this out?"

Elasus's mouth fell open, almost pitying his wife's ignorance. "The Argos are gone; they haven't been seen in decades."

Irelyn changed tactics and placed a warm hand on his shoulder. "Please, Elasus, please don't risk Ruven. If you love me, if you ever loved me, don't send him. Give Sasha more guns and men, but don't risk Ruven. I can't lose both of my children, please!"

His rational mind established long ago that his daughter was dead, likely killed by some murderous exile or a Nein. Irelyn was coming around to this realization, yet coming out directly and saying this to the child's mother gained him nothing. Decades of negotiations with intelligent leaders honed his skills in fabricating statements.

"Ruven has a job to do, but for you Irelyn, I'll consider other options."

CHAPTER 17: YEAR 2400

Syrus leaned over the railing of the two-masted ship, *Challenger*, a cool spray off the Altum Sea hitting his face. He wore dark pants, black boots, a dark shirt, and an oversized overcoat for the upcoming meeting. Already an enormous and intimidating figure, the overcoat gave him a Zeus-like appearance.

A young woman and a younger boy tossed berries to a rusted red-winged phoenix swooping down near the deck, bringing thoughts of his sister and Mea back to his inundated mind. Perhaps twenty sailors worked the upper deck, adjusting jib lines, manipulating rigging, and constantly easing and tightening the forestay and backstay cables. Zakar, a rough-looking man, stood next to Captain Green near the wheel, yelling at the crew in a thick British accent.

The winds were howling, causing Captain Green to grab a second man to tend the wheel. A sailor on the opposite side of ship dropped a premeasured rope with a lead ball into the water, determining the depth.

Syrus didn't much care for taking this meeting aboard an Appian ship, but in the end, he had little choice. To eradicate the Celje, he needed resources beyond what the Nein could produce.

"Welcome to my home away from home, Mr. Tokarek," said Nencia Donato, coming up the stairs and onto the main deck.

Syrus turned around to face the mysterious mafia leader. Her tan body and long black hair meshed perfectly with the dark button-down shirt that left nearly six inches bare between her chest and neck.

"We've been here for almost an hour, Donato. Do you usually keep your guests waiting?" asked Captain Siller, not bothering to hide his irritation.

Nencia ignored him and nodded affectionately toward Andreas. "I work with your man, Andreas, here on occasion Tokarek, which is the only reason I took this meeting. The Nein are one of many clients, not my *only* client. Just to clear the air, I find your entire cult distasteful and do my best to avoid being seen in public with you."

"Watch your tongue, Donato," said Captain Siller.

"Or what?" She laughed. "You'll kill me like you killed those two Celje you met on your way here? Will lightning shoot out of your ass and burn me alive?"

Syrus had indeed killed two Celje on his way from Carendra to Port Naok, but Nencia's spies escaped his notice.

Captain Siller's short stature and patchy beard gave him a peasant look instead of a powerful Nein battle commander. "How about I…" He took two steps toward Nencia, then stopped, for a razor-sharp ice spike was pressed gently against his thigh.

"My aunt doesn't like to be called names, and all this yelling upsets my brother. If he starts to cry, he gets seasick, and we don't want that. Apologize to my aunt, or I'll use what's between here as a fishing bobber."

Syrus looked at the girl whose long, wavy dark hair rippled in the breeze. Very few mystics, especially one so young, had the power to conjure such objects without the use of a staff.

"Easy, Kavil," said Andreas. "I'm not sure how good at fishing she is, but that spike's pointy. Might put a damper on our talks if you took a swipe at Nencia's kid."

Nencia stared at Captain Siller. "Good girl, Bella," she said. "If he moves, cut it off."

Andreas, who knew Nencia well, walked up to the Appian leader. "Nencia, I think this is what they call getting off on the wrong foot."

Syrus's movement toward the girl fixed everyone in their place. He stopped next to her and peered down at the teenage mystic. "Thrust that into him, and I'll give you a place within the people."

Nencia's brows plunged downward. "Enough of this, Tokarek. Call off your dog, and let's get down to business."

Bella looked back up at Syrus. "My aunt, she's all my brother and I have now. I don't want to hurt him, but he needs to be nicer."

The words softened Syrus's heart as he imagined Mea saying them. "Very well. Kavil, move away. This girl and her brother are one of us, and we don't fight our own."

"Of course," replied Captain Siller, and he cautiously backed away.

"This is exactly why I don't deal with you people," huffed Nencia.

Andreas walked over and put a hand on Nencia's shoulder. "Our larger goals are still aligned, Nencia. Give us a chance."

"You need to get away from this crowd, Andreas, and come work for me. I could use someone with your talents." Nencia smiled and slapped his backside. "All right, let's get this over with. Andreas, is my top low enough? I thought I'd show enough cleavage to distract Syrus," she said, moving her torso from side to side.

"Well, I personally haven't stopped staring and don't plan to, but Syrus's more of a gentleman. Don't think that'll work on him."

"Ha! You're many things, Andreas, but gentleman certainly isn't one of them. So, Syrus, how about a bottle of Listo brandy to set the mood, in private?"

Syrus nodded.

Nencia motioned for him to follow. "Andreas gave me the basics, but this conversation should be held in a more private setting. The Celje have spies, just like me. If you don't mind, keep your dog up here where Bella can scare him. Andreas, come with us. I don't often get the chance to have two men in my cabin at once."

Syrus left his staff with Captain Siller and followed Nencia. After maneuvering down three precipitous flights of steps, they pitched from side to side down a damp hallway to Nencia's cabin. The quarters were dimly lit with motion-activated faux lanterns, a small table, and a red velvet sofa against the wall. Folded against the wall was a compact bed, stowed during the daylight hours to make room for Nencia to conduct business.

Nencia sat behind her desk and pressed her chest against the table, pushing up her breasts. "So, Syrus, you want to start a little revolution and need my help?"

Unlike Andreas, who gaped at the provocative pose, Syrus ignored the gesture. "My plan is genocide, the murder of every Celje."

Nencia sat back in her chair and crossed her legs. "Seems like over-kill to me, but even Appian hasn't been immune to their meddling. That moron, Sasha, has been raiding my supply routes for months now, not sure what the hell he's thinking." Nencia lined three glasses and poured a few inches of brandy into each.

Andreas raised his glass. "To friends and low-cut shirts."

Nencia and Andreas downed their drinks in one gulp while Syrus left his untouched. "You smile while my people face the threat of all-out war."

Nencia cocked an eyebrow. "Gotta enjoy it while it lasts. This brandy is our chief export to Earth and the most targeted by Sasha. Ojultan ore and jashinto freight have declined almost fifty percent. Not really a coin-cidence that Sasha assassinated your sister and is now targeting my sup-ply lines." Syrus and Andreas exchanged assenting looks. "Not going to be long before Elasus Reeves wants answers... from me."

"The Reeves baron is a coward who sits behind a desk checking boxes that determine the fate of millions," said Syrus. "The Nein do not fear him."

Nencia smiled. "Not too bright on matters outside Ojult, are you? The Reeves Corporation granted me full control of the economy on this rock, but the corporation takes a thirty percent commission off every transac-tion. The less I trade, the less revenue I bring in and the less profit the cor-poration makes. Since the Celje work for Elasus directly, the finger's gonna get pointed at me for the reduction in profits. Get my drift?"

"Reeves loses money either way," Syrus said, comprehending the sit-uation more fully. "I go to war with Sasha, Reeves loses money. I sit back and do nothing, Reeves loses money. No matter which way this goes, Ela-sus is coming after you."

Nencia poured more brandy into the two empty glasses. "I wouldn't have accepted this meeting if I didn't think I had something to gain. I've been running a well-oiled shop on this five-star penal colony for over a decade; I know what I'm doing."

"Then you need to get to the point where I see the value in this meet-ing," Syrus said.

Nencia swirled her drink. "I don't waste time with pointless meetings either. I've done my homework on you. You're a brutal man, and your definition of justice is borderline insane. But if I say no, I guess you turn me into a frog, or perhaps a pile of dust?"

"Andreas says he's been doing business with you for many years and that you can be trusted. I trust him and thereby trust you, at least for now."

"Did you know when you asked Andreas to find a safe place to stash Mea, he called me?"

The comment took Syrus by surprise and his heart skipped. "No, I didn't."

Nencia nodded. "I say this not as a threat but to illustrate that if you didn't consider me a friend before, you should now."

Syrus already knew the answer to his next question, but he needed confirmation. "The village they're hiding in, those are… Appian people?"

"Correct, and they're very safe. You don't know me, Mr. Tokarek, but believe me when I say I understand your position."

Syrus heard the anguish in her voice and surprisingly believed her, but trust wasn't something that came easy, especially on Ojult. "My family is my life, Donato. If you plan on using them as leverage, then I suggest you rethink that strategy."

"How colorful, but no, that isn't on my to-do list. In fact, I generally try to save kids, not murder them; that's Sasha's new job."

Her casual demeanor toward his threat brought a sudden understanding. "The siblings outside. Those aren't your kids?"

Nencia shook her head.

Andreas, who'd been drinking and staring at Nencia, said, "The girl called you 'aunt' earlier. Her parents work for you?"

"I protect them," she said. "That's all you need to know."

The conversation stalled, and Syrus's patience was nearing its end. "Orphaned children and bank accounts aren't my concern," said Syrus. "Sasha will die by my hand, along with his soldiers. If this helps you somehow, then accept my partnership, and let's get moving."

Nencia thought for a while, then cracked her neck. "All right Tokarek, let's make a deal." She extended her hand.

Syrus ignored the motion and dived right into his next point. "To achieve the Celje destruction, I need more weapons, staffs, armor, and intel."

Nencia took back her hand and walked over to the galley passage. "Pass the word for Zakar!" she yelled down the hallway.

Less than a minute later, a sweaty and rank man swayed down the corridor. "You need something, boss?"

"Zakar, you still have that blacksmith contact in Capintesta?"

Zakar eyed Syrus, hesitant to disclose his information.

Nencia waved him on. "We're partnering with the Nein, at least temporarily, so don't hesitate."

Zakar nodded. "It's possible. It was a family that produced all of it, but the Celje hunted them down. A daughter survived, and she's got the skills to continue the job. Whether she's up for it or not, we'll have to check."

"Okay, then. We'll need to shore up that contact, Zakar. Make that your primary job when we get ashore. You're dismissed." She faced Syrus. "Ammo, guns, and armor I can get you, but that's not cheap. How are you planning on paying for this?"

"When I rule, I'll levy a small tax on the sale of all items. This tax will be used to pay you and my soldiers while things settle down."

Nencia's eyes grew wide. "So… you wipe the Celje off the planet, then Ojult gets, what, a Nein ruler? We might as well toss this whole plan in the sea right now. You realize most people don't even know the Celje exist? They can't resist what they don't know about. People *know* about the Nein, and they really hate you guys. You're going to have to do better than that Tokarek."

"If I may," interrupted Andreas, finishing his drink. "The premier will not rule as you suspect. We want peace, but that peace is on the other side of war. The Nein of the past tried the whole take-over-the-world routine, twice, and look where it's gotten us. We'll work *with* the Thoba, not against them, and we'll kill Sasha and his troops. It's not going to be easy, no one expects that. We also know that the Reeves Corporation will send reinforcements, but if we can stabilize trade and you can get the economy back up and running, this whole thing might work out."

Nencia pondered the idea. "No fascist state."

"I'll give the planet the ruler it needs," said Syrus. "The idea is to eradicate the Celje, not create a dynasty."

"And you'll give me full authority over the economics of the planet, even if that means continuing to deal with the Reeves Corporation?"

Syrus nodded. "Money doesn't concern me, only the survival of my family and returning my Nein to their former glory."

Nencia burst out laughing. "The Nein's former glory nearly wiped out the Argos and Thoba. Not sure that's your best selling point Tokarek. What happens when the PGU stops sending their mystic exiles here? What if they just start executing them back on Earth? What then?"

"Mystics, Nein or otherwise, will not simply lay down and allow the Reeves coward to slay them. Civil war would erupt, bringing devastation rivaling the old wars."

"What, that's it?"

"That's it."

"You're a horrible salesman." She adjusted her posture. "Don't know why I'm agreeing to this, but okay, Syrus Tokarek, you've got a deal. I control all trade on this rock, on- or off-planet, and I charge what I want. In exchange, you give me your grocery list, and I'll start feeding your army."

Supplies, war plans, and other provisions were only one part of Syrus's strategy. When the conversation ended, he asked about the odds of the Reeves Corporation ceasing shipments of mystics to Ojult.

"I know a guy who works for the fleet. For a few hundred tonze per head, he might be willing to smuggle them here," Nencia offered. "I'm not saying they'll be in perfect health, but they'll be alive when they get here."

CHAPTER 18: YEAR 2400

Jayden Vaut pushed through the uneven ground, steering the farming plow carefully behind Certus, the massive draught horse. Thanks to Celine Dubois, he'd recovered from his injuries and now worked for Dalth's mayor, Markus Fonte, plowing fields and doing other odd jobs around town. For months, strangers nursed him back to health, never once asking for repayment or questioning his past. He lived in an abandoned home loaned to him by the mayor on the grounds that he'd clean it up and make it suitable to live in. Jayden stumbled into the small town rather painfully, but he recognized this was the start to the new beginning he'd been longing for.

Sweat trickled down his smooth, freshly shaven face and absorbed into his borrowed clothes as he worked the new plot. The new field rested on the west side of town, relatively close to the small shack lent to him by Markus. It was a good twenty-minute walk to Dalth's town square, but freedom of sleeping without fear was worth every meter. From across the plain, Jayden heard children singing and playing alongside a howling dog. Although Dalth was mostly secluded from the planet's violent culture, predators still roamed the land, and Jayden always kept a watchful eye while the children were around.

"Hello Jayden," said a young girl. "My father said you should take a break and visit him in the pub. Here, I brought you water, it's *so* hot out."

Jayden spun his hat on top of Bélise Fonte's head. She giggled as the hat fell over her nose. The mayor's only child had short, straight hair, plump cheeks, and usually wore large, round glasses.

He gladly accepted the grainy, lukewarm drink. "Thank you, Bélise. Everything okay with you this morning?"

"I think the mail's coming today, so everyone's waiting at the pub. And a zibar was shot last night hunting around the Visconti's house, so that's got people talking."

Jayden gulped down the drink, spit out some of the soot, then handed the cup back to Bélise. He worked another half hour before taking the requested break. After unsaddling and cleaning up the horse, Jayden hiked over to the pub. The town itself sat on the central east side of Capintesta, at the foot of rolling hills. A dense tree line rose from the horizon toward the northeast, giving the town a false feeling of seclusion. When the winds came out of the east, a cool sea breeze simmered the sizzling heat pounding the region.

Spring and fall were pleasant, especially considering the planet lacked electricity for heating and cooling. Sitting so near the coast, Dalth experienced harsh winters with the Altum Sea only a few miles away.

Homes and shops were generally made of wood with the intermittent barn or silo dotting the town. As far as food, beef was not a widespread luxury, but venison was plentiful and frequently a main dish at the pub. When local animal supplies ran low, Markus contracted with Appian to bring in artificial meats. No one was sure who or what these synthetic proteins were made from, and few dared to ask.

Jayden made his away across the relatively flat plains, his stomach rumbling with hunger. His mouth started watering as the eatery came into view and the aroma of cooking meat filled the air.

Jayden opened the faded wooden door to the single-story building and was met with friendly greetings. "Hi Jayden," came a cheerful voice from behind the bar. "Kun shot a buck this morning before he shot that cython. It's on the grill now. Should be ready soon. Ale?"

Jayden stopped in the middle of taking off his boots. A cython was not a zibar. It was part of the cat species and a carnivore, but that's where the similarities ended. At night, a cython's burly hair turned from metallic to black, while their singular eye never blinked. It was not a quiet animal either, hissing like a snake with each breath. It's most dangerous trait, in Jayden's opinion, was its willingness to wait. The cython was known to wait hours, sometimes days, for its prey.

Jayden looked around at the other patrons who appeared unmoved that a cython was killed so close to town.

"Oh, stop," Liao Nguyen said. "For someone so tough, you scare easily. Come, sit."

Jayden swallowed his thoughts on the matter, removed his other boot, and hung his hat on a nearby rack before heading to the bar. He looked from one end of the pub to the other, trying to spot the one person in Dalth who hadn't welcomed him into the city. "No, thank you, Liao. Just water and kaldi. Tell Kun I can smell that grill all the way across the field."

"Coming right up. I've also got phoenix and rice ready if you're in a hurry." Liao was a middle-aged woman with a rail-thin frame. She wore her hair in a ponytail to avoid dirtying the food.

"No thanks, Liao," said Jayden, thinking of pigeons back on Earth. Jayden didn't like or eat pigeons back home and he decided to keep to that code here. A phoenix was a maroon-winged bird with a lava-orange belly that hung around people like pigeons on Earth. Unlike the mythic bird of legend, the phoenix did not regenerate or have any other enigmatic powers.

Liao's husband, Kun, operated the pub full time, with Liao waiting tables a few hours each day. Kun's temper gave way to rumors that he'd killed a man back on Earth, which got him exiled. Some say the man he killed was having an affair with Liao and the couple reconciled after arriving on Ojult, their daughter, Hannah, coming shortly thereafter. As a newcomer and not one to intrude on the private affairs of others, Jayden never pressed for explanation.

The pub's door opened, and Markus came up to the bar. "Morning, Liao," said Markus, holding a brown mug of kaldi.

"The buck isn't ready yet," Liao said. "Another twenty minutes, maybe."

Markus raised his mug. "No rush. Jayden, how's the field looking? It's hot out there and we've just gotten you patched up. Don't go and give yourself a stroke."

Jayden got up from the barstool and shook Markus's hand. "Morning,

Mayor. Got up just before sunrise and been working the plow until a few minutes ago. Put Certus back in the stables."

Markus was older, but aged better than most on Ojult. He spoke with a deep, grating voice that contradicted his consummate kindness.

"I know you think you owe me something, but you don't have to be so formal around me," said Markus. "You were a total stranger when you saved one of us, and it nearly cost you your life. You're a hero, whether you like it or not."

"Markus's right," chimed Liao, delivering his drink.

Markus clapped Jayden on the back. "Well, you just think about what I've said. Now, the mail should be coming today, and supposedly a few dozen carriages were spotted coming down from Worall. You heard who it might be?"

Jayden took too large a sip of the scalding-hot kaldi and burned his tongue. "A few Appian people are delivering supplies. A runner came late last night while you were praying, didn't want to disturb you."

Smoke billowed into the pub from the back door, followed by a filthy, grease-covered man with a pan full of searing meat. "Hello, Mr. Mayor. Ah, Jayden, good day. I have venison. Enjoy it, because it the last of meat and vegetables until we get shipment."

Townsfolk came in and out of the pub while Jayden ate one of the best-prepared venison steaks he'd ever tasted. With lots of work still unfinished, he conversed cordially until excusing himself. He'd yet to run into Serena, the young woman he'd saved from the Celje a few months ago. Typically, they ran into each other during lunch and always for evening drinks. Serena Visconti continued her father's business as a metallurgist, making tools and such for the town, then selling any surplus to Appian.

Remorse, regret, and dejection were all emotions Jayden endured for arriving too late to save Serena's parents. Perhaps his best friend now, Serena made it a point to express her gratitude for saving her life and trying to save her mother and father. He and Serena spent nearly every evening together at the pub, giving way to rumors they were a couple. Yet their close bond never pivoted in the romantic direction.

Jayden detoured on his way back to the stables, recounting the story Markus told of his recovery. Fighting fevers, infection, and surgery to remove bullets, Serena never left his bedside despite her own profound grief. Without hovrol, anesthetics, or nano-treks, many assumed he'd die within a few days of the fight, but Serena never gave up hope. The heartbroken woman wiped sweat from his forehead, changed his soiled sheets, then fed and watered him during his few moments of lucidity. Not even Janice would have taken such care of him.

Serena's home was a good distance south of his own and usually visible by the smoke pouring from the furnace. This morning, however, the furnace was silent. He knocked on the cracked, wooden door.

"V, you in there?"

A grunt came in reply. "Couch."

Jayden walked into the home that had once held the entire Visconti family. He found Serena half naked and face down on the living-room couch. The space smelled of smoked hettle stalks and ale, a common theme since the death of her parents. Jayden grabbed a large water pitcher and filled it up from an outside water barrel, then placed it within arm's reach of his semiconscious friend.

"Hey, V," he whispered. "It's lunchtime. Might think about getting up."

When Serena made no move to sit up, he grabbed the musty ashtray and empty beer mug and emptied them outside. When he walked back in, Serena was sitting up, slurping down water.

"Thanks," she said, picking up a shirt off the floor and wiping her mouth. "God, my head hurts. What time did I get home last night?"

Jayden recounted the previous evening's events that centered on Serena getting too drunk to stand and Jayden carrying her back.

She looked around the room in a fog. "At least I woke up alone."

"Yes, at least," he said, trying not to laugh. "Do you want a shirt or something?"

Serena looked down and realized she was naked from the waist up. "It's nothing you haven't seen before, stop being so modest."

Jayden turned on the solar-powered stove and made fresh kaldi while Serena battled a fierce hangover. "Here, drink this because I need you to start working. I need two discs replaced on my plow, and Victor still needs about a hundred feet of barbed wire for the cattle project. Plus, agents from Appian might becoming, and you know how they get."

At the mention of Appian, Serena seemed to revive. "They're coming today?"

"Yeah. Markus said something about a caravan. Why?" He'd never seen his friend fight off a hangover so quickly.

Serena scolded him for not waking her up sooner, then revived the furnace without another word. Confused, Jayden headed back and continued plowing the fields, breaking only twice to water himself and Certus. The plow's soil analyzer reported plenty of moisture, but calcium, potassium, and magnesium levels were out of range. Even the mellow town of Dalth couldn't escape Ojult's harsh, infertile dirt.

After the sun pitched below the horizon, he called it a day. Jayden inspected Certus carefully before stabling and feeding the workhorse, then cleaned his own equipment and readied it for tomorrow. Jayden locked the barn door and headed toward the pub.

The crushing sound of gravel under heavy weight brought Jayden's attention to the main road into Dalth. Carriage-drawn horses were heading toward the town square. At the front of the convoy was an outlaw-looking woman with a narrow face and black hair jetting out from her hat.

Nencia Donato and Zakar Qualis escorted three large carriages into the center of town. The arrival of both Appian leaders meant Markus would be locked down in conversations until the late hours. That aside, Kun was about to earn some tonze.

Jayden reversed course and headed back to his home, opting to eat in peace. After heating salted beef and beans over the outside fire, Jayden stretched out on his small couch and enjoyed dinner. Relaxing, he read one of the many books Markus had given him, fighting off sleep as the fireplace crackled in the background.

Jayden dozed off under the tranquil silence until a giant roar from outside shook him. With one eye half open, he lumbered outside to relieve himself. High in the night sky, a ship with several dozen red and white underbelly lights flashed brightly. It was an RC-1 Brooks transport ship, the same vessel his father had departed on the last time Jayden saw him. Faded memories of his parents bathed Jayden's tired mind.

"I miss you guys," he whispered.

He stepped back inside, swatting away insects, and ignoring the

Appian party emptying Kun's beer supply across the field. Jayden snatched a half-empty glass of whiskey from the table and tossed it back. He wanted to feel the burn, anything to take his mind off his parents.

Jayden was in a deep, drunk sleep when his bed sheets fluffed upward and a soft, naked body nestled beside him. The smell of perfume, beer, and smoke filled the room.

"The pub too much excitement for you?" said Nencia, draping an arm over his torso.

Jayden rubbed sleep from his eyes and rolled over. "These people saved my life, getting drunk and stupid in front of them is a poor way to repay them. Plus, I worked like a Nein slave today, I'm tired."

She leaned over and kissed him, then wrinkled her nose. "You stink."

Her words were slurred, but Jayden didn't care. "With water rationing, I get one shower a week."

She pushed him onto his back and climbed on top. "You don't try to find me at the pub, you don't shower, and you don't even wait up for me? You're really pretty horrible at the whole courting thing."

His ab muscles flexed as he leaned up to kiss her. "Go find someone else then, I'm tired."

With a joshing smile, she plucked a finger full of hairs from his chest. "That's for being mean." The sting awakened him and he threw her onto her back, then climbed on top of her. Nencia struggled to get up; his weight and strength were too much for her.

Jayden leaned forward and kissed her. "Since I've been in Dalth, you've visited about every other week. Best be careful, people might start to think you like me."

After recovering from his wounds, Jayden had a letter couriered off to the mob boss describing what all had transpired after leaving her at the docks. To his surprise, Nencia showed up a week later, and it took hardly any time for their passion to explode. Since then, they'd seen each other every few weeks.

"I sleep with you because you're young and can keep up, nothing more. I've got one of you in every town."

Jayden suspected she was telling the truth. "I'm sure you do, but you chose me tonight, and that means something."

She adjusted her hips and pulled him close. "Next time you know a beautiful woman is coming over to see you, take a shower Vaut."

CHAPTER 19: YEAR 2400

Nencia woke at sunrise to the crow of preying birds. Dressing and readying herself for the long day ahead, she kissed her boy-toy goodbye and headed out.

"Morning, boss," greeted Zakar outside the home. "Markus Fonte wants a word before you leave. Wagons are loaded, and the special cargo you requested from Visconti is secure."

She rolled a finger over Zakar's shoulder before climbing onto her horse. "You do damn good work, Zakar. I'll go see what the old man wants, but be ready to get out of here when I'm done. I don't want to drag our horses through the heat."

Her mind was distant, fixated on Jayden. He was younger for sure, but he was a catch, especially on Ojult. Her former husband, Garvin, was all right, but that marriage was a disaster from the start. "Marriage, what a con," she whispered, galloping toward the cafe.

The humidity was already thick by the time she reached the pub. Markus was sitting at the bar, drinking kaldi.

"Good morning," welcomed Markus. "I trust you and Jayden slept well?"

She shook his outstretched hand. "You guys patched him up well, no doubt I owe you for that. Before we begin Markus, there's something we need to discuss. It's about the Visconti family."

Markus's welcoming smile flattened. "I was close with Marco and

Erika, good people. Their daughter, Serena, she's not the little girl I once knew, but to lose parents like that, what a tragedy."

Nencia ordered a splash of whiskey from Liao. "Did you lie to me about Marco's operation? Don't look at me like that? I tell it as I see it."

"The loss of Marco and Erika hit our community hard." A dull emptiness fell upon Markus's face. "You're referencing the Visconti's arms dealings back on Earth and now suspect they operated something similar on Ojult? Nencia, if what the Celje claim is true, I knew nothing of it."

Satisfied her new enterprise was still private, she let the matter drop. "You're a good man Markus, I trust you. Zakar said you needed to speak with me?"

Liao delivered Nencia's leaded drink and Markus waited until they were alone again to speak. "Our relationship hasn't always stood on solid ground, but I'm hoping those days are behind us." He pulled out a folded document from his shirt pocket.

"You mean since I'm sleeping with Dalth's hero, you're hoping for a favor?" Nencia knew how this game was played, and whatever feelings she had for Jayden, it wouldn't affect her professional judgement.

"In a manner of speaking. I'm hoping your relationship with Jayden might bring our communities closer together."

Nencia listened and after one more fully leaded mug, agreed to Markus's favor. "I've listened to your sermon, now mind filling me in on all your recent guests?"

"I'm sorry, I don't—"

Nencia slammed her drink on the table. "Damn it, Fonte, what the hell are you doing working with them? If the Nein found out, it could start a war!"

Rumors of Markus's dealings with mystics over the years was no secret, but what she'd heard recently was more concerning.

Markus refused to admit anything, and Nencia left the meeting with Markus's letter. Near the trade caravan, Bella and Logan hovered near Jayden. Nencia moved closer, not revealing herself until she noticed what Jayden was doing.

"So that's how they've been getting chocolate," Nencia blurted, startling the group.

"It helps with my abilities, promise," pleaded Bella. "One bite and I'm ready for a fight."

Logan, afraid his aunt would swipe the valued candy, stuffed the entire bar into his small mouth, turning his cheeks into squares.

Jayden lifted his hat revealing a broad smile. "Like she said, it boosts their abilities, never know when that might come in handy."

Nencia rolled her eyes and motioned for everyone to load up. "Come visit. I don't see myself getting back to Dalth anytime soon."

"Things not go well between you and the mayor?"

"Don't worry about it. You take care of yourself." She winked then started up the path.

Worall was centrally located on Capintesta, roughly ten hours by horse. The path was well traveled, mostly gravel and dirt, with few areas of soaking mud and sludge. The central region was heavily forested with towering trees creating vast canopies over the area. With the humidity thick enough to walk on, the trees at least kept the direct sunlight off the caravan and, more importantly, the horses.

Halfway back to Worall, Nencia checked on Bella and Logan. The twelve-year-old Logan was asleep in the wagon, coming down off a sugar high. Bella by contrast was wide awake, scanning the path ahead for the rumored cython in the area.

With Bella and a half dozen of her people at the ready, Nencia recollected on her visit to Dalth. The trip produced dividends, allowing her to bring back just under twenty-two tons of goods. In terms of tonze, Appian would earn just shy of two hundred million once resold to the Reeves Corporation and other purchasing entities. Reeves would, of course, take their piece, but today's haul, especially from such a small town...

From beside her, Bella's voice rang out. "Watch out!"

The sudden scream caught everyone's attention. "Stop the caravan, Aldrich!" ordered Nencia. "Fan out, kill or capture."

This was not the first time Bella foresaw danger, and the Appian team knew what to do. Like ants scurrying out to defend their mound, they hustled into the brush on either side of the road. Nencia unfastened her pistol and turned to Bella.

"Any details?" asked Nencia.

Bella held her brother close, but both children were calm and composed. "No, nothing, but… there's something bad."

"Right, okay. Keep your brother safe, we'll check it out."

No sooner had Nencia finished the sentence when the first bullets started whizzing by, ricocheting off the wagons and dirt. Trees and rocks exploded, sending splinters into the Appian group.

Nencia looked for casualties, but luckily, the initial volley missed both the horses and her men.

"Fire as needed!" yelled Zakar, and both sides of the road roared with gunfire. The sound was deafening. The nanoprojectiles sounded like a flute as they raced toward their target. The radial energy rifles fired suppressed smart bullets, making it more difficult for the Appian guards to locate them.

The lead bullets and classic rifles used by Nencia's people were much louder by contrast; their bullets mirroring that of a firecracker. Her people only had thermal scopes against the Celje's vital-organ-seeking projectiles.

Smoke and the smell of carbon filled the thick air. With her pistol unholstered, Nencia jumped off the carriage and hurdled forward, keeping low and pistol trained forward. Judging by the number of shots and direction, Nencia figured there were at least four raiders out there.

A bullet whizzed in front of Nencia, missing her face by inches but connecting with one of her men near the road. The bullet caught him in the chest, his screams suppressed by more gunfire.

Her Appian fighters didn't fight like ordinary soldiers. If a man went down, he wasn't tended to until the fight was over.

A flash of movement up ahead, and Nencia fired two quick rounds, doubting she hit the distant target.

Two shots from Zakar's rifle spun her attention laterally.

"Two down, boss!" he yelled from the rear.

"Leave at least one alive, Zakar!?"

Two minutes later, the Appian mob boss stared into the eyes of two injured Celje guards. "We'll interrogate them back in Worall. Keep them alive until then," ordered Nencia. "For now, everyone keeps their rifles out." She caught a glimpse of her men's eagerness. "I want information from these snakes, and dead men don't speak. I'll personally slit the throat of any of you if you hurt them, understand? Take them to the secondary warehouse; I don't want witnesses."

Two of her men were hurt. More importantly, none of their horses or carriages were damaged. On Ojult, replacing a man was easier and less expensive than a horse.

Her column entered Worall through the southwest gate having experienced no other obstacles during the rest of their journey. As soon as the caravan stopped, Zakar pulled his horse around to the front and began issuing orders. "Aldrich, oversee the off-load. Shannon, Berman, take our guests to the barn *quietly*—no need to alert the whole town."

Zakar was loyal, obedient, and anticipated her orders like a faithful shepherd. If anything ever happened to her, Nencia knew the company would be in good hands.

Nencia was off her horse, heading toward a pale-looking Logan, glued to his sister. "Zakar, make sure our wounded get patched up. Fetch Castellani out of Pa'Gran if needed. Then send word for Lacy. Ask her to take care of them when they're better, all expenses paid by Appian."

"On it, boss."

"And get those medical supplies marked with an orange stripe loaded onto a separate wagon. I'll deliver those personally. The ones marked red, get those off to Carendra, but make sure the courier leaves at night. And have a couple extra agents go with him."

After a few words of encouragement, Nencia sent Bella and Logan off with Zakar to organize the off-loaded supplies.

With a wagon full of orange-marked crates, Nencia guided the horse toward a single-story building on the northwest side of town. Outside the building, children of all ages played while an elderly woman in a long skirt supervised.

"Nencia, my dear," said the elderly woman, giving Nencia a warm hug. "How are you? Uneventful trip, I hope?"

"Fine, Barbara. My contact in Dalth procured more supplies, but use them sparingly and it's for the orphans, no one else. There's not much, and it's probably going to get worse until things settle down out there."

A saddened smile brewed across Barbara's hardened face. "Thank you, really. This will save lives. I'm sorry to say we lost little Mary last night. The pneumonia, it was just too much for her frail body to fight on its own. But we'll be able to fight it next time, I suppose."

At any given time, the orphanage housed around eighty children, ranging from babies to teenagers. Headmistress Barbara Roost, alongside several other older women, tended to the kids and took care of the building. Nencia bankrolled the orphanage but with an accord that Barbara didn't agree to easily.

"Yes, well, that's life. I'll send Bella and Logan over once they're done unloading. They haven't eaten dinner yet, so please feed them."

Used to Nencia's hard-hearted attitude, Barbara moved on. "I picked up two more boys this morning outside the launch station. They're fifteen and twelve, brothers, and look like they'll be good fighters."

"Our arrangement is sixteen, no younger. You send the boys to Zakar and girls to Lacy. Keep to the deal, and you'll keep getting your money." Nencia looked around for eavesdroppers, then lowered her voice. "I know you think I'm cold, Barbara, and that's fine, but our arrangement works. The kids get fed, you and the sisters get a roof over your head, and the Nein don't get any more slaves to abuse."

Nencia left the wagon and supplies at the orphanage, then walked back in the darkness toward three large warehouses. From the outside, each building looked the same, painted light brown with multiple docking stations for loading and unloading. The middle warehouse, however, held a cramped, nonventilated basement where Appian's more covert dealings took place.

Inside the basement, Zakar used a soiled rag to wipe the blood off his fists. "Your face is going to break before these knuckles, boy, so you better rethink your strategy. I'll ask again: Why are the Celje raiding Appian supply lines?"

Both Celje prisoners sat side by side, tethered tightly to steel chairs. Both men were bleeding, bruised, shot, and looking at the ground.

"They've said nothing, I take it," said Nencia as she walked into the room.

"No, boss, completely quiet."

The basement was large enough for a billiards game, dimly lit with oil lanterns, and had blood stains splattered over the walls.

"You two know who I am?" asked Nencia, kneeling so she was at eye level with the prisoners. Neither man breathed a word. "My name's Nencia Donato, that name sound familiar? Of course it does because I do business with your boss. I also do business with murderers, rapists, tax collectors, and even the Reeves Corporation. You know what that means? Yes, I'm sure you do." One of the men looked up, giving Nencia what she needed. "I'll ask once more, and if you don't tell me what I need, one of you will die." Her voice was collected and eerily calm.

Zakar reared back and bored into the man still looking at the ground. "Why now? Why start raiding now? What's Sasha up to?"

Nencia kept her eye on the man who'd looked up. "Neither of you want to talk? Okay. I'll be sure to tell Sasha how loyal you were… to the end."

Nencia unholstered her pistol and placed the barrel against the other man's head. She pulled the hammer back slowly, and with a frightening click, the pistol was ready to fire.

Bang.

Zakar sidestepped just as blood, brain matter, and fluids launched across the room. The dead man slumped forward against his bonds. His partner vomited and defecated on himself.

The disgustingly rank prisoner spent the next two hours gushing everything he knew of Sasha's plans and the Celje's next moves. The man was nothing more than a hired gun, not a trained Celje, and didn't offer much that Nencia didn't know already. Still, he cooperated. At the end, Nencia gave the prisoner a choice, something she often did with captives.

"What we do now is simple," said Nencia. "You have a choice. The first option is that I kill you."

The young man's face went six shades paler, and he energetically shook his head. "I'll do anything, Donato, anything! Please, please don't kill me!"

"Thought so. The first thing you'll do is write down the names of the three most important people to you on this planet. Zakar here will verify the list's accuracy. Once verified, you'll begin working for me as a spy, and yes, I'll pay you. You'll tell no one, because if you do, those three people will suffer in ways you can't imagine. I'll hang their limbless corpses in Limeth so you'll know I kept my promise. I'll send various parts of their bodies to every known Celje stronghold. You'll live with that guilt for a while, until I decide to hunt you, torture you, then kill you. Am I clear?"

———————

It was past midnight when Nencia finally reached her apartment and climbed into a warm, freshly filtered bath. The abandoned-building-turned-mafia-boss-apartment was directly behind the Appian warehouses. Her home was one of the few two-story buildings in Worall and housed a shower, toilet, two bedrooms, and a couch, all on the second story. She used the first floor as an office full of special crates and vices she kept out of the official warehouse inventories. Outside, hidden Appian guards kept watch, safeguarding their syndicate's governess from the many enemies she'd made over the years.

With wet hair and a towel wrapped around her, Nencia opened a bottle of wine she'd received from a Frenchman back in Dalth. She relaxed on the couch, sipping the surprisingly good vintage. Despite the day's violent turn, her mind returned to Jayden. There was no doubt the stubborn man liked her, but he was also different. Unlike other men in her life, he was mature for his age and honorable to his core. He liked to talk more than she did and wasn't always trying to get into her pants—what the hell was wrong with him?

A knock on the front door sent her gunning for her pistol on the table top. A visitor at this hour didn't make sense, but how did they get passed her security? Were they dead? She hadn't heard gunshots.

Wearing a brown, ratty bathrobe, Nencia stepped cautiously down the stairs with pistol and wine in hand. The base floor of the apartment was dimly lit by faux, solar candles, and dimmed her profile against a potential assassin.

She raised her pistol, ready to empty her revolver into the door. "Who is it?"

"Hey beautiful, it's me," said a familiar voice. "I know you've got a pistol pointed at the door; don't shoot me."

She exhaled, but it wasn't in relief. Instead, it was a flicker of guilt. Opening the door, she stared at a man wearing a worn black leather jacket and a finely trimmed mustache.

"What the hell are you doing here?" she scoffed. "You realize how damn late it is?"

The cocky captain of the *Night Scope* placed a hand on the doorframe. "You don't look happy to see me. Can't a husband visit his wife every now and then?"

CHAPTER 20: YEAR 2400

Cool, refreshing air off the Altum Sea swept over Dalth and the rest of Capintesta, bringing the first signs of fall to the region. Certus seemed to move faster with the lower temperatures. Landing thrusters off a nearby transport roared over the road, but Certus didn't flinch.

"He's getting old and deaf," said Serena sitting next to Jayden.

Jayden waved the idea away. "Don't listen to her, Certus, you're not old. He's in his prime." Jayden looked up through small rifts in the tree canopy. "I think that's the *Night Scope* taking off."

Serena threw him a sideways glance. "And how the hell do you know that?"

Jayden pointed to the rear of the departing ship. "It says *Night Scope* along the bottom there."

Serena shoved him then crossed her arms. "Look, you may have a mistress buddy, but I don't. I'm not spending the night in that damn saloon again. That place is nasty."

Jayden snapped his head toward her. "Uhh... what?"

"Nencia, you're seeing her tonight, right?"

Jayden momentarily forgot why he was heading to Worall in the first place. "Right. I'm out of it. Still tired from having to drag you home again last night from Kun's."

Serena nestled her head between Jayden's shoulder and neck. "I'm the best friend you have. Admit it, you love me for it. You need me to keep your life interesting."

They were transporting goods to Worall and planned on returning in two days with supplies for the town. Serena would likely stay at the local inn while he hoped to stay at Nencia's place.

They entered through the unguarded gate and headed for the three iconic Appian warehouses. Lines of log homes and mud-brick cottages lined the west side of Worall. Stray dogs fought for scraps in the streets while homeless adults and children begged for money or food. The home-less-child population in Worall was nowhere near as bad compared to the rest of Ojult, mostly attributed to Nencia's questionable recruiting tactics.

With plenty of daylight left, Jayden steered the wagon over to the first warehouse beset with dozens of workers moving and loading crates.

"Jayden, wait," said Serena. "Let's go to the second warehouse instead of this one."

"Why? Are the men more attractive at that warehouse? This one seems just as good as the next?"

"Look over there."

Jayden followed her finger toward the garage heading into the first warehouse. A slender man with a graying beard leaned against the building.

"Wren's not going to start anything with so many people around. Come on, Serena." Yet Jayden didn't quite believe this.

"Second warehouse, Jayden," she persisted. "I know you, and I know Wren. It's never a good mix."

Wren Dikal was the de facto mail-delivery man for Capintesta. He was married to Shari Dikal, and together they had a son named Diego. Shari was nice enough but kept to herself and rarely ventured outside of their home back in Dalth. Diego was a nice kid who attended school but was never seen playing with Bélise or any of the other children.

Wren believed Jayden was a mystic, associating his time with the Nein as confirmation he was a sage. Wren's grounds for hating mystics escaped even Markus, but the man's dislike for Jayden started the moment he set foot in Dalth. Conceding to his friend's persistence, Jayden parked the wagon in the designated offloading area near the second warehouse.

"Serena, good evening," greeted Zakar. "You made good time."

Serena hopped off the wagon and embraced Zakar. "How are you? I see you haven't burned down the place yet."

"Not yet," replied Zakar. "And I see you've brought one of your servants."

Whether it was his past with the Nein or relationship with Nencia, Zakar didn't care for Jayden.

"Good to see you, Zakar," Jayden said, tipping his hat. "It's been a while since you guys visited Dalth, so we decided to make a quick trip up here. Mostly kaldi beans, Victor's wine, and wheat from Markus's fields. There's one crate in there marked with red and—"

"I'll take care of that," interrupted Serena. "It's girl stuff for Nencia."

Jayden climbed down and held his hands up in defense. "Okay, then. Won't go digging in that one. Where's Nencia?"

Zakar waved a few of his workers over and motioned them to begin unloading. "She's got a video link up with the corporation and doesn't need to be disturbed. She wants you to wait at the saloon. She'll fetch you when she's done."

Jayden watched as red, blue, and unmarked crates were unloaded. "And my horse? You'll stable him?"

"I'll take care of Certus when Zakar's people are done," said Serena, keeping an unusually close eye on the marked crates. "I'm going to stay here and catch up with Zakar. You go ahead and have a drink."

"All right," said Jayden, not bothering to question her motives. He pulled a small pouch from the front seat of the coach and walked toward a young boy and teenage girl counting crates inside the warehouse.

Logan noticed him first and rushed him, nearly knocking him over with his hug. "Hi Mr. Jayden!"

"Hey, kiddo, how you doing? Everything okay?"

Bella ambled over, her long wavy hair had lightened from the sun. "Hey Jayden, we didn't know you were coming."

"Did you bring us chocolate?" asked Logan.

Jayden chuckled, then reached into the pouch. "Don't tell Zakar about this, or he'll get grumpy, okay?"

Bella held her piece with a lady's grace while Logan grabbed his with a teenage hunger. Logan chomped into his gift, catching paper and candy in a large gooey bite. He swallowed and hugged Jayden again, leaving chocolate smudges on Jayden's dusty pants.

Jayden promised to see the kids later and set off toward the saloon on the other side of town. Dozens of people littered the streets just outside the launchpad as they normally did after a shipment of new exiles. They looked pale, scared, and confused, and rightly so. Less than half of these people would live, yet there was nothing for him to do. It was a quandary that had no resolution and ravaged Jayden's natural instincts to help.

Avoiding the beggars and street fights, Jayden made his way to Beer, Beds, and Bras, the local saloon owned by Appian. The wood-framed, multistory building featured several windows on each level and tattered benches on the veranda. A malfunctioning virtual sign with neon-blue-and-green lettering hung sideways, sporting the well-known saloon's name. Drunks lay against the sides of the property, passed out while passersby robbed them of what little tonze they had. New arrivals watched holographic escorts flaunt their services through the windows, offering the false sense of reality that awaited them.

A rusted door, made of Ojultan ore, slid open when Jayden approached. Dense hettle smoke whirled over barstools and card tables covering the first floor. Rough-looking, scantily dressed women in sheer, self-tailoring nanofabric hunted young men and women from the corporation or Appian Shipping.

The saloon made most of its business from Appian staff and transport pilots, along with their crew, and tonight was no different. The landing pad in Worall was the second largest on the planet, next to Port Fiesta in Meridone. Three or more transport ships at a time were docked in Worall, lending dozens of crew members to the vices of the disorderly town.

"Mr. Vaut," said the bartender, waving him over.

Jayden squeezed through the crowded floor, drawing an aggravated murmur from two men at a card table.

Jayden shook hands with the bartender. "Evening, Sam."

Sam was an older man with white hair and thick eyebrows to match. He always greeted his regulars with a smile.

Jayden slid over enough tonze for his usual drink. Before Jayden could place his order, a man with a long cloak flagged Sam down. This new customer was about as pale as a ghost, with a thoroughly trimmed handlebar mustache, and wore his hat at a strange tilt.

"Whiskey, please," slurred the stranger, lighting a hettle stalk. He looked over to Jayden, then seemed to notice he'd cut in line. "Sam, I seem to have cut in line in front of this gentleman. My apologies. I'll pay for his drink and his... forgiveness... mister...?"

The man looked as if he functioned well under the influence, minus the slurring. "Jayden. And you are?"

"Well, Jayden, I'm Andreas Palada," said the stranger, tossing back his fresh drink. "I see you have company. Pleasure meeting you."

Andreas headed back into the crowd leaving Jayden baffled by the encounter.

Jayden accepted his drink, but before he continued, Sam's posture went rigid. Jayden turned to see what he was looking at.

Standing in front of him were two men about Jayden's age and somewhat familiar to him. "Can I help you with something?"

The taller of the two men, a man with freckles, a knotty beard, and a receding hairline, whispered, "We seen you coming in with that Visconti woman. She's the one that brawled with Sasha's people a while back."

Very few people on Ojult knew of the Celje, much less their leader. "No idea what you're talking about."

Some of the nearby patrons began to stare, sensing a brewing fight.

Jayden turned back to Sam and leaned into the bar top, but kept his eyes on the two men using the smeared mirror behind the bar. "Sam, another pour if you don't mind."

"Sasha wants information on anyone traveling with that girl," continued the stranger. "Is that your girlfriend? Wife?"

The Celje were secret and shadowy. They didn't advertise their intent to strangers. This meant the fools behind Jayden were either drunk Celje recruits or pretenders. It didn't matter either way, because Jayden was still worried about the Nein. He tried to avoid confrontations, concerned Captain Siller might have spies in the larger towns across the continent. It didn't matter if Syrus had decreed Jayden free if he escaped Listo. Jayden knew the evil in Siller's soul, and that man would never stop hunting him.

Jayden sipped from his fresh pour. "Lots of people look alike on—"

In a flash, the shorter, more muscular man punched Jayden in the side. Jayden spit out his drink as he doubled over.

"Gentlemen, gentlemen, no fighting!" said Sam.

The two men ignored the bartender and stepped to either side of Jayden.

"My name's Broden, and this is my brother Clive. Don't you remember us? You nearly got us *spaced* off the *Night Scope*."

Jayden's side spasmed, but nothing felt broken. He turned, careful not to provoke another attack, and faced the brothers. Ojult had not been kind to either man, and through the grime and hair now covering their faces, Jayden recognized them in a sudden revelation. While Jayden worked with the Nein right off the boat, these two must have got mixed up with the Celje. They probably didn't make the cut as full members and ended up taking odd jobs for Sasha.

"I'm not sorry for what happened on the ship," said Jayden. "I didn't like soras back then, and I don't like them now. Go about your business, and leave me and the woman alone."

The more muscular of the two, Clive, picked Jayden up by his shoulders and threw him back onto the floor. A swift kick knocked the wind out of him, and Jayden rocked back and forth, struggling to bring air back into his lungs.

"No… no fighting in here," continued Sam, still behind the safety of the bar top. "Appian doesn't allow…"

So much for avoiding attention, thought Jayden.

Clive's second kick was met by Jayden's crossed forearms, absorbing the blow, then twisting Clive's ankle. The uncoordinated fool dropped to the floor.

Attempting to avenge his brother, Broden threw a punch that went wide, giving Jayden enough time to stand up and reposition. Jayden readied to end the fight when conscious thought left Broden's eyes, and he crumpled to the ground.

Andreas stood over Broden's comatose body—a pistol in one hand, a drink in the other. He'd pistol-whipped the eldest of the two brothers. "Violence in such a fine establishment is just wrong. Sam, I believe these two will be buying my drinks tonight. And Jayden's, if I'm not mistaken?"

Before Jayden had a chance to respond, the murmuring of the saloon perished, and all eyes went to the entrance.

Nencia headed to the bar. "Sam, who started it?"

"The brothers, ma'am. They attacked Mr. Vaut."

Both brothers were starting to stir when Nencia bent over and lifted Clive's head up by his beard. "Everyone knows the rules of my bar, even Sasha. My people are going to drag you out of this town and off this continent. If any of my people see you again on Capintesta, they'll kill you."

Two Appian guards grabbed the brothers and dragged them out of the saloon. Instead of facing Jayden, Nencia angled toward a woman at the base of the nearby stairs.

"Lacy," said Nencia, giving the enchanting woman a kiss on both cheeks. "I'm sorry for the interruption, they won't be back again."

The enchanting woman of Indian descent wore a long red dress that dragged across the floor and exposed much of her perfectly bronzed cleavage. She brushed her long black hair behind her exposed shoulders. "Lady Donato," replied Lacy in a soft accent, "the actions of a few misfits by no means falls upon your shoulders, but I thank you for your concern. May I be of any service?"

Andreas walked up beside Jayden dusting ash and soot off his clothing. "Ahh, Madam Lacy," whispered Andreas, "a real woman if there ever was one. You know she's run this brothel since it first opened?"

Jayden turned to Andreas. "Not sure why you helped me, but thanks."

The men exchanged handshakes. "Just a friendly scuffle. It's good for the mind. Besides, I know of you more than you might feel comfortable with."

Jayden already guessed who Andreas was, or at least who he worked for. "Nein?"

Andreas nodded. "But don't look so sour, all is well between us. But *Lady Donato* there seems to want a word with you. Have a good evening, Vaut."

———

Jayden's ribs stopped aching by the time Nencia made dinner for the two of them. They were on the second floor of her apartment, the space lit with oil lanterns and the clear-evening moonlight.

Nencia served the finest meal Jayden had seen since coming to Ojult:

imported beef with sides of durian, rambutan, and romanesco decorated his plate.

"Drawing attention to yourself like you did back there wasn't smart," Nencia said before making a second plate.

"Wasn't smart because you don't allow fighting or because the Nein might be there looking for me?"

"Seeing that you're sleeping with me, I'm pretty sure I would have forgiven you for the fight. No, the Nein might still be looking for you. I told you when I first dropped you off on Capintesta, keep a low profile. The man you met, Andreas, you're lucky he owes me a favor."

Nencia poured two glasses of wine, a vintage right out of Dalth, and placed them on the table.

Jayden caught something peculiar about her just then—she had blood underneath her fingernails.

Jayden pushed aside the urge to ask about it and instead answered her original question. He explained his history with the brothers and how they were harassing a mystic on board the *Night Scope* enroute to Ojult.

"You've been seeing me naked for months, and this is the first time I've heard this."

"We have the rest of our lives to catch up, why rush?" The words were out of his mouth before he knew what he'd said.

Nencia shoved a spoonful of beef into her mouth, chewed slowly, and deliberated over her next words.

"Our lives? You want to keep a toothbrush here, maybe a spare set of socks?"

Jayden chased a large mouth full of beef with wine. "I've had a change of clothes here for weeks."

"Come on, Vaut, there's a lot going on right now. My conversation with Elasus and his crew didn't go as planned. With the increase in Celje raids and the Nein not getting along with many folks these days…"

Jayden let her gather her thoughts. It was rare she spoke so seriously. Clearly what she had to say was important.

"It's a game of chess," she continued, "and if Appian… if *I* don't move my pieces precisely, people, including you, become a target."

Jayden reached over and held her hand. "I seem to heal pretty quick. Come on, you're more than just weekend entertainment to me. I'm not saying I'm ready to put a ring on that bloodstained finger, but don't forget that there are people who care about you."

Nencia smiled. "I'm sitting on information that I got off a Celje spy. Sasha would kill me to stop Elasus from getting it. If Sasha found out, he likely couldn't go after me directly, but he could target my friends."

It seemed to Jayden that she'd been wanting to speak with someone about this for a while. "Don't worry about them coming after me. Besides, they'd need to find me first, and Dalth isn't exactly on the main path to anywhere."

She leaned over and kissed him. "You're cute but not real smart, Vaut."

They fell asleep against one another, ignoring the howls of predators resonating through the nearby forest.

He woke up the next morning with his arm draped over her naked body. For some reason, perhaps it was her breathing, but he knew she was awake. "Sleep okay?"

"I'm going to call Elasus today," she said. "He needs to know." Her voice sounded determined.

"I'm guessing you were up most of the night thinking about this," he said. "Can I help?"

With a finesse only she could achieve, Nencia slid on top of him. She let the covers slide off her shoulders, allowing her alluring body to entrance him. An hour later, the lovers were still making no real effort to get the day started.

Wearing only briefs, Jayden rose first. "Kaldi?"

Nencia's long black hair looked disheveled. Her white button-down blouse lay open, fringing against her gray underwear. "Don't you ever get tired of drinking that stuff?"

He came back into the room several minutes later with two cups brewed from Dalth's own beans. "You're the one who told me to find something to trade. All I did was follow the advice from some good-looking, married mob boss."

Just before lunch, the two lovers were awakened by loud banging coming from the front door.

"Who in the hell is that?" Nencia said.

They could hear a woman's voice yelling from the door. "Probably Serena."

He tossed the covers off and struggled to get dressed. Nencia laughed as he stumbled and crashed into the wall. Eventually Jayden, clad in jeans, boots, and a worn button-down shirt headed downstairs.

"Don't forget your hat and gun, *darling*," snickered Nencia.

"Shit," he said, running back upstairs. He snatched up his hat and fastened his pistol belt. "How do I look?"

"Like Wyatt Earp, except younger, clumsy, and not nearly as good-looking."

Jayden leapt onto the bed and kissed her sloppily.

"Yuck!" said Nencia, wiping her mouth. "Get going. And make sure you tell Serena not to forget the extra cargo she promised. Zakar will know what to do with it. And give the old man my best."

Jayden took the stairs two at a time while Serena continued cursing his name. He flung open the door and found his friend upset.

"You two had all night to screw! All I asked is that we get out of Worall before lunch. There's a storm coming. Certus isn't young anymore, and it's going to take twice as long trudging through the mud!"

Jayden flashed his palms in a defensive manner. "Certus is a draught horse, Serena, he'll be fine. I'm sorry for being late."

"Fine. We need to get going."

"Nencia said not to forget the extra cargo. You know what she's talking about?"

Serena didn't make eye contact. "All the cargo was taken care of *this morning*."

Jayden gave her a mock salute, which earned him a punch to the arm.

Zakar walked out from the warehouse with a troublesome scowl. He handed Serena a box. "Give this to the mayor when you see him, and take care of yourself. The roads aren't what they used to be."

"I'll make sure he gets it," Serena replied. "Anything specific I need to be worried about other than the usual?"

A quiet, female voice spoke from the side. "Logan and I were shot at coming back from Dalth last time we visited you guys," said Bella.

Jayden knew about the attack but hadn't heard of any more. "Heard you saved the caravan."

Bella nodded. "My… gifts sometimes do that. They feel supercharged some days but nonexistent others. Must be your chocolate."

"You acted based on your instincts, that's good. A gut feeling can sometimes outdo years of training. I don't know anything about your powers, but don't shy away from them. Ojult isn't forgiving, so take every advantage you can."

"We'll see you guys in a few weeks," said Serena, waving goodbye. "Take care."

With the wagon full of fresh supplies, Jayden and Serena headed back through the southwestern gate of Worall. As they exited the town, Jayden felt eyes burning through him and cautiously scanned his surroundings. On the outskirts of the city, leaning against a large oak tree, was Wren Dikal.

CHAPTER 21: YEAR 2400

Jayden slowed Certus as the horse pulled the seed drill across the churned soil, dropping seeds every two meters. With summer long behind them, the cool breeze and lower temperatures made the back-breaking work tolerable. With Jayden's youth and availability, Markus Fonte decided to plant another full plot of kaldi beans this fall. Between planting the new field and harvesting the older trees, Jayden's days were plenty busy.

There wasn't a trick or special machine to harvest the cherry-colored nuts from the plants, the work was all done by hand. Harvesting, sacking, and storing the beans took every bit of the past four weeks since he'd returned from Worall, and now Jayden looked forward to having the planting season over with.

Movement over the tilled soil to his right caused him to pull Certus to a stop. Pulling out a small knife, Jayden reared back and threw the bladed weapon. The nearest zibar took two more steps until falling over. Seeing the fate of his partner, the second zibar scurried off. Villagers often killed these vermin for many reasons, but chiefly because zibars preferred cats over mice.

He carefully stepped over the freshly seeded soil and added the zibar to the four he'd already killed that morning. He usually gave his kills to Kun, who would clean and skin the carcasses. The furs would likely be sold to Appian and the meat served at the pub. Jayden never asked or negotiated with Kun and accepted whatever payment was offered. His outlook was the same with Markus, accepting whatever payment the mayor offered for working his land. The work was hard and gratifying and didn't involve killing anyone, which Jayden was grateful for.

Jayden looked up to Markus and saw him as something between a mentor, friend, and administrator. Perhaps most intriguing about Markus was the man's vast network of friends throughout the region. One of the more baffling relationships concerned Zakar of Appian Shipping. Implicative of the recent transaction between the two men and a bottle of Listo brandy, there seemed a more intimate meaning behind the gift. Following Jayden's delivery of the gift four weeks ago, Markus unexpectedly and candidly explained the puzzling relationship.

"You'll need to take a drink of this with me one day, Jayden," said Markus, opening the box and admiring the bottle. "It's the best brandy on any planet."

"Thank you, Mayor. I've never tasted it, but everyone seems to think the same."

"Must seem kind of strange, Zakar sending me such an expensive gift."

"I'm not one to pry."

Markus pushed his fingers through his slicked-back hair. "Zakar actually lived in Dalth for a while, he and his parents."

Dalth wasn't that big, and Jayden knew everyone in the town. "No, didn't know that."

"His mother and father were high-ranking government officials within FIAS back on Earth. The Qualis's uncovered a black-market money account between the FIAS minister and the Reeves Corporation. Zakar's parents went public with the information and within a week were found guilty of treason, without a trial. The FIAS sentenced them to exile with the PGU none the wiser. Given the fractured relationship between the PGU and FIAS and the close partnership between the corporation and the PGU, you can imagine the fallout if the secret money exchange was ever exposed. So, Zakar, who was just a young boy at the time, and his parents were sent to Ojult." Markus appeared far away in thought. "Like most exiles, they ended up in Worall with no money, food, or direction and somehow wandered into Dalth. Unfortunately, his parents both came down with pneumonia shortly after their arrival."

Pneumonia, like other illnesses, were a death sentence on Ojult, a subject Jayden was intimately familiar with.

"No, they didn't die, at least not then, if that's what you're thinking," he continued. "At the time, Bianca, my wife, was still with us, and we took care of his parents until they recovered. They lived in Dalth for several years, until both died from the Kupita virus many years later. I still remember that year. It was only the second case of the virus we'd ever experienced. It never spread in town, but the planet experienced a major outbreak. We must have lost a quarter of Ojult's population that year. Of course, that was the same year we had Bélise, but lost Bianca. Bad year for Dalth, bad year."

"I'm sorry," said Jayden, seeing his mentor's eyes imagining a different life in another time. "I wish… I've always heard good things about Bianca. And Bélise, you've done a great job with her."

Markus cleared his throat. "Childbirth, Kupita, pneumonia, stubbing your toe, people on Earth don't think twice about, but it's usually a death sentence here." Markus sighed. "Zakar worked for me for a few more years until he was about fifteen and old enough to look out for himself. He asked me if I could help him get out of Dalth, so I introduced him to Nencia. He's been sending me a bottle of Listo brandy every chance he gets since that introduction."

Focusing on his present duties, Jayden worked the rest of the day, seeding only a quarter of the field. Rains would come during the last half of fall, and he needed to have the land fully seeded by then. Having skipped lunch, Jayden's stomach started gurgling around sunset. After feeding and stabling Certus, Jayden hiked over to Kun's for drinks and dinner.

Jayden wasn't far from the field when a caravan of five wagons headed up the main road. Every so often, Mayor Fonte met with leaders from other towns to discuss trade, security, medical notices, and other management concerns. These leaders always traveled to Dalth, never the other way around, and it seemed to Jayden that these leaders valued Markus's opinion more than the other way around. As a fourth-generation Ojultan, his family and personal experiences far outweighed those of other local leaders. Markus never knew why his ancestors were brought to Ojult, but he understood that his great-grandfather founded Dalth, and the Fontes had managed the town ever since.

"You look worn out, Jayden. The planting going okay?" asked Markus while sipping a large mug of ale.

Jayden hung his coat and hat, then waved hello to those he knew. "Evening, Mayor. Yes, that seed drill's working wonders. The new springs Serena installed did the trick."

"And the mayor here, he has been working hard as well," said Victor Dubois in his customary French accent.

Jayden liked Victor, even more when the handsome Frenchman had a few glasses of his own wine flowing through him. The first-generation Ojultan looked, as well as sounded, French. His graying, frizzy hair blended well with his slender face and green eyes.

"A quick chat with Zakar, nothing new," explained Markus. "Word is murders in Pa'Gran are on the rise, and rumors of mystic disappearances are more prevalent too."

"I do not know, monsieur, Capintesta, it is not so bad. It is better than Meridone, I say. That place, no land for lovely ladies. We should take all the beauties from that continent and bring them to Dalth. I will take care of them and love them like they deserve, yes."

"Not sure Celine would go along with that idea," said Markus. "But you go ahead and try. Dalth is open to beauty, not prostitution. Bring them but make sure they can work and provide for themselves."

Victor raised his glass. "Speaking of beautiful creatures, I do not see Serena. She perhaps had too much of my delicious wine last night?"

"Her furnace is smoking so she's at least up," Jayden said. "Hungover or not, she's the best metallurgist on Capintesta."

Liao walked over from cleaning a table. "Evening, Jayden, what you want?"

Jayden exchanged a quick shoulder hug with the waitress. "Ale please and anything Kun's got hot."

"He's got chicken broiling, that work?"

"All right, but ask Kun to make sure it's not still moving when he puts it on the plate, please." Jayden wasn't kidding, Kun had a habit of undercooking the meat. "Also, tell him I put a few zibars in the back for him."

It was the time of year when the temperatures dropped noticeably as soon as the sun set. Kun lit all three fireplaces in the pub, and Jayden, alongside his friends, ate and enjoyed one another's company, avoiding topics that would stir up the now-intoxicated Victor.

In the middle of a conversation about horse breeds best fit for working fields, the sight of a rider through the front window caught Jayden's attention.

"It's been fun, guys, but it's time for me to head home," Jayden said, tossing tonze on the table.

His sudden change in demeanor fooled no one. "No reason to leave, Jayden, he's just here for dinner," insisted Markus.

Victor stood up, acting as though he wanted to say something, but his wobbly legs gave out, and the Frenchman fell back into the barstool.

A slender man with a gray beard, tattered overcoat, and hat walked into the already chilly room.

"Afternoon, Wren," said Liao. "Hungry, thirsty, or both?"

Wren placed his hat on the rack, then seeing Jayden's, knocked it to the ground. "Both, Liao, and tell that cook to really cook the meat this time."

"I'll tell him," Liao replied, looking insulted.

Wren turned and locked eyes with Jayden.

"You've been gone over a week," Markus said. "Everything okay?"

Markus's injection halted whatever unpleasant statement Wren was readying to fire. "Just finished the mail run on that north side. Lots of detours with the Celje about. Don't know if they're here for us normal folk or maybe hunting *his* kind." Wren nodded at Jayden. "Delivered your tonze, Mister Mayor, just before I got here."

Jayden let the insinuation that he was a Nein slide. "Liao, thank you and Kun for dinner. Mayor, I'm heading home, I'll be back at the fields tomorrow."

Markus's eyes flashed between the two men. "We have enough problems on this planet without you two butting heads every time you meet. Act like adults and work this out."

"We'll do our best," replied Jayden. He got up and walked toward the door, picking up his hat and coat. "But it probably won't be today."

Wren put a firm hand on Jayden's chest, stopping him from exiting the pub. "You're the one who put my kid to work."

"Wren, all the kids pitch in," said Markus. "Diego, Hannah, Monica, and Bélise were all there together, unloading the shipment from Worall."

Wren stepped forward, thumping Jayden's chest. "You don't tell my boy what to do, you get me, wizard man? I'll cut your damn throat if I see that again. That's my boy, not some magician's slave. Mayor, I told you we should've killed him that first night we saw him!"

Jayden kept eye contact and considered knocking Wren to the ground. "Appreciate the warning. I'll be leaving if you don't mind stepping aside."

Wren shifted and shoved Jayden backward into an empty chair. "You're not gonna tell me what to do either, wizard man."

Jayden regained his balance, but didn't think of retaliating, for his respect for Markus was unwavering. Instead, he adjusted his shirt and headed for the door again, intending to avoid the confrontation. He stepped by Wren and reached for the door when Wren grabbed his forearm, and something hard hit Jayden in the head. He fell to the floor, seeing stars, the back of his head throbbing.

Liao whimpered, and Markus said, "Not again!"

Wren's foot came up, but Jayden rolled away and got to his feet. There was a difference between trying to avoid a fight and letting someone play punching bag with your body.

"Stop it, Wren, damn it!" demanded Markus, getting between the two men. "That's enough. Wren, go back to Shari and cool off. Jayden! Get that look off your face!"

The appeal from Markus was clear. He knew what Jayden was thinking.

"You freaking mystics and your pointed hats and sticks. None of us would be here if it weren't for you," Wren seethed. "We'd all be back on Earth if we'd just killed you people to begin with."

"Wren!" Liao said. "Jayden's *not* a mystic, you fool! He was a slave to them, not one of them, and I'm not serving you again until you apologize. Or maybe I need to go to Shari and she can knock some sense into you."

Mentioning Wren's wife usually calmed him down as she didn't share

Wren's views of mystics, at least not publicly. "I'm just gonna eat something at home. This place wreaks of backstabbers and shamans."

The next morning, Jayden untangled himself from the sheets and got out of bed. His bedroom was large enough for a small cot, a few shelves, and a cracked mirror. He'd rigged up a water-pressure system that gave him something like running water for drinking and the occasional shower, but no sewer system. He had an outhouse like everyone else, which became an inconvenience when temperatures dropped.

Wearing only briefs, he stumbled into the small kitchen and started boiling water over a wood-burning stove. Part of Jayden's nightly routine included bringing in logs and setting them up for the next morning.

Jayden collapsed back in bed and fell asleep only to be awakened by the whistling kettle.

Walking back through the living area, he tripped over something soft, which also spoke.

"Ey-w... ouch," said the female voice.

Jayden looked down, vaguely remembering Kun dropping Serena off at his house in the middle of the night.

"Morning," Jayden said to his still-intoxicated friend. "You need a serenade this morning? I know a few good ones."

"Stop talking... need kaldi."

"Just started it," he said, noticing she was shivering. "You cold? Want a blanket?"

"Turn off the kettle!"

Jayden laughed all the way back into the kitchen, allowing the whistling to linger for a few seconds longer just to irk his hungover friend.

"Will you please turn off that damn kettle!" screamed Serena.

Jayden used locally harvested kaldi beans and leaves from a byzantina plant as a filter. A few minutes later, he readied a fresh cup of the caffeinated drink for himself and his headache-stricken friend.

Serena sat cross-legged in front of the couch. "Oh god, that's good," she said, sipping the hot drink and inhaling the soothing aroma. "I'm guessing you dragged me here last night?"

Jayden sat on the couch next to her. "You mentioned something about Kun's moonshine when he dropped you off here. Someday you'll need to explain why you keep coming here instead of your own home."

Jayden suspected she kept crashing at his place because she hated being alone at the home of her deceased parents.

Serena pressed the hot mug to her forehead. "That explains the double vision. What time is it?"

He shrugged. "Don't know, but I probably need to head out soon. Bélise and Monica are helping me with the fields today."

"Don't Diego and Hannah usually help?"

Jayden shook his head. "Hannah's helping her parents around the pub today, and Diego... well, Wren doesn't want him helping out."

For the first time that morning, Serena's eyes opened fully, exposing dry, bloodshot, white slits. "Wren eats zibar poop for breakfast and everyone knows it; don't take his attitude seriously. Not sure how he landed Shari."

Jayden's kaldi-fueled brain thought of how much work still had to be done on the fields. He'd need at least three more weeks to complete the plot before winter blanketed the region. He marched off to his bedroom, leaving his dazed friend to soak in her much needed caffeine. Jayden dressed in his usual garb and brushed his teeth with a cython's hair toothbrush and toothpaste made of baking soda, olive oil, brandy, and salt.

"There's enough for one more cup, but I gotta get the day started." Floorboards creaked as Jayden neared the front door. "You working the mill today?"

She nodded. "I'm still working on that big order Nencia handed me a few weeks ago."

Jayden opened the door, letting a cool draft into the home. "Don't take this the wrong way, but you'd probably get this order done a lot faster if you weren't hungover every morning. I've never seen you work so much on a single sale."

Serena's drinking was something he'd wanted to bring up for some time and understood the topic would intrench friction in their relationship. The conversation was necessary, despite the outcome. Thus, when she didn't yell and belittle him for bringing it up, Jayden got the uneasy feeling something more dangerous was happening.

"I don't drink because of my parents, if that's what you're thinking," Serena said staring at her cup.

Jayden adjusted his hat a bit lower, blocking the rushing wind. It was apparent, even for someone with limited knowledge about the opposite sex, that Serena didn't want to talk about whatever was bothering her.

"I'm not going to try and force information out of you," he said. "You're my best friend, and I'll be here for you when you're ready."

"I've got lots of friends, Jayden, why are you the only one asking me about stuff like this?"

Jayden looked out toward the crops dancing in the gusting wind. "Just trying to take care of the few I got."

CHAPTER 22: YEAR 2400

When Jayden arrived, his two volunteers were already working away in the fields. Several teens volunteered to work the crops when not in school, but Bélise Fonte was different. She had the work ethic of a hardened youth and leadership qualities like her father. If the next generation were to survive on Ojult, it would be on the backs of teenagers like her.

"Thanks for being on time. Everything okay this morning?" Jayden linked Certus to the seed drill, checked the new springs, then turned on the display system's monitor.

The only daughter of Victor and Celine pulled a slimy, opaque worm out of the ground. "This is a toso-worm, right?" She was around fifteen, with plump cheeks like her mother, straight black hair, and close-set eyes.

With Diego and Hannah both out, he'd really be pushing to get the fields done by winter. "Yeah, toso-worm, they eat the seeds and plant eggs in their place."

From above, an intensely loud, ear-blasting roar rang out, forcing the group to cover their ears. Jayden spotted the RC-1 Brooks transport ship buzzing above them at an uncommonly low altitude. The large, dark-gray ship, several hundred meters long, looked like a hybrid between the forward section of a submarine and the aft quarter of a stealth fighter. Six engines covered the rear, while nine landing thrusters lined the bottom.

The ship gained momentum as it reached the lower-level clouds and burst through the atmosphere, leaving a lone white contrail in its wake.

"Probably aliens!" shouted Monica.

Unperturbed by the ship, Bélise continued working. "There's no such thing, right, Jayden?"

"No aliens, just us."

"Could be Elders, though, right?" asked Monica.

"Not aliens, definitely not Elders," assured Jayden. "That's a Reeves Corporation transport ship bringing supplies to Ojult. I want you guys to walk ahead of Certus and pull out weeds, bugs, and other junk that may be in the soil. If you find anymore toso-worms, save them. We can use them for fishing the creek."

"Why can't it be the Elders?" continued Monica.

Bélise pulled a large toso-worm from the ground and tossed it into a leather sack. "Because the Elder's aren't even real. It's just something parents tell their kids to make them feel safe at night."

"That's not true, actually. The Elders were around at one point, around year 2150 or so, but they haven't been seen since."

Bélise looked annoyed. "My father says they weren't real, it was just a bunch of really lucky Argos mystics that defeated the Nein and made the peace."

"Best listen to your folks, then," surrendered Jayden. "But I can tell you that neither the Argos, Nein, or Elders are going to help you clean up this field, so let's keep working."

They worked several feet ahead of Certus, clearing the soil of anything that might hinder the seedlings. If the weather held and they worked daily for the next several weeks, they might have a shot at finishing before winter.

The morning passed and the girls broke for lunch while Jayden worked on the jammed furrower spout. After having to disassemble the funnel to clear the mechanism, he restored the piece and was adjusting the disbursement pattern when the subtle rumblings of nine plain-clothed men on horseback broke his attention. The man leading the formation dressed differently than his counterparts, sporting fashionable sunglasses, slicked-back hair, and a familiarly wicked smile.

"Misora," Jayden said with a scowl. "That murderous *sora.*"

Jayden dropped to a knee, creating a low profile against the open field. Jayden considered his options. From behind him, the noisy giggles of Bélise and Monica triggered his adrenaline.

Jayden scrambled toward them, keeping one hand on his hat, waved for the girls to get down. Bélise picked up on the motion first and pulled Monica to the dirt. He skidded to a stop next to them, peppering them with freshly churned dirt.

"Girls, listen to me. Bélise, take Monica and head back to the square. Find your dad. Tell him there are nine Celje heading into the town from the north and Misora is with them. Tell him I'm going to stall them. Run through the field to the south, then cut over so they don't see you. Got it?"

Bélise nodded. "Let's go before they spot us," she told Monica. Bélise's demeanor was calm, which didn't surprise Jayden in the least.

"Keep Monica close to you, and stay low."

Bélise grabbed her startled friend and set off. Jayden waited until they were out of sight, then reached for his pistol.

"Oh, come on now, what the hell," he muttered, feeling for the weapon that wasn't there. Of all the times to leave it at the house.

The men were within a hundred yards now, and Jayden hastily pieced together his plan. Crouching low, he glided toward the path, aiming to cut them off well before they caught sight of the town square. He took a calm, deep breath and casually walked out onto the dirt path.

A man behind Misora spotted Jayden, mouthed something, then pointed back toward Jayden. Misora and four of his henchmen galloped ahead to confront him.

Jayden and Misora's last encounter had ended with them nearly killing one another, but that was almost a year ago, and Jayden looked completely different, having shaved his beard, cut his hair, and swapped the gunfighter attire for farming clothes.

With only a few dozen feet separating them, Misora pushed his horse up against Jayden in a pathetic attempt to intimidate him. He wore thin sunglasses, a maroon-and-black plaid shirt, and dark pants to go along with his arrogant grin. Having a bit more time to analyze the man this time, Jayden figured he was in his mid-thirties, physically fit and armed.

"Get out of our way, farmer," hissed Misora. "We have business in town."

Jayden's tension eased. If Misora had recognized him, the friendly greeting would have been replaced with a gunshot.

Jayden grabbed Misora's horse by the noseband and gently stroked the animal's cheek. "Just working my farm and noticed you guys coming up the road," Jayden said. "You look a bit out of place. You here for some trading?"

Misora's left hand glided over the butt of his pistol. "We're here to see the mayor. Now get out of the way. I won't ask again."

Jayden felt his pockets for his knife. "Who's your friend coming up the way there? He here to see the mayor too?"

The older man who'd given Misora orders earlier now approached. He wore a thick traveling cloak over his pistol belt and a hood that hid his receding hairline. "Young man, what is your name?" he asked in a thick accent.

Jayden tipped his hat. "Nate... Richardson."

"Well, Mr. Richardson," continued Sasha, "you obviously sent those two girls to warn Mayor Fonte of our visit. Which also means you know we are Celje. Have we met before?"

Jayden gauged the man in front of him and went with the flow of the conversation, remembering his goal was to give Markus time to prepare for their visit.

"Not that I know of. We don't get too many people around here dressed like you two, and I've heard rumors that Celje come around towns doing public-health checks and making sure no mystics are around."

Sasha gave a quick nod to Misora who dismounted. "Well, Nate Richardson," said Misora, stepping so close that Jayden's hat bumped the man's sunglasses, "it's time you moved out of the way."

Jayden needed to give Bélise a few more minutes. "Well, okay, but I always wanted to know, are you guys recruiting? Love what you've done with the planet. Maybe there's an opening?"

Misora looked back at Sasha who nodded again.

Misora turned back and pistol-whipped Jayden, knocking him to the dirt. He took a moment to breathe and gather himself, then got up to a knee, blood zigzagging down from his ear and neck. "Okay then, you're not hiring, I get it."

Misora's nostrils flared, and he plunged a well-aimed knee into Jayden's face, sending him back to the dirt as more blood gushed from his nose and mouth. A blast of wind carried Jayden's hat away, rolling his cherished belonging down the trail.

Jayden rolled over onto this stomach and spat out fresh blood. "Not… not sure that was necessary."

Jayden thought about what he'd do to Misora if they were alone, but the presence of eight other men vanquished the idea.

Misora dismounted and pressed a stained boot into Jayden's throat.

Misora chuckled. "For a simple farmer, you seem eager to taste your own blood. Still, you look familiar. I think Sasha might have been right; have we met before?"

Jayden's lips were shoved up into his nose, giving him a nasally pitch. "I'm… I'm sure I… would have remembered."

"We need to press on, Misora. Put the farmer down, and let's go," ordered Sasha, continuing down the road.

Jayden, fearing he'd pushed the Celje too far, tried to wrangle free of Misora's clamp. He heard Misora click the safety off his pistol and put the barrel next to his ear.

"You're no farmer."

Markus Fonte stepped out of the barbershop, clean-shaven and trimmed. Several years ago, Liao Nguyen unwillingly took over as the town's barber, opening one day a week and leaving her waitressing duties to Hannah. Serena also made money by keeping her friend well stocked with sharpened blades and scissors.

Markus stretched and heard the familiar snap as his back adjusted from sitting in the uncomfortable chair. Stiff, but nevertheless rejuvenated, Markus headed toward Kun's where he'd promised to help fix a drafty window. In front of the pub, Markus stopped and looked at his reflection in the glass. Aging was not for the weak, he reminded himself.

A chill crept down his back, and he looked skyward where graying clouds began to move into the region. "Could always use the rain," he muttered.

He reached for the door handle when a distant yell shot across the field. "Dad!"

Markus glanced toward the southwest, adrenaline pulsing through his system.

Bélise and Monica were sprinting toward him like they were being chased.

Markus walked calmly toward the two teenagers. "Bélise, what is it?"

"Dad," Bélise said breathlessly.

He put an easing hand across her back. "Easy, catch your breath."

"Dad… Jayden said to tell you… the Celje are… coming. They're here…"

At the word Celje, Monica broke into more tears. "Mayor… what is a Celje? Are they from the corporation?"

"Uh… no, honey, no, nothing like that," replied Markus, understanding the girl's imagination was probably running wild, conjuring up all sorts of images of what a Celje might be.

"We… were helping Jayden and he… he said Celje were coming into the town," continued Bélise, finally catching her breath. "Told us to find you, that he was going to stall them."

Markus placed a soothing hand on both the girls' shoulders. "You did a great job telling me. Thank you. Bélise, why don't you walk Monica back to her house. I'm pretty sure Victor's there. Then go find Celine at the clinic, and wait there until I come find you. Okay?"

There was no panic or uncertainty in Bélise's expression, only hushed understanding. Markus kissed her on the forehead and watched her tow Monica away from the square.

Markus had seen it many times over the years, the hardness Ojult injected into men and women striving to survive. It enveloped Bélise at a very young age and would eventually touch Monica in the same way.

Markus wasted no time finding Kun, Serena, and others he'd recruited long ago in case of such an emergency. The five of them, though usually seven when Wren Dikal and Jayden were around, made up Dalth's militia.

Armed with pistols and long rifles, Markus led them up the main road just outside the square. There wasn't time to warn the citizens, generally done by ringing the church bell, but word would spread quickly enough.

"I'm concerned about Jayden," said Kun, still wearing his cooking apron.

Markus pointed toward the northwest. "He was working the fields with Monica and Bélise when—"

Markus's voice was eclipsed by the crack of a BP pistol.

Markus's troop raised their weapons.

"What are they shooting at?" Serena said. "Jayden's the only…"

The ringing gunshot unleashed a splurge of guilt in the hardened mayor. "Let's just pray Jayden's okay and get ready for them."

"Mayor, we… we need to get up there," said Serena. "We… I owe him that!"

Markus raised a calming hand in the air. "Marching up there with weapons drawn, against the Celje no less, is a recipe for an untimely death. Trust that Jayden will do the right and stay calm." Markus didn't want to bring the name up in front of Serena, but he had a suspicion that Misora was with the group. "I need everyone, including you, Serena, to follow my lead and attempt to de-escalate the situation, no matter what. Let's not kick the sarcto in the rear if we can avoid it."

Picking a fight with the Celje was pointless. They were well trained in both ranged and melee weaponry. Decades on Ojult and his father's canon taught Markus that one Celje was worth three militiamen.

Halfway up the northwest road, Markus and his crew finally met up with the intruders. To Markus's disgust, four Celje, Misora, and an unfamiliar man met them, but that didn't add up to Jayden's warning. Thinking quickly, Markus sent two of his militia guards back to town.

"Markus Fonte," said Misora. "It's been too long."

"What do you want, Misora? And who's your friend?"

"My name is Sasha Burmistrov. You and I have not had the pleasure of meeting, but I am positive you have heard of me. Just think of me as Misora's boss."

Markus had heard of the ruthless Celje leader and hoped the rumors of his brutality were exaggerated. Now confronted by the leader diminished those hopes. Serena stomped forward. "Those gunshots—who did you shoot?"

Misora ushered his horse forward. "I… I remember you. Sasha, this is the girl that got away. The daughter of the Visconti couple we brought to justice a while back."

"Brought to justice! You murdered my parents, you son of bitch!"

Markus stepped between Serena and Misora. "Think this through, Serena," he whispered. "This isn't the place for this."

Serena's iris's burned with hatred. Her pupils were half hidden in the corners of her orbits as if masking her next move.

Markus embraced her, then turned to Misora. "Why are you here?"

Sasha adjusted himself on the saddle and pulled his cloak back around his pistols. "Well, Mayor Fonte, since you know of my Celje, explanations are not necessary. I believe smuggled goods are coming out of Dalth and ending up in the hands of the Nein. As the governing body charged with protecting you, I cannot allow this."

The accusation took Markus by surprise. "Dalth is a small town, and while we aren't starving, we don't have anything extra to simply pass around. I'm afraid your information is wrong."

"As he said," blurted Misora, "you've been smuggling stuff to the Nein, like that girl's parents."

Markus locked eyes with Serena who shook her head at the accusation. He nodded and threw both Celje leaders an icy glare. "You were judge, jury, and executioner that day, Misora. None of us believe the false story you spread about the Viscontis. All you accomplished was killing a mother and father in cold blood. You speak of protecting the people, Sasha, but who's protecting us from you?"

Misora let out an irksome cackle. "I think the mayor here is getting bra—"

With a quick swim move, Serena swept past Markus and yanked Misora off his horse. Before anyone uttered a word, Serena's pistol dug into the temple of her parents' executioner.

"I'm going to avenge my parents and spread your brains all over this land they called home!"

Misora kept his hands to the side. Sasha didn't seem bothered.

"Serena, think about what will happen if you pull that trigger," said Markus, keeping his distance. "Think it through."

Serena glanced up, giving Misora the distraction he needed, and the tables turned. Misora reached across his body and grabbed the barrel of Serena's gun, ripping the pistol from her small hand. With a quick hip thrust, Serena was on her back, Misora on top, holding her down.

"Stupid girl," Misora hissed, twirling her hair. "I wonder if the daughter tastes as good as the mother." He bent down and licked the side of her face, groaning with pleasure.

"Enough!" Markus pointed his rifle at Misora's head. "Call off your guard dog, Sasha, and get the hell out of my town."

"Kill him, kill me, it doesn't really matter, Mayor. The corporation will promote someone else, burn your town and hang all of you upon an Amurski tree. Do you want that on your conscience?"

Not only did the Celje sound like he meant it, but something in Markus's gut told him that Sasha had done something like this before. "What do you want?" asked Markus, lowering his rifle.

Sasha took a large gulp from his canteen. "The Nein managed to get arms, munitions, armor, and a few other select items. I am certain they do not have anyone among their sect with this expertise. Naturally I am curious where they came from. Any ideas?"

The implication was clear. The allegations paralleled those against Marco and Erika Visconti. Markus defended Serena now just as he'd done with her parents. "Serena doesn't make weapons, she exports farming equipment and other small supplies."

"What does the girl have to say?"

"I use the mill to make parts for plows, hoes, sickles, flairs. Farming equipment, not weapons."

Misora squeezed Serena's breasts. "Maybe I'll take you with me this time, girl."

Markus raised his rifle once again. "Damn it, Misora, what do you want!? You need to search the whole town? Do it! Just get the hell off her."

"Fair enough," said Sasha who nodded toward his chief henchman. "Misora, lead our men around town. Search every house and barn, question everyone."

Markus's perception of Sasha differed vastly from Misora. Sasha was level, calculating, and probably more dangerous. Misora gave one last perverted grin at Serena before getting off her and mounting his horse. All six Celje followed while Sasha shadowed Markus and the rest.

"Go find Bélise, and get her over to the Dubois," whispered Markus. "She'll be safer there for now."

Serena rubbed her bruised neck and wrist. "What about Jayden?"

"We need to watch these men carefully. We'll have to worry about Jayden once we deal with Misora and this Sasha. If things go bad, I'll need your extra gun—"

"What if he's hurt, I owe—"

"Fine, go look for him, but find Bélise *first*. Get back as quickly as you can."

———————

Sasha relaxed unafraid inside the pub while his henchmen searched the small town. Many of Dalth's citizens congregated in the town square and pub, including Wren Dikal, who was supposed to have left this morning on a three-week mail run.

"What are those Celje doing here?" asked Wren inside the pub.

Markus sipped lukewarm kaldi, keeping one hand near his rifle atop the bar. He was surprised to see Wren but welcomed having another gun in town.

"You've heard of them," said Markus. "Guess I shouldn't be surprised given how much you travel. They seem to think someone in Dalth has been selling guns to the Nein. Know anything about it?"

"Heard rumors of folks making ammo and guns and giving it to those stinkin' magicians. Didn't think it would happen in Dalth, especially with what happened to the Visconti family."

"So, the Nein *have* been making trouble? What have you heard?"

"I've been getting double pay to cross into Listo. Dangerous ground right now. The Celje aren't sneaking anymore, and the Nein are attacking anything that moves up there."

Sasha swiveled on his stool. With Wren's tendency to act before thinking, Markus thought it best to get him out of the pub. "Wren, you better go check on your family. We'll be okay."

"I'd be happy to tell them what I know."

"I'd rather not give them a reason to question you or to stay around here any longer than necessary."

One of Sasha's men walked into the pub, whispered something into Sasha's ear, then left.

"Wren, go check on your family," repeated Markus.

Wren and Sasha exchanged brief looks before the door closed behind him.

Sasha dusted off his cloak and paced toward Markus. "You manage your people well, Mayor Fonte."

"I don't care what you think of me or my town. May I assume you're done here, finding nothing as I told you earlier?"

"Actually, Mayor, we did find something."

Markus hesitated. "What? Where?"

Sasha raised his hand, holding a small brass cylinder. "This shell casing, looks to be made of Ojultan ore, the same casings we've found with the Nein. This particular one was found near the old Visconti mill."

A rush of relief pulsed over Markus. "Are you trying to accuse Serena of smuggling munitions made of Ojultan ore? Are the Celje this desperate? No sane person, let alone a skilled metallurgist, would make casings out of such metal."

"Ojultan ore is indeed poor quality, though the evidence is undeniable."

"No one here could afford to buy extra ore, and you know it. Plus, the skill needed to refine the metal into a casing is complicated, and I don't think Serena even knows the workings."

"It seems we are at an impasse. I need to ensure nothing else arrives in the hands of my enemy, but here I am, looking at a man who tells me he knows nothing of what I speak of."

Markus's normally cool demeanor cracked. "You've done your inspection and found nothing, Sasha. You and your men need to leave."

Sasha grinned, then backhanded Markus. Markus's right cheek split open as the edge of Sasha's ring caught him. The few patrons in the pub, including Kun, tensed, ready to defend their devoted leader.

Smeared blood painted Sasha's hand, which he wiped on Markus's shirt. "I'm a patient man, Mayor Fonte, but I do not like games. Someone in this town is involved with the Nein. Perhaps I shall raze the city or begin executing citizens until the information I need is brought forth. What say you?"

A trickle of blood seeped down Markus's shaven face. "I wouldn't allow this kind of trade in my town. I want Dalth off the grid, yours, the Nein's, and anyone else looking for trouble."

Sasha's heartless gaze turned to the front window. "You have a daughter, Bélise…"

Markus stood tall. "Harm my daughter or any other child in this town, and you won't leave here alive. Choose your next words carefully, outsider."

"My point is to establish a line of communication with you," Sasha explained, opening his palms in a gesture of peace. "My Celje are here to guard against the violence and oppression the Nein represent to mankind. Have you seen what the Nein do to young nonmystic women?"

The crowd around Markus mumbled at the word *Celje*. "There are many evils on this planet, Sasha, the Nein aren't the only ones. My wife died because your Celje decided to hoard medical supplies. Best remember that bullets aren't the only way to kill."

Sasha stepped so close to Markus, he could see the blood vessels in his eyes. "Good and evil do not always see eye to eye in our world, Mr. Mayor. Good guys do not wear white, and bad guys do not wear black. If the Nein come knocking, who will you turn to for protection? Perhaps you believe your small militia can withstand an attack from a mystic horde?"

"You're forgetting about the shades of gray that exist on Ojult. Perhaps you should get out more, make new friends."

"Ah, Mr. Mayor," replied Sasha, chuckling. "Your inference of the Argos is pathetic. Where are they now, or perhaps Dalth is the only town in the entire universe to have seen the Argos in the last fifty years? I can see this conversation is going nowhere. I will leave you with this parting word, Mayor. Mind your business, and make sure I do not see any of these munitions in the hands of my enemies, or my next visit will not go with so few casualties."

Sasha left the pub and led his party up the northern path. Much of the town was now congregated in the square where they peppered Markus with questions. He spent a few minutes retorting the most implausible theories his people came up with, but Markus's mind was on Bélise and Jayden.

———

Inside the clinic, Celine's plump figure leaned over a bloody patient who was either dead or unconscious. On the opposite side of the room was

Bélise, sitting next to a bed where a sheet covered a small object. Her blonde hair was ruffled, her face buried in her hands.

"Markus, she's okay," said Serena, walking over to him. "She was with Victor the whole time."

Markus hadn't realized he'd been holding his breath and let out a sigh. "What's happened?"

"I found Jayden," Serena said, pointing toward the cot behind her. "His ear's bleeding badly, his eardrum is bruised, and Celine says he's got a few cracked ribs. He'll live, but he's gonna be sore."

Celine teetered over and joined the conversation. "He's unconscious, but I gave him a dose of jashinto anyway."

Dark circles encompassed Serena's bloodshot eyes, which was expected given the physical and emotional rollercoaster she'd been on. Facing her parents' killer, then seeing her best friend and guardian nearly killed by the same person.

"It's over, Serena," Markus said, clutching her hand. "He'll be fine, and those men are gone."

Serena buried her drenched face into his shoulder. "I should've killed him, I had the chance. We'd be better off allying with the Nein and helping wipe out the Celje."

He let the comment pass, knowing what his next question must be. "Serena, I need to hear it from you that you haven't been smuggling munitions to the Nein."

She looked up. "Don't let that murderous, pathological liar turn us against each other. My parents—" But she hesitated, holding back tears. "My parents were killed because of that nonsense. You think I'd actually walk that same path?"

He tried to push the speculation out of his voice. "The Celje haven't visited Dalth for nearly a year. They come here, beat the hell out of Jayden, accuse you, then search the entire town. You're the only person here with the expertise, so the question isn't unusual."

Serena moved out from his embrace. "The Celje lie for a living. If they had any real evidence, they'd have gone directly to the person, burned down their home, then killed them. It'd be my parents' situation all over again."

Given his profession over the years, Markus had developed the uncanny ability to detect fibs and fabrications. This conversation was triggering red flags, but the discussion was going nowhere, and Serena was emotionally spent. "I need to go speak with Bélise, but I want you to know that I trust you, so you'll tell me if you hear anything?"

"You'll be the first, I promise."

CHAPTER 23: YEAR 2401

Captain Garvin Donato took extreme care when guiding the *Night Scope* down to the grassy surface of Chden. He stroked his whiskered mustache as he scanned the many monitors across the bridge. The cramped bridge consisted of four crew members, plus himself, who led the other ninety-three crew members who managed the day-to-day operations. Similar to other RC-1 Brooks transport ships, the *Night Scope* measured 433 meters long, 91 meters wide, 60 meters tall, and 6 meters from ground to keel with the landing gear deployed.

Of the numerous displays in front of Captain Donato, he focused on the three directly in front of his ragged captain's chair. "Descent rate is a little quick, FO, slow it down."

First Officer Chelsie Franks sat at the helm, focused on bringing in the large vessel. She wore wired vid glasses that were intuitive and displayed the data needed to fly such a large, complex spaceship. In addition to her inbuilt command, her panel consisted of two monitors, plus all the gadgets, buttons, and control wheels necessary to pilot the ship.

"Aye, sir," replied Franks. "Increasing landing thrusters Alpha through Charlie by five percent."

Franks had a narrow frame, long neck, and flaring ears. Cute but not attractive in the eyes of her captain but for damn sure the best pilot in the entire fleet.

Soft blue lights now illuminated the bridge, signaling the ship was on final approach. Donato watched his ship's descent rate slow from fifteen meters per second down to ten. Without cargo, the *Night Scope* could land at anything under thirty mps with the six main landing gears and their complex shock absorbers taking the impact. However, the *Night Scope* was at max capacity with both cargo and crew and needed to achieve around ten mps for a safe landing.

"Passing through one-zero-zero-thousand feet, Captain. Deploying chutes at forty-five thousand," announced Lieutenant Kass.

Donato glanced at his landing checklist, triple-checking he'd not missed anything. His leftmost display illustrated altitude, vertical speed, and skid indicator. Running quick numbers in his head, descending now at eleven mps, the *Night Scope's* descent rate was still slightly above their target. "FO, even though eleven mps will get the job done, we've got a full ship. Deploy chutes early."

Kass threw him a dissenting look, but he ignored the beautiful woman for the moment.

"No problems here, sir," replied Franks.

Donato rotated his chair toward his engineer. "Brendan, deploy chutes."

"Deploying chutes," relayed Engineer Brendan Hazzard.

If Franks was the smallest member of his crew, Brendan was the biggest and ugliest. The hulk was pushing three hundred pounds and had a face that looked like it had gone through a boxing match and never recovered. Donato took a little bit of shit from the Reeves Corporation higher-ups when he hired an engineer with the last name Hazzard, but the captain's judgement proved right once again.

Donato went back to his checklist, reviewing the many handwritten notes stuck to his mobile touchscreen. He turned and punched the ship-wide-overhead-announcement button. "Attention crew and passengers, we're on final approach, take your seats. Donato out."

Thirty seconds later, the crew felt the familiar lurch as the *Night Scope's* parachutes inflated. Without windows to visualize the landing, the crew relied on their equipment and communication between each other to execute the landing. On Earth, Ojult, and other planets, a control tower or Instrument Landing System generally assisted ships, guiding them faithfully to the appropriate landing grid. On the newly discovered Chden, however, no such amenities existed.

"FO, no course correction needed," reported Kass. "Analysis of landing site still reads green, free of obstacles."

"Roger that, Nav, free of obstacles," replied Franks.

Captain Donato made eye contact with Kass and gave her a seductive wink. Like most of his female crew members, Donato only hired the best, brightest, and most attractive female officers the Reeves Flight Academy offered.

Kass winked back, reminding him of her olive skin that he'd inspected ever so closely last night.

Several seconds later, activity on the bridge increased. "Sixty seconds to landing," announced Franks. "Nav, I'm showing a thirty-meter push from the north due to an unforecasted front coming in through the region. Can you confirm?"

Kass's fingers glided over her keyboard. "Confirmed, FO, you're drifting. What are the odds of that front coming through right now? Where did it even come from?"

Donato remained cool as his tenured crew worked the problem. At this altitude and weight, he dismissed any notion of aborting. While trees and other small objects wouldn't cripple the ship, it would make for a very rough landing.

"Whoa, shit," squawked Franks. "Captain, getting a heavy crosswind." The ship heaved to port, pushing everyone against their seat straps. "Nav, need correctional data."

"On it," replied Kass. "Confirmed, we've got a sixty-knot crosswind, and it's increasing. Uploading correctional data. Captain, the winds are altering our horizontal plane. We'll land within the target zone but not evenly, sir. Thrusters aren't going to have time to balance us."

Captain Donato, who'd spent twenty years in space and seen every problem the profession could throw at him, spoke concisely. "Don't worry about the horizontal plane. Kass, make adjustments for the wind and help Franks stay in the green zone."

"Nav, report on corrected landing data," replied Franks.

Kass's forehead gleamed with sweat as she calculated the necessary course corrections. "No obstacles, FO, landing site classed yellow, repeat, landing site moved to yellow. Margin of error is thirty meters. No way to hit green, not now."

The yellow classification meant the perimeter around the landing site was too close to objects that might damage the ship. It didn't mean damage was imminent but too close for safety protocols.

"Understood. Everyone stay focused, communicate effectively," reassured Donato. In his view, leaders never showed weakness.

Franks continued manipulating her controls. "Ten seconds to landing. Four, three, two, one…"

Donato gripped the arms of his captain's chair. His display monitor still showed a ten mps vertical-descent rate.

"Brace for landing," ordered Kass.

The *Night Scope* landed with a thud, the sounds of bending metal and flexing beams screeching throughout the ship. As the landing gears depressed, the experienced crew waited patiently for the gears to release, seesawing them up and down for several seconds.

Donato unbelted first. "Hazzard, retract parachutes and begin atmosphere equalization, then complete postlanding checklists. Franks, begin postlanding procedures. Nice landing. Comms, broadcast on local frequencies that we've landed safely and will report when off-loading procedures may begin."

The bridge crew worked diligently, preparing the ship for postlanding checks and off-loading operations. Donato made sure to look at each of his female crew members when they bent over at their stations.

"Oh, and Smith, remind the Chden off-loading personnel to stay away from the ship until we give the all clear."

Communications Officer Caitlin Smith replied curtly in her Australian accent, "Yes, Captain." Smith was just plain hot, if you could get past her sizzling personality. She was all business all the time and took her job seriously. She didn't have much to do during the descent, but now that they were on the ground, she was the busiest officer on the ship.

"Captain, I've confirmed main-engine and thruster shutdown," said Franks walking up to him. "Hazzard reports equalization is complete and hull temperatures normal."

"I'll drink to that," he replied, raising a hip flask.

The crew, used to their captain's behavior, prepared themselves for his ritual landing humor.

"You know what they say back on Earth," he continued. "Any landing you can walk away from is a good one!" Eye rolls and tempered giggles rumbled through the room. "Let's look at Chden. Hazzard, open the bridge's armored doors."

"Opening outer bridge canopy, Captain."

Metal latches unlocked, followed by screeching metal. In front of Donato, three-foot-thick reinforced doors moved apart, and Chden's natural light filled the bridge. Donato's eyes took time to adjust but eventually gave way to a gorgeous horizon. A vast ocean dotted with tiny islands filled the window. Within the crystal-clear water bloomed chimerical red robendor flowers. Like hulking trees exploding from the ocean floor and bursting through the rippling waves, the native plants freckled the sea. Two car-sized caerus flew side by side across the bow of the ship. In perfect unity, they banked to the right, landing easily so as not to damage the robendor pedals.

Donato watched as yellow and purple lightning jumped from cloud to cloud in the distance. "We'll be here a few days, so let's get our job done now and enjoy the scenery later. Exploration crews still haven't discovered everything on this garden box, so swim and soak up some real light at your own risk. Ladies, two-piece suits only."

The comment earned him more eye rolls.

Donato picked up his checklist and went to the next item. "FO, get on the horn to Security Chief Bardolf. Have him and his team exit the ship first and walk the perimeter, but remind him of the weather. The rest of you, complete shutdown procedures and post mission checks. Make sure your teams are good, and make time for some R and R. I'll be in my office."

In his office, Captain Donato filed his post mission log report. Over three hundred missions logged without a fatality. No other captain in the Reeves flight department could say the same. His computer started processing the expected off-load inventory report, which he'd add to his own log once the unloading was complete. His fee for this haul was at the standard rate, plus Commodus specifically asked for the *Night Scope*, and Donato never turned down a friend.

By the end of the second exploration mission to Chden, the Reeves Corporation had known they'd landed on a planetary cash machine. With white sands, acceptable weather, and blue oceans, the executives intended to make Chden the vacation mecca for Earth's elite. This meant construction equipment, raw materials, and workers all needed safe transportation, and the *Night Scope's* record for safety put her at the top of the list. The annual massive stat-ten storm that wiped out the first exploration team's infrastructure was still an ongoing issue, but engineers were working the problem.

Donato's computer pinged with a high-priority mission request from the Reeves Corporation. He opened the message, and sure enough it contained a bidding option for an upcoming supply run between Ojult and Earth, except the per-kilo rates seemed way off.

His phone lit up, interrupting his mental calculations on the possible mission. "This is Donato, go ahead."

The voice of Communications Officer Smith came over the phone. "Captain Donato, sorry to bother you, but Commodus Vrabel wants to see you."

"Thanks, Caitlin. Escort him to my office, please."

"Aye, Captain."

Donato continued surveying the bid sheet.

KALDI BEANS   150 POUNDS   6 CRATES
REQUIRES ATMOSPHERE

LISTO BRANDY   4007 POUNDS   20 BARRELS
REQUIRES ATMOSPHERE

JASHINTO PLUMS   1200 POUNDS APX   30 CRATES
REQUIRES ATMOSPHERE

OJULTAN ORE RAW   1,080,611.2 POUNDS   6 CONTAINERS
NO ATMOSPHERE REQUIRED

HUMAN CARGO   2420 POUNDS   11 PERSONS
REQUIRES ATMOSPHERE

TOTAL POUNDS   1,088,388.2
TOTAL WEIGHT KG = (1,088,388.2*.454=49,412.24)

SUGGESTED FEE $14,178 PGU DOLLARS PER KILO = $700,568,354.15

There was no way the per-kilo rate was accurate. Average these days was upward of $20,000 per kilo; someone had messed up.

Two quick taps on his door, and Donato stood, then readied himself to greet his direct boss. "Come in."

Caitlin's slim, jaw-dropping figure glided into his office. "Captain Donato, may I present Commodus Vrabel."

Donato nodded, hoping to get her back in the sack tonight. "Thank you, Caitlin."

"Yes, Captain." The young officer went to attention and walked out.

"Welcome to Chden, Captain. You look like hell!" gasped the COO. "Landing that difficult?"

Donato smirked. "You're not getting any younger, either. I figured with your salary, you'd get rid of all that gray and fix that shriveled dick. By the way, sorry I didn't visit after that last SKIP. I transitioned the personnel into two shifts and doubled the safety checks. Anyways, looks like things are up and running here, congratulations."

Commodus laughed and shook hands with Donato. "Hey now, the ladies love the gray hair."

Donato went over to the wet bar and poured a bourbon for himself and one scotch for Commodus. "You seemed eager to see me, everything okay?"

"Outside of the SKIP, this has been a good flight. No, everything's good."

Both men raised their glasses and sat down. "To old friends, fine ships, and beautiful women," Donato toasted.

"Amen to that. Did we lose any passengers when the SKIP went to hell?"

Donato nearly choked on his drink. "My team did a hell of a job just keeping the ship in one piece. We haven't had a mass-force-generator complication like that in years. The company disabled that MFG as soon as we notified them."

"I'm just giving you a hard time, Garvin. Your ship's safety record is the best in the fleet. Which, incidentally, thank you for taking the bid on this one. We needed all this stuff quickly, on time and in one piece. Plus, I prefer to travel on this hunk of junk rather than any other fleet ship."

Donato acknowledged the gratitude, waving his hand. "I made a couple bucks off the deal, and besides, looks like the trips to Ojult are getting leaner and fewer."

"I know the last couple of bids haven't been great off Ojult, and I'm aware of the latest bid they sent you. I've been speaking with Elasus about it, and I think he's got a good plan to fix it." Commodus took a small sip of scotch. "God, that's good. Hope you brought more."

"You can have the bottle. I only keep that on board for you and the engineering team when they run out of degreaser. I don't mean to pry, but what's going on with Ojult? I'm getting almost a third less than my usual fee out of there."

"Trade on Ojult is in the gutter. I've spoken with Nencia as well, and I know that's a touchy subject, so I apologize."

Donato's lips lingered on his glass. "No apology needed, we get along fine."

"You still talk?"

Donato didn't want to speak about his separated wife but couldn't think of a way around it. "I'll drop by her apartment on occasion when I'm laying over, but nothing regular. We haven't officially divorced but… it just didn't work out. I was traveling nearly all the time and she's busy doing her godfather thing. Anyway, Commodus, what's this about? We haven't even unloaded the ship and you're already in my office acting weird."

"She's a powerful person," said Commodus. "Perhaps, and this stays between us, she may be too powerful. You may not know this, but Nencia's controlling all contracted exports out of Ojult, plus she's getting a chunk off all smuggling operations. Outside of Elasus and the Celje, she's the most influential person around."

Donato thought about the last time he'd seen her. He'd been on Ojult delivering cargo and landed in Worall. He'd tried to make an advance, but she'd told him she was seeing someone and to stop dropping by looking for… companionship. The thought of Nencia with anyone else agitated him. "You mentioned something about speaking with Nencia? What about? Trade?"

"Yeah. This stays between us, but Nencia threw out a pretty strong accusation not too long ago. Claims the Celje are raiding her supply lines all over the planet, cutting down their export business. The execs, we're split on who believes her but thought you should know."

"Commodus, we've known each other for a long time, I can handle Nencia and the downturn, don't worry about me."

Commodus sighed. "Garvin, wish that was all of it. We have reason to believe there's an active intelligence network between Ojult and the Reeves Corporation, or perhaps the PGU."

There were dozens of topics Donato expected, and this was not one of them. "That's pretty big, but honestly, I'm not surprised."

"Some believe Nencia is behind it all."

Donato took the news in stride. "You know my loyalty is to the fleet. I hope you're not questioning that."

"Of course not, and I know if you heard something you'd tell us. Out of respect, I just thought you should know that we're investigating and that the Celje are involved."

That little piece got his attention. "I'm no expert on the Celje, but I thought they were supposed to be unseen? You have them sticking their noses in Appian business, and that's bound to lead to something bad."

"I agree, but the Celje are blaming the mystics, while Nencia blames the Celje, it's a fucking circus right now. The mystics are likely behind all of it. But again, this is all coming from Elasus, and this is the way he wants it dealt with."

"How so?"

"Elasus told Sasha to tighten his grip on the mystics, which should get them off Nencia's back if they're involved. In doing so, Sasha will investigate Appian at the same time. If this doesn't work and the raids don't stop, Elasus might call Ruven to send additional men."

"I thought Ruven was training some sort of reserve army."

"He is, and it was your ship that brought all those Celje recruits to Lent last time, if you remember."

It was a mission no captain would ever forget, transporting a clandestine group of mystic assassins across the universe, all while keeping it from the PGU and other prying eyes. "Correct me, but I thought Ruven's teams were supposed to guard against some apocalyptic Elder attack, not resolve trade disputes and oust spies."

Over the past twenty years under the employment umbrella of the Reeves Corporation, had Donato learned many things about his employer. Foremost, he'd discovered that Elasus Reeves deeply feared the Elder mystics, believing they would appear again and eventually take over.

"Elasus has some weird ideas about Elders," admitted Commodus. "Heck, I'm not even sure they really existed, probably just a myth. But I do know the Celje are real, and they're all business. You can hate the Celje, but they're necessary." Commodus swirled the last of his drink. "Elasus is a smart guy, and he's got my support. But he isn't going to send an entire army to help Sasha. Doesn't make financial sense."

Donato thought the idea made sense: you don't use a nuclear bomb to destroy an anthill. "I noticed that you're sending up bids for additional shipments to Lent. Won't that draw attention from wandering eyes and satellites?"

Commodus tapped his glass for a refill. "You and your questions."

Donato refilled his drink. "I'm just a pilot trying to make his way across space, but come on, if I'm noticing it, surely some of those smart Harvard folks in the PGU will too."

"You're right, and the boss has a plan for that too. He's getting ready to make Lent into an agricultural hub to cover the tracks. Turns out that little planet has incredibly fertile soil that extends six feet below the surface."

"So, we'll be shuttling cow shit and farming equipment to disguise a mystic assassin training camp? My fees just went up, if nothing more than for the smell."

"Greedy fuck," said Commodus with a chuckle. "But yeah, we'll need plenty of ships to transport all the equipment and assets. The money should be good. Elasus wants to send his best pilot as much business as possible with shipping down out of Ojult."

"My crew and I like the Ojult runs—quick, easy, and luckily there's a pub there I like to visit. I get what you're doing on Lent but if it's all the same, I'll stick to the Ojult runs even if it means a few less coin in the meantime."

"Giving up the high-dollar runs? The women on Ojult can't be that good."

Donato stared into the bottom of his glass. "Look, I'll do what you need me to do, but I employ nearly a hundred people on this ship, and I need to think long term. If the PGU ever find out about the Celje, about my involvement, it's probably not going to end well for me."

"Yeah, okay," said Commodus, his eyes narrowing. "Sounds like you have a lady friend back on Ojult that you want to—"

A violent shudder vibrated through the floor, and both men felt the air pop out of their lungs as the ship dropped several feet. Yellow lights, followed by alarm bells, started echoing through the ship.

"Stay here," ordered Donato, picking up the beeping call atop his desk. "This is Donato, talk to me."

The sirens stopped, but the yellow lights continued. Another vibration shook the room, followed by another drop.

Donato managed to stay upright. "Okay, I'm on my way," he said, hanging up the phone. "Commodus, stay here. The ship's breaking in half."

"What's happening?"

Donato grabbed two earpieces and his jacket off the desk. "Soil's collapsing under the ship, some sort of sinkhole. Three of our landing gears snapped, and we've got too much pressure on the aft hull."

"And the cargo? Did we lose any cargo?"

"Cargo's secondary right now; we've got men trapped underneath."

CHAPTER 24: YEAR 2401

For over a year, Syrus's Nein waged small-scale battles against the ever promulgating Celje. The clandestine group continually raided and attacked his people using guerilla tactics across Listo. Casualties mounted on both sides, and even the powerful Tokarek himself was not left unscathed.

Syrus sat motionless on the floor of his tent, focusing on multiple injuries he'd received during the day's battle. A nanobullet had torn into his arm above the elbow, severing the brachial artery. The bullet was still lodged in the muscle, but pride prevented the great Nein leader from seeking help. Telekinetically, his focused mind maneuvered through the fibers of muscle, blood, and bone to find the *live* bullet. With a quick inner tug, the bullet squeezed through Syrus's flesh.

The pain exceeded his prepared body, and he collapsed onto his side. His breathing quickened and sweat lapped his forehead. Blood slithered down his pulsing arm, but at least the worst of the resection was over.

He'd received many wounds in the past, but today was different. The Celje were becoming smarter, more deadly, and better equipped to take on his mystics. Never before had Syrus been unable to finish a battle before its conclusion. Blood loss, pulsing pain, and nerve damage were just the beginning of today's outcome.

The tent door leading into his chambers opened, exposing a young woman, covered in mud and signs of battle. "*Daska,* may I come in?"

Syrus nodded, forcing his body back into a sitting position.

"We interrogated three of them but didn't get anything useful. I already executed them," said Phaedra. She headed toward Syrus, her long, matted silver hair fluttering behind her.

Syrus looked for obvious injuries on his apprentice. "You fought well, though at times carelessly and without regard for yourself. Are you injured?"

"I'll heal tonight. I'm here to deliver your guest, but seeing as you're bleeding to death, maybe I should have them wait."

"Our combined abilities should restore the tissue long enough for the meeting."

It was a command not a request. Phaedra knelt next to him and gripped his elbow. Her eyes closed and their combined strength mended the gushing wound. Minutes later, the wound still throbbed, but a thin scab covered the wound.

"How many did we lose today?" Syrus asked.

He'd sent Kavil Siller to defend their stronghold in Carendra last month, leaving Phaedra in charge of today's assault. She, along with seven other Nein, ambushed a Celje camp. Her squad attacked nearly thirty of the mystic killers and won the day, but not without casualties.

"Lost two before you arrived. Shea and the new kid, Trawl, were badly injured. Lost one more toward the end." Phaedra wrapped a dirty cloth around the wound. "A slight tug and this will bleed like before. You need rest."

Bitterness from losing men combined with her distress over Syrus's wounds. Syrus ignored the sentiment to console the young woman. "Lives are lost during war, but leaders gain experience, making the next battle less costly. It's a tough lesson but one you must adapt to if you plan on leading the Nein once I'm gone."

"Lead the Nein? Do you have a bullet in your head too? I serve you and kill Celje, that's what I do, that's what I'm good at."

"All too infrequently, the call to lead summons those most unwilling to accept it. It's those few who must lead the many into a new era."

"I'm not biting," she countered. "And stop moving your neck, you've got another gash below your jaw. You want me delay this meeting until tomorrow?"

Syrus ran another rag through a bowl of murky water and cleaned up the sprays of blood covering his arm and torso. Content, he put on a black-and-beige robe, then stood behind a temporary desk and waited for his guests.

"Mr. Tokarek, it's good to see you again," said Zakar Qualis, bowing only enough to avoid insult.

Andreas Palada, who'd escorted the Appian supervisor from Worall, leaned in inconspicuously and whispered to Zakar, "Most people call him Lord Tokarek."

"Ah, well, I apologize, Mr. Tokarek. I meant no offense," said Zakar, purposefully repeating the gaff.

"I nearly lost my life today for a cause I care deeply for," said Syrus. "Prefixes and titles mean far less to me at the moment. I trust your travels were uneventful?"

"Your man Andreas made sure I arrived, thank you for seeing to that. I've come under the pretense of a Listo-brandy trader, so my visit here must be brief as I fear I'm being followed."

Syrus checked Phaedra who picked up on the notion. "I'll go send men to make sure he wasn't," she said.

"Ms. Lillea, before you leave, I have a gift for you." Zakar reached into his satchel and unwrapped an impressively sharp short sword with a cherry-red hilt. "My employer asked that I give this to you."

Phaedra cautiously accepted the gift. Someone had put real effort into forging the weapon. The pommel was cherry red with the hilt transitioning to merlot. The guard was dark metallic black, made of sarcto bone. The blade itself measured a little longer than the length from her elbow to her fingertips. The sword's edge concaved nominally until the halfway point where it expanded out. The gleam reflecting off the sword mirrored its perfect balance.

"Admire its perfection later," challenged Syrus.

"Right." Phaedra carefully sheathed the blade into its leather case.

When she left the room, Zakar continued his reason for coming. "Per your agreement with Nencia Donato, I come with information about a small Celje camp to the southwest of Carenda. According to our sources, this is of no particular importance unless you consider that Sasha Burmistrov is currently visiting the area."

Andreas's jaw fell open. "He's hanging out in a camp here, near our stronghold?"

"That's the information I was provided."

Andreas whistled back. "Kavil's gonna wet his pants when he finds out about this, or more likely, hang one of his scouts."

"And what's this information going to cost me?" Insights like this wouldn't fall under his agreement with Nencia, nor did Syrus expect it.

Zakar nodded. "My employer has agreed to provide you the exact location of this camp in exchange for allowing Appian to take over the Listobrandy distillery located near the camp."

Unconfirmed rumors suggested the Celje were secretly taking over businesses across Listo and Capintesta. If Sasha had taken over the brandy distillery, it was probably putting a fair amount of tonze into the Celje bank account.

"Commodities like this distillery are of no importance to my people," said Syrus. "If Nencia wants it, she can have it."

Zakar bowed and handed a small envelope to Andreas. "Pleasure doing business with you, Mr. Tokarek. We wish you continued success."

Syrus looked up at Zakar, rage in his eyes. "Death will strike Sasha soon if this information is accurate. Sheltering so close to our encampment, what kind of game is he playing?"

"The envelope in Andreas's possession identifies the exact location of the camp, though we don't pretend to know how long Sasha will remain."

Andreas handed Syrus the map. "How sure are you of this information?"

"My employer puts significant effort into ensuring the accuracy of our information. Our reputation feeds our business, and we are, at least for the time being, profitable."

The group continued speaking until Phaedra returned. "We've scouted the immediate area; no one followed him."

"Fine," said Syrus, then he pointed to the map. "It seems Sasha has been a chameleon, hiding under our own trees."

Phaedra studied the map, outlining specific areas with her finger. "Assassination under the cover of darkness," she replied. "Let the Celje guess who killed their precious leader and we continue to take them down while they're leaderless."

Zakar coughed, breaking the discourse. "This conversation no longer concerns Appian or my leader. Thank you, Mr. Tokarek, for the hospitality and continued business."

Andreas, Phaedra, and Syrus strategized through the evening, finally breaking for dinner around midnight. With Syrus's consent, they agreed to send a five-man squad, including Syrus and Phaedra, to the Celje camp where, hopefully, one of the four members would assassinate the Celje leader unnoticed.

"Your shield is strong, but you must learn how to deflect as well," said Syrus during training the next day. He launched ice spears from his staff, one after another, and watched Phaedra's conjured shield shatter the incoming projectiles.

With each impact, Phaedra staggered back, and pain rippled through her arms. "This would be easier if you'd just find me a staff," she muttered under the onslaught.

Syrus changed tactics and shot an intense beam of light into her eyes. "Adjust your shield to block out the new attack."

The intensity of the light mimicked those of multiple suns flaring to life. "Aarrggg!" she yelled, now blind.

Syrus released his staff, which continued to stand on its point. Crackling resonated in the courtyard as the Nein leader prepared his next attack. "It will be rare that your opponent will only have one type of attack." Sparks emanated from Syrus's hand, followed by flashes of lightning.

The attack ripped through her fading shield and slammed into her chest, catapulting her into a nearby tree. Syrus's staff drifted back into his hand.

"Staffs are rare, and you must learn to defend yourself using the powers at your disposal, not what you might have in the future."

Half unconscious, Phaedra slumped over.

Syrus knelt beside her and grabbed her wrist, syncing their minds together. A purple arcane aura flowed around them as Syrus used his powers to heal his injured apprentice, an ability that only the most powerful mystics understood. It took mere minutes for Phaedra to regain consciousness.

"I won't always be here to heal you. Get better, be faster, find the power within you." He lifted Phaedra back to her feet and held her as she regained her balance. "We go up against Sasha tomorrow, a real test of your abilities."

The next morning Syrus and his team made their way on horseback toward Sasha's rumored camp. With winter in full gear and a fight looming, all five Nein wore full armor. Syrus wore an entirely black suit resembling a marriage between a modern wizard and an advanced-infantry soldier. Phaedra's battle attire appeared less contemporary with black, lightweight armor partially covered by a jet-gray, ankle-length cloak. Her silvery hair fluttered inside the hood, which rested against her two short swords.

Javier was the group's tracker and knew Listo's terrain better than anyone. His small stature made him difficult to spot as he rode several hundred meters in front of the group. Jenna took up the rear, providing security and ensuring they weren't followed. Much of Listo was flat with a few rolling hills, but nothing Syrus considered rough. That evening, the sun shrunk below the horizon, casting an orange halo in the sky. Javier and Syrus compared their estimated location against Zakar's map.

"Premier," said Javier with a Spanish inflexion. "I believe the camp is just over that tree line. If I may suggest, the cold air and open country tends to carry sounds. Should we tie up the horses here and proceed the rest of the way on foot?"

Phaedra muttered something about her frozen tits, but as usual, Syrus ignored her. "Tie up the horses, but I want you and Turr to stay here. Jenna, Phaedra, and myself will scout ahead. You will not engage unless attacked."

Javier and Turr looked puzzled and nodded, but a proud gleam spread across Jenna.

Syrus started toward the suspected camp using both physical and arcane sight to spot any forward sentries. *Daska* and pupil moved swiftly and silently through the tall grass with Jenna covering their back. Syrus brought the group to a halt just as early morning sunbeams flashed at a distance, exposing frozen dew across the rolling landscape. Syrus figured they'd crossed two miles before entering the tree line beyond the grassy hills.

"This will be our meet-back point," said Syrus. "Jenna, you stay here and protect our fallback spot. Phaedra, move quietly around the perimeter and recon the area. I'll head the other way. We'll meet back here in an hour."

Syrus watched Phaedra glide over the slick sky-grass and through the snow-covered trees. Once he lost sight of her, he set off in the opposite direction, carefully placing each foot to minimize his presence. The aroma of cooking meat caught his attention fifty meters into the forest. He walked more cautiously now, alert for the nearby camp. A clearing up ahead told him what he needed, that Zakar's information was accurate and the Celje leader was possibly encamped here.

Syrus sank into a meditative state, the world turning into swirls of black and white. Fully immersed, he could see the foundation of objects, their atoms and molecules, and could manipulate them with a focused thought. Crouching, he inched toward a large rock to better distinguish a conversation between Sasha and a woman.

A portly woman with black hair stood in front of Sasha wearing a heavy fur coat and a staff across her back.

"This is it, then," the woman said with a Russian accent. "This is what we have been waiting for."

Sasha accepted the document and read it. "Indeed, Achilla. The fools have played into our hand, it seems."

Achilla threw herself into his arms, and the two kissed passionately. "All of the Celje are behind you, my love. You are a god, a king, a leader of the most powerful. We are at your command."

"I will free this planet from Reeves's grip and the mystic plague."

"We will stand behind you," Achilla said. "Come to the tent, and let me show you how powerful men should be treated."

Sasha stopped after a few paces. "Now is not the time for play, my love. Let the men wake and eat, then we leave and proceed with the plan."

Syrus's heart thumped against his armor. The woman's voice and body, he recognized it. Her icy pitch and accent... This was the woman who killed Helia, who tried to kill his family. He watched methodically as Sasha conversed with nearby men, then walked into a tent. The taste of retribution overcame his common sense, and Syrus moved silently toward the small tent. As he neared, two patrol guards approached from across the camp. Syrus scanned the area and estimated that no more than eight Celje occupied the grounds. Yet, unlike Achilla and other Celje he'd encountered recently, these men wore unusually modern armor that covered their entire bodies. Their suits were gray metaflex with slits of white around the joints.

Syrus waited for the guards to pass, then moved hastily toward Sasha's tent. Syrus paused outside, telekinetically calling his staff off his back.

As soon as he entered the room, Syrus knew, even without his powers, that something was wrong. The tent was empty, and Sasha was nowhere to be seen. Syrus's peripheral vision darkened, warning him of impending danger. He pounded his staff into the ground, and a brilliant, shimmering shield surrounded him. No sooner had he conjured the shield when the dome around him began flickering as gunfire tore through the tent.

Syrus had fallen into Sasha's trap, blinded by his hatred for the man. He mumbled several curses until gathering his anger into a concise strategy. Extending his hand, smoke began billowing outside the tent, obscuring his attackers' vision. Bullets continued pouring into the tent, though far fewer hit the shield. Syrus then rammed his hand into the ground, producing an enormous shockwave that rippled violently outward.

The intense gunfire stopped as an unknown number of Celje were tossed to the ground. Syrus extended his staff forward, and his shield evaporated, giving way to a chaotic surge of electricity that tore through the tent and slammed into the nearest guards. Screams of death rang out from the men burning from the electrical charge.

Two men appeared through the smoke with rifles. It was a matter of who saw who first, which Syrus won. Two ice spears erupted from his hand and pierced the chests of the men. Even with advanced armor, the guards fell.

A second group of Celje with guns and energy-blades in hand charged his position. All Celje were expert melee fighters, which Syrus agreed was probably the best way to engage a mystic since it thwarted the time needed to produce an arcane attack.

Syrus took down the first two with silver discs but missed the third. This last man was quick and agile. With swiftness rarely seen in nonmystics, the Celje changed tactics, unleashing a three-strike combo, first going high, then center mass, then high again. Syrus blocked the attack but was completely defensive—then his mystic sense picked up more Celje entering the fray.

"Enough of this." Syrus raged and charged forward launching a six-set combo with his staff. The glowing rod crackled through the air, finally killing the soldier midway through the fourth move.

Syrus's conjured smoke concealed Phaedra's movement near the tree line, and Syrus's acute, arcane sense followed her as she moved in for the kill. Sneaking up behind the four men staging their attack on him, she cut the squad down with an impressive pirouette of precise movements and quick kills.

From the opposite side of the field, Jenna's long rifle kept any reinforcements at bay.

"We've got more soldiers coming up. Where is he?" yelled Phaedra over the sounds of battle. "We can't fight forever."

The Celje had adjusted their fire and were pinning Phaedra down behind a wrecked carriage.

"Lord Tokarek, you're going to be surrounded," came Jenna's voice from atop the hill. "You must leave the battle."

Syrus reversed and jumped through a tear in the back of the tent. More rifle fire from the hill told him Javier and Turr had joined the fight. His smoke screen was little more than a thin haze, and if he didn't act soon, they'd be pinned down.

"Javier, Turr, support Phaedra," Syrus commanded. "Jenna, make sure our path out of here is still clear, and don't let Sasha escape, no matter what."

Syrus darted through the camp, avoiding fights where he could, but more Celje continued to join the battle.

A familiar whistling turned him away from the soldier he'd just killed. Two tents down, maybe thirty yards away, ice spheres were hurtling toward Phaedra. Finding the source, Syrus unleashed three silver discs at the only other staff-carrying mystic, but Achilla was no amateur. She used her own staff and deflected each disc, but Syrus could see the unforeseen attack had startled her.

"My love, it is time to leave!" Achilla yelled.

Following the female warlock's gaze, Syrus found Sasha, and the two locked eyes.

"Filthy mystics," mouthed Sasha and emptied an entire magazine at Syrus.

Syrus rolled laterally, hearing the barrage of bullets skirt over him. His counterattack was averted by rifle fire from a well-entrenched squad on the opposite side of the hill. With few other options, Syrus raised another shield and waited. He'd trained Phaedra well and knew how the young sage would react. She was young and brash, but Phaedra was loyal to the core. With one hand birthing a shield, Phaedra stormed the rooted squad. With no room to maneuver, the Celje stumbled over one another trying to escape her fury.

Blood blanketed her new cherry-handled blade, and she gazed back at Syrus with a killer's grin. A curious silence fell over him, an oddity considering a firefight should be in full gear.

Jenna approached and fell to one knee. "They've escaped, my premier."

Syrus let his shield fade and looked to her. Jenna had a mixture of brown, blonde, and gray hair atop her beaten body. Blood painted her entwined light mail and leather armor.

He'd wasted the perfect opportunity to exact revenge on the two people he wanted to kill the most. Syrus looked into the faces of his followers and pushed aside the urge to obliterate every Celje object in site.

"Get up, search the area," Syrus demanded. "I don't think they expected my involvement in this battle. They've retreated without most of their gear."

He found nothing of interest in the tents, but Sasha's quarters turned up several maps, journals, and notes prepared for dispatch. Syrus started to read one of the letters when Phaedra ran into the ravaged shelter. "We've got two of Sasha's men still alive."

The two guards were on their knees with their wrists and ankles tethered behind them. Syrus pressed the edge of his staff to one of their throats. "You do as I say or you'll die."

Neither man responded, and Phaedra socked both of them in the mouth. "Answer him," she snarled. "Answer him, or we'll jump right to the part where I just kill you both."

In short succession, Syrus identified where Sasha obtained the new-and-improved Celje armor, weapons, and communications equipment.

He also learned that Sasha was getting better-trained recruits, but from off world.

"Drafting the helpless and fools from local towns into his ranks for pointless raids? They're nothing more than bullet catchers. Finish questioning them," said Syrus. "I'm going to look through these documents."

Syrus walked unsettled to a quiet area beneath several trees and pulled out the documents he'd found in Sasha's tent.

> *Commander,*
>
> *Local intel suggests that Appian Shipping may be shipping goods to the Nein. Will submit further information as it becomes available.*
>
> *WD*

Allan thought about the implications of this and pulled out the next letter.

> *Commander,*
>
> *We have confirmed that Nencia Donato brokered a deal with the Nein to supply weapons and supplies for their attacks on our guild. Two separate sources have confirmed. Will await your orders.*
>
> *Misora*

Syrus hastily began reading the last letter.

> *Commander,*
>
> *Received your order to terminate Nencia Donato. Traveling back from Callahan Shores, will conduct this business upon my return. Evidence will suggest the Nein made the kill.*
>
> *Misora*

None of the letters were dated, but surely he would have heard if Nencia Donato was attacked or killed.

"What's that?" asked Phaedra walking up behind him.

Syrus turned. "Our goal of defeating the Celje is now in jeopardy. Did you learn anything else from the prisoners?"

"Nothing. Why?"

Syrus made for the two prisoners. "Sasha, your commander, received dispatches. When was the last delivery?"

The Celje with blood leaking from his mouth said, "I... I'm dead anyway, you shaman trash. My last breath won't be wasted—"

While locking eyes with the other prisoner, Syrus drove an ice spike into the man's throat, ensuring the remaining man heard the gurgling wheezes egress from the dying body.

"You," continued Syrus, bending over the second prisoner. "Sasha received these letters, I need to know when."

The man exhaled. "She's already dead and your kind are done. We're the future of Ojult."

Syrus pulled away, concluding what he'd already feared. "Kill him."

Without even turning to aim, Phaedra's blade cut through the air and sheared the man's head off.

Syrus said, "Sasha knows of Nencia's involvement with us and intends to kill her."

Phaedra shrugged. "She's a tool for our cause. Thoba are meant for such things."

Age, wisdom, experience propagated the notion that Nencia's death would have lasting consequences. "A tool, yes, but a valuable one. We must head this off. Are you well enough to travel? To fight?"

"Of course."

"Leave now. Take Javier and Jenna, find Andreas. He'll be in Carendra. Hand him these letters. I want him to contact Nencia by the most expeditious way possible and warn her. Do you understand?"

Phaedra snatched the papers, tearing one in the process. "You're sending us away from the fight to warn an ordinary she might be killed?"

The ignorance of youth stopped Syrus from punishing Phaedra, from torturing her into the submission he desperately wanted her to see. If Phaedra was going to lead the Nein, she had to see these perspectives for herself.

After Phaedra left, he ordered Turr to collect supplies and equipment off the dead. He paced around the wrecked campsite, noticing small shadows cast by the rising sun. Stopping near an extinguished fire pit, he pulled a leathery water flask from his pocket. A crumpled piece of parchment fell to the ground, and Syrus realized the document must have been part of Sasha's letters from earlier.

Commander

We've confirmed it's the Reeves kid. Not sure how she got mixed up with the mystics, but it's taken care of now. Won't say more in case this gets intercepted. Let me know if you want the kid terminated.

Misora

Syrus read the note several more times, trying to make sense of it. The idea of a Reeves child on Ojult, if that's what Misora meant, was startling. Images of his sister chiding him for such a thought suppressed any ideas of finding the child and using her as a bargaining chip. The child made him think of his own family and how long it had been since he'd written his niece.

"Is this the leader I've become? Soft and unwilling to take risks because of my sister's ghost?"

CHAPTER 25: YEAR 2401

Neighbors were oblivious to the meeting taking place inside Nencia Donato's apartment, despite the frequent pops of champagne corks shooting out the window. Fizzing drinks, roasting garlic, and grilled meat filled the air with an aroma few people on Ojult would ever enjoy.

"Cheers to placing a firm, pointed boot up the Celje's ass," said Nencia, swallowing a large sip of smuggled champagne.

Serena mimicked the gesture. "And for dodging a huge bullet last month with Misora *and* Sasha coming to Dalth."

"No kidding. Your shipment today needs to be the last one for a while, let things settle down a bit."

Serena raised her glass. "Anyone here suspect? Zakar, maybe?"

"Zakar knows what's going on," replied Nencia with a touch of annoyance. "He knows everything that I do, who I do, and why I'm doing it. The rest of my people don't care. How about in Dalth?"

"Jayden and Markus threw a fit when I left, saying I needed an escort here, but I convinced them otherwise. I hate lying to them, but it's for the best."

With champagne in hand, Nencia checked the oven, then looked through her second-story window overlooking the warehouses. "Zakar's got Logan and Bella unloading your stuff, should be done in a bit. You only brought the one horse?"

Serena's long, narrow eyebrows flicked up and down quickly. "Jayden uses him for much heavier work than this." Serena looked remorseful. "I really hate lying to him, but it can't be helped. You heard Misora and his Celje nearly killed Jayden?"

Nencia turned away from the window. "I heard. Don't get too worked up about that. Jayden's much more dangerous than most realize. If he wanted to escape that situation, he could have."

Serena drained the rest of her glass and hiccupped.

The obvious unsaid question both women were thinking hung in the air. Why would the Celje, especially Sasha, risk advertising his supposed clandestine operation by roughing up Jayden?

"You need help with dinner?" asked Serena, breaking the silence. "All I've done is drink your champagne and watch you work."

Nencia probed the pasta and meat inside the wood-fired oven. "You think I made this? Ha! Not a chance. One of Lacy's girls sent it over before you got here. It's almost done. Speaking of Jayden, when you two gonna finally screw, get rid of all the tension? Hell, I can see it from Worall."

"What? Me and Vaut? Never."

"He's great in the sack, single, can hold his own in a fight. He wants a family and a quiet life if you can believe that." Truthfully, Nencia didn't want Jayden screwing anyone besides herself.

"He's cute," Serena confessed, "but no. If he hadn't saved me from Misora and been there when my parents died, it might be different. But we've never so much as kissed. We're kind of like brother and sister. Besides, if I took him, who would you screw? You two are *never* on time when I'm trying to leave here."

"We have a good time together, but he's younger, always talking about a family, settling down. The young fool probably loves me. I don't need that in my life."

Nencia opened the oven door, and smoke rushed into the kitchen, then spilled out the open window. The friends ate like starved zibars, chastising the Reeves Corporation and comparing the men they'd slept with over the years. Nencia was pretty sure Serena was making up all her stories just to keep up with her own promiscuous perspective toward the opposite sex.

"But you've been married, or maybe still are, how can you be against love?" asked Serena.

"Garvin's a good man. He wanted me up in the stars with him and I prefer my feet on solid dirt. We probably could have made the relationship work even with his traveling and my responsibilities here. But love, kids—that's not me."

"What about Logan and Bella?" Serena asked.

"Both of them are hard workers and loyal to the core. I was eating rocks and putting sand in fuel tanks at their age. Those two, they've got a good heart and deserve better."

"You've never discussed their parents, but if they ever needed a home, Markus could probably work something out." Serena seemed self-conscious about the topic.

"You don't like how I treat kids," Nencia said. "If you were in my position, you'd do the same thing. I do what I have to, and that's it. And don't talk about their parents. The arrangement I have with their mother is straightforward. Besides, I think Zakar has kind of adopted them. If anything happened to me, he'd take care of them."

Nencia's appetite left along with her good nature, and she opened a third bottle, not bothering to ask if Serena wanted another pour.

Serena was used to Nencia's nose-diving mood shifts and ignored it. "How do you get this stuff?" slurred Serena. "Dalth is starving, and we're eating like royalty."

Nencia was just as drunk but slightly more adept at handling her alcohol. "I'm the foremost smuggler in the universe." She loosened her blouse and pointed at her chest and head. "Any woman who has these brains and this body can accomplish anything. Dalth's problem is they have nothing to trade, so they rely too much on Appian. I think Markus's got the right idea; getting those other crops up and running next year should really help them out."

Serena looked down at her own chest, absorbed in Nencia's comments.

"Drink up, we've got another bottle to finish," Nencia said.

Serena waved the idea away. "I… I can't even finish this glass. No way are we opening another bottle! Certus is going to have to guide me home as it is, I can't be completely blitzed. Besides, that's going to kill our cover of not liking each other."

"Wait, you're going back tonight? It's pitch black out there and the temp's dropping."

"I've been so wrapped up in your orders that I've gotten behind on my normal contracts. I've got to go back tonight. I'll sleep this off in the back of the carriage on the way back."

"Stay here. I can even make sure you've got one of my girls to keep you company."

Serena blushed and sat back. "What! Me and one of your saloon girls? Uh… no, no, leave them for the boys. Besides, I don't even guide Certus anymore, he just knows the way home." .

Even though the Celje hadn't raided the main road to Dalth in weeks, other dangers still lurked. "You got protection?"

Serena cocked her head.

"Right. You make weapons."

Serena raised her glass one last time. "To strong women, dead Celje, and lots of money."

Nencia toasted. "Speaking of money. Zakar should have placed a crate marked as raw ore. There's about five thousand tonze in there."

Serena raised her glass again. "And you'll let me know when you need another shipment?"

"Of course, but like I said, we need to hold off for a while."

———————

Outside Nencia's apartment, the two women stumbled past an annoyed Zakar and toward Certus who Bella groomed affectionately.

Further up the road to the north, Zakar and Aldrich were speaking somewhat dramatically.

Nencia lumbered toward them. "You boys wearing your burlap underwear again? What's going on?"

Zakar's eyes shot toward the northern entrance of the city. "We've spotted a group of well-armed visitors and they're trying to stay unnoticed. Aldrich sent Berman and his team to investigate."

Aldrich was an older man with gray hair and a handlebar mustache, and he was one of the most reliable men working for her. He was one of the first to side with her when she forcibly took over Appian, and it was a point she made sure to never forget.

"It's either a raid or kidnapping job," grunted Aldrich.

Two quick bursts of gunfire erupted in the north. "Not a raid," thundered Nencia. "If I had to guess, they're here for me." Zakar stepped between Nencia and the cracking gunfire. "This isn't going to be a quick snatch and grab. Get the kids into the warehouse or back into the orphanage. Aldrich, grab Shannon and have her guard the orphanage, then grab the rest of our guys and get them armed. They want blood, then we'll pour it into their dying, mutilated jaws."

She wasn't sure how she knew the Celje were here for her, but there was no doubt. Sasha's recent visit to Dalth, Zakar's visit to the Nein, her recent conversation with Elasus about the Celje, all of this wasn't a coincidence. Sasha had somehow followed the breadcrumbs back to her.

Nencia sprinted toward Serena who was holding Bella tightly against her. "Bella, go with Shannon and get back to the orphanage. Stay there until I come get you. Serena, head south as fast as you can, get the hell out of here before they block the road."

Several pings and snaps rebounded next to Serena.

"Down!" yelled Nencia as more bullets flew over them.

The order likely saved their lives as more volleys missed high.

"What's going on!?" shouted Serena over the gunfire.

Aldrich came running back out, his hands full of guns.

Nencia took a pistol belt and rifle, then started barking orders. "Aldrich, get two teams and start putting bullets down range. Time for them to learn a lesson."

Serena grabbed a short-barreled revolver from inside her carriage, but Nencia blasted the idea. "They're using rifles! Get out of here. They won't come any further into the city now that we've organized. Besides, I've got more guns than they do. This is a warning shot from the Sasha. He's probably found out we've been double-dealing with the Nein."

Worall villagers were joining the Appian men now and putting more bullets down range.

"Nencia, this isn't right, I need to be—"

A shot struck Serena in the shoulder, propelling her backward.

Nencia crawled to Serena. "Hang on!" she hollered as she inspected the gaping wound. The bullet had gone straight through, but it was bleeding badly. Nencia tore off Serena's sleeves and made a temporary bandage.

"Ow, ow! Ahh!" sobbed Serena, thick tears of pain running down her face.

Closer to the warehouse, Zakar fired rounds into the encroaching enemy. "Zak, ZAK! Serena's hit, we've got to get her out of here."

Zakar looked at Serena. "Sixty seconds, we lay down cover fire and get her out the southern gate."

"You up for that, Serena?" asked Nencia.

Serena's brow and cheeks were furrowed in pain, but she managed a quick nod.

A minute later, dozens of rifles roared, and Nencia helped Serena to her feet and clumsily got her into the pilot seat of the carriage. Most horses would have bucked and jolted with the surrounding chaos, but Certus stood patiently, as if understanding his role.

"Markus and Jayden will want to help once they've found out what's happening here," said Nencia, leading Certus toward the south. "Tell them to stay put. We've got more than enough firepower here to take on the entire Celje sect, and we'll get additional support from Rindo and Pa'Gran shortly."

Serena nodded. "Okay, I'll tell them but... but you know Jayden... he'll come anyway Nenc... he's stubborn like that."

"That's for sure but tell him anyways. Keep your pistol out and stay safe. I've got a few guys scouting the path ahead."

Fighting unconsciousness and lancing pain, Serena let the draught horse guide them back toward Dalth. "Certus... I... I don't think I'll be of... of much help on this one. Get us home, old man... Get us home."

CHAPTER 26: YEAR 2401

Markus Fonte poured a healthy splash of brandy into two mugs of kaldi, handing one over to Jayden as the two sat on Markus's front porch. They watched the sunrise in peaceful silence, anticipating the toasty rays to warm their bundled bodies.

A single candle burned in the living room where Markus prayed, as he did every morning, to the God that had seen fit to challenge his faith daily. The single-story, three-room log home, originally designed by his late wife, took a full year to build. Markus and Bianca had planned on having two children, but her unexpected death from pneumonia after Bélise's birth turned Markus's world upside down. Now, his sole purpose for living rested with the teenager that filled his soul with joy.

"The food supply is getting desperate," explained Markus. "Grain shipments from Pa'Gran should have been here by now."

Jayden sipped at the strong brew. Portions of his face were still swollen and bruised thanks to his chat with Misora and Sasha the previous month. "There's enough to get the kids three spreads a day, and if nothing comes today, I'll go hunting again."

The two men had not eaten since yesterday morning because of the shortage. Hunting wasn't a great option either, as many animals had hunkered down for the winter. This wasn't the first time Dalth had run into a food shortage, and the town would come together as it always did, making sacrifices and coming out stronger.

Markus raised his glass in appreciation of his friend, and they sat for a few minutes, enjoying the quiet.

Finishing both the bottle of brandy and the pot of kaldi, Markus stretched his tired body. "Out of food, kaldi, and brandy, what have we gotten ourselves into?"

"Maybe Zakar will bring another bottle and perhaps a wagon full of meat in the next few days?"

"I think you'd rather have Nencia deliver it than Zakar. I don't think he likes you very much."

"He likes me just fine."

Markus laughed. "If you'd stop sleeping with his boss, things might get a bit better between you two."

Jayden rubbed the frost building on his short stubble. "I know you and Nencia sometimes don't see eye to eye, but she's a good person deep down."

"I sense a *but* coming," teased Markus.

A warm tingling rippled through Jayden's nerves, a consequence of the brandy. "Since I left the Nein, all I've wanted is peace and quiet. I've found it here in Dalth, now just need someone to share it with."

Markus smirked. "Have you talked to Nencia about this? Are you sure she wants this perfect life you've conjured up?"

"Point taken," Jayden admitted.

Markus chuckled again. "Want advice?"

"Always."

Markus sat forward, put his mug down, and clasped his hands together. "Enjoy moments like this, what we've got right now. Ojult will kick you when you're up or down. As far as Nencia, or any other woman, just let things happen. God has a plan for everyone."

"Your God's plan and my current situation aren't really seeing eye to eye."

Bélise walked into the room already dressed. "Morning, Daddy."

Markus accepted her hug. "Sleep okay? Need anything?"

Her arms extended above her head while she yawned. "Yeah, thanks. I'm going to help Celine in the clinic today, that okay?"

"You don't need my permission. Breakfast first?"

Bélise gazed out to the fields. "I'm okay. I can cut down on food, leave more for the young ones. I'm heading to the clinic. Hi, Jayden, love you, Daddy."

Bélise strolled across the field leaving footprints in the morning frost.

Markus stood, his back and hips stiff from sitting on the wooden chairs. "Guess it's time to get the day started. I've got a friend from Meridone that should be arriving today, and I'd like to have my work completed early. And if you wouldn't mind, check and see if Serena got back. I'm still regretting allowing her to leave alone."

Markus's small home rested on the southwest corner of Dalth, making it difficult for anyone at the cottage to see guests entering the city from the northern path.

"That looks like Victor, doesn't it?" said Jayden pointing to the east.

Markus's back popped as he turned. "I hate getting old. Yeah, that's him. Don't know anyone else that runs like that."

Jayden laughed. "Is he waving his arms, or is that just how he runs?"

It was tough to see exactly what Victor was doing as the sun was reflecting off the frozen dew.

"Mayor!" came the faint sound of Victor.

Markus spoke first. "Well, this probably isn't good. Wren probably threatened to burn down your home again." Something clicked in Markus's mind. Victor wasn't coming from the town square but from the east, the direction of the clinic.

Minutes later, Victor hunched in front of them, breathing hard, trying to catch his breath.

"Easy, Victor. Don't have a heart attack," consoled Markus.

"No… no time, Mayor," said Victor. "Need you… at the clinic. Serena… she's hurt."

———

Jayden, Markus, and an exhausted Victor rushed back to Celine's clinic where they found her hunched over a bloody and unconscious Serena.

Jayden's stomach tightened in fear. Serena pale and lying on the table, inanimate, stirred memories of the night he'd saved her from Misora and his gang.

Markus approached Celine, careful not to disrupt her busy hands. "Celine, how is she? Do you know how this happened?"

Celine removed a temporary bandage and inspected the wound. "A gunshot wound. Looks like it went straight through. Missed all the major vessels, but she's still bleeding. Oh dear, she's lost a lot of blood. Bélise, hand me another bandage."

Bélise grabbed a stack of clean but recycled white cloths and handed them to Celine.

"I'll need to stitch this up, but… goodness, it's times like these I wish we had a real doctor in this town."

"I'm sorry, Celine, I need to know what you know in case the town might be in danger," Markus said.

Celine looked up. "Victor, you tell him. Jayden, come here. I need you to hold the wound closed while I stitch her up."

This was one of the few times Jayden visited the clinic as a spectator and not a patient. The small building consisted of one makeshift operating room and eight patient beds arranged a few feet of one another. Green sheets lay atop each bed, and the walls were lined with mostly empty shelving.

Markus backed away from the bedside, and Jayden took his place. "My hands aren't clean," admitted Jayden.

"No time," Celine said. "She's lost so much blood. We've got to get this closed if she's going to stand a chance."

Jayden followed Celine's instructions, pinching the skin around the wound while Celine carefully stitched the area. Bone, muscle, and nerves were exposed, but his determination to help his friend suppressed any queasiness.

Jayden eavesdropped on Markus's conversation with Victor behind him.

"There is not much to say, Mayor. I don't think Dalth is in danger, at least right now. I kept telling her not to travel al—"

"Victor!" interrupted Markus. "Please focus, I need details, you can complain later."

"Yes, well, I was delivering some potatoes to Kun, out of the emergency-storage barn, you know, with the food situation, I thought it necessary. Luckily the Celje haven't raided that out…"

"Victor," barked Markus.

"Yes, yes, so I saw Certus walking with two carriages behind him but no driver. So, well, naturally, I went to investigate. I found Serena lying in the first carriage, out cold. I grabbed Kun, who was still in the pub, drinking his own products I might add, and we brought her here."

"Did you see anyone else, perhaps following her?"

"No, my very fine friend. I would have already said so. I would have captured the beast that would hurt such a beautiful, so pretty of a young, single woman like Serena."

"Where's the carriage?"

"Behind the clinic, but Certus is tired, and I would not take him out right now."

The conversation stopped with the frenzied closing of the clinic door.

Celine leaned over, inspecting the gash. "Press the skin there. Hold it, keep it still."

Jayden focused, scared he might hurt his friend. But Celine, she could work medical miracles. He knew both Celine and Victor's ancestors were among the first exiles to reside on Ojult. Victor's descendants were mystics, though the genetic trait apparently died off generations ago. Celine's roots were more straightforward, coming after the PGU declared Ojult a penal colony. Jayden didn't know much else about either family, only that Victor still worked his ancestors' original farm, and Celine continued her family's tradition of medicine.

Five or thirty minutes later, Jayden couldn't tell which, Celine stepped back from the bed. "I've done all I can. I pumped a few milliliters of jashinto extract into her for pain, just in case she wakes up, but she's lost a lot of blood."

Jayden would easily trade his own life for hers if there was any way. "Tell me what you need, and I'll get it. Blood, medicine, you need a doctor from elsewhere?"

Celine walked around the table and whispered, "She's strong, Jayden, really strong. Her body just needs time to heal. We need to change the bandages twice a day and clean the wound. We'll know by tonight if the blood loss was too much. If she survives that, then we need to worry about infection."

Celine's blouse was covered in blood, as she'd not taken the time to put on one of her surgical aprons.

Jayden stepped up and hugged her, kissing both her cheeks. "Thank you. Can I have a few moments alone with her... please?"

Celine replied with a warm smile and left. Jayden slid a small chair next to the bed and sat down.

"Serena... god... what'd you do to get yourself shot?"

He held her pale hand, then with a heavy, saddened heart, placed his forehead on the bed.

A short time later, the clinic door opened and an unfamiliar man glided in.

Celine's expression seemed more encouraging. "Jayden, I'm sorry to bother you, but this is a friend of the mayor."

"My name's Nolan. Pleasure to meet you, Jayden." He spoke with a familiar accent, had a large chin, was very tall, and perhaps was the same age as Markus. He wore a gambler's hat that when removed exposed a mostly balding head.

They exchanged handshakes.

"I don't mean to be rude," said Jayden, "but my friend is hurt, and I need to watch over her."

"Nolan is a medical... err, doctor of sorts. Markus asked him to stop in."

Jayden looked from Nolan back to Celine. "Of sorts?"

Nolan flashed an award-winning smile that card players dashed when hustling one-another. "Jayden, if you could step outside, I'd like Celine to accompany me and see what we can do for your friend."

Jayden didn't know Celine well, but he knew an anxious woman when he saw one. "You all right, Celine? Do you trust this guy?"

"Y—yes. I'm okay. Just tired. I think if anyone can help Serena, it's Nolan."

Jayden kissed Serena on the forehead and reluctantly went outside, keeping a tuned ear to the door.

He paced uneasily for what seemed like hours outside the clinic. With Markus nowhere in sight and Victor complaining nonstop, Jayden's Nein-trained nerves were just about shot.

The clinic door creaked open, and Nolan, followed by Celine, walked out.
"How's Serena?" Jayden asked. He glanced at Nolan who looked exhausted, nothing like the upbeat man he'd seen before.

Nolan walked away, and Celine headed toward Jayden. "The wound is closed, and I don't think we're gonna have to worry about an infection. If she hasn't lost too much blood, I think she'll pull through."

Jayden released the breath he'd been holding.

Celine patted his cheek like a little boy. "Go see for yourself."

Jayden followed Celine back into the clinic, either forgetting or choosing not to ask questions about Nolan's miracle medicines. He sat down in the chair next to Serena's bed, fearful of waking her and undoing whatever hocus-pocus Nolan had performed. Her eyes were closed, but she was no longer the ghostly mirage he'd seen earlier. Jayden continued looking over Serena, ignoring the opening of the clinic door and the voices of Victor and Markus.

They all watched their bedridden friend in silence, some praying for a quick recovery, others pleading for a different god to rip Serena's attackers apart. Serena's head shifted, causing a sudden gasp from her audience. They all watched, motionless, waiting for some other sign of recovery. Seconds later, she opened her eyes.

"Oh… my head hurts… and my shoulder…. My shoulder."

Celine rushed over to a nearby cabinet, grabbing a small, liquid-filled vial. "Hold on, dear. Let me get you some more serum. Try not to move, especially that shoulder."

Serena's crying stopped as the hallucinogenic drug, also used for pain control, took effect. "That's… that's much… much better."

An encumbrance of relief threatened to engulf Jayden. "You're gonna be okay, Serena, just relax. You're safe now."

Markus said, "Serena, I'm sorry to ask this now, but what do you remember? Who attacked you?"

Her eyes were still glossy and still void of cognitive thought. "I'm… sorry, Markus… I was in… Worall visiting Nencia and about to leave when I was shot. I… don't remember how I got here?"

The word *Nencia* and *shot* slammed into Jayden's psyche. "I'm heading there, Markus."

"Hold on a second, Jayden," said Markus, placing a hand across Jayden's chest. "Serena, you're under the influence of jashinto. Please, take a moment to think clearly."

Her head swayed on the pillow. "It's a blank… Mayor, I'm sorry."

"First Misora comes here, attacks Serena, and now she's shot." Jayden waited for Markus to catch up. "He's hunting her. It's time we repay the favor."

"Jayden, please wait just a moment. Let's get all the information we can before making that type of decision."

Jayden placed his hands on Markus's shoulders. "Markus, if Misora wants Serena bad enough to take a pop shot at her, then what's stopping him from coming back here again? If he's in Worall, then best meet him head on. If you're worried about me, don't be. I'm much better at this than farming."

"Ah, but, let me see," came Victor's voice from nearby. "I can fight. I can help you win. I think, yes. I think I shall go with you!"

"No!" said Jayden, Markus, Serena, and Celine simultaneously.

Jayden walked over to Serena, smiled, then kissed her on the forehead. "You okay?"

Serena's frightened, culpable expression told Jayden what he already knew. He leaned over and whispered in her ear, "You have the same expression you did the night your parents died. Whatever's going on, whatever's happened, don't worry, it's going to be all right."

Serena's eyes pooled with tears, but Jayden was gone before she knew what to say.

CHAPTER 27: YEAR 2401

Jayden wasted no time getting his gear together and saddling a tired Certus. Armed with his pistol, long rifle, and short-blade, he left Worall in haste. His appearance mimicked those during his Nein days: dark pants, a hat, and a faded overcoat that covered his pistol. Jayden's black pistol belt held extra ammo for his holstered revolver while his long rifle sat snug in a long leather sheath attached to the saddle.

Jayden kept a watchful eye during the trip, fully expecting an ambush, yet the Celje murderers never showed and Jayden soon found himself within a mile of the Worall gates. The aroma of charred buildings and gunpowder filled the air while dark plumes of smoke rose and drifted off with the strong eastern breeze. The bright-orange glow of the setting sun cast alluring beams through the smoky fallout, an almost picturesque scene if it weren't for the scores of bodies lying dead in front of him.

"Certus, I think Serena left a few details out about her trip here," said Jayden. He dismounted and walked the loyal animal off the main path, opting not to tie up the horse within the dense tree line. "Don't go wandering off, old man. I got a feeling we'll be leaving here in a hurry."

Jayden crept toward the southern gate, finding the lack of gunfire strange considering the smoldering devastation in front of him. The situation in Worall wasn't what he'd expected, and it changed his reason for coming. Killing Misora was now secondary to finding Nencia, Logan, and Bella.

He thought for sure he'd encounter at least a few guards from either the Celje or Appian, but no one, not even beggars, wandered in the streets. Jayden moved parallel to the town, through the forest, looking for a side entrance. The fifteen-foot perimeter fence surrounding Worall was built to keep out unfriendly wildlife, not a man coming to save his friends.

His luck changed when a nearby stack of hay bales on the eastern side of Worall gave him the needed elevation to clear the fence. His knees gave as he landed, and Jayden rolled forward, absorbing the long fall into the hard, dry dirt. Peering up and down the town's main thoroughfare, Jayden suppressed the urge to vomit as dozens of dead bodies came into view. Celje, townsmen, and Appian workers all lay dead or dying in the street. Those still alive moaned in agony with the realization of their impending death.

Among the dozens of low-whirring voices, the distinct sobs of a child caught his attention. Directly across the road, sitting in front of a single-story, heavily damaged home, was a small boy with blond, wiry hair.

"Logan!" Jayden's recognition overcame his common sense, and he dashed over. Once across, he approached Logan cautiously, not wanting to further scare the boy. "Logan," whispered Jayden. "It's me, Jayden… Uncle Jayden."

Logan wiped away his tears and focused on Jayden. Understanding gleamed in the boy's eyes, and he rushed forward, hugging Jayden and burying his wet face into Jayden's shoulder.

"It's okay," reassured Jayden, picking up the boy. "You're safe. Don't worry."

Logan's arms flexed even tighter. "They got Bella… they took her in this house… and told me not to move. I heard screams… I didn't know what to do!"

Jayden listened for movement inside the house but heard nothing. He looked around for a safe place to stash the kid. "Okay," he said, putting the boy down. "I'm going to go get your sister. Take my rifle. Anyone tries to grab you, protect yourself."

Logan hesitantly took the weapon, then pulled his knees back up to his chin.

Jayden unholstered his pistol and peered around each side of the small home, exploring for a window or back door. Unfortunately, the property's only window resided in the front, giving him no advantage. Seeing only one option, Jayden clicked the front door open and quietly entered.

A single lantern dimly lit the empty front room and kitchen. The floors were made of wood which squeaked with heavy footsteps. With no apparent sign of Bella, Jayden tightened his grip and headed toward the left-most room. He pressed his ear against the door and heard the moans of an injured person. Was it Bella or someone else? Seconds might cost Bella her life, and Jayden reacted, ready to kill.

Inside the bedroom, two candles on either side of an undersized bed shined over a gruesome scene. Splattered blood covered the mattress and a fractured dresser. Jayden counted three people in the room. One man, a Celje, was on the floor, dead, blood pouring out of his neck. The second person, a deceased male, lay face up, his eyes open. Allowing his eyes to adjust to the limited light, Jayden looked below the man's waist where both femoral arteries were exposed, severed by the transparent gleam of ice spikes.

The third person, Bella, stood at the head of the bed, legs and arms bent in a rapacious position. Her clothes were torn and covered in blood, but the passion thundering from her eyes left no doubt she was ready to continue the fight.

"Bella, it's me, Jayden." He lowered and holstered his pistol.

Bella fell to her knees in surrender.

He carefully reached over and lifted the young girl into his arms and carried her away.

"Logan," whispered Jayden when they got outside, "come here." He tenderly put Bella down on the porch and surveyed the streets.

Logan flinched at the sight of his sister, then nearly knocked her over with an intense embrace.

Jayden's adrenaline started to ease, giving him a different perspective on the situation. The two Celje in the other room were killed violently—by a mystic. Jayden came to the simplest conclusion.

"Bella, are you injured?" The question was awkward for him, especially since he knew what those men intended on doing to a teenage girl.

Bella sniffed and wiped away tears. "I… I killed them before they could… you know."

Jayden nodded. "Do either of you know where Nencia is or what happened here? Where is everyone?"

Logan said, "Aunt Nencia? She and Zakar were in her apartment."

Bella finished the explanation. "The fighting, it left the town a while ago. They all headed that way. Zakar shuffled us from the warehouses to the orphanage, then to Aunt Nencia's apartment. Nencia and Zakar were surprised and fought back, but captured." Some semblance of strength was returning to Bella's voice as she pointed up the northern path. "They were asking questions, then hitting them. Aunt Nencia was hurt. I don't... I don't think she could answer."

"You think they're still there?"

"I think so," replied Bella.

Jayden looked toward Nencia's apartment window where a faint light glimmered. "Logan, give Bella the rifle. I know Zakar taught you how to use it, so I won't ask. I know you don't want to, but take your brother back inside and hide in the other room, the one on the right. I'm going to go get your aunt and Zakar, then come back. If I'm not back by sunlight, take Logan and head to Dalth. You understand?"

"Yes," said Bella. "Logan, you keep the rifle, I have other ways of fighting."

Jayden expected the kids might beg him to stay, but they knew the stakes and understood what had to be done.

He crossed the vacant streets and headed for Nencia's apartment. Smoke billowed from homes and businesses, but Nencia's home appeared untouched. He circled and approached from the rear, staying silent and using the moonless sky to his advantage. Concealed behind a stack of empty crates, Jayden spotted a guard at the door. The Celje wore a dark, modern combat suit that fit reasonably tight against his body. Jayden didn't recognize the material or design.

Jayden had serious doubts if his pistol could penetrate the man's armor and decided against firing on the man, mainly because of the noise. Jayden withdrew his dagger and inched closer. With fewer than ten feet separating them, the guard turned and walked toward a pile of wood.

Jayden stood still until the man reached up to adjust his helmet. The fight was over before it began. Jayden cleared the distance and plunged the blade into the guard's pliable neck coupling. The dagger punctured the guard's voice box, preventing the man from screaming. After laying the man gently to the ground, Jayden turned to the apartment. Nencia used the first floor as a makeshift office and storage for off-the-books inventory. He entered quietly over the carpeted floor and through the first room where Nencia conducted meetings. A round wooden table surrounded by eight straight-back chairs filled the room. Bypassing this, he glimpsed upward through the small gap in the L-shaped stairwell where several men conversed.

"You will name those allying with you," said a man's voice.

Jayden sneaked slowly up the stairs.

"I'm a smuggler, you idiot, of course I'm working both sides," said Nencia, spitting on the ground.

Hearing her voice was jarring. Jayden paused for a moment.

"Not good enough!" yelled the interrogator, and Jayden heard several smacks as the man struck her. "Names, Nencia. I suggest you give me the information instead of forcing Misora to carve it out of you when he gets here."

Jayden reached the landing and proceeded up the next flight of steps.

"There are other, more invasive ways. You don't want that, now do you?"

Nencia struggled against her bonds. "Keep touching me, and when I get out of here, I'm going to kill you, your family, and anyone that's worth anything to you. You have my word."

Jayden reached the last step, which opened into the kitchen. He lurked closer toward the main bedroom.

"Fine then," said the man.

A gunshot rang out, followed by a painful roar from Zakar.

"You *cad*!" snarled Nencia. "Zakar, I swear I'll kill him, I promise!"

Jayden could see into the bedroom. The interrogator had a fistful of Nencia's hair, yanking her head back over the chair's backrest. The next blow sent her and the chair crashing to the floor, but now she was facing into the hallway, toward Jayden. Nencia was a pro and gave nothing away as the Celje yanked her and the chair back up. Jayden snuck up behind the guard, reached around, and slit his throat.

The man floundered for several seconds. Blood gushed, and the sickening sounds of gurgling filled the room.

"Jayden!" shouted Nencia. "Behind you!"

Jayden ducked, turned, drew his pistol, and fired. The bullet struck the knife-wielding guard in the forehead, dropping him at Jayden's feet.

"Holy hell am I glad to see you," said Nencia. "Hurry up and get me out of this."

Jayden used his bloody dagger to free Nencia and Zakar.

Nencia snatched bandages from the kitchen and slapped them over Zakar's right leg. "We need to hurry. Misora will be back any minute. Zakar, can you walk?"

Zakar winced. "N-no, boss. But, you… you need to find Logan and Bella."

"I found them, they're safe," said Jayden, peeking out the kitchen window. "I need to get you all out of here. The streets are empty, so I think we can make a clean escape."

Nencia reached over and kissed him, then pushed him away. "Don't be stupid. Most of the Celje went chasing after my men who tried to lure them away from the town, but they'll be back any minute. Misora was leading them and you can bet *he'll* be back. He found out I've been double-dealing with the Nein and he's pissed."

"Okay, let's deal with one problem at a time. Evacuate Zakar and the kids, then find your people and retreat to Dalth."

Nencia didn't argue, and together she and Jayden managed Zakar down the steep stairwell and across the street to Logan and Bella.

"Bella, can you help Zakar? Can you get that bullet out?" asked Jayden.

"Logan, turn away. You don't need to see what happens next," said Nencia. "Jayden, I need intel. Tell me what have you seen so far?" She pulled Logan next to her.

"Two Celje got hold of Bella, dragged her away from Logan, and into a bedroom."

This statement iced Nencia's expression. "Did they…"

"No, they didn't get a chance to," said Jayden.

"I'm going to cut off their—"

"And Logan doesn't need to hear the rest of that," said Jayden. "I found her right after she… handled them. She was upset, but you can see her handiwork for yourself. Beyond that, I've killed one guard outside your home, plus the two in your apartment."

A low-pitched roar came from Zakar inside.

Nencia said, "He'll be all right. Bella's done this sort of thing before. And this is Aldrich's place. He's gonna be upset. You seen him?"

Bella pushed open the front door and handed a bloody bullet to Nencia. Then she stole Logan away and guided him back inside.

Jayden found himself alone with Nencia. "God, I'm glad to see you," he said, embracing her. Feeling her warm body against his was proof she was still alive.

"We probably would have been killed if you hadn't shown up. How's Serena?"

"Rough, but Celine says she's going to be fine."

"Good," she replied. "I want you to lead Zakar and the kids back to Dalth. I'm going to round up as many of my people as I can, then counterattack."

"Seeing as you just lost the battle, were captured, and now your *army* is trying to lure them away from the town you just lost, how does that make sense? And why the hell have you been double-dealing with the Nein! Didn't think Ojult's intelligence spooks would find out!"

Nencia shoved him. "I would have told you, but I've been busy with all the other men in my life. Just slipped my mind, I guess. And I'm not leaving my men."

Jayden helped Nencia attach the wagon to the two horses in the stall. She gestured for him to take the reins. "Go pick up Zakar and the kids, I'll meet you in a minute. There are documents back in the apartment that I want you to take to Markus. No, don't look at me that way. Zakar can't fight and Bella's too inexperienced. You're going with them, Jayden!"

The kids eagerly jumped into the wagon while Zakar gingerly hoisted himself into the driver's seat. Jayden was tightening Zakar's bandages when rebounds of shattering glass grabbed both men's attention. Jayden was quickly off the wagon and ran toward Nencia's apartment. He cautiously walked up the stairs. Beyond the kitchen were three bodies, two belonging to the men he'd killed earlier.

"Nenc! Come on, baby, wake up!" Jayden said, rolling Nencia onto her back. He checked for a pulse and found a strong heartbeat.

The floorboard behind him creaked, and Jayden spun, pistol ready, but even his reactions couldn't overcome a prepared enemy. The baton struck him square in the temple, and he was unconscious before his head hit the floor.

The pulsating pain inside Jayden's skull brought him back to consciousness with a nauseating jolt. He was on his side with his hands and feet bound. Blurred lines veiled his vision, but he made out Nencia lying beside him.

Blood dripped from her mouth as she spoke. "We're still in Worall. I think Zakar and the kids got out, so tell these bastards nothing, no matter what. This is bigger than us."

It sounded like a prepared statement, like she'd be waiting for him to wake up. Her voice must have alerted their captures as he heard footsteps skidding across the dirt. With a hard thrust, Jayden was lifted off the ground and slammed back onto his knees, execution style.

"What the hell?" he slurred, his throat parched.

A man walked in front of him and knelt. "Good to see you, Nate Richardson. How long has it been? Your face says it hasn't been long enough."

Misora's face was still blurry, but Jayden recognized his arrogant tone. "Where... where am I?"

"I need a bit of information," said Misora in a casual tone. "Come to find out, it seems you and Ms. Donato have the answers. You two are lovers, so I figure threatening one of you will empower the other to speak. And did you know she was still married? My spies tell me you've been tasting this lovely lady for some time. You little playboy."

Jayden's wits were slowly coming back. Misora had called him Nate Richardson, so he still hadn't connected their first encounter.

Wham! Jayden hit the ground hard. "Errgg. Didn't... we... already... play this... game?"

Misora laughed. "Ha! A comedian to the end." Misora paced back and forth while a nearby guard sat Jayden upright. "I know that Nencia has been providing the Nein with guns, ammo, supplies, and anything else needed to fund their little war against my peacekeeping force." The surrounding Celje laughed. "But she didn't make all this by herself, so I need to know who helped. Sasha and I thought our culprit was in Dalth, though our first visit turned up little."

Jayden's eyesight adjusted, and his surroundings came into focus. It was nighttime, and they were in the middle of a street in Worall.

"I work for... for Markus Fonte. I'm a farmer and... deliver supplies on occasion. I don't deal in anything else."

Misora's heel plunged into the tender region just below Jayden's rib cage. Fracturing bones popped under the onslaught, though Jayden refused to submit.

"No!" screamed Nencia. "I'm going to cut your guts out and use them to grease my pistols when I get free! Cut me loose and fight me, you coward!"

Misora rubbed his hand against her cheek. "Oh, patience, my girl. You refused to tell me anything, and now he refuses to tell me anything. Odd that he mocked us last month in Dalth, and now I find him here with you. I suppose I should kill one of you, perhaps that might get the other to talk?"

A guard hoisted Jayden back to his shaking knees. A feeling arose in his gut, suggesting only one of them was getting out alive.

"I sold it," Jayden blurted. "I'm the one you want. I made the ammo. Kill me."

"You!" exclaimed Misora. "You admit manufacturing all of it?" Misora paused, then laughed. "Ah, Mr. Richardson, you couldn't clean a rifle let alone make one. You might have played a part, but you're not the main supplier. No... no, you are not the main con here, so stop wasting my time. And speaking of time," said Misora looking at his watch, "I'm about out of it. So, here's what's going to happen. Nencia, tell me who's supplying you."

Nencia's eyes went snakelike, and she spat blood on his shoes. "Screw you, pretty boy."

Misora shook his head. "I'm afraid that's the wrong answer." He plucked a pistol from his belt and aimed it at Jayden.

The round tore through Jayden's shoulder and the pain flooded his consciousness even before he heard the shot. He wanted to scream but found his voice paralyzed.

Misora's unwitting smile flipped into a cold, dark glare. "You aren't understanding the position you're in, nor the gravity of the consequences. Put him in front of her; I want her looking at him."

Jayden was dragged and set directly in front of Nencia. "Kill... me, I... don't care. You're not... get what you want." He felt blood washing down his shoulder.

"We'll get to the killing part in a minute." Misora was no longer smiling. "Tell me who's supplying her, and I let her live. Do not, and I kill her."

"He doesn't know anything," recited Nencia.

Misora seemed to consider this. "So, he knows nothing, and you're unwilling to speak? Then why did you come here, Jayden? A rescue mission gone bad? Yet you came alone. Surely you didn't think you could take us out by yourself. Like you said, you're a simple farmer. Ahh, but perhaps love has guided you here?"

Jayden's pain tolerance was high, but the pounding was making it difficult to speak. "Just... kill me, I'm the one you want. Let... let her live." He swayed back and forth, blackness threatening to take over.

Nencia's mouth dangled open. "He's delusional. Let him go, and let's make a deal."

"Do you think he loves you?" mocked Misora. "Could anyone love a traitorous tramp like you? I want to know why he's here."

Nencia looked at Jayden. "I suppose he does love me, like a delusional puppy. He doesn't know Ojult, he doesn't know me, he doesn't understand the things we've done and have to do to make it on this planet."

"Well, tell you what. Because I'm such a giving person, I'll let you say goodbye to each another." Misora motioned with his pistol to hurry up.

Nencia and Jayden locked eyes, knowing this was the end.

Jayden managed a smile. "Remember our good times."

Misora pressed the pistol to Jayden's temple.

Tears streamed down Nencia's cheeks. "I... I will. I love—"

Misora redirected his pistol toward Nencia and pulled the trigger.

The zing of the projectile was distinct over the short distance. Jayden's breaths were short and shallow, bursting from his nose in shock. Nencia's dead body swayed for a moment before falling to the ground.

Whatever goodness Ojult hadn't already sucked out of him left Jayden at that moment. His heart turned black, no longer accepting anything but hate and revenge. He fell gently on top of Nencia.

A sinister laugh erupted behind Jayden, yet the voice sounded different. Jayden had just enough time to look behind him and see Sasha Burmistrov. There was a slight pain in his neck, then everything went dark.

CHAPTER 28: YEAR 2401

Syrus Tokarek walked through the city of Carendra wearing his usual winter clothing, but unlike years past, he always kept his staff on him. The street curved, taking him by the slave quarters, then below his own home. Slaves, servants, and mystics bowed as he passed, but he gave them no attention.

The safety of his niece was on his mind, as was Nencia Donato's fate. With no real destination in mind, he loomed toward the combat-practice area, skirting the glassy pond his sister so often visited to clear her mind.

Helia was the only person allowed to enter the crystal-clear water. The town used wells for washing and drinking, but never the lake. He'd posted guards at the lake for the first few months after her death, ordering the lookout to turn away anyone who dared go near it.

Syrus drifted toward the lake, the water mirroring the stillness that swallowed his soul. He walked to the water's edge and sat down. A small sand bank surrounded the pond, and the harsh winter had turned the nearby grass brown.

Fond memories of his sister flashed through his mind, bringing a momentary flicker of peace to his hardened spirit. Hours went by until the sun began casting magnificent orange beams across water. Flashes of light from nearby florescent insects brought memories of Mea trying to catch them.

The guards bowed as he entered his home and walked along the carpeted walkway toward his desk. Fireplaces lining the building cracked as servants placed more logs onto their only heat source. With time on his hands, Syrus began writing.

Dearest Mea,

This letter will find you well and in good spirits, I am sure. Our war against the sect who murdered your mother goes well. My Nein are eradicating their existence off Ojult, town by town. As I have said in previous letters, you have nothing to fear. Listen to your caretaker, learn from your preceptor, take in all that you can. We will be making our push into Capintesta soon, which will give me the chance to come visit. But for now, the risk is too great. I know things are tough, but keep your mind focused on what you can control. I miss you dearly.

Love,
Syrus

"Writing to the kid again?" asked Phaedra, standing in the doorway, wearing dark pants and a heavy black coat that reached all the way down to her boots.

"I am," he said.

"When will you see her?"

"Our work here takes precedence. Our efforts against the Celje require all of us, especially now. But you haven't come to chat about my niece."

"No, I haven't. I'm nervous about Andreas. It's been almost two weeks since I relayed your message. He should have been to Worall and back by now. Why haven't you sent someone to check on him?"

Syrus's tranquil mood morphed into agitation. "Andreas is a senior member of my council and an intelligent man. He will accomplish his mission. For now, I want our efforts spent on the Celje and Reeves child."

Phaedra helped herself to a platter of vegetables and wine on a nearby table. "Elasus Reeves sending one of his kids to a planet full of violent exiles and mystics doesn't sound like something the richest person in the universe would do."

Syrus motioned for a glass as well. "I agree, but the intelligence is solid.

The Celje are shortsighted and will probably just kill the child while I would use him as a bargaining tool."

Phaedra slurped and wiped her lips on her sleeve. "Of course, all those papers could have just been a plant, phony leads to draw us off course."

"You're smart and deadly. Yes, all of this is a possibility, yet none more likely than the next. Once Andreas returns, I plan on putting him in charge of finding the child."

Phaedra seemed indifferent, ready as always to follow his orders. Obedience was a struggle for her, but her blindness to the bigger picture concerned him. She would kill Celje for as long as it took to eradicate them, with no thought to an eventual peace between the two sects. Syrus was certain this war would kill him, and he planned on leaving the Nein in Phaedra's capable hands. He hoped her immature attitude would change in time.

Loud footsteps clanked near the chamber's entrance. "Premier, may I interrupt?" asked Kavil Siller stepping through the door.

"What is it?"

Siller rubbed his patchy black beard. "One of our scouts picked up a suspected Celje a few hours ago. The woman is from Worall and was forced to flee after the Celje launched an attack on the town. It appears Nencia and her followers put up a tremendous fight but in the end were defeated."

Phaedra stole a quick look at Syrus.

Sasha's note had suggested taking out Nencia, not attacking an entire town. "And what of Andreas? Was he caught up in the ordeal?"

"By the woman's reports, the Celje killed anyone who fought in the battle. Andreas's body wasn't discovered, at least not yet. It's believed that Nencia is dead, executed by Sasha. By all accounts, Appian Shipping is destroyed, along with our supply line.

Phaedra walked to Syrus's side. "The Celje attacked Worall, and you want to launch an obvious counterattack?" Her way with words was not her best quality, but she had a point. Sasha would expect a powerful counterattack, likely at their strongholds in Limeth or Port Naok.

Siller's hand went up. "Quiet your tongue, girl. I'm the captain of our guard; strategy is my job, not yours."

The outcome of his war with the Celje could very well rest in the strange dynamics of their supply chain. Any disruption might turn the tide of the war. "Kavil, you'll accompany me to Worall," said Syrus. "We need firsthand knowledge of this, and perhaps we'll find evidence of Andreas during our visit. Phaedra, you take care of things here until I return. Lead the raids we've previously planned but nothing more. Kavil, we leave at first light."

Syrus left with Siller the next morning before sunrise, riding along a lesser known path to the southeast toward Port Naok. Under the deception of traders, they boarded the sailing ship *Challenger* and made for Rindo. From Rindo, they paid forty tonze each for a wagon ride to Worall.

Syrus glanced at the impressive defensive barriers around Port Naok as they passed through the main gates. Nine-foot-tall wooden fencing surrounded the village, reinforced by a gigantic iron gate. The driver steadied his horse down the steep hill ahead of town, yet another defensive characteristic.

"This town would be difficult to overcome if invading from the south," said Siller, mimicking Syrus's thoughts. "By the time foot soldiers and horses reached the gates, they'd probably lose half their number against a dug-in foe."

Forty-five hours after leaving Carendra, Syrus and Siller arrived in battle-torn Worall: smoldering buildings, burning pits of dead bodies, and a dirt road checkered with dried bloodstains. Few people noticed their arrival, as they were busy repairing their shops or homes.

They made their way down the dirt thoroughfare, ignoring the child beggars parked on every corner. Large, wrecked warehouses ahead marked their target, and the two men disembarked on foot. Syrus pretended to use his staff as a walking stick to fool onlookers. Though down the road, a shabby-looking man with soiled clothes took special notice of them. Glancing once, then twice, the curious man grabbed a nearby cane and limped toward them.

"I see the rumors are true," said Syrus in recognition.

Zakar Qualis limped toward them, his face exhausted and eroded. "Mr.

Tokarek, not a good idea for us to speak in the open. Head over to that warehouse across the way."

Zakar limped off and continued bellowing orders to the nearby Appian workers.

Syrus placed a hand across Siller's chest, foreseeing his captain's concern. "Zakar's been through much, Kavil, let the grievance go. He's got more important things to worry about than bowing or calling me by a title he doesn't believe in."

Soon Zakar met them behind the appointed warehouse. His voice was dry and frustrated. "Coming here was a mistake, Mr. Tokarek. The Celje still have eyes on us. You may have invited more attacks upon the town."

"Watch your tone, simpleton," chastised Siller.

Zakar stood still, unphased by the provocation.

"Touch my uncle and your blood will join those of my friends."

Syrus appraised the familiar dark-haired girl. "Bella… is that right?" said Syrus, raising his hands. "Kavil, you remember her. No harm will come to your… uncle. Zakar, our presence here is not intended to disrupt your operations or provoke you. I wish to speak with Nencia."

"She's dead," snapped Bella.

Syrus looked to Zakar for confirmation. Zakar limped to a nearby empty crate and sat. "Your expression tells me you already know. Might as well tell you everything." Zakar spent the next hour explaining the past few days, their struggles against more raids by the Celje, loss of infrastructure, supplies, men, and foremost, Nencia.

It was much worse than Syrus had imagined. Thinking about the massive consequences of the Celje attack, Syrus placed his palms against a nearby wall, his chin falling to his chest.

"My deputies survived the attack. Bella and her younger brother, Logan, escaped too. I received a note from Misora today threatening more raids and even taking over Appian."

Siller anxiously peered around the warehouse. "All leverage Appian had is now gone. They're of no use to us. We should leave."

Zakar gestured toward the road. "Smartest thing your associate has said so far."

Syrus pushed himself off the wall. "The Celje will not destroy Appian for the same reason they have not invaded Meridone. Sasha needs human capital, people to run the businesses, execute the contracts, manage the wagons and supplies across the region. He can't do it with a bunch of trained assassins."

Zakar gestured to the Appian workers in the street. "I'm pretty sure that's why I'm still alive along with many of my people."

Syrus leaned on his staff, thinking of his next move. "I grieve for your friend and I'm thankful the kids made it out. My fight against Sasha, Misora, and the Celje will continue. For you, Zakar, I'll try to take Misora alive so you can carve him up like the *sora* he is."

Zakar shook his head. "Killing isn't my business, Mr. Tokarek. We're in the business of making money and new friends. Obviously I can't keep up the agreement you had with Nencia, at least not now. If they'd just hit Worall, it might be different, but with all our operations marauded, it's not possible."

"I understand," replied Syrus. "I'll pay my respects to Nencia and leave."

Syrus followed Zakar and the children down to the graveyard situated on the far southeast side of town. Mounds of freshly shaved dirt over recently dug graves lined the area.

"Over there, the one with the three wooden blocks beyond the tree," said Zakar, resting on a nearby wheelbarrow.

Syrus ordered Siller to stay put while he approached. He knelt next to the mound, reflecting on how much the woman had meant to the Nein. Memories of his sister raced through his mind as he thought about Nencia, who had also died at the hands of the Celje. Kneeling in silence, Syrus contemplated how her death would change the war against these cowards.

Away from Syrus, Siller conversed quietly with Zakar. "You were injured but managed to escape?"

Zakar adjusted uncomfortably. "An old friend of Nencia's had heard about the attack and came to help."

"This friend, he fought through the Celje lines just to find Nencia?"

"Just a guy trying to save his girlfriend. I'd have rather seen Jayden Vaut die with the rest. Instead, the Celje captured him after they executed Nencia."

Syrus approached, interrupting their conversation. "One of my men,

Andreas Palada, I believe you know him, was here around the time of the battle. Would you ask your people if they've seen him?"

Zakar looked up into the night sky in contemplation. "Sorry to tell you this, but I think the Celje captured him as well."

"You sound like you know more than you're saying."

Zakar massaged his healing leg. "Rumors only, nothing confirmed. But we've been hearing about Celje taking mystic prisoners for months. Started with a mystic a few years ago, apparently a powerful one, but the guy vanished. A few accounts of him being dragged away. Same with your friend, Andreas."

Syrus waved Siller over. "I want you to head back to Carendra and task a group with finding information about this prison."

Siller had dedicated his life to the service of the Nein. When one of his own was in danger, Siller would commit everything he had to the task.

Zakar pushed himself off the tree. "Keep in mind, these are just rumors."

"The rumors you hear are probably more accurate than the facts I typically get," remarked Syrus. "I'll respect your wishes and not return to Worall unless necessary, but I trust you'll notify me if you come across anything important?"

Zakar nodded. "The Celje made an enemy of Appian, and Sasha doesn't know how much this is going to cost him. Give me time to rebuild and you'll have an ally, Mr. Tokarek, I promise you."

―――――――

Kavil Siller had set off for Carendra intending to put the resources he'd just been granted into full use. Of course, the news about Jayden Vaut dominated his mind. Rumors of that *cad* on Capintesta had reached his ear before, but this confirmation changed everything. With dozens of Nein at his disposal, he'd find Andreas, and if Jayden inadvertently died during the rescue attempt, well, accidents happened.

PART IV

CHAPTER 29: YEAR 2401

For the third time this week, Irelyn Reeves woke up in a familiar bed, though not in her own home. She was naked under fine silk sheets, her blonde hair tangled from a hard night's sleep. The room was pitch black despite the hour; surely it was morning. Blackout shades and other luxuries bejeweled the finely decorated master bedroom of Prime Minister Joshua Kennedy.

She had many reasons for sleeping with Kennedy; first on the list was the incredible sex. Sure, the first few times she felt guilty, wishing Elasus would miraculously apologize for being the world's worst human, and they'd rekindle their marriage. Alas, it would never be. Elasus's passion for money and his whore secretary overshadowed any thoughts of repairing their marriage.

Joshua hired a personal chef last night, and the two adulterers dined in. The minister's back patio overlooked the broken Las Vegas skyline, but the view was nevertheless stunning. After two bottles of some very hard-to-pronounce pinot noir, Kennedy hoisted her onto an enormous lounge chair where they made love. Despite the dry, hot summers in Nevada, the night brought cooler air, and they retired to Joshua's bedroom where they slept soundly.

Joshua lived in Las Vegas during the week, then commuted to Napa Valley on the weekends where his wife and two children lived. He made it known early on in their affair that he loved his kids more than life itself, but his wife, well, that was a different story. Once money started really flowing in, Amy Kennedy let herself go. She gained weight, drank from sunup to sundown, and let the nanny raise the children. She was too expensive to divorce, and the negative publicity that might come out of the ugly episode wasn't worth it.

Irelyn relished in the passion of the affair, fulfilling her fantasies while enjoying none of the relationship responsibilities. Neither partner deluded themselves, focusing instead on their passions rather than any sort of intellectual connection. Of course, that was until last week when Joshua threatened to end the affair if she didn't agree to start spying on Elasus for him.

For several months, Elasus had spent less time with the PGU and more time with the Free and Independent African States. At first Irelyn thought the threat was some sort of bad joke, but Joshua had tossed her out of the house when she refused.

If being married to Elasus had taught her one thing, it was to never give up anything for free. The next evening, Joshua's chef had prepared another meal, and they ate in cool silence.

"Joshua," she'd said, making the first move. "I'll do it, I'll give you whatever you want. I'll pass along what you need on Elasus, but I want you to reopen the investigation into my daughter's whereabouts."

Joshua pondered the request. "I have spies everywhere who do important work. I'm not about to take them off their assignments to look for a runaway."

Another rule from Elasus's handbook: always call their bluff. Irelyn methodically pulled down her already low-cut blouse, first off her shoulders, then her chest, then down around her waist. Like peeling an orange, Joshua's eyes followed the seductive dance all the way.

She waited until he was fully engaged, then stood and leaned over the table. "Then I guess it's over," she whispered. Without waiting for a response, she pulled her shirt back on and headed for the door. She'd only gotten to the patio before Joshua started backstepping. He fumbled over his words, unable to focus.

The next morning, after an endless night of passion, they sat at the breakfast table, Joshua reading the headlines while she scanned through messages on her 3DI. She'd tidied up the kitchen and the bedroom beforehand, clutter and disorganization being one of her biggest pet peeves.

"Your husband's dealings with the FIAS keep ramping up. Last time this happened, it involved an arms deal that resulted in two peculiar, high-profile deaths," Joshua explained as if continuing a long running conversation. "He exiled the Visconti family and cut off all business agreements with the FIAS. Rumors of these Celje warriors on Ojult alongside all this FIAS talk—is there anything you want to share?"

Irelyn had neither confirmed nor denied the existence of the Celje to her lover, despite his questioning. This had nothing to do with protecting Elasus and everything to do with protecting her son. There was something to Joshua's thinking, however. Her husband's renewed interest in the FIAS was confusing, and Elasus had not confided his plans to her. "I'm heading to his office this morning. I'll find out what it is, even if I have to screw it out of him. How do you plan on upholding your end of the bargain?"

"Elasus has done an excellent job keeping the PGU out of his business, especially when it comes to Ojult. In fact, to my knowledge, we don't have a single spy on the planet." Joshua's eyes fixed on her breasts. "But we've got plenty within his transport fleet. I'll contact Secretary Madigan this afternoon, have him start digging up information. Tell me your daughter's full name again?"

Brycor Madigan was new to the Planetary Governing Union, recently selected as the body's security secretary. Irelyn had met him a few months ago, but from what she could tell, he was a private man. Madigan never attended the required social events, nor the well-attended conferences and meetings the more prominent members of the PGU frequented.

"Marilla Eve Reeves," replied Irelyn. "And, yes, just her. Ruven is on Lent as the planetary resource governor. I still think she's on Ojult, despite Elasus's opinion."

"You've got a fine ass, Irelyn, but you're naive. You really think she's been on Ojult this whole time?" Joshua stared at the floor. "Look, I'm sorry, but I tell it how it is, and it's hard for me to turn that off. If she's been there all this time, she's probably dead. But I made a deal, and I plan on keeping it. I'll get my people on it, but don't set your expectations too high."

Irelyn dressed in the spacious black sedan on their way to the Reeves Corporation headquarters. The family driver, Hewitt, had seen Irelyn dress a hundred times and didn't flinch as she exposed her body. She trusted Hewitt to keep her secret, just as she expected him to keep Elasus's.

The short black-and-tan dress exposed her back and complimented her wavy blonde hair exactly the way Irelyn had planned it. Her high heels would lift her ass and thin her legs, giving her the disposition needed to con her husband out of the information she needed.

"What time did Elasus get to work this morning, Hewitt?"

Hewitt was pushing seventy-five, but he looked in good shape. He always wore a suit, which complimented his thinning, slicked-back gray hair and clean-shaven appearance. Hewitt was the consummate professional, charming, and above all, delightful.

"Yes, ma'am. I dropped him off last night at his office after a dinner meeting with a PGU member. To my knowledge, Mrs. Reeves, he stayed the night."

"Of course," murmured Irelyn.

Hewitt kept his hands near the wheel as the sedan turned the corner onto Reeves Corporate Boulevard, and the enormous building came into view. Pulling up to the main entrance, Irelyn's plan started falling apart.

"Hewitt, stop the car here. Don't let them see us."

Hewitt engaged the manual stop. Perhaps two hundred yards ahead stood Elasus and Tayla Cruz in front of two parallel-parked vehicles. She recognized the first as Tanner's vehicle. Irelyn didn't recognize the second, a small, white two-door sedan, but the matter resolved itself as Tayla kissed Elasus then entered the car.

"I'm sorry you're having to see this, Mrs. Reeves," said Hewitt. "It also seems that Elasus is on his way to a meeting, escorted by Security Chief Sands."

Not even her perfectly applied makeup hid her angry, blushing cheeks. "That's it, time to face this head on. Follow the white car, Hewitt." She'd spat the irrational idea without giving it a second thought. Why, after all these years, did this affair suddenly bother her?

"Mrs. Reeves, I'm not certain that's a good—"

"I can't do anything about what he does in his office, but in broad daylight, it becomes my business. Do it!"

To Hewitt's credit, he didn't argue the point and kept a safe distance from the white sedan. They eventually stopped in front of a small apartment complex on the east side of Las Vegas, just short of Henderson City. The complex was secured by a double-gate security fence that allowed for one vehicle at a time, using separate transmitters to open each.

Irelyn watched her husband's mistress walk up a single flight of stairs and open the door to a second-story apartment. "I'll be back. Stay here until I return."

It was midmorning, and the apartment complex was empty aside from a few maintenance workers. Irelyn felt their filthy eyes following her as she walked up the stairs, but this conversation needed to happen.

Irelyn stood in front of the plain door, no welcome mat or friendly plants in sight. *Unwelcoming whore,* thought Irelyn. She took a moment to reassess her decision, then knocked twice and waited.

Tayla opened the door wearing workout attire, her hair in a ponytail. "Mrs. Reeves? What are you doing here?"

Irelyn pushed past her. "Shut the door, it's time we had a chat."

"Excuse me," replied Tayla, shutting the door. "I understand that I work for your family, but barging into my home is ridiculous. What have I done that called for this?"

"Cut the bullshit! You and I need to chat about Elasus, *your* relationship with my husband." Irelyn took a moment to look around the living room. It was spotless, no signs of toys or the usual mess a working mother of two would ordinarily walk into. A bookcase along the far wall stored youth trophies while digital family pictures covered the adjacent wall. "I can't do anything about what you two do behind those pristine office doors, but in public you *will* not embarrass my family!" Her breathing was erratic, and she fought the urge to punch the woman.

"Mrs. Reeves, I'm sorry, but my… my contract with Elasus spec—"

"Don't give me that contract bullshit! Does *your* husband know what you're doing!? I know you've been staying at the office apartment with Elasus. You've been slowly tearing apart my family for years, it's time it stopped!"

Tayla kept her distance. "Mrs. Reeves, I really can't say anything to you about my contract with your husband, but I can promise you I've done nothing to intentionally invade your family."

At headquarters, no one entered Elasus's office without first passing Tayla's desk. Over the years, Irelyn had passed by the desk hundreds of times, and she made it a point to look at the woman's pictures. Almost all the pictures included her husband and young children which explained trophies in the bookcase. The pictures in this living room, however, were different; none of them showed Tayla after her numerous cosmetic procedures.

"Is… is this apartment Elasus's too? Is this another one of your play-houses where you get away from your spouses? Play make-believe while your children are at school and your husband's at work? Do you two do this often? How about I just drive up to the local school and let the kids in on your little secret?"

Irelyn expected Tayla to hit her, but Tayla looked dejected rather than upset.

"Mrs. Reeves… please… just leave," replied Tayla, falling onto her sofa.

Taking another look around, Irelyn surveyed the entire apartment. Living room, kitchen, adjacent dining utility room, and one bedroom. "You're a sick woman," spat Irelyn, heading for the door. "I'll leave you to your guilt, but the public expo stops today!"

Irelyn let herself out, and Hewitt pulled the car so it was next to Tayla's sedan. Before getting in, Irelyn peeked through the secretary's car window. The inside was clean—no clutter of toys, candy wrappers, or snack bags.

"Can the phone here connect to Chden?" she asked, getting into her own car.

Hewitt turned around. "I'm sorry, ma'am, you want to call where?"

"I need to speak with Commodus, it's important. Can this car call another planet?" The admission she knew where Commodus was felt embarrassing.

The tenured driver punched three buttons on the car's heads-up-display. "Ma'am, a soundproof barrier will soon appear between us, and the call will connect to Commodus shortly. Depending on certain factors, you may experience a delay when speaking."

Less than a minute later, the barrier went up, and Commodus's face appeared. "Mrs. Reeves, I can see you're calling from the car. Is everything okay?"

Irelyn felt the tension in her back suddenly release. "Commodus, it's a secure line. How are you? You... you look well."

"You're all dressed up and looking... wait, it's morning there, isn't it?"

Irelyn smiled. "I'm sorry to bother you, but I've just visited Tayla Cruz's home, and we had an argument."

"Oh hell, Irelyn, please tell me you didn't drive over there?"

Irelyn looked down at the floor. "I did and... I'm... well, what's done is done. But I'm calling because something is off." She explained her encounter, plus the weird pictures, trophies, and small car. "For a working mother of two with a husband, something isn't adding up. What am I missing?"

"You need to leave that place and forget what you've seen. Don't tell anyone else about this. Do you hear me?"

For several years now, Irelyn expected that Commodus liked her, but given her marriage to his boss, he'd not really come out with it. She couldn't tell if Commodus's warning was out of his liking for her or something else.

"Commodus, I'm here now, not two dozen feet from her front door. We've had an argument, but I need to know what else is going on. She kept mentioning a contract."

"Ah shit," said Commodus. "I can't say anything about that, Irelyn."

"Can't or won't," she countered. "I can just ask Joshua if you won't tell me, he has the resources—"

"That's low, Irelyn."

Rubbing her affair into the face of a man who probably wished it was he having the affair wasn't fair play. "I'm sorry. I didn't mean it like that. Tell me about the contract."

"Elasus will hang me by the cojones if he finds out I told you." But Commodus spilled the details anyway. Irelyn sat in horror listening to the account of her husband's deal with Tayla that basically made her Elasus's concubine, her children used as collateral if she didn't obey.

"Irelyn, you still there?"

Torn between vomiting and punching the video screen, Irelyn dabbed the tears running down her cheek. "Did you have anything to do with this, Commodus? Are you... *involved* with her too?"

"Hell no I'm not," he responded. "I'm no saint and I've probably got a first-class ticket to Hades himself, but not when it comes to women. Where I come from, we don't do that type of shit."

She nodded. "Call me tonight," she said and ended the call. The sound barrier drew down. She was aware of her wet cheeks, but Hewitt had seen worse.

Hewitt handed her a tissue. "Ma'am, what can I do to help?"

She wiped the tears from her face and opened the door. "Stay here. This may take a while, but please, don't come up."

Contrary to her earlier stampede up the stairwell, Irelyn took the steps one at a time. She knocked softly on the door, like a friend. She heard Tayla weeping on the other side. When the door opened, Tayla stepped back, her eyes wide with bewilderment. Both women stared at one another. Shame, guilt, anger, and repulsion fell with each tear. Irelyn stepped over the threshold and shut the door. Words failed them, and Irelyn reached out and embraced the baffled secretary.

"I'm just finding out things, and for what it's worth, I'm so, so sorry."

Tears flowed freely now but words were in short supply. For many minutes they embraced, pent-up emotions finally escaping out the only channel which the world they lived in allowed.

Tayla broke the hug, her nonwaterproofed mascara smudged over her face. "I don't know what to say, Mrs. Reeves. I'm… I'm lost."

"You don't need to say anything right now. I'm going to work up a plan, and we'll figure this out together. But first, you need to clean yourself up and make us a drink."

"There's tea or coffee in the… the cupboard there."

"Yeah, I'm thinking something a bit stronger," replied Irelyn, believing they'd both benefit from a stiff drink.

Tayla pointed toward a cabinet above the refrigerator. "There's vodka and soda there."

Irelyn smiled. "We're already speaking the same language. You and I, we're going to get through this and find our damn kids."

CHAPTER 30: YEAR 2401

Waking up from unconsciousness, pain coursing through his every nerve, Jayden wanted to scream but the link between his mind and voice hadn't come back. The room smelled damp, with the overwhelming stench of urine, vomit, and feces.

Wham! A blow jerked Jayden's face to the side.

"Time to wake up," said a familiar, jovial voice.

Another blow jerked Jayden's head to the other side, and this time he felt warm blood seeping from his nose. He tried to open his eyes, but his lids were sealed shut from dehydration and lack of use.

Suddenly his eyes were wrenched open. "Arrrgggghhhh!" Jayden felt like a paper cut just sliced through his eyeballs.

"Ah, there we go," said the man's voice again. "Look at me, Mr. Vaut, look at me. There... there you go, focus on me. No need to look around, she isn't here. And yes, she's dead, in case you forgot that small detail from earlier."

Jayden looked up at Misora from where he was hanging in chains in a small room lit by a single light in the corner.

Jayden gasped, each breath a hollow struggle. "You... she... Nencia didn't deserve this. You... executed her for nothing." Jayden used what little energy he had left and threw himself against his bindings, but the metal chains gave only a few inches.

Misora inched closer to his face. "We can spend all day reminiscing about Nencia, how great she was, the people she killed, the men she screwed, and the trillions of tonze she's smuggled. But no, Mr. Vaut, we're going to focus on you. More specifically, your time with the Nein and with Nencia."

Jayden suddenly recognized Misora's use of his *actual* last name. How had Misora figured it out? "Finally figured it... out... did you? Not much of a... story. I was a slave. I don't know anything about your... smuggling or helping the Nein. Kill as many of them as you want, I don't care."

Misora pressed his thumb into Jayden's wounded shoulder and shouted over Jayden's yells. "Yes, I figured it out, or shall I say a mutual friend of ours filled me in. Interesting story, really, but not for today. And please, don't insult my intelligence. A simple slave with the Nein? No, Vaut, you're a mystic. You're one of them and I think you would care deeply if I found, for instance, Mea Tokarek?"

They were looking for Mea, which meant she and Helia were okay. Jayden showed no sign of knowing the girl, afraid the admission might endanger the only people he cared for within the Nein. Through watery eyes, he looked to his shoulder, covered in white bandages and medical tape. "I'm... not... a mystic... you *cad.*"

Misora pulled up a small metal stool and sat. "The Celje are here to protect humans from your kind, Vaut. We know the Nein are in Carendra, but what we don't know is who's making all the ammunition, armor, and guns for them. I have a little friend who told me that Nencia is... err... *was* the broker. Nencia's dead, so all that's left is the manufacturer, and you're going to help us find him."

Jayden looked him in the eye and smiled. "You're a lunatic if you think I'm going..."

Misora reached out and clamped hard on Jayden's shoulder, pulling the stitches apart and forcing blood up through the bandages. Jayden groaned, forfeiting any sense of composure.

"You see," continued Misora, still moored to Jayden's shoulder, "I have a friend who believes the supplier is in Dalth. You saved Serena, you're a Nein, and you're both from Dalth. You can see the connection we're drawing. So, who is it? Who's making this stuff? Is it Serena or perhaps the mayor?"

Jayden's silence brought on more pain as Misora bashed his shoulder.

Misora smiled, enjoying the thrill of torment. "Where are the Nein staging points and campsites on Capintesta?"

The agony was too much, and Jayden vomited, barely missing Misora's boots. "I was... a slave... of the Nein... kill... them all... I don't... care."

Misora slid a thick, armored black glove around his hand and stretched his fingers in front of Jayden. "You ever seen one of these? It's a shock gauntlet or, as I like to call it, a mystic breaker. It's made of African ore and sends an electrical shock through the target while breaking whatever it contacts." The Celje leader reared back and let loose, shattering Jayden's cheekbone.

The explosion in Jayden's cheek was deafened by his nervous system igniting in a blaze of never-ending torture.

Misora slid the bloody gauntlet off and tossed it on top of a pile of other torturing devices. "In truth, we've already checked out Serena Visconti and the mayor—both are clean. I couldn't believe it myself, but even I'm wrong sometimes. So, Mr. Vaut, help me out here."

With his remaining strength, Jayden spit into Misora's smiling face. "I... I'm do... done speak... ing... with you."

Misora leaned in closer. "Oh, Mr. Vaut, we're so far from done."

"Put him on the table," demanded the redheaded nurse. "Don't bother chaining him up; you've beaten him into unconsciousness. He's probably closer to death than life by now!"

The taller of the two guards backhanded her. "You don't give us orders, girl. Misora says all these freaks will be chained, so they'll be chained."

She took the blow on her right cheek, which was already bruised from a similar hit yesterday. "Just leave so I can try and save his life!"

The prison infirmary wasn't big, nor was it well supplied. She had two procedure tables, six side-by-side beds, and only a handful of portable lights and overhead lamps illuminating the dull room.

The nurse slapped electrodes all over Jayden's body and turned on the scanner. It was an older version of the panoramic 3-D InPathaScan, but it beat using the tradition stethoscope hanging around her neck. The small holo-projector created a pop-up representation of Jayden's body for the practitioner to review. "You're in bad shape."

He looked pale, like losing another drop of blood would kill him. But what really concerned her was his stomach, swollen from massive internal bleeding, all while blood continued leaking from his mouth, nose, and ears.

She'd seen worse patients, but none had ever lived. "Okay, nothing I can do for the internal bleeding," she uttered. The young woman started bandaging and stitching his wounds, starting with his shoulder. She'd already stitched this once, but the guards had torn it back open.

The man's hemoglobin levels were in the toilet, but with no way to measure those vitals, she worked feverishly to stop what bleeding she could. Banding and stitching took over an hour and cost her half of her already limited supplies.

"Is he going to live?" came a man's voice.

"Misora, I need to work."

Misora walked up behind her and yanked her hair, forcing her toward him. "I need him alive or you'll share the same fate as your patient."

"We both know that isn't true, now let me work."

Misora leaned over the motionless patient. "Sasha wants an update soon, fix him. He only needs to live through a few more sessions."

Misora sneered, slapped her rear, then hummed with mirth as he left. She ignored the abuse and checked her patient's heart rate and the scanner again. "Forty-two—you're getting worse not better, mystic, come on, help me out!" Having worked on dozens of sages over the past years, she knew the incredible healing powers of the sect. But they had to be aware of their situation and knowingly enter the healing trance.

An idea flickered in her mind, but if Misora found out… "I hope you're worth it, like you're going to save the planet or something," she remarked, and she reached into the bottom drawer of a nearby cart and pulled out a syringe. "Okay, you can't hear me but listen up…" She paused, staring at her patient's chest, which was no longer moving. "Damn it!" She set the rare syringe aside and quickly started CPR on the mystic. "One… two… three… four… five… six… seven… eight… nine… ten" she counted, compressing his chest, then paused and roared breath into Jayden's lungs.

Her hands and arms cramped after several minutes, but she refused to lose her patient. "Come on!" she said. Finally, her labor bore results.

Jayden started breathing on his own, but his blood pressure and heart rate were still at dangerous levels. She took the syringe and injected a combination of erythropoietin and nano-treks into his leg.

Misora had made it very clear that the very expensive and rare drug was only to be used on injured Celje, never prisoners. The erythropoietin helped the body generate red blood cells via the kidneys while the broad-spectrum nano-trek would ward off infections and speed up new tissue growth. It wasn't a miracle drug, but it was the only medication she had that might do any good.

She didn't know if it was the injection or his mystic healing, but during the night, her patient stabilized. If he survived, he would need weeks, if not months, of rest, which Misora would never allow.

The next afternoon, she performed her hourly vital-sign check and found he'd not progressed like she'd hoped. Most of her mystic patients usually showed faster restorative development by this stage. Before dinner, Misora and two guards barged into her office, startling her as she'd tried to catch a few minutes of sleep.

"What are you doing? He needs rest!" The two guards ignored her and dragged Jayden off the stretcher. Alarms from the scanner starting whaling over the arguments of its user. "You move him now it might kill him!"

"Back off, or I'll black that other pretty eye of yours."

There was nothing she could do but watch in disgust.

Misora scoffed over her objections. "It's okay, don't worry. Look, clean yourself up," he said, gingerly touching the side of her face. "Why don't you sleep in my quarters tonight? You need a good rest, and these guards won't bother you in there."

CHAPTER 31: YEAR 2401

Jayden dreamed vividly, introducing Nencia to his mother and father on Earth, explaining to his parents they were engaged. The illusion suddenly jumped ahead, and Nencia was wearing a slim white wedding dress, her long black hair skirting the small of her bare back. The formfitting dress looked immaculate against her tan skin.

Outside the church, wedding bells chimed alongside cheering friends and family. In the distance, clouds clustered and turned gray, then green. A storm was brewing, and the clouds rotated. Lightning flashed across the sky, but instead of hail, silver discs rained down. Jayden hesitated, having to choose between his parents and Nencia. He decided quickly and leapt to cover his bride, but he couldn't move. In front of him, silver discs cut through Nencia, his best man, Rystral, then his parents.

Jayden woke to intense, pulsating pain. His first thought: *Dead people don't feel pain.* He was naked but for a pair of briefs and lying on his back upon a cold metal bench. Heavy chains weighed down his wrists and ankles, but the slack allowed him some freedom to move.

The cell was small, lined with metal bars, a bench, and a bucket. The entire ward was dark except for a few candles. Jayden tried sitting up, but pain jolted through his ribs, shoulder, and most of his body. He was sweating despite the moderate temperatures inside the noxious room. With multiple lacerations and deep wounds, his body was fighting multiple infections.

Another set of chains rattled near him. "You need to heal. Don't talk

or try to move. You're in bad shape. I don't think you're a mystic, but if
you are, then heal."

Another man spoke, but his cadence was forceful. "If he was a mystic,
he'd have already healed himself. This Thoba has somehow managed to get
himself locked up in a mystic-only prison. Congratulations."

"Charming, Levi," said the calmer voice. "Look, stranger. The first couple days are the worst. You'll be interrogated again soon. Heal up as much
as you can. Don't give in to these butchers."

There was something familiar in this man's voice, but his eyes hadn't
adjusted to the dark room. Jayden didn't know if it was day or night, but
his body told him to sleep, so he did.

The thud of a metal door staggered Jayden awake. Misora and two
guards dragged him out of the cell.

Hours of questions and torture made up Jayden's next few days, more
than surpassing his will to live. Misora's line of questioning was always the
same, but Jayden, having nothing to hide, answered the same way every time.

"I thought for sure they'd break your weak mind," said Levi. "Now you
get to live out your life in a small cage. Feel better now? Maybe you've beat
the system?"

"Levi was dropped a lot as a child, then dropped again, and perhaps a
third time" retorted his other cellmate.

Time meant nothing to Jayden. His neighbors, like the Celje, believed
he was a mystic, and Jayden felt it best to keep up that illusion until his
position became clearer. For the first time since arriving, he wasn't being
tortured and had found a moment for himself. Jayden did a quick check
over his body and found dirt, blood, and his own excrement covering him.
His beard was long, fostering his theory he'd been in prison for months.

"Not even a thank you, newcomer?" said Levi. "I admit that perhaps
I deserve nothing, but Andreas here, you could at least acknowledge his
willingness."

"Perhaps we haven't found the right topic for chitchat," retorted
Andreas. "Of course, the other possibility is maybe he's been beaten, feels
awful, and doesn't want to talk?"

Jayden pushed himself up to a sitting position, resisting the drum-
ming urge to vomit.

Andreas's mostly naked body leaned into his own cell bars trying to get a better look. Andreas's body glimmered in the faint light. "Didn't much think it was appropriate before with you half dead and bleeding, but I know you. Jayden Vaut, is it?"

Andreas, the guy in the Worall saloon from months ago. He'd jumped in when Clive and Broden Carter had tried to rough him up. But Andreas was a Nein, and Jayden wasn't about to let his guard down. "Why are we here? The Celje don't take prisoners."

"Fate's a sour mistress," continued Andreas. "They're questioning us about someone smuggling to the Nein. Which, of course, is true, but narrowing it down to just one person is a bit unreasonable."

"They asked me the same," Jayden replied, not seeing any reason to deny it. "I don't have a clue, but they're willing to kill for the information." Jayden paused, letting the memory of Nencia's death pass. "I was a farmer in Dalth. They picked me up in Worall while trying to help a friend, that's all."

"Isn't this sweet," scoffed Levi. "You and Andreas, two long-lost friends finally reunited. There's probably enough room between these bars for you two to hold hands."

Jayden turned, taking his first good look at Levi. The smartass mystic looked old and worn out, but Jayden imagined this prison wasn't fully responsible.

"You're a real joy to have around, in case no one's ever told you. I feel like we've met before, but I'd remember a gentleman like yourself. What's got you thinking I'm not a mystic like you?"

Levi looked him in the eye. "Unless you're just completely stupid, which my money says that you are, any other mystic would have healed himself by now. And no, we haven't met. I've been in this prison for years, so unless you've been here, escaped, and then managed to get yourself captured again, I doubt we've met. I'm also pretty damn sure I've never had the pleasure of hanging out with a nonmystic peasant farmer from Dalth."

Andreas pretended to kneel toward Levi. "Levi here thinks he's some sort of demigod mystic. An all-powerful sage who can't be defeated… most of the time."

Jayden's mind started to clear. "If you two are mystics, why haven't you escaped? Create an ice spike and prance on out?"

Levi sighed. "Real chatterbox now that he's awake. Look, everything in this prison is made of African ore, a metal combined with the asteroid particles that leveled Earth."

Jayden didn't understand how that answered his question.

Levi rolled his eyes. "You really aren't a mystic, plus it seems you've been gifted with a touch of ignorance. Asteroid dust, particles, whatever you want to call them, from Earth's Event in 2049 is like kryptonite to Superman, except it doesn't kill mystics. We can't manipulate it or anything it's combined with. And there's very little of the element left on Earth, thanks to the Reeves Corporation."

Andreas raised his chained hands. "Elasus and the rest of his spectacularly dressed cohorts hoarded it, apparently giving some of it to the Celje."

Levi began clapping. "Congratulations on such a fine answer."

"Does he have an off button?" asked Jayden.

Andreas shook his head. "Unfortunately not. Oh, but don't worry, he's way crazier than this. Just wait until he starts talking about how some Elder of old is going to sneak in here and rescue him; that's when his crazy side really comes out."

CHAPTER 32: YEAR 2401

Two weeks after Tayla found her new friend, the two women were once again in her apartment. They'd just put down their second drink, and Tayla was mixing them both a third while Irelyn shared stories of her own children.

"I've gone through the official records, but there's not much else. What Elasus has on file matches the public database. I'm only now figuring out what my husband has put you through, it's... it's indentured servitude."

Knowing that Irelyn was also looking for her daughter, Tayla tried to think of anything that might help. "The day I signed my contract, Elasus executed a man in front of me to test my loyalty. He executed him because of your daughter, but I didn't get all the details."

"From what I've seen and heard, it's clear my husband is a deranged sociopath. Elasus and Marilla's relationship was never great, but it turned worse after she got serious with Cadoc."

Bile rose in Tayla's throat. "Oh... oh no... my god, Irelyn. Cadoc, that was the prisoner... that was him. Cadoc, something. I think it started with *A*. Atl, Abi—"

"Alzer. His name was Cadoc Alzer. Elasus killed him? Was... was Marilla there?"

Three drinks, maybe even thirty, were not going to make this conversation any better. "No, I think she was already gone by that point, but I'm not sure. There were a bunch of executives in the room, but Tanner Sands actually killed him." Tayla pushed through the fog in her mind. "Elasus and Tanner claimed the man was only dating Marilla to get close to the family. I'm sorry, I feel like I'm just unloading on you. Are you okay?"

Irelyn nodded and rubbed her forehead. "I'm okay. Can you tell me, if you don't mind, why you keep sleeping with Elasus? What was in that contract?"

Tayla explained that Elasus threatened to accidentally "lose" her children if she ever violated the contract. He then paid for all her body upgrades, her outfits, and her apartment.

Suicide, or perhaps slitting Elasus's throat in the middle of the night, crossed Tayla's mind. "I never knew what to do. I've been trapped."

"Why were they exiled? What happened? And where's your husband?"

Tayla sat a bit straighter. She looked Irelyn in the eyes. "Grylo was an MFG fleet tech with the corporation. He was blamed for a malfunction that cost the corporation one of their ships. As punishment, they exiled our children. That's when I begged the corporation for mercy. It's like Elasus expected it because I met with him a short time later, and he stipulated within my contract that as long as I served him, Grylo could accompany the children to Ojult."

Irelyn cupped her mouth. "My god…"

"I found out through a fleet friend that Grylo died shortly after arriving on Ojult. I haven't heard from my children since."

Irelyn set her drink down on the table and placed a consoling hand on Tayla's leg. "I have nothing to say that can possibly forgive my husband for what he's done. Don't think you're the only one using her body to try and get her children back. You want the truth, then here we go. I'm sleeping with Prime Minister Kennedy so he'll help find Marilla."

Tayla's head fell into her hands. "We shouldn't have to do this."

Irelyn refilled their glasses. "When we're in this deep, everything has a price. I've agreed to spy on my dear husband in exchange for Kennedy helping find Marilla. Apparently my body wasn't enough."

"Irelyn… I hope I can trust you."

"Honey, you're the only person on Earth I trust right now. We're in this together, and we'll get our kids back."

Tayla nodded, not fully encouraged, but went with her gut. "I was in the corporation's cyber-defense division before being transferred to the fleet as a network administrator. If I can get full access to the dispatch and communication systems, I might be able to break in to the grid. Maybe there's some tight-beam comms between Elasus and Ojult discussing my children. If I can gain this access, I can find out about Marilla too. It's a long shot, but it's all I have."

Tayla could tell Irelyn didn't have the same confidence in her plan.

"I'm not even sure Tanner has that kind of access." Irelyn took a long drink, staring at the wall over Tayla's shoulder. "Kennedy told me he's got spies in the Reeves fleet. I wonder if he could help?"

Tayla wasn't sure how much to reveal. "I… I don't think so. I don't want anyone else knowing about this. I just need Elasus to trust me enough, give me more responsibilities, and maybe I can get access."

Irelyn raised her fifth glass. "Good or bad, it's a start. You do what you must Tayla, don't give up. I'll keep screwing Kennedy to see what I can find out. There's one more thing, something I hope you can help me with. Kennedy asked me to relay information about Elasus's dealings with FIAS. You think you could help me out there?"

Tayla didn't like the PGU any more than the Reeves Corporation, but difficult times often created unforeseen friends. Tayla raised her glass and touched Irelyn's. "To the end of Elasus, the PGU, and to finding our children."

––––––––––

Despite his age, Hewitt managed the stairs with the spring of someone half his age. He'd placed the voice-enhancement ring on the door lock and placed the wireless earpiece around his ear. Despite the technology, he struggled to hear the entire conversation, gathering only bits and pieces. He didn't get the entire plan, but these women were conspiring against the man that had given him everything. Back in his car, Hewitt dialed the first person he thought of. "Mr. Sands, good morning, sir, this is Hewitt. I'm sorry to bother you, but there's something you need to know."

CHAPTER 33: YEAR 2401

Days passed with neither of the neighboring inmates taken by the Celje interrogators. Guards brought them large bowls of mold-covered vegetables and water once a day, enough to keep them alive, barely. Andreas and Jayden conversed occasionally, but Jayden didn't fully trust him and limited the details of his past. Contrary to Andreas, Levi said nothing, not even a rebuke to Jayden's naive comment about the Amurski staff.

"Yes, that's pretty much how it works," explained Andreas. "And, mind you, I've only seen two mystics with a staff. A mystic with that tool and the inner power to command is nearly impossible to defeat."

Jayden knew one of the staff wielders. "Other than Tokerak, who else has one? Any way we might be able to contact them, help us get out of here?"

Levi suddenly came out of his muted coma. "A staff-wielder isn't some commoner with a stick. If another sage had one, every mystic would know about it."

Jayden's skeletal frame didn't have the energy to rebuke the incoming attitude. "What about mystics who aren't aligned with the Nein? Could one of them have a staff?"

"Please inform our baby brother here the reality of our situation?" said Levi.

Andreas twirled his out-of-control mustache. There was something he didn't want in the open. A secret, perhaps? "While it pains me to say this, Levi's right. Over the past decade, the Celje have come for us, Nein or otherwise. There's only a couple hundred mystics left on Ojult."

Jayden thought of the conversations he'd had with Nencia, talks where she was reluctant to confide in him everything she knew. *Nencia knew about the Celje attacks and was going to tell the corporation, that's why the Celje came after her.* Jayden's thoughts were interrupted by the opening of the main cell-block door.

"Ah, breakfast. I can only wonder what the chef cooked up for us this time," said Levi, sitting up from his bench.

Like every other morning, the guard pushed a cart full of large bowls and cups for the few dozen inmates. Today however, was much different. Instead of a heavily armed guard, a distinctive female figure walked through the glimmering lantern light.

"Who's that?" asked Jayden.

The woman worked counterclockwise around the room, unlocking cell doors, delivering breakfast, then conducting what looked like physicals on each inmate. From Jayden's vantage, the woman looked homely, with shoulder-length red hair, soft features, and glowing green eyes.

"That, my friend, is Misora's mistress," said Levi. "After he tries to kill you, that woman patches you up just enough so he can beat you some more. She gets high seeing us beaten half to death, then gets more thrills sleeping with Misora. Don't let her charm fool you, she's one of them."

Jayden looked to Andreas for confirmation. "I think he's probably right. She seems nice enough, but she's not a mystic. Just watch yourself around her."

Jayden nodded. He wasn't a mystic either, and their description of the woman's character didn't match her appearance or demeanor. Jayden watched her make her rounds until she came to Andreas's cell.

"How are you, Andreas?" she said. "All your old wounds have healed it seems. Anything hurt? All okay?" Using a digital stethoscope, she listened to his chest and back.

"I'm good enough to go a few rounds with your boyfriend," Andreas said. "That's if he doesn't tie me up and beat me to a pulp first."

The woman's demoralized expression didn't change. "Make sure you drink all the water and eat everything they give you," she continued in the same soft tone.

She locked the cell and moved on to Jayden. "I'm Eve, the prison's nurse. You're Jayden Vaut, correct?"

Jayden looked from Andreas back to Eve. She was shorter than him, with a perfectly sketched round chin and a strange aristocratic flare to her movement.

"It's okay, you don't have to answer," she said, adjusting her scope around his chest. "Do you have any allergies or conditions I need to know about? Anything your abilities might struggle to heal? Our blood analyzer stopped working so I'm relying on you to tell me."

If everything Levi and Andreas had said about this woman was true, she was one hell of an actor. Her humble expression gave way to a strikingly pristine charm. Jayden contemplated telling her that he wasn't a mystic, but if she shared a bed with Misora, the Celje leader might use that information against him somehow.

"Other than getting beaten, nearly dying, and your boss executing my girlfriend, I'm fine."

"I'm sorry for your loss. Misora, this organization, they kill without regard."

Jayden wanted nothing more than to reach out and strangle her. "Organization? You do realize this is a prison and not some corporate retreat, right?"

Eve retook his blood pressure.

Jayden said, "Where are we? What can you tell me about the prison?"

A guard at the main door shouted, "Quiet!"

Eve looked at Jayden and placed a finger to her lips. "No questions. They'll hurt you if they suspect anything."

Jayden leaned closer and whispered, "Tell your boyfriend that something worse than hell is coming for him."

Eve ignored his needling. "You're not healing like a normal mystic. Your wounds aren't infected, but you need to heal tonight. They could still fester into something worse."

"After you're done with the guards, can you visit me?" said Levi as Eve entered his cell. "Hey, don't look at me that way. I know you'll be tired, but I'll be gentle."

Eve finished the rest of her checkup and reminded them to eat up and stay hydrated.

Jayden stared at his meager meal. He swirled his cup of cloudy, green water.

"Not sure they completely purified the water this time," said Levi, swirling the liquid with a finger. "Waiter, waiter," he yelled. "I'll be writing the corporation about this."

"Still think you're going to break out of here one day?" remarked Andreas, already finished eating.

A guard opened the cell-block door, peered into the room, then left.

Levi likewise finished his meal. "As much as I enjoy our chats, yes, I'll be leaving soon enough. It's been foretold. The purpose of my life lies beyond these walls and the company of you fools."

Jayden pushed his empty bowl and mug outside his cell. "And we can't go? Not room for two more?"

Andreas rubbed his eyes. "Oh no, it's a single-seat flying wagon. Remember, he's been chosen by God to… to do *something*."

Levi reached down and checked his pulse. "The Elders will free me."

Jayden's head started to ache. "The Elders? You mean the ones who saved Earth from the Nein then bargained all mystics to Ojult?"

"The very ones," replied Levi. "I'll be recruited into their ranks."

Jayden laughed, but the movement caused his head to hurt. "I need to sit down. Any… anyone else feeling strange?"

Levi and Andreas agreed.

"Well… that's not good," slurred Andreas, slipping off his bench. "That… that beautiful, betraying… she… pois… poisoned us."

"Position yourself better on that bench, Vaut, you only got a few seconds left," said Levi.

Jayden heard Andreas slump onto the concrete floor. Then he felt the darkness overcoming him. What little part of his humanity that believed the nurse was just another victim of the Celje left him along with consciousness.

———

Jayden woke feeling hungover. He gazed around, expecting to be in Misora's torture room.

"He's gone," said Levi.

The haze overlaying Jayden's mind took a moment to process. "Who's gone?"

"Come on, graduate, look around you."

Jayden slowly propped himself up on his elbows, feeling every pulse in his aching head. He looked at Levi. "Andreas?"

Levi laughed. "He's probably dead. No reason to drug him if they're just going to interrogate him. Not sure why she knocked out everyone in the ward."

"Has she done this sort of thing before?"

Levi shrugged. "Not since I've been here. My powers repel such meager toxins."

Jayden doubted his neighbor's candor. "And you have the ability to fight off poisons, drugs?"

"Yes."

"How?"

Levi was getting frustrated. "Because I'm the most powerful mystic on this planet, and you ask too many questions."

"Good thing you're not egotistical too," said Jayden. "So, how does a demigod like yourself, with infinite abilities, get captured by a mere mortal group like the Celje?"

"She was no mere Celje. Her trap was cunning, well timed, a work of perfection."

For the first time, Jayden heard truth in Levi's voice. "You sound envious. That or maybe grief?"

"I don't expect a simpleton, a Thoba, to understand."

The ward door opened, and two guards dragged Andreas's limp body back into his cell. The guards dropped Andreas onto the floor, then secured his bonds before departing.

"Because he needed another broken bone!" Jayden yelled. "Andreas, you okay?

Other than the modest motion of Andreas's chest vacillating up and down, the mystic remained motionless.

When Jayden woke the next morning, he rubbed his eyes and found Andreas sitting up. His body looked like he'd been introduced to a meat grinder, twice. Both his eyes were swollen shut, and his bottom lip looked three times its normal size. In the dim candlelight, Jayden gaped at Andreas's chest, which had a massive dark-purple bruise. Both his wrists were heavily bandaged with scarlet blotches covering the white mesh.

Andreas twisted uncomfortably. "I don't remember much. They found out who I worked for and asked a few questions, but it's all a blur. I think... the Nein are in full rebellion against the Celje. Syrus is still alive and leading the fight. That's how I ended up here. He sent me to warn Nencia Donato about an attack. I was picked up by a Celje scout team before entering the city. They shot me with a rivea dart, and I was done."

Levi whistled from the corner. "Syrus Tokarek is a powerful Nein, perhaps more powerful than me. He's also intelligent, but he will need more to defeat the war that is coming. Perhaps he needs his banished assassin to aid him again?"

Jayden turned and looked at Levi. "I'm a farmer, nothing more."

Levi's smug smile widened. "Afraid of your past, assassin? Even within these cells, I've heard about Tokarek's butcher. Yes, I know who you are. Tell me assassin, how long has it been since Tokarek banished you?"

CHAPTER 34: YEAR 2401

The overnight downpour forged deep ruts and hazardous traveling conditions for the twelve-foot-tall Ardennes workhorse. He was eight years old, bred and born within the confines of the Appian Shipping organization. Nencia had bought the horse for breeding purposes after creating the logistics company, and now dozens of the breed helped transport supplies across each continent.

With Nencia dead and Appian in the midst of rebuilding much of its infrastructure across Capintesta, leadership fell on Zakar Qualis's shoulders. He and Nencia often spoke of a situation where she was either killed or indisposed, and she'd told Zakar what he should do in such a circumstance.

The recent rain atop the harsh winter freeze made for an uncomfortable trip, yet the visit was necessary. The morning sun did little to warm him under multiple layers of clothing. On a positive note, Zakar hadn't seen a single insect in weeks.

Behind him in the covered white canvas, Logan and Bella slept. With Nencia gone, he'd taken up the position of caretaker, which was another point Nencia cited in case of her death. Bella's aura of just another teenager abated after she killed two Celje and accepted the role of keeper over her younger brother.

Logan, on the other hand, was a thirteen-year-old boy with adventure on his mind. The loss of Nencia hit him the hardest since she was all he'd known growing up. Logan hadn't shown any mystic talents in his young life, and Zakar believed the mutation must have bypassed him.

Zakar knew nothing of their parents. Only Nencia knew of their heritage, and she'd fiercely guarded that secret. With a weighted carriage and muddy road conditions, they moved south, rarely encountering other travelers. Dalth desperately needed the food supplies he was transporting despite Mayor Fonte's strides this past year in making his town self-sustaining. Recent raids by the Celje on shipping caravans and scheduled food runs left Dalth, much like other towns, to fend for themselves.

As the carriage made the first turn into Dalth, Zakar noticed the fields Jayden Vaut had worked prior to the attack. The assault on Worall occurred months ago, and weeds were already starting to take over the untended fields. A young, tan-skinned woman with wavy brown hair and her arm in a sling stopped him in front of the pub.

"We've been waiting for you," said Serena. "Glad you made it. Any trouble?"

Zakar's body language gave nothing away. "No trouble. I have Logan and Bella with me, and we've been traveling all day. I have bandages, syringes, jashinto serum, hovrol, and other supplies smuggled away from the Celje. Let's get unloaded, then catch up."

With the help of many hands, the food allotments and other trade goods were unloaded into a supply shed.

"I've had my reasons for not allowing you and other friends into Worall," said Zakar, heading off Serena's icy glare. "It's been only in the past few days the Celje have lessened their presence in Worall and other towns."

When Serena spoke, her voice didn't match her fierce expression. "The Celje have raided us as well. It's been a mess. We've been wanting to look for… for *him*, but getting out of town has been impossible. Misora's got the roads locked down."

"Let's find the mayor and speak plainly. The situation is far worse than you think."

Zakar limped next to Serena toward the mayor's home. Smoke from the fireplace smeared the horizon as the sun sank.

Markus looked tired and stressed but managed a smile as he opened the door. "Hello, Serena… and Zakar. Please, come inside." The over-abundance of strain and lack of food was clearly taking a toll on Markus. He was frail, slow to react, and his eyes seemed to have lost hope.

Serena's impatience intruded on the men's pleasantries. "I know I sound curt, but delaying the conversation about Jayden isn't going to make it go away. What's going on?"

Zakar sat and propped his gimp leg on a chair. "I know you've been through a lot recently. The Celje have done the same thing across Listo and Capintesta. They've attacked different towns and leaders, but we don't think it's random—they've been looking for something or someone."

Markus folded his hands in his lap. "We've tried several times to make our way up to Worall but were pushed back by the Celje. Very little news has reached us, even through Wren. So, please, tell us what happened. And Jayden, where is he?"

Though Zakar had never liked Jayden, delivering this news would give him no pleasure. "I believe he's dead. I say *believe* because I'm not sure. He rescued me, Nencia, and the kids before being captured. On Nencia's orders, I escaped with the children. Shortly after, Misora showed up and executed her. He found out about the smuggling arrangement Nencia had with the Nein."

Serena fell into the couch next to Zakar.

"The recent chatter about a Nein rebellion is true, most of it is anyways," continued Zakar. "Prior to the attack, Nencia never actually chose a side. Appian was trading with both sides, seeing the Nein rebellion against the Celje as a business opportunity."

Markus looked out his window toward the open pastures. "Jayden traveled up there to find Misora. I shouldn't have let him go."

Zakar proceeded to give a full account of the attack. "My network believes Misora killed Jayden after interrogating him."

Serena's body deadened into the couch. "Jayden… dead?" Serena said. "He's… gone?"

"Nothing's confirmed, but I think I'd be giving you false hope if I said I thought he was still alive."

Markus knelt next to Serena and held her. "I'm so sorry. Jayden would have wanted to go out like that, helping his friends and fighting the Celje."

Serena looked up into Markus's eyes. "What... what have I done."

Zakar said, "I know what burdens you Serena, but now is not the time."

"Something you care to share?" asked Markus.

Zakar shook his head, encouraging Serena to keep her mouth shut.

"Markus," she said with tears trickling down her cheeks.

Zakar's austere expression did nothing to deter her.

"My parents, they... when Misora killed them, he was right. My father was dealing arms to Nencia."

Zakar of course knew all of this but thought it unwise to tell Markus of all people. Serena spent the next half hour explaining about her parents' involvement in trading arms to Appian, along with the smuggling strategy she and Nencia had devised to moonshine arms, ammunition, armor, and other supplies to the Nein. Her guilt overcame her better judgement, and she left nothing out. Zakar took particular interest in the story involving the Visconti family's original exile to Ojult. Marco Visconti evidently developed and sold prohibited armaments and weapons to the FIAS government until caught and nearly executed. Presumably PGU Prime Minister Carter was involved but never convicted.

When Serena finished, an intense silence fell upon the room. Zakar watched Markus carefully, unsure how the mayor would react to a confession whose implication put his entire town in jeopardy.

Serena's emotional rollercoaster was only just beginning. "I'm... I'm so... so sorry, Markus. I never thought it would lead to this. I was trying to do the right thing, I wanted Misora and his soras dead!"

Markus stood and went back to the living room window. He peered out toward the hidden sun. "I've known you for many years, Serena. Your parents were my friends, and with their absence, I think our bond has grown even stronger. But I'm also the mayor of this town, and it's very important that I know everything, so I'll ask only once: Is there anything else I need to know?"

"No, that's it."

Markus turned away from the window. "We've lost an ally with the death of Nencia. Serena, you knew her better than you led on, and your parents' dealings with Appian is not relevant now. With Jayden, well, Dalth lost a son." Markus paused, swallowing hard. "Serena, you're young but have experienced great loss in the past few years. I grieve for you and will pray that God heals your soul. I need to think all this over, determine who should know these details and how to avoid further conflict with the Celje. Serena, I need to speak with Zakar alone, if you don't mind."

"But… but, I've… I'm responsible for all this. I should—"

"You made a mistake that has cost you dearly. There's nothing you can do to fix it. I surely don't want to add to your suffering by belittling your error, so please, do as I ask."

Serena's words now sounded more composed. "Zakar, do the Celje suspect me?"

When Zakar sat or stood for too long, his leg stiffened. He stood awkwardly, rubbing the wound. "I believe the Celje know that arms are either coming out of Dalth or passing through it. The recent attacks on Dalth along with their border patrol support this idea." He leaned hard on his walking stick, giving some reprieve to his leg. "We all took a risk getting involved with the Nein. Nencia, along with your parents, understood this. Not that it's any comfort now, but the rebellion is making a difference. It has the Celje nervous, and Nencia and Jayden's deaths are proof of that."

Markus approached the front door and opened in, gesturing toward Serena. "I need to speak with Zakar, alone."

Serena placed a hand on Zakar's shoulder. "I know you could have sent someone else to tell us about Nencia and Jayden. Thank you."

The two men waited until Serena's narrow frame dissolved into the darkness before speaking.

Zakar's large eyes searched Markus's alarmed face. "You let her off light."

"It's a bit much to take in at once. But I assume there's more to the story?"

Zakar nodded and sat back down, admiring the old man's insightfulness. "I believe you have a spy in town. One that's well hidden and in a position to know about the town's business."

"That's a bit vague."

"When Misora tortured Nencia and me, he shared details about the smuggling operation that no one on the outside could have known. Then, a few days after the attack, Misora sent me a note, giving me *permission* to continue running Appian. In the message, he reiterated that he has eyes on me."

"He's giving you permission to continue the company, that's thoughtful," said Markus bitterly. "Still doesn't mean there's a traitor. Could Nencia or Jayden have broken under Misora's torture?"

It was a fair question and one that Zakar had considered already. "Jayden knew nothing about the operation, and Nencia didn't break. None of Appian, aside from me and Captain Green, knew anything about the deal with the Nein. I believe someone's actively working against us, and I think they're in Dalth."

"I'll heed your warning, but we should consider all our options, including Nencia breaking. Let's go back to Misora *permitting* you to keep running Appian. Seems like an odd play."

Zakar had his own ideas about Misora's long-term aim, but now wasn't the time to expose those notions. "With the caveat that I don't trade with the Nein, Misora told me to get trade back up and running. Of course, he'll probably continue raiding our lines or try to take over the company once it's back up, but for now, I'm trying to get everything in order. All my satellite offices were hit the same night Misora attacked Worall. It's a mess."

"Hardly anyone knows the Celje exist. If Misora or some other sect of the Celje took over Appian, it'd be hard to keep their little organization a secret, and I don't think they're ready to go public."

"Good point, but a lot more people know about them now."

"Is there anything I can do to help? I can keep Bella and Logan here, though we don't have many resources to offer, especially in winter."

"The kids will stay with me, at least for now. Nencia made it clear they were under her personal protection, no matter what. I say *protection* now knowing Bella can take care of herself. She's grown up a lot over the recent months." Images of the dead Celje she'd killed flashed in front of Zakar. "To be clear, I don't plan on working with the Nein anytime soon, but that's not to say never. And when that time comes, Serena won't be involved."

"Thank you," said Markus. "Are you sure working with the Nein again is a good idea?"

"Yes."

Markus folded his hands again. "Zakar, please forgive me, but this dispute between the Celje and Nein has the opportunity to spill over into our lives, into the small towns that have no interest in either sect. My family has been here for generations, and someone is always trying to take over; it never works. I won't try to talk you out of anything, but please be careful."

Markus wasn't just a mentor, he was the ultimate strategist who never gave advice without careful consideration. "You and my father were friends, I consider you a great ally now. Your words carry weight with me."

"That means a lot Zakar, thank you for saying that."

It was time to change the subject again. "Nencia had a husband—or technically had one. He's a space-transport pilot who frequently comes to Ojult. Misora destroyed our long-range communication equipment, so after I leave, I'm heading to Callahan Shores to use our backup. I think I should call him, give him the news, you agree?"

"He'll be working for the Reeves Corporation?"

Zakar nodded.

"No broadband then. Send a tight beam only. Better chance of avoiding dark eyes in the sky."

When Zakar nodded, Markus's disposition changed. "Then it's decided, you'll need to stay the night. Please, you, Bella, and Logan, sleep in Dalth. I'm sure Kun's already using some of the supplies you brought in to make dinner."

"We accept. And in exchange, I have something for you." Zakar reached into his satchel and pulled out a hazy-looking bottle with a dark-brown liquid rippling inside.

"Despite everything, you still bring gifts. Thank you."

They left Markus's home after a quick drink and headed toward the pub, one lingering question hanging over both men.

Zakar decided to ask before they reached the tavern. "I'm sorry to bring this up, but what of the funeral arrangements for Jayden? If you plan on having it soon, I can attend. I didn't like him, but the kids enjoyed his company. Bella will want to say good-bye."

"If there's no body, then there's no funeral. Jayden's a survivalist, and if Misora didn't execute him, then there's hope."

Zakar slid his boots against the bent brown grass, scraping mud from his soles. "Elders protect Misora if Jayden's still alive, because if he escapes, Misora will live just long enough to regret what he did to Nencia."

"And if he were alive, you have no idea where he's at?"

Zakar wished he'd had more to give instead of rumors and conjectures, but the information just wasn't there. He wasn't going to talk about the alleged mystic prison and shouldn't have told Syrus in retrospect. "I've given you all I have. I've sent word through Listo and Capintesta, but with Appian in disarray, getting actionable information isn't likely."

CHAPTER 35: YEAR 2401

I t's a waste of my time to remind you all that our objective on Ojult is to improve our financial footprint, not create unwarranted expenses that will undoubtedly lead to additional budgetary shortcomings."

For the past hour, the exceptionally dressed executive of the Reeves Corporation reviewed Ojult's weak quarterly results with Sasha, Misora, and Commodus via video conference. The conference camera followed Elasus as he paced the room. The generally mild-mannered executive tore into his audience when a woman's voice came over the speaker.

Elasus cleared his throat. "Gentleman, this call is private."

He wasn't surprised when Sasha's pompous voice came back. "A companion of mine, Mr. Reeves, nothing to be concerned with. She has no secrets to share nor friends to share them with. She is here at my invitation."

"You must be hanging out in the thin-air regions of Meridone!" shouted Commodus. "Get that damn woman out of the conference, Sasha!"

Commodus was still on Chden, overseeing their economic-development strategy.

Background audio picked up Sasha asking for the woman to leave the room.

"Focus, gentlemen," Elasus ordered. "The volume of exiles entering Ojult is steady, but imports are down. Microeconomic data indicates consumption has dipped but not enough to explain these financials. On top of these financial statements, Sasha, the number of reported Celje deaths is up significantly. I need an explanation."

"The Nein are attacking us from everywhere," blurted Misora. "They've attacked our supply lines, assaulted our people, and they're going after the Thoba. They've gone crazy!"

Elasus hated the tone in Misora's voice but accepted the man's presence since he usually produced results. "I hear excuses. Sasha?"

Sasha sipped some sort of clear liquid from a glass, then puffed upon a hettle stalk. Smoke blinded the camera, but his voice came over clear. "He is correct. Circumstances on Ojult are volatile and fluid, changing daily. Our lives are at risk even now, as I speak to you in your comfortable office."

"You got jashinto in that hettle stalk," hollered Commodus. "I sure hope that's the reason you've gone stupid all of a sudden. Cut the crap, and tell us what's going on."

Misora cut across Sasha again, and this time the leader's demeanor showed frustration. "Look, we know the money isn't flowing like it used to, but that's on Appian, they just haven't shipped much recently."

The smoke cleared from Sasha's screen, and he spoke with unusual placidity. "Nencia Donato is dead, and we are seeing the repercussions."

Elasus knew Sasha as a strategic man, perhaps cocky, but never one to exaggerate. "Nencia Donato is dead?"

Sasha took another long drag, this time having the courtesy to vent away from the camera. "The Nein attacked Worall a few months ago. My spies believe they went after Nencia because of her commitment to you and the Celje. Terrible tragedy."

Commodus's whole head filled the screen now. "So this happened a few months ago and you're just now telling us!?"

"Like I said, things are not easy on Ojult right now. We are constantly fighting with the Nein, and news like this takes time to verify. The Nein, like I have stated before in these lovely meetings, have been raiding shipments for some time." Sasha licked his stinging lips after another sip from his near empty glass. "I've requested additional resources to help combat this but have only recently been granted such assets."

Elasus was skeptical. "So… Nencia, who commands a sizable militia, perhaps the same size as your own, decided to suddenly cut ties with the Nein, then the Nein leadership declared war on Appian because of a trade deficit?"

Elasus and Sasha locked eyes, playing a mental game of chess.

"Strange, yes?" replied Sasha. "And yet that is the current state of your planet. If given more resources, we might—"

"Resources for what, a war?" Commodus said. "You planning on assaulting the Nein in a blaze of glory? You realize that preventing war is the plan, right? Fighting is bad for business, and starting one is a really bad way to prevent one."

Sasha's hettle stalk was nearly consumed, as was his drink. "Tensions are high, and people are nervous. Attacks on both the Celje and Thoba are more frequent. To protect your investment, Mr. Reeves, I need more resources."

"Mr. Reeves," interrupted Misora. "About the financials, listen. I spoke with Nencia's second-in-command a few days ago. My people are helping him get Appian rebuilt, plus I've put additional guards on all major supply routes on Capintesta."

"Well, at least you did something right," chided Commodus. "There's, what, a couple hundred mystics on Ojult? And at last count, a couple thousand Celje? You guys are still having problems with them?"

Sasha leaned in closer to the camera. "A thousand Celje? No, my good man, no. My people number less than five hundred. Most of those are not actual agents but exiles hired as spies. There are nearly fifty thousand non-mystic exiles on Ojult, and perhaps two hundred mystics. The problem is the Nein leader has a staff."

"A problem you've been failing to resolve for some time now," Elasus said.

One of Sasha's primary assignments stated that he and his agents were to prevent, at all costs, any mystic obtaining an Amurski staff.

"My team captured the Nein's leader on Capintesta," added Misora. "He had a staff as well, and we destroyed it. But Listo, it's a different theater."

Elasus ignored the statement, his mind working quickly to cipher through the different outcomes this might bring upon the corporation. "The presence of a second staff on Ojult is concerning but not knew. It explains your defeats and my financial losses, but I'm not hearing solutions."

Sasha diverted from answering the question. "The staff-wielding Nein leader attempted to assassinate me only weeks ago. I barely escaped. All of which underlines the importance of my request for more agents."

"With that staff hanging around, nothing will get better," said Commodus. "Looking at the odds, it's not good."

"Listen to me, all of you," said Elasus. "Misora, Sasha, reduce your presence in the streets, specifically in Worall. You've become too visible. Get back into the shadows, observe the actions of the Nein, particularly their leader. Identify his plan, whether it pertains only to eliminating you and the Celje or something more inconspicuous. Am I clear?"

Misora spoke first. "Yes, Mr. Reeves."

"Of course, Elasus," said Sasha.

The monitors showing Sasha and Misora went black as soon as Elasus terminated the connection.

"Thoughts on the meeting, Commodus?" asked Elasus.

Commodus sat back down in his chair with a sigh. "That call revealed a lot. Biggest concern for me is the loss of Nencia. For the Nein to go after her seems audacious."

Elasus caught the hesitancy in the COO's tone. "You don't believe it either, I assume?

"No. Something in his tone, his demeanor, it's not adding up. And since when did he ever call you by your first name?"

"Sasha misrepresented the Celje numbers as well. Ruven sends me weekly reports on recruiting, training, and deployments."

Commodus's eyes widened. "Sasha even admitted to hiring some of the locals. You think there's a power play going on?"

"Speculation on the matter gets us nowhere, but keep the premise of this conversation fresh. You're with Captain Donato, correct?"

"Yes, ship's fixed minus a few minor repairs. Ship sank about ten feet, broke three gear shafts and tore up the underside."

Elasus made a mental note to have the Chden mapping geographer exiled for not reporting on the poor soil conditions at the primary landing field. "I want Donato to chaperone you to Ojult. Nencia was conniving but produced the monetary results I needed. Give the captain the opportunity to say goodbye to his wife."

Commodus said, "I'm sensing a *but* coming."

Elasus nodded. "Head to Lent first and pick up another Celje team. I'll call Ruven and have him make the arrangements."

Elasus felt confident that his son, planetary resource governor on Lent and commander of the Celje training post, would provide the most competent agents for the job.

"You're thinking something is about to happen on Ojult?"

Elasus grabbed a stylus and wrote a note to call his son tomorrow afternoon. "Running a business based on incomplete information or incompetent midlevel managers is a poor way to reward our shareholders. I want you there to identify what we're not being told."

"Understood. We'll get off the ground as soon as possible. Anything else?" asked Commodus, reaching for the termination switch.

"Keep your travels discrete. The situation on Ojult may be more than just a temporary escalation between the Nein and Celje. If Sasha's putting together a power grab, then you will need to resolve the dispute."

Elasus ended the conference call and sat back. He looked around his office, peering at the portraits of his ancestors, many of whom also ran the Reeves Corporation. Something in his gut told him to stay alert, like a shadow of uncertainty creeping into whatever plight was afoot.

The office door opened, exposing Tayla Cruz, who walked into the room. She wore a short, sleeveless, low-cut dark-blue dress that contoured to her body with each stalking step.

"I noticed you were off the call, Mr. Reeves. May I get you a drink?" she asked, already heading toward the bar.

"Yes, please."

She stooped to reach the crystal glasses, forcing her hindquarters to shift in the tight dress. The visual landscape took his mind off Ojult and the real possibility of civil war. Of course, there was another problem. He'd charged Nencia with other responsibilities, not just running Appian. He'd need to address that problem at some point.

"Here you go," Tayla said, handing him his usual bourbon on the rocks.

She placed her own drink on the desk, then inched up her dress to comfortably sit on his lap. It was four thirty in the afternoon and Elasus didn't mind the sudden switch.

"You seem tense. Everything okay?"

Elasus waited for the burn trickling down his throat to fade before

speaking. "The updated report you put together illustrated declining revenues coming out of Ojult. I'd hoped it was a lull in the normal business
cycle, but something more complex is brewing."

Tayla adjusted herself so she sat directly on his groin. "Guess I should
make room in your schedule for the prime minister?"

"Perhaps. For tomorrow. I want a full communications log on Sasha
and Misora on my desk. Go back twenty-four months. Have Commodus give you full access to the communications and security grid. I don't
want anyone else knowing about this, so do it independently. If I'm correct, they'll have tried to hide some of their discussions, so be thorough.
Do not assume Sasha's eyes do not reach back to this office. I'll be heading
home early today, so use the rest of the afternoon to work on this."

"Is everything okay on Ojult? Are my children in danger?"

He never allowed contact between Tayla and her children, allowing
only periodic updates on their well-being. Naturally the assignment he'd
just given her would arouse her anxiety. "No danger, but the economic
situation is deteriorating, and my spies on Ojult suggest a different story
than the one I was just told."

His cool demeanor put her at ease, and her IT background should
make simple work of the assignment. "I'll start on it immediately," she
replied.

Elasus finished the bourbon and pulled Tayla back on his lap. "No
need to rush off so quickly, Ms. Cruz."

Garvin Donato lay in bed, his sheets scattered on the floor. The night's
activities were coming to an end as he stroked the olive-skinned back of
his navigation officer.

"At some point I'm going to have to get up, Captain," said Alanah,
brushing back her black-and-pink hair.

"You said that three (cough) hours ago. Admit it, you can't get enough
of my piloting skills."

"If you weren't my boss and—"

"Romance aficionado."

"Yeah, whatever. Just remember that I use you for sex, just like

Chelsie and Caitlin, but at least with me you have something to brag about."

"Excuse me, but I only employ the most attractive and physically fit officers on the *Night Scope*. It's blasphemy to say anything to the contrary. It's even written in the ship's hiring manual." Donato actually *had* written that in the procedure manual, unbeknownst to the Reeves Corporation.

A yellow light flashed on his nightstand. "I need to grab this, it's probably my… next appointment." Over the phone, he listened carefully to his communications officer, Caitlin Smith. Halfway through the conversation, Donato started dressing, much to the dismay of his current companion. "Okay, thanks, Smith. Have him escorted to my office. I'll meet him there in fifteen minutes. Wake up the senior officers and have them on the bridge within the hour. If he's waking me up this early, then something's up. Oh, and don't bother calling Kass, she's with me."

A pillow glanced off his head and hit two empty glasses. "You're such a dick."

Donato hung up and turned to her. "That was Caitlin. She said you're taking too long with me. Sorry, but you need to leave."

"Could you be any more arrogant?"

Thirty minutes later, Captain Donato walked through the bridge, tapping each person on the shoulder as he passed. The crew was tired, and he felt certain something big was about to come down. He didn't have time to shower but wore a clean, pressed shirt, pants, and polished boots. When Donato opened his office door, Commodus was already sitting on the couch with a heavy expression.

Donato decided to play the easy, cool captain, and wait for Commodus to drop the shitty news that undoubtedly awaited him. "Good morning. Did Caitlin set you up with some breakfast or coffee?"

"She did, thanks."

Donato noticed his friend's subdued tone. "Ship repairs are almost done. Don't worry, the corporation will still have money left over after the repair bill."

"Garvin, take a seat. I've got something to tell you."

For the next hour, Commodus explained the situation. His coffee rested on his knee, untouched during the entire conversation. "It's mostly internal financial relocation that will impact your fee schedule, but it's probably temporary. No, no, sit down for a moment Garvin, I'm not done and this is the part that sucks. During the Nein raid on Worall, it seems they targeted Nencia. They found her and, I'm sorry to be the one to tell you this, but she died during the fight."

"The Nein killed her!?"

"I've investigated and confirmed it. I'm sorry, Garvin. The details are weird, I know, but that's all we've got right now."

Donato expected Commodus to bring bad news, like taking away a future contract on some big shipment to Lent. "Why would the Nein go after Nencia? They probably had the most to lose from her death."

Commodus walked over to the captain's bar and poured scotch into his lukewarm coffee. "Elasus agrees that something's off, and that's why he wants us, and he specifically asked for you and your ship, to head to Ojult and investigate."

Donato hid his face in his palms. "What the hell were the Celje doing during all this? Aren't they supposed to prevent this from happening?"

Commodus downed his fiery morning pick-me-up then poured straight scotch into the cup. "We don't think we have all the information, that's why we need the *Night Scope* ready. You said repairs are almost done? Is she ready to fly?"

Garvin lumbered to his office desk-panel and depressed a white button. "FO, what's the status on repairs this morning?"

A moment later, Chelsie came back. "Captain, they've dug trenches around the gears and we still need to inspect all the new struts, gears, and new retractor arms. Probably take a few days."

Commodus motioned toward him. "I also need you to pick up a few passengers on Lent, maybe thirty or forty. We need to be on Ojult in the next few weeks."

Donato made a few notes then did some quick mental math. "The safety of you and my crew come first, you know that. We can complete the inspections, pick up your friends, and get to Ojult within your time-frame and still not risk the ship." It was Donato's ship and his decision, and he didn't need Commodus's approval. He reached over and dialed for his FO. "Chelsie, we need to be airborne in seven days."

Donato gripped the ends of the desk, letting his chin fall to his chest.

Commodus placed a hand on his shoulder. "I'm sorry. I'll leave you alone. Call me at the Chden station when the ship's ready."

Garvin heard Commodus exit, then another set of boots enter.

"Captain," said Chelsie. "You... okay?"

Donato turned around, displaying his wet, flushed face. "Is Commodus gone?"

"He just walked off the bridge. I can come back..."

Donato wiped his eyes and smiled. "I'm fine. Just had to act surprised in front of Commodus. He came to tell me about Nencia."

Chelsie shook her head. "You're one hell of an actor. I thought someone else had died."

"Nah, we're good. Don't get me wrong, Nencia was a good person and utter perfection in the sack, but even our priest gave up on her. But she was mine, imperfections, and all. Someone's going to pay."

"Wonder who finally told Commodus?"

Donato shrugged. "Who knows? Zakar said I was the first one he called, and I doubt he'd lift a finger to help anyone with the Reeves Company now."

Chelsie fell behind him and rubbed his shoulders. "Do I need to start reconnoitering cannons for the ship?"

Donato turned around and leaned back into his desk. "Damn, I love it when you talk dirty." He got the eye roll he'd seen a hundred times before. "I think Sasha and his band of professional lunatics took out Nencia. If that's the case, then Elasus was part of it too."

"I've always thought the Celje were a bad lot, so you know where I stand on all this."

"Thanks, Chelsie, that means a lot." The solidarity that had formed between him and his crew was unbreakable. They had each other's backs, and nothing could break that. "The chief wants us to pick up some *passengers* on Lent before heading to Ojult, probably more Celje."

Chelsie leaned in as if to kiss him, then started fixing one of his lopsided collars and straightened his jacket. "Maybe the Nein are finally giving the Celje what they deserve?"

"According to Zakar, the Celje, not the Nein, attacked Worall. So, either Elasus is with Sasha, or Sasha's conning everyone. Either way, I'm done with the corporation. From this point forward, we do what's best for us."

CHAPTER 36: YEAR 2401

Syrus Tokarek paced the auditorium inside the town hall of Caren-dra, the small building now the headquarters for the Nein rebellion. A heavy black sarcto pelt fell over his shoulders, keeping his body warm as winter swept through the continent.

Syrus stood near one of four fireplaces, the smell of smoke and incense offering euphoric vibes through his tranquil body. Until evidence suggested otherwise, Syrus chose to believe Andreas was still alive, which kept his demeanor calm and methodical.

Earlier in the day, Turr, a trusted and formidable sage, passed along a message indicating Captain Siller would return by late afternoon. Since receiving the message, Syrus had not left the hall.

"May I get you something to drink or eat?" asked a servant girl.

Syrus ignored the young woman's chattering teeth. "Quiet," he ordered.

The door to the main chamber opened, and Captain Siller entered, Phaedra following close behind. Siller was a formidable warrior, but he looked tired and rugged from his recent journey. He'd adorned himself with his usual dark-maroon two-piece armor ensemble with a fur neck guard and black boots. Phaedra, on the other hand, looked nearly frozen, wrapped like a mummy in cold-weather gear.

The troop commander bowed, and Phaedra went to the nearest fireplace.

"What news?" asked Syrus, his temper already flaring.

"We investigated the last site to the west of Rindo, but the grounds

305

were abandoned, except for a few hunters. We interrogated the hunters but found nothing useful. This was our last lead." Siller's eyes darted around, avoiding eye contact.

Syrus sat back in his chair and conjured a black sphere of erratic energy in his open, chafed palm. "Jayden, Helia, Andreas… how many more will we lose before ending this?" Syrus had failed to protect those counting on him, and the burden was weighing on him.

Phaedra stood next to the fireplace, thawing her numb limbs. "We're backing the Celje into a corner. When they start to feel desperate, that's when we'll lose the most. *Daska*, you can't save everyone."

"During our excursion," continued Siller, "we came across many who were sympathetic to our cause. While most were Thoba and useless, some were mystics. We've bolstered our numbers by almost a dozen. Your war against the Celje is gaining support and notice."

"Definitely wouldn't have mentioned that," whispered Phaedra, her back still turned.

Syrus's calming orb vanished along with any patience he had left. "Our current objective is to find Andreas; I thought I made that clear! Running into a few children who show magic tricks to their friends isn't worth our attention. If you can't accomplish the tasks I've set before you, then I'll find someone who can. Clear?"

"Yes, Premier, very clear. May I add one more piece to my report?"

Phaedra shook her head. "Yes, keep digging that into that hole."

Syrus waved his hand.

"Your name has spread throughout Listo and Capintesta. The people of both factions, mystics and Thoba, are calling you the king of Ojult."

"King?" questioned Syrus. "Titles, wealth, power… we fight for the survival of our kind, not a commoner's dreamworld."

Phaedra pulled herself away from the fire. "*Daska*, it's you who are trying to free us from the Celje. If the people, especially the Thoba, want you as their king, why not?"

Syrus stood. "Titles and riches are for the masses, not the Nein. Finding Andreas and defeating our enemy is the priority. To move forward, you both must understand this. Now listen, for we are shifting our plan against Sasha."

Phaedra shook her head. "Shifting? We need action not more idle scouting parades. Send Kavil against the Celje, put us on the offensive. He's been wasted as a search hound, and it's time to regroup. Release him, let him do his job, and have me take over the search."

Syrus raised his hand and created another black sphere, shooting the globe of energy toward Phaedra. The sphere stuck to her torso and surged electric shocks into her body. While his pupil fought the electrocution, Syrus cast another orb at Siller, who took the orb in the neck.

"You both speak to me like I'm your companion. As if we're merely friends contemplating our next gathering." Syrus walked up to Siller, whose teeth vibrated with each electrical charge ripping through his stupefied body. "I do not seek your counsel on the plan I've constructed. Learn your place or suffer."

Syrus ripped the spheres from their targets with a jerk of his hand. The spheres returned, orbiting his extended hand. Siller and Phaedra were on the floor, convulsing with fading spasms.

Syrus maintained a savage expression as he walked toward her. Phaedra expected another attack and attempted conjuring a shield with a twitching hand. Syrus's arcane-infused fist blasted the shimmering shield into nothingness.

Syrus clasped her by the throat and lifted her. Phaedra's smoke encircled eyes closed, refusing to give him the pleasure of victory.

"You'll learn your place, my pupil. Your position is behind me, not beside or in front. Do you understand?" His voice was losing its previous venom.

Phaedra remained still, but her wild eyes showed she understood.

Satisfied she'd learned her lesson, yellow and blue energies flowed from his hand into Phaedra's disabled body. Syrus released her, and Phaedra absorbed the healing energies.

Syrus turned and retreated to his pew. "Both of you, come, stand before me." Siller and Phaedra lumbered to the head of their master's seat. "Phaedra, you're my apprentice, and the Celje know this. If you were to take up the search for Andreas, you'd do it alone. Captain Siller needs every warrior if he's to carry the fight to our enemy."

Phaedra rubbed her throat. "I wouldn't have suggested it if I didn't understand the risks."

"Your attitude says otherwise. The Celje know I carry a staff and surely have spies following me. This means they know who you are. Captain Siller, please inform my underling what the Celje will do to her if she's caught."

Siller slumped despite his efforts. "Once your body is used to their satisfaction, the interrogations will begin. The Celje are masters of torture, invoking pain beyond imagination. They've been known to peel skin off mystics while they scream for mercy. After you give them what they want, because you will break, eventually, Sasha will likely remove your limbs, one by one, while you're conscious, and send them to known Nein strongholds."

Phaedra, unphased by the speech, said, "This *is* a good plan."

Was he sending Phaedra to her death like he'd done to so many others? Was she going to be another Andreas, never to be seen again? "Kavil, proceed with the offensive against the Celje. Take a few days, gather the men and supplies. Don't go haphazardly. Phaedra, continue the search for Andreas. If successful, we might find more of our brothers and sisters."

Phaedra's alluring eyes narrowed. "I will not fail."

Syrus stepped closer to his pupil. "I'm giving you liberty to find Andreas using whatever means you think necessary. Don't make me regret this. You're worth far more to the Celje alive than to me dead. Mind this if you're captured. Now, go."

––––––––––

Phaedra set off the next morning, hitching a ride from a passing farmer. She wore plain clothing, impersonating a wanderer. She tucked her hair up into her inconspicuous hat and pulled the brim low over her brow.

Whipping winds from the east brought bitter temperatures throughout the six-hour trip to Port Naok. She boarded a large sailship and soon bathed in relief as she set foot on solid ground, but her abatement lasted only a short while as she began to scrutinize the Rindo harbor. Hundreds of people occupied the port making it difficult to spot Celje spies.

She walked alongside other passengers, counting at least two groups of Celje as she headed for the main gates. Dense wooden security fences surrounded the port, giving way to only one main entry point into the city. She walked toward the access portal, feeling the spying eyes of Celje agents.

She recognized an Appian supply wagon and walked up to the driver. "You heading to Worall?"

Six hours later, with a stiff back and no sleep, Phaedra reached her destination.

"Welcome to Worall," said a clerk standing outside his shop. "Your boots look worn. The town may look a little beat up but our wares aren't. Come inside!"

Phaedra flashed the salesman a faux smile and continued down the main road. More than half the buildings were either crumbling or showed signs of recent fires, no doubt the result of Sasha's handiwork. She continued walking south until finding the third warehouse on the left, a large unpainted building bustling with activity. It didn't take long for her to find her contact.

"The rumors are true then," Phaedra said, sneaking up behind Zakar.

Zakar pivoted on his cane and smiled. "Phaedra Lillea, left yesterday from Carendra, almost drowned crossing the Altum Sea, then almost got snagged by the Celje in Rindo. No, pupil of Syrus Tokarek, I am not surprised to see you."

"Nothing wrong with your spy operation," she retorted. If her disguise wasn't fooling the Appian's spies, then the Celje were sure to have spotted her. "Maybe you should point those spies toward finding Andreas Palada?"

Zakar ignored the sarcasm. "Did you come all this way to give me guidance on my own business?"

"Of course not. Syrus sent me here to find Andreas. Do you still have Celje on your payroll?"

The ends of Zakar's mouth lifted in a caustic grin. "How do you think you got out of Rindo?"

"You've taken to your new role quickly. Child labor, though, seems a bit underneath you," said Phaedra, pointing toward an orphanage down the road.

"Youth and inexperience, not a good combination if you want to live to grow old on this planet. The people I lead, Logan and Bella specifically, are important to my operation. But I am done trading insults with you, speak your mind or leave."

Phaedra gave the situation a second thought and calmed herself. "I let my mouth get the better of me sometimes; Syrus calls me a work in progress. I was hoping with Appian's network back under your control, maybe you've heard something about Andreas's location?"

Zakar remained silent, perhaps gauging her sincerity. "Come. Let me show you our progress."

Phaedra followed Zakar through the maze of boxes filling the warehouse. She noticed a complex set of lines and pulley systems attached to large horses that helped lift heavy crates, one atop the other. Conversely, rats were everywhere, scurrying away from the frequent foot traffic of warehouse workers.

"Inside my office, please," gestured Zakar, allowing her to enter first.

Zakar opened a small vent in the side wall of the office, letting in a refreshing blast of cool air. The office housed a wooden desk and two chairs, a bookcase full of multi-era literature, along with bunk beds in the corner. However, most intriguing was a metal cabinet behind Zakar's office chair.

"Interesting room. Mind explaining why we're here?"

"Home and office decor was never my strong side, and neither, I'm afraid, was it Nencia's. I would like to show you this." The Appian leader Zakar opened the metal cabinet behind the desk and retrieved a small box with two antennas sticking out. "You asked earlier if we had everything up and running. This is a big piece of that puzzle."

Phaedra scanned the device. "Am I supposed to know what this is?"

"It's what Nencia used to contact the Reeves Corporation and, more recently, what I used to contact her widowed husband."

"She was married?"

Zakar shrugged. "Technically yes, though they had not been on good terms for many years. She had relations with other men, but that's not the reason I'm showing you this." Zakar closed and locked the cabinet. "The organization Nencia built relied less on technology and more on information coming from human capital. And of those people, not all of them are here on Ojult."

Phaedra picked up on the innuendo. "You have spies inside the Reeves Corporation?"

"As you said earlier, *a work in progress.*"

"Okay, so you *can't* chat with Earth, that's great. How does this help find Andreas?"

"It doesn't, directly. If Andreas and other mystics are alive and being kept somewhere, someone out there will be chatting about it. This device listens to those communications."

Phaedra's patience was wearing thin. "I'm guessing the Reeves people and Sasha aren't talking about imprisoned Nein."

Zakar shook his head and stepped closer. "It's not what they are speaking about that concerns me. What concerns me and should be interesting to you is that they're not speaking at all."

Phaedra grasped the problem. "You're saying Sasha and Reeves are not getting along?"

"Precisely."

Phaedra felt no closer to finding answers.

Zakar said, "We'll continue to listen for information, but pledging additional resources isn't possible. I must focus on the company."

"Great. So you've got nothing on Andreas. My trip here was a waste."

She'd been certain that Zakar was going to lead her to Andreas. A foolish notion to believe Siller hadn't already contacted the biggest spy on the planet. A knock on the office door interrupted them, and an older man with gray hair and a handlebar mustache entered.

"Sorry, but received this message, thought you should see it."

Zakar accepted the paper. "Thank you, Aldrich. Stay for a moment."

While Zakar read the letter, Aldrich addressed Phaedra. "Name's Aldrich, I run the warehouse here."

"Phaedra," she replied. "A simple warehouse hand who passes secret notes to the new mafia boss?"

Aldrich looked taken aback by the sassy response. "I also discipline little girls who don't respect their elders and their place."

"Touch me, and it'll be the last thing you ever do."

"Hmm," uttered Zakar, drawing Phaedra's attention back to the letter. "Phaedra, there is a large contingent of Celje now encamped outside the city."

Phaedra thought about Siller's stern and gruesome warning as she headed for the door. "I need to get back to Carendra if there's nothing here that will lead me to Andreas."

Aldrich said, "It's nearly dusk, and a young pretty woman, despite her attempts to blend in, will attract a lot of attention traveling at night, never mind that you're a mystic. If the Celje come upon you, even by accident, it's not going to end well."

"He's right," said Zakar, setting down the letter. "I doubt the Celje know you're here, this is likely just a coincidence. I can put you up in a safe house in town."

Phaedra again thought about Syrus's warning and the risks. "Okay, then. I'll leave at first light."

She followed Aldrich to a large three-story saloon called Beer, Beds, and Bras. The inn was adjacent to the stores she'd walked by on her way into town. Inside, a haze of hettle smoke coasted above the patrons. Dozens of people littered the saloon, mostly drinking, smoking, and playing cards. An older man played an out-of-tune piano in the corner. Scantily dressed women loomed over young men, hoping to draw in business.

Two deep voices from the other side of the room supplanted the background noise as two men stood from a card table, pointing pistols at one another. Phaedra suppressed her instinct to join the fight and followed Aldrich away from the fray.

Aldrich said, "Don't worry about them, ole Sam, the bartender there, he'll take care of them in a few minutes. Worall is the frontier for new exiles and it's dangerous, but at least not like Meridone. Wait by the staircase, I'll go get your key."

Although the crowd seemed preoccupied with their own vices, Phaedra assumed all customers were heavily armed. Standing in a crowded saloon possibly infested with Celje agents was not her idea of staying incognito. She still wore her hat and coat, her long silver hair hidden. She remained vigilant, avoiding eye contact with nearby patrons.

A man of about thirty walked down the staircase, accompanied by a woman many years older than Phaedra. The male was attractive and well dressed, probably a freighter pilot or bridge officer from one of the docked spaceships. He was good-looking, but the older woman attached to him was gorgeous. Her bronzed skin gave her a Persian semblance. She glided down the stairs artistically, her arm curving around the man for support. The woman flashed a well-practiced smile to the crowd now eyeing her with reverence.

"You're one of a kind, Lacy," the young man said into the escort's ear.

Lacy smiled. "Yes, I am, and so are my girls. Come back next time you're in town, and bring your crew."

As they passed, Phaedra noticed the woman's long sleeveless red dress was made of real silk, an extremely rare material on Ojult.

"Phaedra," came Aldrich's voice from behind. "You'll be on the third floor, last room on the right. It's a suite if you can imagine such a thing on this planet. It's quiet, long as the transport ships stay away. You need anything?" Aldrich handed her the key to the room.

She appraised the old man, wondering if she could seduce him like the whores that worked the bar. "No, I can find my own way from here." Finding no reason to stick around the bar, Phaedra headed upstairs. As she passed the second floor, the unmistakable noises of prostitutes performing their craft echoed through the stairwell.

The third floor was strangely quiet. Her room was decorated artfully, unlike anything she'd ever seen. Small, scented candles lit the room, and the single window faced the Worall landing pad. A bathtub in the corner, near the window, sat empty with minimal grime. Adjacent to the porcelain tub sat an actual toilet and fully stocked bar. On the opposite side of the room was a large bed with blankets, comforter, and, to Phaedra's great surprise, another woman.

"My name's Bella, and I know why you're here. I think we should work together." Bella's voice was soft but guarded. She wore plain clothes, and her curly hair hadn't seen a brush for some time.

Phaedra meandered around the room, checking to see if anyone else lurked. "A little presumptuous."

Bella slid off the bed and into the candlelight. Her clothes were stained, and the teenager was in desperate need of a bath. "You want to find your friend?"

"I have lots of friends. Don't know what you're talking about."

Bella's expression remained void of emotion. "I'm not prying, but

I think I can help if you don't mind doing things that are sometimes frowned upon."

Phaedra took off her hat and coat, tossing them on a nearby chair. She shook out her sweaty, silver hair. "People frown on most things I do. How do you know me and what'd you have in mind?"

Bella stepped over to the wet bar and poured what looked like scotch into two glasses. "I need your word that what we discuss stays between us. Zakar can't know."

Intrigued by the forwardness of the girl, Phaedra accepted the drink and raised it in salute. "I'm already starting to like you, Bella, now convince me you're right."

CHAPTER 37: YEAR 2401

Tayla—dry, red lips a few centimeters apart—sat gaping at the message on her screen. For over a decade, she'd been working toward the goal that now rested effortlessly upon her screen. Full security and communications access across the corporation, excluding only those permissions involving the most senior executives. For now, her assignment demanded that she use these new capabilities to find communications to or from Sasha Burmistrov.

Logging on with her normal credentials, the home screen produced several new subject lines to choose from. Her background in the cyber-defense division of the corporation gave her advanced knowledge of the system, but on a fraction of the scale she now inherited. There were few satellites in orbit above Ojult thanks to the dense asteroid field surrounding the planet.

Urged on by her new capacities, Tayla worked through the night, rummaging through return files illustrating conversations concerning the Celje leader. By the end of the second day, it was obvious to the cyber aficionado that Sasha had not used satellite communication methods to conduct his unofficial business.

Three more days of near nonstop work, ciphering through tight-beam communications and short-wave radio interceptions picked up by fleet ships, all produced nothing. If Sasha was working against Elasus, he was doing a thorough job masking his transmissions.

"Tanner produced the same results," Elasus said, reviewing her report.

"Yes, I had you both working on the same project. Your background in cyber defense along with his security experience would have produced results if there was something to find. It does not mean Sasha is innocent, only that he's not using modern means to comunicate."

The news of Elasus utilizing two of his most well-resourced assets to accomplish the same objective didn't surprise Tayla. What interested Tayla was that Elasus didn't tell her and perchance never informed Tanner either. What did this mean? She used an untraceable defense portal to burrow through the network, so there was no way Tanner would know what she'd seen.

"My research into the project turned up almost no communication from Sasha off planet. I collated this against previous years and the trend is significant. He's avoiding generally used communication methods."

Elasus zoomed in on one paragraph in her report. "This suggests you found something off one of our fleet ships not related to Sasha?"

Tayla stood up and leaned over the desk, allowing her shirt to fall open. She tapped her 3DI watch and produced a small holo-image of a firewall and network model. The image flickered into focus above his desk.

"I'm sure Mr. Sands has already informed you of this, but during my analysis, I found a gateway transmission adjoining a tight-beam message back to Earth."

Elasus's eyes surfed up from her neck line. "You found a cloaked message hiding within a normal one? Was it from Ojult?"

As much as Tayla loathed him, she was surprised Elasus knew what she meant. "The channel came from a ship, a fleet ship for sure, but it's impossible to tell. The buried line jumped from one message to another, so it's difficult to even fathom where it originated. The only thing I can tell you for sure was that it came from one of our ships and ended up on Earth."

For all Tayla's hard work and findings, Elasus rewarded her by allowing her to spend the night with him. Her assignment was complete and yet Elasus hadn't rescinded her credentials; the plan was working.

The next morning started off like any other workday after she'd spent the night with him. She strutted around in her towel, composed herself with the most expensive makeup, then with sublime grace, pulled on a fitted, sleeveless maroon dress. It was critical that Elasus believe this day was as routine as any other.

An impromptu surveying trip of northern Michigan came up, and he wanted his schedule cleared for the next three days. She wouldn't get the days off but he didn't ask her to accompany him. Perfect.

Elasus left shortly after lunch, and Tayla embarked on her long-awaited crusade. Using the same network ciphering tool she'd used as before, Tayla manipulated the watchword to match that of her husband and two children. The result was instantaneous. Grylo Cruz, Gabrielle Cruz, and Aaron Cruz, all came up as exiled in 2388. The return values were listed by date, oldest to newest. Tayla tapped on the first file.

File Corrupted, unable to retrieve.

Used to incompetent database managers screwing up their own archives, Tayla tapped the next line.

File Corrupted, unable to retrieve.

She went through the entire first page of returns, each the same as the next. Experience told her even the most inept database managers couldn't have fragmented every file with her family's profiles on them; something else was at work. Without thinking, Tayla ran a subquery on the original returns, looking for similarities in their structure. This time, the search took almost half an hour to yield results, but it was worth the wait.

Each of the files were accessed on the same date, almost eight years ago, by the same analyst.

Tayla swiped over to the security software and searched for Marquise Babbage, the analyst who'd taken an interest in her family. Whether grocery shopping, watching the net, or walking into a corner market to take a leak, a FOCC always sent your location to the PGU. By law, the PGU was supposed to delete the information after twenty-fours, which of course they did. Naturally, the Reeves Corporation purchased the information from crooked slicers working for the PGU, then stored it on their own secure server.

Tayla pinged Babbage's last known location and the result didn't surprise her a bit. He'd just entered the Dark Souls Lounge six blocks away from the Reeves building. The lounge was not for the faint of heart, nor was it for someone dressed in a short skirt with half her chest falling out.

Black sweatpants and shirt, disheveled hair, no makeup, and too much perfume is what the gamer girls wore into the lounge, and that's how she showed up. Tayla changed in Elasus's office apartment, double-checked Babbage was still in the lounge, then headed out to meet the man who could give her answers.

The lounge let people in based on their gamer card that kept reputation points with the lounge. The more you visited, the quicker you got to the front of the line. That logic applied to most, but not the personal assistant to the most powerful man in the universe. One swipe of her FOCC, the bouncer's screen went gold, and she was ushered in like a virtual goddess.

Drinks were free as long as you were playing, and the games here weren't your run of the mill, play a couple hours until vertigo set in, and then let a CAV take you home. Customers rented virtual-reality rooms for hours that allowed them to escape their shattered world. People like Babbage didn't rent the simulation rooms for gaming pleasure, but for jobs. An avatar milling around on a virtual plane didn't attract much attention from the PGU. Hackers, slicers, tech punks, and gearheads generically touted their skills to the highest bidder. The Dark Souls Lounge was a closed network, so unless you were playing their games in their club on their network, you had no chance of finding these pandering wonderers.

One of the details Tayla researched before leaving the office was Marquise Babbage's employment status and wealth. Babbage's employment status terminated with the Reeves Corporation days after he accessed the Cruzes' files. Less than two weeks after that, the PGU changed his official employment status to retired. His banking records appeared forged, but whoever falsified those records forgot to alter his tax records, or at least his tax rate. In less than a year, Babbage went from a mid-tier tax rate to the highest tier allowed under the PGU. Someone had paid this swine a lot of money to destroy her family.

Whether it was her status within the corporation or Tayla's quick flirt with the handsome bartender, she found Babbage with little effort. He sat inside a digitally translucent wall, wearing custom eye contacts, earbuds, body suit, and gauntlets. The digitally shadowed wall evolved into a crystal-clear window after she paid off the tech supervisor managing that side of the lounge.

It was hard to tell Babbage's ethnicity because he looked like he spent all his time indoors, perhaps in this lounge. The virtual-reality contacts showed his bloodshot eyes, dark tattooed eyeshadow, and erratic wide pupils. His head was shaved on the sides, but the top looked freshly colored with a barber's touch.

"Tayla Cruz, born December 5th, 2351, husband to Grylo, mother to Gabrielle and Aaron." Babbage hadn't moved his head, or made any gesture showing he knew she was there. "Personal secretary to Elasus Reeves, former cyber-defense administrator and dispatcher for the fleet department. Nowhere does your profile suggest the Dark Soul Lounge is a place for your… kind, which tells me you're looking for me."

Tayla considered flirting with him, a skill she'd become quite good at in Elasus's company. Threatening the lowlife also crossed her mind, but in the end, she let the fool talk himself into trouble.

"You know who I am and who I work for," Tayla said while keeping her hood pulled up. "Why don't you guess why I'm here."

Babbage turned his head, fully exposing his face for the first time. His sallow skin was covered in busted blood vessels and patchy, flaking skin. He was looking directly at her, but not quite seeing her. "You know I'm the one who put together the cast of what you'd look like after a makeover? I wasn't far off, but I'd need to see you naked and with a little more makeup. Based on the way you're dressed, I'd say that Elasus didn't order you here, which means you found out that I'm the one that erased your family's files once they got to Ojult. Congratulations, you caught me. Now, leave."

"Actually, Tanner Sands sent me."

Babbage's reaction was immediate. He took off his gauntlets, ear pieces, then finally his contacts before reaching for a drink. "This is a suicide— the drink I mean, not you coming here. It's made of jashinto juice, diluted rivea, and tonic. Want to try it?"

Tayla was good at reading men and particularly adept in knowing when they were nervous. She went out on a limb, trusting her intuition. "I know what you did to my family's files, but like I said, I'm here because of Tanner Sands. This place is too public to snatch you out of, so he sent me. We work together when his operations require a little bit more finesse. So, tell me, Marquise, how long you been working against the corporation?"

His tough-guy pretense shattered in one quick gulp. "The PGU, they threatened to take all my money, all the money Elasus gave me to take care of certain files. All I've been doing is jumping into the corporation's systems and deleting the messages they tell me to. I swear, I haven't read them, I don't even know what's on them."

"Tanner already knows all this, but he wants more. He wants names of those in the PGU and the backup files of everything you deleted. You do this and maybe you'll be able to leave this lounge in one piece."

Babbage ordered another drink trying to control his teetering composure. "I own this lounge. I bought it after Reeves paid me, that's how I knew you were in here. And look, I don't want any trouble with Tanner, even if I don't like Elasus and his iron grip over our society."

Was this dirtbag trying to get sympathy from her? "You've got ten seconds to tell me what you know, then we do things the hard way." Tayla pretended to tap buttons on her 3DI.

Babbage's drink arrived and he clumsily drank the exotic liquid. "I've been helping a PGU spy send messages back to Earth. All I do is update and reroute the portal that dumps the communications back on Earth. And no, I don't know who it is, and I don't know who within the PGU is reading it. I'm working as a contractor, on a need-to-know basis."

"Just like you did with my family? You were just a simple contractor?" The words were out of her mouth before she knew it.

"What? No, totally different." Babbage took a more elegant drink this time. "Your husband was framed for the inaccurate NAV data inputs to the MFG system; I thought that was obvious. There was a spy on board that ship, and Elasus wanted them eliminated without it looking like an assassination. It was an expensive hit, but it got the job done and no one ever raised any questions."

Grylo was a fleet technical specialist within the corporation who flew out to MFGs to update or fix navigation hardware. The first SKIP after one of his repairs resulted in the ship being launched off course, getting sideswiped by an asteroid, and spinning out of control into the endless universe. Grylo was sentenced to death and his two young children condemned to Ojult. Only by Tayla's contract with Elasus was Grylo spared death and permitted to accompany their children to Ojult.

The news Grylo was set up as part of an elaborate assassination scheme put Tayla into a psychological, nerve-splitting trauma. Her family, ripped apart because Elasus needed an informant eliminated. Her world, and the lives of those on board the destroyed ship, were shattered because of Elasus's abominable conscience.

Tayla worked through the agonizing fog sailing through her cognitive mind. "So… you altered the MFG's charts after my… after Grylo fixed it?"

"I guess so, yeah. Look, I'm not proud of it, but Elasus tossed a ton of money at me. You know how he gets when he wants something."

Killing the lunatic in front of her, even if she could manage it, wouldn't do her children any good. Tayla needed to focus and consider her options. "If Tanner finds out you've been covering for the PGU, they'll make your homicide look like another accident. You know that, right?"

"I wish I knew how the hell he found out," Marquise uttered. "This is the part where you and I broker a deal, right?"

"That's right. You do what I say, and I'll keep Tanner off your back, for a while. First thing, you're going to input a tunnel into the Reeves corporate finance department and release his life insurance funds into a dummy account in the FIAS region. Second, can you create a false video file? I need a fake picture and voiceover on a recording."

Babbage didn't react to the first request, but the second caused him to order another drink. "Can I create it, sure, it's not that hard if I've got enough voice data to plug in to the file. But look, I'm not going to create a false video showing the PGU minister admitting to being a spy or anything like that. Hell, lady, just shoot me now if that's what you're thinking."

Tayla stood and glanced around the flashing neon-lit building. "No, that's not what I have in mind. From this point forward, we communicate in this lounge, no external messages. Get that account set up and the funds wired. We'll be in touch."

CHAPTER 38: YEAR 2401

Y ou put an ice spike into his balls," exclaimed Phaedra.

As if it were an everyday event, Bella replied, "He threatened Nencia, and it wasn't called for. What would you have done?"

Phaedra tossed back her third scotch, only half of which fell into her open mouth. "Ha! I wish you'd done it, Kavil's an ass." She refilled her own glass and topped off Bella's.

Bella took a small sip and set the cup down. "You want to know my plan?"

"I didn't get cleaned up and drunk for nothing," replied Phaedra. Her freshly cleaned hair fell over her new blouse, which she hadn't bothered to button.

"The girls here work for Lacy, not Appian, and they're professionals. They have their regulars, mostly officers from arriving ships, but sometimes we get outsiders."

Phaedra already knew where Bella was taking the conversation. "And by regulars, you also mean the Celje?"

"The Celje work in rotating shifts, and one of them, a regular, let it slip that he was being rotated to another camp."

"Where?"

It was Bella's turn to refill their glasses. "He didn't say. Almost sounded like he didn't know yet."

Phaedra jumped to her feet, only to trip and land back in her chair. "Okay... I have ways of extracting information, I just need to know who he is."

Bella leaned back in her chair. "That's a dumb idea. Lacy can't have her girls being snitches; they'd all be killed. I was thinking we might use someone a bit chicer."

Phaedra looked from the bottle of scotch back to Bella, wondering if she'd heard her correctly. "You want me to sleep with him?"

"Lacy knows of your problem and wants to help, but it can't be known. She thinks with a little help, you could get whatever you wanted out of the agent, without killing him."

Phaedra threw back another drink. "I can't believe I'm even considering this."

Bella sipped at her own potent drink, showing no signs it bothered her.

A soft knock on the door diverted their attention.

"Hello, Lacy," greeted Bella, unsurprised by the visitor. "We were just speaking of you."

Lacy and Bella embraced. "Hello, my dear. How's the evening going?"

For the second time that day, Phaedra appraised the mistress. She'd changed dresses, going from red to a sheer, calf-length dress. Her long black hair was folded neatly over her shoulders and her chest. She looked nothing like a prostitute but had the seduction powers of Aphrodite.

Lacy turned to Phaedra, extending her hand. "And this beautiful young woman is Phaedra Lillea. It's a pleasure to meet you."

Phaedra's eyebrows nearly reached her hairline. "Hello."

Lacy glided around Phaedra, as if inspecting her. "Our mutual friend here says that you have a piece of information you need extracted from one of my clients?"

Phaedra's brows landed back just above her piercing eyes. "Yes, that's the gist of it."

Lacy stopped behind Phaedra. "Our way of life here depends on a very specific service we provide our clients. We must always meet the expectations of our client or we risk them leaving unhappy, unfulfilled. So, in meeting our obligation to our clients, we develop a unique bond with them. One that assures they come back, again and again. Do you understand my meaning?"

"I can't just give him a great night and ask for the location of the prison," blurted Phaedra.

Lacy was too eloquent to reply to such a jest. "Have you been with a man before?"

Phaedra's face turned red. "I… it's not…"

"The question wasn't meant to offend, only to identify how we can help you succeed in your goal." Lacy's tone was reassuring.

"No… I mean, yes, but, not… not like what you're asking, I think."

Lacy took Phaedra's hand. "Allow me to sit with you, and together, I'll teach you how to prevail over the simplistic male mind."

———————

Phaedra met with Lacy and many of her cohorts over the next two days, discussing the most agreed-upon services Phaedra might provide to obtain her goal. She tried dozens of loungewear and shoes, then nearly called the whole plan off when two older women forced her into a bathtub and scrubbed her down like a child.

"You see that brown grime around the tube, missy, that wasn't there before," blasted one of the maids.

Seeing the brown ring left Phaedra speechless, but the body detail wasn't over.

"Oh hell no!" Phaedra tried springing out of the tub, but slipped.

Lacy smiled and glided toward her. "There are areas that must be finely shaven, and then there's makeup, my dear. A man's mind is simple and driven by violence and sex. A woman's face is a strong motivator toward the latter and is the first feature he'll see. It can make or break your goal from the start."

Phaedra's eyed grayed over. "I'll just shoot his ass then, I'm not painting my face."

Lacy replied tenderly, "Corpses tell no truths or lies, and I cannot help you extract what you need from a dead man."

———————

Phaedra sampled her new talents on unsuspecting men for several nights, finding it much easier to control the opposite sex than she'd expected. The more time she spent with Lacy, the more Phaedra liked her, absent the outfit demonstrations and makeup sessions. A knock early the next morning gave way to a brief conversation with Bella and Lacy. Her target, a Celje guard named Sherman, had reserved a room at the inn.

Phaedra stayed in her room during the day, practicing the lines Lacy had provided that would surely distract Sherman's mind as she played her part.

Just before sunset, Phaedra met with Bella. The teenager always looked the same, wearing worn-out dirty jeans, dingy work shirts, and out-of-control hair.

"Lacy will be here in a minute," said Bella. "She's got your makeup and a dress picked out. I've seen the dress. You'll look… well, not like you normally do."

An hour later, Lacy and her cohorts transformed the grievous Nein into a lady of the night. The housemaids washed and straightened her silver hair, which reached well below her chest. Lacy handpicked a lightweight dark-blue dress of Lent silk that skimmed the floor as she walked. The ravishing dress exposed Phaedra's bony shoulders and lifted her exposed cleavage. There was still one tiny hiccup.

"There's not many women on this rock with silver hair. Given I'm wanted by the Celje and this Sherman guy works for them… damn it! I can't walk in these things," said Phaedra, stumbling around.

Even with Lacy's cool touch, Phaedra's balance faltered. After dozens of attempts, Lacy gave up and found a clean pair of house shoes for the temptress to wear.

"This is going to work," said Bella from across the room. "For all he knows, you colored your hair. Nothing about you now shouts famous Nein sage."

Phaedra looked into the mirror, barely recognizing herself. "You know, I'm helping find Andreas because he's vital to our goals. But why are you helping? Why get involved?"

"Because the Celje took something from me and my brother. It's not really about getting your friend back, more like taking something away from the corporation."

Phaedra adjusted her smashed breasts inside the garment. "Fair enough."

The plan called for Lacy to promise Sherman a surprise, something like a going-away present. After a few drinks, Lacy would take him to see Phaedra and let the Nein enchantress work her magic.

Faux lanterns lit the hallway while scented candles and a crackling fire-place brightened the borrowed suite. Phaedra paced the room, wanting more than anything to finish the bottle of scotch sitting at the bar. Foot-steps approached, and Phaedra took a deep breath and sat down. The entry-way opened, and Phaedra regarded Lacy, who wore a stunningly beautiful black dress, her arm wrapped around Sherman's. "Good evening, Carmella. This is Sherman, our guest. Sherman, my special gift to you, Ms. Carmella."

Phaedra remained seated, seductively uncrossing her legs while sip-ping on a wine glass filled with grape juice. "Thank you, Lacy. Sherman, please, come in. A drink?"

Lacy kissed Sherman on the cheek, then shut the door behind her. Phaedra quickly evaluated him. Throughout Lacy's description of the Celje, she'd left out the part about him being handsome.

"When Lacy said *surprise*, I thought maybe a nice dinner and free drinks. You… you're stunning." His accent—British, maybe? He sat down and took the fresh drink. Sherman was probably twenty-five, clean-cut, freshly shaven, and smelled like a touch of cologne.

"Lacy tells me tonight is your last visit with us for a while and suggested we provide something of a going-away present for you." Even Phaedra was impressed by how tempting she sounded.

"Yeah, my… friends and I are heading to a place, not too far from here. But the… the work will have me grounded there for at least a year."

This was going to be easier than she thought. Though, admittedly, a small piece of Phaedra liked being this close to an attractive man.

Phaedra sipped her fake wine, then placed a well-aimed hand on the inside of his thigh. "You've got me all to yourself, Sherman. The lady told me your work is dangerous. I like men who are fearless."

Several hours later, Phaedra sat atop the bed, the covers scattered, and Sherman's gift bestowed.

"I'm really going to miss this place," slurred Sherman, attempting to pour another shot but missing the glass and dumping it on the floor. "I've been working for the… my company since I was fifteen. I'm good at what I do. Now, all of a sudden, I'm babysitting a bunch of cons."

Into the night, after sex, idle chatter, and multiple scotches, Phae-dra launched into the real work. "I have to admit something, Sherman. I really liked tonight and not just because Lacy's paying me. Are you sure I can't, maybe, come visit wherever you're going?" Her hand glided across his bare chest.

"You'd do that?" he said excitedly. "I mean, actually travel away from here. It's really not that far from here, and I'd... well, it'd be great to see you again."

"We're not supposed to. Lacy doesn't like us leaving the protection of Worall, but if you think it's safe, then I'd really like to."

"Well, what I've heard is that... someone is cleaning house. Trade passages are going to be safer, and those mystics will finally get what's coming. You'll be fine. When do you think you can come?"

Using a trick Lacy taught her, Phaedra snuck her hand underneath the sheets and caught Sherman's attention. "I don't like traveling alone, but if you tell me it's safe, then okay. How do I get there?"

After Sherman explained the complex maze of roads and barely noticeable paths to what he called "the facility," Phaedra wasn't surprised no one had found it yet. With her mission complete, Phaedra contemplated her next move. She could kill the young man and be done with this whole mess.

She threw him onto his back. Phaedra was on top of him before he could grasp what was happening. During their first encounter, Phaedra had focused all her efforts into satisfying his needs in order to extract information. This go around, it was about her.

As the sun rose, Phaedra left Sherman sleeping soundly on the demolished bed. She passed by other courtesans in the stairwell, many of whom helped her prepare for her mission. A distant part of her brain understood why the job appealed to so many.

Bella was asleep with a pistol atop the nearby nightstand when Phaedra came back with the news.

"That you?" said Bella. Still half asleep, she sat up, trying to focus on her new friend. "Did... did you get the information?"

"There's a prison, and it's not far from here. One problem: it's heavily guarded. I don't think we have enough girls to sleep with every one of them."

Blood and alertness flashed back into Bella's disposition. "When do we leave?"

CHAPTER 39: YEAR 2401

Months of malnutrition, sporadic torture, and frequent infections took its toll on Jayden's body. He was little more than skin and bones with clumps of hair falling from his scalp. His nerves were either dead or numb because he couldn't feel the chains clamped around his wrists and ankles. The smell of waste and death was so commonplace now, he barely noticed their signs smeared across the interrogation-room walls.

Footsteps approached the room, and even in the dim light, he recognized the man. Sunglasses rested atop Misora's long black hair, suggesting he'd just come from outside, something Jayden had not seen for a long time.

A wide smile appeared on Misora's face. "Well, hello, Mr. Vaut. How are we doing?"

Jayden stayed silent, having neither the energy nor the care to respond.

Misora's sweaty palm popped hard against Jayden's cheek. "Oh, come on now, give me a smile. I've got a special surprise for you. A guest you know well, one I call friend."

Another set of boots splashed in the hallway, and a slender bearded man entered. A murderous betrayal filled Jayden. "What... what the hell?"

Wren Dikal, courier for Dalth and Mayor Fonte's associate, stepped forward. "You mystic filth," said Wren, then he sucker punched Jayden in his already bleeding nose. "If it was me, I'd just kill you and be done with it."

Jayden felt a stream of blood traverse down his ratty beard. "Why...
are... you here? What have you... done?"

Misora stepped up beside his ally. "We've had a spy underneath that
narrow-minded mayor of yours for years. We know more than you could
possibly imagine."

"Mystic freak," spat Wren, slapping Jayden across the face. "I know
you were with the Nein, I know you're a mystic. Tell us what you know
about the revolt."

"I... I told you, I don't... know anything. I'm not part of... it."

Wren knelt so close that Jayden smelled the stank of molded meat on
the man's breath. "I've been a watching you, Vaut, for so long. Don't give
me that about not knowing nott'in. I followed ya to Worall. I saw you
with that whore Nencia. Keep refusing to talk, and I'll find someone else
to play witt. Like Serena."

With his remaining strength, Jayden reared and headbutted the Dalth
traitor. Wren's nose cracked, and blood exploded everywhere. "Traitorous
bastard," croaked Jayden. "Leave... her... alone."

Wren staggered back.

Misora's smile vanished. "Ah, fighting to the end. Perhaps I need to
chat with Mayor Fonte again."

Wren stroked his blood-stained beard. "Go after his daughter, Bélise,
that'll get him talking."

Wheezing and unable to breathe from his nose, Jayden clung to what
little life he had left. "You... have a wife, a son... what are you doing?"

Wren reared back and punched Jayden. "Leave my family outta this!"

Jayden's vision blurred. "I'm no... mystic... you fool."

Wren removed a small knife from his coat and slowly pushed the tip
of his blade into Jayden's shoulder, relishing in Jayden's screams. "For your
sake, you better be."

Jayden screamed. The pain was too much, and he began to beg for
death. Wren left the knife in his shoulder, intensifying the pain.

Misora laughed, then paced the room. "Finally, a reaction from Dalth's
most infamous farmer."

"Farmer," smirked Wren. "He's the worst farmer on Ojult. Half the crops he worked on died." Wren yanked the serrated blade out, and Jayden felt something snap and curl up inside his neck.

"Ah damn it," scowled Misora. "You've cut his damn artery!" There was blood everywhere now.

Wren wiped the blade against Jayden's arm.

Instead of fearing the darkness enclosing around him, Jayden welcomed it. He was done being a prisoner, done putting up with Misora. Eagerness to see Nencia and maybe his parents numbed the pain.

Misora looked nervous. "We can't kill him yet. Sasha says he and a few others have to stay alive. You two!" he yelled at two nearby guards. "Grab him, and take him down to the infirmary. Tell Eve he'd better live!"

———————

Jayden hardly recognized the woman before him. His body felt cool, yet he knew it was summer. A soft, gentle hand tugged on his neck.

"If… this… is heaven… I've got… a serious… bone… to pick… with Markus." Even in his drug-induced state he knew his words came out unintelligible. The room around him was blurry and dark.

"Shhh," Eve said. "I'm stitching your neck."

"Oh great, it's you" mumbled Jayden.

"I said be quiet," demanded Eve. "Whoever stabbed you almost severed your artery. I've been able to stop the bleeding, but it's delicate. And you can't see because I've got you drugged up on jashinto. You're in bad shape, I mean really bad shape, so please, be still."

Why did Misora's whore keep saving his life? Did she enjoy seeing Misora break him time and again, satisfying some sort of sick fetish?

There was more tugging and pulling on his neck, but there was little pain.

"There," she said. "I've stitched you up the best I can. Don't move. You've lost a lot of blood again, and if anything rips, I don't think you'll make it back here in time."

Her words sounded kind and sincere, opposite of what he expected. "You washed your hands before touching me, right?" His words were slurred.

"If pain begins to creep up, let me know. I can't give you any more jash-into for another few hours. You've probably only got a few liters of blood in you right now, so more drugs might lead to an overdose."

"You didn't have a problem… drugging us all… a few…"

Eve leaned over him, her long red hair falling against his chest. "My job is to heal people, not hurt them."

"Nurse," came the guard's voice from afar, but Eve ignored him. "Hey, witch doctor! I need to go take a piss. I'll be back in a few. Can you handle this magician for a minute?"

"He's a jerk but he's chained, I'll be fine."

Why would Misora allow his own agents to belittle his mistress?

"At least I'm not the plaything of a psychopathic killer." Jayden wasn't completely sure he made sense.

Eve glimpsed over her shoulder toward the unguarded door. "I don't know why you think I'm Misora's girlfriend, or anyone's girlfriend for that matter. I drugged all of you because I found out Misora planned on laying into you guys. I didn't know who he planned on questioning so I drugged all of you so at least you wouldn't remember. I've been treating poisons in you guys for years, so if I wanted you dead, it wouldn't be hard. So, if you don't mind, I'd appreciate a little more respect."

She was so close to Jayden's face that he thought about reaching and grabbing her by the throat. Enough slack in the chains might allow for it. Jayden blinked away the blurriness. "What's on your neck?"

Eve pushed back and pulled her hair over her neck, tripping over a large blue-branded crate. "That's the greeting I get from Misora. You know, the guy you called my boyfriend a few minutes ago. Whenever I lose a patient or resist his… his invitations, this is my reward."

Jayden didn't shy away from the rising guilt. "Or maybe that's… from a prisoner who was trying to escape this place?"

She cocked her head and looked pitifully at him. "Believe what you want, mystic, but my job is to save your life, not to justify it. Speaking of, you need to start using your powers to heal yourself. I might not always be just around the corner to keep saving your life."

A burst of pain leapt through his neck, and the right side of his body flinched.

Eve examined his shoulder and neck. "The jashinto shouldn't have worn off this quick. I'm sorry, but it's too early to give you more. I know it hurts, I'm sorry I just can't give you anything else for the pain."

It was impossible not to hear the sincerity in her voice. "So... why are you here? Looks like the worst you've suffered is a simple bruise while the rest of us are having our nails torn out and arteries severed."

She paused. "Misora's impulsive but not stupid, he's not going to push his luck hurting me."

"Cryptic. So, you don't like the Celje, aren't sleeping with the devil's right-hand man, and save people's lives on a routine basis."

Eve leaned in closer and whispered, "Stop probing me for information. I don't know anything, and I can't leave, okay?"

"You're a prisoner?"

She shook her head. "Not exactly. Just stop asking me about it."

Either the meds were messing with his ability to think or Eve wasn't making sense. "So... you work... for Reeves then?"

"God no," she yelled, then covered her mouth and lowered her voice. "I don't think the corporation even knows what's going on here."

"I thought the Celje worked for the Reeves Corporation?"

"Technically yes, but something is going on. I've seen more prisoners in the past few months than I have in years." Echoing footsteps outside the door. "We need to stop talking."

Jayden looked toward the hallway and immediately regretted moving his neck.

"Stop moving, or you'll tear the stitches!"

Jayden yielded. "What... what about Levi and Andreas? Are they... what do you know about them?"

Jayden liked Andreas well enough, perhaps not Levi as much, but he still hadn't confided much in either man. With Wren Dikal coming out as a Celje spy, it would push Jayden to further distance himself from anyone inside the facility. Less than an hour ago, Jayden had yearned for death. Now he was alive and beginning to think this woman was as much a prisoner as he was.

"My name is Jayden Vaut. I'm from Earth, but found a life in Dalth."

Eve scowled at him. "So what, *now* you believe me?"

"Hey, sorry, just thought…"

"You didn't think, that's the problem with all you men. You keep trusting the wrong people."

"Um, are we still talking about me," Jayden challenged. The emotional switch from uncaring, dispassionate nurse to crazed, melodramatic stranger threw him off.

Incoming footsteps were just outside the door.

"Look," replied Eve, "I don't want to get involved in your wizard revolt, but if it helps, Misora seems afraid of the guy in the cell next to you."

"Levi? Why would he be afraid of him?"

"Yeah, him, and I don't know, but Misora constantly talks about him."

The guard wandered back into the infirmary. "Did this lag give you any trouble? Do I need to beat him? Surprised you didn't cut him loose yourself. Shame, I might have enjoyed beating you as well."

Eve checked Jayden's pulse again. "He wasn't trouble. He can barely move. He'll need to stay here for a while under my supervision."

Andreas and Levi had it wrong, all wrong. "Eve," Jayden whispered. "I'm not a mystic, I can't heal."

CHAPTER 40: YEAR 2401

Jayden spent weeks in the clinic. With special ointments, rest, and a small dose of nano-treks, his wounds scabbed without signs of infection, seemingly relaxing some of Eve's tension.

Jayden was still substantially malnourished when the guards hauled him back to his cell. The corridors leading back to the main hold were dimly lit with sporadic lights forged into hastily built cement walls.

They dropped him onto his knees as they opened his cell door, unafraid he would escape in his weakened state.

"You've got more bandages than Levi with a Meridonian hooker," said Andreas after the guards left. "I've been saving water for you."

Jayden graciously accepted it through the cell bars. He finished the cup in seconds, then set it down, exhausted from the effort of staying conscious. "Thanks."

Andreas grasped the adjoining cell bars and leaned in. "Don't be thinking about giving up on me now. For god's sake, don't leave me alone with his highness over here."

Jayden gave him the thumbs up. "I was interrogated by a man I've known for years. A spy in Dalth this whole time. A lot of people have suffered because of him."

"You trust easily, Vaut, and you're an idiot for doing so," interrupted Levi. "You have no one to blame but yourself."

"Shut it," said Andreas. "We've all been screwed by someone we've trusted, including you. Syrus Tokarek is coming for us, we just need to hang on."

With a grunting effort, Jayden sat up. "You think he's going to come riding in on a white horse and rescue us? Why, to save a few mystics? He'd sacrifice a dozen of his own people just to prove a point. He's got no reason."

Andreas gave a sorrowful expression. "Reason? Sasha and the Celje killed his sister. It's not just revenge, he wants blood, Sasha's blood, and this planet's going to give it to him."

Jayden's tired body downshifted, sending his heart into a pulsating overdrive. "They… they killed Helia? She's dead?"

Andreas met his gaze. "You knew her?"

Rattling chains from Levi's cell cut through the room. "Syrus's sister is… dead?"

Jayden listed then fell to his haggard knees. "Did… did Mea make it?"

Andreas inclined his head and looked down. "Yes, she survived. Syrus sent her into hiding with Nencia Donato."

Tears mixed with dirt and welled in Jayden's parched eyes. "He sent them with Nencia, oh… oh… no…"

Andreas's voice swelled with questions. "What do you know that I don't?"

"I knew Syrus and his family."

"Yeah, we've gathered that," said Levi, unusually involved in the conversation. "You are more notorious than you realize, Thoba. What about his sister and niece? What do you know?"

Jayden nodded. "Did you know I was the slave who saved Helia and Mea? And his great reward was teaching me how to kill mystics, how to be the perfect assassin."

"Seems you used those skills to remove a couple of Kavil's guards," muttered Andreas. "Yup, Kavil didn't like you very much. But to Levi's astonishing moment of insight, what is it that you know? I mentioned Nencia and you went all funny."

Jayden shot him a shrewd glare while images of Janice fluttered through his mind. "Don't believe everything you hear. That bastard set me up, tried killing me and a friend one night."

"Why would Kavil do that?"

"Thoba are second class, unworthy. Beyond that, I have no idea."

Andreas stayed quiet for a moment. "Kavil hasn't changed much then, but Syrus, he's not like that anymore. He's changed. Losing Helia, it changed him."

Jayden realized he was treating Andreas like some sort of enemy. "Changed or not, he still banished me."

Andreas gripped the cell bars like he was fighting a conscious thought. "I took over protecting Mea after you left."

"You're a mystic, Andreas, let's not pretend you took my spot as a slave to Syrus."

"My point is that I know Syrus, and he's changed. Catch us up on how you knew Nencia."

"Long story," replied Jayden, unsure if he was ready to talk about his former lover.

Andreas tapped on the cell bars, the hollow sound echoing through the ward. "Clearly you two were close. She's helping Syrus defeat the Celje and when it's over, things will get better."

"Let's all bow down to the almighty Syrus," injected Levi. "Sounds like a deal; trade the Celje for a repurposed Nein leader."

Jayden ignored Levi. "You asked how I knew Nencia. We were good friends. When I heard Worall was under attack, I came to see if I could help. She'd already been captured by the Celje. I got caught, and Misora questioned us, then executed Nencia."

The three cellmates remained silent until Levi spoke. "You said Helia was murdered by the Celje?"

Andreas spoke first, saying what Jayden was thinking. "This isn't the time for one of your sneering taunts or backhanded comments Levi."

Levi's gaze fixed on Jayden, who worked his body slowly into a more comfortable sitting position. "Tell me Thoba, did you love Helia like you loved this Nencia?"

In the many months Jayden had known Levi, he'd never known the man to ask personal questions. The self-declared dark mystic usually teased, ridiculed, or taunted his neighbors, never vesting himself into a conversation.

Jayden returned Levi's watchful gaze. "Helia was special to me in a different way, like a sister." When Levi broke eye contact, an absurd idea occurred to Jayden. "Levi, were you…"

"I what?"

The ward's main door opened, and two Celje strutted toward Andreas's cell.

"Well, gentlemen, I'm off for caviar and champagne again with the duke of this fantastic establishment," chided Andreas.

What was there to say? They'd each been dragged off similarly, and they knew what was coming. When the door closed behind Andreas, the room echoed only with the squeaks of rats.

"They won't kill him," said Levi, breaking the silence. "They'll torture him and then toss him to that harlot to get patched up."

Jayden was beginning to solve the mystery behind Levi. "You were the Nein leader on Capintesta years back. You fought Syrus, I was there."

Levi burst out laughing. "Just figuring that out?"

Levi's interest in Helia's death, the compassion he'd shown for her back in Carendra. "And Helia… you were lovers?"

"Like a child piecing together a puzzle."

The statement about being lovers was a guess, but it was one more answer to a bigger question. "Andreas doesn't know, and Syrus sure didn't."

"Know what, exactly?" spat Levi, showing an energy Jayden had never seen. "That I was the leader of the Nein on Capintesta, husband to Helia, and father to Mea? Or perhaps one step further, knowing that I was mis-led by a sage working for the Celje, who left me to rot while Helia decayed underneath Ojult's blood-soaked earth. We aren't friends, Vaut, so mind what you say next."

The threat was genuine, but Jayden battled on. "You were betrayed? By whom? How did they defeat you if you had a staff?"

"A staff is only a tool, not a lifeline to immortality. Syrus defeated me after I led my camp to Listo for a final confrontation. I should have sus-pected after Genest went after Helia that he wasn't acting alone. Genest was my man you fought inside Helia's tent."

The memories of Jayden's first days on Ojult flew back. "Who was Genest working for?"

"After Helia begged her brother to spare my life, I headed back to Cap-intesta, abandoned by my Nein followers. I was in a healing trance when a sage visited me, and conned me into believing she could reunite me with Helia. Blinded by my passion to see my beloved, I walked into Achilla's trap. When I woke, I was a permanent resident of this place."

The belief that a former Nein adviser suddenly betrayed her own leader and defected to the Celje didn't jive with Jayden's understanding of either sect. "But who was he working for? Who is the woman working with?"

"I told you, I've been locked in here since it happened. Listen, Vaut, there's more going on than your tiny mind can comprehend. What do you think Misora might do if he found out I, Levi Anjou, one of the most powerful mystics alive, had a living child?"

Having seen firsthand what Misora did to Nencia, Serena's parents, and the hundreds of other stories he'd heard, he knew exactly what Misora and Sasha would do. "They'd use her for leverage against you, force you to fight with them, and probably execute her regardless."

A cold bluish torch flared in Levi's eyes. "I will not permit the Celje to harm my child."

Although Andreas suggested earlier that Mea was safe, there now seemed a very real possibility that she was in significant danger. If three prisoners with no outside communication figured this out, then Sasha's network of spies surely knew.

"Levi, your daughter is under the protection of a woman who's dead. If this Achilla woman is really working with the Celje but can pass as a mystic, what's to prevent her from doing the same thing to Syrus and finding out where they are?"

Levi took a reluctant step away from the cell wall. "My time here is coming to an end, and I'll soon be with the Elders. When this happens, I'll find my daughter."

A light on the far side of the room flickered out, bringing even more darkness to the windowless room. "You keep putting your faith in the Elders, but I think we may have another way out." Jayden was thinking of Eve. "You might be callous, Levi, but we're gonna find Mea. I let Helia down, and it won't happen again."

Levi shut his eyes and looked as if he was meditating. "You were a friend of Helia's and a champion to my family; it would seem I owe you a debt, Jayden. I will not forget that."

CHAPTER 41: YEAR 2401

Elasus Reeves poured a fresh cup of coffee into his usual black mug. Except this wasn't coffee, at least not his traditional drink of choice. Tayla notified him when he'd gotten back from the survey trip that she was switching to kaldi, a cousin of coffee grown on Ojult. Elasus drank it black, with an occasional splash of bourbon. He liked the new variety, mostly because it was exclusive.

Elasus enjoyed spring in Las Vegas, very little rain, moderate temperatures and, most importantly, the woman in his life wore shorter skirts. Peering out the window of his building, he gazed at his reflection in the glass. His custom black suit magnified his dark beard and hair, an image he purposefully advertised. Beside him, his phone started flashing.

"Yes, Ms. Cruz?"

"Mr. Reeves, Prime Minister Joshua Kennedy just arrived and insists on seeing you."

Elasus processed the many reasons for the visit. "My office is always open to the PGU minister. Please, escort him in."

Elasus turned and watched Tayla and the prime minister enter. Even from a distance, he could spot the minister's knife-edged nose.

"Mr. Reeves, how good to see you. I hope I'm not intruding, but it was necessary that I speak with you."

Despite Kennedy's efforts, he came off anxious. Elasus dismissed Tayla and addressed the minister more forwardly than usual. "Good morning,

Mr. Prime Minister. It's early, and you're unannounced. What problem can I help you resolve?"

"You can start by offering me a cup of coffee."

Elasus sipped at his own cup. "This is why I have assistants. But she's already left, so let's move on."

Kennedy's eyes widened. "The gentleman as always. I'll get to the point. Many PGU members opened their distribution check this morning, and I must say, I've heard a lot of rumblings about the amounts. It's almost half the usual, and it's got everyone talking."

"And you felt the need to come to my office first thing this morning, unannounced, to impart this inconsequential knowledge?"

Kennedy sat down. "These men are politicians. They have to answer for their votes, and if the money stops flowing... So, *why* are our checks so low?"

Elasus felt the question was reasonable. "The violence on Ojult isn't settled, which has hindered commerce. Our staple revenue, which emanates from the transportation of exiles, mystics, and criminals, has also slowed, owing to the political infighting within FIAS."

"Violence? That's just great. What are you doing to resolve it?"

"Minister, the FIAS infighting is a PGU matter and doesn't directly concern the Reeves Corporation. However, I'm working with another PGU member to provide aid in resolving the dispute."

"And what of the situation on Ojult?"

"Let's stop wasting each other's time. Why are you here?"

"I've already said—"

"Don't waste my time, Minster," Reeves demanded, his voice rising only slightly.

Kennedy sat forward and locked his hands together. "I want to know about a group called the Celje, and don't try to snivel your way around this."

Elasus's expression remained unchanged. Internally, however, his blood pressure spiked. "They're a defense force that helps keep the peace on Ojult." There was no sense hiding the group's existence if Kennedy already knew their name.

"I'm told they're like a gestapo, arresting without warrants, killing without regard, like a vigilante group for hire, and you're their boss."

"Then you've heard wrong, and I'd like to know who's been feeding you this nonsense."

Kennedy ran a shuddering hand through his thinning hair. "Elasus, some in the PGU think you're developing your own army. This isn't just about Ojult either, it's about Earth."

"You believe I have aspirations of conquering Earth with this fictious army? The Celje numbers are small, and they're trained to defend against mystics."

"But—"

"Let's speak no more of this, Joshua. It's a private security force that protects PGU interests on Chden as well as Ojult."

Kennedy's eyes shot up. "You've got them on Chden too?"

Elasus let his full threatening figure hover above the uncertain minister. "And they'll remain there until I see fit to remove them."

"Elasus, you've… you've got to listen to reason. Rumors will spread. I've already heard about the kidnapping of children. Exiles with various skills, like engineers and scientists, gone missing. Then there's talk of you covering up assassinations. I'm just trying to help you make informed decisions based on all available information. This type of security force has never worked out well for any government, you need to reconsider."

Elasus moved to put down these ridiculous ideas when the door to his office banged open. "Ah, Irelyn," said Elasus, clearly not appreciating the interruption. His beautiful spouse wore a thigh-high skirt with her brown hair up. Tayla, who appeared distraught with the second interruption of the morning, was close behind.

"Mr. Reeves, I'm sorry, but your wife insisted—"

"I don't need permission to enter my husband's office."

"Ms. Cruz, thank you. That will be all. Mr. Prime Minister, my wife, whom you already know, of course."

Kennedy jumped to his feet, and instead of shaking hands he embraced Irelyn, perhaps a little too long. "Mrs. Reeves, how good to see you again."

Irelyn smiled. "Thank you. I'm so sorry for interrupting, but when I heard you were here with my husband, well, I just couldn't stand outside. I had to come in and say hello. How are your wife and children?"

Kennedy and Irelyn spent a few minutes catching up with Elasus closely monitoring their body language. In a public setting such as this, he'd seen his wife develop relationships and create lasting friendships that even Elasus would admit benefited the company. This exchange was different, more casual than intellectual. He let the conversation continue until the white light on his phone flashed again. Elasus inserted his earpiece.

The timing of this interruption was perfect. "Escort him in, Ms. Cruz." Elasus lowered the phone and interrupted his wife. "I'm sorry, but Treasury Secretary Zhang is here, and I have a prearranged meeting with him. I must ask that you two continue elsewhere."

Kennedy looked outraged. Irelyn grabbed him by the wrist before he could respond.

"Of course, dear. I'll escort the prime minister, but may I have a quick moment alone with you first? You won't mind, will you Joshua?"

Kennedy bowed and walked away from the desk, out of earshot. Irelyn hugged Elasus.

"How the hell did you let it slip about the Celje to the PGU?" she whispered.

Elasus returned the hug, giving the appearance they were indeed sharing a loving moment. "The source of the leak is under investigation."

Irelyn pulled away. "The PGU doesn't like armed security forces. Remember the FIAS debacle? Ruven's life is in danger every moment you let this linger. Fix this mess and take care of the leak. I won't lose another child to your incompetence." Irelyn turned to Kennedy with a pleasant, welcoming smile. "Have you had lunch, Minster? I'm starving, care to join me?"

Elasus watched his wife parade down the hallway with the minister walking loyally behind her. They passed Treasury Secretary Zhang, exchanged pleasantries, then Zhang continued on his way. Elasus appreciated Zhang's talent for leadership, a mid-thirties up-and-coming PGU member who was as good-looking as he was smart. Elasus did a lot of research on the young man before investing time and money into grooming him. Zhang wore finely tailored suits, was always kempt, and wore a cologne that smelled like a winner, strong and lasting.

"Mr. Reeves, thank you for seeing me. I feel that I must apologize, it seems you were in another meeting when I arrived." Zhang spoke perfect

English, though it was only one of many languages the aristocratic man spoke.

The two exchanged a firm handshake. "That meeting was not scheduled, simply old friends catching up. Thank you for coming. I know your time is limited, Mr. Secretary, and I'll be brief."

Zhang sat and crossed his legs. "I'm thankful for the meeting, Mr. Reeves. Your empire is quite the marvel. I'd be foolish not to take advantage of the opportunity to speak with you."

Elasus accepted the well-timed flattery. "I believe it's time for the PGU to head in a different direction. While Prime Minister Kennedy has led the PGU into prosperity, his successes are owed more to my personal achievements than his leadership. Do you agree?"

Zhang cracked his neck before giving a well thought out politically correct response. "I certainly have different views on how the PGU should be led, but I by no means believe he's done a poor job."

"A young, brilliant, single man like yourself has a lot to offer the PGU. I am a powerful person, this isn't bragging, it's just a fact. I want to put my resources behind you and make you the next prime minister of the PGU. I believe we're heading for turbulent times, and it will require a man of significant cunning and intelligence. In short, I believe your resume fits what our society will need in the coming decade."

"Forgive the sharpness, but it seems as if you're requesting a puppet instead of a leader."

Clearly Zhang admired him but wasn't afraid of his power, a rare combination. "If I wanted a puppet, I'd keep Kennedy. No, what I need is a political warrior who knows where the real power of the PGU comes from. My distributions to various members of the PGU have served me well, but it's time to narrow that circle."

Zhang's elliptical eyes advertised his calculating thoughts. "A crisis is coming, I agree. And I also believe we share a common fear that involves the Elders. Taking this one step further, Kennedy doesn't share our views on this and thus puts our entire institution, our race, all that we have built and restored at risk. Am I wrong?"

Elasus listened intently. How long had it been since he'd found a potential equal to his own intellect? "Correct on all fronts. Protecting the planet my ancestors rebuilt is the priority. Contrary to circulating rumors, I have no delusions of power."

"Then, in principle, Mr. Reeves, we have an accord. I'll consider all we've discussed, perhaps in a less intimidating environment, then hopefully we'll meet again?" Zhang flashed his practiced smile at Elasus who saw yet another ally fall in beside him.

Tayla escorted Zhang back to his car where, upon her earlier instructions from Elasus, she had placed one of the company's well-known courtesans. According to Elasus, the only vice Secretary Zhang enjoyed centered around beautiful women.

Back at her desk, Tayla analyzed various network and intelligence reports upon Elasus's orders. Like before, she suspected him of giving the same assignment to Tanner. Of course, she still had all her permissions and already knew who the culprit was who was sneaking the corporation's private matters into the hands of the PGU. Turning Babbage in meant losing her children forever, and that wasn't an option.

Pictures of her children along her desk gave her both motivation and solace during the week's long hours. With Elasus buried in meetings, Tayla closed the spy report and began entering the long, sequential characters needed to access her private portal. Once her concealed connection opened, she pulled up the file she'd been working on for days.

In front of her was a list of fleet ships and crew members, sorted by tenure to include only those who might have served during Grylo's tenure with the corporation. Trying to work with the PGU mole was out of the question, as was trying to contact someone on Ojult directly. The option with the best chance of success lay in front of her, somewhere on the long list of names scrolling on the holo-screen in front of her.

Tayla's rumbling stomach woke her just past midnight. Written on a small paper lay four names: Horatia Buell, Brion Argaez, Corbett Tesar, and Garvin Donato. Out of the thousands of names she'd sorted through, only these four were possible contacts that might be willing to help.

Tayla took a bitter gulp of stale, cold kaldi and wiped crusty sleep from her eyes. With a worn-out vitality, she opened her secure messaging portal and typed in the first name. Horatia Buell was a pilot for the *Gambia* who flew Grylo to the actual MFG station. Tayla chose Horatia because he was the first person to send the corporation a message volunteering to vouch for Grylo's work ethic and dependability. Using the code name Pamela, she typed her message.

> *Horatia:*
>
> *Many years ago, you served with Grylo Cruz, an MFG fleet tech who was exiled to Ojult because of an accident concerning an MFG he had worked on previously. Grylo and his two children were exiled, but his wife remained on Earth and to this day works within the corporation. Recent evidence has surfaced that suggests Grylo was innocent and the search for his children now begins. Would you be willing to put your ship's resources to use and help find Grylo's children?*

Tayla wanted to say more, to put more emphasis on the details behind *why* she thought Grylo was innocent. Yet putting those details into even the securest of encrypted communications was unwise, as was attaching her real name.

The second message went to Brion Argaez, the primary dispatcher who assigned Grylo his missions. Brion was based in Las Vegas and had even come over to dinner occasionally before Elasus decided to shatter their family. She sent a similar message to Brion and with astonishment received a reply almost immediately.

> *Pamela:*
>
> *I'm not sure who you are or what your motive is, but don't contact me again. Grylo was a nice person, so was his wife, but that was a long time ago. I've lost three more techs since then, none more or less special than Grylo. Tell that wife of his that I wish her all the best, but no way am I sacrificing my job for that hunt.*

Tayla slumped back into her chair. Whether it was because it was her first rejection or because Brion had lost other techs, Tayla couldn't determine. The risks were high, and she knew the odds of rejection were just as bad, but it was too early to give up.

She went on to her third possible confidant, Corbett Tesar, captain of the *Observer*, who attended the fleet academy with Grylo during their freshman core classes. Less than twenty-four hours after the MFG accident, Corbett put together an expedition to find the missing ship. According to Grylo, his friend did this for two very public reasons. First, Corbett was good friends with the captain of *Duraturo*, the ship that was slung off course by the MFG and was lost. Likewise, finding the missing ship might help clear Grylo's name.

After Tayla sent her message, the communications portal paused. *Searching... Searching... Searching...*

Corbett and the *Observer* were tasked with exploring potential locations for new MFG stations along with high-orbit scans of newly discovered planets. It didn't surprise or concern Tayla that mass communications relays were having difficulty locating his ship. Tayla went on to her last and least hopeful option. Captain Garvin Donato of the *Night Scope*. Along with a reputation of being a womanizer and egotistical jerk, Garvin also carried the best safety record in the entire fleet. His standing with Elasus was very high, and rumors reached Tayla's ear that he and Commodus Vrabel were good friends. Why then was she reaching out to a man who might just as well turn her in instead of helping?

Grylo had only held two captains in high regard. Hundreds of ships scattered throughout space with attentive leaders at their helm, and her husband only trusted two of them. Grylo had told her during their infrequent times alone that Garvin, for all his faults, earned the trust of his crew and those around him. On the surface it seemed inconsequential, but now, looking back, Tayla believed there was something more behind those pillow-talk conversations. It wasn't much to go on, but Grylo trusted Garvin for a reason, and now, with hope teetering, it was time to take a risk.

All this prancing around in ridiculous outfits, fake breasts, over-the-top hair, and sleeping with the abductor of her children had maxed out Tayla's nerves. She wanted to know where her children were and to speak with them. She needed sleep, she needed closure, and she needed to send this message to Garvin, but it could wait a few minutes.

Frustrated, she bounded into Elasus's office. With practiced hands, she fixed a vodka tonic into a large glass, gulping down the drink. With slightly more self-control and less tonic, she elegantly sipped at the second drink.

She grimaced at her reflection, tears in her eyes. "I made a deal with the devil at the expense of my children; what kind of mother am I?"

"Ms. Cruz, are you okay?"

Startled, Tayla dropped the glass and the fine crystal shattered into a thousand pieces. "Why the hell would you... Tanner? I'm... I'm sorry, you scared me."

Tanner Sands looked down at the shattered glass, then back up to her sodden face. "Didn't mean to scare you. I was working late, and my workstation indicated you were still online. Wanted to make sure everything was okay."

Tayla's earlier scare transitioned to alarm. Tanner never came to this floor unless Elasus was around, and seeing how she'd just sent encrypted messages across the universe, the timing was too convenient. "I'm... sorry. It's just... I needed a drink. All this nonsense on Ojult has me so worried about my children."

Tanner stepped closer, his large figure crushing the bits of broken glass beneath him. "It's understandable. Is there anything you'd like to talk about?"

Fear blossomed within her core.

"No, thanks. I'm going to finish up a few things, clean up this glass, then head home. I'm such a mess right now, please don't tell Elasus I broke one of his glasses, please." She'd lifted her dress up slightly hoping the thought of what lay beneath might distract the glowering man.

Tanner stepped closer. "I won't tell him you broke his glass, nor about your attempts to seduce me by hiking up your dress. You're his property. You'd do well to remember that in *all* your activities." He held her gaze and let the moment linger for several seconds, before he turned, and left the office.

Tayla waited for the door to click shut, then calmly walked over to the trash can, and vomited.

CHAPTER 42: YEAR 2401

Commodus Vrabel sat in one of three vacant seats, only just remembering how bad his feet swelled in space.

"Gonna have to saw these boots off when we land, Garvin," said Commodus.

Blue lights illuminated the bridge, casting a meticulous vibe upon the crew. Since leaving Chden, the *Night Scope's* troubles continually snowballed, and for the first time since knowing Garvin, he felt the crew's uneasiness with the upcoming landing.

"We're on target, Captain. Velocity looks good," said Lieutenant Kass, hovering over her station.

Short, precise reports came in from the crew, narrating the end to the *Night Scope's* worst voyage to date.

"Copy that, Kass," replied Donato.

As with previous landings, Donato perused his checklist several times, though Commodus was pretty sure it didn't include how to land a ship with a giant hole in its side.

"Still no tower communications, Captain," repeated Caitlin Smith. "Worall's dark. Getting chatter from Pa'Gran, hold one."

Commodus watched the communications officer speak with someone over her headset. A violent shudder vibrated through the ship, and Commodus gasped.

"Hazzard, what the hell was that?" asked Donato. "We still have a mostly whole ship?"

Kass who spoke first. "Windshear from the west, hit…"

Another fierce vibration, followed by a breathtaking drop, sent the crew into weightlessness for a moment. "It's weather, sir."

Only Donato's reputation as a safety-first captain kept Commodus from losing his breakfast. His faith in Donato was unwavering, even after the explosion that nearly destroyed the ship.

"Stay focused. Kass, how's our trajectory? Chelsie, slow our descent to five meters per second. Deploy chutes when appropriate. Smith, anything from Pa'Gran?"

"Captain, Pa'Gran's tower is ordering us to land," replied Caitlin. "They're insisting that all cargo-bearing ships land there for inspection."

Commodus and Donato exchanged looks. "First I've heard of that," said Commodus, genuinely surprised. "Play along. Let's see what they're up to."

Donato didn't like last-second changes, and his enduring scowl backed up the notion. "Acknowledge their request. Tell them we're coming in damaged, but in control, and give us a wide berth."

"Aye, Captain," Caitlin responded.

Donato swiveled. "Chelsie, Alanah, work together, and plot us a new route to Pa'Gran."

Another thump, and the ship lurched to the stern, hurling everyone against their restraints.

Donato peeked around the bridge. "If you're not buckled in, get to it. That blast took all our medical supplies, and all I've got is Alanah's dirty thongs for tourniquets."

"Don't forget Chelsie's tampons for bandages," retorted Alanah.

Chelsie waved her middle finger like a pageant winner to the crew, but quickly thrust her hand back down to her controls. "Sir, Charlie thrusters are sputtering, she's starting to fight me."

Brendan Hazzard confirmed the problem. "Got a major pressure change in the primary and secondary fuel line. Safety systems kicked it and shut it off. We didn't get a notification of the issue beforehand because of all the damage. One of those lines runs near cargo bay ten, sir."

The ship was still leaning hard, and Commodus's harness started digging into his neck. Last week's explosion occurred right as the ship exited

FTL and entered Ojultan space. The blast was still under investigation, and Commodus knew little more than what he and Donato had discussed. The explosion occurred in or near cargo bay ten, the main region housing the Celje agents they'd picked up from Lent. The Celje agents were asleep in their bunks when the explosion occurred, sweeping them out into space before they knew what had happened.

"All right, let's do our job here," said Donato. "Hazzard, find a way to give Chelsie enough power to land this bird without sending us all to the chiropractor."

Engineer Hazzard didn't immediately acknowledge the order. His hands raced over his screen, then onto a digital notepad, then to a hand-held calculator. "The best I can get you is twenty meters per second on the descent without risking overheating the remaining thruster regions."

"That'll do," replied Chelsie, fighting to keep the ship level.

Thirty seconds later, Commodus felt the ship even out and his equilibrium return.

"Clearance received from Pa'Gran, Captain," relayed Smith.

From this point forward, the bridge crew worked in silence. Twenty-five minutes later, the *Night Scope* landed hard, but good enough to walk away from.

Once satisfied the ship was safe, Donato escorted Commodus outside to examine the damage.

Some type of hydraulic fluid or fuel, Commodus guessed, flowed onto the ground from multiple holes under the ship near the explosion site. Commodus looked carefully at the gigantic, jagged hole in what used to be holds nine and ten.

"Still no idea what could have caused this?" said Commodus, amazed they'd survived such a devastating blast.

Donato hissed, "No, but I don't think this was an accident. This was designed to take out these cargo holds. The odds that your people were in here is just too coincidental."

Commodus believed his longtime friend, the viciousness in his tone leaving nothing to the imagination.

Donato starting talking through his chiming earbud. "Go ahead, Smith."

Donato's face reddened, then contorted in anger.

"They'll go through this ship right after my boot goes up their ass!" yelled Donato. Another moment passed as he listened. "Okay, get the ship squared away, then follow up with them. No one boards without my permission, and get Lewis patrolling. Donato out."

"What's going on?"

"I asked Caitlin to check with the tower and figure out why the Worall pad wasn't available. Apparently the Celje are inspecting all cargo, in and off planet. They're forcing all ships to pass through Pa'Gran for the inspection. Bullshit if you ask me. Bet you they're asking for kickbacks."

Footsteps approached from behind. "Pardon me, gentlemen," interrupted the *Night Scope*'s security chief, Lewis Bardolf. "Mr. Vrabel, your surviving security detail are equipped and ready to go. They're just outside the rear ramp."

Commodus looked over the newest member of Donato's crew. Lewis was an old-timer, having served in Reeves's fleet for forty-plus years. He had graying hair and enough scars on his neck and face to play chess.

"Good, I'll be over there in a minute," answered Commodus, then he turned to Donato. "Garvin, I'll get the Celje off your back. Nobody from corporate authorized them to do this. Unless you need me, I'll leave you to your ship."

"You've still got a heavy contingent of guards there, Commodus, you really need them all? That's going to draw a lot of attention."

Commodus felt the pistol hanging from his shoulder harness. "You're probably right. Might be more going on here than we know."

Donato seemed only half engaged in the conversation, his eyes still surveying the damaged area. "Well, if you see any Argos, let me know. I've got a bet going with Alanah that we see one."

"The Nein decimated the Argos, they're all gone. But, if I see any, I'll be sure you win that bet. Should I ask what the stakes are?"

Garvin replied with a perfect poker face. "She's got to wear a bikini on the bridge for a week. If I lose, I have to wear one."

The imagery of that statement would forever be cemented in Commodus's mind. "Thanks for that image. You sure you don't want to come with us?"

Donato pointed at the big hole in his ship. "In case you didn't notice, chief, I've got a big-ass hole in the side of my girl here. If you want me to haul your ass you back to Earth, I have to find a way to patch her up."

"You and your crew did a hell of a job. Elasus will know about your heroics." Commodus meant every word. The fact they just didn't blow up in space was a miracle in his mind.

"We still lost a lot of your people, and I'm sorry. My crew and I pride ourselves on safety, and—"

Commodus threw up his hands. "Stop, Garvin. Space travel is dangerous, and so is being a Celje agent. Shit like this is going to happen, and no one blames you. Now, if you're not coming with me, then get your shit together and start duct-taping this hole. Since your puddle jumper isn't flying right now, I might be a few days, maybe a week. I'll call if anything comes up."

Garvin again pointed to the hole in his ship. "Damn near everything in a hold on this side of the ship is at risk right now, chief. I'm not taking any chances with you or anyone else. We'll get working on fixing the ship, then the puddle jumper."

When it came to safety, Garvin never budged. Commodus shook hands with Donato, then headed toward his own men. At the front of the formation stood Jeder Vanderkamp, the head of his security detail. Jeder was every bit as vicious as he looked. Lean and muscular, he wore his blonde-to-gray hair high and tight. His teenage days had been spent street fighting to make money, and his cauliflower ears were a constant reminder to everyone around him that he wasn't to be screwed with.

"Mr. Vrabel, the team's ready," said Jeder.

The two men shook hands. "I want you and two others for now. Choose who you want, and let's get going."

Commodus ditched his sport coat and assumed a more mundane look to better blend with the locals. Jeder and his two guards did likewise, though their modern rifles would give them away to a trained eye.

They exited the north end of the landing pad, expecting to see the usually robust trade epicenter full of people and supply wagons. A much different sight greeted them. Dozens of empty shops lined the streets where only a few dozen people wandered. Rangy dogs fought over scraps while a silver avis circled high above the town. At the far end of town where the grove met the cattle pens, three men hung from a large tree.

"Something wrong, sir?" asked Jeder.

The sight of malnourished children begging for food on practically every corner didn't bother Commodus. What did was the lack of business, the scarcity of people bartering. If trade was bad before, it was surely in the shitter now. Elasus had given him specific instructions to speak with Zakar Qualis upon arriving and get a better read on the situation.

More starving children littered the street as they headed to find a wagon to Worall. More closed shops and empty warehouses as they exited town. Unattended farms and homes met them as they crossed a bridge over the Connery River that cut through the entire continent.

The wagon that took them to Worall was backbreaking, but they arrived in half a day. They'd entered through the southern gate, near Appian's offices where three bullet-ridden warehouses lined the street. Further down, sounds of gunfire and screams pulsated.

"Beer, Beds, and Bras is up that way," said Commodus. "The people that hang out there don't like folks from the corporation. Pilots are okay, but us, they'd probably shoot on sight."

Echoes of thunder reverberated off the nearby warehouses, affirming his earlier supposition of an approaching storm.

Commodus said, "Let's get to the warehouses and find…"

Three men appeared in front of them, each shouldering a seasoned rifle.

"My name's Aldrich," said an older man with a handlebar mustache. "Tell me your business here." His bottom lip bulged slightly and he spit out dark brown saliva.

Commodus didn't appreciate the rifle-bearing greeting, but his options were limited. "My name's Commodus Vrabel. This is Jeder and his security team. Point those weapons someplace else, and tell me where Zakar Qualis is."

Aldrich's eyes opened wide with recognition. "Commodus Vrabel, from the Reeves Corporation?"

Commodus's eyebrows raised with anger, "Yes. Now point those weapons someplace else if you want to live."

Aldrich motioned for his men to lower their rifles but didn't show any sign of giving ground. "Things are a bit tense around here, so tell me what you want."

"He's either here to kill me or he needs my help," came a familiar voice from the dark side of the warehouse.

Commodus peered into the shadows. "Zakar?"

Zakar limped out of the darkness. He looked dirty and tired. "Not sure it's a pleasure to meet you, Mr. Vrabel. You'll understand if I keep my team around while we figure out why you're here."

Commodus surveyed Zakar, his men, their surroundings, and pieced together an idea of what was going on. "You've got an interesting way of making introductions. Maybe Sasha was right about Appian after all."

Zakar's expression was that of indifference, or was that malice. "Misora gave me this limp, and he also executed my predecessor."

Even when it started to rain, Zakar didn't invite them into the warehouse or offer any shelter. He explained the events leading up to today. Whenever Commodus tried to poke a hole in the man's story, Zakar's explanation put the query to rest. Commodus had no choice but to accept Zakar's word.

Jeder inspected the area, then asked the very question Commodus was thinking. "Why does Worall seem in better shape than Pa'Gran?"

The exhausted Appian leader replied, "Because of me. Appian's been rebuilding and keeping up trade as much as possible. The Celje now inspect every crate Appian ships, including the smuggled medicine to shelters and orphanages."

Commodus did some quick math. "You stealing meds is costing the corporation money. Sounds like Misora has the right idea—you need someone watching over you."

"Mr. Vrabel, how much money do you think it will cost you when disease spreads through Capintesta or when the Celje genocide wipes out the very people you profit from? No, Mr. Vrabel, you might sound like the war chief, but I'm the master here, and what I do is for the good of the people."

Commodus paced considering the situation. Sasha and Misora were clearly up to something, but the Nein had a staff-wielder. Nencia was dead, trade was down, and Appian was at its wits' end with the Celje.

Jeder glared at two siblings dragging a crate into the warehouse. "That girl just lifted that box off the ground… without touching it. You're employing mystics?"

Zakar waved a finger and Aldrich's team placed themselves between Commodus and the teenagers. They kept their rifles down, but the implication was clear.

"I care for them," said Zakar. "Mr. Reeves asked Nencia to keep them safe, and if it weren't for an annoying farmer, Misora would have killed them as well."

Elasus had exiled family members to Ojult while blackmailing their relatives back on Earth. Yet there was only one set that his boss gave to Nencia.

"So, those are the two he sent to Nencia? Surprised she kept her word."

Zakar saw through Commodus's lie. "Instead of seeking out information that doesn't concern you, perhaps you should focus on Sasha, or more specifically, his mistress, Achilla."

Jeder positioned himself between Aldrich and Commodus. "Who Sasha screws isn't relevant. What about Nikoli on Meridone?"

Zakar looked surprised. "Nikoli, the leader on Meridone? Appian never had a strong presence on that continent, even less so now. As Sasha's cousin, Nikoli resisted our attempts to set up operations there."

Rain started to fall harder, which hastened Commodus's next words. "Nikoli's isolation seems to have worked, and he doesn't have the mystic problems you have here."

Aldrich stole a quick glance that Zakar did not return. "Perhaps, but my point is the same. We have very little insight into Nikoli's operations."

Commodus was piecing together an ugly picture that put the corporation and Sasha at odds. "Zakar, I need to use your long-range station. While you're setting that up, tell me about this Achilla woman."

CHAPTER 43: YEAR 2401

Donato finished the third scan of the damaged section, triple-checking the data ensuring no other valves were leaking and the integrity of the interior hull was undamaged. He estimated the repairs would take at least three months, and that assumed the fleet management division could deliver to the contested planet.

"How's it looking, Captain?" asked Chelsie from behind.

Donato handed his first officer the datapad. "I've spent the better part of this week making sure I didn't miss anything on the scanners. Hazzard was right, looks like damage was kept within bay ten, though nine and eleven suffered moderate damage and decompression. I'm surprised the blast didn't take out more sections."

Chelsie studied the report. "Other than losing the medical supplies, it turned out all right. I'll begin working with Appian and the corporation tomorrow morning, we'll get her back up and running soon. I'm glad you killed those bastards. I would've aired all three cargo bays, killed the whole damn squad."

Donato unbuttoned the top of his sweat-soaked shirt, the heat of the day taking its toll. "There was a time when I would have sacrificed a lot to stay in the good graces of Commodus and Elasus, but those days are gone. Commodus isn't a bad guy, he's just a company man manipulated by the system he helped create. But for us, we move forward from here, no room for regrets. Take over repairs, and get Hazzard or another engineer down here to check everything. Don't rely completely on the fleet to get us what we need. Have Alanah chat with some of the locals; there's plenty of crashed ships around here, we can loot some hull material from. Ojultan ore won't work, and we also need some sort of nano-tube alloy."

"Repairs are on me. Get engineering to verify, plunder some hull metal. Anything else?"

Feeling the continuous stare, Donato returned the look with a bite. "We aren't going rogue. We continue our jobs for the corporation and take advantage of situations when we can." He paused, realizing how enraged he sounded. He took a deep breath and collected himself.

For years, he'd played both sides of the galactic wheel of fortune. He'd gained the trust of the most powerful man in the universe, earning him wealth and the largest ship in the fleet. Even recently, Donato had helped smuggle weapons to both the good guys and not-so-good guys, aiding those the Earth's governments called "criminals."

"You lead, I follow." Chelsie's tone was unoffended, but Donato still felt guilty.

"I'm sorry. Let's keep our focus on repairing this old girl, and if another opportunity comes flying cross our bow, then we take advantage of it. But let's not go looking for trouble."

"Understood. Where you going?"

A strong gust of wind forged a dust devil that sent specks of dirt cracking against the exposed bays.

"To check up on the puddle jumper, make sure it isn't damaged. I gave Zakar the heads-up Commodus was coming, and we agreed to meet tonight."

Chelsie laughed. "Commodus is going to be pissed if he catches you in that ship."

Donato's plan was to wait until nightfall, take the puddle jumper to Worall, meet with Zakar, then make it back to the *Night Scope* with Commodus and his cronies none the wiser. The creek and grind of the cargo doors panged loudly in the night air, but only his crew noticed the activity. A special platform extended from cargo bay three, allowing the low-altitude, short-range ship to lift off from the structure. The CV-55 rotary-wing ship was built for personnel transport with a 750-mile range. The sleek vessel used four alternating, lightweight carbon-fiber main rotors and six smaller tail rotors, all combining for a smooth and quiet ride. The land-slides pulled up after takeoff and could also be used for water landings, if necessary.

Donato climbed the ladder to the platform, ducking against the amass-ing winds and walking around the ship multiple times, checking for safety oddities. After conducting preflight checks and receiving all green indica-tors, the engines roared to life. Donato kept the ship low and under the scopes of Pa'Gran tower, not that anyone was manning it as this hour of the night. Other than terrifying a flock of phoenixes, no one would know of his flight. He landed the craft on the outskirts of Worall, well out of earshot of the townsfolk or Celje spies. Ensuring the highly valuable ship was locked and secured, he set off toward Worall.

Donato passed Beers, Beds, and Bras, only briefly considering stop-ping in to see his old companions.

"Is he gone?" asked Donato, walking up to the last Appian warehouse.

Zakar looked around, holding a mug in one hand and a cane in the other. "Would I be speaking with you if he was still here? Thank you for letting me know about Vrabel, he wouldn't have appreciated my earlier visitors."

"Don't mention it. Place looks like hell, you guys still picking up the pieces?"

"And will be for quite some time, but we're surviving." Zakar winced and sat down on a nearby crate, then sipped the foam off his ale.

"You got another one of those?"

"It's the strongest ale you've ever had. One might do you in after all that space travel."

"Only if I'm lucky," said Donato.

"Bella, grab an ale from the barrel for our guest."

Donato hadn't seen the girl sitting in the shadows. "Girlfriend?"

Zakar rolled his eyes.

"Here you go," said Bella.

"This is Garvin Donato," introduced Zakar. "He's a space-transport pilot and a good person to know, though if anyone asks, he wasn't here."

Bella appraised him but didn't seem particularly impressed. "I know who he is and his relationship with Aunt Nencia."

Donato sipped the room-temperature ale, leaving a thick barrier of foam across his mustache. "Thanks for the beer. And, Bella, don't believe everything you've heard about me. I can't be that bad." There was no telling what the young woman had been told about him.

"They work around the warehouse. Bella's a mystic. Her brother might be too. They'll be good to have around in the future."

Donato thought about the name, swallowing the unusually warm ale, and feeling the liquid sit heavy in his gut. After their official marriage ended unofficially, Nencia mentioned she'd taken in two kids. Nencia gave no information on them other than she'd made a promise to keep them safe. "So, she's Bella, and she's got a brother?"

"Logan, a few years younger. You seem more curious than usual, what's your interest?"

"Nothing, just rehashing old memories. On to more exciting news, the PGU now know about the Celje."

Zakar's mug sat motionless against his lips. "I bet Elasus and Commodus weren't pleased."

Donato raised his glass. "I'm starting to play a slightly larger role in the activities Elasus and Commodus may not agree with. Maybe you and I can work on a few things together."

Zakar raised his mug. "Taking advantage of a weakened enemy? What do you have in mind?"

Donato wiped beer froth off his mustache. "I hear this Nein leader has a staff?"

"Your ex-wife was the one responsible for getting it to him."

Garvin choked and ale spewed from his mouth and nose. In the rarest of scenes, Zakar laughed out loud.

Barely able to breath, Garvin started his rebuke. "Nencia was smarter than that. If the corporation found out, it would have been the end of her and the operation."

"And yet, here we are. Nencia's dead, the Nein are rebelling, and her operation was nearly destroyed. Don't be naïve, Garvin, she had relationships with the FIAS, which also happens to have the largest Amurski forest."

The FIAS region housed the largest Amurski tree population on Earth. Unfortunately, the FIAS governors were ruthless, even compared to Appian standards, and not a group to trifle with.

Hearing Nencia's name brought up his other reason for coming to Worall. "Did Nencia get a good burial? Did anyone show up?"

"Nencia had just as many friends as enemies. I laid her to rest a few hundred yards behind this warehouse, if you'd like to see her. Logan cleaned up the gravestone yesterday."

Donato's relationship with Nencia was complicated. They loved and cared for one another at various times in their lives, but they had different goals. His aptitude for sleeping with other women, combined with long trips away, didn't lend itself to forging a strong marriage. "Let's grab a couple beers for the trip, I'd like to pay my respects."

With mugs filling all hands but one, Zakar led Donato to the grave site, then left the widowed man alone. Donato said nothing, but sat down in front of the simple grave. The cement slab had a small, square hand imprint made of Ojultan ore on the top. A few tears fell into Garvin's mustache, but not so many that the ground puddled below him. He downed two mugs like a young fleet officer, then accepted two more brought by Bella. He imagined what might have happened if he were on Ojult the day of the attack. Might his presence have saved her life? Guilt and dozens of "what if" scenarios tugged at him. They were friends, lovers, spouses, then friends again, but never close.

On his third trip to a nearby tree to relieve himself, Garvin looked up into the night sky, seeing two of each constellation. The powerful ale was starting to affect him now, and he felt woozy and dropped to a knee.

Soon Bella came to check on him. "You need help, Captain?"

Garvin took a deep breath, pivoted, then fell face first into the dirt.

Small soft hands rolled him over. "I got you a room at the nearby inn and found a way to sneak you up there." Bella tugged but struggled to move the much larger man. "Listen, Captain, I can levitate you, but I'm not that good at it and I might just catch you on fire…"

Though Donato shook his head, he put his arm around Bella, and she helped him stand and walk through the dark. He wouldn't remember making it to Beer, Beds, and Bras, nor the struggle getting up the stairs.

Bella had to be up early and passed him to Lacy. "He just visited Nencia's grave for the first time. He's not in good shape."

At the name Lacy, Garvin's ears perked up, but he was too drunk to move. "Lacky... Luca... that you, babe?"

The inn's madam stood tall and rigid, her beautiful tan skin reflecting the dancing candlelight. "Yes, Gabrielle, thank you for bringing him in. We'll take care of him and ensure he is not discovered."

Donato heard the name *Gabriella*, then the door shut. He wondered why he should care about that name, but then a cool voice took over his mind. "You're a mess, and you smell like space. Time for a bath."

"Ahh, Lukey, it's been a long time" he said, unaware of his unintelligible words.

Lacy started unbuttoning his shirt. "Garvin, whatever *experience* you're imagining needs to first start with a bath, then we'll see."

Garvin smiled, murmured something unintelligible, and passed out.

CHAPTER 44: YEAR 2401

Warren Vaut piloted the Boeing AMS-11 mining ship toward the Webber-James Asteroid Belt, a day's travel from Ojult. The bridge crew manned their stations, but their eyes, why did everyone have their eyes closed? Warning sirens and flashing lights blazed across the bridge, but no one seemed to see or hear it. Jayden sprang up from his seat and started shaking the crew, but they were paralyzed. Collision bells roared to life, and Jayden turned to his father, trying to warn him.

The rear of the ship exploded. Flames hurdled over oxygen molecules, racing through the ship and detouring as decompression forces took over. Jayden's feet cemented into the metal flooring, stopping him from reaching his father. Warren unbuckled his harness and walked toward the flood of flames heading for the bridge.

A flash of green and yellow light blinded Jayden, who now found himself aboard a transport ship next to his mother, Helen, adorned with dark-blue scrubs. She reached up with bandages and medical tape to cover an open wound above his forehead. She smiled but wasn't showing her teeth. A gust of wind blew her shoulder-length hair across her face, covering her green eyes. But… they were on a ship—why was there wind?

Jayden tried to speak, but his tongue seemed glued to the roof of his mouth. A cup of water appeared next to him, and he tried drinking, but the cup slid out of reach.

"I have bad news," said Helen, now stitching a new wound on his arm. Her voice sounded hollow and faint, like speaking inside an endless cavern.

"The corporation called," she continued, looking into his eyes. "Your father's dead. He flew into an asteroid. I'm sorry."

But Jayden was just there, he could have stopped it. Why was he suddenly with his mother?

She placed a cold palm to his cheek. "Don't worry, my son, I'll be with you for a while, but then I must leave as well."

"It's more than just a dream," said a cold voice from nearby.

Jayden slid out of sleep trying to separate his dream from reality. Pins and needles ran up and down his left arm. He used his right arm to push himself up. "What… what did you say?"

Levi looked at Jayden. "You have two arms, perhaps using both may help? Or are you just practicing being weird?"

Jayden flashed a phony smile and gave Levi the middle finger, using his right hand. Jayden shook his head, flushing the cobwebs and images of his parents. Sweat trickled down his forehead from the oven-like temperatures. The heat, among other things, enhanced the disgusting odors of sweat and feces.

Next to him, Andreas snored, unaware of the conversations echoing around him.

"He sleeps like that every night," commented Jayden.

"Perhaps the nurse poisoned him again," challenged Levi.

"You're up early. That magic fairy bus finally coming to get you today?"

But Levi had already closed his eyes, starting his ritualistic meditation that he'd been practicing for months.

"A focused mystic sees his surroundings in shades of gray, even with his eyes closed," explained Levi. "The other prisoners, I can interpret their physical well-being, their heart rate, injuries, and emotions. A well-practiced sage may see objects at their molecular level and choose to manipulate those materials if desired."

"Great, so can any of that get us out of here?"

"Perhaps, if I acquired a staff. Like fuel on a fire. The fuel by itself does nothing, but add fire and the molecules greet one another, ending in a reaction."

"I'm ready to leave whenever you are, let me know if you find any *reactions* around here."

Levi opened his eyes. "A staff cannot burn, nor can it break once taken from the tree."

"I'd prefer a steel pistol over shooting a firecracker from a piece of wood. Not to mention, a pistol still works even if I'm in chains made from special metals."

Levi stood and stretched, ending his meditation. His mostly naked body was scarred and dirty, just like everyone else in the ward. "Bullets, knives, cannons, and whatever else you Thoba use won't defeat the coming enemy."

"You say you're leaving, but here you are. You promise an enemy is coming to kill us all, yet it doesn't seem they can get through the front door. Why didn't they, whoever it is, come last night or last week?" Jayden was tired of Levi's murmurs of hope when none existed.

Andreas's snores gave way to normal breathing. "Since you two can't keep your mouths shut and let me sleep, I'm gonna go ahead and ask you to take me with you, Levi."

Jayden's starved stomach pinched when he began to laugh. "I think it's a one-passenger flight, Andreas. No room for you."

Jayden didn't like Levi, though the mystic had grown on him since they'd first met. Less than friends, Jayden couldn't help but shake the idea that there was something unique about the strange man.

Andreas stood with a slight hunch. "I've got an idea. Levi, you should open a school to pass on your knowledge. I can be a fellow teacher; Jayden, you can cut the grass."

"A school would require competent staff, so you two wouldn't be involved. You're the companion, an afterthought, something less than average. Your place in history will be a forgotten footnote. Stay with Jayden, he'll need your guidance."

Andreas slapped his hand over his heart. "My friend, I'm shocked you'd say such a thing."

Jayden felt guilty for not sticking up for Andreas, but Levi had a point. Andreas didn't exemplify the makings of a great sage.

The cellblock door opened. Eve glanced at Jayden before walking toward the other end of the ward to start her rotation. A single guard stood at the main entrance, resting his rifle across his chest.

"Well, we all know who she's here to see," chastised Andreas.

Jayden watched the nurse as she rounded on the prisoners. Cells bordered the perimeter of the square room, meaning he, Levi, and Andreas would be the last to see her.

Each month, there were fewer prisoners in the ward, many dying from disease, malnutrition, or succumbing to old wounds.

Other than Levi, none of the inmates gave Eve any grief; even Andreas had come around to Jayden's way of thinking.

"Hello, Levi," said Eve. "How are you feeling? Anything hurt?"

Levi sat with his eyes closed. "No worse for wear, though certainly not as well as Misora. Speaking of him, how's his boss and your parents?"

Eve listened to his heart and lungs. "You're dehydrated. I'll have the guards bring more water. Are you drinking your full ration?"

Levi nodded. "I'm getting my rations, just as you give Misora his."

Eve cleared her throat. "Always a pleasure."

She locked his cell and continued to Andreas, bypassing Jayden.

"Hey there, good lookin'," said Andreas's parched voice. "You thought any more about what I said last week?"

Eve smiled. "Andreas, I don't have a sister or a twin. How are you today? Hurting? Feeling different?"

"Only my heart and pride, goddess. Your continued rejection, one day, will be too much."

"Right," she replied, handing him a bowl jashinto leaves. "You've got a cut on the back of your neck that's infected. If it starts hurting, mix those leaves in with your water rations, but you need to heal yourself, okay?"

She closed and locked the cell, then walked toward Jayden.

It took several months for him to trust Eve, but he'd seen enough to convince him she had a good heart. "Hey Eve, how's the job? Volume been good?"

"Funny how Eve always visits Jayden last and spends the most time with him," said Levi with his eyes still closed.

"I think you're right," Andreas agreed. "She ditches the guards, leaves him for last, always tries to drug me. I'm starting to get suspicious."

Eve's cheeks reddened. "He smells the worst, and in my profession, you always save the worst for last."

Jayden tossed a glance over her shoulder. "Not as many guards as usual. Misora losing interest in us?"

She started checking him. "Not as many, no, and they won't let me travel to Pa'Gran anymore for supplies. I have to give my list to a guard now."

"Maybe Misora's giving up the game, or he's got another prison."

She put her finger over her lips. "Your blood pressure is really low. Have you been eating all your rations?"

"Every teaspoon."

Eve felt Jayden's forehead and pulled down his cheek to look more closely into his eyes. "High blood pressure may also arise from lack of sleep. I know it's hot down here, but have you been getting enough sleep?"

Between the heat, nightmares, and fear of torture, it was enough to keep any man up. "Enough I suppose, but I could do without the nightmares."

"Your father again?"

Jayden looked at the ground, feeling vulnerable. "Yes, but this time, my mother entered the dream. It's been a while since I've dreamed about her."

"Your mental health is just as important, Jayden. If you need to talk, I'm here."

He tried to smile. "Thanks, but the last thing I want is to relive the nightmares."

Eve placed a warm hand on his shoulder. "You can talk to me about things like this, I hope you know that."

"My mother, she died of the virus a long time ago. My father died in an MFG accident. Nothing else to talk about."

Eve scooted next to his rank body. "Do you have any other family?"

"No. I was practically a kid when I got here." Since arriving at the prison, only now did Jayden feel the impulse to explain Nencia's importance to him.

Eve looked sickened. "I'm so, so sorry."

Feeling he'd been talking too much about himself, he turned the tables. "So, how about you? Family, husband, kids?"

Eve's back stiffened, and her expression tightened. "My family situation is complicated, but no, nobody special for a long time. It's hard to find a date when mom and dad don't let you out of the house."

There was an obvious backstory that Eve didn't want to bring up, so he kept the conversation light. "Oh, come on, there's plenty of available men in here. Except for maybe Levi, you could clean a lot of these guys up."

"Trying to sway the good nurse into conjugal visits, are you, Vaut?" murmured Levi.

When Eve smiled, Jayden thought the gentle expression fit her. She stopped grinning when she locked eyes with Jayden, then quickly looked away.

Loud snores suddenly took over the conversation. To Jayden's left, Andreas lay face down, arms hanging over each side of the bench, with an empty cup on the ground.

Eve got to her feet. "He didn't mix the leaves with water? Why does he do this to himself. Jayden, make sure he drinks all of his water rations when he wakes up."

"All right. Thanks for checking in."

Eve leaned in and whispered, "I've got a past, just like you and everyone else. Having a flawed family, or one that no longer exists, can mess with you. Don't be afraid to talk to me, okay? This world, it's a lot to handle."

Jayden exhaled. Her perspective on the situation wasn't wrong. "Before things heated up with Misora, I worked a farm in Dalth, had a quiet house away from the Nein and Celje. It was good for the soul."

"And now?"

"And now I'm going to kill Misora, Wren Dikal, and every Celje I see until they're gone from this planet."

Eve didn't flinch. "And then what? Go to Earth, kill Reeves, everyone in the PGU?"

Jayden caught Eve's point. "A killing spree isn't what I had in mind."

Eve walked out and closed the cell door behind her. "I'm glad to hear you say that, Jayden. We need less brutality and more compassion on this forsaken planet."

Jayden watched Eve leave the chamber, the Celje guard following behind.

"If you're so inclined to kill Celje, why not have stayed with the Nein?" asked Levi.

"I was a slave, not a volunteer. I've seen the Nein ways, I've seen the mind of their leader. You think it's just the Celje with blood on their hands?"

"Manipulate it however you want, Vaut. You'll be free one day, and then what will you do? Pick potatoes while your friends die? You'll be forced to choose between the Celje and the Nein; apathy isn't an option."

———————

Jayden again dreamed of his parents. They were at home on Earth, sitting on a couch, watching cartoons. His mother looked happy, her gentle aura giving Jayden peace.

His dream was interrupted by the click of a door latch. He woke, his internal clock knowing it was the middle of the night. From the head of the dark ward moved a heavily armored figure.

"Andreas, Levi, wake up."

"Say nothing," ordered Levi who was already standing and facing the incoming figure.

"Wha... what's going on?" said Andreas.

The figure thumped forward. All lights in the room extinguished. Jayden's adrenalin kicked into gear, as did his survival instincts. He caught a brief glimpse of the figure's armor.

Jayden looked at Levi. "What's going on?"

"Quiet. All is well."

Andreas stood. "I'm starting to wonder what Eve put in those leaves. Are you seeing this?"

The figure stopped, looked at Andreas, then Jayden. The visitor wore heavy leather armor and metal plating over key impact points. A clean but obviously worn metal mask covered his face alongside a dark hood that draped over the shoulders.

"Are you ready?" said the figure.

Levi nodded. "I am, *Daska*."

The hooded figure waved a hand, and Levi's bindings unlatched and fell to the ground.

"It's time. Come with me."

Levi looked neither frightened nor surprised. "As you command," he replied, and turned to Jayden as he stepped out. "You've been a friend to me. I'll not forget."

Jayden was dumbfounded. This hooded man looked more like a courier for Guy Fawkes than an angelic liberator.

Levi followed the man out of the prison door.

Andreas picked up the empty bowl previously full of jashinto leaves. "Did that really just happen?"

Jayden's weary mind swam with questions. "Those chains were made from African ore... I thought mystic powers couldn't affect that?"

"We've got a bigger problem now. What do you think Misora's going to do when he finds Levi gone?"

CHAPTER 45: YEAR 2401

Tayla closed the door to the conference room adjacent to Elasus's office. Another closed-door meeting between him, Tanner, and someone within the FIAS government. Meetings with the African region were more frequent and mysterious. These interactions corresponded with fewer talks with the PGU, an interesting link at the very least. Whatever deal Elasus was brokering with the PGU's largest competitor, he was keeping it guarded. Tayla hadn't been invited to take notes, run follow-up reports, or schedule the meetings.

The days following Tayla's run-in with Tanner were the most stressful of her life. Everything she'd hoped to accomplish teetered on Tanner's true knowledge of her undertakings. Perhaps he'd discovered her meetings with Babbage or broken through her encryption and ascertained her communications across space. Tayla hadn't logged back into her private portal, and only now, with some of her previous conviction returning, did she resolve to carry on the fight.

Elasus was having dinner with Irelyn and Secretary Zhang tonight and wouldn't be back until later, if at all. Under the pretense of staying at the office to hunt down more chatter from Sasha, Tayla bid goodbye to her owner. Tanner exited with little more than a glance, adding more concern to Tayla's shattered nerves.

She spent a full hour researching outbound, tight-beam communications from Ojult. Consistent with her previous attempts, Tayla found no communications to or from Sasha. With this certainty, Tayla logged into her second life.

With no reply from Horatia Buell, she quickly dived into the remaining option on her contact list, Garvin Donato. Weeks ago, Tayla was minutes away from sending the prideful, well-connected captain a message before Tanner surprised her. There would be no interruption this time, and Tayla transmitted the scrambled memo without hesitation.

The fleet-management system had the *Night Scope* on Ojult, hence a reply might not come for days if there was significant asteroid activity in the region. Tayla had wasted valuable time waiting to see if Tanner was onto her scheme, and she wasn't about to squander more precious time.

Tayla's next aim was to help locate Marilla Reeves. To do this, she needed Babbage's help, and that meant another visit to the Dark Souls Lounge. She'd already pictured the outfit needed to enter the veiled building when an arresting chime brought her eyes back to the display.

Pamela

If we're going to chat, then I want to see who I'm speaking with.

Garvin Donato had taken only minutes to respond, suggesting he had nothing better to do or her offer was tempting in some way. Her mind adjusted from befuddlement to implementation. How could she secure a video tight beam stemming the exorbitant distance? The bandwidth alone would alert every meddling satellite within tracking distance. Pondering her options, Tayla thought about the number of ships in the fleet. If she could use the traveling ships between Earth and Ojult to rebound the transmission, the signal might be taken for just another fleet video-conference update. Of course, a nosy comms officer with an annoying tendency to check conference schedules might realize that nothing was scheduled for today, but it was the only option Tayla could think of on short notice.

There were twenty-three ships that could relay the video calls, each with a cyber-defense shield with unbreakable codes. Having been on the coding side of the fleet's cyber-defense program, Tayla knew the systems and their shortcomings. Naturally occurring radio waves produced by intense astronomical phenomena traveled throughout the universe, passing by the planets and ships without harm or notice. However, all fleet ships operated by the Reeves Corporation employed standard operating procedures mandating the full processing of all intercepted radio waves, organic or otherwise.

Frequencies deemed organic were dumped into a cache server for deletion while encrypted or manmade radio waves were transferred to a secure server. Just before deletion, the mainframe transferred the cache files to another folder behind the main firewall. This was done so the system could log the deletion. Tayla's plan was so obviously simple, she verified her method five times before putting it in play.

Placing a nonencrypted signal onto the back of an organic wave, her executable file would jump from the cache file into the secure network one-eighth of a nanosecond before the cache folder emptied. Since her program wasn't encrypted, the mainframe would overlook the program until its weekly systems check.

Vessels identified, transponder numbers verified

Searching for radio noise... Searching for radio noise

Wide-band radio frequencies discovered...
Wide-band radio frequencies discovered

Pamela files sending... Pamela files sending

Waiting... Waiting... Waiting...

Files attached to wide-band radio frequencies...
Files attached to wide-band radio frequencies

Waiting.... Waiting... Waiting...

One of twenty-three uploaded... Six of twenty-three uploaded... Thirteen of twenty-three uploaded...

Connecting... Connecting... Connecting...

Lines of rainbow-colored interference sliced through her monitor before evening out and displaying a mustached captain with stress lines over his brow. Donato squinted as he scrutinized his caller. "Grylo's wife turned assistant to Elasus Reeves? I want an explanation, *Pamela*, or this meeting's over."

"Y-yes, of course, and I'll… I'll do one better. Please, hear me out, Captain." Desperation, fear, and surprise came through her stuttering voice. She uploaded the files she'd prepped earlier, never expecting to share them so soon.

"I wanted an explanation, not a data dump," Garvin snapped as the transfer completed.

"The files are proof that my husband was set up. Please, all I'm asking is for you to look at them. I'm a slave to Elasus, not an assistant. I'm here because… because he's got my children."

Garvin's malicious eye eased. She could tell he was reading the files off to the side of his display. His hand swiped across thin air. "Grylo wouldn't have screwed up this bad, and there's not a brain cell throughout the universe that would believe you'd have volunteered to work with Elasus after he exiled your family. The official records only have Grylo being exiled, nothing about your kids. Christ, what a mess."

Tayla's lungs filled with a refreshing coolness, then exhaled much of her anxiety about the call. "Thank you for understanding, Garvin, it means a lot. I've reached out to a few people who can help, but it's been… difficult."

Garvin massaged his mustache. "So Elasus used the crash to cover up an assassination? Two years ago, I wouldn't have thought that possible. So, I get it, Tayla, I really do, but I've got to be honest, there's not much I see you can do about it. You're better off trying to use those pretty new looks and get yourself in with someone in the FIAS region. They've got spooks everywhere and might be able to smuggle them out, if they can even find them."

"Getting the FIAS involved is a mistake. Elasus has been working with them a lot lately. No, I need someone on the inside, Garvin, someone like you. I've got money, if that's what it takes."

"It's not about the money. This is borderline lunacy and—"

"What about Nencia? Your wife's dead because of Elasus. What happens when he decides to use the *Night Scope* to cover up another one of his assassinations!? The evil strolling leisurely through humanity right now can be traced back to him. We have a chance to push back. Maybe not push him out completely, but we have to try!"

Garvin waved away her idealistic plans. "If someone like me wanted to exact revenge on that son of a bitch, I could. For instance, expunging a bunch of Celje troops out an airlock. And don't lecture me about Nencia. I know the Nein weren't involved, so please, stop trying to be the gorgeous hero that saves the day. We've been on this call long enough. I'm not saying I'm in or anything, but if I were you, I'd find a way to cover your ass before the corporation's security teams find out about your little escapades. Forget about revenge or somehow getting even. Take baby steps, Tayla. We'll be in touch, but no more video chats."

With a potential ally standing on Ojult's surface, Tayla's spirits rose, and her resolve hardened. She decided that for all the talking Donato did, he made one very important point: Someone within the corporation would find out eventually, and she needed to prepare for that moment. It was time to chat with Babbage again.

Several days passed before Tayla had another evening free and Babbage was visiting the Dark Souls Lounge. During a middle-of-the-night venture, she trekked back to the gaming palace wearing homely clothes and no makeup, but this time, an invaluable key rested comfortably in her hand. Tayla bypassed the dozens of tech addicts waiting to enter the lounge and bribed the nearby supervisor guarding the door.

Tech and gamer junkies weren't her thing, but when it came to cyber campaigns, she was the authority. Clear of guards and suspicious eyes, Tayla headed straight for her reserved mech room and pressed a sweaty thumb to the wall mounted dispenser. Framed to the right of the automatic door, the machine flashed green and dropped two, finger sized wrappers onto a small tray fitted below. She placed one packet in her pocket, and opened the second. Familiar with the delicate technology, Taylor peeled back the thin packaging and placed the nerve monitoring patch on the back on her neck. A quarter sized portion of her neck numbed, then Tayla watched as the automatic door slide open.

The dark room smelled of sweat, smoke, and illegal vices, much like the club itself. Inside the digitized room, Tayla pulled the second packet from her pocket. Two wireless earbuds and contact lenses dropped from the wrapper. She inserted the opaque optics first, followed by the earbuds, and then slid on the body suit and gauntlets that lay over the cybernated seat. The instant Tayla sunk into the networked chair, her virtual avatar zoomed into being.

Tayla blew through the introductory course showing new users how to manage their avatar. With two simple commands and a quick change in the privacy codes, Tayla opened a closed network channel to Babbage.

"We need to talk," demanded Tayla. Her voice was altered through her avatar's profile, coming across like an old housemaid who had smoked all her life.

Babbage didn't immediately respond. "The guards out front said you came alone. Is Tanner with you? Does he know you're here?"

She ignored the question and went head first into her purpose for coming. "I need to know what data you covered up on Marilla Reeves. She disappeared around the same time as my files. What did you do with them?"

"Who told you I was involved? I didn't touch that case, and believe me, Elasus threw some crazy dollars at me. That girl's gone, off the grid, and if you ask me, probably dead."

"If you didn't look into it, how do you know?"

"I didn't say I didn't look into it. I said I *didn't* take the case. Of course, I looked into it. Anyone with my skills would have, and my curiosity got the better of me. But I found nothing. If she's alive, she covered her bio signatures."

Babbage had been honest with her so far. Granted, he believed Tanner was after him, so the cyber thief was motivated. There was nothing more to gain, and Tayla moved on. The docuchip in her palm suddenly felt greasy and slick.

"Babbage, listen to my next words like your life depended on it, because it does."

CHAPTER 46: YEAR 2401

Syrus Tokarek stood in full battledress, peering through a thick layer of thorn bushes at a compound surrounded by several hundred acres of open fields. There was no evidence Andreas was inside, but Syrus planned on freeing any captured mystics and ripping apart the Celje responsible.

When a man with unkempt, dark-black hair, sunglasses, and a cocky edge walked through the door to the centermost building, Syrus knew they'd found the right place.

Behind Misora were two Celje dragging a young redheaded woman by her hair. Blood zigzagged behind the woman who clawed and kicked against the guards' armor.

Syrus felt no power emanating from her and brought his attention back to the compound in front of him. It was spread out with few defensive positions between his current emplacement and the center building.

"Premier," said Captain Siller, "one of our forces encountered a Celje squad while positioning to the other side of the compound. He was killed, but it doesn't appear the compound went on alert."

"Fool," said Phaedra. "Why did you send him alone?"

Siller sounded as mad as Phaedra looked. "He left his brothers at his own discretion, not by my orders."

Syrus turned to his senior leaders. All too frequently his Nein were seeking glory against the Celje and giving into their own cravings for blood. Troop discipline cannot always overcome a warrior's lust for revenge, and Syrus needed his commander to understand the lesson.

"Captain, learn from this," Syrus said. "One of our own wasted his life and may have also jeopardized this entire force. We must incessantly remind our brothers and sisters of the larger vision. Remember this. You too, Phaedra. We also know Commodus Vrabel is on the planet, likely hunting us with reinforced agents. Many of our own know this and may seek to kill the executive for their own satisfaction. They must be compelled to see the goal for our people. As for our attack today, it must be swift and merciless, or we'll be defeated by their numbers and our prospects for a moored society expelled."

Siller stood tall, flattening his armored gear. "Our troops are prepared to die for you, just give the command."

Phaedra said, "You've already proven that today."

"Our goal is to liberate our brothers, not toss snide remarks that do nothing for our cause." Syrus's voice remained collected, but the inference was clear.

Phaedra's keen eyes flashed toward the compound. "Another patrol's coming."

Unlike traditional Celje, who preferred to blend in with the population, these guards wore full armor similar to what they'd encountered at Sasha's camp on Listo months ago. The uniform was thick and formfitting, meshing dark colors of green, brown, and black. They wore high-tech headgear that displayed various digital information on their visors.

The lead agent in the patrol lifted his visor to wipe his sweating face.

"Well, if it isn't Brass Balls himself," rasped Phaedra. "That's Sherman, the guy who gave me the information on the compound. The big one on the left."

Syrus wasn't happy about how Phaedra had extracted the compound's location from the soldier, but she'd succeeded.

A messenger knelt next to Siller and whispered in his ear.

"What is it?" asked Syrus.

"All three squads are in position and awaiting your command," said Siller.

Syrus looked to Phaedra and made his decision. He marched through the brush toward the patrolling Celje. The density of the grove provided the cover he needed before unleashing the full might of his power.

Phaedra followed while Siller sent messengers to the other squads.

At the end of the tree line, Syrus looked back at his pupil, then with a quick mental command, a large fireball erupted from his erect staff. The intense orb covered the distance in seconds, detonating in the center of the unsuspecting squad.

Sherman looked up and unslung his rifle just as the orb erupted into an incendiary wave, engulfing the four men, turning their bodies into scorched flesh.

Syrus looked over his shoulder once again, gauging Phaedra's reaction. To his malicious satisfaction, her expression would have burned a whole through a lesser man.

Celje started popping out of tents and buildings. With practiced skill, the agents bolted toward preassigned defensive positions and sprayed the tree line with energy bolts that auto-targeted the vital organs of their targets. Syrus, Phaedra, and other Nein soldiers deflected the incoming fire with conjured, glowing shields that rippled with every impact.

Siller's prepositioned squads rushed down the uneven slope toward the guards. His soldiers attacked with daggers, energy-blades, and rifles, wearing light armor for improved quickness and dexterity.

Syrus launched a barrage of ice spikes, gyrating discs, and fire orbs at the enemy, watching most fall dead in the onslaught. The back and forth of projectiles lit up the morning sky in a beautiful spectacle of raining death. As anticipated, the Celje adapted to Syrus's tactics, ordering their frontline units to separate.

"More coming in from the woods on the far side!" yelled Phaedra.

Syrus surveyed the additional Celje troops. Lowering his shield, he launched three massive fireballs, each landing ahead of the reinforcements. Syrus glimpsed the blackened earth, cursing he'd not killed more.

Zing.

A bullet whizzed past Syrus's ear.

He quickly conjured another shield and reassessed the situation. "They repositioned, we're in a deadlock," he muttered, then noticed two men stumbling out of the center building. The first was an unfamiliar slender man, though the second man Syrus easily recognized. The Celje leader's sunglasses were broken, and gray dust covered his bloody face.

Wisdom on the battlefield was an element not all leaders possessed. For every Nein lost, it would take Syrus months to recruit, train, and replace just one fallen warrior. This knowledge made Syrus's next command difficult, foreseeing what consequences would follow.

Syrus raised himself to his full height and pointed at Misora. "Kavil, take troops, advance on the compound. I want Misora alive."

To fight off the hunger that gnawed at both men, Jayden and Andreas sought refuge in arguing the existence of the Elders.

"Elders don't exist, Andreas. They haven't for decades, and maybe they didn't exist at all. Most people still believe the stories were made up by the PGU to give people hope after the Event."

Andreas's ribs, collarbone, and shoulders showed through his frail body. His head now looked odd atop his frail body, but he still somehow managed a smirk. "They're real, Jayden, and what we witnessed is proof. Normal mystics can't do what we saw."

Jayden was on the fence about the Elders' existence, but he felt reasonably sure that if the powerful mystic sect was still around, they wouldn't have allowed the Celje to torture their own kind for so long.

"Okay," Jayden said, trying to be reasonable. "Why would the Elders, defenders of righteousness, choose *Levi* of all people to speak with? Why did they only release him? What about you and the dozens of other mystics down here?"

Andreas shrugged. "Levi's been saying for months this would happen. How did he know? I'm not saying I have the answers, but I'm telling you that guy was an Elder, no other explanation for it."

"The easiest explanation isn't always the right one. Whenever Mea asked about them, Syrus would brush them off as a powerful Argos that got lucky."

"Well!" exclaimed Andreas, then paused. "Well, all right then, I don't know what to say to that!"

Both men laughed, but their debilitated bodies ached with each chuckle.

Their jovial attitude vanished with a thunderous crash as the ward's front door banged open and Eve walked swiftly toward them.

"Eve, what… what happened?" Jayden asked, looking at her beaten face.

"Good god, Doc, you alright?" Andreas asked.

Eve walked up to their cells, giving both men a clearer picture of the beating she'd received. Hints of dried blood underneath her nose alongside a black eye, a swollen lip, and cuts along her forehead and cheekbones.

"I'll be okay, but you both need to listen." She spoke in a hushed tone, although guards accompanied her. "Misora's back and he's got dozens of troops with him. He's raging mad about Levi and thinks I had something to do with it."

"It's okay, we know," assured Andreas. "It's going to be a long day for us."

Jayden began twirling his ratty beard around his finger. "He thinks we used some sort of magical power to release Levi, but decided to stick around?" It was the logic of a psychopath, and Misora pretty much fit that bill.

"I'm sorry, I don't have more information, but I don't have much time. The guards will be down here soon. Take this." Eve took two small pouches from her coat pocket and handed one to each of them. "Jashinto serum, the same potency as the ones I gave you when—"

"When you knocked us all out?" finished Andreas.

"Yes. He's irate, and… well, I don't want you guys to suffer through what's coming. Please, inject yourself when they come for you. Once in your bloodstream, it will only take moments to put you under."

There was controlled fear in Eve's voice. Jayden was burning up with anger. Abusing this woman was one of the many crimes Misora would eventually pay for.

They heard snoring from Andreas's cell.

"Did he already take it?" asked Eve.

Jayden looked down and noticed the empty pouch next to his friend's bench. "Seems he did."

Eve put a hand over her mouth. "But it's too early, he might—"

Eve stopped midsentence and Jayden understood why. "Did you feel that?"

Eve shook her head, trying to listen. "Earthquake maybe?"

Two loud bangs reverberated throughout the ward. Eve clapped her hands over her ears and shut her eyes. Andreas stirred.

"Eve, go!" Jayden demanded.

"Jayden, I… what's going on?" She shrieked as more booms echoed through the ward. Footsteps rushed through the main entrance.

"Eve, run!" Jayden peered at the ceiling, feeling confident the structure wasn't strong enough to withstand much more of whatever was crashing down on them.

A guard rushed into the room and grabbed Eve. "Come with me, now!"

Eve resisted, and the guard knocked her down and dragged her out by the hair.

"Hey! Leave her alone!" Jayden shouted, but he was powerless in his cell. Soon Eve was gone, and the door slammed shut. Jayden turned to Andreas. "Andreas, wake up!"

The unmistakable pops of gunfire burst from inside the building, followed by the screams of casualties. Other prisoners inside the room started yelling and chanting, convinced the gunfire was a sign of impending freedom.

Several bullets caromed against the prison entrance, and Jayden dove behind his bench. The ward door flew open, and two guards entered, weapons out.

"Misora says kill them and then regroup at the north building," said the leading guard.

Realization among the prisoners spread quickly. Cries of mercy and panic bleated from their worn bodies. The guards fired several rounds into each cell, relishing the screams of their victims.

Jayden turned to Andreas, screaming his name over and over.

The Celje approached the cell adjacent to Levi's. The prisoner inside stood rigid, frozen in fear, then six bullets slammed into his chest and head. The body slumped forward, crashing into the concrete floor as the shackles around his wrists pulled him back toward the bench.

The guard was now in front of Jayden. The barrel of the rifle squared on chest. A commotion from the entry door distracted the guard, granting Jayden a temporary reprieve.

Dozens of shots rang out, and the guard toppled to the ground.

"Two down but check the room," whispered a strange, new voice.

Armor-clad men stepped into the room. The first, a short man with a patchy beard and balding scalp, the second, a young woman with silver hair.

Siller scanned the room one last time before unhooking a large key ring off one of the dead guards. "I'll check for survivors. Phaedra, cover the escape."

Phaedra nodded and proceeded back through the main door. Jayden watched as Siller opened each cell, checking for survivors, finding none, then moving on to the next. Soon enough, Jayden and Siller stood face-to-face.

Jayden pushed himself upright, exposing his gaunt figure. Though he'd kept his beard and hair short while in Dalth, Jayden now resembled his look while with the Nein.

"Hello, Kavil."

Siller looked at him closely, then to the cell next to him, recognizing Andreas. "Is he…"

"No, just drugged."

Siller unlocked Andreas's cell, kneeled, and checked for a heartbeat. "I suppose you're responsible for him being here?"

"Actually, no, he was here when I arrived, but those are just facts, nothing you'd be interested in."

Siller unlocked the impermeable shackles cutting into Andreas. "Are there other prisoners, other sites?"

"No idea. They kept us down here except for their little one-on-one sessions." An idea clicked, and Jayden couldn't believe he'd not thought of it before. "But there's a nurse here, a nonmystic, who's friendly toward—"

"We care only for our own Vaut, you of all people should know that. I came for Andreas and our other devoted followers. You forget that your kind are beneath us. You serve us, not the other way around. If you had understood that, maybe you'd still be with the Nein."

Jayden stepped toward the cell door until his shackles caught. "Her name's Eve, and she's been helping us, including saving Andreas's life multiple times. All I'm asking is that if you find her, get her to safety."

Siller turned toward Jayden and methodically edged his sword into his cell. "The night you left, Syrus gave me permission to kill you as long as you were on the island. I searched for days, not stopping for food or rest. And now I have you in front of me."

Jayden stared at the bloodied sword that rested against his chest. He refused to let the savage see him beg for mercy. He would not show fear, not in front of this man.

Siller looked down at Andreas, conflicted. "You chose to fight for the weak rather than stand with the strong, the rightful rulers. Ten years with us, and you learned nothing."

"I learned the difference between right and wrong, the gray that exists between good and evil. No, Kavil, I learned a lot, it's you who sees only black and white."

Silence filled the space between them until Siller withdrew his sword. He hoisted Andreas over his shoulder, then turned again to Jayden. "This girl you mentioned. You're asking me to save an ordinary woman when I'd just as soon keep her as a slave? Tell you what, I won't kill you, but I'm not going to help you either. If you escape this place, stay away from the Nein and from Syrus. You're not welcome. If we cross paths again, I'll kill you."

Siller carried Andreas out of the room.

"Godspeed, Andreas," Jayden whispered.

Hours of explosions took their toll on the room. The ceiling was caving in as the walls buckled on the far side. Seeing his life ending soon, Jayden lay down comfortably on his bench, thinking of Nencia, Helia, his parents, and countless others he'd known over the years. In truth, he'd never expected to leave the prison alive, but dying under the crushing weight of an underground bunker...

"Jayden, are you there!?"

A large concrete block slammed against the top of his cage spewing dust all around him. "I'm over here!"

"I... I can't see much."

Jayden's heart lifted. "Eve! What are you doing!? Get out of here! The building is coming apart!"

A large section of the ceiling crashed down near the foyer.

"Eve!" Jayden scanned the area, trying to glimpse her through the dust.

"I'm here!" she said, climbing over pieces of rebar and metal from Levi's old quarters. "I… I thought you'd be dead! Where's Andreas?" She looked around, then realized all the prisoners were dead. "The two people who ran in here left you… to die?"

There wasn't time for talk. "Eve, the keys are gone. I can't get out. Please, save yourself!"

"I've kept you alive for this long, I'm not about to abandon you or anyone else down here now. I've still got my keys."

She pushed and prodded the key. "I think the latch is jammed or broken!"

An enormous detonation above them sent the remaining ceiling thundering to the ground. A jagged cement slab tore through the ceiling, edged its way through the narrow railing above the cell, and smashed into Jayden's shoulder.

The impact slammed Jayden into the floor, leaving him bewildered and chasing white stars. Fervent, straining, grunts from nearby, told his rattled mind that Eve was trying to reach him. Dust and debris continued to rain down while Jayden's body refused any command to move. He felt calloused hands fasten around his wrist. The grip was tight, but tender. Someone began pulling him across the rocky floor, stopping, then pausing to catch their breath. Dirt and other rubble cut through his ankles as his body was dragged outside until coming to a rest on a grassy incline.

"E… Eve?" he gasped, his throat dry and sore. "You need… you need to escape. If they… find you…"

"Jayden, your shackles, they're broken. Come on, get up!"

Weak and severely injured, Jayden hadn't noticed the heavy metal shackles had ripped off when the ceiling crashed. With an effort, Jayden smiled. "I'm… I'm really not… a mystic. I can't just float out of here."

A man suddenly appeared in his view. Eve was thrown to the ground, sending the bag she was carrying careening near Jayden's body.

"You little tramp!" flamed Misora. He'd climbed on top of her, punching and slapping her. "I gave you protection and a place to sleep, and this is how you repay me!? Ojult would have put you into the ground if it wasn't for us!"

Jayden heard Eve screaming, but his senses were crossed. Rolling onto his side, he felt wet grass between his fingers and toes. Actual wind flowed over his back, sending chills up his spine.

Jayden heard the sound of ripping clothes. Beaten into submission, Eve was no longer putting up a fight.

A brown bag lay next to Jayden. He fumbled with the bag's latch, feeling the familiar leather that adorned his back during many journeys. His hand quaked until brushing against an intimate metal object. Jayden struggled opening the partially rusted cylinder. Misora was ten meters away, perhaps more, but Jayden's hunger to kill this man once and for all overcame all other burdens. Using both hands to lift the pistol, he took careful aim and pulled the trigger.

The impact tossed Misora like a sandbag and rolled him several feet. Eve moaned and lay still, her hands over her face. Tears mixed with blood trickled down her nose and lips. Jayden pushed himself to a knee and readied for another shot. Misora twisted onto his back, revealing a smoking hole in his shirt and a pistol in his left hand. The two men fired in unison. Jayden's second bullet tore through Misora's right rib cage and exited near his collarbone.

Jayden's physical capabilities were spent, and he dropped the pistol into the grass. "Eve… you… run. If the Nein… if they find you…" Jayden collapsed, hearing only Eve's terrified sobs, which turned to screams just as Jayden's peripheral vision narrowed. Jayden probed his chest with numb fingers. Misora's energy bolt had left a tonze-sized hole in him, and blood was fleeing his body. Jayden's last vision was of Eve, screaming for help.

CHAPTER 47: YEAR 2401

Syrus moved around the prison's perimeter, killing the dying Celje as he passed. A dozen of his Nein were lost, and he had two bullet wounds himself, but the battle was worth the cost.

They'd recovered Andreas, though he was starved and overdosed. Much to Syrus's dismay, Siller had failed to secure Misora or any other high-value Celje.

As Syrus approached, Phaedra ignored his presence as she'd done since the battle. Syrus surmised she was still upset at the death he'd given her brief Celje lover. Using her honed powers, Phaedra worked on Andreas, healing his more visible injuries.

"What's the final count of our dead and wounded?" asked Syrus.

Siller hesitated. "Still twelve, with six under the care of healers."

The Celje were becoming more advanced with their tactics, causing more casualties than ever before. The casualty rate was unacceptable and unsustainable.

Syrus said, "The Celje today had advanced weapons and armor. Why? What makes this group unique compared to others we've faced? These are questions you will find answers to Captain. Have you cleared all buildings?"

"Yes, my premier. Most of the buildings on the exterior were holding facilities for Thoba. Mostly specialists, engineers, scientists, doctors. The central building, the one holding mystics, we've not been able to enter since the roof collapse."

Syrus glimpsed the razed building. The only recognizable part, the main entrance, looked surprisingly untouched. "Kavil, continue searching for stragglers, kill on site. Phaedra, have Giles look after Kavil. Follow me."

Syrus and Phaedra stood at the entrance of the primary compound that had housed Andreas and the other mystics. Syrus hesitated, for even his unparalleled power couldn't keep the structure standing for much longer.

"You're sending me in there?" seethed Phaedra.

They walked down the uneven hill, hearing the faint trickle of water from the nearby river. The stream was part of the Connery River that forked at the northern side of Capintesta. One segment drifted south near the prison compound, the other flowing just north of Worall, then through Pa'Gran, and eventually emptying into the Altum Sea.

"Wait," said Phaedra, her voice recognizing danger ahead. "Stay here a moment."

Ahead of them, just outside the main compound, Syrus felt what Phaedra had observed. The strange aura permeated through his senses, leading them both to the same spot. Phaedra jogged ahead, swords in both hands.

Several hundred feet away, Phaedra relaxed, then knelt next to a red-headed woman who worked frantically over a motionless man.

Syrus approached, stopping near enough to see the dying man.

"Jayden," hushed Syrus.

The redheaded woman looked back, then continued compressing Jayden's chest.

"He's barely alive," said Phaedra, using her abilities to aid the nurse.

"He was a prisoner here. My name's Eve. He escaped, but a man named Misora caught us and shot him. He's got a collapsed lung, and he's bleeding badly. I don't know if he can heal himself or not. Please, I don't have any of my equipment or supplies, if… if you can heal him, please, I beg you."

"He's not a mystic," replied Phaedra. "Syrus, something's wrong. My powers aren't working. He's not healing."

Syrus peered around the grounds. "Misora found you? Where is he now?"

Eve stood and faced Syrus. She was several feet shorter than him but boosted a strong presence nonetheless. "Please, there's a doctor in Pa'Gran named Kevin Castellani. He—"

"Quiet," Syrus said. "Pa'Gran is a foolish option. You mentioned Misora, where is he?"

Misora, Andreas, and now Jayden, all at this prison at the same time. The questions were endless, and the odds of such a thing astronomical.

Eve's cheeks were turning purple. "I... don't know. Jayden shot him just over there. Please help me!"

Syrus waved both women away. "Step back, both of you."

Jayden wasn't just white, he was nearly transparent, not to mention malnourished to such a degree that Syrus could clearly discern each of his ribs and the faint thumping in his chest. He had a long beard and hair reminiscent of his days with Syrus, minus the lice and other insects living all over his body.

Syrus focused his healing abilities on his former slave, allowing his staff to enhance his restorative powers. He felt Jayden's lungs heal and spleen mend along with the entry and exit wounds.

Continuing to use his powers, Syrus spoke softly. "The bullets, they've left a trace that doesn't respond to our powers. He's beginning to slip beyond my reach. I've given him a fighting chance, but whatever caused these wounds is blocking our abilities." Syrus opened his eyes and looked toward Eve. "You said your name is Eve and that you are a healer?"

"Yes, why, what's wrong?"

For the first time in a long time, Syrus felt helpless. "We might take him back to Carendra, but—"

"No," Eve interrupted. "That's too far. He'll never make it. If your powers can't heal him, then we need to operate, remove whatever fragments are still inside blocking your abilities."

"Interrupt him again, sister, and you'll be the one needing an operating room," threatened Phaedra.

Syrus clinched Phaedra's shoulder and pulled her away. "I need him to survive. Eve, you seem to have thoughts on this, explain?"

Why he couldn't heal Jayden was a question for another day; for now, he needed answers.

"Dalth," replied Eve. "That's where he's from. He told me of a practiced nurse there who sounds like—"

Syrus didn't care for the specifics and there was something about this woman that he trusted. "Then he will go to Dalth under your charge. If he dies, so do you. Phaedra, put together an escort, and make sure they reach the town. I'll convene with the others and ensure Andreas's returned to Carendra."

Syrus spun and headed back up the hill, leaving the two women in surprised silence. In the far corner of Syrus's mind, he considered that Kavil already knew of Jayden's presence here.

———————

After overseeing the cleanup of the battlefield, Syrus rested his marred body inside his personal tent. The temporary canopy provided space for everything he required, including a hot-water tub where he soaked and healed. Indentured female slaves came in sporadically, bringing hot water, food, and wine. He dwelled on the battle, the number of Nein lost, the recovery of Andreas, Kavil's strange behavior, and the discovery of Jayden, the man who'd saved his sister.

Then there was Eve, a prisoner herself who seemed to wallow while treating his people. With no extraordinary abilities, she saved not only Jayden but also Andreas and apparently countless other mystics.

Syrus slid underneath the water line, his eyes staying open as his body relished in the euphoria of hot, clean water. He lingered underwater until feeling the presence of another mystic. The powerful presence stood in front of the tub, wearing full armor, a metal mask, and a staff sheathed to his dark-blue-and-maroon garments.

Syrus's chin ascended above the murky water line. "Sneaking up on me isn't wise," warned Syrus, keeping his eyes focused on the intruder.

The man bowed, acknowledging the rudeness of the intrusion. "You're Syrus Tokarek."

"Courage or foolishness brought you into the tent of the most powerful mystic on the planet. You had the element of surprise and might have killed me, but you didn't. So, tell me, why are you here?"

"My name is Melron, and you will listen to my words."

Syrus rose from the blazing water and readied himself for combat. Melron made his move, tossing a coin into the air. Syrus caught the coin, confused. "Sneaking into my chambers, then making demands is not the way I do business." Syrus mentally reached for his staff leaning against the far wall, but nothing happened. He glanced at Melron, who raised a hand, and Syrus suddenly found himself flung over the tub and onto the floor.

Melron made no other move other than to kneel beside him. "I have no time for games, Tokarek. The fate of our kind is at stake. You'll listen to my words or I'll kill you and move on to another."

Syrus's hands were cuffed behind him, though no metal bound them. "You've made an enemy today," Syrus retorted, using every ounce of power within him to break free.

Melron placed a hand on Syrus's forehead, pushing him into a dream-world of pictures playing out a story in his mind. Violence and blood filled the nightmare, mystics and Thoba sharing the same frenzied death. The nightmare abruptly ended, and Syrus found himself free of the invisible bonds. Dazed, he raised himself to a knee. "What... was that?"

Melron stepped back and spoke with distress. "That is the present and future of our kind, Syrus Tokarek. If you value your life and the lives of those who serve you, listen to me."

Whomever this Melron was, his power was undeniable and overshadowed Syrus's. "I'll listen, but I need to know what that was you just showed me."

Melron gave a slight bow. "That tonze in your hand is why our people suffer. I'll explain this and much, much more."

PART V

CHAPTER 48: YEAR 2401

The first rays of the morning sun brushed the treetops of Dalth, signaling the parade of roosters to wake up anyone still sleeping. One such crow perched atop a fence post outside Serena Visconti's small home, and sang much to the dismay of the hungover woman still trying to sleep.

"You're dead rooster, you're dead!"

Serena fumbled around her nightstand looking for her pistol, but only managed to knock over a three-day-old mug of ale, a glass of water, and an empty lantern.

"Oh, come on!"

Naked, and not completely sure which room she'd passed out in, she stumbled into the kitchen. Head pounding, room spinning, and after ten minutes of early-morning effort, Serena finally got the furnace and kettle going.

Sheet creases still lined her face as she ventured outside, quickly finding the barrel of freshwater and plunging her head into it. She let the water run off her face and onto the porch, grimacing slightly as her previously injured shoulder ached with stiffness. Letting out a sigh of resentment at life, Serena walked inside and readied herself for the day's work.

An hour later, she was melting Ojultan ore and molding metal frames for Kun's new wood-burning stove. She rested frequently, drinking whiskey-laced coffee, and puffing on a hettle stalk.

Once the six sides of the new oven were complete, Serena stepped away from the furnace, took off the heavy protective clothing, and sat down at her desk to begin putting the finishing touches on a new type of ammo she'd been working on. Using a combination of two different heating furnaces, Serena believed that she'd created one of the most efficient rifle-caliber bullets yet. She planned on testing the ballistics on three newly finished armor pieces she'd created last week, and if successful, she expected Appian might pay a handsome price for the new projectile. The idea of smuggling anything through Appian brought Serena nothing but pain and guilt, but the war against the Celje raged on regardless of her guilt. By now, Dalth had given up hope of ever finding Jayden even though Zakar sent messages every few weeks about possible leads.

Serena bowed her head and considered praying, like Markus, but the moment passed. She smashed her fist on the wooden table, spilling bullet casings onto the ground. She inhaled a large puff of smoke, letting it out slowly. She wanted to kill Misora.

Shuffling gravel pushed Serena's remorse aside for the moment.

"Hi," said Bélise, letting herself in through the screen door. "Whoa, what died in here?"

"I had a rough time last night, haven't had time to clean up. What do you need?"

Bélise took a wary step back, uninterested in discovering what was causing the smell.

"How refined," muttered the teenager. "My father said I should come get you. He said it's important."

"Probably another one of your father's speeches about me drinking too much and how I should find god."

"Uh, it probably should be," Bélise said, gesturing to the mess that surrounded them. "But no, I think it's about the visitors that showed up."

Serena headed toward the town square with her pistol strapped to her thigh. It didn't take but only a few dozen steps to figure out where everyone, including Markus, was heading. She changed direction after seeing Markus lead a pack of newcomers toward Celine's clinic. The newcomers carried a stretcher. As she neared the clinic, Serena identified the newcomers as Nein based on their armor and style of clothing.

"This is going to end well," she murmured, lighting another hettle stalk.

Why the Nein were here she couldn't guess, but Markus kept some strange friends, why not add these lunatics to the list?

Soon Serena walked past a Nein guard and into the dimly lit building. Celine and a redheaded woman worked feverishly on a thin, bloodied man lying atop a surgical bed. The man was naked but for his underwear and looked about as pale as her drinks from the night before. Serena crept closer, not wanting to attract attention from the accompanying Nein or Markus. An image of her past, like a reality she'd not known for decades, flashed before her. She faltered into Markus, catching his shoulder so as not to fall.

"It can't be…"

"It's okay, I've got you," said Markus.

Celine and the ginger haired woman were speaking rapidly and using medical terms she'd never heard before. "What happened? Why are the Nein here, with… with Jayden? Is… is he alive?"

A woman with long silvery hair and black armor stepped near the bed. "Keep quiet so the healers don't screw anything up."

Serena felt her pistol's weight against her thigh, paused, then discerned what the woman really said. "Why is a Nein trying to save Jayden?"

The woman's eyes narrowed on Serena. "I was sent to safeguard him."

Markus interjected. "Serena, this is Phaedra. She's the one who found Jayden and escorted him to Dalth. The attending nurse is Eve. She was held captive and forced to work at a prison operated by the Celje." Markus turned his attention to Phaedra. "Phaedra, this is Serena Visconti, a long-time friend of Jayden. In fact, Jayden's the reason Serena's with us today."

Serena's thoughts were finally catching up with her emotions, but so were more questions. "What happened to him?"

"Come over here, and I'll tell you." Markus led her to a medical cot.

Her blood pressure jumped with every new detail, and now it seemed Dalth was playing host to a Nein guard detail tasked with protecting Jayden.

Serena noticed something peculiar about Phaedra. "You there, Phaedra, that sword with the red grip, where'd you get that?"

Phaedra's hands went to her sword handles bordering her neckline. "What the hell does it matter?"

Serena paced coolly toward Phaedra. "You make that yourself?"

"It's not for sale, if that's what you're thinking."

"You're an idiot, but let's pretend it's not the first time you've heard that," continued Serena. "I'm the one who sold that and other pieces to Nencia who sold them to Syrus. I'm the metallurgist Syrus's been working with the past couple years."

Phaedra eyed the weapon. "What of it?"

Serena moved on. "The war against the Celje, are you winning?"

Phaedra turned to look at Jayden. "We're killing more of them than they are of us."

Celine murmured to Eve. "We can remove whatever's in him later. If we don't sew him up soon, he's going to bleed to death."

"He's lost a lot of blood then," Serena guessed.

Phaedra nodded. "He was shot with some sort of energy weapon designed to take down mystics. I've already tried healing him, as did Syrus. The bolt may have been poisoned with something, but no one really knows."

Serena's knowledge of different alloys and metals, everything her father had taught her, culminated at this point. "I think I may know why your powers aren't working."

Before Phaedra could reply, Serena pushed past her toward Celine.

Celine didn't welcome the intrusion. "Unless you've got some miracle cure, let us work."

"Celine and… Eve," Serena asked the redheaded woman.

Eve, a medical person of some kind, didn't seem any more welcoming. "Step away if you can't help!"

"Look, Celine," continued Serena. "Have you found fragments of black residue, almost like gravel?" Celine nodded. "It's African ore, extremely toxic to mystics but also acts like a blood thinner to us. The mystics can't heal tissues that've been polluted by it. Remove all the fragments, then see if one of these mystics can heal him."

Celine and Eve exchanged glances.

"I thought we got it all out, but this makes sense," said Eve. "At the prison, the Celje used African-ore-laced chains to keep the mystics from using their powers. This isn't a huge leap. If we're gonna do this, we need to do it quick."

Celine stole a peek at the blood-soaked floor and rags around them. "Then let's do this and pray we're not too late."

Serena, Phaedra, and Markus watched as the two nurses worked to save Jayden's life. Blood dripped off the surgical table while Jayden's body went chalk white. During the procedure, Jayden stopped breathing twice, sending the team into a CPR cadence.

Tears filled Serena's eyes, and she turned away from Markus as to avoid his sympathetic gaze. She'd do anything to save Jayden's life but felt helpless standing there, hands in her pockets, hoping that Markus was doing enough praying for the both of them.

After an hour, Eve turned to Celine and the group. "I don't think there's anything else we can do."

Celine nodded. "We need one of the mystics to try again."

Phaedra stepped forward, arms crossed. "Well, what are you waiting for? Get out, all of you."

Understanding this was Jayden's best chance, Serena tugged on Markus's arm. "Come on, let's leave them to their business. Plus, we need to talk."

Once out in the open and away from prying eyes, Serena opened up. "Having the Nein here is dangerous. If the Celje haven't noticed them already, they soon will, and we'll have another Worall on our hands. As soon as they fix Jayden, you need to get them out."

Markus's eyes were swollen and bloodshot, but his voice was steady. "I have assurances from the young lady that the Celje won't likely be coming here."

"The young lady? You mean the crazy one in there who seems like she'd rather attack all of us than be here? No, Markus, you're risking the lives of everyone in Dalth. The Nein are just as dangerous as the Celje. Use them, and get them out."

In hindsight, Serena knew better than to taunt Markus into some sort of witless retort. His wisdom and experience didn't lend itself to taking her bait. "You'd use these people to save Jayden, then cast them out? Is that what I've taught you? Is this the leadership I've shown?"

She would have preferred a slap across the face than his reasoned response. Her apology hung on the tip of her tongue when Phaedra marched out of the clinic.

"You may think you're whispering, but the entire damn clinic heard you." It wasn't hard to pick out who Phaedra was admonishing. "For the record, we think the Celje are nearly defeated. The last of their guards are fleeing west of Pa'Gran and probably headed for Meridone. Syrus wants Jayden safe, and leading the Celje here wouldn't accomplish that, now would it?"

"Meridone?" said Markus.

Phaedra faced the surprised mayor. "We think Sasha and Misora are headed there. There isn't much left for them here, and Sasha's got a cousin over there—Nikoli."

The news the Celje might be off the continent lifted Serena's spirits, but quickly sank back to reality by the report of Misora's escape. "I owe Misora a long, painful death."

Phaedra shrugged. "I imagine your friend in there will want a piece of him too."

The clinic door opened again. Eve said, "I'm sorry, I didn't mean to interrupt—"

"It's okay," said Markus.

Serena said, "Thanks for working on my friend in there."

Eve was covered in blood and looked like she'd not slept in days, yet she still managed a smile. "Your advice might save his life."

Phaedra pushed past the group. "Watch for infections, and come and find me if he gets worse."

"Eve," said Markus, watching Phaedra leave, "was Phaedra able to heal Jayden?"

"She stabilized him, but he's in bad shape. Mystics can't create blood, he'll need to regenerate that on his own. Serena, you were right about the ore. There were two fragments lodged inside."

Serena fell into Markus's open arms, vowing never to leave her home without a flask again.

Eve stepped back from the heartwarming moment. "I was told that your pub had rooms available. I'm going to head there for some rest. I don't have any money, but I can—"

"You've brought back one of our own, Eve, you're a welcomed guest to an indebted town. Please, stay as long as you'd like. You'll pay for nothing as long as you're here."

The bags under Eve's eyes seem to grow by the second. "Thank you, Mayor. I know it must be disturbing to have so many Nein suddenly show up on your doorstep."

"Understatement of the day," said Serena.

"What we mean is that it's the least we can do for you. Stay at the local pub or Serena's home, whichever you prefer," offered Markus.

Markus hadn't said anything about this to her, and Serena instantly thought of Eve drinking her stash of whiskey. "Well, Markus, let's not get ahead of…"

"Thank you," said Eve, yawning. "That's awfully kind of you, but the pub will be just fine."

Serena picked up on Eve's *too* quick reaction. "I'm not buying that. I just met you and I can tell you're not just tired. What aren't you telling us?"

Eve had more to say. "I'm sorry to unload this on you, but we've been so rushed that I haven't had a chance to really sit down and think. It was something Jayden told me that you probably need to know. In the prison, Misora brought another man in to… to interrogate Jayden, and they seemed to know one another. If I remember correctly, his name was Wren Pelt, maybe Potts, or—"

"Dikal!" blurted Serena. "Wren Dikal, yes?"

Eve nodded. "Yes, that's him."

Serena looked in the direction of Wren and Shari Dikal's home. "Markus, I haven't seen Wren in over a month, but I know Shari and Diego are still there."

"He checked in with me three weeks ago," said Markus. "Wren travels a lot this time of year, but Eve, this… this is significant. Please, before you go, I must know everything."

Serena listened in horror as Eve recounted Misora and Wren's torture sessions with Jayden and the other prisoners. One particularly nauseating report detailed Wren pummeling Jayden with a shock-gauntlet, then thrusting a knife into his shoulder. The episode had nearly killed Jayden, and Eve admitted she'd still thought Jayden a mystic at that point.

If a man's heartbroken soul had a face, Markus wore its mask just then. The idea of someone betraying his trust was implausible to the man's genuine nature. "It seems your escape from that place was nothing short of a miracle. Thank you for sharing all this. Perhaps when this is all over, you and I can sit down to discuss God's plan for you. For now, though, both of you keep this quiet until I've had a chance to deal with the situation. If this is true and Wren has played us for fools, we could all be in danger. Eve, I think it more appropriate that you stay with Serena until this issue's resolved."

CHAPTER 49: YEAR 2401

Ten tons of Ojultan ore weighed down Markus as he walked away from the Dikal home. The conversation was short, and Shari admitted she'd known Wren was double-dealing between the Celje and those who opposed them. This explained why Wren kept Diego away from the other children and why Shari never grew close to any of the other women.

Markus needed to pray for Jayden's recovery, to seek wisdom from his God in the trials that would come, then spend time with his gifted daughter. The silence of his home revealed his daughter was nowhere around.

Markus took advantage of the solitude and kneeled before a single white candle in his bedroom. Religion had always played a role in his life, his father and grandfather instilling the notion of a higher being in him since he was young. Now, as a single parent, leader of Dalth, and quickly approaching old age, those ideologies played an even more prevalent role in his life.

"Amen," said Markus, rising stiffly from the floor. His stomach growled, and with some hope of finding Bélise near the town square, Markus headed for the pub.

———

"Hello, mon amie, how are you?" hailed Victor Dubois, motioning Markus to sit down. Three glasses and an open bottle of red wine rested on the circular table. "You missed an excellent brew this morning. We had the most wonderful rambutan and real plump, moist oranges with a small glass of white wine, delicious. You've been working too hard, so I grabbed my best bottle and opened it. Kun has already partaken in this fabulous vintage, and we have snacks as well."

Markus looked over the table. "What snacks? All I see is wine."

Kun raised his hands in resignation and headed toward the kitchen. "The French are weird," he said, then started frying bacon and toast for Markus.

The mayor did his best to keep the conversation with his friends casual, but his mind was elsewhere, unable to part with the idea that Wren Dikal was a traitor to his town and his own kind.

"Well, I heard about that despicable Wren Dikal. Should have known it from the beginning," spat Victor in an intoxicated accent. "Never liked him. Horrible taste in food, and my wife, don't even get me started. Celine never liked him, and she knows bad men. What of Shari though? Fine woman, she needs a man, a French man in her life."

Kun reached across and refilled all three musty glasses. "Sounds like Shari just needs a different man, or maybe just some time away. If you think Liao can help, just ask, Mayor."

It was possible Shari was colluding, but so far, the facts didn't lend to that conclusion.

"What is this?" said Victor. "This is not from Dalth. What have you done, Monsieur Nguyen? Are you trying to poison us!?" Victor stood in disgust, tripped over his chair, and crashed to the floor.

"It's ale from a new barrel you drunken fool," replied Kun. "Mayor, any chance Wren was working with others within the city?"

Victor struggled back up to the table only for Kun to push him over again.

Victor propped himself up on his elbows. "We must not start such rumors. They snowball into disgusting things, like makeup on a beautiful woman. We cannot stoop to this."

The men were practically speaking over one another, giving Markus little room for thought. "I prefer to stick with the facts, and nothing leads me to believe anyone else in the town was working with the Celje."

Kun's even manner slid into something dark. "If you need anyone taken care of, let me know. You, my family, even Victor, I'll protect them."

Markus figured this was the closest thing to a confession he'd get from Kun about why he and Liao were exiled to Ojult. Kun had supposedly killed a man for having an affair with his wife, but Markus never broached the subject. The man looking at him now, this was a killer.

Bells chimed as the front door opened. Kun rose to greet the patron, then froze. Markus's back was to the door and thus didn't initially see what rooted his friend to the floor.

Turning slowly, Markus found a very large, very intimidating man wearing distinguishable Nein armor and a sheathed staff across his back. Behind this godlike figure stood Phaedra, her silvery hair coming to rest across her shoulders.

"I'd like to speak with Mayor Fonte," said the large man.

Victor's unexpected hand shot up from the floor. "See, Mayor, I told you. Bad vintage, and when you choose such horrible spirits, this, this is what you get."

The inebriated farmer received curious looks from everyone in the bar, including the Nein. Markus slid off his chair and greeted the newcomer as he would anyone else.

"Hello. I'm Markus Fonte. Welcome to our town."

Syrus closed the distance between them in two long strides, then stuck out his hand. "My name is Syrus Tokarek, leader of the Nein. I wanted to meet you and thank you for saving Jayden Vaut."

Markus reciprocated the handshake, then looked at Phaedra. The young woman's eyes were narrow slits of anger, but why?

"The pleasure's mine, Mr. Tokarek. We had lost hope of finding Jayden but are certainly glad to have him back. Your protégé here deserves praise as well. Rumors have reached me that the voyage from the prison was fraught with Celje, and her healing abilities ultimately saved him."

"She did her job. Perhaps you can find a suitable place for us to speak... in private?"

Markus agreed and led them toward his own home, the quietest place he could think of. Kun followed the men with ale and small samples of food.

Syrus explained how he knew Jayden and his significance to Syrus's deceased sister. It was here when Markus noticed a shift in Syrus's demeanor. Was it regret or perhaps shame? Whichever, speaking of Jayden clearly stirred something within the notorious leader.

As quickly as Syrus started the conversation, he ended it, leaving a stillness between them.

Markus crossed his legs and sipped his mug, enticed by Syrus's account. "I must admit, our time with Jayden wasn't nearly that interesting. I first met him when he saved a young woman from our town but was badly injured in the fight. Celine Dubois, the same woman taking care of him now, saved his life. Since then, he's been a simple farmer and a much-needed resource to our town."

Unlike Markus, who appeared relaxed, Syrus sat rigidly with perfect posture, his staff leaning against the wall. "I must change the focus of our conversation, Mayor, to the reason I'm here. The past few days have been☒ educational. Finding Jayden alive, along with one of my senior council members, has brought about new perspectives. My war with the Celje is nearly complete. I've defeated them on Listo and nearly driven them off Capintesta. Once I've rid the planet of them, Ojult will know freedom."

"Freedom from whom, exactly?"

Syrus sneered at the remark. "The Nein never seek the opinions of lesser people. Yet my sister saw something in Jayden and other Thoba. In many ways, she was beyond her time. She never agreed with the Nein way, nor my rule, but her love toward family never wavered." Syrus sighed. "Jayden risked his life for Helia, and that act, along… along with other things, has weighed on me especially hard. Fate has brought me back to Jayden, and by consequence, to you. I don't think it a coincidence that a man whom my sister trusted now lives under your domain."

Markus felt like he was being ridiculed, thanked, and mentally hijacked all at the same time. "Again, Mr. Tokarek, you mentioned freedom, but those offering that freedom may define it differently. For example, you and I may see this liberty in very different terms."

"You're associating the brutality of the Celje to the Nein, yes? You believe that Ojult is trading one dictator for another?"

Markus sat back on the stiff couch and folded his hands in his lap. "That's exactly what I'm thinking, and while I appreciate the company, I'm not sure why we're in my home, eating together, and acting like our peoples have somehow reconciled. In truth, I despise the Nein and have hoped for many years the Argos might reorganize and finish you off. So, let's do away with the idle chitchat and get to the point where you tell me why you're here."

Any Nein of the past would have struck him down right then for such a remark. The fact he was still alive told Markus something very, very important.

There is something he needs from me.

Syrus extended his palm and created a black-and-purple orb. "Conversations I've had recently lead me to believe that a fight, beyond our comprehension, is coming. Alone, our peoples will not survive."

Markus heard uncertainty in Syrus's voice. "A fight? From whom? You just assured me the Celje are defeated. If you are looking for soldiers, well, I'm no warrior, and neither are my people."

"I came here to plant a seed of trust. Like any seedling, it will take time to grow, but it must start somewhere."

The next morning, after sending Bélise to Celine, Markus made his way up to the pub where he hoped to begin a new frontier with the Nein. He didn't trust them, but now they shared a common enemy. Beyond this, however, Markus wanted to learn more about Syrus's thoughts on the Elders and how much he knew about the Argos living on Ojult.

The morning was already humid and damp, stifling Markus's mood from the get-go. His hopes of forging this peculiar new relationship with the Nein turned sour almost immediately.

"Additional fighting will be met with severe punishment," said Syrus over the howls of the crowd.

Echoes of "Yes, premier" and "Of course, Sir Tokarek" were heard, followed by "Who the hell are you to tell us what to do?"

Markus made his way through the small crowd and into the middle, placing himself next to Syrus in a show of support. "Please, everyone, calm down," pleaded Markus.

In front of him, a Nein, short in stature with tanned skin and a patchy beard, raised his sword. Kun was next to the man, recognized the motion, and reacted. In seconds, Kun had Kavil Siller on his back. Feet away, Phaedra launched an energy wave that tossed Kun and Kavil into the air, slamming them into bystanders. Syrus stepped into the fray and used his massive form to separate them.

Markus suspected the crowd would soon morph into an unruly mob. The fight took an interesting turn when Serena skidded into the scuffle to help Kun. With quick reflexes, Kavil carved the air with a side strike. Kun rolled but left Serena exposed. The blade grazed her torso, tearing her blouse and opening a small wound. The brawl was halted when a Nein dived into the riot, and placed himself between Serena and Kavil.

"Care to play with me, Kavil?" said a cool, confident voice. "It's been a while since I've danced with a proper opponent." The Nein man stepped in front of Serena and produced a semitranslucent shield in one hand, then lit a hettle stalk in the other. His armor exposed a sheathed short sword and holstered pistol, both positioned for a swift draw. The newcomer looked emaciated and many stones underweight, but ready to battle.

The two Nein put their weapons down and went into an all-out melee.

"What are you doing, Andreas?" roared Siller. "They're the enemy!"

Andreas snapped back, "The enemy? They're farmers and schoolteachers, not agents of some super-secret empire."

Siller snuck in a quick kick, which put Andreas onto his back.

Andreas rolled back to his feet, wiping blood on his pants. "I've spent over a year under the control of someone else. We have an opportunity to change Ojult, and the first thing you do is attack a woman who's done nothing to you?" His frail body was unable to continue the fight, and Andreas turned, then knelt next to Serena. "I'm Andreas Palada. You okay?"

"I… I'm fine, just a small cut, it's not bad."

Concern draped over his eyes. "If you'll permit, I can heal that."

"I don't need to take… my shirt off or anything, do I?"

"I usually prefer the ladies in my life whole and not bleeding from the stomach. Perhaps, if you let me fix that, you can show me around your lovely town?"

Serena nodded, and he placed a gentle hand over the wound. It wasn't pretty, but the bleeding had stopped and the wound scabbed. "I'm afraid

I don't know how to fix the tear in your clothes, but the injury shouldn't give you any trouble."

In the many years Markus had known Serena, this was the first time he'd ever seen her lost for words. Wounded and stunned, Serena stared warmly into her healer's eyes.

"Phaedra!" interrupted Syrus, his booming voice causing everyone to jump. "Lead our people to the outskirts of town. No one re-enters without my approval."

Phaedra began pushing and grabbing Nein, forcing them away from the cooling crowd.

The crowd kicked up dust as they divided, murmuring empty threats to help dispel their unease. As the square cleared, two people remained, whispering within their sphere of isolation. It was a small, perhaps inconsequential moment, but Markus prayed the exchange between Andreas and Serena was the spark needed to bring the two peoples together.

CHAPTER 50: YEAR 2401

Inside the clinic, Syrus's calloused hand glowed as it hovered over Jayden's chest.

"Let's give him some space," suggested Eve.

Celine, Eve, and Markus watched as the faint glow grew brighter. Syrus's eyes glossed over, and Markus got the impression he was seeing into Jayden at a level even Earth's medicine couldn't achieve.

Syrus freed himself from the healing trance and addressed his audience with deep undertones. "The earlier situation with my guard captain will not happen again. I am here for many reasons; brutality is not one of them. Captain Siller is a battle-tested mystic worthy of his title, but inaction doesn't suit him. For Jayden, I believe he'll survive. Mayor, please find me if his condition changes."

Markus offered up Jayden's old home for use and Syrus accepted with goodwill. A cool breeze off the Altum Sea surfed through the open windows of the neglected home. Syrus spent most of his time outside, surveying the town, watching children tending crops or playing, men hauling dirt and supplies from one side of town to the other, women gathering food and chickens or, in one case, casting iron for armor.

It was the first time he'd observed the workings of the Thoba in a free setting such as this. Could the two peoples unite and defeat the inevitable challenge by the corporation, the PGU, and the threat Melron spoke of?

Just outside Jayden's home, Syrus pondered a different reality. Helia, the one he trusted above all, taken from him, leaving his niece orphaned and in hiding.

An approaching presence nudged his psyche.

"Premier," said Siller.

Syrus turned to see his disheveled commander adorned in plain clothes. "Speak."

"Our spies along the coast have confirmed that Sasha and Misora left Capintesta on a ship bound for Meridone. They seem to have taken the remnants of the Celje with them." He paused, apparently expecting some sort of praise for delivering the news.

Syrus's eyes bore into the captain. "The story of Misora's injuries were exaggerated then? Interesting. Convene Phaedra and Andreas. We must plan our next action."

———————

Hours later, Syrus leaned against his temporary desk, staring at his three advisors. "Know that I plan on inviting Jayden Vaut back into our ranks." Syrus paused, watching for any signs of debate over this sudden announcement. "He's still unconscious, and we cannot wait. With the Celje off Listo and Capintesta, it's time we moved forward."

"Absolutely!" shouted Siller, knowing better than to argue the point about Jayden. "Your reign will be marked by scholars as the greatest in history!"

"Scholars? Who says *scholars* anymore?" mocked Phaedra. "And why the hell are we waiting on Vaut? He's an ordinary and a nobody. Not to mention he's not very good in a fight."

Syrus continued. "Vaut, is a skilled killer, don't let his mild temper fool you. And Helia saw something in Vaut when I did not. A mistake I don't plan on repeating. The corporation will soon send more reinforcements to Sasha. Because of this, we must ally ourselves with the Thoba. Such a partnership will not sit well with our Nein warriors, so those who disagree are to consider themselves banished."

The muscles in Phaedra's face tightened. "Should I prep a speech for the kids or are we passing out fliers?"

"Despite the girl's usual chastising comments," said Kavil, "we already know who in our group will not stand for this, best we put them down now."

After decades of working with the man, Kavil's attitude surprised him. "The cold-blooded killing of our brothers is not part of my strategy. The corporation hasn't shipped exiled mystics to the planet for months. For now, we keep to the plan. Kavil, you will head back to Listo and assist in tightening up security."

Phaedra's spying eye left no doubt what she was thinking. "You're putting our battle commander on guard duty, again?"

"Andreas, your absence from my side was noticed," said Syrus. "Trade and security are your priorities on Capintesta."

"Of course," said Andreas, blowing smokes rings off a hettle stalk. "If I may add a small fact. I understand everyone's thoughts on Jayden, but I've had the fortunate opportunity to spend some time with the man. He is no fool and he can take a beating. If we're serious about joining with the Thoba, he can help bridge our two peoples. Plus, he's loyal as a puppy to the mayor here. Win one, you might get the other."

Out of his three advisors, Syrus trusted Andreas's leadership the most. "It will take more than just Dalth's mayor. Widen your search, contact all continental leaders. Garner their support and help them prepare for a counterattack."

Andreas mentally tugged on the smoke rings turning them into spinning discs. "What of Appian? Zakar might be ready for a little payback."

Syrus's lips landed together in a contemplative line. "Zakar's spy network along with his trade base will be a great benefit. He has been rebuilding and might be ready to rejoin our effort. Try to enlist their help."

Kavil's tense posture gave way to his dislike for the plan. "The Nein are hated amongst the Thoba and we expect them to join us? And Appian? The Celje watch Zakar's every movement. My premier, if we send Andreas to Worall, we risk losing him again."

Phaedra spun and stomped away from the two men. "I'm going to go paint a big red target on my chest, be right back."

Syrus caught her in a telekinetic clamp and yanked her back. She skidded until grinding to a halt in front of him. "I am not oblivious to the risks, but my commands will be carried out. One last item before you are dismissed. All Thoba slaves are free from Nein servitude unless still under contract or serving because of a crime."

Phaedra gave an unrelenting glare. "You do this, and there'll be riots on top of the ones we're already going to have. Don't get me wrong, part of me wants you dead, but just not like this."

"The lady's right. You'll have a lot of former slaves with pent-up hostility," said Andreas.

"Lady?" questioned Phaedra, turning around.

Andreas curtsied, knowing fully how Phaedra obtained the prison location in the first place.

Syrus raised himself to full height, towering over his council. "The decree goes out tomorrow."

———————

Syrus strode passed the Nein guard posted outside Dalth's clinic and found Eve at Jayden's bedside. He thought her intelligent and her devotion to her trade was admirable, uncaring of what or who her patient served.

Syrus previously questioned her about other missing Nein, suggesting they'd ended up at the prison, but outside of Andreas and Jayden, she didn't seem to befriend many of the inmates. When he'd asked how she came to be on Ojult, she retold a story he'd not heard before. The Reeves Corporation exiled her because she supported equal rights for mystics and was apparently very outspoken.

Eve looked rested, though her bruises and cuts were still healing.

"How is he?" Syrus peered over Jayden, who looked more ghostly than yesterday.

Eve brushed her red hair behind her ears and folded her arms. "His heart rate and blood pressure continue to improve, but I'm concerned about his nutrition and hydration. I don't have IVs or anything to force fluid into him. I don't suppose you mystics have any alternatives?"

"Unfortunately not. How much time do you think he has?"

Eve placed her palm on Jayden's forehead. "Thanks to your handiwork, his fever is gone, as is the internal bleeding. But he hasn't eaten in a week."

Syrus turned to Eve. "Thank you for helping him and my people, it won't be forgotten. If you think he'll come around soon, then I shall prepare to depart. Please send for me if his condition changes."

He had turned to leave when Eve blurted, "I hear you're trying to unite our two people. That's pretty bold."

Not since Jayden and Markus did a nonmystic speak to him so informally. "News travels fast I see."

"Yes, it does. Am I going to become another prisoner for a different master this go-around?"

Syrus walked back up to the young nurse, unafraid of the debate. "I serve a cause that will benefit both our peoples."

"Deceit and ulterior motives are what your kind are known for. Is everyone just supposed to accept this radical change?"

"My ancestors did what they felt was right, just as I do now. Times are changing, as are the threats we face. We must adapt to survive."

"Doesn't matter anyway, does it? Most people don't even know what the Celje are, and the others will think the Elders are going to come and save them."

Syrus peered deep into Eve's green eyes and surmised she was holding something back. "Perhaps. Send for me if his condition changes."

Syrus walked out of the clinic and spotted Andreas conversing with a Dalth woman.

"He dead yet?" Phaedra was leaning against the wall. He'd not sensed his apprentice, a sign of her growing power.

"If he doesn't wake soon, his body will perish."

Phaedra picked kerns of food from her teeth. "The redhead seems pretty optimistic."

Syrus didn't find the jest amusing. "You are thinking about Kavil's reaction? He will not disobey me, and if he attacks Jayden, he will be banished." Phaedra waved the idea away, but Syrus was not to be ignored. "Thinking ahead is something you'd do well to learn if you're to lead the mystics one day."

Phaedra pushed off the wall. "I've told you before, I don't want to lead mystics, people, or anyone! I was put on this destitute planet to kill. That's my purpose."

"Yes, well, the universe has a funny way of wrecking plans. For now, put this nonsense out of your mind. I have a private mission for you."

Phaedra raised an eyebrow. "I'm speechless, do tell."

"Do you recall the conversation about the Reeves's child possibly on Ojult?"

"Of course."

"I want you to find out if there's any truth behind it. Work behind the scenes like you did when searching for Andreas." His young, brash apprentice, despite her many faults, brought back Andreas when all others had failed. Gratified by her efforts, Syrus viewed her perfect for this new task.

"I've proven I can fight. I'm reliable. Send me to the front lines where my training can actually do some good!"

"Don't get caught lusting for battle, Phaedra. I've taught you many things, bloodlust isn't one of them. We fight when we must for a cause we believe in, not for the fight itself."

"I'm not going anywhere," said Phaedra, palms fastening to her hips. "I know when I'm being manipulated. Tell me what's going on, really. No more garbage, what's your end game here?"

Youth was always stubborn but probably not as consistent as Phaedra. Was now the right time to convey the truth? Time was getting shorter, and he needed his apprentice for this mission. "Last year, when we raided the small Celje camp where we found the notes telling us about the Celje attack on Worall, Sasha's journal was also discovered. Much of it was encrypted, but the parts I could decipher told me more about the man than I ever knew. He's cunning, deceitful, and he thinks he's been wronged by Elasus Reeves."

"So, you're feeling sorry for him?"

Syrus knelt and drew what looked to be a chess board in the dirt. "Sasha's not thinking three or four steps ahead, he's dozens. He's got plans to revolt against Reeves, and I think Nencia found out about it; that's why she was killed. Sasha wouldn't risk this much unless he already *had* the upper hand."

"They ended Nencia because of something she found out about?"

Syrus finally had her attention. "Perhaps it was this child."

"You want to capture this child for… leverage? If I remember right, Elasus has a son. I think the daughter died a while back."

"Son or daughter, if they're killed, then our leverage is gone along with any chance of negotiation. They'll come after all of us, to extinction."

"I should've seen this coming. When did you become—"

"See the bigger picture, Phaedra! Our people face extinction! See past the Celje. See the threat of the *real* hidden enemy that *will* come for us. If we aren't ready, our people will die." Phaedra had no idea how important she was, how much her strength meant to the Nein. In a practically unheard-of gesture, Syrus placed a rare consoling hand on her shoulder. "Our people will need you. I can't predict the future, but my time here is short. People like Jayden and you will lead Ojult beyond the defeat of the Celje and the corporation."

"Right," said Phaedra, shrugging off the comment and his hand. "This kid better be worth it."

The world around Jayden gradually came back to him. He realized he was naked, very sore, and starving. The sounds around him were muffled, but hearing people talk was a good sign.

Dead people can't hear, can't wiggle their toes, and aren't hungry.

He wiggled his fingers and toes, then tried to use his left arm, which was tingling and asleep. Using his good arm, he rubbed crusty sleep from his gummed eyes. The room was dark, blurry, with only a few lanterns for light. For one anxious moment, he thought he'd been brought back to the prison.

He managed a croaked, "Hello." His throat hurt from thirst. He tried to swallow and choked on what little saliva was left in his mouth.

A soft hand pressed against his forehead and cheek. "Don't move," said a familiar voice. "You've been through a lot."

His faculties weren't firing on all cylinders yet, but the voice and those green eyes.

Eve's warm smile reached into his core. "You're recovering from surgery. Don't move, you're still in bad shape."

"Everything's... a little... fuzzy."

She checked his vitals. "Eat something and let me get some fluids in you, then I'll tell you everything."

He ate small bits of bread and vegetables, hydrated himself, and listened to Eve's explanation. He'd nearly died again, and extreme efforts were made to save his life.

Jayden was lost for words. "Saying thank you doesn't seem like enough."

Eve's grin forged dimples in her flushing cheeks. "You have a habit of getting shot and beaten more than anyone else I've ever known. But listen, I need to tell you something first. Someone from your past is here, in Dalth."

Jayden already suspected where she was heading. "Syrus Tokarek," he said, trying to avoid the bitter taste that name left.

"I know you don't like him much, but hear me out. He ordered his people to bring you here, then sent an escort to ensure your safety." Eve's voice trailed off, suggesting there was more to be said. "Syrus is still here, in Dalth. He's been checking on you daily and seems genuinely concerned."

Jayden swallowed his first thought as calmer words came to mind. "The important thing is that you and Andreas got out." He noticed her posture shift. "You look tense, anything else you need to talk about?"

Eve ran two stained fingers through her red hair, pretending to untangle an imagined knot. "Just in case people ask, you've been mumbling in your sleep about Nencia. I know it's none of my business, but you've had a lot of visitors who also heard it."

"She was an important part of my life, I won't deny it."

Eve turned away, overly focused on looking for something on a nearby shelf. "Yeah, good, that's what… exactly. So, a few people wanted to know when you woke up. I don't want a lot of people here at once, but a few wouldn't hurt, if you're ready for it."

Soon the clinic door opened, followed by a bright light and a teenage girl with glasses.

"Bélise," piped Jayden, his voice still recovering. "My gosh, you're tall. Didn't think I was gone that long?"

"Jayden! You're up!" She rushed over and choked him with an affectionate hug. "Why do you get beat up all the time? And, Ms. Eve, my father is having lunch soon and wanted to know if you want anything. I guess Jayden might want something too? He should eat, he looks dead."

Eve turned away laughing. "I'll eat later on, but could you tell your father that Jayden's awake?"

Bélise was already halfway out the door with her exciting news. "Sure!"

Seeing Bélise stirred thoughts of the other children in town, then an anger painted his battered face. "Wren Dikal, is he here? Did you tell them about him?"

Eve shoved a firm hand into his chest, keeping him in place. "I already told Markus about him. I don't think he's been in Dalth for weeks. Markus also spoke with Wren's wife. I don't know all the details, but he made it clear that she wasn't part of it. Markus also reached out to someone named Zakar to keep an eye out. And before you ask, Misora escaped. You shot him, but somehow he slipped through Syrus's net."

Jayden relaxed back down. "Looks like I failed on all accounts. Wren's gone, Misora's alive, and Syrus's in Dalth."

Eve placed a firm grip on his wrist, checking his pulse and looking at her watch. "A few more days of rest and food for you. You're not out of danger, Jayden, so please, rest. The problems of Ojult aren't going to be solved by a half-dead man who continually manages to get himself shot." Eve pulled the covers over Jayden's chest. "I'm going to get Celine, then maybe you can help me figure out where to go after here."

"Wait... you're leaving?" There was much he didn't know, but Jayden was sure he didn't want her to go. "Eve, there's... maybe a lot of Celje out there looking for you and... you'd probably be safer here."

His argument was weak and her crooked eyebrows told him she agreed. "Since you're begging me to stay, I'll consider it."

She was out the door before he dared reply. "I... I didn't beg."

CHAPTER 51: YEAR 2401

The bow flawlessly kissed the violin, ringing soft, tranquil music through Elasus Reeves's master bedroom. He woke peacefully with the calming music.

"Jay, wake-up alarm off and home alarm off," ordered Elasus to his artificial-intelligence home system. A soft chime dinged in response. "Play Chopin, any song." Chopin's Ballade No. 1 in G Minor began to play, one of his favorites. He folded the covers down and sat up, resting at the edge of the bed. Unlike his younger days, he'd pass right out if he just hopped up out of bed. Flattening and adjusting his gray silk loungewear, he gave his blood pressure time to adjust, then stood.

He set off for the kitchen where his favorite coffee, an Ojultan bean, topped the filter. It was the last bag of this particular bean, the crop apparently no longer in business or unable to get it off-world.

"Jay, where's my wife?"

"No record of Mrs. Reeves entering the home on record," replied the AI.

The perfectly brewed coffee leisurely brought his consciousness into full awareness. The past few years were difficult for his family, financially and relationally, and he admitted that not even his brilliant mind could fix everything.

The sound of running water caught his awakening mind. With coffee in hand, he followed the sound back toward the west hallway, near the kids' old rooms. The culprit was a leaking toilet that hadn't been used for years. "Jay, send a reminder to Irelyn to have a plumber come out and replace all the toilets."

He next headed to the front door, whose panel just above the door-knob displayed the weather: *39 Degrees / Wind Southwest 19 Knots / No Precipitation*. He looked down at his thin garments. The gate guard would have brought the *Journal* to his doorstep, but Elasus still disliked the cold. The twenty seconds needed to retrieve the paper brought memories of his decision not to relocate the corporation to Florida. If Florida wasn't a smoking, ruined disaster area, things might be different.

He owned the most technologically advanced company in human history, yet still preferred the paper version of the *Journal* and opted not to gather important news from television outlets. Being Saturday, the paper was thinner than usual, but the weekend was just another day in his busy life. Walking back into the kitchen, he sat down with coffee and paper in hand. Elasus meticulously scrutinized every word, front to back, while finishing exactly two cups. Of course, this was his usual routine, and today wasn't going to be usual. He'd only gotten past the headline when the phone rang.

"Incoming call from Tayla Cruz," said the AI.

Good news never ensued from a call this early. Elasus double-tapped the kitchen table, and the holo-display illuminated above his hand. "Good morning, Ms. Cruz."

"Good morning, Mr. Reeves. My apologies for the early call, but I have information that requires your attention."

Elasus flipped the paper over and grabbed a nearby pen. "Go ahead."

"Mr. Reeves, the Las Vegas police have reported, and both the PGU and coroner's office have confirmed, that Prime Minister Kennedy was found dead of an apparent suicide in his home this morning. I say this because yesterday evening, Hewitt picked up your wife and took her to the prime minister's residence. Hewitt just contacted me and indicated that he'll drop off Mrs. Reeves at your residence shortly."

Elasus wrote down the times mentioned by his personal assistant. "Thank you for the call. Please message Commodus and let him know of the minister's death and that I will need to speak with him in the next few hours. Contact me if any additional information should come to your attention."

After the call, Elasus showered, shaved his head, trimmed his beard, and dressed.

"Side garage door, open," chimed Jay.

The stunning female figure of Irelyn Reeves entered. Her high heels tapped against the tile floor as she rounded the corner. She wore a purple tank top, black nano workout pants, and her hair up in a bun.

"Hello," she said, walking past Elasus and into the kitchen.

Elasus reached over and adjusted the paper so Irelyn could read the front page. "His death is tragic, don't you agree?"

Irelyn glanced at the paper and stopped reaching into the cupboard. In shock, she dropped into the chair next to him. "My god, what… how?"

Elasus examined his wife's body language. He knew she'd slept with Kennedy last night, but how she reacted now told him much. "I need to know where you were last night."

She rose from the chair and shuffled to the other side of the kitchen. "You son of a bitch. How long have you known?"

Elasus calmly sipped a fresh cup of coffee. "It's important I know all the details about your whereabouts last night so when the PGU and local investigators eventually find out you've been sleeping with the now-deceased minister, I can protect you."

She turned her back on him and started fixing herself an energy drink, with more than a touch of vodka. "I… I spent the night." She turned and looked at him, her face pale with dark circles around her swollen eyes. "Don't pretend you didn't already know that. So… you… you had him killed?"

He often thought his wife's intuition was her strongest attribute. "Yes, I had him killed," he replied idly. "Poison was dripped into his workout shake yesterday afternoon. The poison, when exposed to sulfites in red wine within a certain time frame, induces a heart attack. Now, what time did you leave his home and where did you go?"

She refilled her empty glass, spilling more on the counter than into the glass. "I suppose I'm next? Family is everything to you and once you're out, then you're out, right?" She strode toward him. "Bet you don't have the balls to do it yourself."

"I think we're beyond the point of consulting with one another about family commitments. And no, I have no plans to remove you. Now, what time did you leave his home?"

Irelyn looked at her watch and tapped a few buttons. "I left around four-thirty this morning, went to the gym, got my nails done, then came home. So, if you're not going to kill me, I guess you're planning on pinning his death on me? That's nice. Well, if I'm going to jail, I'm not going looking like this."

She walked off without giving him a chance to respond, so he followed her into the master bath. Her emotional state was out of sorts, but Elasus could sense there was something else floating in that double-crossing mind.

"No one will hurt you," Elasus said as Irelyn undressed and walked into the shower. "Investigators will find Kennedy died of natural causes, and you'll be cleared after questioning."

She leaned against the steamy shower doors. "You killed him because I was sleeping with him? You're either suddenly jealous or a psycho."

"Ending a life isn't a simple matter, and I don't take it lightly. Kennedy's death served me in many capacities, none of which I care to explain."

Irelyn showered close to the glassy door so he could see every detail of her sculpted body, but to what end? Moreover, she'd not shed a tear over the death of her lover. Why?

Irelyn propped her leg up as she shaved. "Zhang will be nominated and confirmed as the new minister, I guess, then it's back to business as usual?" Irelyn stopped shaving and looked at him through the mist. "The Celje, right? Kennedy knew about them? You killed him because of what he knew, not because he was sleeping with me! But you've killed others for less. All for the family, right?"

Irelyn was putting together this puzzle faster than he'd anticipated. "Your insight into this is just as sharp as your body," he conceded. "All but the part about blaming you."

She had the big picture but was off on the details. If the former minister ever knew the true nature of the Celje, then Kennedy would have used the PGU's security force to shut down the Reeves Corporation or perhaps take it over. Elasus would have had no choice but to retaliate with his own Celje teams to defend the corporation, and war would have ensued, costing trillions of dollars, countless lives, and sending the economic state back into turmoil.

Irelyn's demeanor changed. "You... do you still find me attractive?"

He nodded. "You possess both intelligence and beauty, a rare duet."

She pressed her body against the dripping shower glass. "It's been a while since we've been together."

"Yes, it has," said Elasus, who turned and walked out. "Jay, have my car brought out front." He needed to find out more about Irelyn's relationship with Kennedy. Her behavior didn't match someone who was simply having an affair.

The AI chimed, acknowledging the order.

Lining the large circular driveway were beautiful tropical-colored flowers and plants imported from all over the globe.

"Good morning, Hewitt," said Elasus, stepping into the open car door with briefcase in hand. "Busy night, I take it?"

Hewitt's pressed suit collar flared as he bent over to shut the door. "Good day, Mr. Reeves. Yes, long evening, but this old body can still handle it."

The local news channel flickered to life in front of Elasus. The stations were shelling out details of Kennedy's life, family, commitment to the continuity of mankind, and the usual bullshit the news feasted on.

Inside the Reeves building, Elasus made his way past the security desk and into his private elevator where Doug Kranzer pressed the button for the thirteenth floor and wished the executive a good day.

Elasus acknowledged the gesture with a nod, and the glossy steel doors closed between them. A few seconds later, he was looking at Tayla beside her desk in a dark-green pantsuit, black high heels, and an off-white undershirt that exposed more than it covered.

"Mr. Reeves, good morning. I've contacted Commodus, and he's ready to accept your call when convenient."

"Ensure that I'm not disturbed."

Elasus walked down the long hallway, feeling the stares of his ancestors protruding through their ancient portraits. He mashed two buttons on his display, and Commodus's face beamed into focus. On the rightmost monitor, Elasus scrolled through dozens of names until he found his chief security officer, then clicked the send-message icon:

Tanner: Put eyes and ears on my wife until otherwise told.

Commodus's face appeared as Elasus whisked off the message. "Morning, Elasus. Tayla said it was important."

Elasus explained the last twenty-four hours to his COO, ensuring he included all details of the situation. "Steps have been taken to prevent additional ripple effects, but that may not be enough," Elasus warned. "You'll have daily updates about our progress in handling the situation, but your efforts on Ojult have now become imperative if the worst-case scenario plays out here. Do you follow?"

Commodus stroked his goatee. "War between us and the PGU, plus all the regional authorities, the FIAS, Asian Alliance, Provinces of South America, and Unified Western Powers. Yeah, they'd be upset if they found out about the Celje. Definitely a worst-case scenario. Things here are getting better, but the ship is still a mess. Garvin's doing a good job piecing it back together. Don't think I'm going to be back on Earth anytime soon, though."

"I've already submitted a bonus to Garvin and his crew, no need to bargain on his behalf. What else?"

"I've held two more meetings with Zakar. He's gotten trade back up, at least locally. There's no doubt Misora and Sasha have really stirred things up around here. I'm beginning to think those two were behind the supply raids and Nencia's death. Motive undetermined."

"Leverage."

"Against you?" Commodus whistled in wonderment. "Thought we had smarter guys running the show down here. In any case, I don't think they're still on Capintesta or Listo."

"And why's that?"

Commodus lifted a cup to his mouth and slurped. "That fight between the Nein and Celje a few weeks ago, turns out Sasha was running a mystic prison there. Information says they were holding a top Nein advisor. The Nein won and liberated the prison, but Misora and Sasha escaped, supposedly headed to Meridone. What's got me confused is the Nein don't seem interested in ruling or taking over."

Elasus thought of Sasha's request for supplies a while back and connected the request with the prison. "Liberations and Nein leaders don't concern me. I want Sasha and Misora found. They've stolen from me and left behind an economic mess."

"One last thing about that prison."

Elasus was no longer listening but instead reading an old secure tight beam.

> *From Wren Dikal: Nein raided a Celje prison. Tokarek led the raid. He's going to kill Sasha. My cover is blown. Hiding for now.*

Elasus read the message two more times before permanently deleting it from the database.

"Elasus, is our feed still on? Hello?" continued Commodus, hitting the camera with his knuckle.

Elasus turned his attention back to his COO. "I'm here."

"We found two injured guards hiding in the rubble outside the prison. We questioned them about what they knew, and they mentioned a woman. A nurse actually, interned by Sasha at the prison, showed sympathy toward the mystics, and their description made it look a hell of a lot like Marilla."

"People see ghosts, Commodus, and it's none of my concern or yours. I want you focused on finding Sasha and Misora before Tokarek does. I don't want a war over this, but keep in mind that a mystic with a staff isn't good for business. Settle things down, get trade up and moving again."

Commodus gulped the rest of his beverage. "What if the PGU find out about everything? They aren't going to be happy, especially about the Celje. I think you're right; they'll assume we created the Celje for a private army. It'll lead to conflict."

Elasus looked at a portrait of his father and grandfather hanging on a nearby wall. They were staring into him, judging his actions, his strategies, daring him to make a mistake that would bring down the empire they'd created. "I'm working on a backup plan."

CHAPTER 52: YEAR 2401

Jayden cursed and moaned while struggling to get comfortable on Markus's old couch. "Still can't believe you loaned my home to the Nein. You could have burned it, sold it, made it into an outhouse, but loaning it to the Nein?"

His friends filled him in on everything that had gone on over the past year. Victor supplied wine while Kun brought up hearty meals for the recovering hero. For three days Serena, Markus, Victor, and Kun rarely left his side.

"I'd invite you over to my place," replied Serena, "but I like Eve more."

Eve stopped in every now and then to check his vitals but stayed noticeably clear while his friends were visiting.

Victor poured dark-red wine into Jayden's chipped cup, then drank from Jayden's and his own, then refilled them. "I know it's faux pas," Victor said in a drunken mumble, "and I'm sorry to bring it up, but what of Wren Dikal?"

"I think the Celje hired him to figure out who was smuggling to the Nein. For some reason he thought it was me."

Markus glanced at Serena, then back to Jayden. "We're all friends here, so I feel it's appropriate to tell you something. After the battle of Worall, Serena confessed that she and Nencia were in business together. Serena was making munitions and a few other supplies, then selling them to Nencia who transacted the deal with the Nein. She feels horrible about it and she and I have already discussed the matter, so please, don't be mad."

The room and perhaps the whole world stood still, waiting for Jayden to hand out his judgment. Yet Jayden said nothing, unable to verbalize all the questions and emotions soaring through his mind.

"I am not a good judge of such things, but I don't think Jayden expected that," said Victor swirling wine around in his glass.

How could the daughter of Marco and Erika have gotten involved in the very trade that got them killed? Jayden forced his eyes to meet Serena's, neither knowing what the other was thinking. When it was obvious Jayden wasn't going to respond, Serena scowled and slammed her glass on the table before bolting out the door.

"I'm sorry to have been the one to break that to you, Jayden," continued Markus. "It seems Misora already knew Nencia's part in the deal, but apparently not the manufacturer. Please, don't be too hard on Serena."

Victor held his glass to his lips, his eyes flashing between everyone. "I think it was Dikal."

All eyes turned to Victor. "I'm sorry?" said Markus.

Victor's accent was becoming heavier with every sip. "It was Wren Dikal who betrayed our beloved Visconti friends oh so, so many years ago."

It was a statement not a question and Markus took it as such. "Perhaps, but that's speculation. And Jayden, believe me when I say that Shari Dikal had nothing to do with it. I'm convinced Wren was treating her more like a servant than a wife."

"And since we're on the topic of trusting people," said Kun, "can we trust Eve?"

"Eve's good," assured Jayden. "She saved my life more than once."

"The Dubois trust her too," said Victor. "Celine, my lovely Celine, she thinks Eve is an angel, a sign of things to come, a princess blessed with curing hands."

"I want to see Shari, I need to speak with her." It was an idea that kept nudging Jayden's consciousness.

Markus said, "Perhaps when things calm down."

———————

Using the couch as leverage, Jayden stood for a few seconds before wobbling and crashing back into the couch. Eve had told him to give it time, to let his body recover at its own pace, but patience wasn't his style, and he was growing restless.

"You don't look sturdy," said a female voice from the other side of the screen door.

He looked up to see a middle-aged woman dressed in a faded gray dress. Her hair was untidy, her eyes bloodshot, and she had scars across her face and neck. "Shari?"

Her fraying dress dragged on the floor as she stepped inside holding a small blue-marked box. "Before you say anything, I know about my husband, what he did to you, and what he's capable of. If you're looking for a shoulder to cry on, go find some other shabby woman to confess to. I've got work to do."

There was anger, fear, and perhaps resentment in her voice, but Jayden forged on. "You and I share—"

"Spare me your feelings, your sympathy, and all that other Earther stuff. I'm sorry for what he did to you, but if you try to hurt me or my son, I swear I'll skin you."

"Hurt you? No, my god, no Shari, that's... I'm sorry, that's not why I wanted to speak with you."

She seemed to believe him because her tense, vertical posture relaxed. He stared at the scars around her neck.

"I understand Wren hurt you, but I don't have much to offer and frankly, I don't know why you wanted to see me. Besides, if he comes back and it's—"

"Comes back?" interrupted Jayden, the mere suggestion reigniting his anger. "Look, I can't promise anything, but Wren coming back to Capintesta, let alone Dalth, isn't likely. There's a long line of people who want him dead. I was going to ask if you knew anything about his relationship with the Celje."

"You think that maybe I'm in league with them, yes?"

"I think that you're about as much in league with the Celje as I am." He'd heard enough. The tone, anguish, everything about her being in front of him screamed sincerity.

Her eyes foretold a tale of abuse and courage. "He forced me to make drugs for him, and I guess he sold them to the Celje. If I didn't have enough or ran out, he'd… Sometimes he'd take it out on Diego, threaten to kill both of us if we ever talked."

Never in his life did Jayden want to kill a man so much. The bastard had made a slave out of his own wife and deserved a slow, painful death.

Grinding dirt outside the screen door broke their attention.

Shari made toward the door. "You have company, and I don't think we have anything else to talk about, but here." She set the small box on the table. "There's hovrol and jashinto serum in there. If my husband really isn't coming back, then he won't need it. Give it to someone who can do some good with it."

Eve stepped through the doorway wearing a one-piece, calf-length dress common among the working women in town. Her usual inviting smile warmed the room. "I hope I'm not intruding, but I wanted to meet…" Her smile morphed into an expression of shock. "That box, where'd that come from?" She pointed toward the crate.

"It's a gift from Shari just now, why?"

Eve swept away the cords of unwashed red hair covering her face. "That blue mark on the box, where did you get that?"

Shari's earlier defensiveness returned. "It's how I mark the medical supplies I sent out. Blue is for healing, red is—not for healing. I'm an alchemist of sorts."

Eve knelt and wedged open the box and began sifting through its contents. "Shari, I've used these crates for years, with the blue and red marks."

Shari looked unimpressed. "I'm not surprised. I've made them for years while my husband cashed in. You use the red-marked boxes too? Some not-so-nice stuff in those, like ambar and SMD."

As a slave, Jayden had learned of these drugs. SMD (Silvery Myst Dancer) was a combination of wolfsbane and hemlock seed. Depending on the dosage, it could kill instantly or over time when ingested or injected into the bloodstream. Ambar was a plant extract that when ingested created a severe hallucinogenic reaction. Mystics had a more severe reaction to ambar, somewhat blocking their mental fortitude needed to conjure their powers.

"We've all been forced to participate in things we're not proud of," said Eve. "But I've used your drugs, and you have an amazing gift that many good people could benefit from. Dalth, even the whole continent, could use your talents. I realize I'm new to this town, but I think we could work together, do some actual good."

Minutes after the ladies had left, Markus arrived, then Syrus's large frame squeezed through the door. He looked strong and confident, wearing raven-black garments with his staff slung across his back.

"Good afternoon, Syrus," greeted Markus.

Syrus nodded. "Mayor Fonte, I wasn't expecting you here."

"Well, it is my house, and I thought I might supervise the conversation, keep the peace."

Jayden sat forward, elbows over his knees. "I'm unarmed but beating him over the head with a tire iron crossed my mind."

He didn't know what to expect, but somehow a giant hug and apology didn't seem on Syrus's agenda.

"You're recovering quickly, I'm glad to see it. Many of your peers didn't think you'd make it," Syrus said.

"Glad to know you're so concerned. Now, say what you need to and leave Dalth. You bring violence and death everywhere you go, and this town deserves better."

"I plan on doing just that. Much has happened since we last spoke, and for my part, I hope I've become wiser for it. Your banishment from the Nein was a mistake. You deserved better, and I handled it poorly."

"Everyone already knew that. Now tell me why you're here."

Despite Jayden's cynicism, Syrus's tone remained steady. "Save your anger for the real enemy, Jayden. Helia's dead. Mea's in hiding, and the Nein you once knew are no more."

"She's dead because you're a fool, and it's only luck that Mea is alive. You're evil, pure and simple. The Nein and the Celje are the same in my book."

Markus raised a cautioning hand. "Jayden, hear him out. Despite his reputation and your history, he's been a pleasant guest. Also, remember that he saved your life."

"Helia and others are dead because of my lack of foresight," continued Syrus. "I didn't come to rehash my mistakes but to foretell of something beyond our knowledge. Jayden, you have insights into the nonmystic realm. I seek to unite our people and believe you can help."

Jayden's pupils narrowed. "Unite our people, are you crazy!? You're speaking as if we aren't enemies. The Nein are horrid, and history's got a clear record of it!"

"Yet again, I agree. The Nein under my command have done evils of which we cannot atone, nor do I plan on it. But there are dangers coming that even my people can't stand against. I have a plan that you should consider when you're ready."

"Why the change? You could have done this years ago. And why are you asking me? I'm a simple farmer now."

Syrus strode over and knelt in front of him. "There's something out there, unseen, unknown. I don't know where it lies, but it's there and threatens all of us. Survival is the goal, and the unification of our peoples is the only way."

"I don't forgive you or your hell-hound captain. I'll listen, if only because I respect Markus."

Syrus nodded.

"I assume Andreas neglected to tell you that Levi Anjou was with us in the prison? Yeah, thought that might grab your attention. The first thing you need to know is that Levi admitted to being Mea's father. Helia and him were in love and met in secret for years, too afraid to make their relationship public, which is why he kept trying to duel you and unite the two continents. After you beat him the last time, Levi was captured and thrown in that mystic prison. Chew on that for a moment, because it gets better."

Syrus turned and leaned against the wall. Part of Jayden enjoyed seeing the proud mystic brought down.

"We weren't rivals in the usual sense," said Syrus. "We were like brothers until he left for Capintesta, strengthened his forces, then tried to take over Listo. My powers, alongside those of my legion, were too great for him. But now, it seems power wasn't his goal. Why didn't we find him in the prison?"

"Yeah, for one, I'm pretty sure he would've destroyed you, but he was holding back because he didn't want to kill you. Killing the brother of your girlfriend probably wouldn't have gone over well. Why wasn't he there when you raided the place you ask, that's because another mystic broke him out weeks before."

"Explain."

"For months he talked about how someone powerful was going to free him, then one day a figure in a cloaked mask broke him out. He unlocked the mystic-proof cuffs like it was nothing." Jayden studied his former captor with a speckle of premonition. "You aren't surprised by what I'm saying, why?"

"Listen," said Syrus, speaking to both Markus and Jayden. "I believe I know who this cloaked figure is. I'm not certain which side this man plays, and I don't consider him an ally."

Jayden's eyes drew down as he smirked. "You're not my ally either, and this cloaked figure rescued one of your rivals who, by the way, was Helia's lover. Right now, I'm siding with Levi."

Syrus pulled several letters from his pocket and laid them out in front of Jayden. "You gave me information about my sister, so let me repay that service. You and Nencia Donato were close. We found these dispatches from Sasha after a raid. One of them tells how he was intent on killing her all along. I know your soul, Jayden Vaut, and you have laid her death at your own feet. These letters say otherwise."

Jayden snatched the letters and scanned through them. They confirmed what Syrus had said. It also lined up with Serena's dealings with Nencia.

Jayden grabbed his cane and got to his feet. Markus rushed to his side with surprising quickness and put himself between the two foes.

"Zakar told me the events leading up to Nencia's execution. Whether you join me or not, I promise Misora, Sasha, and the rest of the Celje will pay." Syrus leaned forward, emerging more vengeful than before. "Those letters speak of a bargaining chip Sasha is trying to use. For now, I see only two outcomes. The first, Sasha wins and gains complete control of Ojult with limited interference from Reeves. Second, Elasus Reeves brings in the remaining off-planet Celje, and wipes Sasha and his team off the planet. If you follow either option to its conclusion, it doesn't end well for our peoples."

"You mean it doesn't end well for the Nein," rebuked Jayden.

"Helia wasn't a mystic, neither was Nencia. Think about Zakar and his underlings, Bella and Logan, or perhaps Andreas and your friend Serena. Then there's Mea, who will get snatched up when this evil spreads."

Images of everyone Syrus named passed through Jayden's weary mind. "Ten years ago, this conversation wouldn't have happened. I don't know whether to call your bluff or be terrified that something has you so spooked it jarred your mind back to sanity. I hate you, Syrus, I really, really hate you. You've brought nothing but pain into my life. I think I'd rather shoot you instead of working with you. We've got too much history, and any sort of partnership wouldn't work. I'll help Markus and Dalth, and if our goals overlap, then so be it."

"Then this is where we part," said Syrus, extending his hand without reservation. "I'll leave Dalth tomorrow morning, and for your sake, I hope things work out."

The moment of solidarity was broken when Syrus's grip tightened so hard Jayden felt his hand might break. Looking into the mystic's eyes, Jayden recognized his former master's rigid expression. The glossy look, as if he was looking into another dimension—Syrus had felt something, a ripple of danger.

Phaedra burst through the door holding in her arms a young girl covered in blood.

"No!" Markus took Bélise's limp body and placed her on the couch.

Syrus looked to his apprentice, his fiery eyes revealing his only question.

"Jenna and I were about a mile outside of Dalth on the north side when we ran into a squad of Celje questioning her. She refused to cooperate so they started thrashing her. We killed all of them but didn't recognize who she was until after. *Daska*, it's a good bet the Celje know we're here."

CHAPTER 53: YEAR 2401

Bélise was going to live, thanks to the heroic efforts of Phaedra, Celine, Eve, and to everyone's surprise, Shari. Several finger-length gashes covered the teenager's face, neck, and shoulders, most requiring stitches.

When Jayden stepped inside the clinic, an unfamiliar Nein guard introduced herself. This Nein, unlike the others he'd known, never showed any attitude toward him or the other townsmen. In fact, it seemed to Jayden that Jenna went out of her way to show her likeness toward his kind.

"Glad to hear that girl's going to live," said Jenna. "The innocent always get caught up in matters like this." Her scared face, battered armor, and peppered hair put twenty years on her otherwise youthful figure.

In the far corner of the candlelit room, Eve, Celine, and Markus stood next to a small bed. Markus's sagging posture rested next to Bélise, and a small candle burned on the nightstand.

"Can't believe they went after her," said Serena.

"She's floating in and out of consciousness, but Phaedra and Eve say she'll be okay in a day or two."

Jayden walked over and hugged Serena. It was the first time they'd seen each other since Markus revealed her part in the smuggling operation with Nencia. The unexpected gesture caught her by surprise, and her arms just dangled.

"The smuggling aside, I'm glad to see you're okay." His earlier anger and resentment melted away, finally realizing how close he'd come to losing her. "Last I saw, you were bleeding like hell and in rough shape."

"I really missed you." Serena was fighting back tears. "I didn't want to lose you too, and I never gave up. Never. All I kept thinking was those bastards got my parents, but they couldn't get you too. I thought you'd hate me."

Jayden stepped back, rested his hands on her shoulders, and looked into her watery eyes. "I wish things were a bit different, but we need to make the best of the situation now."

Her eyes darted to Bélise. "Kun and some of the militia went out to scout for more Celje. I think Phaedra went with them. What if more show up? We can't fight them all."

Jayden inhaled, surrendering the idea of living the rest of his life in peace. Thoughts of dusting off his old tracking attire and asking Serena to forge more ammo for him traversed his conscious mind. "We kill as many as we can, to our last breath."

"You've got that look, Jayden, the one you get when you're angry. If you're gonna fight, you'll need supplies. We both know the quality of casings I make, so don't argue. What about your girlfriend over there, can she fight? She's damn good with a scalpel for sure."

"She and I, Eve I mean, we aren't…"

Serena elbowed him hard in the groin. "You aren't rubbing thighs yet? Well, that's not surprising. You've got as much game as that Phaedra woman. Don't look at me like that either. I'm good at making weapons, armor, and pretty much anything that deals with metal. I am also a woman, which means I am an automatic expert at relationships. And there's definitely something going on between you and the pretty nurse."

"Moving on from Nencia isn't…"

"Nencia's dead, and don't go giving me the sob story that there's some kind of hole in your heart. She was my friend too, then the Celje almost got you! I know how you feel. You need to move on, Jayden, it's been over a year and she's not coming back. Don't walk away from something good."

"Hole in my heart, what the…"

"Sshhh," came Celine's voice from across the room. "Take your bickering outside."

Serena threw her hands on her hips but spoke softer. "The light bulb doesn't shine real bright with you when it comes to women, does it, Jayden. And speaking of bright things, tell me about Andreas."

Serena was changing topics faster than a ship going through an MFG. "Andreas, the mystic? He's one of Syrus's top advisors and a Nein. Why?"

"Is he planning on sticking around or anything? I haven't seen him today."

"I think Syrus asked him to help get Capintesta back in order. If you need to speak with him we can…"

"No," she shouted, catching the attention of both Celine and Eve. "Sorry, sorry."

But it was too late. Eve and Celine got up from Bélise's side and headed toward them.

Serena's eye roll was as loud as her voice. "Ah dammit!"

Celine launched into them. "You two! Bickering like siblings while Bélise lays here fighting. We're lucky Phaedra arrived when she did! Serena, you're not staying here any longer, come with me."

Celine grabbed Serena by the wrist, marching her out the door with long, furious strides.

"She's strong, like her father," said Eve, now alone with Jayden. "It's important for daughters to have a father, someone who can be firm but loving. We should leave too, let Markus have some time alone with her."

Jayden followed Eve outside. "Thank you for doing so much for Celine and this town. Lots of people owe you."

They walked south through tall grass, stopping occasionally to untangle Jayden's walking stick.

"Celine has the hands of a healer. Not sure how you guys found her, but you're lucky. Most towns don't have a clinic or healer, yet you have both."

"She patched me up when I first came here, a great woman and excellent with kids. Not sure how she keeps them all in line. Victor's a good guy too, likes his wine, but he's harmless."

Eve stopped in the middle of the field, brushing her hand over the tops of the grass. "It's a shame what the PGU and Reeves Corporation have done to families. Breaking them up and condemning them here for life. I guess people find ways to manage."

Jayden regarded her closely, noting the contempt in her voice. "It's called sky grass, grows everywhere around here."

"Because it grows so tall?"

"You guessed it." Jayden yawned, then rubbed his eyes. "You hear that Syrus asked me to join his little band of merry men? I already told him no, but this whole thing with Bélise has me walking back a bit. Syrus's evil no matter what façade he's holding over everyone, but I think he's got the best chance of getting rid of the Celje. What do you think?"

"Do you think he could defeat the corporation if they send reinforcements? If you join, will you stay in Dalth or live elsewhere?"

Jayden stroked his long beard. "Dalth is as good a place as any, I guess. Can Syrus defeat the corporation, anything is possible with that staff on his back."

"You told me back in the prison you weren't really sure if you wanted revenge against the Celje, PGU, or Reeves. You also said you wanted to live a quiet life. Joining this war doesn't fit into those plans."

Jayden plucked some of the sky grass and chewed on its ends. "Sky grass has a sweet taste if you bite the ends but tastes horrible if you cook it. Kun makes tea out of it, not too bad either."

Eve stepped closer, gripping her hardened medical hands into his. "You're a good man with a good heart, that's a miracle considering everything you've been through. I like you, Jayden—just remember that you are *not* immortal. One day you're going to get shot or stabbed or something else that I can't fix. That's going to be a sad day for a lot of people."

"I'm not a good person, Eve. Believe me, Syrus doesn't want the nice guy in me, he wants the killer who feels nothing when he takes a life. I've done my best not to let *that* Jayden come out of its shell. You've only seen the one side to this beaten man."

"Sometimes the hero we need doesn't fit the typical profile. Just do me a favor. If you join Syrus, make this world a better place, don't just ally with the next conqueror."

They walked aimlessly through the fields while he explained all that Syrus had told him.

"I can't make this decision for you," she reasoned. "The Celje, or one of their agents, took someone close to me once years ago, so if you need encouragement, look no further. I'll be here to sew you back together but know that I come with lots of baggage. Being close with me isn't going to be easy."

They walked and talked until Eve seeded a sublime kiss on Jayden's cheek before walking back toward Serena's home. Vowing never to wash that side of his face again, Jayden walked back to his old home to speak with Syrus.

———————

Phaedra looked up from stitching her armor. "Jayden Vaut, still afraid of the dark? Come to snuggle up next to your guardian angel for the night?"

Jayden raised his hands. "If I'm interrupting something important, I'll just… oh wait, you're in my home, so I think I'll just stay."

Syrus rose from his meditation.

"So long as our goals align, and you don't do anything stupid, like I suspect you will, I'll join," Jayden said.

Phaedra stood and began to clap. "Sounds good to me. We need as many Thoba as possible to catch the Celje bullets for us."

A single glance from Syrus ended Phaedra's theatrics. "I'm glad to hear of your decision. Come, let us strategize."

Syrus offered Jayden titles, troop commands, and dozens of various missions, but Jayden refused them all.

"You're not getting it," snapped Jayden. "If Misora finds out I'm working with you, he'll target Dalth, go after the people I care for. I can't let that happen."

Syrus's eyes danced for a moment before resting on a decision. "I have reason to believe that a child of Elasus Reeves is on this planet. I need to find him or her and—"

"Absolutely not," rasped Jayden, quickly assessing the unfinished statement. "See! You don't even need to finish that sentence because I already know what you're thinking. This is exactly the kind of thing we need to avoid! Have you not been listening? I'm not going after an innocent child, young or old!"

Phaedra shot back, "He's not planning on killing the kid!"

Jayden shoved his walking stick into Phaedra's chest. "No, he's going to use the kid as bait or a bargaining chip. And when Elasus calls his bluff, what do you think will happen?"

Phaedra looked at the rod pressing against her chest. "Unless you want to be crapping splinters for the next week, you better take that off me."

"I have one last undertaking that may interest you," said Syrus. "I must identify with certainty that Sasha and Misora fled to Meridone before I commit to the region. Zakar's information is generally reliable, but in this case, incontestable verification is required. I need a small group to travel to Meridone and confirm their whereabouts."

Jayden said, "That's it? Just spot Misora and come back?

"Yes, the objective is straightforward," concurred Syrus.

"I'll need some time to heal."

"Phaedra will accompany you on this mission, along with Jenna and anyone else you wish to bring. A mystic can also heal you on the way."

"What!?" exclaimed Phaedra.

"Don't be scared, I've played this game more than you can imagine," said Jayden.

"Enough," barked Syrus, raising his voice. "Phaedra's a capable agent I trust. Too many of our number have left us recently, so I have no other options. Phaedra, you need guidance from a vantage point I cannot give. Use this experience to learn from someone who has talents different from your own."

There was something off between Phaedra and Syrus, like the calm before a storm.

"All right, let's leave in a week," Jayden said, leaving no room for debate. "We find Sasha and Misora, pick up any additional intel we can find, then come back. If I'm going, I'm leading the mission."

Syrus nodded, but Phaedra was furious. She walked up to Jayden until they were nose to nose. "You're going to get someone killed. Better hope it's not someone I like, or you'll be begging for death."

Jayden took a step back. "This is my team, and I won't do anything to jeopardize you or the others."

Phaedra turned to Syrus. "First you don't give a second thought to killing one of their kind, now you want to work with them. And I thought I was supposed to be looking for that Reeves kid? Now I'm babysitting this frail skeleton."

"This takes precedence," replied Syrus. "I'll consult with Mayor Fonte about the Reeves child and see if there's another, more acceptable way of going about it."

Phaedra ran her fingers through her silvery hair. "Guess I'm not going to win this am I? Fine, I'll just go freshen up, powder my nose, and make sure I'm all pretty for this one-way disaster."

CHAPTER 54: YEAR 2401

The transition from summer to fall was more subtle than in years past. Jayden hoped the mild weather would hold throughout their mission. Six days ago, he said goodbye to Serena, Markus, and Eve, then set off for Meridone by way of Worall, then Port Rindo.

Leaving Eve in Dalth wasn't the nervous experience he'd anticipated. She was spending much of her time tending to Celine's clinic and working with Shari Dikal. Shari's aptitude for compounding drugs and other medical remedies was astonishing according to Eve. Jayden's guilt for leaving his friend behind faded knowing she had friends and a renewed purpose.

"Just don't get shot, stabbed, or poked please," Eve said, only half teasing. "Your luck is going to run out eventually." She hugged him, turned, and headed off toward the clinic without another word.

Markus was preoccupied with Bélise's recovery. The morning Jayden left, Markus sat down in front of him, sipping a steaming cup of kaldi. "What you're doing is important, Jayden. I hope you can see God's plan, how he's working through you."

"Can't say I agree with his way of doing things at the moment."

Markus put down his cup. "I'm not unfamiliar with Meridone and its people. The land's reputation is well deserved: home to violent, uncaring, and dangerous people. But there's another side to that continent that is... less known. Your journey will take you to Port Fiesta and perhaps further east toward the middle of the continent. But if you find yourself in the mountainous regions on the far eastern side of the continent, be cautious.

The planet's jagged surface and no atmosphere are not the only dangers that you may face."

Markus didn't elaborate and Jayden couldn't help but latch on to the crater-sized cliffhanger. "So... don't go too far east, that's it?"

Markus nodded. "Avoid the mountains, especially with the company you are bringing."

With the assistance of Appian Shipping, he'd set off with Phaedra, Jenna, and Turr under his lead. Jenna and Turr were friendly enough, but Phaedra's obstinate silence remained steady. Under the cover of a supply ship, Captain Green of the sailship *Challenger* took them toward Meridone.

"Bella's coming with you," explained Zakar before they departed. "The port authority knows her and she'll get you past their inspection."

The last time Jayden saw Bella, she was covered in blood. Yet seeing what she'd done to the assaulting Celje would change any leader's mind. Once on board the *Challenger*, Bella helped keep Captain Green in check, plus her familiarity with the ship came in handy. She saw to all their needs and kept the peace between his team and the ship's crew.

Belowdecks, Jayden assembled his team while Bella distributed hot kaldi, bacon, and toast.

"When we arrive on Meridone, Turr and I will scout the city first, then regroup back at the ship and disperse according to what we find."

"I agree," said Phaedra with bacon hanging out of her mouth. "You boys should do all the work while Bella, Jenna, and myself just stay here, perhaps do laundry, clean the ship, get dinner ready?"

"It has nothing to do with—"

"We all came on this little voyage for the same reason, and it wasn't to screw around on the ship. Bella stays here, the four of us head out at the same time, plus we cover more ground."

Treading with obvious prudence, Jayden maneuvered the conversation away from the looming confrontation. "How exactly do you know Bella? I get the rest of you, but not Bella. You act like sisters almost."

"We've worked together a few times here and there," chimed Bella. "But our biggest job was finding Andreas. And by finding him, we found you."

Jayden looked to Phaedra, but words struggled to come out. "I had no idea. I mean I knew you and Syrus raided the place, but I didn't know it was you personally, Phaedra."

"Please, don't thank me or start groveling," Phaedra sneered. "Oh, for hell's sake, don't start crying either, I wasn't looking for you anyways. Bella, tell him the whole story so he doesn't start nagging us, but you might want to leave out the part where I wanted to kill him."

Bella told their story, prompting Phaedra to head back up to the main deck.

"Chivalry died the moment you stepped off that transport ship from Earth," said Bella, reading his addled expression. "Don't think too bad of Phaedra, she accomplished what Syrus asked of her. The end justifies the means with Phaedra, which also explains why Syrus's new strategy isn't sitting well with her either."

Similar to the previous days, Jayden stood on the foredeck, contemplating their mission. He wanted a quiet, peaceful life, which meant getting rid of the Celje. True, the planet was full of rapists, murderers, and some of Earth's most ruthless criminals, but the Celje were a different breed.

Behind him, Captain Green's voice boomed over the boat. "We've caught good winds, lads! Tomorrow, boys, you'll have enough *arse* around you that you'll forget you live on this homicidal planet."

Their time aboard the *Challenger* was coming to an end, and Jayden wanted to smooth things over with Phaedra before landfall. He eventually found the mysterious sage in the crow's nest, high upon the second mast. Not a big fan of heights, Jayden climbed the rope ladder until reaching the protective cage around the lookout.

Phaedra watched in delight as he struggled up the narrow passage. "You looked like a drunk monkey getting up here. First time on a ship?"

With a white-knuckled grip on the cage, Jayden said, "When we're out there, on the mission, I need to know that we're on the same side. I can't be fighting the Celje and looking over my shoulder the whole time."

The wind blew hard, whipping Phaedra's hair around like sky grass in a storm. "First, this is a scouting mission, you shouldn't be fighting anyone.

Second, mystics don't need help from your kind. So maybe it's best you keep looking over that scrawny shoulder of yours."

There was more on his mind, and he wouldn't get a better opportunity. "So that night I was banished from the Nein, was it you who tried to hunt me down? Did Syrus ask you, or did you volunteer?"

"Wouldn't you just love to know, but sure, why not. Kavil asked me to lead the hunt, but Syrus vetoed it and ordered Kavil to lead it himself. Guess he didn't really want you dead after all."

But Jayden knew better, knew why he didn't send his protégé. "Sounds like he didn't want *you* to die."

Phaedra snorted. "You got altitude sickness up here? You better climb down before you start believing your own bullshit."

His shaking hands let go of the ropes, and Jayden stepped close to her. "You mean more to him than you know. Back in those days, had he sent you, you wouldn't have survived. I tell you this so you'll understand that Syrus cares for you. Helia told me he thought of you as a daughter, which is why he never bothered marrying or having children. Syrus's a first-class prick but he loves you like his own kid."

"It would have been a good fight, you and me," she said, hurling one leg over the rail. "But a daughter or love? No, I'm as much a slave as you were, just with different titles."

Thirty minutes later, Jayden gathered Bella, Turr, Jenna, and Phaedra around him on the foredeck. It was the most private area on the ship, and with the threat of Celje spies, everyone understood his caution. He still wasn't sure if Phaedra was with him, but he'd appealed to her in the only way he knew how.

"Bella, I invited you here in case things go poorly. I want someone other than Captain Green to know our plan. We need to stay hidden and avoid any sort of encounter with the Celje. We blend in, ask around, see if Misora and Sasha are in the region, then get out."

Phaedra laid out a rough sketch of the town. "Appian spies think they're in Port Fiesta, so that's where we'll focus our search. We'll split up, then meet aboard the ship each night. Jayden and I will be on their watch list, so be on alert. Hoods and cloaks are common on Meridone, so wear them." Out of an old pack, she pulled five small pouches. "Syrus gave us tonze. Each of us takes a bag, spend as needed."

Bella reached across the map, pointing out various locations. "I've been here many times. We'll dock in Port Fiesta on the west side of Meridone. Then you have Trebia, the capital city to the northeast, then Dorwood to the far east. Mountains cover the entire east side of the country, but it's also where the planet pretty much drops off, becoming a spiked, uninhabitable, toxic wasteland. The south is uninhabitable marsh with pockets of nomads," Bella apprised the group. "Port Fiesta and Trebia are dangerous but no matter what, don't head any further east than Trebia. You get anywhere close to Dorwood and the people get strange. Some say it's the thin atmosphere, others think the people are just insane. Appian's tried to send their people to Dorwood, most didn't come back, and those who did all tell the same story."

Markus had told Jayden the same thing, avoid the mountain regions at all costs. He was about to relate this when a slow rumble vacillated through the ship.

From the west, an enormous black spaceship crept over the horizon. It's contrail bloomed down and away from its massive engines, leaving a thick layer of fog in its wake. For reasons unknown to Jayden, the *Challenger*'s crew moved as if the flying ship might collide with them.

"All hands brace for a jet wash," roared Captain Green. "Get the royals tied down! You in the crow's nest, hold on!"

CHAPTER 55: YEAR 2401

The gargantuan ship zoomed over the wide sea, its nine underside thrusters kicking up thick walls of mist. Jayden recognized it as a Reeves transport ship used to ferry exiles and supplies to and from Earth. The ship passed to the port side of the *Challenger*, immersing the sides of the ship into the disturbed sea. Jayden's team, the crew, and accompanying cargo were thrashed from side to side. Sea water flushed over the sides, spilling into the *Challenger*'s main and lower decks. Jayden snagged Bella's arm as she skidded uncontrollably toward the starboard-side railing. Looking up through the stinging spray, Jayden spotted the spaceship's name: *Night Scope*.

"Get up! Get up, you lazy dogs," yelled Green. He was still standing, unlike the rest of his crew. "Get the rigging untangled damn it! Why aren't the bilge pumps going yet? I'll throw you all off this ship, all of you! Jayden, get your people out of the way or you'll be the first one swimming. Wait until I get my hands around that captain!"

The violent rocking slowly diminished, and Jayden checked on his team. All were accounted for except Phaedra, who was thrown belowdecks, unharmed.

"Captain Green," asked Jayden, impervious to the captain's annoyance. "Why was that ship so low? Landing?"

"You some sort of physics professor, Vaut? Keep those airhead comments to yourself. That's Donato, captain of the *Night Scope*. He sat his ship down in Pa'Gran not too long ago, probably for repairs. Why the hell he decided to take his entire ship instead of a jumper across the sea here is beyond me. Must have cost him a fortune in fuel."

Jayden's stomach twinged. "You said Donato, as in Garvin Donato?"

"Yes, that's the *Night Scope*."

Jayden spun and found Phaedra coming up the steps, cursing every slipping step.

"I think we've got a problem," warned Jayden, pointing toward the departing ship. "That's the *Night Scope*, and her captain is Garvin Donato. He's known for being in the corporation's good graces. If he was in Pa'Gran, there's no reason for him to have flown that huge ship to Meridone. He's got someone important on board, or maybe a full load of troops."

"I can confirm that," admitted Bella. "Zakar met with them."

"They were on Ojult, and you're just now telling us. And what do you mean, *them*?" said Phaedra.

Bella shrugged. "Appian doesn't blurt out all the information it comes across. And before you ask, no, I don't know exactly why they're here."

"A spy agency with a big mouth wouldn't stay in business long," said Turr.

Phaedra paced the deck. "Okay, let's go back to what Jayden said. Moving a ship that size over such a short distance isn't normal."

"And Captain Donato is famous for putting safety first," added Bella. "That maneuver is dangerous and unnecessary, not something the captain would have done voluntarily. Not to mention the ship is badly damaged."

Phaedra turned and addressed the group. "Syrus was right then. Either the corporation is here to reinforce the Celje and restore order, or they're here to get rid of Sasha and Misora and put in new leadership."

The timing of this wasn't adding up. Syrus had only recently defeated the Celje on Listo and Capintesta. The odds of the higher-ups getting to Ojult this fast didn't seem likely.

"All good points, but our mission hasn't changed," said Jayden. "We scout the region, try to confirm Sasha's whereabouts, and report back. If we find any Reeves people while we're out there, we report it."

The next morning, Jayden confirmed with Captain Green that Port Fiesta had the only spaceport large enough to hold the *Night Scope*. By noon,

they had spotted the outline of the *Night Scope* near Port Fiesta's shore-
line. While the winds were ideal for Captain Green to traverse the open
sea, they were bad for docking in the harbor, and Green was forced to
anchor in the bay.

Not being able to tie directly into the dock irritated the already wound-
up captain. "Once these forsaken winds calm down, we'll attach a few lines
to the dinghy and tow the ship in. Bella's got permission to take the blue
dinghy into shore, so stop bothering me about it, Vaut."

Jayden's getup resembled his days as a Nein with his overcoat, brimmed
hat, and pistol belt. Bella and Jenna looked like farmers, while Turr borrowed some of the midshipmen's garb. Phaedra had borrowed clothes
from Serena before leaving and looked like any other trader coming from
Capintesta, donning jeans, boots, and a worn-looking shirt.

Phaedra, Jenna, and Turr were assigned the eastern region of Port
Fiesta while Jayden focused on the town itself. The port was bustling with
people, prostitutes, gunfighters, and beggars. Outside the docks, Jayden
encountered shops, pubs, and several other stores. Malnourished children,
many sick with dysentery, begged for food and money.

Gunfire erupted frequently, followed by faintly distinguishable
screams, and calls for a doctor and a priest. The scene brought Jayden
back to his first moments after arriving on Ojult. Now, instead of uncertainty, fear, and terror filling his mind, only a slight scent of sorrow arose
in his deadened core.

With his hat pulled low, Jayden walked down the nearest street until
coming across an unusual-looking pub. The sign read Lost P̶i̶n̶e̶s̶ PANTS,
with the middle word intentionally crossed out. Ahead of him, two men
with holstered pistols cut in front of him, muttering something about the
pub having the best two-deck blackjack tables on the continent. Reaching down, Jayden loosened his pistol held tightly in its leather holster, then
followed them inside.

Jayden coughed as he inhaled the dense hettle smoke that layered the
pub. Scantily dressed women stood next to nearly every table where deal-
ers dealt cards. Just inside the door, a sign read: "All mystics are required
to register with the local government representative. Failure to do so will
result in public hanging."

The sign looked new, perhaps something Sasha had recently installed. Jayden headed to the bar.

"Welcome," said the bartender wearing a stained long-sleeve shirt and black vest. "What can I pour ya?"

"Just arrived from Rindo," he said. "I'll take a kaldi."

The bartender looked at him and laughed. "I've got half-priced liquor if you work for Nikoli, a one-tonze beer that might or might not be mostly water, and a twelve-ounce hops for six tonze. I've even got half-priced women and free beds if you pay for more than two at a time, but I don't have any kaldi. And before you ask, I ain't got water either unless you want to visit the stables."

Jayden looked up and down the bar. "Seems like a busy place. I take it you get plenty of Reeves people in here?"

"Not these days. Either order a drink or a girl; but questions aren't on the menu."

"Fine. Whiskey."

The bartender slapped the table and smiled. "Now you're talking!"

Jayden put down six whiskeys in as many hours, taking every opportunity to speak with newcomers. Prostitutes of all races, young and old, fat and thin, offered their services. He acted flattered and asked them questions before politely declining their offers of companionship.

Undeterred by the late hour, Lost Pants still quartered dozens of gamblers and escorts when Jayden decided to give up for the night. Exhausted and none the wiser for his efforts, he tossed enough tonze to cover his tab plus a small tip for good will in case he needed information from the bartender in the future.

The coins rattled for a moment, then came to a deadening stop. In the far corner of the bar, Jayden caught a peculiarly dressed man staring him down. They locked eyes, but the stranger kept his stare, unperturbed by the awkward moment. The man dressed like a card dealer and wore circular, wire-rimmed glasses with purple lenses.

Jayden let the moment pass, refusing to push his luck. He excused himself through the remaining crowd, parting smoke clouds until leaving through the main doors. Jayden made certain he wasn't followed and found the *Challenger* tied up to the docks. Like him, his team had found nothing.

For several more nights, Jayden and his team's presence garnered no information or attention. On the fourth night, under a heavy blanket of fog and disappointment, Jayden's warrior discipline pricked his senses into awareness. Following the same path back to the *Challenger*, two men dressed in farm clothing stepped in front of him.

"We hear you've been asking about the Celje," said one of the men. "Questions like that get you killed around here."

Jayden pegged them as Celje agents. "I'm just a deckhand trying to find my boat. No idea what you're talking about."

The second man reared back with a hidden baton. Jayden stepped back just in time as the weapon grazed his overcoat. He grabbed the Celje's wrist, using the man's momentum to twist and flip him over. With the baton now in his hand, Jayden clubbed the man's head.

Click.

The familiar, unnerving sound of a revolver's hammer clicking into place.

"You're either a man of many talents or a Nein who's full of shit." The agent's voice was cold and resolute.

Jayden dropped the baton next to the unconscious agent and raised his hands. "Like I said, I'm just a sailor who's been in one too many bar fights. Come on, man, I just want to get back to my ship. How about we forget about all this and head our separate ways?"

The barrel of the pistol pressed into the small of Jayden's back. "The boss will decide what to do with you."

Out of the shadows, something whistled by Jayden's ear. The impact mimicked the pop of a suction cup, followed by the scant huff from the armed agent. Jayden peaked over his shoulder, finding a dull-silver dart hanging from the agent's neck. Minute beads of blood trickled down the befuddled man's neck before his nervous system went into shock.

"Quick, follow me!" His savior spoke quickly in a Meridonian accent that placed a heavy emphasis on the last letter in every word. She started to run off before he got a good glimpse of her. Looking back toward the ship, Jayden marked more men heading toward their fallen companion. With few options, he followed the woman up the road. They took several turns until comping upon a red-brick building with three triangle windows on the first floor and three circular windows on the second. On the upper floor, half-nude women strutted in the front of the windows.

"My employer asked that we keep an eye on you," said the woman. "Ask me no questions about him and we'll get along just fine. Besides, it's not often I see such fine young jacks come into my establishment. Do you have tonze or another way to pay?"

"Wait, what?" asked Jayden, perplexed. He looked at the half-nude women above him, then back at his new friend. "Uh, no, I don't really need this kind of service. What… why did you knock that guy out, why save me? Have you been following me? Who are you?"

The woman laughed like she'd not just attacked a trained mystic killer. "It seems you have attracted unwanted attention. Come inside, my owner would not like to see you in the hands of those brutes."

Six agents, dressed exactly like the ones from before, were coming up the street. He looked across the way and up the street, but no other building looked any more secure than this one. Jayden stepped up to the door.

"Fifteen tonze."

"You save me and now you're charging me?"

"My girls are hungry and we don't find many jacks like you with money. Besides, I can always tell my boss we didn't get to you in time. Fifteen tonze or get away from our splendid establishment."

The woman took the money, counted it twice, then motioned for Jayden to follow her. "Welcome to Duggan's Lodge. Finest ladies and cleanest sheets on Meridone. Our owner had a run in with Nikoli not too long ago, didn't go well, but we're still in business. Now, the fifteen is only a cover charge. Our girls are six hundred tonze. Can you pay?"

Jayden nodded, already assessing how to turn this situation to his advantage.

"Good, my girls will make sure your money is well spent. My name is Daria. Enjoy your evening."

Jayden handed Daria fifty tonze. "No girls, just keep my name off that log book on the desk. Who's your boss?"

Daria took the money and nodded to the half-dressed hostess. "You can keep passing your money to me, Jayden Vaut, but my employer asked that he remain anonymous. Enjoy your stay."

Daria wasn't going to budge and he needed to vanish before the other agents came into the building. Upstairs, his room was clean with an unsoiled bed, a red-cloth couch, and two red-tinted lanterns. The window used sage-tint that auto cloaked the glass with a single touch.

Partially unveiling the window, Jayden peered out and viewed the town around him. His vantage point gave him a perfect view of the Meridonian spaceport. Only one ship lay berthed. A flashing thought made Jayden think Daria stashed him in this room *because* of this angle.

He kept a steady eye on the well-lit ship. Daria put him here for a reason, and his gut told him that something big was going on, so he stayed up, ordering kaldi from the unrelenting escorts. Well after midnight, the *Night Scope*'s skyward lights flashed on.

After allowing his eyes to adjust, Jayden spotted a large group of men approaching the ship. Most of them wore green-and-black armor with RERs slung over their backs. Then another group entered his line of sight, this time exiting from the rear of the ship. This new group appeared to be guarding a single man who looked out of place, wearing a light-brown coat and hat.

The two groups met, exchanged handshakes, then headed off toward a single-story building. Jayden grabbed his gear and flung open the door.

Jayden froze, face-to-face with a short, curly-haired young woman.

"Bella?"

CHAPTER 56: YEAR 2401

Y ou following me too?" asked Jayden. He looked into Bella's soft, prominent cheeks. There was the glow of youth colliding with the strains of responsibility emanating from the maturing mystic.

"Daria was the original owner of this place and used to work with Appian. I'll explain later. You spying on the *Night Scope*? Notice that group leaving?"

The child-mystic spy never stopped exceeding his expectations. "Guess I shouldn't be surprised you knew that. I was heading out to follow them, but you didn't come up here to tell me that."

"No, you're right," Bella chirped back. "I figured you might think about following them, and probably get yourself arrested. It's not a good plan."

Like Syrus and Nencia, Bella didn't speak just to hear herself. If she came all the way to see him, there was a reason. "All right then, what's your advice?"

She accepted his invitation and walked in, withdrawing a small paper. "There's a meeting happening tonight, but we're not sure who's involved. This is a map and *X* marks the meeting spot. It's not too far away. Too many holes in Appian's intel to say more, but this is definitely the meeting spot."

Jayden unfolded the paper. "Only a few blocks away, some sort of abandoned building?"

"A *friend* placed an old carriage on the side of the building. When you get there, use the carriage to climb up to one of the windows. It should give you a good vantage point to listen in."

"If Appian has enough spies on the ground to get this, why not just send one of your people?" The idea of Zakar sending him into a trap wasn't farfetched. "Aren't the Celje looking for me now, especially after I sent one of them to the clinic?"

Bella's usual impassive countenance intensified. Starting with a single bead of sweat, her plump cheeks dotted red; something had the teenage woman concerned. "The agents from the docks work for Nikoli, not Sasha. They headed back to Trebia a few hours ago on his orders, no idea why. To your other question, that's actually why I'm here. Phaedra, hasn't checked in. The few spies we have think she might have left town. I've sent what few people I have to search for her, but they've turned up nothing so far."

Phaedra's responsibility was scouting the eastern region of town. Not checking in wasn't a big deal, but Bella didn't share his outlook.

Jayden stepped back into the bedroom and pointed toward the cloaked window. "She's probably drunk and sleeping it off somewhere. What time does that meeting start?"

"Not for another hour," said Bella.

Bella's confident, natural voice had morphed into defeat and Jayden reconsidered the situation. "You told us earlier that heading east was a bad idea. Are Turr and Jenna searching for her?"

Bella walked toward the cloaked window and pressed the *illuminate* toggle. "Turr and Jenna have already started searching. They don't sense her presence in town, and neither do I. That's not good, Jayden, I'm… worried."

Overlaying Phaedra's sinister nature was a beautiful woman with silvery hair, attraction to danger, and win-at-all-cost personality. If she'd been causing trouble, it wouldn't take long for the locals to figure out who she was.

More beads of sweet coasted down Bella's face, and Jayden tossed a consoling arm around her. "Phaedra's your friend, what can I do to help?"

Beneath her rounded cheeks and warm smile, was a teenager with intelligence beyond her years. When Bella spoke next, Jayden found it difficult to see the child who wanted nothing more than chocolate bars when he'd come to visit.

"I'm okay, Jayden, thank you. I'm tougher than I look and don't forget who raised me." They shared a quick laugh, then Bella pointed to the map. "I want you at that meeting for the mission, of course, but for another reason. Whether Nikoli's goons or the Celje, both consider Phaedra a valued target. If she's been captured, maybe it will come up in this meeting."

Not fully understanding the plan but trusting in Nencia's acolyte, Jayden set off for the meeting. He traversed the dark streets cautiously using Bella's hand drawn map. He felt the darkness watching him, waiting for him to turn his back one last time before striking.

The creeping shadows never struck, granting Jayden their consent to move through their gauntlet of unease. A few more furtive steps placed him near the map's marker. Wood framed buildings, abused, rotted, and empty, speckled the area. Only two guards stood ceremoniously outside the corner property that would surely crumble with the *Night Scope*'s next rumbling takeoff.

Jayden kept his hat low and overcoat open, ready to draw his pistol with a gunfighter's ease. Keeping to the shadows, he walked toward a carriage parked against the back side of the building.

He settled one boot, then another into steady crevices, then lifted himself atop the carriage. Jayden questioned if his scarred shoulder could lift him onto the narrow second-story ledge. Careful not to allow his pistol to grind against the cracked brick, he fought through the aching limb and hoisted himself onto the platform. Jayden rested for a moment and watched for alerted guards.

At the end of the ledge, a beautiful stained-glass window overlooked the building's interior. Several bullet holes littered the unique glass, allowing Jayden to peek through and glimpse dozens of people sitting around a circular wooden table.

"I'm here because you and Misora decided to take a bunch of stupid pills," said the man in the brown sport coat.

Jayden recognized Sasha and Misora but not the woman sitting with them. Her black hair was pulled back, her back toward him. Along the interior walls, several squads of armed guards watched the perimeter.

"Oh, come on," said Misora, standing and flashing his pompous smile. "Everything we've done has been in the best interest of you and Elasus. We'd never do anything to upset you."

"And I've ordered nothing that contradicts the goals of Elasus," added Sasha, sitting with his legs crossed.

Even from Jayden's vantage, he heard Commodus sighing, trying to control the outbursts readying for takeoff. "Really? Misora, care to share why you're bandaged up? No, shut up and don't waste my time. You killed Nencia Donato, then let things get so screwed up that you allowed Syrus Tokarek, staff in hand, to push you off two continents. Trade's down so much that the PGU is starting to ask questions. Overall, I'd say you've earned a visit."

"Perhaps if you'd sent me the additional guards I'd asked for, our efforts might have succeeded," countered Sasha. "I requested more men and resources over a year ago, and now look at our situation. If you had done your job, all would be under control."

"And we didn't kill Nencia, that was the mystics," said Misora, adding to the already rising tension in the room.

The rustling of someone stumbling on the road behind Jayden pulled his attention away. He turned in time to see a shadowy figure weave in and out of the lantern light.

Just another drunk finding his way home, thought Jayden.

"Let me make myself perfectly clear," bellowed Commodus, bringing Jayden's attention back. "The *only* reason you two are still alive is because Elasus thinks you can still salvage the situation. Blow this opportunity and you'll be executed. Of course, you probably already figured that out, right? Explains why you didn't take this meeting on the *Night Scope.* Right?"

Shouts from the meeting were loud enough now to carry through to the street. "Shut it! Everyone!" yelled Commodus, his voice exploding over objections. "You've deceived the corporation once and you're lucky that didn't put you six feet under or out an airlock."

The screech of a chair pulsated through the broken window. "State your terms so this pointless meeting can be over!" roared Sasha.

"These aren't *terms,* they're orders," said Commodus. "Get your people in normal-looking clothes and out of their armor. We intended the Celje to be inconspicuous, not prancing around like armored ninjas. Some of the more informed locals now think the corporation is trying to organize Ojult into some sort of new world government. We know the PGU has spies everywhere, including Ojult. They suspect the Celje exist, *don't* give them walking proof! Get back into the shadows. The raids on supply lines, regardless of who's operating it, will stop. Ojultan ore, jashinto plums, Listo brandy, all of it needs to get back into production. Money makes this operation work. With Prime Minister Kennedy dead and rumors of the Celje popping up within the PGU, we have to tread carefully. We've already had to stop the export of exiles, and I don't have to tell you how much that's hurting profits. Getting trade up and getting you two off everyone's radar is the priority."

"And what of my men?" asked Sasha. "The mystics, not just Tokarek, are slaughtering us. You tell me to order my men out of their armor, yet they're hunted like zibars. Shall I just leave them for the massacre?"

"You both deserve death for picking this fight to begin with. Letting Tokarek get this organized was your fault. What the hell did you expect would happen?"

The woman held Sasha's hand and looked him in the eyes. "Apparently this fool does not understand the power a staff-wielder possesses, or he might change his tone. Yes, darling?"

"But, my love, Mr. Vrabel does not care about the how and why, only the result. Right, COO Vrabel?"

With a swift kick, Commodus smashed the chair next to Sasha's girl-friend. He acted quickly, moving behind the woman, brandishing a knife to her throat. "I'm not sure why you're here, woman, but rest assured, this is no joke. We're messing with the fate of the human race, there's no room for error!"

Sasha reached for his pistol but kept it holstered. Commodus's guards had their rifles trained on him within seconds. Sasha breathed hard through his nose, seething. "Put that knife down. You may have the upper hand here, Commodus, but Ojult is mine. If Achilla's even scratched, you will never leave this planet alive."

Commodus pressed the knife harder into her throat, drawing blood. "Because threatening me will get you what? Elasus is giving you a second chance, don't screw it up. Fail him again or ignore his commands, and you're all dead."

CHAPTER 57: YEAR 2401

The evidence was undeniable. Sasha and Misora were on Meridone, and the Reeves Corporation was ready to kill them both. Elasus Reeves and his thugs weren't directly responsible for Nencia's death, but their hands were still bloody.

Jayden shifted away from the stained-glass window and into the darkness as the meeting adjourned. Commodus and his group left first, heading back toward the *Night Scope* in silence. Sasha's gang opted to loll around the building, sending Jayden further into the shadows.

Misora exited first, sending expletives with every step. "I could have that greedy bastard killed on his own ship if I wanted. He comes here, accuses us of everything under this dead sun, threatens to kill us, then just leaves! Send Achilla, send her Sasha. Her staff could take down that ship in nothing!"

Staff? Jayden's overcharged mind couldn't have...

Sasha hooked his arm around Achilla's. "Our situation has not changed, neither has our plan. Killing Commodus would only bring more off-planet agents to fight us. Let the Reeves man think he has won. Let us continue down our chosen path and let the corporation come crawling back to us after we've taken everything from them."

Achilla stopped, then pulled Sasha in close. Her lips pressed hard into his, only releasing after an endless moment. "My one love, we have the corporation in one hand, Tokarek in the other." Achilla's passion flooded every word. "Now that we have his student, Tokarek's rule is at an end.

Let me kill her, slow and raw. It shall be repentance for all the Nein have done to us!"

"Oh no, no, no, no." Misora leaned in between them. "My people captured that silver-haired witch, and we'll be the ones who decide what to do with her. I've got Garret heading down there in a minute to give us a final tally on the contracts. Can you imagine how much some idiot Earther would pay for a night with her? Plus, we've got two or three others that will draw in some serious tonze. This piece of the business stays with me."

Jayden listened to the rest of the conversation, fighting the urge to leave Phaedra to the fate she deserved. His instinct to leave her wrestled against the urges of his heart. The smart decision versus the right decision. Phaedra was part of his crew and like it or not, she was Jayden's responsibility.

Sasha dismissed his crew after agreeing to leave Phaedra in the *comforting* hands of Misora. The smirking vermin paced until his man Garret arrived with his ploy. Lingering in the shadows, Jayden listened while the two men detailed their plan of moving the *girls* tomorrow morning. Whatever that meant, it was clear Garret was returning to where Phaedra was being kept.

The Altum Sea's crisp, cool breeze picked up as Jayden climbed off the overhang. Sand mixed with trash glided down the street, bringing images of Texas tumbleweeds to his distant mind. The Celje were gone, and Garret was half a block ahead of him, unaware of his pursuer. They were at the eastern edge of town before Garret entered a worn-down log home with busted-out windows.

Jayden stopped in a dark corner across the street, checking for possible lookouts. Satisfied, he crossed the street, his gun hand near his pistol. There was no lantern near the door or signs of life coming from within. The door latch hung from its hinges and opened with a quick turn.

The entryway was dark and still, yet it was the odor that nearly pushed him back. Jayden knew what it was, had lived in this essence of death for over a year. Voices from a stairwell ahead refocused him, and he moved toward the descending staircase. Foregoing the search of the first floor, he stepped covertly down.

The staircase opened to a dimly lit hallway with lights above doors that lined each side of the corridor. The first door on the right was cracked with just enough light seeping through to make out two beds and a chamber pot, but the room was otherwise empty.

The next door was closed, but the floorboards inside groaned with heavy footsteps. Jayden depressed the latch and the door opened quietly.

A grungy man with a syringe made for a dinosaur stood above a bound woman laying atop a stained bed. She was young, perhaps in her twenties, rail thin with disheveled hair and dark eyes. The man jabbed the needle into the terrified woman's arm. Before the killer depressed the syringe, Jayden was behind him, knife in hand. Jayden drew the knife's edge across the man's throat, severing the carotid artery. Blood pumped from the open wound, covering the man's feet in a few short seconds. Jayden settled the man quietly to the floor, then looked to the frantic woman, placing two fingers to his lips.

"I'm not one of them," he whispered, then eased the syringe from her neck. "I'm going to free you, but I need you to stay silent. I don't know how many there are. Do you understand?"

When Jayden cut her free, she embraced him without fear. She trembled against his chest, so much that her teeth chattered.

"What is this place?" he asked when she'd calmed enough to speak.

The woman's face kept to his shoulder. "It's a... trade shop for the... the Celje. They trade us to different... towns... for..."

"Slave trade," he answered.

The woman nodded. "Appian, the Nein, and the Celje all have agreements. They trade us like... like used tools. Before they send us up for auction, they drug us so we'll cooperate."

He looked down at her arms which were dotted in yellow and red marks. Purple bruises and black scabs lay atop past injections. Appian and the Nein, both involved. Jayden seethed at the thought. Syrus and Zakar would answer for this, at the business end of his pistol.

"Are you well enough to walk?" asked Jayden. She nodded. "I'm guessing there's more of you in here, including one of my friends. I need you to get out of here and head for the docks. Find a ship called the *Challenger*, find Captain Green. Tell him what happened and that you met a guy named Jayden. Tell him they've kidnapped Phaedra. Can you do that?"

The woman's eyes went wide. "My sister... she's, I think she's in here... we've got to find her."

"I'll get everyone out of here, but I can't do it stepping over you. Now, repeat what you're going to tell Green?"

"You're Jayden... find Captain Green on the... the *Challenger*. You're looking for Phaedra."

"Good, now follow me out of here, head up the stairs, and run."

Jayden peeked into the hallway, then pointed her up the stairs. He waited until she was out of sight before moving on down the hallway. There were three more rooms to clear, each with shut doors. He stepped up to the next door, pistol in hand, and listened. Hearing nothing but the sound of his own heart pounding, he entered. The room was like the last, two beds, a chamber pot, and a lone, lifeless woman. The innocence of her vacant eyes should have fueled more rage, but Jayden's anger was already maxed.

Back in the hallway, a door squeaked open.

"Misora wants the witch for himself," said Garret. "After he's done with her, he wants her sold off planet. Wonder how many of us she's killed. How'd you get her anyways?"

"Your friend Waylin told me they'd spotted some *mako* heading toward Trebia. I followed her, thought she might be a mystic." This second man spoke in disconnected English. It sounded just like... "She got to the outskirts of town when I hit her with a rivea dart. Had to hit her twice, she's a tough one. Had her stashed at an apartment overnight before bringing her here. Nah, don't worry, she's going to be hallucinating for a week."

"You gonna take her before putting her on the board?"

"Huck yeah," said the second man. "Go check on the other ones, make sure they're secure and drugged."

The top half of the Garret's head exploded as he stepped into the hallway, sending brain matter back into the room and along the wall. Jayden had his gun cocked and at eye level when the door opened, but at close range, tissue sprayed back into Jayden's eyes. Then a powerful blow sent him skidding back, slamming him into the wall. The impact cleared his eyes but sent his pistol skidding down the hall. It was Wren, Wren Dikal. He moved quick and landed on top of Jayden, connecting two hard blows to his face. With a quick hip thrust, Wren was thrown to the side but quickly rolled up onto his feet. Dikal raised his fists. "Vaut! How did you find me?"

He didn't wait for a response and instead rushed Jayden. The narrow hallway didn't allow for maneuvering. Dikal's shoulder crashed into his ribcage. Jayden twisted away and threw Dikal against the torn sheetrock. The already-crumbling wall cracked, sending dusty chunks to the floor. Jayden landed three unimpeded punches, followed by a knee strike.

"You traitor! You betrayed your own people! Markus, Serena, Victor, Kun. What are the Celje giving you?" Jayden let his rage take over. "Why did you torture me? Why did you try to kill me? Why!?"

Blood dripped from Wren's nose and mouth. "You mystics, you're a deformity upon humanity. I joined Reeves to help exterminate your kind. And that's exactly what I plan to do."

"Joined Reeves?" Jayden had a split second to digest the comment before diving back into the room as Wren drew and fired a small pocket pistol. The bullet soared inches above Jayden's head, then ricocheted off the back wall. He spun on his back and kicked the door closed, pressing his whole body against it.

"I'm not a mystic!"

Two bullets splintered the door above his crouched body.

Wren pounded the frame, but Jayden's weight held.

"You *are* a mystic, and you'll die today! I should've hung you in prison!"

There was a pause where neither man moved nor said anything.

"Who the hell are you?" Dikal said.

"Drop the gun," said a cool voice from the hallway.

Jayden jumped to his feet and swung the door open. Wren's pistol was aimed down the corridor in the opposite direction, giving Jayden the perfect angle. He went for Dikal's gun hand and slammed it against the wall. Wren's forearm fractured with a gratifying crack. He dropped to his knees, clutching his forearm, screaming in pain.

If Wren expected mercy, he'd sorely underestimated Jayden's hatred for him. A perfectly directed punch sent the traitor sprawling onto his back. Using his own body weight, Jayden pushed his knee into Wren's throat and watched. The traitor's legs and arms flailed, but the struggle was brief.

Jayden felt another pair of eyes watching him, but nothing would stop him from finally killing this bastard. Wren's eyes rolled back and his heart gave one final thud before ending.

"I hope hell spits you back out so I can kill you again."

His rage vanished when he sighted silvery hair inside the far room. Phaedra was on her back with her hands bound behind her. Her face and neck were bruised but she was alive. A heavy glaze covered her eyes as he pulled her lids back. "Phaedra, you've been drugged. Wake up, come on, wake up, we need to get the hell out of here."

Her eyes wandered left and right, seeing but not understanding. "Jayden... I'm... something isn't... right... I'm not... drugged."

His bloodstained knife cut the ropes binding her. "Yeah, you're drugged, but we need to go, can you stand?"

She nodded and tried to stand but fell back onto the bed. Jayden pulled her up and threw her arm around him. "Use me for support."

"This... this isn't... I need... focus."

If they ran into the Celje, he couldn't shoot and hold her at the same time, so he let her drift into a healing trance while he walked into the hallway to grab his hat and pistol.

"Are you okay?" said a voice from down the hall.

He'd completely forgotten about the other person who'd showed up during the fight. Jayden raised his hands in a surrendering motion, seeing his own pistol in the hands of the stranger. The man wore purple-tinted glasses and dressed like someone with influence.

"I don't know who you are, but I'm not your enemy," said Jayden.

"You're Jayden Vaut."

Seeing no reason to lie, Jayden nodded. "I'm not a Celje, if that's what you're thinking."

The stranger limped forward through the dim light. His stringy hair and swollen eyes gave the appearance of hard living. He slid his purple glasses into his coat pocket and twirled Jayden's pistol like a professional gunfighter. "From Texas, right?" The stranger shuffled closer. "Didn't think I'd see you again after we got off that ship. You look like you've seen better days."

The purple glasses, unusual horizontal hairline, but Jayden still couldn't place him. Jayden took the pistol and paused before holstering it. "It's been a rough few... days and we're kind of in a hurry."

"Not ringing a bell? My brother and I sat next to you on the trip over from Earth. Name's Rystral if you recall?"

A flood of memories from a different life swirled into view. "Rystral, yeah, I remember. You made it?"

The acquaintances shook hands.

"Rystral, we're in deep here. This is some sort of trade shop for... people. My friend's back there. She's hurt." Jayden pointed to Dikal's corpse. "That... man down there, he deserved death and anything else hell gives him."

Rystral bent down and tossed Jayden's hat back to him. "Look, pal, it's worse than you think. There's a bounty out on you and your friends. Nikoli Sokolov, the governor on this continent, put a price on your heads. You remember the Carter brothers, Broden and Clive, the one's that attacked us on the exile ship? They work for him on a contract basis sometimes, and rumor is they're on your trail. I've been using my girls at Duggan's Lodge to keep tabs on you. You and your friends need to get off Meridone."

Jayden recalled Daria's unwillingness to give up her employer. "Let me check the rest of this place out, make sure there's no one else tied up, then we'll leave."

"Jayden, I'll do it. Take your friend and get out of here. Once the sun comes up, you're going to find out how popular you've become in this town."

Jayden didn't know Rystral beyond what he'd witnessed ten years ago, but circumstances didn't allow for a background check. Jayden rushed back to Phaedra. Her voice was slightly stronger, but she couldn't fight if it came to that.

Jayden gently pulled her up. "We've landed ourselves in a bad spot, Phaedra. We've managed to catch the eye of the local governor. We need to get out of Meridone."

She nodded and let him help her up the stairs. "Who's that guy?" she asked.

"Long story, focus on walking... faster."

They climbed the stairs one at a time, and after carefully scouting the

street, lumbered out of the building, turning west toward the docks. The
sun was beginning to glow over the land, and Jayden recalled his friend's
warning.

Phaedra was more or less walking on her own now, but she continued
speaking in sentence fragments.

The harbor finally came into view, but, following the same luck they'd
had since arriving, so did a squad of Celje. The plain clothed agents
blocked the path to the boat, then raised their rifles as Jayden and Phaedra approached.

"Get behind me, and say nothing," Jayden whispered.

"You there, stop!"

Jayden kept his hat low and tried to sidestep the men. "Sorry, sir, sorry,
just trying to get back to the docks. She's had too much to drink. You
know how it is."

"Sure looks like them, Waylin. What do you think?" asked one agent.

Waylin looked at Phaedra, then Jayden. "The woman is the Nein witch,
let me see him."

Phaedra stumbled over her own feet, then her muddled mind sealed
their fate. "See, Vaut… you're notorious… all over the planet."

Jayden looked with horror into his partner's glazed eyes.

"Well, isn't this your lucky day, Jayden Vaut?" Waylin stepped closer,
pointing his rifle at Jayden's chest.

They were close to the docks, but there were too many Celje to even
think about fighting.

Waylin pushed the barrel into Jayden's sternum. "Both of you get on
the ground. West, go tell Misora we've found Vaut and recaptured the
witch."

A small blonde kid dressed in clothes two sizes too big came up from
the back of the group. "Okay, I'm on it."

"Pursuit of peace, ha," said Jayden, trying to steady Phaedra. Still,
maybe the situation wasn't completely lost. In his peripheral vision, Bella
and several others were positioning themselves behind several stacked
crates near the *Challenger*.

Wondering if it was just luck or that woman he'd rescued from Dikal
got word to Green, he didn't much care. As soon as Captain Green raised

his rifle toward them, Jayden dived on top of Phaedra. She cursed as the first bullet whizzed above them. Suddenly both sides were exchanging intense gunfire. Green's men had too much time to ready themselves and took down the Celje agents in one precise volley.

"You okay? You hit?"

Phaedra pushed him away. "… off me!"

"Well, don't just stand there on top of her you lazy buffoon! Get up and get on board," Captain Green's voice boomed across the harbor.

It was the first time Jayden ever genuinely appreciated hearing him speak.

Jayden tossed Phaedra over his shoulder and made for the ship. "How'd you know we were coming!?" shouted Jayden across the bow.

"Our girl Bella said she felt a fight coming, told us to get our guns ready."

Jayden kept pace with Green's long strides back toward the ship. "A thin woman, black hair, did she ever get here, deliver a message?"

"No women have come aboard Vaut. Why? You trying to bring back a lady friend?"

He'd never even gotten the woman's name. Why hadn't he at least asked? Was she okay? Had he freed her only so she could be captured again?

Bella's alarmed voice snapped his self-pity. "More coming, Captain!"

Everyone, including Captain Green, looked toward the town. "Okay, ladies, let's get my floating princess out of here! Bella, set up a defense while we prep. Vaut, get your friend down below, then get back up here with something loud."

Jenna was the first to take up position. "Better hurry, Vaut, a lot of them coming this way."

Jayden carefully navigated the stairwell into the crew quarters and placed Phaedra into her bunk. She collapsed into the hardy cushion, dashing any hope she might be able to fight.

He tossed his overcoat and hat onto the ground. "Phaedra, we're in a bad spot. Put yourself in a healing trance; we're gonna need you."

Her middle finger told him she understood.

Rushing up the stairs with his long rifle and backpack, the scene unfolded into chaos. The Celje had taken up position near their fallen comrades. Roughly three dozen agents opened fire, bursting eardrums as their barrage tore into the ship.

Captain Green sent the majority of his crew to defend his ship while the rest prepared the *Challenger* for sea. Bella, Turr, and Jenna supported the crew with conjured shields and their own firepower.

"Ha!" cackled Captain Green. "I told you she'd be okay, didn't I, Vaut? Come on old girl, flash them your pretties. Show them that steel chastity."

The odds weren't good, but they had the Celje at a choke point on the dock. Rushing up to the bow of the ship, Jayden dove into a prone position and joined his rifle with the others. He took calm, steady breaths, briefly holding as he squeezed the trigger. His marksmanship, combined with the range of the rifle, should have been good enough, but the motion of the boat sent many of his shots wide.

Bullets glanced off the hull around him as he fired shot after shot, yet even his sure strikes weren't taking them down. "They've got armor!"

A squeal from his right jolted his focus as Jayden saw Jenna dragging Bella away.

"Turr, she's hit!" shouted Jenna. "Shoulder and forearm."

The Celje were using RERs with vital-organ-tracking software, but the swaying of the boat was working against them.

"Get her inside, I'll hold them off,' replied Turr, redirecting his conjured shield.

The Celje were creeping up the dock.

"Green!" shouted Jayden. "We need—"

A ricochet sent a splinter into the side of his face. "Ah!" Jayden flipped onto his back, feeling for the fragment. The piece was too large to yank out. What concerned him wasn't the fragment but the amount of blood covering his hand. "I'm hit!"

"Stay there!" roared Turr. "Wait… what the…" Turr pointed toward the approaching Celje. "More reinforcements coming!"

Jayden rolled back onto his stomach and looked through his scope, pushing the pain away. Behind the Celje approached six men in dark-gray-and-brown garbs. They walked fast and confidently and didn't look like the other agents. One man, walking casually behind the rest, wore purple-tinted glasses.

"Turr, Green, don't fire on that new group! Don't fire on them!"

Rystral's team looked more like mystics than brothel bouncers, and it didn't take long for his theory to play out. The new group produced shields on the heels of a simultaneous swarm of rifle slugs. The attack took down five soldiers before the well-disciplined agents adapted to the new front.

So Rystral had bounty hunters and mystic mercenaries to go along with a brothel. It was a testament to what Ojult did to good people.

Rystral's mystics continued their fight, but their advance was quickly halted. Fighting through the sting in his face, Jayden pulled his rifle back to his shoulder.

Bullets were screaming everywhere when Captain Green walked up to him and stood, fearlessly. "If you plan on living today, we need to take advantage of this distraction and get out of here. You willing to leave your friends out there?"

No way Rystral and his men were going to fight their way through the Celje line. Jayden nodded. "Both groups need to retreat in unison."

Green began barking orders.

Jayden turned and waved at Rystral, trying to get his attention. After a few moments, Rystral gave him the thumbs-up, then started gesturing for Jayden and his crew to get out of there. It gave Jayden only mild comfort that his newfound friend understood their position.

Green gave the order to unmoor, and within minutes the smaller rowboats were towing the *Challenger* out to sea. Four fully manned dinghies with heavy ropes attached to the *Challenger*'s bow pulled the large ship out of the docks. Jayden felt sick leaving Rystral on the mainland to deal with the Celje, but the situation couldn't be helped. They'd accomplished their mission, organized a retreat, and rescued Phaedra, but took casualties along the way. Jayden's team wasn't in any condition to continue the fight and retreating was the right call.

Below deck, Bella and six of Green's men were receiving medical attention from Turr and Jenna. Bella looked to be in a healing trance, her shoulder and forearm bandaged. Lucky for them, Shari Dikal had sent along vials of hovrol and jashinto serum.

Kaboom! Kaboom! Kaboom!

Jayden jerked down and smoke started to billow through the ship.

"Now that's what I call a good old-fashioned dustup," said Captain Green. "Had a friend of mine make these cannons. They're old school and I love 'em! And, Vaut, stop bleeding all over my deck and get downstairs. And stay away from the maps!"

CHAPTER 58: YEAR 2401

Donato drifted through the depths of an unknown world looking at the most horrifying demons and mythical creatures he'd ever imagined. Of course, he was dreaming, and somehow felt he needed to stay in the dream. With his "Stick of Destiny," he plowed through the demons, hacking and slicing his way through to a dark tower. Lightning struck a nearby tree, setting it ablaze and forcing him to leap over the moat leading into the tower. Flaming arrows flew by his head as he climbed the circular stairwell. Finally seeing the door leading into the models' chambers, he bashed the door down and—

"Garvin!" said Chelsie, shaking him awake. "Damn it, you're dreaming again and your thing's poking out. Wake up."

Garvin awoke. "Oh… come on now. Darn it! That was a good one too. I was using my Stick of Destiny."

She laid her head back on his chest. "More like a Stick of Wishful Thinking. We've gotta get up soon. What were you dreaming about?"

"Naked blondes in bikinis."

She pinched a handful of chest hair.

"Ouch! You asked!"

"Lie next time."

A low hum rang from the nightstand. She tapped the "off" button on her watch and rolled out of bed. "Told you, time to get up. Can't be late or the captain might not sleep with you for a month."

She wasn't as attractive as Alanah, but Chelsie was something special in the sack. He watched her naked body walk off and turn on the coffee dispenser.

"I'll never look at that coffee maker the same way again," he said before three knocks on the door interrupted the couple.

Chelsie slid on one of his silk robes before responding. "Come in."

Alanah walked in, took one look at Chelsie, and rolled her eyes so far back that Garvin thought she was seeing yesterday. "Good morning."

"Well, good morning to you too," he said, flashing a preemptive grin. "You know, with the two of you here, I can think—"

A stirring spoon came hurtling from the direction of the bar, missing Garvin by inches and bouncing off the headboard.

"Don't finish that thought," Chelsie warned.

Alanah said, "We got an early start on repairs this morning. Our trip to Meridone caused two more fractures in cargo bay ten. Did I already mention that was a bad idea? I'm about to finish the overnight watch and noticed that Commodus didn't come back until a few hours ago. I just checked out a report about a fight on the docks, and it's getting bigger. Slugs are being tossed by each side, seems the Celje are involved."

Chelsie sat back on the edge of the bed with a steaming cup. "Launch a few drones. Let's get a better picture as to who's involved. Have Caitlin check the waves for chatter."

Donato thought of a conversation he had with Commodus a few days ago. The chief said he was ordering Sasha and his team back underground. Donato also knew that most of the docks on Meridone were operated by Nikoli or Appian, neither of whom would ever openly fight on their own business tract.

Five minutes later, Donato was dressed, on the bridge, and over-looking the fight. Alanah hadn't been exaggerating, and he realized why the Celje were involved. Mystics were intermixed with the crew of the sailship.

Donato needed a closer look, but the surveillance drones were offline. Hazzard was working on them but didn't have an ETA. The fight was getting bloodier by the minute.

The bridge door opened, and a freshly dressed first officer entered, followed by a tired-looking COO.

"I've had a long night, Garvin, what do you need?" Commodus's eyes were bloodshot, and his lips were dried and cracked.

Donato pointed out the bridge window. "If I'm not mistaken, Misora and Sasha are viewing the fight from that corner building. Can't tell for sure since none of my damn drones are working."

Chelsie handed Commodus a kaldi. "Any idea how it started?"

Lewis Bardolf walked up from the front of the bridge with his professional opinion ready. "I've had my guys keeping an eye on the situation all morning. The Celje apparently stopped a couple trying to make it back to that sailship there. One, if not both of them, were on Sasha's capture list. When the Celje attempted to detain them, the sail ship's crew opened fire."

Commodus took several sips before replying. "I'd ask you to intervene, Lewis, but I don't want locals associating the corporation with any side here. Let's see how Sasha handles this."

Lewis leaned into Donato's ear, careful not to attract Commodus's attention. "Hazzard got the drones launched, but he's not putting them on display."

Donato nodded then caught the wondering eye of Alanah looking at the wordless exchange. He locked eyes with her, daring her to say something.

"Are those your people firing from town?" demanded Commodus.

Donato pulled a pair of antique, non-networked binoculars from a small compartment near his chair. "No, not mine, chief."

The Celje weren't bothering to cover their rear and the first volley from a new group took down a third of Sasha's agents.

"Jesus," shouted Commodus. "Garvin! You sure those aren't yours!"

"Not mine," answered Lewis. "That new group are mystics. See there, they've conjured shields. Those people on that ship, they look just as confused as we are."

Seconds passed while Garvin considered his options. "Bet those wizards would pay a fortune for a staff right about now."

Commodus slammed his hands down on the window's frame. "Each time I lose a man it costs the corporation insurance dollars plus the expenses needed to train and recruit their replacement. This battle is bleeding us by the minute."

Chelsie was next to Commodus now, pointing at the sailship. "That brig is about to pull out, see the boats going over the side. And that new group is getting ready to retreat. Anything we did now would only give away your association with those agents."

Small boats began towing the much larger ship out of the harbor. The Celje adjusted their fire toward the second group until the brig let loose cannon fire. Besides the bloody devastation, the smoke covered the ship's retreat. Commodus turned back to the bridge and set the empty cup down on the ledge.

"Keep me updated on any changes. I need to make a call." Commodus left the bridge, muttering something about hanging Misora and Sasha.

Alanah drummed over her navigation display. "Ship's moving too slow to figure out where they're heading."

Lewis walked to the bridge exit and locked the door. "Doesn't much matter at this point, Kass, but Captain, I've got something. Didn't think you wanted me to shout it out in front of the exec, but our drones found something pretty interesting."

The security officer selected a file on Hazzard's computer, and a video started playing. It was drone footage of the fight, zooming in on a young female mystic fighting on the docks. There was too much smoke to get a clear view, but then Lewis pulled up another video from three days prior. The new video showed a clearer picture of what seemed to be the same girl escorting cargo from the docks to the *Night Scope*.

"The drones sent her facial signature to the fleet database," said Bardolf, pulling up the catalog. "She's obviously a mystic, but she's in the employment of Appian. Did Nencia ever employ mystics?"

Donato looked at the two pictures, then downloaded the images to his personal datapad. His head swiveled between the two graphics. "Lewis, delete those images from the main computer, all the backups too. Smith, make sure Commodus can't find a link between that girl and Appian. Hack into any database you need, but make it happen. Kass, don't lose sight of that ship. I want all the data you can give me on who owns her and its captain." He could feel the crew's sudden tension, surprised by their captain's angst over something as trivial as a mystic girl.

Donato was at a crossroads, pulled apart by a game of double agent that required his officers to come on board to continue the gambit. He glanced at Chelsie. His conversation with Tayla Cruz not long ago and now seeing the unmistakable resemblance between this girl and Tayla… "Soon, we're going to miss the days of being a simple transport crew with nothing but time and tonze to worry about."

———————

Tayla Cruz finished her makeup, slipped out of her Lent silk bathrobe, and put on a red square-neck pencil dress that amplified every curve of her body. Her heels were tall and pointed, hair curled and falling over ears and in front of her shoulders. She paraded like a fashion model into the bedroom where Elasus sat in bed reading the morning journal. "How do I look?" she asked, flashing her recently whitened teeth.

"Ravishing." His voice was mechanical, and his eyes never left the paper.

For the second night in a row, she'd slept at the office, unable to escape the psychological torture that rained down on her.

She turned slowly, permitting him to see the expensive dress. "Thank you again for the dress, Mr. Reeves. Unless you require anything else, I'm heading to my desk. I'll have your morning brief shortly. Is there anything—"

The nightstand phone rang twice, then flashed white. Tayla answered. It was the doorman letting her know Mrs. Reeves was heading their way.

"Mr. Reeves, your wife is on her way up. Would you like me to leave?"

A loud clambering came from the main office door. Elasus took a long slurp of coffee. "I suppose she won't stop until she's let in."

Tayla set off down the long gallery, her backside advertising perfection while she mentally cursed every portrait she passed.

"Good morning, Mrs. Reeves, how may I help you?" she said, opening the door and winking at her ally.

Irelyn nodded but continued the facade by tossing a shoulder into Tayla as she walked by. "Take your sweet attitude and shove it. Where's my husband? And why isn't my code working on this door!?"

"Your husband is in his bedroom suite. Would you like me to escort you? May I get you something to drink? Tea?"

"I'll call you later," Irelyn mouthed, then marched off.

Tayla kept pace with her, noticing the screen of Irelyn's datapad displayed the front page of the local paper.

"Hope you had a relaxing night," scolded Irelyn as she entered the bedroom. "Were all your needs taken care of?"

Elasus locked eyes with Irelyn. "Good morning. What can I help you with?"

Irelyn slid her hand across her 3DI and a holographic image resolved over Elasus. "Read the journal today? Have you gotten to the page where the new opinion polls say you're a god!?"

"Just page fillers. Polls are nothing but attention-gathering nonsense publishers use to sell their product. Now, what can I help you with?"

Irelyn crossed her arms. "Attention gathering! That's precisely what you don't want! Have you read the opinion section where rumors are circulating about the conflict on Ojult? Oh, and by the way, Zhang called this morning asking why there's a full-scale war going on there!"

"And what did you tell him?"

"Elasus, you're thinking like a broken MFG. If Zhang knows, then the PGU will know. The news will then drop an asteroid-sized story on the public, leaving Zhang with little choice; he'll go after the corporation and Ojult. I know you like him, and god knows he thinks you're a corporate deity, but Zhang still has to answer to the PGU."

Elasus slid out of bed, his silk robe fluttering as he walked toward his desk. "And what do you suggest? Kill Zhang? Send in more agents? Of course, that would imply sending Ruven to finish the job, which puts our beloved son in harm's way. Then again, Ruven's force is still unknown to all but a few and sending that size of a force to deal with a few dozen mystics is like putting a grenade on an ant hill. No, my strategy for dealing with the situation will work."

Tayla continued to watch the exchange from afar, uncertain whether to stay or go. Regardless, she knew the mention of Ruven would infuriate Irelyn.

"Let's just be honest. Ruven's *force* shouldn't even exist! You've got some delusion that the Elders are going to come back and try to destroy Earth or turn us all into mindless arcane slaves. You're putting our son in danger for a purpose only a deranged sociopath would believe!"

Elasus turned to face Irelyn, leaning slightly against his neatly arranged desk. "Does the name Cadoc Alzer ring a bell?"

Tayla's perfect posture went rigid as did Irelyn's.

"Why... why would you even bring him up?" replied Irelyn. "You act like you don't even remember our daughter, why would you bring up her dead boyfriend?"

Elasus dialed four numbers on his phone, then put the call on speaker.

"Tanner here, Mr. Reeves, what can I do for you?"

"You're on speaker with my wife present. I'd like you to give me a brief explanation on Cadoc Alzer."

"Yes sir, no problem. Years ago, Secretary Madigan provided video surveillance, along with a firsthand transcript between a mystic hit cell located here in the Unified Western Powers region. The PGU and the corporation had been tracking the cell for years. The cell's goal was simple but genius. Plant someone of the opposite sex with one of your children, get them to become close, even romantic, then assassinate you. We aren't sure who they tried to pair with your son, Ruven, but Cadoc Alzer was assigned to Marilla. We intercepted a message from the main cell the day we arrested him. He planned on killing you, then your wife. I've got the file, or I can have the secretary call you to speak more about it."

Elasus looked at Irelyn. "Send a copy of the file to my wife. Thank you." Elasus ended the call and glared at Irelyn. "You mentioned a potential war with the Elders? Perhaps the Elders will come again, perhaps not. But the mystics *are* here, and the war has already started. Elder involvement or not, the sages are stirring, and something's brewing out there. I must be prepared."

Tayla's stomach tightened as she digested his declaration. What was brewing? Coming from any other person, this sort of announcement would have sounded insane, but not today, not from Elasus. This man didn't exaggerate, and he never lied.

"If we can put the theatrics to rest," continued Elasus, "I have a business to run. Ms. Cruz, please escort my wife out of the building."

Tayla heard him but didn't answer. Were her children in danger because of this hidden threat? Why hadn't she already known about this? She had been secretly monitoring all inbound and outbound calls, along with Elasus's private correspondence.

"Ms. Cruz, did you hear me?" he repeated.

"I... I'm sorry, Mr. Reeves. Mrs. Reeves, please follow me."

Irelyn's answer was just as distant. "Of course, Tayla... let's... I'll follow you."

Tayla led her by the arm into the elevator.

Neither woman dared speak until they were outside the closely monitored building. "Marilla's boyfriend... an assassin?" said Irelyn, walking toward her awaiting car. "Is this, how can, but... Why haven't I heard about this before? What did he mean by a *new threat*? Zhang's said nothing about it."

"This is the first I've heard of it too, but we need to hang low for a while. I think we were a bit too casual in front of Elasus just now. He might suspect something. I'll contact you when it's safe."

After Hewitt drove off with her only friend, Tayla headed back into her office to continue the already-exhausting day. Despite a thousand worries about her children, she had to stay focused and started putting together Elasus's reports.

Tayla had just finished her first brief when an icon appeared at the bottom of her screen. It was an inbound call from an unrecognized, encrypted caller. She removed a docuchip from her purse and inserted it into her computer, then entered her password. She launched her own customized codebreaking program, and the cypher was uncoded in seconds. The inbound call was coming from the *Night Scope*, which could only mean Donato was trying to contact her. With Elasus getting dressed, Tayla inserted her earpiece and accepted the call.

"Calling me like this is dangerous, Garvin, what's wrong?"

"Well, calling me by my first name probably isn't that smart either," Donato snapped. His tone was less charismatic than usual. "Call me Canine, and you're Pamela, got it?"

The captain's tension surged through the call, and Tayla's neck tightened, fearful of what Garvin had discovered. "What's happened?"

There was rustling on Donato's side, then a file transfer came through. "Pamela, I've sent you a file. Is this someone you recognize? If so, don't overreact; people might be listening."

Tayla ran a quick script over the file, checking for oddities and viruses.

When the inspection completed, the image opened. The long bushy hair, soft features, and homely look were impossible to mistake. "It's her, that's Gabrielle." Tayla's voice was sturdier than she'd imagined. "My little girl, alive. Yes, absolutely, that's her."

"Snap back to reality, there's a lot you need to know. First, your *little girl* is a bona fide mystic badass. Our system doesn't have her listed under Gabrielle, so she's likely going by another name. And before you ask, no, I haven't seen her brother."

Gabrielle, a mystic? She never showed any sign of it. "This picture? When was it taken? It looks as if she's surrounded by a shield."

Prolonged silence.

"Gabrielle was traveling with a group of Appian and Nein scouts. The Celje attacked them as they were leaving the port. Gabrielle was producing the shield that was protecting the group."

Tayla's little girl was in the middle of a fight, with real bullets aimed to take her life. "I want them dead, Garvin. I don't care what you have to do, kill them. I'll pay whatever you ask!"

"I'm no soldier, and you're no killer. Just relax. I don't think she needed much help. But listen, this isn't the only reason I called, so I need you to breathe and take in what I'm about to tell you. I'm tracking your daughter's ship, and we'll keep looking for your son. But I did some digging around on Grylo, and I can't find him."

"This is a lot. Wait, what do you mean? He's not there? Maybe he's with Aaron? Why can't you just fly over and pick her up? What's going on!?"

"You want me to park a stadium-sized ship over a sailboat? Come on, Pamela, I need you to think clearly. The records on Ojult don't show him ever getting here. It's like he boarded the ship on Earth but never got off."

Another encrypted message flashed across Tayla's worktop signaling Elasus was at his computer. "Garvin, I don't have much time. I don't know what you want me to say. Grylo was *on* that ship with my children."

"Stop using my real—"

"Oh, shut up! If anyone's listening, then they'll connect Grylo to me, which will lead back to you, so you're already screwed. Now, please, help me find my family!"

CHAPTER 59: YEAR 2401

Ship on the starboard side, Captain!" yelled the lookout from the crow's nest.

No one needed Captain Green to tell them what to do this time. They were five days into their journey back to Rindo, and everyone on board was ready to fight for their ship.

"Get to quarters. Man your stations! Jayden! Get your people up there, I want you picking those bastards off if they get close!"

Every ship was a potential threat, and Green took no chances. Jayden was the only member of his team in good enough shape to fight. Turr and Jenna were still tending to the injured.

Having climbed up to the crow's nest several times a day, Jayden had overcome his fear of heights and rocketed up the rope ladder to the crow's nest. With his rifle and backpack in tow, he vaulted over the railing and started scanning for the enemy.

"Captain!" shouted the lookout next to him. "It's the *Sparrow* out of Listo!"

The third false alarm of the day and just another of the dozens they'd encountered on the way back. With the trade winds failing, the trip back to Capintesta was taking longer than expected and the number of false alarms was beginning to wear on the crew. Jayden spent nearly the entire trip home on the bow of the ship, keeping an eye out for the Celje. Captain Green cursed him less since the two had fought together on the docks.

When the *Challenger* docked in Port Rindo after six days at sea, there was a new bond between the two men.

"I still don't like you, Vaut," shouted Green with far less enthusiasm than usual. "If you ever get on my boat again, I'll drag you behind it like bait!"

"Looking forward to it, Captain. Thanks again for everything, you pulled us out of a rough spot."

Green continued his threats even as Jayden followed Bella and Phaedra onto the dock. "You going to be okay?" asked Jayden, helping Bella into a carriage.

Bella accepted the help and gazed back at him. "I'm good, don't worry about me. Got my best friend Phaedra to keep me company on the way home."

Jenna tossed their rucksacks into the carriage and extended her hand. "Fun fighting with you, Vaut. Hope we get the opportunity again soon. Turr says goodbye. He nearly missed the wagon heading to Carendra. Apparently Kavil wants him up there assisting in whatever he's doing. Once we get Bella settled, we'll meet up with Syrus in Pa'Gran. Good luck."

"I know you're upset about Appian's involvement in the slave market," continued Bella. "It almost took my best friend from me; I'll see that it's ended."

He believed her and knew Bella would get her message across to Zakar, even if it meant forcing him at the sharp end of an ice shard. Bella might have been acting indifferent about the situation, but almost losing Phaedra, was fueling a silent rage within her.

Jayden was in the middle of waving when Phaedra walked by. She said nothing and stepped up into the carriage, taking the reins. The two-horse carriage trotted away, kicking up dust. Bella poked her head out the back and waved. Jayden returned the gesture, losing sight of the wagon as they passed through the gates and headed down the hill.

"Better to have hated and survived, than never to have survived at all," sang a man with a familiar drawl. A hettle smelling of chestnuts and sweet stalk filled the air around them.

Jayden turned and extended his hand. "Andreas? You here on business or pleasure? Thought Syrus had you wrangling in security around Pa'Gran."

"Brothers in arms to the end, or perhaps brothers in cuffs? I'll need to work on that axiom, but I digress. Forgive me, Jayden, but you look like hell, or like someone who's been shot at a lot lately." Andreas handed Jayden his flask. "It's Listo brandy, only the best for my semi-Celje-proof friend."

Jayden cocked an eyebrow. "I gave more than I got this go around." He took a long drink from the haggard flask, waiting for the burn to dissolve. "Being shot at is one of the few things I'm good at. But Bella, Phaedra, and a handful of sailors were hurt, no deaths, but still …"

"That explains Green's foul mood."

Guilt over Bella's injury sprayed his nerves, and Jayden took another swig from the flask, then handed it back. "I also had to rescue Phaedra from a slave trader who worked with the Nein."

Andreas drank, then locked eyes with Jayden. "Some of us are less Nein than others. I'm not part of that despicable crowd and hope the devil finds their soul before my pistol does. Now, moving on to much more agreeable topics, did you find Sasha?"

"Yeah. Looks like there's a Reeves executive on the planet, goes by Commodus. He's not too happy with them, and I've got something else you might be interested in."

"Do tell."

Jayden couldn't help but smile. "Wren Dikal's dead."

When Jayden finished his account, Andreas's flask was empty. "You're putting together quite the resumé. Congratulations on putting that demon scum into the ground."

"Thanks. So why are you here?"

Andreas tipped his hat. "At your service. I'm your escort back to Syrus. He's in Pa'Gran and looking forward to your debrief."

Jayden took a calming breath. "Phaedra's in rough shape, and Jenna hasn't slept in days, but let them rest and they can update Syrus. Tell him the next Nein I find dealing slaves is going to end up with a very special Visconti bullet between their eyes."

"You know, I have this wonderful lady friend who—"

"No thanks. Consider this my resignation. I'm done with Syrus and the Nein. I'm going back to Dalth to spend more time with Eve, friends, work Markus's farm, and try to forget this mess. It was a mistake to trust Syrus. Tell him not to visit, but I hope you do. I know Serena would like to see you too."

"Thank you, Jayden, and I will visit if for nothing more than to see you work a farm, that's got to be entertaining. But if I may, we're fighting the very group that murdered Nencia and Helia, what of their legacies? What of revenge?"

An old but familiar wrath engulfed Jayden. "I've killed a lot of people, most of them on Syrus's orders. Nencia and Helia's deaths are both linked to Syrus. I don't trust him, and neither should you."

Jayden arrived in Dalth as the sun rose, the fresh daybreak glistening the morning dew. With backpack and rifle in tow, Jayden walked to Shari Dikal's cottage. The screen door was shut, but the main door was open revealing Shari and Diego eating breakfast. The conversation wasn't going to be pretty, but Jayden had to be the one.

He knocked on the screen door. "Shari, it's Vaut." The smell of frying meat, baking bread, and chemicals filled the locale.

She approached wearing a red-patterned dress and white apron. "It's early, Mr. Vaut, but a good morning nevertheless. What can I do for you?"

He was quickly losing his nerve now that the widow was in front of him. "You... your medicine, it worked."

"I'm sorry?"

"The medicine you sent with us to Meridone. I wanted you to know it saved lives. Just... wanted to say thank you."

She folded her arms and raised an eyebrow. "I'm glad to hear that. Now, why have you really come?" She turned and called toward the kitchen, "Diego, go fetch two more buckets of water. I need to speak with Jayden."

Jayden sat across from her, around a chipped table made of scrap wood and metal. He sipped at the bitter kaldi Shari offered, biting back the tang that threatened to scrunch his face. Taking a flying glance, he noticed most of her bruises were gone, but she still bore the signs of a tortured life. Jayden struggled to start his story. How does one go about telling a woman she's now a widow?

"I was recently sent to Meridone to look for the men responsible for making life on Ojult difficult."

Shari pulled out a hettle stalk and scratched the match underneath the table. "Not sure why you had to travel all the way to Meridone. There are plenty of evil men on Capintesta. I happen to know one. Did you kill him? You wouldn't be here if you hadn't found my husband."

"A friend of mine was captured by a human trafficker, then brought to something like a prison in Port Fiesta. I found her and a few other women, freed them, and yes, Wren appeared to be running the place. He'd already killed one woman before I got there."

"I don't care about your story. Did you kill him or do I need to still keep a blade under my pillow?"

Jayden forced himself to look into her eyes. "Yes, I killed him."

Despite her earlier sharp tone, Shari seemed lost for words. Her hettle continued to burn, her jaw clenched tight.

Jayden got up, leaving his mostly untouched kaldi on the table. "I'm sorry it came to this."

He was halfway out the door when she finally responded with a sad and empty tone: "I don't know if it's possible to love and hate someone at the same time, but he was my husband and gave me Diego. You killed a wicked man, I know that. Sounds like you saved a few girls too. But, Jayden, I know your kind. You may not be the demon my husband was, but you're just as bloodthirsty. I see it in your eyes. Stay away from me and Diego. Don't come by trying to play catch with my son like some pretend father who feels guilty for what he did. He'll know the truth one day, but that truth will come from me, not you. Understand?"

CHAPTER 60: YEAR 2401

Elasus leaned back in his oversized office chair, exhaling the day's frustrations. According to the computer projections, the Reeves Corporation was going to miss their targeted revenue goals.

"Ojult's bringing the entire bottom line down," said Elasus, pointing to the graphs. "My strategy on Lent and Chden are only making up for a portion of the shortfall. Then, of course, there's the mounting death toll."

Tanner and his overly styled hair sat across from him, wearing a gray suit and blue turtleneck that reached to his jawline. "The violence seems acceptable if not slightly irregular."

"If by *acceptable* you mean reaching levels not seen since the mystic civil wars, then you're correct. But for our purposes, violence breeds higher expenses and lower revenues, neither of which I desire."

Since taking over the corporation, Elasus dreaded the day the Elder's would come back. Many thought the idea was crazy, which was fine by him. While the PGU and regional authorities danced around the apocalyptic scenario, Elasus prepared for it.

"You suspect the Elders will show themselves soon?" asked Tanner.

Elasus closed the financial application, tired of the reminder. "We need to stick to facts and learn from history. Historical accounts show us that when mystic deaths begin to mount, the Elders appear. What many don't know is when these infamous sages show up, violence and death increase elevenfold. It's a piece of the past our schools tend to leave out of the textbooks. These Elders instigate violence and perpetuate disorder, which quickly induces an economic bomb. You asked me over the phone why I called the meeting with the FIAS leadership? This is why."

A message from Tayla appeared on his computer.

Escorting FIAS Regional Governor Kadeem Drohar and FIAS Defense Minister Dagara Igwe to the conference room.

Elasus stood and buttoned his suit jacket. "It's time we formalized the next piece of our plan to protect the corporation."

Governor Kadeem Drohar and Defense Minister Dagara Igwe acknowledged the executive's presence as they entered the conference room but did not stand to greet them. It was the reception Elasus expected given their history, but they would be allies by the time this meeting adjourned.

Governor Drohar was overweight with a wide mouth and short graying hair. He looked more like a teacher or storybook grandfather than a powerful authority.

Defense Minister Igwe was the polar opposite. He was younger, muscular, with a shiny shaved head, and a peppered goatee. If Drohar looked like the friendly negotiator, then Igwe was the disobliging enforcer.

Elasus sat at the head of the rectangular conference table, Tanner adjacent to him.

"Good afternoon, gentlemen," said Elasus. "Thank you for making the trip to the Unified Western Powers."

Igwe sat forward and took off his glasses, seemingly trying to hold back his temper. "You know the FIAS doesn't recognize the UWP or the PGU, why would you insult us like this before this meeting even begins?"

"What he means," bellowed Drohar, flashing a gigantic smile, "is we appreciate the plane you sent and have enjoyed our trip thus far. Thank you for the warm reception, but it's been a long journey. Our meetings and conference calls have sufficed thus far, so, please, tell us, Mr. Reeves, why are we here?"

Both men spoke with a British accent though the language was not natural to them.

"The story I have to tell is long but necessary." He didn't wait for questions, but dived right in to the escalating situation on Ojult, conveniently leaving out any mention of the Celje.

Drohar's eyes were wide by the time Elasus finished. "I'm surprised you shared this with us, given our history. Our relationship has grown over the past few years, but we are far from allies. As much as I appreciate the information, you're an astute businessman, and I'm sure you'll solve these problems. For our part, I'm still unsure why we're here."

"Isn't it obvious?" interjected Igwe. "The infamous Elasus Reeves believes another civil war between the mystics and Thoba is coming."

"Is this true? Surely you are not expecting our help. The incident between your corporation and my former defense minister is still a contentious topic in my region."

Tanner swiveled to face Drohar. "Still think we iced Okiro? Despite his under-the-table arms deals that nearly caused a war between our two regions, the corporation had nothing to do with his death."

"You deny killing him? Do you also deny exiling the Visconti family?" asked Igwe.

All eyes turned to Elasus who, like usual, showed no signs of stress. "The Visconti family was under contract with my company to make reinforced armor for my space fleet. They were caught brokering arms to the FIAS, and such deals are prohibited by the PGU, thus their exile was legal and warranted. Regarding the late Minister Okiro, I didn't find out about his involvement until after his untimely death."

Minister Igwe shot forward, ready to respond, but the cooler and less abrasive governor cut across him. "Rehashing this isn't going to change anything. So, Mr. Reeves, tell us why you brought us halfway across the globe to your conference table."

"I want to broker an arms deal between the FIAS and my corporation for eventual transportation to Ojult and any other world, other than Earth, that I choose."

The stunning statement had its intended effect. Igwe's eyes turned snakelike with speculation, and Drohar fell back into his chair in disbelief.

"You... you are absolutely mad!" yelled Igwe. "Why would we ever agree to such a request!?"

"Because it will make you rich and add a powerful partner to your region. I am also not unfamiliar with the disagreements between you and the PGU. The new prime minister is a close partner of mine and it would not be inconceivable to see the three of us working closely together at a point in the future."

Drohar sat forward, folding his hands on the table. "I have never known you to jump into a deal that was not favorable to your bottom line. This time, however, I do not think we are talking money. I believe Dagara is correct. You are thinking of the Elders. Your belief in these phantom mystics is well known. I think you are wanting this deal because of them, you want some sort of defense against them, which also means you already have the personnel, perhaps a private army, to allocate these weapons. Am I correct?"

"A highly condensed version but accurate nevertheless," admitted Elasus.

Igwe lifted out of his seat again. "You are certifiably crazy! The FIAS will not stand for this!"

Drohar said, "The defense and safety of our region rests in my hands, not yours, Defense Minister." There was suspicion yet interest in his voice. "I do not share your belief in the enigmatic Elders, Mr. Reeves, but I do not care much for the PGU and their overreaching views either. I am hopeful Mr. Zhang can rectify many of these headaches, but that time has not yet reached us. Undermining the PGU's authority while putting money into the pockets of my countrymen, I can begin negotiating on this premise. So, tell me, where do we begin?"

Elasus tapped a button under the table. Tayla walked through the door, carrying drinks tailored to each man's tastes. She handed out the refreshments, then placed a docuchip in front of each member. All eyes were on the excessively attractive assistant as she exited the conference room.

"Power is the key to peace, prosperity, security, and wealth. The strategy detailed in the docuchip in front of you will annex new power into our future partnership." Elasus raised his glass, and everyone but Igwe followed suit. "To the future."

Drohar and Sands replied in unison, "To the future."

Igwe ignored the ovation and his drink, choosing instead to pick up the docuchip and stroke the small device. "Keeping this on a need-to-know basis will be difficult. There are already rumors of spies within the PGU and the corporation. How do you plan on dealing with this?"

Tanner's eyes zeroed in on Igwe's caustic comment. "Spies are part of every organization. If we find out about one, we take care of it."

"Like you took care of the Visconti's?"

"Yes, like the Viscontis," replied Tanner. "Like Mr. Reeves already said, the Visconti family was legally exiled. Your partnership with them, while illegal, was strategic. The armaments we're willing to purchase from you all aren't small in quantity. I hope finding another Visconti within your region won't be difficult."

When the meeting finally adjourned, Tayla escorted the two FIAS members to a fleet of armed personnel waiting in the parking garage. Back in Elasus's office, another meeting was taking place.

"From a risk-tolerance perspective," said Tanner, "I'm not sure a deal with the FIAS leaders is wise. Some in their government are sympathetic to the mystics, and we regularly seize Amurski staffs off smugglers trying to moonshine them to Ojult."

Elasus sat behind his desk, a victorious hand wrapped around a glass of bourbon. "For a deal to succeed, each side must gain. I've been purposefully mediating with them for some time now, each meeting just as strategic as the next. I have no doubt that our African friends will try to take advantage of their position, perhaps bribe one of our pilots for intelligence. I trust our fleet captains, men like Donato, who'll protect our interests."

"I understand. Speaking of Captain Donato." Tanner slid his hand across his digital screen and a document resolved in front of them. "The bullet points list concerns I have and the evidence to support them."

It took Elasus only moments to read over the summarized document. "I see one of your concerns is a topic Defense Minister Igwe brought up."

"The PGU security division has made some very specific inquiries into our operations over the past month. The information coming from our moles inside the PGU support the idea we've already discussed. I believe we have a spy deep within the corporation, and they're feeding Secretary Madigan sensitive data."

Elasus deliberated over the evidence and came to the same conclusion as Tanner. "I agree with your assessment and know where you're going with the accusation. I'll handle the leak. Now, the last bullet you have here concerns me."

Tanner pulled out a black cylindrical object. He showed the object to Elasus, who nodded, and they began listening to the recording.

With a secure connection to the corporation's archives, Tayla searched tirelessly for the name Visconti. If FIAS and Elasus were partnering, it seemed logical to figure out who the Visconti family was and what got them booted off Earth. After hours of searching, the only name she was able to find dated back over twenty years ago.

Erika and Marco Visconti, born in Venice, Italy, migrated to the UWP under an employment agreement with the Reeves Corporation with no children or other relatives to speak of. According to the file, the wife and husband had violated the PGU statutes of dealing arms outside the region and were exiled to Ojult. The corporation made it clear this family violated the arms-exportation ordinances, but there was nothing in the file that demonstrated how the corporation found out about the deal.

She continued reading through the file, making mental notes of important facts. The entire incident took place over ten years ago, and there were obvious deletions and modifications to the file. Getting to the bottom of the mystery didn't seem likely, but one thing was certain: the Viscontis were no fans of the corporation.

Even with nothing actionable, this was information her allies needed. With Tanner and Elasus still meeting, Tayla pulled up her secure-messaging system and started writing a summary of the information she'd learned.

Last time she'd messaged Canine, he'd found Gabrielle but not Aaron. He'd also suggested that Grylo never made it to Ojult, another puzzle she'd not been able to solve. This glimmer of hope had reignited her resolve in taking down Elasus and getting her children off Ojult. As she pulled up the blank message, Tayla's secret audio link to Elasus's desk suddenly turned off. She'd not been paying attention to what the men were saying, but for the device to suddenly turn off...

She typed furiously.

> *Canine: Evidence suggests that FIAS and corporation are considering a partnership, arms trade is part of it. PGU was not invited. The name Visconti was brought up, but I've been unable to find anything current on the family. Something big is happening within the corporation.*

Tayla sent the message, then typed a second.

> *Babbage: I think the time to take down our mutual "friend" is upon us. Upload that cypher file we've been working on. Once I see it on my 3DI, I'll transfer the funds. Better keep a low profile for the time being, and if you're still working with that mole, I'd stop.*

Tayla breathed a sigh of relief as she shut down the hacked link. Maybe the audio chip had simply stopped working, but she'd not received any alerts suggesting the device was malfunctioning. Had she been caught? Was Tanner finally wise to the spy within the organization? In the end, Tayla decided it didn't matter. She had to act normal and continue her duties like any other day.

She was midway through her second report when Elasus's office door opened. Fully expecting to see Tanner, she was caught off guard by the site of Elasus.

"Hello, Mr. Reeves, what can I help you with?"

Elasus knelt next to her, his eyes shifting between her low-cut blouse and hiked-up skirt. "Ms. Cruz, something's come up, and I won't be staying the night. When you're finished here, no need to come back."

Tayla's blood froze, and every sense in her body told her she was in danger. His tone, his mannerism, something was off. "Okay, Mr. Reeves, but I was looking forward to tonight."

He stood and headed back into his office. "No, Ms. Cruz, you've already done enough."

CHAPTER 61: YEAR 2401

Physically exhausted and emotionally drained, Jayden slept hard and undisturbed in his own home, finally empty of the Nein. He'd not lit a fire the night before and woke up seeing his breath linger above him. He slipped on chilled clothing, then prioritized his morning. First, get firewood. Second, get something warm into his stomach.

Stumbling into the kitchen, a note lay by the stove.

> *Jayden,*
>
> *We heard from Shari that you were back and stopped by twice yesterday, but you were asleep. We wanted to leave you this note to let you know we're delighted you're back. Everyone sends their best, and please stop by the pub when you wake.*
>
> *Markus*

"Jayden, bonjour, come in," greeted Victor inside the much-warmer pub. "My goodness, I am so glad to see you. You missed, well, what can I say, one of my best harvests. It was small but its beauty, its plushness, its art! It will make the most beautiful, most excellent red. But come now, have a seat, have kaldi, yes, you need kaldi. Kun, please my good man, a cup of kaldi. I am sorry, Jayden, to leave you in such boring company, but I am just going. Monica is not feeling well. Until tonight!"

The outpouring of good tidings and salutations lifted Jayden's meager spirits.

"God, Jayden, what took you so long?" She smelled like whiskey, but Serena's bearlike embrace reminded him he was home.

"I'm gone for three weeks and I miss a harvest, then my best friend nearly forgets who I am."

Eve stepped through the crowd, her embrace different, expressing anxiety, fear, and relief.

"I'm so glad you're back," she said, coiling her arms around his neck. "Everything okay?"

Jayden turned so the stitches in his neck weren't visible. "No injuries this time," he said smiling.

Her warm cheek brushed against his. "We've got a table in the corner. Go sit, and I'll get you something hot."

He spent over an hour explaining his adventure to Meridone to the group. It seemed Markus had already spoken to Shari and gotten the scoop on her late husband. Eve, on the other hand, seemed concerned about Bella and Phaedra's injuries, offering several times to ride and check on them.

When Jayden finished, Serena poured the rest of her flask into her kaldi and raised it. "Well, cheers to Wren finding his way to hell, and may Misora follow."

Eve offered a compelling theory. "You might get the chance to send him there yourself if the Celje decide to retaliate."

Markus pushed himself upright. "Sorry to cut our reunion short, but I need to check up on Bélise and take care of a few things before the morning gets away. Eve, if you don't mind, I may take a few moments of your time later today. You know Misora better than any of us and if there's a chance he may seek revenge, it may be worth discussing further."

———

Jayden enjoyed the next few weeks more than any other time in recent memory. With the help of Eve and a few others, they salvaged most of the dead kaldi plantation that had been neglected during his long absence in the prison. It was too late to plant new seeds, but he trimmed off the dead branches and cleaned up the soil as much as possible. With luck, some of the plants might produce tradeable beans next year.

Times were good, but Jayden and Markus continually clashed on topics concerning Syrus. Jayden stood his ground, refusing to assist Syrus regardless of Markus's pledge.

Outside of this, Markus met with Eve several times before sending word to Syrus about Misora's possible revenge ride. Despite the unpopular theory, Syrus supported Markus's counterattack theory, and preparations throughout the continent began. One unintended consequence of these measures was the massive influx of arms and ammunition orders to Serena and those with similar skills.

The nights in Dalth were becoming colder, with smoke billowing from every fireplace. At the end of laboring days, Jayden often met up with his friends. With encouragement from Eve, even Shari Dikal occasionally showed up at the pub.

With supply lines safe and winter stores high, there were plenty of reasons to celebrate. Kun experimented with multiple new brews on his inebriated patrons, who gave mostly honest feedback. Nomadic musicians even stopped by every so often, giving the cheerful crowd a tune to dance to, a rare treat on Ojult. During these carefree evenings, Jayden discovered something he possessed that Eve did not.

With music coming from two six-string guitars played by a traveling duo, Jayden grabbed Eve and dragged her onto an open area of the pub.

"What kind of dancing is this?" she asked, turning bright red while trying to follow his movements.

In the background, Celine and Liao, alongside many others, clapped to the beat of the music, encouraging the only two people on the dance floor.

"Just follow me," Jayden said. "You're doing great!" The two guitarists played random tunes and by the fifth song, Eve was moving like a professional. When Serena butted in and started dancing with Eve, Jayden declared victory and moved to the bar. Everyone in the room was smiling, laughing, and immersing themselves into the euphoric energy.

The fun went on for many weeks, and the citizens of Dalth enjoyed peace. The real surprise was the relationship blossoming between Eve and Serena. If Serena and Jayden were like siblings, Eve and Serena were now sisters. They cursed men, spoke of Andreas a lot, laughed over drinks, and seemed to understand one another.

On the coldest morning in recent memory, Jayden treaded over the frost-covered grounds toward Kun's place. Wind whipped over the northern tree line, piercing through his heavy overcoat and hat.

"Good morning, Jayden, a bit cold out there," said Liao, still sporting a heavy coat inside the pub. She handed him a steaming cup.

"Thanks, Sara, morning, Markus."

Jayden joined the mayor, as he did most mornings. "This chair and our mugs are about the only thing not frozen."

"Very true. At least we're in better shape than last year and the year before." Markus leaned back and stretched. "Cold weather wreaks havoc on these old bones. Speaking of old, I was up early this morning and had a pleasant chat with Eve while she was on duty at the clinic. We talked about your time in that prison. She mentioned there was a third man in the cell near you. I knew about Andreas, mostly because of Serena, but who was the other person? You know this town is always open to helping out strangers if he or she needs help."

"He sort of escaped while we were there. His name was Levi Anjou."

"Levi Anjou? The former Nein leader?"

"Yeah."

Markus stiffened, raising his cup to his chapped lips. "He's one of the most powerful mystics in Ojultan history. You spoke with him? He's still alive?"

Just outside the pub, a man and woman were arguing, but Jayden couldn't make out the conversation. "A few months before Syrus's raid, he escaped with a mystic who managed to waltz right into the camp, break the African-ore cuffs holding Levi, then the two just walked out."

The front door of the pub whistled as Eve walked in. Markus and Jayden waved her over, exchanging hugs and salutations.

Pale white blotches dotted her face from her recent walk in the frigid air. "I don't mean to intrude on your breakfast, but a Nein named Turr just came and picked up armor from Serena. He mentioned the Nein are looking for a child of Elasus Reeves, here on Ojult. Have you heard about this?"

"I heard Phaedra and Syrus talk about it once," said Jayden.

"Syrus mentioned it to me when you and Jayden first arrived from the prison," added Markus. "I haven't heard anything since. The idea of a Reeves child on Ojult seems unlikely. That child would be in tremendous danger."

"You look like you're about to pass out, Eve. Go sit by the fire to warm up." Jayden fell short of volunteering to sit next to her.

"Everything's happening so fast." She started roving between the surrounding chairs. "Markus, Jayden, I... with everything happening... you need to know something."

"Speak when you're ready, Eve, no rush," said Markus. "You're with friends, remember."

She pressed her face into her hands. "Eve isn't my first name, it's my middle. My first name is Marilla, and my last name, well, my full name is Marilla Eve Reeves. I'm the daughter... I'm the one they're looking for."

Jayden glanced around for eavesdroppers.

After a few seconds, Markus reached over and grasped her trembling hands. "Dalth loves you, and I consider you my friend. Nothing has changed with this admission. We might want to rethink our security for you, but that's all."

"I'm so sorry, Jayden, I didn't want you to think... differently of me. And why is... is Syrus looking for me?"

Jayden wasn't upset over the deception, far from it. He liked Eve and knew the goodness that lay within her healing heart. Whatever evil had overcome her father, Jayden was certain Eve hadn't inherited the trait.

He reached over and brushed a gentle hand over her shoulder. "I'm not going to guess why you decided to come to Ojult, but your reasons must have been pretty serious. Whatever you were escaping, it's a good bet the Nein know about it. Syrus must never find out about this, ever."

Markus's support for Syrus came up once again. "I disagree, Jayden. He should be the first person we tell. The longer—"

"I said no, Markus!" Jayden's voice carried across the bar and caught the attention of several patrons, including Liao, who looked over from the kitchen.

"Okay, why?"

Jayden pushed his cup out of the way and leaned across the table. "You don't know Syrus the way I do. He doesn't care about friendships, integrity, character, or mistakes. He doesn't forgive, nor will he understand. If he or any of the Nein find out, they'll take Eve and dangle her like a carrot in front of Elasus until Syrus either gets what he wants or shows Elasus that he's not screwing around."

"My father doesn't care about me or my life, if that's what you're referring to. I didn't leave under the best of circumstances. He pretty much disowned me." Eve dove into the story that eventually led her to Ojult and into the mystic prison.

Jayden glared at the table, imagining Eve's life like a giant jigsaw puzzle. "Sasha knew who you were to begin with and was going to use you as bait. When I overheard that Reeves executive on Meridone, he was jumping all over Sasha and Misora for revolting against the corporation, like they were rebelling. This can't be a coincidence."

"No, it's not," agreed Markus. "But I don't think Sasha has shared this with Elasus yet."

"And why's that?" asked Eve.

"Because we've not been attacked. It's no secret you're here, Eve."

Eve shook her head. "No, it's not like that. My father isn't like most people. If you, a family member, go against the family, you're done. There's no coming back."

Disturbing flashes of Syrus executing Eve sent chills through Jayden. "Which makes it even more important that we hide you from Syrus. There are too many unknowns here. If anyone starts poking around, we take them out."

"I've placed all of you in danger. I'm so, so sorry."

Jayden inched closer to her. "Victor's gonna give up his vineyard before we let anyone lay a hand on you."

Eve laughed and snorted, bringing her face to a new shade of red. "I feel awful about this. I was planning on telling you all at some point, just not like this."

"Dalth is home to many people with many different backgrounds. This doesn't make you a bad person, it just tells me you're in the right place," said Markus.

"Thank you, that means so much to me. I…" She turned to Jayden. "Please, don't judge me for this."

Jayden's eyes were soft with compassion. "You're forgiven. We'll figure this thing out together. You won't be alone, I promise. I guess this is what you meant by having a lot of baggage?"

CHAPTER 62: YEAR 2401

Irelyn was no stranger to the Medallion steakhouse, but she was usually accompanied by her husband or girlfriends, not the prime minister of the PGU. Relations such as these were best kept veiled from the public eye, so Zhang came in via the private entrance in the back.

Irelyn meanwhile waited patiently in the private dining room large enough for two dozen people. Zhang pranced in, pulled her close and examined her physique. An invisible smirk shared his satisfaction with her figure, then Zhang gestured for her to sit. They sat close, Irelyn's ringless left hand resting on the inside of his thigh while his eyes idled below her neck. Tonight was a big step in finding Marilla, yet another matter continually interrupted her attention.

After the main course, Zhang ordered a second bottle off the restaurant's exclusive wine list, but the leader looked more exhausted than intoxicated. Despite his endless responsibilities, he was freshly shaven, hair meticulously combed, and suit finely pressed. Irelyn needed her man mostly sober yet distracted, so she decided to wear one of her more revealing dresses. Flawlessly hemmed slits followed up her thighs while her fake breasts made even the most confident man blush.

"I enjoyed our evening the other night," said Zhang, rimming the top of his wine glass with his finger. "Describing you as exquisite doesn't seem to do you justice."

Irelyn smiled while thumbing her phone. "Keep those types of compliments coming, and you might just get lucky again tonight."

They'd spent nearly the entire dinner conversing about the future of the PGU, the Reeves Corporation, and then, toward the end, why she'd scheduled this dinner in the first place.

When she'd caught him staring at her breasts again, she struck. "Vijay, darling, it's time to start fulfilling our arrangement. I know you know where Marilla is, and now I have something you want. After tonight, you'll make good on your end, because if you don't, never having this 'exquisite' body again will be the least of your concerns. Am I clear?"

Zhang pulled back, shocked she'd threaten such a thing. "And this information has something to do with those Celje people we spoke of earlier?"

"Very much so."

"Okay then," he said, struggling to focus. "I can agree to this on a contingency basis. When do I get this information?"

"Right now." She pressed two buttons on her phone. "Ruven, dear, how's the reception, can you see us?"

"I can see your hand on the minister's crotch, if that's what you mean."

"Elasus's son! Are you drunk? What game are you playing?"

Despite her misgivings about Ruven's involvement with the Celje, she needed something to dangle in front of the minister. With help from Tayla, the two devised a plan, and after thoughtful modification, it was time.

Looking into the camera, it was hard for Irelyn not to see Elasus in her son's face. That confident look, thick beard, calculating smile, and now his ruthlessness.

"Relax, Minister," said Ruven. "I already know you're keeping my mother warm at night, and she's already told me what she wants in return. I think it's foolish, but I've got my own reasons for being here."

Zhang's confused face matched his annoyed tone. "Your reasons better be good, or I'm done with all of you."

"Look, you've heard the rumors about the Celje and some sort of phantom war against the mystics on Ojult. The rumors only scratch the surface of what's really going on. The Celje are real, their power ten times what you believe it to be. But there's something much worse we need to focus on."

Zhang gave no hint of surprise. "Confirmation of the Celje's existence is hardly anything new. Do better."

Irelyn crossed her legs and sipped the pricey wine. "The Celje are real and my son is at their helm."

"So I should have your son arrested and put into a cell next to his mother. What else?"

Irelyn ran a soothing finger over Zhang's wrist, showing she was in control. "Ruven, like his father, believes the mystical, all-powerful Elder Nine from the past will one day return and destroy Earth. I personally think it's rubbish."

"I'm sorry, a war with the Elders?" said Zhang, not following the strange turn.

Irelyn's lustful overtones quickly vanished as she dived deeper into her ploy. "My dear husband believes the mythical Elders will one day return and conquer us. He's got my son playing soldier, training an army on Lent to defeat them when they come jumping out of the sky with their flaming sticks and glowing eyes."

"That's not exactly how I'd describe what we're training for. We train to fight mystics, and we're good at it. We recruit loners, people no one will miss, and train away from Earth and any official government agency. Secrecy is our greatest weapon, but make no mistake, we're preparing for the Elders."

Irelyn refilled her wine glass and sipped from the crystal. "Elasus has an army, Vijay, that is well trained and already battle tested against mystics. We're sharing deeply held secrets in hopes you'll understand our concerns."

Recognition was beginning to show on Zhang's face.

"It's gets more complicated," continued Ruven. "I believe my father's growing tired of the PGU and beginning to cut deals with the FIAS for additional arms and ammunition. So even if you don't believe us about the Elders, what do you think he might do with a private army that has nothing to do?"

"You believe Lent is a staging ground for an assault on Earth?" concluded Zhang.

Ruven said nothing while the screen rebuffered and came back into focus. "The mystics have all but beaten the Celje on Ojult. But these guards weren't my tier-one soldiers trained on Lent, they were trained locally on Ojult. My guys here are bigger, stronger, and better equipped.

Our numbers alone guarantee victory on Ojult, but what if they're not meant for that planet?"

Zhang relaxed into his chair as if he were back in control. "But if you believe in these Elders, Ruven, why tell me?"

Irelyn steadied herself as she anticipated the approaching summit of the conversation. The next few minutes were crucial.

Ruven's camera adjusted and refocused as two women glided behind him, brushing their hand over his neck. "My father always has a plan and three more plans as backup. I believe in the Celje's original purpose, to protect humanity from mystics. My father's intentions aren't clear right now, but I won't support my soldiers moving against Earth."

Irelyn focused on Zhang over the rim of her lipstick-stained glass, already knowing they'd added another ally to their cause. "This is the information I promised you, Vijay, and unless I've vastly misunderstood our conversation, I think I've lived up to my end of the bargain."

But Zhang's experience as a politician proved invaluable, and he delayed any outright acceptance. "Neither of you have offered up ideas as to what you'd like me to do with this information. You assume that Elasus and I have not already spoken about this. Humanity nearly lost itself after the Event, and I will not be the leader who sees mankind dive back into that rift. I'm ceasing this insane conversation but will leave you with one small note. The Nein are a known threat, and if you believe the Elders are real, that means the Argos exist. Why haven't they jumped into this yet? Have you at all considered that Elasus is actually on the *right* side of this issue?"

Zhang got up from the table and left through the back door.

The question about the Argos came up from time to time, especially among the conspiracy theorists of Earth, but no one ever had a good answer. The question in this context, however, was odd, and it took Irelyn slightly off guard.

Careful not to seem overzealous, she waited for the back door to close before speaking with Ruven. "I'm proud of you for coming to me with this information. Really, it's valiant and proves your heart is on the right side of this fight. Your father has to be reined in somehow, and the PGU is the only one that can do it."

Ruven reached over to end the communication. "Mother, don't pretend like all's well between us. I'm not doing this for you. The Celje have a purpose, one that I believe in, and I won't see them misused for some fantasy power grab. If the Elders come walking in the front door and try to spiral humanity into another war, I'll stop them. But you have no place in that discussion. You're standing, perched upon some weird, demented altar you've created in your head. Take a step off and look at the bigger picture, the bigger threat."

The screen went blank, and Irelyn considered her options. Zhang was upset and probably stunned, but he'd gather his senses by morning and come groveling back.

———————

Irelyn's new driver rolled the black, unmarked sedan to a gentle stop at the front gate. Irelyn scanned her ID and provided the necessary thumb scan, which prompted the guards to open the barricade. She was tired and wanted to get into bed.

Elasus was probably spending the night with Tayla like he did most nights. Before discovering the truth, Irelyn despised Tayla. Now, it seemed the more Tayla slept with him the more information she was able to pump to their circle of moles.

Through the front windows, Irelyn saw the lights were off in the kitchen and living room.

"Front door, open," chimed the AI.

"It's eleven-thirty, Irelyn, I was beginning to think you were going to go home with the minister," said Elasus's icy voice from the darkened kitchen.

Irelyn stopped and grabbed the wall for support.

"Elasus? What the hell, you scared the shit out of me. Turn on the damn lights!"

Elasus knew she'd been with Zhang, but had the minister called him to tell of their dinner conversation?

"Come over and sit," he continued, "we have a few things to discuss."

CHAPTER 63: YEAR 2401

Nigel knocked on Syrus's door. It was the middle of the night, but news like this couldn't wait. "Lord Tokarek, please, your attention. Another message has arrived."

Syrus rolled to his side and sat up. The third-story fireplace still burned hot inside his Pa'Gran bedroom. The long-abandoned and rough-looking building wasn't spectacular but served an important purpose. The condensed four-story home, built of white stone, extended spacious balconies off the second and third stories. The fourth floor was attic space, long neglected by its previous owner. The ground floor housed maids and servants, while the second and third chambered the kitchen, sitting room, dining room, and bedrooms. Small square windows dotted the exterior while a wide staircase allowed guests to walk to the second floor, avoiding the housekeepers. Pushing sleep from his wary mind, Syrus tossed off the covers.

Candlelight reflected off Nigel's bald, sweaty scalp. "My apologies, but we've received another message from the north. An unidentified vessel has docked in Rindo."

Since putting his entire arcane guard on alert, Syrus received messages like this nearly every hour. With tensions high, his people were seeing Celje ghosts at every corner.

"And did any armed Celje rush off the boat and attack?" asked Syrus, growing annoyed with false alarms.

Anxious sweat dripped off his servant's head. "It's unknown, but the message was from Captain Siller who was near Limeth at the time."

"Hand me something to wear," said Syrus, getting to his feet.

For six weeks now, Siller had sent countless messages, giving accounts of unknown or unscheduled boat arrivals on the northern continent. Since Jayden's botched mission to Meridone, Syrus ordered all senior leaders on full alert in case of a Celje counterattack, but that was almost two months ago. With winter in full force and the tendency for the Altum Sea to form massive underwater ice floes, the likelihood of an attack now was near zero. Instead of spending time chasing ghosts, he'd hoped his senior leaders might have the wherewithal to spend their time a bit more productively, like searching for the Reeves child.

Syrus walked up to the fourth-floor attic, overlooking the capital city of Capintesta. Even without the first snowfall, the ground shivered against the frigid wind. He opened the small window and let the chilly air brush over his body, fill his lungs, and awaken his tired mind. The streets were empty save a few dogs searching for scraps. On the outskirts, he made out security patrols walking the area.

Andreas was working tirelessly across Pa'Gran and the rest of Capintesta, trying to form hybrid defense forces consisting of mystics and Thoba alike. As a strictly volunteer group, sign-ups were sluggish, but Syrus felt confident the popularity of the idea would grow when warmer weather arrived. Andreas also found a creative way to put the old mystic prison to good use. He'd begun construction to convert the facility into a mystic training ground. Some Thoba blasted the idea, claiming a hidden agenda to build and train a massive mystic army, but Syrus persisted that defending the planet was a priority, and this served the greater good.

Appian Shipping was also fulfilling a major role. Medicine generally reserved for Celje was now reaching children and the critically ill across Capintesta and Listo. Zakar also promised to smuggle vaccines from Earth to those born on Ojult who weren't already inoculated.

Captain Siller, on the other hand, faced stiff resistance from his Nein brothers and the Thoba on Listo. Siller's personal struggle with Syrus's new direction didn't help matters, and his poor administrative decisions frequently clashed with Syrus's directives. Moreover, Siller was running his defense teams night and day, which alarmed the locals. Fearing an attack from the Celje, Siller blanketed Listo in scouts and blockade teams, furthering the locals' dislike for the mystics. Indifferent to their opinions, Siller was convinced the Celje might still attack, irrespective of the weather.

From the floor below came the creaking of old boards.

"My tits are about frozen off," complained Phaedra, climbing the last step. "And here you are, soaking it all in like you're at the beach."

"You're in full armor; expecting something?"

Since recovering from her trip to Meridone, Phaedra continually wore her custom-stitched armor.

"Those of us who've seen combat recently have been, yeah, but you wouldn't know about that, would you? Besides, Serena's stuff is pretty comfortable."

This wasn't the first time she'd brought up the Meridone mission, and he was becoming tired of her petulant attitude. "My directives were clear: go in and stay hidden. Next time, follow my instructions, and you will see better outcomes. It is time you put that mission behind you. We have important trials ahead."

"Trials? More cryptic passages from a book no one understands. What aren't you telling me?"

The streets of Pa'Gran grew slightly more active as the sun grew brighter.

"I have told you everything you need to know, all else is nonsense. Whatever the mice have been whispering in your ear, shut it out. Or is this Jayden Vaut?"

"Vaut? No, it's nobody, but I can tell when I'm being mind-shagged, so tell me what I am not supposed to know!"

Phaedra was no longer the young girl he'd mentored, or at least tried to mentor, and if he really was turning over a new chapter, lying now wasn't an honorable start.

"When things calm down, I'll tell you everything, but for now, we must stay focused. I can't have my apprentice, perhaps the most powerful Nein in the group, distracted."

Nigel's head appeared halfway up the staircase. "Premier, I'm sorry for interrupting you again, but I have another message from Captain Siller, marked urgent." Nigel handed Syrus the note.

My premier, Surprise attack in progress by Celje. Limeth has fallen, and I'm retreating to Carendra and will launch a counterattack once regrouped. I'm sending civilians and the injured to Port Naok. Initial attack, crippling.

—Captain Siller

Syrus reread the hastily written note, ensuring he'd not missed details that might impact his next decision. Calculating several options at once, he'd forgotten about his interrogating pupil standing next to him.

She peered at the note, shaking her head in disgust. "Guess you're not going to admit blame for this one either?"

"Nigel, send word to Andreas at the training grounds. Inform him to gather what forces he has available and prepare to move. I'll meet him in Worall, then we'll head to Port Rindo as one unit. Tell him the Celje have started their attack."

Syrus turned to Phaedra, his eyes glowing in fiery contempt. "Find Jenna and Javier, then bring them here. I want us on the road within the hour."

On horseback, Syrus led Jenna, Phaedra, and Javier to Worall at a steady pace. Syrus wore his traditional black-and-blue heavy armor with his staff strapped across his broad back. Phaedra wore her hood up, keeping the frigid wind from burning her flustered face. Every so often, Syrus looked back at his three companions.

They passed several of Andreas's hybrid patrols along the way, a tactic Syrus approved of, especially now. The journey across the central region of Capintesta was otherwise uneventful, arriving in the inmost town in less than a few hours. Syrus expected to arrive well before Andreas and his militia but found he was mistaken. Andreas, along with two dozen militia, sat just outside the main gates of Worall, dressed and ready for battle. Behind them, six carriages with accompanying horses stood ready, carrying supplies and other necessary wartime equipment.

Syrus approached the rebuilt gates of Worall, surveying the scared but eager soldiers adorned in various combat gear, no doubt assembled by Serena Visconti. Recognizing Syrus, the militia stood, the mystics bowing while the Thoba stood near attention. Swords, knives, pistols, and rifles reflected dully in the cloudy sky.

"Good evening," greeted Andreas, bowing low. His dark-green-and-brown armor blended perfectly with the natural landscape. "Seems like our old friends decided to pull one over on us, but we're ready. If I may, there's a guest who would like to speak with you and Phaedra."

From around the nearest carriage a curly-haired teenager appeared.

"Hello, Mr. Tokarek," said Bella. "Zakar sends his best and apologizes for not being able to come, but he asked that I bring you a message."

Syrus knew what those soft girlish features hid. "Hello, Bella. Are you here to join us or something else?"

She pulled a small map of Meridone from her pocket. "Our crews came across information about recent Celje movements. Everyone on Ojult is aware of the attack on Listo, but those ships were part of a much larger force that departed Meridone at the same time."

Syrus reviewed the surprisingly detailed hand-drawn map that illustrated dozens of boats departing Meridone. "If I'm reading your map correctly, it suggests Captain Siller will be flanked by another Celje landing party if he's forced to the south, toward Port Naok?"

"Yes. I should also mention that Callahan Shores to our south is also a suspected landing zone, but we believe those ships will be delayed several weeks due to weather and glacier activity."

Phaedra came up from the rear and gave Bella a hug. "Wish they would have attacked during the summer," she complained. "Where's Zakar and your brother?"

Bella pointed at the map, which Syrus handed to his apprentice. While Phaedra studied the alarming picture, Syrus formed a new strategy. The Celje were overzealous. Dividing their forces like this was foolish, and he wouldn't make the same mistake.

With Andreas, Bella, and Phaedra around him, he outlined his plan. "We first head north to Kavil's location and eliminate the threat. We'll leave a small garrison on Listo and go back across the Altum Sea toward Callahan Shores to meet that force head on. Phaedra, I know you want to take your own force to the south now, but I need you with me. The force to our north is unknown, and your power may tip the battle."

Phaedra looked around at the militia, then back at the map. "I get it. You're not sure if we're going to win this one, are you?"

"I must be off," said Bella, breaking the silence. "Phaedra, take care of yourself, and by the way, how's Jayden?"

"Jayden and the almighty here had a spat. He's playing farm boy with the redhead in Dalth. I haven't seen him since Meridone."

Bella looked woefully at the soon-departing soldiers. "I'm sorry to hear that. Stay safe, and please send word when this is all sorted out."

Once Bella was out of earshot, Phaedra whirled on Syrus. "You're leaving Dalth to the sarctos. We need to at least send someone to warn them."

Syrus was studying the map again, trying to identify any other possible landing zones that might jeopardize their position. "There's more at stake than one simple town of no strategic value to the Celje. Calm down and see our situation through a leader's eyes."

"Calm down? No strategic value? Where the hell do you think I got this sword!?" She pulled her red-hilted sword partially out of its sheath. "Where do you think most of our armaments came from?"

She was right. He'd brought her up in the old traditions of the early Nein mystics who were bloodthirsty and leaderless. They'd lacked vision and brought about their own demise by foolish, nearsighted behavior. Was it unfair to ask his apprentice to change everything she knew only because he'd demanded it? There was something much larger at play that he'd not found time to discuss with her, but now, on the eve of battle, was not the right time.

Andreas jumped in before either replied. "Premier, with the introduction of our guests to the south, perhaps I should head back to Pa'Gran with a small contingent?"

Syrus agreed. "When they land in Callahan Shores, they'll head to Pa'Gran. Take what you need to defend the city and hold them off until we're able to return."

Andreas bowed and began plucking men from carriages.

If Bella's information was correct, they couldn't waste any more time. In a last-minute adjustment, Syrus dispatched Nigel.

"Nigel, scout ahead to Rindo and ensure the boats are ready by the time we get there. Use whatever means appropriate, but I want us departing for

Naok as soon as we arrive. I know most captains won't leave until first light but convince them otherwise."

––––––––––

Phaedra led the column while Jenna covered the rear and Javier scouted their flanks. Enormous trees hung over the path with leaves and dirt zipping by in the intense winds. Their slow pace against the harsh winds gave Syrus time to analyze the battle plan. The aggressiveness of the Celje and their multistaged attack didn't concern him at first. His spies suggested the Celje lacked the numbers for such an attack, so what had changed? Did the Reeves executive Jayden spoke of bring reinforcements? Or was their initial intel on the Celje numbers wrong? With either scenario, the fate of his Nein was in jeopardy.

Three hours into their journey, Phaedra halted the column. Javier rode ahead to scout whatever danger lurked. Syrus's senses quivered around his awareness, forewarning of impending danger as Javier road back with his sword unsheathed.

Phaedra road close behind, yet her weapon remained holstered.

"I'm not sure what's going on, Syrus, but Zakar and a few others are up ahead, just off the main road." Phaedra shifted on her saddle. "He wants to speak with you."

Seeing as they just spoke with Bella a few hours ago, Syrus didn't think this was a coincidence. "Stay here and be on alert," he ordered.

Syrus galloped until coming upon a large, covered carriage with two saddled horses. Zakar loomed next to the larger wagon. Surrounding them were seven heavily armed Appian men, casting even more confusion.

"You're looking old but well, Mr. Tokarek," said Zakar, extending a hand. "I'm glad to see you at full strength."

Syrus leapt off his horse and greeted his friend. "My servants pay me enough empty compliments, Zakar, and we're in a hurry. What's happened?"

Zakar gestured toward his own carriages. "Unfortunately, I have more troubling news. Your contingent in Listo is defeated. I'm not sure how many made it across, but my sources suggest very few. I came here to scout Rindo for myself, and what I've seen isn't good."

Syrus knew better than to question the planet's foremost spymaster. Captain Siller was a pain but an elite mystic and competent field commander. For the Celje to have defeated him so quickly meant they'd overwhelmed him with numbers, confirming his earlier assumption.

"I see. This is the second time you've provided me with essential information, thank you." He looked carefully at his ally's entourage. "You said you're heading south, but judging by the amount of supplies you have in that carriage, you're not heading to Dalth or Callahan Shores."

"A short time ago, just after I sent Bella to find you, one of my couriers found me. He reported seeing a large group of Celje land in Callahan Shores last night. They're marching south, probably to Pa'Gran, which was your last known location. The threat is serious, so much so that I'm shutting down operations and going into the shadows until this mess settles."

There was a lot to unpack from this, but something caught Syrus's attention. "You said 'probably' heading to Pa'Gran; why the hesitation?"

Zakar shrugged and tapped the top of his walking stick. "There's only one main trade road that cuts through the continent. It connects Callahan Shores to Pa'Gran, then to Worall and up to Port Rindo. These Celje are taking back roads that push them more east than necessary. Those roads are narrower and difficult to navigate when wet. They might be trying to avoid detection. Then again, Sasha was never the brightest."

Syrus unfolded a map of Capintesta and traced the main road from Callahan Shores to Pa'Gran.

"Phaedra, up here, now!"

Zakar's eyebrows raised. "You've figured something out?"

Syrus studied the map, looking for another possible explanation. "Our situation has become more complicated. The Celje have already landed in Callahan Shores, but they're not heading for Pa'Gran."

Phaedra focused on Syrus's map and pieced the situation together. "Dalth?"

"Yes."

"Zakar," continued Syrus, "you're going into hiding?"

Zakar looked back at his troop. "I'm sorry to cast doubt on your odds of winning, Mr. Tokarek, but the Celje are reinforced, probably by that Reeves ship that landed last month. I'm taking Bella and Logan, along with others to a safe place. Once I'm convinced how the war will end, I'll leave Aldrich with them and return."

Logan wasn't a mystic and was too young to fight. Bella was more than capable of defending herself, but Zakar knew this. If he was taking Bella away, then it foretold Zakar's belief in his chances of winning. Yet there was still the question as to why Sasha would go to Dalth. The best idea Syrus imagined was the need to rid him of supplies, the need to kill Serena Visconti.

"Phaedra," Syrus said. "We're going with your original plan. Take Jenna, and head toward Pa'Gran. Tell Andreas about the incursion, then ride to Dalth. Inform Markus Fonte of the situation."

Phaedra's piercing eyes gave way to real despair. "Jenna and I are the two most powerful guards you have. Keep Jenna, I'll go alone."

Syrus walked back to his horse, mounting the large beast. "Use your instincts, Phaedra, why Dalth?"

It wasn't difficult to follow his logic. "The Reeves kid?"

Syrus nodded and pulled his shoulders back. "You're a mystic, by far my most-prized protégé. Where others might fail, you will succeed. Believe in yourself, trust your knowledge."

A gust of wind picked up dirt and leaves, tossing them between pupil and *daska*. Phaedra pushed the hair from her face and locked eyes with Syrus. "I'll kill them quickly, then come back to Rindo." She sprinted back toward her horse.

Syrus trotted closer to Zakar. "You're heading west into the mountains?"

"After a slight detour, yes. West or northwest, depending on the terrain. The mountains to the northwest may provide better concealment from prying eyes."

Syrus imagined Logan and Bella going into hiding, bringing images of his own niece to mind. "No chance of getting the kids back to her parents before all this breaks out?"

"Nencia left no clues to who their parents were, so I will see Bella, Logan, and others to safety."

The situation was bleak, and Syrus thought for a moment. What would Helia do if she were here? His current position called for compassion. "I know of a hidden enclave that will guarantee their safety, but I need your assurance on something."

Zakar bowed. "If the arrangement is satisfactory, you'll have my word."

Syrus felt out of place speaking in such benevolent terms. He leaned back in his saddle, trying to muster up the right words. "Travel to Dalth, ensure you get there before Misora's troop. Meet with Markus, offer to take his child, I forget her name, but offer to take her with you to my safe house."

Zakar smiled. "Mr. Tokarek, I'll do this regardless. Markus is my oldest friend, and Bélise is like my own child."

Syrus wasted no time explaining his plan. "To the southwest, between the mountains and the sea, there's a small village called Pallio Valley. From Worall, head to the western coast, then south. When you see a jashinto farm separated by a large field of sky grass, head east. The town is about half a day's journey. If you hit the mountains, you've gone too far north. If you run into the river, you've gone too far east."

Zakar's eyes widened. "Mea, she is there now?"

Syrus pulled the reins sideways, directing his war horse up the road. "If I'm defeated to the north or Phaedra fails in the south, we'll be overrun. Sasha won't take prisoners nor show mercy; make sure Markus understands this."

CHAPTER 64: YEAR 2401

K un jumped to his feet and rushed out the front door of his pub. "Don't hit store, you break windows!"

A choir of apologies came from the two groups involved in the snowball fight. Dalth was seeing its first snowfall of the season, and the kids, plus a few adults, were enjoying the scene.

Kun sat back down with Markus and Jayden. Looking out the nearby frosted window, Jayden grinned as Serena, Eve, Celine, Liao, Bélise, Diego, Monica, and Hannah pelted one another with freshly packed snowballs.

"I've got my money on the kids," said Jayden, putting a single tonze on the table.

"You never seen my wife in competition," replied Kun. "It will not be long until Celine and Eve are patching someone up."

"Dalth's own civil war, fantastic," joked Markus. "Survival of the fittest, I suppose."

Laughter followed from the mayor's rare joke and Kun snagged another pot of Meridonian kaldi for the group. "I doubt I receive more shipments from Meridone until after winter, so we drink brandy soon."

Outside, Liao flung a well-aimed snowball at Bélise; it smacked her in the nose before exploding into tiny flurries.

Eve's back was toward the window, oblivious to Jayden's stare. "Kaldi may be running low, but the word's getting out about Shari's medicine trade. Now that Wren is dead and not forcing her to sell her entire stock to Appian and the Celje, a lot more people are being healed."

Markus winced as Bélise took another snowball to the face. "Zakar's done a good job getting it shipped across Capintesta and Listo. Nencia offered better rates back in the day, but Zakar... I'm sorry, Jayden."

"Don't worry about it, Mayor, I'm a big boy, I can talk about Nencia. But I think Bélise's heading to the clinic. Looks like a bloody nose."

"See, see," said Kun with a touch of pride. "My wife, she wins."

Sometimes Jayden didn't understand Kun or his culture. "Bélise's a kid!"

The smell of the crackling fireplace reminded Markus of earlier times when he and Bianca would nestle next to one another during the winter. "Not anymore, Jayden. She's almost a woman. I can still remember when she was still diving into my arms after a scary dream."

Kun came over with several slices of bacon. "This the last for today."

The sizzling meat cooled after Victor walked into the pub, a cold wind following him through the door. He dusted off his snow-covered coat, exposing red-wine stains across the front.

"What is all this fighting outside? Snow, it is so beautiful, and to use it with such savagery!?"

"Not exactly Charles de Gaulle are you, Victor? Besides, your wife seems to enjoy it," Markus countered.

"Yes, well, my wife, she is magnificent in everything she does, you all have seen it. Shall we have a toast to her good health? Come now, lend me your mugs."

The snowfall faded as the sun peeked and retreated through the dense layer of gray clouds. The battling adults called for a ceasefire, and the children dispersed toward their homes. Liao and Celine were the first to walk into the pub, followed by Eve who resembled a half-melted ice sculpture.

"Where is my husband" asked Celine, warming her hands near the fire.

Jayden pointed behind the bar where Victor was pouring a bronze liquid into his mug. "He seems to be consulting with his second love?"

"Ah yes, my husband's other lover, Brandy, that deceptive whore."

Jayden got up and tapped Markus on the shoulder. "I need to get back to work, see you all later."

Bundling his heavy coat, Jayden headed home. With his chin dug into his collar to guard against the wind, he just heard the thud of hooves and rustling neighs of ahead. Peering ahead, the sight of arriving visitors emitted a shiver down his spine that had nothing to do with the cold.

Phaedra ranged toward him. "I need to speak with you and Markus now."

———————

Everyone was gathered back inside the pub with Phaedra summarizing the events.

Phaedra flipped a chair around and sat with her arms draped over the back rail. "So, there you have it. The situation looks bad, but I think, with a little bit of preparation, we can hold them off long enough for reinforcements."

Markus's commendable leadership was on full display. "Phaedra, you and Jenna risked a lot to bring us this news. Leaving Syrus's side probably wasn't easy, so on behalf of Dalth, thank you. You two are valuable warriors, and any guidance you wish to offer is welcome. My family has been in Dalth for many generations and have fought many battles on this land, but I don't have your experience."

Phaedra's shrewd eyes softened. "Jenna and I are at your disposal."

A man behind the counter coughed. "I'm sorry," implored Victor. "Please, hand me a biscuit, this… this wasn't brandy at all. I'm battling a horrible vintage, horrible, disgusting."

Kun launched a biscuit across the room. Surprisingly, Victor caught it.

Jayden stood next to Markus and watched the experienced leader prepare his threatened town for battle. Phaedra took Jenna and headed south to scout the Celje's movements, but when they returned in only a few hours, the reality of the town's situation sunk in. The news was grim. The Celje were already camped and liable to arrive within twenty-four hours.

Kun and Victor prepared supplies while Celine and Eve readied the clinic. Serena and Liao busied themselves making ammo, sharpening weapons, and mending armor. The town's militia consisted of two dozen men and women, each having little to no experience in combat. Markus asked Jayden to try to educate them on what they might encounter.

Crammed inside Serena's heated mill, Jayden spoke candidly with the militia. "Many of you are just now coming to know what and who the

Celje are. I've been fighting them for over eleven years, and I know them. They are well-trained experts in long-range marksmanship and close-combat melee. They're trained to attack fast and kill quickly."

"Fantastic pep talk," chided Serena.

Nervous chuckles came from the audience, but Jayden got the point. He moved empty shell casings around the center table to illustrate the town and its defensive positions. "They'll expect us to have more mystics than we actually do, which means they'll rush us as quickly as they can. Engaging them in melee is a bad idea, so our best bet is to bring them in close, then open with well-placed shots. After the first or second volley, they'll figure out we're not imbedded with mystics and start lobbing bolts our way. Make sure your fighting bunkers are reinforced because their rifles use organ-detecting auto targeting."

"Clear as mud," replied Serena. "I'll have seven armor-penetrating bullets for each of you. That's six or seven *per person*, so make them count. We'll also have chest armor for everyone. May not fit perfectly, but it'll do."

Inside the deserted pub, Jayden popped the cork off one of Victor's red wines. The wine enthusiast figured many of his best vintages might either be destroyed or raided and passed the fine spirits out to the few who came to the pub that night.

Eve clinked her clay mug against Jayden's. "Serena told me your speech to the militia was a real hit."

"I just told them what I knew, maybe it'll make a difference."

"The people around here look up to you too. Maybe not for farming advice, but they know your past, what you've done, and what you're capable of. That rage, the brutality you've buried, the town is going to need that."

Jayden redirected the conversation. "I've been thinking and please, don't take this the wrong way, but I think it's better if you left Dalth before the battle tomorrow. Celine is more than capable of handling the clinic by herself, and it could get pretty dangerous."

Eve leaned in, resting her tired head upon his shoulder. "Was that... are you flirting with me, Jayden Vaut?"

"I'm just worried about—"

Eve closed a comforting arm around his waist. "I've made Dalth my home, and I plan on defending it. I may not be very good with a weapon, but I can save lives. Plus, given your propensity to get hurt, you should be glad I'm staying."

With the bottle nearly empty, Jayden needed to say what they were both thinking. "The Celje aren't coming for Serena. If things go badly, you need to find a way out. Can you promise me that?"

Their conversation was disrupted by a loud cough behind them.

"Zakar," said Jayden, choosing not to stand and greet the older man.

Several citizens and Appian workers walked in behind them including, to Jayden's surprise, Bella and Logan.

Markus motioned toward Kun behind the bar. "Zakar's people could use something to eat and drink, I'll pay for it."

Kun started digging through supplies, tossing kettles and iron pans onto the nearly extinguished wood stove.

Zakar sat down near the fireplace and waved the mayor over. "Thank you, Markus, but our time is short, and we must speak before the Celje arrive."

"Everyone, everyone, settle down!" yelled Markus, stepping onto a chair.

Zakar gazed around the familiar room, returning smiles and greetings. "Ladies and gentlemen, as you know, the Celje are camped less than a day from here. They appear to have been reinforced by the Reeves Corporation, and we don't have long until they begin their assault. I'm taking children to a private location until this war is settled. I will not give this location away, nor allow anyone to follow, but I'll take any children who wish to go."

Markus addressed the crowd. "We knew the Celje were coming, but now we have an opportunity to protect the most valuable among us. I understand it's late, and you'd usually want time to consider this, but that time is gone. Talk to Zakar now, ask questions, but just so you all know, I plan on sending Bélise with him."

Around midnight, only Hannah Nguyen, Bélise Fonte, and Monica Dubois were in the pub with backpacks and terrified expressions. Tired and nervous tears streamed down the teenagers' faces while their parents feigned confidence. Celine and Liao probed Zakar about where they were going, its safety, and how they'd communicate once things settled down. Zakar gave them little comfort and even less information other than the location was safe and well hidden.

On the other side of the pub, Jayden minded a slightly more robust conversation.

"I can fight, Phaedra, I've already proved that. I should be at your side rather than hiding in some cave," said Bella.

"I agree with you, but who's going to protect the kids if you run into trouble? And what about Logan? Zakar's too old and gimpy, his men too few to resist any coordinated attack. Face it, you're going to have to protect this group."

"Come with us, then. You're my friend, and it doesn't look like Markus and Syrus are going to win this." It was hard not to hear Nencia's candidness as Bella's spoke.

Part of Jayden wanted Phaedra to accompany Bella if only to calm the young woman's fears, but Dalth needed her.

"And what of the other children?" asked Zakar from the other side of the room. "I count only three, and we can carry more."

Markus could only shrug. "Those who knew you and your parents no longer see that young man who carried much of the town's needs on his shoulders. You stand before them not as a citizen, but as the Appian leader. That title is gives people... pause."

"What of Shari Dikal and Diego?" asked Kun, kneeling next to Hannah.

"She's opting to stay in Dalth as long as possible, then evacuate to Pa'Gran if things go bad," said Markus. With watery eyes he looked at Zakar. "This... this is it. You're not going to get any more volunteers. It's time."

Jayden thought back to his final goodbye with his own father and mother so many years ago. Everything had happened so quickly, he'd not realized he'd said goodbye for the last time. Watching the trembling hugs and cries of families being separated was difficult to stomach.

Next to him, tears of empathy fell from Eve's eyes, and Jayden realized she must be thinking of her own parents. Even Jayden shed a tear watching Markus say goodbye to Bélise. His only living relative, the decision to hand her over for protection, even to a trusted friend, broke him.

For Bélise, encountering the Celje again was probably bringing back memories of violence and murder, experiences someone so young should not have had to live through. She was like her father, strong, smart, and understood the dynamics of their situation, but still, she was only a teenager.

With everyone outside, Bella and Logan helped get luggage into the wagons, reassuring their new passengers they'd see their parents again soon.

Boom! Boom! Boom!

The sudden and intense explosion rattled the windows and sent everyone diving over one another and under the wagons. Snow, dust, and insects fell from the pub's roof as the thunderous roar rippled over the town. Phaedra and Jenna, who'd concealed themselves away from the gathering, stood calmly, like it was nothing more than a clap of thunder.

The night sky flickered orange with strands of yellow. Zakar limped over to the already anxious crowd. "Meteor, my friends, just another rock, nothing to worry about."

Of course it was, and Jayden mentally thumped himself for not recognizing the sound.

"You need to get going, Zakar." Phaedra was gently separating the teenagers from parents. "The whole point is to leave *before* the Celje get here. Come on, let's move."

Almost ready to leave, Zakar sidestepped in front of Jayden, nearly causing a collision. "A quick word?" Zakar leaned in, his voice part contempt, part plea. "You and I, often, have not been on good terms. I don't regret this and still believe Nencia would be alive if not for your relationship."

Jayden swallowed his initial comeback. "Nencia's dead because of the Celje, not me."

Zakar eyed his cane. "She liked you and even more importantly, trusted you. Faith in a person is not common on this planet. With this, I think she would have wanted me to trust you during this plight, so listen, Vaut. If Syrus and I should both fall, remember the town Pallio Valley. Tell no one, not even Markus, but know that Mea is also there."

Zakar walked off before Jayden had the chance to take in what he'd just heard.

"Jayden, are you okay?" Eve said, walking up beside him.

Jayden looked into her captivating green eyes. "If your mother and father knew you were here, do you think they'd order Sasha's men to stop their attack?"

She seized his arm and pulled him closer. "If it were up to my mother, I think so. But Elasus, the only voice he listens to is his own. Why ask that now? What do you know?"

Jayden wrapped his arm around her and pulled her in close. The reassuring embrace betrayed his true feelings about their future.

"I've lost battles, killed men, and had those closest to me killed before my own eyes. During all that, I've never doubted the outcome of the bigger struggle. The fate of the war was always a given—the good guys would win." He moved his chin and placed it atop her spirited red hair. "Eve, we're not going to win."

CHAPTER 65: YEAR 2401

Y ou slept with your servant!? You had a slave, and you forced her to sleep with you?"

"What? No, it's not like that at all," Jayden pleaded.

Eve's cheeks now matched her hair. "You've been preaching against Syrus and his slaves, and all the while you had one of your own! You hypocrite!"

Jayden had just walked into Kun's pub when Eve started in on him. She was still staying with Serena, who didn't know about Janice, so who'd told her?

"Eve, please, let me explain. My job while with the Nein gave me certain amenities, like my own quarters and a servant. I was young, alone, and yes, I slept with her. It's not like I ordered her to do it, it just sort of evolved. But I promise I treated her as an equal, not as a slave."

Eve walked past him, thumping him with her elbow. "Liao, whiskey… please."

Liao handed her a three-finger pour. "No charge."

The two women exchanged understanding glances, and Eve tossed back the stinging liquor in one gulp.

"I thought you were different Jayden. A complicated guy who'd just been handed a bad deal."

Jayden expected to wake up to gunfire this morning, not Eve tossing back whiskey.

"What do you think I did while with the Nein, do laundry, give massages? Syrus gave me targets, I eliminated them, that's it."

Eve took a frightened step back.

"Everyone has a past, even you. Don't judge me for what I did when I was young, enslaved, and had a young attractive woman as my only friend. I care about what you think of me, but this isn't what it seems. I'm not even sure Janice survived. When Syrus banished me, the first thing they did was go after her."

Her agitation retreated for a quick beat. "I never knew that's what you did with them, with Syrus."

He shrugged off the pity in her voice. "I don't like fighting; in fact I hate it. I keep clear of it these days, even if it means getting bruised from time to time. Who told you about her anyway?"

Civility was returning to the conversation when a small but firm hand landed on his shoulder. He turned to see Phaedra, her forehead creased with stress. A quick glance at her pulled-back hair and unfastened swords told him everything he needed to know.

Outside the pub, Eve hugged him tightly and smashed a hurried kiss on his cheek. "I'm sorry I exploded in there. I had no right, so just forget that happened. Please be safe, I… well… just come back in large enough pieces that I can put you back together."

Goosebumps hip-hopped down his neck and arms. "You too, and remember what I said. If things go bad, get out of town, and hide. Don't wait for me or anyone else. Meridone will be the last spot they'll suspect you to head. Find the *Challenger*, get to Meridone, seek out Duggan's Lodge. Daria's the… supervisor and Rystral owns it. They'll look after you."

Eve rushed off to the clinic, and Jayden went back home and dressed for battle. He geared up just as he had when he worked missions for Syrus. Pistol, rifle, and short-blade, all sheathed in familiar places. He flipped up the collar on his black overcoat to keep the icy wind out, then pulled his wide-brimmed hat low.

Why did simply changing clothes make him feel like a killer again? He didn't like the sensation and wanted to burn everything that suddenly reminded him of his former life. Yet Dalth needed his skills, today more than ever. Retreating wasn't an option, neither was surrender.

By the time Jayden found the mayor, Markus was already giving orders and positioning the town's militia. Fathers and sons old enough to fight hugged and kissed their loved ones, some for the final time. Serena went from person to person checking weapons and armor, occasionally exchanging a piece for something of higher quality. Victor gathered small children, the elderly, and anyone unable to fight, then led them north. Many years ago, Markus had built a small cabin in the forest for such an occasion. It wasn't big, but it was well hidden and stocked with enough supplies to get them through what was to come. If the battle went poorly, it was Victor's job to keep them safe.

Markus turned to Jayden and ordered him to the southern line to meet the enemy head on. The men and women tending the front line were already in their designated firing positions by the time Jayden walked up. They looked scared but in control of their fears. They'd fight, and many would die, but he didn't think they'd run.

Their bunkers were covered in wood, old mattresses, rocks, and other sturdy objects, providing both cover and concealment. Jayden's post gave him a perfect vantage over the wheat field and sky-grass, all the way down to the southern tree line.

Markus made his way to the front lines, and as the minutes passed, the waiting became nerve-wracking. When Phaedra and Jenna returned from another scouting mission, it was the first time in memory Jayden wanted to see that silvery hair.

"I still count about thirty," advised Phaedra. "Suspect about a dozen more somewhere that we can't see. They're wearing upgraded metaflex suits, definitely has the corporate touch."

Markus stood and surveyed the open land in front of them. He wore a black button-down long-sleeve shirt, tan hat, and his usual brown heavy coat that barely covered his belt and holster. He kept his rifle slung over his shoulder with the barrel pointed at the ground.

"We're the blood of Dalth's defense. We go down, the town falls with us. Watch one another's back, and we'll get through this."

The bell-tower sentry near the town square yelled something unintelligible, then started ringing the bell. Looking south, a dozen black figures marched toward town, kicking up snow in their wake. They were aligned in two rows, some with energy-blades, others with RERs.

"The front have rifles," clarified Phaedra. "Expect them to take up a firing position soon."

Jayden unslung his rifle and scoped the incoming enemy. "Mayor, time for you to get off the front lines. We've got this corner covered."

Serena came skidding in next to Jayden, rifle in hand. "You seen Misora or Sasha yet?"

"Not yet."

Behind them, Markus bellowed orders up and down the main line, inspiring his people to remain calm and steady.

As Phaedra predicted, the first row of Celje knelt and raised their rifles.

Jayden's heart somersaulted. "Everyone, down!" The first volley of energy bolts zoomed inches above them. "Stay down!" Additional rounds came their way.

Jayden looked around for casualties and found none. Their cover had done its job. In front of Markus, a subtle glow shimmered.

"They didn't even ask for a surrender! Mayor, now might be a good time to retreat back to the square," advised Phaedra, angling her shield in front him. Bullets pinged off the impressive shield, but the display also gave the attacking Celje their confirmation that Dalth had mystics among their ranks.

"Running away from the front line in an open field doesn't seem like a good idea," replied Markus. "What about their armor, can our bullets get through it?"

A bullet struck a few feet in front of Jayden, splattering snow into his face. He turned to Serena. "Probably take a point-blank shot with no problems."

"Tell everyone to aim at the joints," said Serena. "Probably the only vulnerable spots on that gear."

Markus relayed the information through the line, hearing iterations of his order shouted from one person to the next.

"This is it," said Jayden, seeing the enemy shift formation. "They're getting ready to charge!"

At fifty meters, Jayden, Serena, and Jenna unleashed Dalth's first wave. Serena's improved bullets cut through the enemy's reinforced gear. Their effectiveness took the charging Celje by surprise, and the advancing line dove for cover.

The main lines of both forces were fully engaged now, bullets flying everywhere. Two screams on Jayden's left pulled him away from his scope. One of Dalth's guards was dead, and next to him, his battlemate, bawled in agony.

To Jayden's horror, he saw Eve running out from behind a wagon toward the injured man. "No, Eve, stay!" But the Celje were already taking aim at the defenseless target. "Cover fire, cover fire!" he screamed in panic. Dalth's line responded, sending several dozen rounds downrange.

Phaedra whacked him behind the head. "You're wasting Serena's ammo!"

Jayden didn't care about the special ammo, he needed to protect Eve. He fired continuously until Eve, with the help of Kun, pulled the injured soldier away. Her heroism might have saved the man, but the militia had used up their armor-piercing munitions.

The Celje appeared to notice this dilemma and resumed their charged. They were within Dalth's lines in seconds, the sounds of colliding metal reverberated across the plains. Terrified howls whistled over the main line as energy-blades and swords found flesh.

A young man stationed at the far-eastern side of Dalth's line was engaged in a sword fight with their armored enemy. In two calculated moves, the Celje disarmed him and went for the killing strike. The crosshairs of Jayden's scope centered on the Celje's chest just as the sword came down. The bullet struck and exploded the soldier's neckline, catapulting him back.

From slightly behind, Markus leaned around a rock, firing his rifle with precision. "Jayden, where's Phaedra? We need her in this fight!"

Jayden looked around. "Been a little busy here, haven't seen her." Taking precious seconds to survey the field, Jayden eyed two important details. First, Jenna was also gone and second, Kun was rushing toward their position carrying a thin sword with blood dripping from it. The middle-aged man, who normally wore a friendly smile, now looked like death's servant. He wore light-leather armor, dyed dark green and black, matching the paint that striped his face. Kun's smile was gone, his eyes probing, giving off a predatory vibe.

Markus's head peeked up. "Kun, glad to see you. What's the clinic look like?"

"The ladies have hands full, Mayor. What do you need?"

Markus glanced up and down their line. "Looks like that Celje rifle team is starting to advance toward our flanks. Go reinforce them and get the injured to Celine. Jayden, Serena, make sure he gets there!"

Kun was up and dashing down the line before his cover fire began. Jayden and Serena laid down continuous fire, but two sword-wielding Celje found their way close to Kun. Serena took a risky shot and hit the nearest, staggering him.

Kun reacted, taking a step forward and decapitating the man, his blade cutting cleanly through the mesh around the neckline. Facing the second man, the two sidestepped around the dead body at their feet.

Kun let out a chilling battle cry and went on the offensive. Sword and energy-blade clashed, and both men parried in perfect sequence. Kun received two deep gashes to the shoulder and thigh before retreating. For a moment, it looked as if the two men were speaking, but the respite didn't last. Kun feigned a quick jab, then executed a three-strike combo, ending the dual. The Celje guard took one last look at the blood spilling from his belly before collapsing into an empty foxhole.

"Not everyone fights like him," asserted Markus. "We're losing two for every one of theirs, can't last."

Jayden was about to tell Markus not to give up when the bell tower rang again. Peering up at the lookout, Jayden followed his signal toward the west, but Serena was one step ahead.

"Mayor, to the right!" she yelled, swiveling her rifle.

Jayden did likewise, putting his scope on the newest group. Six Celje with raised rifles advanced. "They've broken through!"

Jayden and Serena engaged the new group, doing little more than staggering them.

Yet Markus didn't react, or at least react the same way everyone else did. "What are they doing in the open?"

Jayden thought back to his conversations with Eve and his theory on Misora's true intent for coming to Dalth.

"You think it's a diversion?" responded Jayden while reloading. Then an idea hit him. He swiveled his scope to the other side of Dalth, toward the clinic. Jayden's trained eye spotted the two Celje whose armor had transitioned to blend in with the tall sky-grass they were sneaking through.

"Mayor!" shouted Jayden. "It's Eve! They're going after Eve! Two Celje coming up from the south. I'm going after them!"

Jayden was up and out of the foxhole before Markus or Serena had the chance to protest. Bullets flew by him from what seemed like every direction. He moved fast, catching himself as his boots slipped in the grimy soil.

He could see the agents at the door of the clinic, and Jayden made his move. He skidded to a knee and shouldered his rifle. At fifty meters, he was an expert marksman. Jayden lined his crosshairs on the neck of the second man, then midway through exhaling, squeezed the trigger and watched the projectile strike true. Expecting the man to crumble, Jayden lined up the other man, but it was too late, he'd already entered the clinic.

The soldier he'd shot was back on his feet and wasted no time returning fire. Jayden dove into the prone position and put two more bullets in the man's chest, knocking him to the ground. Unsure if the agent was dead, Jayden jumped to his feet and charged. He needed to kill this man and take down the second before he was able to get to Eve. The injured Celje was shakily getting to his feet, looking for the rifle he'd dropped. Since bullets weren't doing the trick, Jayden tossed his rifle aside and unsheathed his short-blade. Of course, heading into melee combat with a trained Celje agent was the exact thing he'd told Dalth's militia not to do. However, Kun's earlier display proved one very important point: the Celje's upgraded armor was purposed to absorb high velocity bullets and energy bolts, not conventional bladed weapons. The metaflex armor was expensive, and adding that additional layer of cross-weaved casting likely put the executives over budget.

The Celje unsheathed his energy-blade and came up in a controlled attack that sent Jayden diving sideways. Jayden rolled, narrowly avoiding a sparking saber that slammed into the ground where he'd been seconds before. Jayden sprang to his feet, aware he'd just missed death by inches.

With a well-practiced aim, Jayden sent his blade end over end toward the soldier's soft neckline. The blade missed by inches, leaving Jayden defenseless. The Celje moved with speed and finesse despite the full body armor. His attacks were controlled and precise, never overextending or losing his balance. The agent's first pair of strikes connected with Jayden's ear, shoulder, and forearm. Jayden rolled backward, clearing the next combo, but the soldier was relentless. With a long stride forward, the agent thrust a killing strike toward Jayden's chest that would have finished the job if not for the muddy terrain. The agent's foot slipped, and his jab went wide. Jayden slid toward his half buried short-blade and scooped it up in one nimble maneuver. Armed, he countered sideways with his blade, disarming the agent, but failed to inflict any real injury.

His foe went back on the attack, tossing punches and sidekicks that Jayden struggled to deflect. Soon Jayden landed a lucky strike into a vulnerable area near the kneecap that stopped the onslaught, giving him a much-needed pause. Jayden checked his wounds, finding a steady flow of blood from each.

The Celje retrieved his slimy sword, and the duel started once more. Jayden charged, but the Celje anticipated the move and swung upward, hoping to end the battle in one swing. Jayden danced away from the arching sword, then swung his short-blade upward, into the man's face.

The agent's screams were horrific, but short. Jayden extracted his blade from his enemy's jaw checked his surroundings. To the north, he spotted three of Dalth's militia running from the enemy. To the west, he saw Serena and Markus fighting for their lives. Then, to the south, a lone hooded figure atop a grassy knoll near the tree line. Something protruded from the cloaked figure, a rifle, perhaps. Regardless of the direction he looked, the battle for Dalth was coming to an end, and they'd lost.

He gathered his rifle and limped toward the clinic where the second agent had already entered. Jayden was a dozen meters away when his worst nightmare came tearing out of the clinic. With his helmet visor up, Misora flung open the door dragging Eve by the hair.

The mortal foes locked eyes. Jayden resisted the urge to draw his pistol with Eve in front of his target. Behind him, Jayden registered the rapidity of increasing gunfire.

"Release her, and I promise they'll find enough of you to bury." Jayden hobbled toward his rival, his body cool and shaky.

"Oh, this *is* a surprise! Jayden Vaut, you've saved me the trouble of finding you. What are the odds, locating both my targets in nearly the same spot?" Misora held Eve in front of him, raised the butt of his pistol, and knocked her out in one turn.

With Eve on the ground, Jayden drew and fired two quick rounds into Misora's chest. Unfortunately, Misora also fired off a well-aimed round that caught Jayden in his uninjured shoulder. The impact threw him into the dirt, knocking the wind from his lungs. Jayden fought through the mind-numbing pain and rolled over. Jayden had just pushed himself onto his knees when Misora's foot found his jaw. The blow rolled Jayden across the cold ground, and white stars filled his vision.

"God, that felt good," said Misora's cool, cocky voice. "How you been, Vaut?" Misora drove the side of his boot into Jayden's shoulder, pushing him to the limit of consciousness.

A radio transmission came through Misora's helmet, and he eased off the pressure. "I don't care about the people, we're here to grab the Reeves girl. Kill anyone who resists. I'll meet you north of town."

Jayden rolled onto his side again and spit blood onto Misora's boot. "Get this over with, Misora, I'm tired of trying to figure out if it's your face or ass I'm looking at."

"Such language! Didn't think I hit you that hard."

Buried images of Nencia's last moments fueled Jayden's contempt for the Celje leader.

Misora reached down and grabbed Jayden by the collar. "You know I'm not supposed to be here, attacking Thoba. So, sshhhh, don't tell anyone. We're only supposed to kill Tokarek, but took a wrong turn, and here I am! Hey, by the way, how is ole Tokarek?"

Gunshots in the distance gave Jayden hope his friends were still in the fight. "Syrus and I had a bit of a falling out, or hadn't your spies told you yet?"

More gunshots and Misora's helmet lit up with more chatter. His smile dived into a wicked frown. "Regroup, and take them out! They're just farmers!"

Jayden's vision was getting worse, and he was shaking uncontrollably. "Problems?"

"You've been a real pain, Vaut. I'm beginning to think I should have killed you instead of that whore, Nencia. Guess I finally get to kill you properly this time." Misora readied his sword and moved to thrust it into Jayden's chest.

People often say that a person's most vivid memories flash before them right before death. Others describe seeing a bright light with an angel at the other end. Jayden had been close to death several times and experienced none of these supernatural events. Facing death once again, he saw nothing but a blurred battlefield and a sharp blade heading for his heart.

Over Misora's shoulder, a small figure with a silvery outline rocketed up the path, and with lightning speed two shiny edges poked through Misora's chest plate. His eyes glazed over through his visor, then his vile smile turned to shock.

With a sneer Phaedra slowly pulled her blades from his chest and shoved him onto his back. She straddled his squirming body, then leisurely wiped her blades clean across the collar of his armor. "You've killed people I've liked, and now you're going to die a slow, endless death choking on all the blood you've taken."

Jayden was still on his knees, swaying with his weakening heart. It wasn't the firm hands of Phaedra that laid him down but the gentle hold of Jenna. "Eve... what about... find her..."

Inside the clinic, Jayden lay mostly naked atop a coarse bed, surrounded by the dying. He'd woken up a few minutes ago, his wounds bandaged and a cup of water next to him. His forearm and leg hurt like hell, but it was his nearly severed ear that kept him from getting comfortable. In the bed next to him, Eve lay semiconscious, suffering from a concussion.

A few rows away, Shari worked with the clinic volunteers, ordering bandages, medications, and surgical equipment as she rotated to each bed. At the rear of the building, Celine rolled the teenager Jayden had saved into the operating room, but his body wasn't moving. Through the room's window, Jayden watched Celine work forceps over the young man's chest.

"You awake?" It was Phaedra, perhaps the last person he wanted to speak with.

"Guess you're not going to tell me where you went during the battle? We needed you at the beginning."

She sat on the side of his bed, sending vibrations through the feeble bed that in turn agitated the wounds. "Jenna and I found another squad coming around to the north. We took them out before they ambushed you, then we went south to check something out. I saved your puckered butt, so how about you just thank me. Besides, I think we have more important things to worry about."

"You cost lives. If it weren't for Zakar's crew, we'd all be dead by now."

"I had to check something out, but like I said, it doesn't matter. By the time I got there, whoever it was had left. And stop talking about the Appian people like they did you a favor. Zakar's probably going to send you a bill for the mercenaries he sent. He does nothing for free."

Jayden was tired of talking to her. "I'm wounded, Phaedra. It's been a bad day. What do you want?"

She smiled, but this wasn't a cheery, let's-hug-it-out smile. She was about to give him news that wasn't good.

"How long have you known she's the Reeves kid?"

Blocking out the fiery burn in his shoulder, Jayden grabbed Phaedra by the throat. Even her mystic reflexes weren't fast enough to pull away. She had one of her swords out, but Jayden could crush her windpipe in seconds. Jayden pulled her face closer, his jaw clenched so tight he thought his teeth might crack.

"I don't think I heard you say anything about a Reeves kid, did I? Because if I did, I'd need to kill whoever started that rumor, wouldn't I?"

Phaedra's smug expression melted into concern. "Let go of me, and I might let you live," she seethed back.

"Save your threats for someone who hasn't killed mystics for a living." He squeezed her windpipe tighter. "If you value your life, you'll leave this town and never come back. And if I get even a whisper that you've talked about Eve, I'm coming for you."

CHAPTER 66: YEAR 2401

Syrus steadied his horse on the outskirts of Port Rindo, watching as fog and plumes of smoke rose together and sailed off toward the east and over the forest. Less than thirty soldiers stood behind him, ready to fight, ready to give their lives for Ojult. Yet something in the cool air told him the fight for Capintesta had already begun.

Giles inclined his head in a hasty bow. "Premier, I tried to find Nigel, but there was no sign of your servant. However, your feelings about the town were correct. The town is burning, and the Celje are already in the harbor. No doubt they're expecting us."

Syrus felt the eyes of his soldiers upon him just as he could feel the wind upon his face. "Zakar's intelligence was correct then. Very well, Giles, heal and return to the line. Until we confirm Kavil made it back, you command the arcane guard."

Syrus considered asking about the size of the enemy force, but it didn't matter at this point. His forces were already committed to the fight, and Siller's squad appeared totally decimated. Syrus moved his forces up the large hill that bordered the main entrance into Port Rindo. Thick trees and brush bordered the path, bottlenecking his troops during their approach. If the Celje decided to launch an attack now, Syrus's troops would follow the same fate as Siller's.

They reached the top unabated, giving Syrus his first clear view of the town. The Celje had not just taken the town, they'd destroyed it. Smoke billowed from every building while bodies scattered the street. Those who lived were running past Syrus's force with whatever possessions they could carry.

Syrus's forces stopped a hundred meters in front of the main gate where the tree line ended and opened to a grassy plain. "Captain Giles," said Syrus, "I want three rows, and put the Thoba in the rear."

Syrus dismounted and walked toward the main gate with his troop falling in behind him. After a few dozen steps, his senses told him what his eyes confirmed. Up ahead, just outside the main gate, a man in black armor holding a spear with flashing electrical pulses rested upon a forti-fied horse. Syrus unsheathed his staff, then watched as the stranger flung his lance toward him. The inflamed spear landed well short of Syrus's line, sparks cracking out from the three elongated forks. At the end of the protruding weapon was the guillotined head of his servant, Nigel. Syrus breathed out his initial emotion, his nostrils flaring with open disgust. He slowly turned his attention back to the spearman. Syrus's first impression was the man in front of him wasn't part of Sasha's regular army. The sol-dier's blood-orange shield, metaflex armor, energy-sword, and RER sug-gested this warrior was anything but regular.

From behind the black-armored fighter appeared a man dressed not for battle, but for a more civilized action. He wore a wide brimmed hat and a heavy winter cloak that barely covered his pistols.

"Syrus Tokarek," boomed Sasha's voice over the field. "Take note that your steward is dead, as is your guard captain. Do I have your undivided attention?"

Syrus's enhanced vision zoomed just beyond Sasha to a spike where Kavil Siller's head sat. Siller's eyes were open but rolled back, and flies swarmed his rotting flesh. At least he died in battle, the way destiny always planned.

The man responsible for his sister's death and countless others now stood within striking distance, but Syrus's wisdom prevailed over his desire. He knew Sasha wasn't here to negotiate and briefly wondered why he'd not attacked from the beginning.

From inside the gate, Celje troops poured out of the town, forming row after row of lined fighters. Sasha gestured to the arcane guard. "If you value the lives of your fellows, I suggest you listen. I have more than enough forces to eradicate you from this planet, but my only interest is you. Surrender yourself Tokarek, and I will let your sages go."

Syrus didn't believe that nonsense for a moment, and neither did his arcane guard. "My sister and the others were innocent, yet they lie within the dirt of this banished planet. You put the heads of men I respect on spikes and you ask that I surrender?" Syrus yearned for the fight, but the aura of a trap also lingered.

"Fair enough," said Sasha. "An executive form Earth is here, on Ojult, right now. He wants this war to end and, unfortunately, he also wants you dead and that stick of yours destroyed. Surrender yourself and the staff, then tell your people to scatter. If all this happens, then the Celje will go back into the shadows. Agreed?"

Syrus estimated Sasha's numbers, armament, and possible reinforcements. "Something's off. There's more going on here than what we see."

"I feel it too," Giles agreed.

Sasha's vexatious voice boomed from ahead. "Syrus, are you surrendering, or do we fight?"

Syrus's voice boomed over the entire region: "My people will not be slaves to you or the *soras* you serve."

Sasha's forces didn't hesitate and fired just as dozens of coarsened shields forged along Syrus's line. After the initial hail of bullets, droves of black-armored soldiers carrying various bladed weapons and blood-orange shields marched toward the awaiting mystics.

"Hold here, Captain," ordered Syrus. With focused rage, he stepped several meters in front of his troop and channeled the full power of the Amurski staff. The ground around him shook as wheel-sized chunks of rock, leaving craters behind them, launched like mortars toward the advancing enemy. As the mortars found their mark, Syrus rocketed groups of flat, razor-sharp discs from the end of his staff. The projectiles whistled through the air before smoothly cutting through their armored targets.

Sasha's melee troops were advancing faster, leaving Syrus time for one last large-area attack. Syrus gripped his staff and focused every ounce of mental willpower before unleashing. The well-trained Celje recognized the attack and raised their shields. Hundreds of tiny, sharp, purple barbs rained down upon Sasha's army. The darts penetrated their improved armor but not the shields, killing far fewer than Syrus had hoped.

Syrus's devastating barrage erased dozens of the enemy in less than a minute. Sasha's men were advancing again, and Giles ordered his front-line mystics to attack. An intense tsunami of energy waves buckled underneath the ground and collided with the advancing enemy. The maneuver knocked many of the approaching Celje off their feet. Giles issued a second order, and bullets sprayed the fallen and disoriented enemy.

But keeping the enemy at bay wasn't realistic, and within seconds, Sasha's men met Syrus's in melee combat. Blood, limbs, and weapons began peppering the battlefield.

Syrus jumped into the fray with the ends of his staff glowing lava red. Syrus's first victims were run through, his staff easily cutting through their armor.

Three Celje surrounded Syrus, trying to overpower the mystic with numbers, but their efforts faltered. He killed the first two with two quick ice spikes, then eliminated the third with slightly more effort.

Only minutes into the battle and already dead bodies filled the hillside. To his left, Giles fought fiercely with battle-axes in each hand, bringing down Celje combatants.

"Premier, the battle is going well!"

But Syrus pointed toward Sasha who'd not joined the battle. "Look carefully, Captain, Sasha hasn't released his entire force. These are his gladiators, his pawns."

"They're taking too many losses. Perhaps he's reconsidering?"

Syrus reached out with his senses, trying to gauge the aura of the battle. A familiar presence he'd not felt before waned nearby. Looking back at the tree line, a tall man with slicked black hair, hallowed eyes, and an oversized sword charged into the fray.

Turr's giant steel blade met the Celje's improved armor, hacking off limbs and exposing organs with deadly efficiency. Turr had been part of Siller's defense on Listo; if he survived, perhaps others did as well.

"I apologize, Lord Tokarek," said Turr, his chin touching his chest. "I was injured and in a healing trance. I just realized what was going on."

Syrus's connection to the battle caught the subtle change just as Giles tackled a soldier attempting to spear Syrus from the side. Yet Syrus's presage extended beyond, touching something dark and imminent.

Turr stepped in front of Syrus, raising his sword in defiance. "Premier, Sasha has a mystic within his company. He unleased her at the beginning of their assault on Listo, giving Captain Siller no chance. She wields a staff and contains power I've never seen. I'm sure she's among us on the battlefield."

Dozens more men rushed from the front gate to join Sasha's main force. The tide of battle was turning.

"They will not get to you, my premier!" yelled Giles, struggling to fend off two soldiers.

The Celje were closing in, but his mystics greeted them in kind. The lurking presence he'd been feeling since arriving, it must be Sasha's mystic assassin. The woman responsible for his sister's death was here, and Syrus hungered for the revenge that had so long evaded him. His heart pulled him toward the sage assassin, but the mystic leader's steady mind asked if vengeance was the reason for today's battle. He was fighting for the future of the entire mystic race, not just the Nein. If his people fell today, who would be left to carry on their lineage?

"Turr, Giles, stand before me," demanded Syrus. Giles was struggling to breathe, thanks to a welling chest wound. Turr joined them with sweat trickling down his large forehead.

"You both will retreat from this battle and head to Pa'Gran where you will tell Andreas of our defeat. News must also reach Dalth, do you understand? Stop for nothing, for no one."

Turr's hollowed eyes stared shockingly at Syrus. "Premier, we'd rather stay and fight."

For the first time in Syrus's long life, he felt the end creeping near. "Now's not the time to argue. Go now, before our perimeter collapses."

Giles was hurt and torn between his duty and the order. "Turr, I'll follow behind. Don't wait for me. Go!"

Turr's eyes darted between Syrus, Giles, and the tree line, then he sprinted down the path.

Syrus's fury helped hold his mental focus as he launched ice shards into the soldiers following Turr. As Turr began to outpace Giles, several gunshots rang out near the rear of their line. The first hit the slowing Giles in the shoulder, and the second struck the top of his skull, killing him instantly.

There was nothing to be done. Giles was dead, and his troop needed a leader. Syrus trudged down the broken line, thrusting ice shards and discs into the backs of soldiers engaging his troops. Halfway down the battle line and fully baptized in mystic energy, Syrus touched the presence he'd been waiting for. Rapt in arcane power, Syrus pushed the racing knife away from his back, spun, and readied a counterattack when, to his confusion, he missed the second blade spinning through the air. The velocity and speed of the attack was blurring even to Syrus's profound powers. The sage followed her initial attack with a knee into his stomach. Air ejected from his lungs, but he still had the wherewithal to counter with a quick jab of his staff. The woman sidestepped, landing a disarming kick that sent his staff flying. From one knee, Syrus looked up in time to see the woman somersault over him, then he felt the end of a small blade in his shoulder.

Syrus rolled forward, evading the next attack, but the move pushed the embedded knife deeper.

Achilla slammed her first into the ground, permeating the largest shockwave Syrus had ever seen. Everyone within twenty meters was launched into the air. The impact with the ground drove the dagger all the way through Syrus's shoulder, the tip coming out the other side.

Achilla launched into the air, intending to land a double-knee strike. Syrus rolled away once again, but he'd lost all feeling in his dominant arm. He didn't have time to consider the injury before she launched more hand and leg strikes. Even with only one arm, Syrus held his ground, blocking and parrying the attacks.

When Syrus found an opening, he pressed his own attack, landing a side kick that sent her floundering backward. She skidded and recovered her balance, an evil grin spreading across her face. "This will be the second staff I've taken."

He'd launched the assassin right next to his fallen staff.

Syrus produced an energy shield, but the screen shattered against the might of her energy blast. His limp body flew backward until slamming against a half-fractured rock. The force broke something in his back and sent him spiraling into a dark, endless oblivion.

———————

Syrus was conscious enough to feel the rocky terrain tear into his legs and knees as he was dragged across the battlefield. Time was a blur, but the sounds of battle were gone. Both his shoulders were out of socket, and his spine was numb.

His bearer carelessly dropped him to the ground.

"His staff, my love," said Achilla, kissing Sasha. "He was far easier to defeat than I expected."

Sasha looked at the staff in wonderment, gazing up and down at the legendary weapon. "Thank you, Achilla. Today will see the end of the Nein and peace on Ojult."

A mystic working with the Celje?

"Let my... people go, it... it's me you want. You won, you have me. Let them go."

"Let them go!" mocked Sasha. "Your people kill over half my agents, and you think I am letting them go? No, I think not. I have the great Nein leader kneeling before me, before the Celje. It is a wonderful day, and you are in no position to ask for anything."

Achilla broke away from her lover and knelt beside Syrus. "We should kill him now and move on to the next plan."

Syrus eyed both staffs clinging to the woman's back. "Where... did you get that other staff? Why are you... working with the people... killing our kind?"

Achilla slapped him across the face. "What have the Nein ever done for me? You can't even save your own sister. You are pathetic. My loyalty is to power, to Sasha, to my love."

"You're my sister's killer. You're the one who murdered her."

Achilla looked to her lover, the ends of her mouth curling up in a carnal grin. "Yes, I am the one that outwitted the great Nein ruler."

Sasha walked up close to Syrus. "I must admit that I have been lying to you. You asked that I let your people go, your remaining force. I am not sorry to say it is not possible. You see, with a very small exception, they are dead. Every, single soldier you brought is dead."

Reaching out, Syrus no longer felt the courage and strength emanating from his people. He'd led the Nein into a slaughter, and all but him had paid the price.

"And now I am taking my army to Pa'Gran, then south," continued Sasha. "And then, Syrus, would you like to know where I am going from there?"

Syrus's expressive eyes burned into Sasha. "You have no idea... what's coming."

Sasha smiled, then leaned closer. "Yes, I am sure. But you did not answer my question, so let me tell you. We are taking a little trip to Pallio Valley. Perhaps you might know who I will find there?"

CHAPTER 67: YEAR 2401

How many more scars would mark his body before this conflict ended? Or would he even make it to the end? These ideas freckled Jayden's mind as he sat alone in his home. His ear, shoulder, and forearm were mending nicely, thanks to Eve's stitching and Jenna's healing.

He'd come home from the clinic yesterday; his only visitor since, Shari Dikal, delivered hovrol and jashinto serum. Jayden declined the valuable pain pills but accepted the hovrol. He could handle the pain, but infected wounds on Ojult didn't end well.

For now, he needed rest. He was lying near his fireplace, keeping warm with a heavy blanket.

Someone knocked at the door.

"I'm tired, half naked, and injured!" yelled Jayden, not in the mood for company. "Come back in the morning."

Eve opened the door and walked inside. "It's freezing out there."

Eve was the only person he remotely felt like seeing, but he wasn't anywhere close to presentable. "Sorry, been a hard few days."

Her nose was glowing scarlet and her red hair flared out from under her brown beanie. "I came to check on you. How are you feeling?"

Jayden sat up, giving her a spot to sit. "Your handiwork and Jenna's magic tricks got me in pretty good shape. How's your head?"

The entire front part of her pants and blouse were caked in dried blood, thankfully not her own. "I'll have a lump but the headache's gone. I'm in better shape than most in the clinic."

Feeling he needed to do something for her, Jayden went to the kitchen and retrieved a small bucket of water, soap, and rags. "Here, let me help." He gently pried her hands away from the warm fire and began scrubbing.

The small bucket quickly turned a grimy brown as she let him clean the crusty blood off her coarse hands.

Jayden continued scrubbing, ignoring the throbbing in his forearm, while she explained the latest news. Serena and Kun were cleaning up the battlefield, gathering equipment off the dead and burning the enemy corpses. Markus visited and prayed with those who'd lost loved ones and did his best to restart the town. Victor, who looked after the children and elderly, came back from the small bunker outside town. Besides a few of the kids being upset, they were all okay.

Eve's eyes were bloodshot from fatigue and when she yawned, Jayden thought she'd pass out on her next breath.

"You're tired and been through a lot. If you want to sleep in the other room, don't feel embarrassed. The room's got clean sheets, I think, but I'll have to cancel plans with all my other ladies tonight."

Eve rubbed her eyes, looking relieved at the offer. "Not that I want to offend your lady friends, but I'm going to take you up on that offer. Misora knew exactly where to find me and attacked Dalth because of me. People are dead because I'm here. I… I don't want to be alone tonight."

Unable to lift his shoulder, he patted her leg. "You're the daughter of the most powerful person in existence, so yeah, you're going to draw some attention. But all those people out there, they don't know who you are. They volunteered to fight against a malevolent, conquering gestapo and they knew what might happen. This isn't about one person, it's about free-dom from tyranny. Bullies like Misora, they pop up throughout history and people like you, they stand up against them."

Her head fell against his injured shoulder. "Thank you. I just can't… I'm terrified it's not over."

They stayed up talking until finally falling asleep. The crackling fire-place and heavy blankets kept the frosty night air at bay. Eve slept soundly, but Jayden stirred most of the night. His arm throbbed while his mind spun around the idea of Phaedra knowing Eve's real identity. When she'd finally tell Syrus, there'd be a fight, one that made today look like practice.

When the slightest glow of the sun started to leak through the window, Jayden heard heavy, excited footsteps outside. When he heard a knock, he was ready to defend his friend.

Wearing heavy winter clothing and a rifle over her shoulder, Serena opened the door and pushed her way into the living room. "They're here, Jayden. I don't know how long they've been here, but they're all here."

Even Jayden's semi-drugged mind knew what she meant. "Any sign of Syrus's forces?"

"None, but Jenna and Phaedra are scouting the area. They think we're already surrounded, but it's not looking good. Markus said to come get you."

Phaedra and Jenna were supposed to be gone already. "Did he say anything about Eve?"

"Yeah, he said she should stay hidden. Why would we hide her? What don't I know?"

"If we're surrounded, fighting isn't an option, but maybe we can get the kids out."

Eve sat up and yawned, unaware of their situation.

Serena said, "Get to the pub as soon as you can," then dashed out the door.

Jayden quickly explained the situation to Eve.

"Then Sasha's here, for me?"

"It's possible. What's concerning is if Sasha is here, then Syrus's offensive didn't go well, but there's no time to think about that. I need to connect with Markus. I'll meet you in the clinic after I speak with Markus."

"And if Sasha comes to the clinic looking for me?"

Jayden had already considered a handful of different outcomes, all of which concluded with their capture. "If we're surrounded, then it probably won't matter much. We'll figure something out."

———

Jayden holstered his pistol but deliberately left his rifle since his mending limbs would not support the weight of the heavy weapon. He took long, quick strides across the field, scanning the faint horizon for any sign of trouble. Outside the pub, he encountered Phaedra and Jenna.

"Morning," Jayden said, keeping his hand near his pistol.

The two mystics were atop horses, scanning the edges of town. Phaedra ignored his presence, but Jenna greeted him.

"Didn't think we'd see you so soon, but here we are again, ready to fight. Phaedra and I were riding north when we ran into Sasha's army. We tried sneaking away, but they spotted us. We killed two, but there wasn't any way around them, so we came back. I know we won the first round with Misora, but this isn't looking good."

The Nein were trained to fight, not run. The mere mention of retreating or bowing out was near blasphemy. "Thanks, Jenna" he said. "Any sign of Syrus or Andreas?"

"Sorry, we haven't heard anything, but since Sasha's here, that's not a good sign."

An ear-piercing horn ripped through the crisp morning air. Then, to the north, Jayden spotted a cloud of snow being kicked up by a horse carrying a black-armored soldier.

Phaedra whirled her horse around. "I'll take him!"

The pub door opened, presenting a tired but determined man. "Please, no," said Markus. "It looks like a messenger from Sasha. It'd be poor form to kill their courier."

Many townspeople gathered around the pub, anxiously awaiting the messenger.

"My name is Kain," said the armored soldier in a British accent. "I have a message for Markus Fonte."

Markus stepped up in front of the crowd. "I'm Markus Fonte. You may deliver your message to me."

Kain's jittery horse made a full turn while its rider tried to speak. "The message is from Sasha Burmistrov, protector of all Thoba and leader of the Celje. We have you surrounded and will not hesitate to kill every last one of you. You will bring all mystics, plus Jayden Vault and Marilla Reeves, to the northwestern perimeter. You have until noon, or we will march on the town."

Without awaiting a response, Kain spun and rode hard back toward his own line.

"Not much for talking was he," interjected Jenna.

"We aren't surrendering," blurted Phaedra. "I will not be a captive to that maniac."

"I'll surrender myself now," appealed Jayden. "I won't let them hurt anyone because I was too cowardly to surrender."

Phaedra tapped her head several times. "So, you're just going to walk up there and hope for the best? You're just as stupid as you are crazy."

"Please, calm down." Markus's gift of pacifying a rowdy crowd was needed now more than ever. "We have time to think about our decision, yet I agree with Phaedra. Surrendering might not gain us the advantage you think."

Jenna raised her hand like a classroom student. "Sorry, Mayor, but that rider mentioned Marilla Reeves. Did I miss something?"

"That can be addressed later," replied Markus. "Right now, I think the best course of action is for me to speak with Sasha."

"That rider was referring to Marilla Reeves, the daughter of Elasus Reeves!" shouted Phaedra over the crowd. "She's here, in Dalth, being protected by the mayor and Jayden. She's using the name Eve and she's the reason your people have died, and it's the reason the Celje keep attacking Dalth."

Jayden pulled his pistol and fired two rounds that ricocheted off Phaedra's shield. Her startled horse bucked her high into the air, and Jayden had his blade to her throat before she regained her footing. Jenna leapt at him, the collision sending Jayden's blade flying. Both he and Jenna rolled across the ground. Jenna and Jayden had their pistols aimed at one another before the dust began to settle.

It looked as if Jenna was going to fire when Jayden heard an unexpected voice. "Drop gun, or I end Phaedra's life." It was Kun and he was holding a sword to Phaedra's throat. His ruthless expression mirrored what they all had seen on the battlefield.

"This foolishness is going to stop," Markus said. "Yes, Eve is the daughter of Elasus Reeves, and yes, I've known for some time. She's not in league with her father and is a former prisoner of the Celje. Your selfish arguing goes against everything I thought this town stood for. And now, look what its cost you. I might have been able to work something out with Sasha, but he's drawn a line that I cannot bargain with."

With her chin up and shoulders back, Eve walked up from behind the mayor, defiance pulsating from those pure green eyes.

"Put your weapons down," she said with contempt. "I'm turning myself in, along with Phaedra, Jenna, and Jayden. Walk with me now, and leave your weapons at the pub."

Phaedra's defiance ignored Kun's blade shaving her throat. "Why the hell would I ever do anything you say, princess? Your father's why we're all here!"

"He's also why I'm here," Eve countered. "You want to fight Sasha? Go ahead. We'll wait here while he kills you and tosses your body behind a tree. Of course, the other option is to honorably surrender for the sake of these people because they're innocent, and maybe we should put their lives before our own."

Jenna and Jayden continued leveling their weapons at one another.

"I'll surrender, but Phaedra, we do this together," pleaded Jayden. "Let's do the right thing and make a difference."

Eve walked up to Kun and gently pushed the curved sword down from Phaedra's neck. She looked at Phaedra then gestured up the road. "I know you hate me, my family, and my kind, but the real enemy is up on that hill. I beg you, Phaedra, please, help me save these people from certain death."

Phaedra's hands were still resting on the handles of both hilts, her hard expression and posture reflecting that of a hunting tigress. Dozens of tense people waited on her next move.

"We're probably all dead anyway," Phaedra said. "Jenna, lower your pistol, Jayden, do the same. Let's go see Sasha *with* our weapons and see what he wants. If it's not a trap, which I'm sure it is, then we'll give ourselves up."

Led by a conflicted Markus, the soon-to-be prisoners, plus dozens of curious Dalth citizens friendly to Jayden, walked up the trail. The two mystics were still armed, as was Markus and a few others, but Jayden carried only his integrity, opting to leave his pistol with Kun. The mass of people were silent, save for the frosty gravel crunching underneath their footsteps.

Nearing the edge of town, three figures sat on horseback in front of a line of armored soldiers.

"That's Sasha in the middle," said Jayden. "Not sure of the others. Any idea what those rods are sticking up from the ground?"

"Heads," snarled Phaedra. "Ours will probably be joining them soon."
Eve's eyelids fluttered. "That's revolting."

"Don't puke on me, sunshine," warned Phaedra. "Remember, this was
your idea. Suggest you put that pretty hair of yours in a ponytail, it'll look
much better when it's run through and sitting up on that hill for everyone to see."

The scene was grotesque. As they neared Sasha, more impaled heads
lined the road. Immediately recognizable atop the lances were Kavil Siller,
Nigel, Giles, and Javier, along with other familiar Nein sages.

Most interesting were the captured and bound mystics resting on
their knees behind Sasha. Syrus, Andreas, and Turr were each shackled in
heavy black chains, their faces bloody and bruised. The Celje had defeated
Syrus's guards at every turn, and they were now in Dalth to recapture Eve
and end the rebellion for good.

Jenna tapped her senior on the shoulder as they continued up the trail.
"Phaedra, that hooded figure on top of the horse next to Sasha, she's got
a staff."

Judging by Phaedra's reaction, she'd already seen it and processed what
that meant. "That's Achilla, a mystic, and she's got two. We've seen her
before at that mystic camp back on Listo. She's been doing the dirty with
Sasha for a while now. Those two staffs are gonna be a problem."

Jayden had a pretty good idea where this Achilla woman got one of
the staffs, but that wasn't going to do them any good right now. They were
walking into the sarcto's den, and it brought back memories of Nencia and
Worall. The Celje never negotiated, so why would they now?

When they were within speaking distance Jayden could see the oppos-
ing force. Sasha looked thin, almost gaunt, yet sat with a confidence of
someone who knew his superiority. He wore a heavy black-and-brown
overcoat with a hat that had not seen much wear and tear.

"Mr. Vaut, Phaedra Lillea, and Jenna Dimare," said Sasha. He then
turned and tipped his hat toward Eve. "And, yes, there she is, Ms. Marilla
Reeves."

No one, least of all Markus, was in the mood for small talk. "Against
my advice, the four people you've requested are here. They're giving themselves up in exchange for you and your filthy goons leaving Dalth in peace."

Sasha's sinister eyes peered over the top of Markus toward the town square. "Part of my plan included sending Misora here ahead of my main force. May I ask what you have done with him?"

"They're planning something," spat Achilla. "They have him prisoner, we should attack now."

A wiser man would have kept his mouth shut and let the more experienced leader handle the accusation, but Jayden's lips were moving before his brain could shut it down. "You think we would've taken that trash prisoner?"

Sasha said, "My number-two man is dead then?"

"I burned his body personally," said Jayden.

The dark circles around Sasha's eyes seemed to blacken as he took in the news. "According to Misora, you killed Wren Dikal, a dear friend of mine. Is this true?"

"You need to pick better friends," goaded Jayden. "But we didn't come up here to compare body counts. You asked for us, and here we are. You going to live up to your end of the deal and leave Dalth alone?"

Sasha turned and looked at Achilla. The two seemed to agree on something.

"Misora's death was not part of my deal," explained Sasha. "The terms must change now. Mayor, you will surrender all the town's weapons, armor, and anything confiscated from the soldiers you killed. You will do this now, without comment."

Markus huffed, clearly not surprised by the sudden amendment. "Your genocidal escapades will catch the attention of the corporation, Sasha. My family has seen generations of your kind on this planet, and the corporation never accepts this type of brutality for long. Your days are numbered, butcher."

Jayden didn't know what exactly gave it away, but he knew Sasha's next move. Jayden's gaze drifted into the beaten eyes of Syrus who returned the stare. Even though the mystic leader was gagged, his eyes did all the talking. Even after today, whatever happened, the fight would continue.

Sasha fired two bullets into Syrus, both entering his chest and exiting his back. Syrus gave no sign of pain or surprise and remained steady on his knees for a few seconds before falling backward. His rule ended at the barrel of Sasha's pistol, but the Nein rebellion would continue.

"No!" It was Jenna, in something between a whimper and a scream.

Jenna and Phaedra unsheathed their weapons and attacked. Jenna's rifle swiftly centered on Achilla while Phaedra went for Sasha. Jayden tackled Eve to the ground, trying to protect her from whatever happened next.

Achilla's lethal reaction focused on Jenna first. With both staffs unsheathed, the seditious assassin launched two mutated ice spikes into Jenna's torso, hammering her into the ground. Then, with little effort, an energy wave erupted from Achilla's second staff, suspending Phaedra in midair before hurling her over the gathered crowd.

After a few seconds, Jayden looked up at Sasha who was aiming a pistol at his head.

"Your reputation as a killer has not escaped me," warned Sasha. "Do anything other than what I tell you, and you will die."

Jayden didn't resist when Kain wrestled him to his feet and put him in the same shackles as the others. He was gagged and pushed onto his knees next to Andreas and Turr. To Jayden's other side was Syrus's lifeless body still holding the same defiant expression.

To Sasha, Syrus was another dead mystic, another notch of power to his oversized ego.

"West, put Ms. Reeves into the carriage, and be gentle. We don't want our only leverage against Elasus damaged." Sasha turned and regarded Phaedra with contempt. She was conscious but unable to push herself to a knee. "Kain, bind the witch, and put her with the others."

Markus knelt next to Jenna's static body and placed two fingers to her neck. It was a fruitless gesture, but Markus's whole being rested on the shaky foundation of hope.

Behind Markus, many of Dalth's citizens were murmuring, and tempers were beginning to flare. Markus rose and raised a calming hand to the angry crowd.

"Listen, don't do that," Markus commanded toward two men who looked ready to charge the Celje leader. "Our friends have selflessly turned themselves in to Sasha so we may live. Don't waste their sacrifice by doing something stupid. Please, return to your homes, and we'll gather in the square."

As the crowd turned, a refreshing tingle of relief fell over Jayden. He watched the pack walk down the empty road, but strangely, one person remained. She stood defiantly with clenched teeth and hands resting at her hips with holstered pistols Jayden didn't remember her wearing on the walk up.

To his left, Jayden watched Andreas's stern narrow eyes spring open in panic. His head shook, and he grunted desperately through his gag.

Serena stood alone, looking down the still-smoking barrel that had already killed two people today. Her eyes spied Sasha, then back to his gun, then back again as if she was considering her options.

"What do you think you are doing? Go back to… oh, but wait, could this be," remarked Sasha, guiding his horse up next to her. "You are the Visconti girl? So, we meet again after all these years. I must say, you have filled out quite nicely."

Markus tenderly hooked his arm around Serena's elbow and kindly pulled her back. "Come, Serena, now is not the time." Markus's voice cracked with worry. "Please Serena, I don't want to lose anyone else today."

Andreas and Serena locked eyes for a sobering moment until an odd shift in the air brought everyone's attention toward the sky.

The whoosh and chuff of helicopter blades soared over the tree line. The CV-55 helicopter hovered over the crowd before the side hatch slid open exposing four men with assault rifles pointing down on the crowd.

"Sasha!" The voice rang out through an amplifier, but it was coming from the ground, not the aircraft. A squad of two dozen men with metaflex camouflaged armor advanced through the nearby forest with rifles raised. An older man wearing Earther clothes marched at the front of the line. "Put that damn pistol away!"

Sasha's horse stomped nervously, moving from side the side. "Commodus!" gasped Sasha. "What are you doing here? I have everything under control."

"Sure you do," scoffed Commodus. "To the men under Sasha's command, put down your weapons. And you there, holding the woman, let her go, or you'll be the first to drop."

Kain let go of Eve who rushed over to Jayden and embraced him.

The first shot rang out from Sasha's troop, the sole sound distending the entire region. When both legions opened fire, the explosive concussions paralleled that of a departing space ship at close range.

Up the road, Serena and Markus jumped into a ditch near the side of the road.

Jayden and Eve, alongside the other prisoners, tipped over into the snow as the battle flared into a massacre. Achilla and her horse toppled to the ground. The horse squirmed for a brief second before succumbing to several bullet wounds. Achilla managed to roll away, but her legs were riddled with bullets.

Seeing his lover injured rattled Sasha who began yelling for his men to cease fire. It was too late. The battle was raging, and the hundreds of discharging weapons drowned out the Celje leader's commands.

Commodus faded to the rear of his troops while his team overpowered Sasha's outgunned agents. The executive's men were disciplined and carried more advanced weaponry, putting down Sasha's men in droves.

Sasha continued waving his hands, trying to get the attention of his team leaders when his horse took several rounds to the abdomen. The brown warhorse hurled his front hooves into the air, then launched Sasha. He landed in a nearby thicket, imitating the stillness of his dead horse.

The intensity of the battle continued for several minutes until nearly all of Sasha's men were dead or wounded. Commodus returned toward the front lines where Achilla and Sasha both lay unconscious.

"My resolve should not be tested," threatened Commodus, eyeing any who dared to disagree. "Any of Sasha's men who remain, drop your weapons and surrender."

Of the few left, Sasha's men emerged from concealed placements with rifles held over their heads. They were immediately disarmed and handcuffed, then placed under guard away from the main road.

Commodus stepped over Sasha's unconscious body and headed down the road toward Markus and Serena. As if knowing exactly who to speak with, he approached Markus like he was late for a meeting.

"My name is Commodus Vrabel, chief operations officer of the Reeves Corporation. That man back there, Sasha Burmistrov, acted without my consent and will be dealt with. You're Mayor Fonte?"

When Commodus extended his hand, Markus rejected the offer. "I'm Markus Fonte."

Commodus placed his hands back into his pockets, unoffended by the mayor's reaction. "Go back to your people. Tell them not to venture outside the city until I get this mess figured out. Sasha probably still has men ready to fight to the death, and the area isn't safe. Those prisoners over there will remain under guard. I'm having my ship brought over, and if prudent, they'll be returned to you."

Serena tramped in front of Commodus. "But those prisoners are our friends, you can't just take them!"

"What my brash friend is trying to say," said Markus, "is that we'd appreciate it if perhaps you could just release them back to us? They've done nothing wrong other than oppose Sasha."

Commodus eyed Serena with suspicion, then recognition. "What's your name?"

"Serena Visconti."

Commodus folded his hands in front of him and looked Serena over. If this was a game of poker, Jayden would have bet that Commodus was hiding four aces behind this bluff.

"I see. For now, they'll stay in my custody. They will be treated fairly; you have my word." He didn't wait for another snarky reply and waved toward a muscular man with deformed ears. "Jeder, when Garvin gets here, put those prisoners on the ship. Treat them with respect, but they are not allowed to roam."

"Understood." Without orders, Jeder marched over to Jayden and the rest of the prisoners and removed their gag and leg shackles. "You'll be escorted to the *Night Scope* momentarily."

Eve's chin rested on her collarbone. "Jenna's dead… because I convinced her to… surrender. What did I do?"

Kavil, Javier, Jenna, and Syrus were all dead. Phaedra was injured and the heads of the Nein were dead. The Celje were now all in handcuffs thanks to the corporation, an ironic turn.

Away from prying eyes, Sasha and Achilla were restrained. Commodus wasn't giving Achilla much attention, but he was slapping Sasha around like he'd just insulted his mother.

"No, Jenna died because Achilla put ice spikes through her chest," said Jayden. The battle was over, but the day was far from done. "Keep your eyes open, I don't think we're any safer with Commodus than we were with Sasha."

CHAPTER 68: YEAR 2401

A distant, deafening roar grew louder and louder until an enormous starship barreled over the trees. The sound was ear shattering, forcing everyone in Dalth who didn't have their hands tied behind their back to clasp their palms over their aching ears.

Burnt-orange flames shot out of the *Night Scope*'s hovering engines thousands of feet above the northwestern region of Dalth, then descended gradually until touching with a grinding thump.

The ship's landing lights flashed red for several minutes until flickering to green, indicating it was safe to approach. Commodus stalked through the hibernating crops until coming to the edge of the *Night Scope*'s side entry ramps.

Jeder stood behind him, one hand on his sidearm. "What's left of Sasha's men are cuffed and under guard, Mr. Vrabel. What else do you need?"

"What I need is a time machine so I can go back ten years and kill Sasha before he created this mess," blasted Commodus. "The corporation will be in deep if this leaks. Bring Sasha and the other prisoners onto the *Night Scope* for questioning. I want them away from the town."

Thudding footsteps from the ramp brought their attention to Captain Donato and Alanah Kass. Alanah stepped off the ramp first and regarded Commodus. "I'm going to survey the landing area and the gears, Captain. Look for any problems that may affect takeoff. Don't want a repeat of Chden."

"Let me know if you find anything significant," replied Donato. He wore his black jacket unzipped, exposing sweat marks on his green shirt. "Hope all this was worth it, Commodus. Not sure why I couldn't have just landed in Worall or Pa'Gran. We'll be lucky if we don't torch half the forest trying to get out of here, and that's if our landing gears haven't plunged halfway to the core by now."

There weren't many situations that made Donato anxious, but risks concerning his ship and crew were enough to get the man's blood pressure up.

"The company will pay for any damages," Commodus conceded. "Things here are more complicated than I realized. Once we're done, I want us lifting off as soon as possible. I'm going to transfer prisoners to the ship, and I want a briefing room put together for an interrogation, can you handle that?"

"Should I get the mop out, or is this going to be a friendly chat?"

Commodus knew Donato's way of releasing stress was either by sleeping with women or joking. This was the latter, but Commodus was in no mood.

"I said interrogation, not torture."

Commodus and Jeder made their way back to the temporary encampment where several of the corporation's guards surrounded the fenced area. Marilla's friends were no longer gagged or shackled around their feet, but all of them still had their hands chained together.

The guard captain came to attention as Commodus approached.

Commodus looked around until finding one particular woman with gently bobbing red hair. "Jeder, coordinate with Garvin, and get Marilla's friends, plus Kain, Sasha, and Achilla ready for questioning." How many decades had he worked for Elasus and not once was a situation so utterly mishandled? "On top of everything else, we find Marilla in this mess. I need to speak with her, then I'll join you."

Jeder entered the camp with a practiced hand resting on his sidearm, spoke briefly with the captives, then led them out the front gate toward the *Night Scope*. Sasha still didn't have all his wits about him but was able to help Achilla limp her way with the others. Another one of the prisoners, a man with messy brown hair and a week's worth of stubble, hung back and spoke with Marilla. There was an obvious connection between the two, a sentiment reinforced when they embraced.

Once Jeder had all the captives marching, Commodus waved Marilla over. He had no delusions about how this reunion was going to start.

"Too afraid to look me in the eye?" hissed Eve. "I know my father doesn't care about me, but you, I thought you actually had a heart."

Commodus thought he probably deserved that and let it go. "After everything I've seen today, I should be more surprised to see you mixed up in all this, but I'm glad you're okay. It's been how many years, Marilla? And you still look the same. Your mother, she's never lost hope. You want to call her now?"

"I go by Eve around here, and I don't know if it's good to see you or not. Certainly your timing was impeccable. Your plaything Sasha was about to execute a friend of mine, and no, I don't want to speak with my parents."

Sasha executing Marilla, Christ, that would've been the cherry on top of this mess. "I'm sorry. Sasha went too far, but I'm here to make things right. I hope you can see that. Your mother is part of the reason I'm here. She's sacrificed a lot trying to bring you home."

"You just took my friends away in handcuffs, and you're asking me to see all the good you're doing? I don't care about my mother and certainly not my father and the verdict's still out on you. If you want to help, then release my friends and get some medical supplies to all the towns, starting with Dalth. Sasha's been on a rampage and lots of people have been killed or injured."

Giving away medical supplies or purchasing them for the exiles would surely catch the attention of Elasus. The corporation was already seeing significant downward shifts in revenue, and Commodus couldn't justify the charity.

"I can't release your friends until after I've spoken with them, and you know the rules governing Ojult, I can't just give medical supplies to you. Right now, I need you to come with me, and we need to contact your—"

"Release my friends and—"

"Damn it, Marilla, this isn't a negotiation!" roared Commodus. "You have no idea how much money the corporation stands to lose if we don't fix Ojult. You're going to contact your parents, and then we're getting you off this planet!"

"Oh, I'm sorry, you're right, profits before anything else. How foolish of me! And leave Ojult? Oh, okay, let me just go pack my bags so I can go live happily with my parents, that is until they decide to kill me like they did my fiancé."

There was a side of Commodus that agreed with her and wanted to see her stay on Ojult and do some good, heal the sick, that sort of thing. Of course, his other side wanted to drag her by the throat and toss her into a holding cell until they got back to Earth and never set eyes on Ojult again. Luckily Garvin decided to stroll into their conversation at that moment, giving him a few more moments to consider his options.

"Damn, chief, I'm pretty sure everyone across the Altum just heard you," teased Garvin. "If you're having lady problems, I can probably help." He turned to Marilla and shot his best smile toward her. "My name is Captain Donato and that big ship over there is mine. Perhaps later on I could show you…"

Commodus stepped in front of his old friend. "Shut up and show some respect, Captain. This is Elasus's daughter, Marilla Reeves, the one who's been missing for over a decade!"

Garvin paused and studied Marilla, not sure if Commodus was for real. "Well, can't take back what I said. You are beautiful, Marilla, much like your mother. Will I have the pleasure of escorting you back to Earth?"

"All right, Garvin, time to shut up," said Commodus with zero humor. There was something ominous in the air, and Commodus wanted out of here. "Marilla, I need to know how you got here, what you know, and anything that might help us stabilize the planet. We can talk about the other stuff later."

"I want my friends released and any medical supplies you have brought to Dalth's clinic first."

Like her father, Marilla understood when she was negotiating from a position of power and didn't seem willing to budge. She'd been in the thick of Sasha's plans for years, and Commodus needed her assessment of the situation.

"Fine, tell me what you know, and I'll release your friends *after* I've spoken with them. I'll also have a separate shipment of medical supplies delivered to Dalth. You have my word."

Marilla didn't trust him, but her friends were the golden chip that finally persuaded her to describe what all had happened. She gave a detailed account of what she'd been through since arriving on Ojult. Her time with Dr. Castellani, then as Misora's prisoner, her escape, and finally her time in Dalth.

Commodus didn't think he could become any more enraged with Sasha than he already was, but that sentiment faded with every new detail Marilla shared. When her voice trailed off, Commodus thought very seriously of marching up to the *Night Scope* and executing Sasha.

"Marilla, I'm sorry. You need to know that I, and your father of course, we didn't know about this. We've relied on Sasha for decades, and he's never failed us, at least until now."

Marilla took a sharp step forward, her forehead only inches from his chin. Her lips were clamped shut, and every breath she took sang with anger. "I know you don't care about me or the people here. The money is all you and my father care about, and that's fine, I don't expect I'll be able to change your mind. But the people here are suffering because of it, so if you want anything else from me, release my friends, and help these people out. They didn't ask for this and certainly don't deserve it."

"I can't do anything about the past, and I'm not here to soak up tears. Most people here are dangerous criminals, but you're wrong, I do care. I'll fulfill my end, and I'll get Captain Donato to have quarters ready for you when we head back to Earth."

"You think I'm heading home? Are you insane! Sasha planned on using me as leverage over my father, and I'm pretty sure he'd have just thrown me back to these wolves. I'll fight to my last breath, but I'm *not* going back to Earth!"

A short olive-skinned woman with pink highlights came up from behind Commodus. She wore a green-and-khaki uniform that signified she was a member of the Reeves Space Fleet. "Pardon me, Mr. Vrabel, but the captain wanted me to tell you the prisoners are ready for you. I also walked around the ship; it's not looking good. Landing flats are already about a foot into the soil. Captain says we only have a day at most before we need to lift off."

Commodus drew in a sedative breath. "Thank you, Lieutenant Kass. I'll finish up here, then head up."

Alanah inspected Marilla for a moment, then spun and headed back toward the ship.

"If your friends are innocent, they'll be released. Kain, Sasha, and that weird girlfriend of his will not be, you have my word." Marilla didn't think much of that promise judging by her sour look. "You're free to go where you please, and once I finish, we'll talk more about you leaving."

Further debate would get them nowhere, and Commodus turned and headed back for the ship. There was the chance she'd make a run for it and go back into hiding, and Commodus weighed that idea. He had her friends under supervision, and at least one of them meant something special to her. All he had to do was squeeze that pressure point and Marilla would come running back.

The stars were beginning to shine brightly against the clear night sky, which was also bringing freezing temperatures. The picture above him was stunning, and if it weren't for the bloodstained soil encircling them, he would have stopped to enjoy the hypnotic moment.

Commodus was nearing the ship now, close enough where white and green lights nearly blinded him. At the bottom of the closest starboard ramp stood Jeder, carefully scanning the grounds ahead. When Commodus approached, his security head hesitantly handed him a report.

"Sir, I've summarized the entire report. I'd read it before you walk in there. I've got Sasha, Kain, and the woman ready for you in bay six."

Commodus took a few minutes to read over the summary. Anxious sweat started to build on his freezing neck. What this report suggested was nearly impossible to believe, but Jeder was as thorough as they came. His contacts inside and outside the PGU were vast, and he could find anything on anyone given enough time. What really made the report crucial, if not chilling, was that Tanner Sands had verified all of it.

Retribution sat on the tip of Commodus's next move as he tramped into the secure cargo hold. The extensive corridors leading to the various cargo bays were empty save for a few soldiers on guard duty. The guard attending to bay six went to attention and opened the door for his two superiors. The room consisted of a few crates, empty water bottles and food wrappings, and three captives, sitting on the cold metal floor, chained together with African-ore metal secured to the wall.

Kain, Sasha, and Achilla were covered in dirt and bandages but otherwise well enough to withstand questioning.

"You fool!" shouted Sasha upon seeing his boss. "Release us! I am the leader of the Celje on this planet and have earned more than this! You have no idea what you are doing!"

Sasha's voice fell flat against the metal walls.

"Are you really demanding something, from me," growled Commodus. "You're done Sasha and according to these notes, you're in way over your head."

Achilla looked like she wanted to stand, but both her legs were heavily bandaged. When she spoke, her voice was raspy and tired. "We eliminated Syrus, quelled the rebellion, and this is how you treat us? We should be honored as heroes, not prisoners."

Commodus stepped closer, fighting the urge to kill the woman. "You're the wolf inside a red cloak." He knelt and read a brief line from the summary. "Achilla Alzer, sister of Cadoc Alzer, from the FIAS region, both gifted mystics. Tell me, have you spoken with your brother recently? Has Sasha met him? Have you been to see one another's families, shared a holiday dinner perhaps?"

"I do not know what you are talking about."

This was bigger than anything he'd come across since joining the corporation, but he had to refocus on why he wanted to talk with the two lovers in the first place. After that, he'd take them back to Elasus who'd figure out what to do with them.

Commodus pushed his shoulders back and erect. "The three of you will answer my questions, then spend the rest of your lives in prison, if Elasus doesn't order me to execute you. So, my first question, which Elasus himself will surely ask, did you plan on using Marilla in your scheme to control the planet?"

Sasha leaned back, snorted, and spit on Commodus's shoes. "Go eat a cython, Vrabel. You and your golden crown, you aristocrats and your ships and skyscrapers. You have no idea what is going on out there, lurking beyond the border of the few planets you know of. I have seen what is coming, and me, my Celje, we know how to kill them. Achilla knows of this, and she is powerful, perhaps enough to bring us through to the other end. But no, instead of thanking me, you kill my men!"

Commodus wiped the mucus-covered shoe against Achilla's injured leg, then stepped in front of Kain. The clean-cut man had a large gash across his forehead that was already stitched. Unlike Sasha, who smelled like the wrong end of a zibar, Kain smelled like used gun oil and death.

"You're Kain, one of Sasha's senior advisors." It was a statement, not question, and Kain stayed silent. "How did this war with the mystics come about? Did Sasha provoke the conflict? What was his plan?"

Kain looked up, speaking with genuine hatred. "I've served Sasha and the Celje loyally for many years. I'm not about to throw that away for some businessman that has no idea what he's stepped into."

Commodus looked over his shoulder and nodded toward Jeder. Kain folded his hands in front of him, putting up no fight. The security officer paraded forward, grabbed Kain by the collar, and dragged him out of the bay.

Commodus knelt next to Sasha. "You kidnapped the daughter of the most powerful person in history, what the hell were you thinking? Why did you start this? What was your end game? I'll get the answers I need, and I don't care who I have to kill to get them."

"You don't have the balls, Vrabel. You wouldn't get that pretty coat of yours dirty. Kain is loyal and good at killing mystics, something you are going to need soon, I think."

A short yell from Kain down the hallway was silenced by a single energy bolt. Sasha's brow creased. "You'll live to see the day where all of Ojult, all of Earth bows before me! Elasus, the PGU, even you, Vrabel, will beg me to take you in!"

Commodus smiled with a touch of gratification. He saw four of his guards rush down the hallway, rifles in hand, but he discounted them. "Now that I have your attention, I'd like a thorough explanation as to what you were planning and who was involved. If I'm not satisfied, Achilla's next. If you love her, I suggest you cooperate."

From behind Commodus, Jeder entered, whispering over his earpiece. The blood covering the security chief's boots and the threat against Achilla sobered the Celje leader at once.

Sasha's eyes locked onto his lover. "What guarantees do I have that you will not harm her?"

"The fact I haven't killed her already should be enough."

Sasha appeared ready to narrate his entire plan when thumping footsteps down the ship's corridor seized the group's attention. From beside Commodus, Jeder's earpiece buzzed into overlapping warnings. The security leader's hand dashed to his sidearm as a tremendous boom walloped the ship, throwing the group into the metal plied floor. The metal landing gears holding the ship ground and screeched under the new pressure.

Booms of faraway gunshots and shouts of team leaders repositioning their squads filled the air.

"Is it the prisoners?" asked Commodus, getting back to his feet.

Jeder was up and jabbering into his microphone, already halfway out the cargo bay. "No sir. We've got an unknown group of mystics near Dalth."

Commodus lunged toward Achilla and yanked her small body up. "Friends of yours?"

Achilla didn't shy away from Commodus's snarling look, but her next question threw him. "I have no mystic allies. These mystics, what do they look like?" Her eyes suddenly turned glassy, seeing the world through a different lens.

Yellow alert lights flashed through the ship, followed by a woman's voice over the loudspeaker.

"This is First Officer Chelsie Franks, preparing for emergency takeoff. We're under attack by an unknown force. Captain Donato has ordered an immediate takeoff."

Commodus released Achilla, and her mutilated legs crashed under the pressure.

"Jeder, wait!" Commodus ordered, calmly thinking through the situation. "If the mystics are in Dalth, what the hell hit the ship? That's over two miles."

"Not sure," conceded Jeder. "Could have been a rocket or something with some range."

"What is it?" asked Sasha, but he wasn't speaking to Commodus or Jeder. Instead, Sasha was looking at Achilla who was staring up at the ceiling, fixated on a single spot.

Achilla's head jerked back down, and she grabbed Sasha's arm as her silky eyes came back into focus. "Sasha, something is wrong, I can't see them. The mystics, I should be able to see them."

Commodus processed her warning and thought this might all be part of a ruse the two lovers put together to escape.

"What do you mean?" Commodus asked, peeking down the hallway.

"You may think we are the enemy, but you are wrong. You need to free me now and allow me to heal. Where are my staffs?"

Jeder's voice sputtered between radio messages. "Reports suggest several mystics have come through a gate or portal. They're marching toward the ship. They have staffs, our people are engaging."

Achilla jerked her head toward Sasha. She was breathing rapidly. "We are too late, my love. They are here."

Jeder had his hand cupped over his ear, listening fixedly to the reports coming in. "Charlie four this is Bravo one, calm down and repeat that last transmission." Jeder took in the message and raised his head slowly, clearly overwhelmed. "Sir, more mystics have just come through a portal of some kind. That makes nine of them."

CHAPTER 69: YEAR 2401

I told you something felt off!" shouted Phaedra over the ship's sirens.

Jayden rammed his good shoulder into the locked cargo door. "This door isn't budging, and I bet you the locks are made of African ore."

Andreas, Turr, Phaedra, and Jayden were in cargo bay two, eerily similar to the bay Jayden traveled in over ten years ago. This time, instead of wearing virosuits, he wore metal chains. He could feel the refiltered air, smell the gamma-sterilized walls and ozone from freshly welded metal.

Behind him, Andreas and Turr exchanged quiet thoughts on the situation.

"Not that I'm as tuned as you, but I feel one, maybe two of them," said Andreas, squinting like he was trying to see through the wall. "I can feel their power."

Turr was still trying to heal from the battle of Worall and looked the part of a beaten prisoner. He'd healed for much of the day, but his body was far from recovered. "Like all three of us with our powers combined," corrected Turr. "Like seeing two of Syrus but richer."

Phaedra was scouting the bay for another way out. Her normally straight hair was frizzy, and she wore simple pants and a long-sleeve blouse lent to her by their new caretakers. Jeder had made it clear that she wasn't wearing anything resembling a Nein while in custody.

Phaedra was on the other side of the bay when she stopped and looked to the exit. "We've got bigger problems. I think more of those new mystics just showed up."

Faint pops of gunfire reverberated down the corridors separating port from starboard. Jayden ignored Phaedra's blabbering and focused on how to get them off the ship or at the very least, out of this room. According to the overhead speaker, the ship was about to take off.

His answer came when Commodus's head appeared in the small square window a little more than halfway up the door. The executive popped the latch and opened the door. The stifled gunfire grew louder with fresh air now circulating the cargo bay. The scared-stiff appearance of the executive paused Jayden's demand to be freed.

"All of you, get over here, now!" demanded Commodus.

Jeder was behind him, still in the hallway, speaking rapidly over his earpiece. Groups of soldiers rushed by every few seconds, rifles raised.

Turr and Andreas ushered in front of Phaedra's laggard pace.

"Nothing to drink or eat, no bed, chair, or something to rest our legs upon. You should know I'm filing a complaint with the corporation when this is over," said Andreas, trying to catch his breath.

"Shut up and listen to me." Commodus's pistol harness was poking out of his jacket, unstrapped, but the safety was on. "There are nine mystics, all with staffs, heading toward the ship, and my guess is they're coming for one of you. Did you set this up? Is this some sort of escape plan?"

All eyes went to Phaedra, who met their gaze with cold fury. "No, this isn't my doing. But if they're here to rescue us and kill you, then sign me up."

There was always the possibility she was lying, but the truthfulness in her voice swayed Jayden enough to take a stand.

"We don't have anything to do with this, Commodus, but free us, and we can help fight," assured Jayden. "Where's Eve? Is she on the ship!"

"We're cut off from Dalth right now, and she's still there. I'm letting you four go on the condition you fight your way through that new group and bring her back. Agreed?"

Jayden had the perfect angle to Commodus's unstrapped pistol. He considered taking the weapon, killing him and his bodyguard, then going after Eve. Yet the ship was full of armed soldiers loyal to Commodus, and each had just proven their fighting proficiency against Sasha. Killing Commodus would only get him shot before stepping foot off the ship.

The foolishness of the plan prevailed over Jayden's mind, but not Phaedra's. She either didn't care or hadn't thought it through because she had Commodus's gun out of its holster in one quick move.

Andreas sidestepped Commodus and twisted Jeder's pistol to the side, disarming him and launching him over his shoulder. Within seconds, both corporate men were on their backs, disarmed, looking down the barrels of their own weapons.

"Vaut, get the keys to these cuffs," said Phaedra.

Jayden didn't move. "They've got Eve, and if you think you're going to fight through their entire security team, you're dreaming. Come on, you two, think this through. This isn't the way to do this."

Her lips came together in a long, hellish smirk. "You've always been soft, like Syrus without the power. Things are changing, Vaut, and you can either join us or I can bury you with these two when we're finished."

Andreas edged over Commodus and retrieved the fob that unlatched the powered cuffs. He waved the device over his own bonds, then unlocked Phaedra and Turr. "Come on, Jayden, these guys are bad business, no chance of compromising with them. Let's sneak out of here, find the ladies, then trek to a sandy beach away from all this."

"We're not finding anyone," Phaedra countered. "We look out for our own, no one else. Syrus made that mistake and look where we are. Andreas, help Turr, we're leaving."

When Andreas didn't make to comply, Jayden grasped what his friend was feeling. It was the same connection he had to Eve. Was it love, friendship? Perhaps both or neither, yet something was compelling the men not to leave their friends.

Jayden lifted his hands slowly. "We can accomplish both goals here if we work together. You kill either one of these men, and you'll bring down the corporation upon everyone. Let's at least try to work out a deal with them so everyone walks out of this ship alive."

"I wasn't planning on killing these men," said Andreas, leaving no room for interpretation. "You're not killing them either, Phaedra. We toss the cuffs on them and lock them up in this room. Come on, Phaedra, help us find Serena and Eve, then let's get out of here."

From the floor, Commodus and Jeder recovered to their feet.

"We've got no reason to kill you," Commodus said. "If I wanted you dead, I wouldn't have wasted the time bringing you here. And your friends are mostly right. You kill us, you won't have a chance getting off this ship. In fact, without us walking you out, my forces will assume you've escaped. You want to negotiate, I'm all ears, because whatever's attacking my men out there is beyond anything we've ever encountered."

Jeder looked to Andreas, then to his pistol. "Whatever you plan on doing, make it quick. Those mystics out there are plowing through my men. They'll be at the ship within minutes."

Phaedra's eyes blazed into Jayden, indifferent to the corporation's opinion. "Why did he choose you?"

Jayden leaned his ear closer, not understanding the question. "What?"

"Why did Syrus choose you? He had piles of his own people to choose from, yet he chose you to become part of his family? I was his apprentice, but he *chose* you. You were with Mea and Helia while I was running errands like a slave. Why?"

"We can talk about—"

"Talk now, Vaut!"

The barrel of her pistol now aligned between Jayden's eyes. He needed to choose his next words with care. "I... don't think he trusted me to the extent you think. If I had to guess, I expect he saw us working together... at some point in the future. Syrus knew, somehow, that he wasn't going to see this war to its end. Maybe he hoped we would be able to bring some semblance of peace to Ojult. He wanted Mea to live in peace, something maybe he thought you and I could bring to the planet after he left. I don't have a good answer for you."

"There's more truth in that statement than you realize," Andreas said. "He did see his own demise. On the surface, Phaedra, you're difficult, but Syrus saw beneath this brashness. He groomed you to take the reins of the Nein during the difficult times he envisioned. The future Syrus imagined always had his family in mind. He wanted them safe, beyond all things. Jayden's right. In some oracular manner, I believe he wanted you two to partner up, for the sake of Mea, Helia's legacy, and for *your* future, Phaedra."

Bursts and cracks of weaponry were becoming more defined.

Opinions and verdicts processed behind Phaedra's cold, penetrating eyes. "We can't beat the corporation by ourselves."

It was a question, and Andreas took it as such. "No chance. We need pathfinders like Jayden to help. Not killing these executives will also help us live a bit longer."

Phaedra kept the pistol centered on Jayden, but an arresting warmth swirled in her cunning eyes. "You, Commodus. Our gear, where is it?"

Outside the ship, Jayden and company were outfitted and ready to confront the foreign mystics. Things were far from cordial between Jayden and Phaedra, but an unmentioned evolution had occurred in their relationship. Phaedra's hardened hostility toward him submerged beneath her duty as the new Nein leader.

Commodus and Jeder, who remained bullet free, escorted them to the ship's defensive perimeter.

"I have men in the field, and Marilla still isn't on board!" Commodus yelled. "Keep your cool, Captain, and don't move the ship!" Whatever idea the ship's captain had about leaving was crushed with Commodus's orders.

"Pretty sure that ship isn't going anywhere," suggested Turr. "Think we better just wait here, make sure these staff-wielders don't perceive us as a threat."

Jayden's body tensed. His mystic companions were anxious, if not outright scared. Phaedra tapped her blades together while Andreas held the butt of his holstered pistol.

The team's first trace of the arriving sages came with the soft-white glimmering of their shields, which soon gave way to cloaked shapes. Each carried a staff, and dark cloaks covered their masked faces. The innermost sage wore thick dark robes with dashes of deep blue and maroon across the shoulders and torso.

Jayden scrutinized the metallic mask that exposed the man's toxic black eyes and misshapen narrow face. Something familiar about this sage spurred a flashback.

With an unannounced change, the other eight mystics stopped while the lead sage continued forward with an elongated staff at his side.

"Stop!"

It was a deep, masculine voice, daring anyone to disobey. Even without Commodus's orders, every soldier ceased their onslaught.

"Commodus Vrabel," continued the sage. "My name is Melron, and as of this moment, your persecution of mystics is over. Pull your soldiers back into the ship and collect your dead."

The sage's rumbling voice careered through the night air, reaching across the entire planet. The power these sages had just displayed was beyond anything Jayden had ever seen. Up ahead, Commodus spoke softly into his earpiece giving instructions to Jeder. The powerful executive was stubborn, but at least he knew when to admit defeat.

What was left of Commodus's men began an organized retreat toward the ship, filing in by squad with Jeder issuing more instructions as they boarded.

Phaedra, Andreas, and Turr did nothing but watch these omnipotent mystics force their will over Ojult's regulators. Even Jayden agreed these newcomers were, at minimum, not their enemies.

As the last of the soldiers entered the ship, another of the sages stepped forward and stopped at Melron's side. The newcomer was tall and slender with white, green, and black layered robes. His silver mask covered everything from his nose to his chin, leaving his lavender-speckled eyes in clear view.

Whereas Melron faced Commodus, this man turned to Jayden.

"Andreas and Jayden, you are alive?"

Nothing prepared Jayden for that familiar, condescending voice.

"Levi?"

CHAPTER 70: YEAR 2401

Levi secured his staff and removed his mask and hood. Back in the dimly lit prison, Jayden never completely discerned Levi's features, but tonight, he fully regarded them. Levi was in his mid-forties with dark hair that had a natural cowlick in the front. His lips turned naturally downward as if they weren't meant to smile or show happiness. What really confounded Jayden was Levi's lavender-freckled eyes that looked as if they belonged to some sort of exotic sea creature. For the life of him, Jayden didn't remember this unique feature on the man.

"Levi," said Melron. "Now is the time for resolution, not greetings."

Levi pivoted. "As you say."

"Commodus," continued Melron, who stood in total control of the situation. "Finish gathering your men, and prepare to depart this world. While doing so, bring Sasha Burmistrov and his female companion to me."

Commodus uttered more instructions to Jeder over his receiver, then approached the intense man with caution. Until now, Commodus had been the only one in charge, and everyone on Ojult knew it. The sudden caution and change of tone did not pass unnoticed. He wisely kept his sidearm holstered, but Jayden could tell he was uneasy approaching the sage unarmed.

"You've proven your point," said Commodus. "I'm gathering my team, but leaving this place permanently isn't happening. For one, Elasus Reeves won't stand for it, and two, I'm not even sure who I'm speaking with. And what do you want with Sasha? He's the corporation's prisoner, and we'll deal with him."

Melron raised a gloved hand, took off his mask, and pulled back his hood, revealing an old man with aged lines painting his face. The front of his head was shiny bald, giving way to a gray mane. His mostly absent eyebrows sat above pure-black eyes that reminded Jayden of ancient paintings of Lucifer he'd seen in schoolbooks.

"We represent the last of the ancient Argos, apostles to our mystic brothers that you have wronged for so many decades. I am Melron, leader of the Elders, and you will do as I command. Elasus Reeves will pay for what he's done to the mystics of this world, but not today. Now, bring me Sasha and the woman he travels with."

As if backing away from a hungry lion, Commodus pitched his hands up in surrender and backed cautiously to the ship.

Stories of old described the Elders as a beacon of light, sent to purge the wicked after the Event. What Jayden witnessed now was like seeing Syrus again with a fancy mask. Jayden didn't know if he'd ever believed in the Elders, but this didn't seem like the grand entrance of the most powerful beings to ever walk the Earth. Pictures of the Elders he'd seen in school had them wearing robes, smiling, healing the sick, and chatting pleasantly with nonmystics. The scene unfolding was greatly… underwhelming.

The other eight Elders, including Levi, stood in formation with staffs out, no longer producing shields. They stood static, keeping their masks on, waiting for the unexpected. Adding to the mystery was Levi himself, an Elder? Levi had a complicated past and was by no means up to the level of evil that Syrus was capable of, but joining the purest of the pure, joining the good guys? The idea seemed to cheapen the story of the Elders and all the good they'd accomplished over the centuries.

The reaction of Andreas, Phaedra, and Turr was more cryptic. None of them reacted toward Melron's sudden announcement. Instead, each of them appeared in a meditative trance. Jayden suspected each of them were probing these newcomers for some deeper purpose.

Clusters of townspeople, led by Markus, walked up from Dalth. Between the fighting, the booming sirens from the ship, and Melron's amplified voice, it was hard not to notice the sudden silence covering the region.

"Jayden… Jayden!"

That voice placated all of Jayden's worries. He turned toward the dozens of citizens who now approached more cautiously after getting their first look at the unique sages. Jayden made out Eve pushing through the crowd.

Soon, they locked eyes, and Eve halted with her hands covering her mouth, overwhelmed by everything.

Careful not to alarm the Elders, Jayden took quick strides, and in moments he was embracing her. He pushed away the pain in his shoulder and held her firm while her body shook.

"We heard so much gunfire, I didn't think we'd find anyone alive up here," said Eve, her voice quavering.

They continued clutching to one another as if letting go might bring back the reality of their situation. Markus, Victor, Kun, and others were now around them, gawking at the strangely erect sages.

"I'm okay. We're all okay," replied Jayden. "Phaedra convinced Commodus to let us go, but when we stepped off the ship, the battle was raging." Jayden kissed her forehead and addressed the group. "That guy up there in the blue and maroon, he's claiming to be an Elder, as are the rest of them. All I know is that the power I witnessed, I've never seen any mystic with that mastery. They're something else."

The idea of the Elder Nine coming back passed through the crowd. Nearly all the townspeople were on their knees, like worshipping an army of gods that had just saved them bondage. Many were bowing at the feet of the Elders, grasping and kissing their robes.

"I wonder if they like wine…" inquired Victor. He held a bottle and two glasses like he was expecting to toast the newcomers. "I brought my best vintage, but only two glasses. Let's see, there are… let's see, yes, nine of them. Here, Mayor, please hold these. I'll be back."

Markus's half grin acknowledged Jayden and the pleasure in seeing him alive, but the mayor was clearly distracted. He ignored Victor, who kept nudging him with the wine bottle, and spoke with underlying skepticism. "This sage, he calls himself Melron? They all claim to be Elders?"

Jayden's response was checked by Andreas whisking between the group and dashing toward Serena. Andreas held her by the waist, her arms wrapped around his neck. He plucked her up off the ground, and the two kissed in a graceless passion.

Jayden looked away from the fervid moment and caught the mischievous grin of Eve whose cheeks were rattled with relief. Phaedra and Turr now seemed to be missing. Jayden scanned the area for Phaedra's silvery hair.

"Sorry, Mayor," said Jayden, realizing he'd been ignoring him, "but you seen Phaedra or Turr?"

Markus placed a gentle hand on Jayden's shoulder and shuffled closer so others wouldn't hear. "I don't think we're going to see Phaedra and Turr again for some time. That man in the green-and-white robes keeps stealing glances toward us. Do you know him?"

"That's Levi. We've talked about him before." Jayden's earlier feeling of concern pooled with Markus's clear presumption that something was off. "What is it you're not saying?"

Abrupt shouts, boos, and hisses sprang from the crowd as Commodus came out with Sasha and Achilla. A few of the crowd threw pebbles and other nearby objects. Commodus shoved the two prisoners at the feet of Melron, then retreated several meters.

Melron arched his back and spoke to the crowd with his earlier resounding voice. "To the people of Ojult, hear me now." His voice once again reached the furthest edges of the planet. "My name is Melron, Peritus of the Elder Nine, master of the sages who protect you now. For too long we've watched and hoped our accord with Earth would bring peace to mystics and Thoba alike. Our brothers and sisters, exiled to Ojult in hopes of keeping the peace on Earth, have been corrupted by the likes of Elasus Reeves and his followers. Today, I bring an end to the deception."

Sasha and Achilla knelt, looking at the red glow emanating from the top of Melron's staff.

Sasha looked at the glowing staff, knowing death was upon him. "I go to my death, not ashamed to face my maker," Sasha vowed. "You will not succeed, Peritus. I may die today, but someone else will rise in my place."

A harsh white light jetted from the top of Melron's staff. He leaned the staff over Sasha's head, and the glow engulfed his contorting body. There was a brief cry before he devolved into a smoldering pile of ash.

Gasps and utterings of delight flowed from onlookers. Not only had the Elders saved them from the corporation, but they'd shown they were willing to protect the people and administer punishment as they saw fit.

Jayden and Eve exchanged uneasy glances. There was no doubt Sasha deserved death, but the power suddenly displayed now gave them cause for alarm. Nothing but the reputation of the Elders of old kept them, and everyone else, from running for their lives.

Melron looked to Achilla, but his words were for Commodus. "You know our history and have now seen our strength. Commodus Vrabel, the corporation's reign over this planet and my brothers and sisters is over. Take this sage, imprison her as you intended, but death shall not befall her or it will be your pile of ashes the people see next."

Melron strapped his mask on and headed toward the other Elders. When all nine sages were together, Melron knelt. Moments later, a swirling mist resembling a circular gate appeared in front of them. It was a portal to somewhere, elusive. Melron entered first, followed by seven other Elders, until only Levi remained. Levi's purple eyes locked on to Jayden, and something unsaid passed between them—a forewarning of danger. Then Levi followed through the gateway.

Commodus yelled to his remaining troops to board the ship, then the defeated executive scanned the crowd. He found Eve but made no move toward her. Jayden wasn't armed, but Kun and Markus were, so if it came to a fight, if Commodus tried to take Eve from Ojult, she wouldn't go quietly.

Yet Commodus made no movement toward them and instead smiled and spoke loud enough for only a few to hear. "Not sure if leaving you here is any safer than taking you with us. I'll get word to your mother. Just know that she loves you and never gave up." Commodus trudged through the thick grass and onto the ship's ramp, never once looking over his shoulder at the bloody ground he'd created.

Andreas stepped up beside Jayden. "A wolf and its sheep just left us."

Jayden wasn't sure if he was speaking of Levi among the Elders or the Elders among the people. Perhaps he meant both. But Jayden was already taking a gigantic leap forward within his mind. Phaedra and Turr didn't disappear by chance, and Levi's weird conduct was a message, not his usual eccentric behavior. Jayden turned and looked at Serena and Eve who were holding one another in comfort as were many other friends and family within the crowd. He knew that Dalth's troubles weren't over, and his mind went to Bella, Logan, Mea, Bélise, Monica, and Hannah.

"Mayor," said Jayden, knowing what needed to be said. "Zakar told me where he's hiding the children, but he's not going to bring them back, and I don't think we should go looking for them. Sasha might have thought he was in control, but I think we just witnessed the planet's newest challenge."

EPILOGUE: 2401

Midmorning in August, and Las Vegas was already a sauna. Few clouds littered the morning sky, and the outer edges of the sun blushed incandescently through the thirteenth floor of the Reeves Corporation building.

One hour ago, Commodus sent a priority message that requested all senior executives to conference on the corporation's secure line.

"We're all here, Commodus," said Elasus into the speaker. Commodus's image flared in and out. "Tanner will be here momentarily, and I've brought in Rico Crouse, as you requested."

Rico sat on the other side of the desk, stroking his mustache and trying not to look annoyed. He'd developed a slight hunch from too many hours at the desk and in the airplane, mostly working on their renewed contract with the FIAS government.

Elasus relaxed back in his chair, his black suit flawless and creased in all the right places.

"Thanks, everyone. This is going to be worth your time," said Commodus.

"Just flew in from the FIAS region, so your timing was good," replied Rico. "So, what couldn't wait for our weekly meeting?"

Commodus inhaled deeply, then spewed out information. "Less than twelve hours ago, nine mystics appeared and decimated my forces. Afterward, their leader, a sage by the name of Melron, declared they were Elders, returning to bring order and peace back to their people. They executed

Sasha, turned him into a pile of dust, then ordered me to imprison Achilla. We're in the process of lifting off. They made it clear we aren't welcome."

Elasus looked at his watch, then to the screen. "These Elders, they showed up shortly after you defeated Sasha's insurgence?"

"They came through something that looked like a portal, defeated my forces, then left through another portal. It looked almost like a gate."

Tanner came through the main door and strode down the long hallway, gesturing toward his ear that he was listening in on the conversation.

Rico arched forward, and the chair grated under the heavy load. "Commodus, these were probably just a bunch of mystics who got lucky and are trying to scare us off. Commodus, get back down there, and show them the corporation won't be pushed around!"

"Nine mystics, each carrying staffs, walk through a magic portal, eliminated over three dozen of my men, turned Sasha into a pile of ashes, and you think this is some sort of prank!?" Commodus was yelling so loudly that the auto-volume feature kicked in to lower the sound.

"They all had Amurski staffs?" asked Rico with sudden angst.

"All of them!" exploded Commodus. "And there's more. We found Marilla. She's been mixed up in the fight between the mystics and our people. She's safe but not on the ship."

Elasus typed quickly on his computer and let Commodus's announcement hang momentarily. Everything he'd done since taking over the corporation from his father was in preparation for this moment. Deep inside, Elasus always knew he'd be the one to fight the Elders when they returned.

"Gentlemen, calm down," Elasus ordered. "There are two possible scenarios at play. First, these are the Elders of old come to bring balance to Ojult." Elasus stopped and drew in a measured, deep breath. "Or, we are dealing with a contracted, employed group; *mystics of fortune* if you will. For the time being, both situations call for the same action. Commodus, your flight plan suggests you're heading back to Earth. Redirect to Lent. You have the mystic witch Achilla on board, and it's unwise to bring her back here where she might have allies. I've informed my son that you're on your way. He'll have suitable accommodations for her when you arrive."

Tanner sat next to Rico and handed the intelligence officer a docuchip.

"What's this?" asked Rico.

"It's the file on Cadoc Alzer with a few updates. After we eliminated Cadoc and Marilla went missing, we started investigating his family for any clue that might have led us to Marilla's whereabouts. The Alzer family is somewhat nomadic, never staying in one place for too long. We do know they originally lived somewhere in the Sovereign Asian Alliance region, probably Thailand or Philippines. What we discovered a few days ago confirms he had a sister named Achilla. We've compared surveillance pictures, and it's a match. Commodus has already been provided this information, but your team Rico, failed us again."

Elasus continued typing while Rico picked his jaw up off the ground and gathered his faculties.

"How did we not catch this sooner?" As the chief intelligence officer of the corporation, it was Rico's job to notice such things. This oversight was huge, and what made it worse was Tanner discovering the facts before he did.

Elasus pushed himself away from his desk and walked over to the wet bar. "The how can be investigated later. Right now, we need to assume the corporation is compromised with mystics like Achilla and Cadoc. My son will interrogate Achilla when she arrives, and we may get leads from there." He turned and looked into the display. "Commodus, you're carrying a dangerous passenger in a partially functioning ship with a defeated troop. Get to Lent, repair, regroup, and let me know when you can get back to Ojult. The Elder's may be there, but we still have a business to run. We'll need to open negotiations with the local leaders and with the Elders, if it comes to that."

Judging by the strain in Commodus's neck, the COO was clearly unhappy. "Elasus, I just told you the Elders destroyed us and that I found your daughter, but you want me back there to... what? Put together a trade show? And what if you're right and these are some sort of hired, super mystics."

Careful not to spill his drink, Elasus walked back up to his keyboard. "Marilla chose to live among the mystics instead of helping her own family. Her path is her own. To your other question, the answer is simple. Soldiers, or in this case, *mystics of fortune* are nothing more than mercenaries. If one group hired them, then reason suggests they can be bought again."

In a few short minutes, Elasus had already calculated his next move. "You have your orders. Contact me when you're on Lent."

Elasus tapped a key, and the display went black.

"Just in case Achilla's got any more relatives around, we've increased security at the building and your home." Unlike Commodus and Rico, Tanner wasn't going to let emotions get in the way of his job.

Elasus sipped the cool bourbon over ice, feeling the burn, then the chill, then finally the rapturous delight that engulfed his nerves.

Elasus turned to Rico who still looked disgruntled by his department's failure.

"Mr. Crouse, we need to expedite our deal with our FIAS friends. Be mindful their hands may be intertwined in recent events."

"I'll schedule a call with them this afternoon," said Rico.

Elasus glanced outside, watching a crane reconstruct one of the many buildings wiped out centuries ago. If the Elders were back for a fight, the battles would occur far from Earth. No, his ancestors had spent too much money rebuilding this planet just to have those magicians destroy everything again.

"You have your orders, gentlemen, carry them out," Elasus said. "As you do so, remember the fate of the corporation, as well as humanity, may rest in the decisions we make. History will remember me as the victor in this match, it is the only way."